THE WORLD FROM BELOW

For a full list of the books in

Jules Romains's series

MEN OF GOOD WILL,

please turn to end

of this volume.

Translated from the French for the
first time, by GERARD HOPKINS

THE WORLD FROM BELOW

by **Jules Romains**

Alfred A. Knopf · New York · 1944

THIS BOOK HAS BEEN PRODUCED
IN FULL COMPLIANCE
WITH ALL GOVERNMENT REGULATIONS
FOR THE CONSERVATION OF PAPER, METAL,
AND OTHER ESSENTIAL MATERIALS

Published September 23, 1935
Second Printing, October 1944

Originally published as
LES HOMMES DE BONNE VOLONTÉ
VII. *Recherche d'une Église*

VIII. *Province*

Copyright 1934 by Ernest Flammarion

Copyright 1935 by Alfred A. Knopf, Inc.

Contents

7. THE LONELY

Contents

8. PROVINCIAL INTERLUDE

DRAMATIS PERSONAE

DRAMATIS PERSONAE

Since a number of the characters of *The World from Below* were introduced in the earlier volumes of *Men of Good Will,* the reader may find it convenient to refer to a list of Dramatis Personæ, with a short summary of the antecedent action in which each has participated. It is suggested that the best way to use the Dramatis Personæ is to refer to each character in turn when the reader reaches the point in the narrative where that character makes his first appearance (as indicated by page numbers following the names below). The characters who appear for the first time in *The World from Below* are not included in this list.

JERPHANION, JEAN (p. 3), has come to Paris in the fall of 1908 to study at the Normal College in preparation for a career as a teacher. He is of a peasant family in the mountains of the southern provinces, and he brings with him the honest ruggedness of his background. Even six years before its outbreak he is conscious of the danger of impending war; but in general he is a healthy optimist, a tolerant sceptic. On arriving at the Normal College he has met Jallez (see below), who is to become his closest friend. In long walks through Paris they discuss their early lives, their ambitions, their ideas; they see all too clearly the shadows of coming events that may immerse Europe in chaos, and their conversations are centred in the question that has occupied the minds of thoughtful young men everywhere: What can we do about it? Jerphanion tutors young Bernard de Saint-Papoul (see below), whom he has taken on an educational walk through the slums. He has announced his intention of joining the Socialist Party, and has written to Clanricard (see below), to

DRAMATIS PERSONAE

express appreciation of an article by the latter—"We Are So Much Alone"—and to suggest a meeting. Meanwhile he has begun a casual, satisfactory love-affair with a young milliner.

CLANRICARD, EDOUARD (p. 3), is an idealistic young Parisian school-teacher. Out of his genuine goodness of nature, which might be mistaken for naïveté, he has been a good Samaritan to one of his pupils, a poor boy whose father is unemployed. (This is Louis Bastide, who does not appear in the present volume.) At a political discussion group he has met and been attracted by Mathilde Cazalis (see below); he has also become interested in Freemasonry. His article on the loneliness of the young intellectual has attracted the attention of Jerphanion.

JALLEZ, PIERRE (p. 3), has been introduced as Jerphanion's fellow-student and roommate at the Normal College. On first acquaintance Jallez thought Jerphanion provincial; Jerphanion suspected Jallez of cynicism. But the discovery of opposite temperaments—Jallez is of an introspective subtlety—leads quickly to mutual admiration. In many long walks together Jallez has shown his friend the Paris which he genuinely loves, and has evoked, from a lyrical memory, the story of his childhood friendship with Hélène Sigeau, which ended in Hélène's disappearance. With Jerphanion he has many discussions about life, literature, and politics; they go together to a literary party for Paul Fort, and to a Socialist meeting presided over by Jaurès. Although Jallez is less successful in love than Jerphanion, because less spontaneous, he has revealed a deeper emotional nature.

JEANNE (p. 3), the little milliner who has a love-affair with Jerphanion.

LAULERQUE, ARMAND (p. 12), is one of a group including Clanricard which meets regularly with Sampeyre (see below) for political discussion. He has spoken in advocacy of violence in political action, and is interested in the possibility of joining a secret society.

DARNOULD (p. 12), another member of Sampeyre's circle.

SAMPEYRE (p. 17) is an intellectual liberal in middle age, a follower of Jaurès, and mentor of a group of young idealists who meet at his house on Wednesday evenings to discuss peace, politics, and labour.

JAURÈS, JEAN (p. 17), one of many actual characters introduced in *Men of Good Will* under their own names, is the famous Socialist. He is frequently in the thoughts and conversations of many of the other characters—particularly Jerphanion, Jallez, Sampeyre, and Gurau (see below).

HONORÉ (p. 19), professor at the Sorbonne with the reputation of a pedant.

CAZALIS, MATHILDE (p. 29), is a girl to whom some of the young men of Sampeyre's circle become attracted. She also frequents the Wednesday evenings.

MICHELS, ROBERT (p. 32), a German radical who has spoken to the group at Sampeyre's.

ROTHWEIL, LÉON (p. 43), a successful shoe-merchant and a friend of Sampeyre, though not a regular member of the circle; important in Freemasonry. He attempts unsuccessfully to assist the Bastide family (see Clanricard, above).

LIGUEVIN (p. 44), associated with Rothweil in Freemasonry.

SAINT-PAPOUL, BERNARD DE (p. 46), Jerphanion's young pupil, who is unimpressed by his tutor's revolutionary idealism on their walk through the slums.

SAINT-PAPOUL, JEANNE DE (p. 46), Bernard's sister, a shy, nervous girl of eighteen who attends a convent school.

DRAMATIS PERSONAE

GURAU, MAXIME (p. 53), is an honest politician with slightly tarnished ideals. A member of the Chamber of Deputies and an independent journalist, he has been politely blackmailed by a group of oil monopolists headed by Champcenais and Sammécaud (see below) into dropping his opposition to their activities; in return, they have bought for him the control of a newspaper, the *Sanction*. Gurau's attempts to justify this to himself indirectly produce a strain on his relations with his mistress, Germaine Baader (see below), who has been playing the market; Gurau declines to help her out of financial embarrassment, for fear that he might be accused of selling out to the oil-magnates to meet her debts. However, his importance grows in the political picture; he is in frequent contact with such men as Jaurès, Viviani, Briand, Clemenceau, Caillaux. His ambition is to become the leader of the Syndicalists in the workers' revolution which he anticipates—a bloodless revolution leading to a better order. His first step into national prominence is as Minister of Labour in Briand's Cabinet.

SIGEAU, HÉLÈNE (p. 62), the little girl whom Jallez loved in childhood, enters the story only in his recollections.

CAULET (p. 63), student at the Normal College, acquaintance of Jallez and Jerphanion; a practical joker.

BAADER, GERMAINE (p. 68), mistress of Gurau, is a successful actress, past the first flush of youth as her affair with Gurau is past its first rapture. She has been playing the stock-market, is much concerned for her investments, and has been still more concerned by the threat of the oil-magnates to take over the theatre where she is under contract, in order to control Gurau through her. Pressed by her broker to put up more margin on her securities, and denied financial assistance by Gurau, she sells out.

AVOYER, JACQUES (p. 68), has gone as an emissary of the oil-dealers to see Germaine Baader. He tries to blackmail Germaine by informing her that the oil-men have gained control of Gurau's newspaper and can do the same with the theatre where she is under contract. He subsequently becomes dramatic critic of the *Sanction.*

TREILHARD (p. 68), editor of the *Sanction,* the newspaper which the oil-magnates control and on which Gurau supersedes him in authority.

SAMMÉCAUD, ROGER (p. 70), one of the leaders of the oil-magnates, has been instrumental in sidetracking the opposition of Gurau. He conducts a long and elaborate liaison with Marie de Champcenais, wife of his friend and partner (see below), which ends in her having an abortion. (Marie de Champcenais does not appear in the present volume.)

RICCOBONI (p. 70), Germaine Baader's broker.

MARQUIS (p. 72), manager of Germaine Baader's theatre.

ALLORY, GEORGE (p. 98) (real name Abraham David), is a snobbish and empty novelist, introduced first at the Champcenais' dinner-party, later in a literary and half-amorous interview with a woman writer.

BERTRAND (p. 98) is a motor-manufacturer affiliated with the oil-magnates.

DUROURE, LIEUTENANT-COLONEL (p. 98), has made one appearance at a dinner party with the oil-dealers, where he holds forth on artillery in modern war.

MACAIRE (p. 106), a small dog belonging to the Saint-Papoul family; he has an amorous and whimsical disposition.

DRAMATIS PERSONAE

SAINT-PAPOUL, BERNARDINE DE (p. 107), eccentric old-maid sister of the Marquis (see below), who studies the lives of the saints with a mixture of piety and secular curiosity. She somewhat maliciously misleads her niece, Jeanne, as to the nature of the sexual act.

BRIAND, ARISTIDE (p. 109), one of the actual personages introduced into the narrative under their own names, has been instrumental in furthering Gurau's parliamentary career.

EZZELIN, JULIETTE (p. 135), is first introduced as a casual customer of the bookbinder-murderer Quinette (who does not appear in this volume). The young wife of a humdrum office clerk, she is passionately in love with Jallez, who breaks off their affair and fails to re-establish it, leaving her desperately unhappy.

MARJAURIE (p. 148), advanced student at the Normal College, who leads the traditional rite "Quel Khon for the Pot"—a demonstration of protest in the college dining-hall.

LENGNAU (p. 151), authority on Freemasonry, is tangential to the Sampeyre circle.

BARTLETT, STEPHEN (p. 154), an English journalist, of whose travel diary one chapter, similar to the present one, has previously appeared.

TORCHECOUL, ERNEST (p. 155), Bartlett's friend who introduces him to Paris; an amateur economist.

EZZELIN, MAURICE (p. 164), Juliette's husband.

VÉRAND, MADAME (p. 166), Juliette's mother.

HAVERKAMP, FRÉDÉRIC (p. 178), is an opportunistic but not dishonest business man who opens a real-estate office on small capital.

He is the nearest French equivalent of the American Babbitt, but with important differences: he is unsentimental, systematic, fond of the pleasures of the flesh, and genuinely in love with the city of Paris. With a keen eye for the main chance, he has his own system of ethical scruples. He is approached by a group of Catholic investors to act as intermediary in an undercover deal in the disposition of disestablished religious properties. This leads to his most ambitious scheme, the promotion of his "health" spa outside Paris, Celle-les-Eaux, where he builds a fashionable hotel and casino; he obtains a chemist's report on the local waters, which are not remarkable for distinguishing mineral properties; but he proposes to advertise their medicinal value.

SCHARBECK (p. 178), one of the Catholic financiers who become associated with Haverkamp.

LOMMÉRIE, MONSIEUR DE (p. 178), spokesman for the group of Catholic financiers; it is he who first establishes contact with Haver-kamp.

CHAMPCENAIS, HENRI, COMTE DE (p. 178), leader of the oil-magnates; a man of considerable wealth and position, although his title is recent in origin. He has used his influence to obtain access to the files kept by the police on public servants in order to look up Gurau. When his wife, who is conducting a liaison with Sammécaud, goes to London, he sees her off under the impression that she is making the trip to find a school for their son Marc, a subnormal boy who is being brought up in the country. Champcenais organizes a large party at their château, which coincides with the time when his wife has her mechanically induced miscarriage.

TURPIN, RAOUL (p. 179), architect at Haverkamp's watering-place, Celle-les-Eaux.

DRAMATIS PERSONAE

MIONNET, ABBÉ (p. 241), a priest in his early thirties, has been introduced at a dinner-party given by the Saint-Papouls (see below). He is a graduate of the Normal College. In conversation with Jerphanion he emerges as a man of considerable intelligence and reserve.

MÉZAN, COMTE DE (p. 241), a Catholic financier unconnected with Haverkamp's group; a friend of the Marquis de Saint-Papoul (see below), with whom he has discussed the career of Mionnet.

SAINT-PAPOUL, MARQUIS DE (p. 241), is a comfortable landed proprietor from the provinces who has married money and has developed political ambitions. He has been introduced in the bosom of his large family in their Paris apartment. His political views are leftist.

SICHLER, FATHER (p. 256), a minor character who, in a conversation with Mionnet, expresses concern over the relations of Church and State.

DUPUY, PAUL (p. 314), is a professor at the Normal College who has been friendly to Jerphanion and found him a tutoring job in the Saint-Papoul family.

SAINT-PAPOUL, MARQUISE DE (p. 315), is content to back her husband's political venture, and is concerned for the protection of their daughter.

LAVARDAC, ROBERT DE (p. 331), a cousin of Jeanne de Saint-Papoul, whom she romanticizes in her imagination.

SAINT-PAPOUL, RAYMOND DE (p. 339), elder son of the family.

DANIEL, ABBÉ (p. 371), a fashionable priest.

DRAMATIS PERSONAE

STRIGELIUS, MARC (p. 424), a minor poet and essayist, introduced briefly at a literary party which Jallez and Jerphanion attend.

ÉTIENNE (p. 497), manservant in the Saint-Papoul household.

MONTECH, MONSIEUR DE (p. 500), father of Mme de Saint-Papoul; wealthy chain-store proprietor in the south-west of France.

DUCATELET, PROFESSOR (p. 526), of the Academy of Medicine, whom Haverkamp consults about the analysis of the mineral water at Celle-les-Eaux.

JANITRESS AT 142 A FAUBOURG SAINT-DENIS (p. 528), whose disappearance is noted herein, has previously rented an apartment to Quinette, the bookbinder who commits a sensational murder.

The foregoing paragraphs have been prepared by George Stevens.

BOOK SEVEN:
THE LONELY

BOOK SEVEN:

THE LONELY

Chapter

1

JERPHANION GETS TO KNOW CLANRICARD

Jerphanion had replied at once to Clanricard. He suggested Wednesday the 12th, at half past five, and named a meeting-place.

Re-reading his letter, he had a moment's uncertainty: "Wasn't Wednesday the day he told me he was engaged?" He turned again to Clanricard's note. "Yes, just as I thought. . . . Only after dinner, though, and it's before dinner that I'm suggesting."

It would have been better to postpone the meeting for a day, but Jerphanion was impatient to find out what sort of a fellow this potential new friend might be. Besides, the day after would have been the 13th. "I'm not superstitious—much less so than Jallez—but, other things being equal, I'd rather not begin a friendship on the 13th. Jallez, on the other hand, pretends that the 13th is his lucky day."

He had chosen as meeting-place a little bar on the boulevard Sébastopol, not far from the Grands Boulevards. He knew it from having been there several times with Jeanne, the dressmaker's assistant, and memories, even of the lightest of love-affairs, cannot but give a fragrance to the possible birthplace of a friendship.

"If Clanricard is coming from Montmartre, he can get straight there by subway. I get out of the Sorbonne at five and can be there, walking, in twenty-five minutes."

He suggested that Clanricard should carry a copy of *La Flamme*.

On his way to the rendezvous Jerphanion thought of many things. At first he was obsessed by the memory of the first time he had passed that way, aimlessly, and a prey to desire; but once past Potin's grocery, his mind turned to Clanricard. "What kind of man am I expecting? To what extent should I be prepared for disappointment? I'll play a betting game with myself: on one side the figure of my imagination, on the other the vacancy in which the man of flesh and blood will materialize."

But he found his imagination working without conviction. The boulevard was too full; so many people made anticipation difficult; the present was too noisily insistent. As he approached the bar he thought it dim and shabby. "Well, he can't complain that I'm trying to dazzle him," he thought. "Poverty and obscurity are good omens of birth. Bethlehem has taught us that."

Five thirty-five: the walk had taken him longer than he had reckoned. Perhaps he had unconsciously slowed his pace.

Suddenly he saw, sitting at a distant table, a young man who, with a red-coloured leaflet spread before him, was watching the door. The young man was thin and, even though he was seated, gave the impression of alertness. His head was small, the thick hair cut short. He had round, wide-open, slightly protuberant eyes, a small moustache, and gave the impression of confidence and a sort of shy intensity. He wore a decent suit of dark clothes and sat with his hands carefully spaced on either side of the leaflet, as though at once to exhibit and protect it. Despite his appearance of shyness he had "Paris" stamped all over him—that Parisian "attitude" which Jerphanion, with all his self-assurance, knew that he himself was not yet master of.

"I know perfectly well," he thought, "that I'm less awkward than he is, but that doesn't alter the fact that some kinds of confidence remain provincial, while some kinds of crudity are unmistakably Parisian."

Clanricard got up, bowed slightly, gave the newcomer a charming smile, and deliberately moved his overcoat from the bench to a chair. He shook the hand that Jerphanion offered him, and the two men sat down side by side. Jerphanion noticed that his breath was slightly sour, though not offensive.

"Obviously he's a decent sort, and he seems to be looking to me to take the lead, which is odd, because by rights it's I who ought to defer to him. He's a bit older than I am, and he's got a job, a job of his own, while I'm still a student. To be a student, no matter how advanced, is to be still a child; socially, one isn't grown up until one has a job. I may pretend as much as I like, my knowledge of life is hearsay compared with his. I don't even know whether I could have written those four pages."

Their conversation at first, if not deliberately cautious, was clearly feeling its way. Jerphanion apologized for the possible inconvenience of his meeting-place. Clanricard protested, and once more deplored the fact that the offices of *La Flamme* were as slack about forwarding letters as they were in noticing proof corrections. Jerphanion assured him that the printer's errors in no way obscured the sense of his article.

After a few openings of this sort and a few compliments from Jerphanion, there came that moment of silence which is the sure sign that a conversation is about to reach its real point.

"Yes, I was enormously struck by your essay," Jerphanion repeated. "It so obviously wasn't just a literary exercise. What you say echoes something that I have been conscious of feeling for a long time. That's why I was so anxious to meet you."

Clanricard's response to his companion's phrases showed itself not only in his face, but in the whole attitude of his body. It was as though he were experiencing an almost intolerable pleasure.

"The only merit," he stammered, "to which I can lay claim, surely, is—is sincerity. I don't pretend I'm a writer. I know that, from the point of view of style, this little effort of mine's nothing much."

"No, no. . . . Besides, style that's nothing but style isn't worth bothering about. You can pick up that sort of thing at every street-corner. Why, your very title's exciting: 'We Are So Much Alone.' "

Clanricard blushed, and hung his head.

"I'm afraid that wasn't my own."

"You found it somewhere?"

"No, a friend of mine used the phrase one day when we were talking. I don't think he attached much importance to it; he certainly didn't read as much into it as I have done. . . ."

Clanricard on this point was not strictly truthful. Each time that

5

he spoke, it was clear from the tone of his voice that he was struggling with the twin fears of making too much of himself and of being misunderstood.

"In that case," Jerphanion said bluntly, "the title is certainly your own. . . . You're a teacher, aren't you?"

"Yes, in the eighteenth arrondissement. I was a student at the Auteuil Training College."

By thus mentioning the Training College for elementary teachers, Clanricard clearly wished it to be understood that he belonged to a privileged class. At the same time his reference was intended to convey a discreet compliment to the more distinguished institution of which his friend was a member: *the* Training College.

"My father was a teacher too—in the provinces," said Jerphanion.

They both smiled. They looked at each other as might two people who have just discovered that they are related, alert for some sign, for some family trait, that would pass unnoticed by a stranger.

"I've got a lot of questions to ask you, not about the meaning of your essay, which is perfectly obvious, but about its general relation to your ways of thinking; that's to say, if you won't think me a nuisance."

Clanricard could answer this only by a polite gesture and a slightly worried look. He saw a difficult time ahead, though he feared Jerphanion's curiosity less than his own inability to satisfy it.

Chapter

CHURCH AND ANTI-CHURCH

"I should like you to realize that your article came to my notice, or, more accurately, was shown me by a friend, the very day on which I had decided to join the United Socialist Party. I will tell you later, perhaps, the stages by which I reached that decision. The point is that it's now the 12th of January, and I'm still not a member, largely owing to you. You're surprised?"

Clanricard did indeed look astonished, but also rather confused. His expression was almost one of guilt.

"At this point," the other went on, with a frank glance of his brown eyes, "I am going to commit my first indiscretion. Are you a member of the Socialist Party?"

"No."

"Do you mind my asking why not?"

Clanricard hesitated. Wishing to help him, Jerphanion went on in a tone that already combined friendly intimacy with a subtle deference:

"I'm putting this blunt question to you because your example, the precedent of your own action, would strongly influence me. That the man who wrote these pages has not seen fit to join the party which I was about to join myself is, for me, a fact of fundamental importance. But to feel its full weight I must first know your reasons."

Clanricard looked straight before him, as though he were staring at a reflection in the big front window. He had the constrained expression of a man who is marshalling his ideas to deal painfully with some unforeseen demand. Again and again he made a movement as of joining his hands on the brown oak of the table-top, a groping movement like that of a man who is trying to sweep together something that lies before him. His fingers seemed aimlessly at work making an invisible pile round the little red leaflet.

Jerphanion, meanwhile, was busy pressing, crushing, the base of his beer-glass into the damp felt mat on which it stood.

He was insistent:

"It's not, I think, that you belong, in any real, living sense, to a religious community, to any regular church. If you did, you wouldn't have so acute a feeling of solitude."

"No," Clanricard said, "I have practically no religious faith. Socialism, however, is another question. In many ways I feel that I am a Socialist. There have been times when I have actually taken part in Socialist demonstrations. All the same, I'm not a member of the party. I belong to no party."

"As a matter of principle?"

"Oh—for many reasons; among them the influence of one particular man."

"Will you tell me who he is?"

"His name will probably mean nothing to you: Sampeyre. He was one of my masters at Auteuil, a historian; a splendid type of man, for whom I have an enormous admiration, for whom a lot of us have an enormous admiration. If he were a member of the Socialist Party, I should probably be one too."

"Let me change the form of my question: do you know his reasons for not being a member? But before we go further into that, do you think he has the same sense of spiritual loneliness, the same craving for some kind of church, that you have, that we both have?"

Clanricard smiled and shook his head.

"Do you know, you're making me think, really think, about something I've never been more than vaguely conscious of before. No, on the whole, I should say that he hasn't that sense of loneliness. I don't believe that it's ever been a dominant feeling for people of his generation. . . ."

He stopped, thinking.

". . . Not that they haven't from time to time formed leagues

and associations, but, looking back on their activities, I should say
that when they did so it was always in order to fight certain definite,
strongly entrenched tyrannies, such as the Army or the Church, in
order to protect human rights and human liberty from the violence
of the caste spirit. . . ."

"In fact," Jerphanion observed, "one might say that their attempts
at union, at solidarity, sprang from a need that was pre-eminently
negative. . . ."

"If you like to put it that way. . . ."

"While the need that we feel is definitely positive. . . ."

Jerphanion, as he spoke, suddenly felt his ideas arranging themselves neatly in his brain. It was as though, at a word of command,
they had been drawn up in two perfectly dressed ranks, facing in-
wards like soldiers on parade. Along the alley-way thus formed the
inspecting officer would briskly advance, pleased by the symmetry of
their alignment, by the perfect balance of their polished brightness.
Like most young men, Jerphanion liked thought to be symmetrical.
He knew no delight more intoxicating than that which he derived
from such meticulous perspectives of the mind. He would have had
no hesitation in ranking it higher in his scheme of values even than
sexual indulgence. The pleasures of the senses may be more solid,
may convulse more violently the very roots of one's being, but those
of the mind operate in a higher region of the consciousness, where
they attain a sort of crowned sublimity. This natural preference of
his had been developed by his College training. He had been taught
to think that the essence of a literary or philosophic thesis can be
found only when the first rich confusion of thought can be checked
and bounded by some semi-mathematical formula. The text of a
thesis offers a problem. The important thing is not to fish up a few
mangled answers from the limited experience of life which is possible at eighteen or twenty, since such answers will probably be
inconsistent and may even be mutually contradictory. Any conclusion
they offer will be hesitating, handicapped at the outset by a sense
of immature audacity. The important thing is to begin by demon-

strating an opposition—whether true or false doesn't much matter—between two groups of fundamental ideas. Once that is done, the seam of the problem is truly visible, the incision can be made and the whole question at issue opened out. Symmetry ensues by a sort of natural process. The particular ideas involved, delighted at this opportunity to advance along their ritual paths, move towards their set positions. The conclusion is duly reached at the end of the ordered progress, sure of itself and duly founded, ready to welcome the pilgrim with the rhymed couplet and the three trumpet notes prescribed by decent usage. Only by observing these rules can the competitor hope to make his papers stand out from the ruck and wake a show of interest in the jaded examiner. Although, in the case of examinations, Jerphanion had not allowed himself to be altogether taken in by this conventional method of approach, he had never been at pains to free himself from the fundamental rigidity of thought which it presupposes. So poignant was the delight which he derived from the construction of this sort of mental symmetry that he was inclined to regard it as a kind of natural touchstone by which the intellect recognizes the sudden revelation of truth. The whole history of the human spirit serves to excuse and encourage such an illusion in the mind of a young man who is engaged in serious study. He can hardly avoid regarding the central tenets of the great philosophical systems, even the fundamental discoveries of science in the great periods, as having been produced by some such manipulative process. He recognizes that, for their authors, the sure sign that what they have seen is indeed the illuminating flash of truth, the unshakable message of God or of Universal Reason, is just this moment of incomparable pleasure, this bright apotheosis, this crowned and sceptred intoxication which can be produced by such pompous simplicity of thought. He doesn't really believe that the human spirit has found other methods of attaining the truth. It is only by slow degrees that we come to realize that the pleasure given by a sense of intellectual symmetry is, in itself, no argument. What counts is the proof, and for the proof we must wait. Meanwhile the mind is the prey of old habits, alert for the first hint of symmetry in its working, ready to set out along the newly drawn perspective with something of the old delight. For this is the condition of fruitfulness in the human spirit, the central law of its creativeness. And if reality is not, in fact, bound by the rules of such intellectual games, it is well that we should recognize their observance as the only chance we have, be it no more than one in a thousand, of finding ourselves surprisingly upon her track.

It was, therefore, with a certain voluble enthusiasm that Jerphanion set himself to explore the vista which had just been revealed to him.

". . . So much so," he continued, "that no matter how much one generation may bequeath to another, the fact remains that there is a fundamental opposition between the generation of your master Sampeyre and our own. We are all of us in some sort looking for a 'Church.' According to our various tastes we are attracted by the Socialists, the Sillon,[1] the Action Française."

"Or Syndicalism."

"Yes, perhaps; while what dominated our elders was a feeling against 'Churches,' a desire to destroy 'Churches.' Their very attempts at solidarity were founded upon an opposition to solidarity. In joining parties they abrogated their individualism, but only in order to reassert it with an added sense of security. We are the generation of 'Churches,' they, fundamentally, of the 'anti-Church.'"

Clanricard smiled. He saw no reason to contradict the argument, since the argument was his own. He half admired, was wholly dazzled. Trained only as an elementary teacher, he was not intoxicated to the same extent as the other by the achievements of symmetrical thought. His education owed less to the Humanities, from which that heady wine is mainly pressed. He found himself thinking: "How

---

[1] *Le Sillon* was a politico-social movement founded by a rich and eloquent Catholic modernist named Marc Sangnier. It preached a sort of primitive Christianity, tinged with humanitarianism, and, despite its patriotic leanings, aimed at a vague fraternity of peoples. About this time it had a large following, but later fell foul of the Action Française and finally came under the Papal ban. It still exists in much reduced form, and no longer bulks large in French life.—TRANSLATOR'S NOTE.

brilliant these Sorbonne fellows are! With what alertness, what sureness, they can marshal and illuminate the headings of a problem!"
His attitude towards such dexterity was one of respect, but also,
faintly, of mistrust. He almost found himself wondering whether
this theory—which, after all, he had been the first to formulate—
was really as right as all that.

His accurate mind found and voiced an objection:

"Don't let us forget Freemasonry."

"What about it?"

"Only that it bears a remarkable resemblance to a Church, and that,
according to some people, it was never in a more flourishing condition than during the period we are discussing."

Jerphanion had only the vaguest and most conventional ideas about
Freemasonry; ideas vaguer, indeed, than those with which Clanri-
card had been satisfied prior to his evening walk with Darnould and
Laulerque.

"Do you believe that?" he asked cautiously.

"Yes, I do."

"What about Sampeyre—is he a Mason?"

"No. At least I've been assured that he isn't."

For a moment Jerphanion hesitated over his next question. But in
matters of this kind he was not particularly shy, and scruples of
politeness almost always, with him, yielded to the demands of curiosity. He therefore added:

"What about you?"

"No, I'm not, either."

Clanricard flushed slightly and hurried on:

"But the fact that Sampeyre is not a Mason proves nothing about
the general tendencies of his generation. Many others of his age are
not only Masons, but active Masons, and they seem to have found in
Masonry exactly what you were talking about—a 'Church.'"

Jerphanion appeared to be plunged in reverie, a little bit put out,
perhaps, by the flaws which this objection had caused to appear in
the fine new symmetry of his argument.

Meanwhile the chill which was spreading upwards from the black and white tiling of the floor became more and more perceptible. The winter, held at bay by the warm and smoke-filled atmosphere of the bar, was making its way in by the circuitous route of the ground, catching the feet and ankles as in a trap. The vitality of the brain, its quickness in the discovery of fresh arguments, was not immune from this onset of cold. "That everlasting bad circulation of mine," thought the young man. "A lot of good I get from coming of mountain stock." Still intent on repairing the damage done to the fine edifice of his argument, he began to move his toes about irritably in his shoes in an effort to get warm.

But Clanricard had a kind heart and was too keenly conscious of the pleasure of finding himself in agreement with this brilliant friend to mind sacrificing some of his advantage.

"I must admit," he said, "that I have heard people use, in discussing Freemasonry, exactly the same word which you found just now to express your sense of the generation to which Sampeyre belongs. The word I mean is 'anti-Church,' and it is used in the connexion, as no doubt you understand, in order to stress the fact that the main object of Masonry, at least at one period, was to support the struggle against what is usually meant by 'the Church.' . . . If you've never come across this particular use of the phrase, the coincidence is all the more remarkable."

Jerphanion was conscious of a slight sense of relief. But though he was willing enough to be deceived by a symmetrical arrangement of ideas, he was not so easily taken in by words. He was perfectly well aware that Clanricard's concession did not really contradict his former objection. He tried, however, to consolidate the advantage he had gained.

"You must at least admit this, that even when they formed themselves into a clearly defined and permanent party, they were driven to find the reason for their association, its moving spirit, in some sort of opposition to another party that was both older and more extensive. What held their Church together was the hatred of another

Church, of the most powerful of all Churches. It seems to me that, regarded in that light, their anti-clericalism takes on a new and profounder significance. It ceases to be something merely temporary. Don't you think so?"

Clanricard made no direct reply to the question.

"I'll say this much," he ventured, with an air of rather shamefaced confidence, "that—well, take Sampeyre, for instance; he's the most tolerant of men; in his lectures he used to go out of his way to be fair, as a historian, to Catholicism. All the same, when we're having one of our serious discussions at his house, he'll now and again slip in a malicious little aside at the expense of the Church. We juniors laugh just to please him; but that means nothing; we don't really understand what he's after. . . ."

They agreed that on this point and on many others there was a considerable difference, and much ground of mutual misunderstanding, between their generation and its immediate predecessor. Jerphanion, in particular, maintained that in many respects this generation of elders was bankrupt. It had succeeded in constructing nothing positive, had bequeathed to the young no heritage of any value. It had left them without a pilot. Among those who were middle-aged now, some —the most sincere—had abandoned the struggle, from a sense of disgust. One must admit, whether one liked it or not, that they were failures. Others, less pure in intention, had become mere placehunters. It was men like that who were the pontiffs of the modern world. No matter where one looked, in every department of public life, it was the old or the middle-aged, lazy and gorged with success, who were in control. They lived by outworn formulas, and carried a responsibility of which they were not even fully aware. Not content with being deaf to the aspirations of a new age, they were heading straight for some sort of violent upheaval. And it was the young who would suffer the destructive effects of this inevitable catastrophe, the young, who could do nothing to divert it or to lessen the force of its impact.

Clanricard supported his friend's indictment, warmly at first, but later with reservations. He set himself to examine his conscience. Perhaps there was no great harm in blackguarding a whole generation like this, but one ought to be careful about being unfair to individuals. It is so fatally easy to let oneself go. Hadn't Jerphanion's violence of condemnation sprung from some passing remark of his own about his old master?

He continued, almost defensively:

"I oughtn't to have spoken as I did about Sampeyre before you've had a chance of judging him for yourself. I blame myself for letting you get such a bad impression of him. You must realize that at bottom he's the purest of pure democrats. When you go into his study, the first things you see are portraits of Michelet and Hugo. No one is more vividly aware than he of the vices of our present social order. But that they exist is due, according to him, precisely to the fact that society today is only partially democratic, that it carries within itself the legacy of the ages of oppression. In a real democracy he would be perfectly at home, nor does he think that such a state is impossible of realization. All it needs is a little goodwill. He doesn't suffer as we do from a sense of the disproportion between this enormous society and the individual. He doesn't feel what I tried to express—so unsuccessfully—in my little bit of an article: this excess of space, of empty space, in which each one of us moves, this—this aimlessness. Surely what is tormenting us is just this feeling that we are wandering vaguely in a huge mass of humanity, that we are lost in it. We are too far from the shore. For him, on the contrary, and for the men of his generation, that was what was meant by liberty, the free movement of human beings. Perhaps it is we who are deficient in strength and courage. The men of his generation, and of those that went before, had courage. Only think of what they achieved."

Jerphanion seemed to be surprised. He tried to remember what it was that these men had achieved. "The Third Republic?" he thought, but found it difficult to be enthusiastic about the past of the Third Republic. He saw nothing but a long perspective of top-hats and frock-coats and paunches; of the triumphs of bad oratory, of party

15

bargainings that hadn't aspired even to the dirty distinction of intrigues; of bourgeois cunning. There had been no planning on a grand scale, no real dangers overcome.

He said aloud:

"Are you really so much impressed by what they have done?"

"I'm thinking of the separation of Church and State, and, earlier still, of the Dreyfus affair. If you want to go still further back, what about the struggle with Boulanger, the consolidation and organization of the Republic? What about compulsory education?"

Jerphanion suppressed a smile and looked at his neighbour out of the corner of his eye. He was amazed at Clanricard's seriousness, at his solemn mention of these matters, as though there was something magnificent about them. He was, however, sufficiently honest to say to himself: "It may be that I'm not sufficiently aware of tradition, that I'm out of touch with the world of yesterday. Perhaps there are living waters of enthusiasm at which others, brought up under influences of which I know nothing, slake their thirst."

"Oh, quite," he said; "but it doesn't seem to me that there was anything very heroic about it."

"It's easy for us to say that," Clanricard observed quietly; "but don't imagine for a moment that those things just happened."

"Oh, quite," said Jerphanion again.

But his thought had lost definiteness. He plunged into reverie. He felt lost.

Chapter

3

REVOLUTION: THE SUPREME NECESSITY

Suddenly, without his being consciously aware of the connexion, the drift of their discussion and the atmosphere of the restaurant combined to recall to his mind the meeting in the rue Foyatier, the smoke, the babble of talk, the voice of Jaurès.

"I was just thinking of Jaurès," he said. "I've never met your master Sampeyre, and I've only the most passing acquaintance with Jaurès, but wouldn't you say that he, too, was a pure democrat in the sense that you used the word?"

"I think so, yes. As a matter of fact, Sampeyre and Jaurès used to be friends—still are."

"Nevertheless, Sampeyre has never become a member of his party?"

"No. . . . He has watched the growth of the Socialist Party from the beginning, and its increasing strength has been a matter of pleasure to him."

"But he has done no more than watch?"

"He probably argued that they had no active need of him, that any service of which he was capable could best be rendered if he remained free."

"That's as may be. I'm beginning more or less to understand Sampeyre. But I'm not so clear about your case, which I find much more interesting. You have just proved to me that the influence of your master has not stood in the way of your having your own view of things, of your feeling certain misgivings, formulating certain demands, which are foreign to the outlook of his contemporaries. You're not going to try to persuade me that if you've held aloof from the party, it's entirely because of Sampeyre?"

Clanricard had a moment of acute distress. It seemed to him that he must appear guilty of hypocrisy, almost of bad faith. Since the beginning of the present interview he had desired above all things to be worthy of the confidence of this bearded student with the frank and open face. He had swept aside all purely personal considerations of caution. His hesitations, his qualifications, had been entirely due to motives of disinterested honesty. He was not conscious of having allowed himself to be influenced by any selfish motives.

He pulled himself together, urged his brain to still greater efforts —if such were possible—of clarity and truth, and said in a sudden burst of confidence:

"I know that you must think me inconsistent—yes, inconsistent. . . . There was a time, some years ago, when I could have joined, when I ought to have joined, the party. I was in the right mood, and you're perfectly correct in assuming that it wasn't Sampeyre who stood in the way. But with me there has always been a big step between feeling that I ought to do a thing and doing it. I know perfectly well that I lack energy. In many respects I'm one of those people who only half wish things."

There was something appealing in this confession and in Clanricard's expression as he made it. "Could I," thought Jerphanion, "speak of myself with such frank humility?" He hastened to interrupt the other.

"But surely that's so with all of us, at times. . . ."

"Not with you, I think. You give such an impression of energy, of being quite sure of what you want."

"No one is energetic all the time, except brutes or madmen. If I were really what you think me, I should have joined the party weeks ago; there was one evening in particular when I definitely decided to take the plunge. . . . But it's you we're talking about."

"Well, a few years ago I *ought* to have joined. Things are different now."

"You have lost your faith?"

"In Socialism generally? . . . Probably no. But the question has become more complicated. I've come to see the emergence of new tendencies. You see, the group which centres in Sampeyre is a concentration of various attitudes, a point of meeting, in an atmosphere of extreme intimacy. The people who frequent his house are people who know each other very well; but it's the exact opposite of a clique. We know that he himself is completely independent, that he will listen to anything, that he holds himself accountable to nobody, with the result that friends who might otherwise avoid one another, or who, elsewhere, might hesitate to talk with perfect sincerity, are delighted to get together under his roof. Everybody is free to say exactly what he thinks. In other circles, even in the most advanced, there is a tone to be observed. One keeps a watch on oneself and tries to avoid heresy. Every group has its own idea of orthodoxy, and the nature of the orthodoxy changes with the group. . . . It's really rather funny, when you come to think of it."

(Jerphanion was conscious suddenly of a series of pictures conjured up before his mind's eye. He saw men debating in dim-lit rooms, holding forth, dominating the company: schoolmasters of the Revolution, quick to frown in disapproval, ready with bad marks for the vagaries of free opinion, doling out the small change of authority, excommunicating one another at long range; bores, all of them, and as empty as Honoré at one of his Sorbonne lectures—less informed too, if it came to that. He pondered his own ignorance of politics. How little, up to now, he had suspected the existence of these petty, self-sufficient worlds!)

Clanricard went on:

"I'm not the kind of man who is always persuaded by the speaker who has been last on his feet, but one can't help seeing that on certain points the Socialist doctrine has been left behind. I'm not sure that 'left behind' goes quite far enough. To hear some of the younger, more live men of the vanguard, one would think that the official program of the party is already a matter of history, and that even in questions of pure tactics, of revolutionary action, the future will have to take a line of its own. I don't deny that some of those who criticize the party most harshly, who represent tendencies that are quite irreconcilable with its theories, still call themselves Socialists; they don't much mind what they call themselves—nor that the party, afraid of being left in the ditch along with the respected parliamentary institutions of the Republic, tries to hang on to their coat-tails, going out of its way to be polite to them and sweating blood in an attempt to prove that everything can be comfortably arranged, and that they are really its own darling sons. But no one who listens as I do, no one who doesn't wilfully blind himself, can help having doubts and feeling a bit discouraged. If I became a member of the party now, it wouldn't, you see, be any longer on a wave of enthusiasm. It would be a cold-blooded, reasonable, disillusioned sort of business, like regularizing an old liaison because one's got nothing better to hope for. But God knows I yield to no one in my personal admiration of Jaurès!"

Jerphanion was still all attention, but it was about himself that he was thinking. His sense of humiliation had grown until it was almost bitter. "So this is what comes of all my boasted shrewdness! We agreed that Jallez should take the lead in matters of literature and modern art, but in politics it was to be I who held the lantern, I who was to have the last word. I can just see him laugh! Why, he'd know at once that I was out of my depth, that I didn't know what the fellow's talking about. Although it's annoying to feel that I'm a baby in arms compared to Jallez when it's a matter of discussing Moréas or Mallarmé, I'm ready to accept my inferiority. But to be beaten by this shy suburban schoolmaster, and on my own ground! The calm way in which he tells me that the Socialist Party, which, up to an hour ago, I had always thought of as the spearhead of revolution, is nothing, for those really in the know, but a decent old bundle of respectability suitable for a steady young man with a career to make, a safe, academic, carpet-slipper affair! And it's not that he's trying to make an effect; I don't believe for a moment that it's a pose. If only I had a clear idea what these new tendencies are which he talks about. But I can't very well ask him; I should look such a fool! Besides, it would be a fine advertisement for the College, wouldn't it? Is it really my fate to be one of those fellows whom Jallez is so scornful of, whom I'm so scornful of, full of second-hand knowledge, and when it's out of date?—the sort of fellow who's always thinking, and getting excited, about the day before yesterday. Perish the thought! What was that he said to me once about the stars?—'I don't want to dream about the stars like a young woman in a novel by Francis Jammes.' It would be far more stupid for me, because my ignorance wouldn't have the saving grace of fragrance."

But Clanricard, whose desire to think straight and communicate his thoughts increased with achievement, added in a lower voice:

"It's not only that there's been an evolution of theory; it's I who demand more. What is membership in a party? It's no more than going into a mill. One's bound to it by what? By having a card in one's pocket, and one's name on a list. All parties are very much alike. They take your subscription, and what do you get for it?—a candidate to vote for at the elections. I don't think one's going to get cured of solitude that way."

"I agree. It's exactly what I've been thinking lately."

"I want to receive, and, still more, I want to give. I suppose you'll say that there doesn't exist a Church for a man like me. Perhaps you're right. I'll bury myself in my work. I've found comfort in the children before now; they warm my spirit. You quoted a phrase from my article in this connexion which seemed to you to be true. As for the rest, well, I'd rather stick to my democratic liberty and make the most of that gift of the times. I'll try to capture Sampeyre's secret and use it for my own ends."

"Awhile back," thought Jerphanion, "he seemed to me a decent enough chap, but not quite up to his writing. Little by little he's drawn level with it, quite unconsciously. He's really fine; I wasn't wrong about him." And he breathed a prayer of gratitude to the vague divinity who, in such various ways, presides over the friendships of mankind.

Clanricard was once more the prey of scruples:

"You'll say," he observed, with an air of contrition, "that this is all very egotistic, and I suppose you're right. I'm only thinking about the comfort of my own miserable little conscience."

"Isn't that what everyone thinks of who belongs to a Church?"

"More or less, but one ought also to be concerned about ends."

Clanricard seemed to be addressing a question to himself. He opened his eyes wider than ever. He was one of those men who, when they ask themselves questions, appear to seek the answer not by frowning their way into the recesses of their being, but by trying to focus it in the vibrations of the atmosphere around them.

"And in the matter of ends, too, one wonders whether there aren't matters of still greater urgency."

"Than what?"

"Than the economic reorganization of Society."

"Economic—and moral."

"Certainly—things which can't wait."

"I find it difficult to follow you there. . . . This reorganization is surely something that can't wait."

Jerphanion saw again in imagination the slum district he had visited, the street where the boy in the velveteen trousers had been squatting, the corner in which he had seen the half-starved titan.

"I can think of nothing more urgent than the need of getting some minimum of justice into this frightful state of chaos."

"Please understand me," Clanricard said earnestly; "I don't want to see this state of chaos, this reign of injustice, last one minute longer than is necessary. . . . But you yourself alluded just now to some catastrophe that threatens us. . . . Well, if you had a farm, I don't care in how bad a state, and you thought that somebody was setting fire to your barn, which necessity would seem to you the most urgent: to clean out the stable and improve your equipment or to run and see what was happening in the barn?"

Jerphanion listened with astonishment, with a curious sort of emotion. He was too much afraid of showing his surprise to ask at once what exactly the other meant, nor was he altogether displeased at the vague, half-solemn sense of apprehension which the schoolmaster's words caused him to feel.

Clanricard continued:

"I don't say that the party hasn't some intuition of the danger—Jaurès certainly has, a strong one. But while we wait for all the machinery of propaganda, of tactics, to get going, all the old business of precedence, the whole parliamentary ballyhoo—anything may happen."

He went on suddenly, as though he were following a new train of thought:

"This evening, as every Wednesday, I am going to a little meeting at Sampeyre's. I shall see my friends there; among others a certain Laulerque—the man, as a matter of fact, who suggested my title. . . ."

" 'We Are So Much Alone'?"

"Yes. A man of quite exceptional vitality, much better informed than I am, more inquisitive, bolder. I should like you to meet him. . . ."

"Nothing I should like better."

"I'll speak to him at the meeting—something might be arranged. Look here, if you're free, later on this evening, he and I could slip away about eleven and meet you somewhere. Tomorrow's Thursday. Neither he nor I mind a late night, but perhaps you—"

"No, I love going without sleep occasionally. I'll meet you wherever you like. I could go farther afield than you because I shall be free earlier."

"Really? So much the better, then; I'm willing. There are some things that Laulerque can explain much better than I can. He's got very clear ideas about the dangers that threaten us, about what he calls the hierarchy of ends. Anyway, he'll interest you."

They agreed to wait for each other, from eleven onwards, in a café on the Place Clichy.

On his way home Jerphanion walked briskly. He was pleased at the

solid way in which this new friendship had begun, at its promise for
the future, at the readiness it showed to throw out new shoots, pleased,
too, to feel in a budding intimacy that sense of haste which urges new
friends to see one another again as soon as possible, to put everything
else aside so that they may finish the uncompleted sentence, go on
with the interrupted discussion. In such a mood of impatience he
recognized some quality of generosity, of nobility, although the well-
known wariness of the mountaineer, for which Jallez was fond of
giving him ironic praise, sometimes counselled caution.

Chapter

IN THE COLLEGE DINING-HALL

The stewed beef lay like greasy slabs of dark-brown chocolate at the bottom of the plates. The meat and the sauce seemed to be two related states of the same substance, two stages in a progressive transformation. The shrivelled carrots looked like the bodies of dead birds. The smell was crudely pleasant. The three classes gathered round the tables would pay dear for being twenty and hungry. Their senses, long accustomed to such fare, had no illusions about the abuses to which they were to be submitted. They knew perfectly well that three minutes' beggarly pleasure would be paid for by two hours of sluggish digestion. But this bitter knowledge remained localized as far as possible, like bad news in a country ruled by a dictator. It was assumed that the digestive organs knew nothing about it, and the glands, obedient to the call of optimism, discharged their fine, vigorous juices, in an eager rivalry to accomplish the back-breaking task of assimilating the heavy brown sauce. Draughts came through every crack and cranny of the doors. The smell of cooking impregnated the chill of the atmosphere like a stain, without lessening it.

"Well, have you seen your schoolmaster?" Jallez asked.

"Yes."

"Was he there before you?"

"About two or three minutes. Why do you ask?"

"Oh, nothing. . . . What was your impression?"

"Good, on the whole."

"I'm not surprised. Did you recognize the author in the man?"

"Not at first, but little by little. I ended by completely identifying them."

"Well, then, you ought to be pleased, and so ought he. There must be in the world of schoolmasters certain habits of thought, certain fundamental conventions, references, which I know nothing about, but which you've probably inherited."

"Oh, not to that extent. You mean my upbringing—well, there may be something in that; and talks with my father? I don't see him very often, and he never says much except when he's gossiping. He never speaks openly to me, or before me, about his view of life. Besides, a man of my father's age, who took his diploma in a provincial city and has done all his teaching in villages and little market towns, doesn't really belong to the 'world of schoolmasters.' He remains a countryman, with the same interests as the local magistrate, the postmaster, the gamekeeper, the publican, and two or three local landowners who shoot their own coverts. The only difference is, perhaps, that he goes about with the more radical element. He belongs, let us say, to the definitely republican wing of the local middle class, to the party that doesn't include the clergyman. Any connexion he may have with the 'world of learning' is purely administrative and formal, a matter of promotion, of official circulars, of being bothered or not, as the case may be, by inspectors. For the younger generation, many of whom have been through the local training college, things are already a little different. I think that they do take back with them to the coldness of their mountain villages some recollection of their three years of warm comradeship. They keep the memory of some master of repute who influenced them, who interrupted his lessons to speak of contemporary affairs, who injected a little idealism and enthusiasm into the peasant brains that came to him for a sure job and a pension. Later on, when they meet one another on some examining body or at a club dinner, they don't forget those things. . . . But that's not the sort of life I knew with my father. I've only had glimpses of it at second hand—had whiffs of it, so to speak. And even that's pretty far removed from what I take to be Clanricard's background."

"Ah, so he has a definite background?"

"I should think so! And from what I've seen, I should say that it wasn't the general background of the Paris schoolmaster, but something much more privileged and exclusive."

"And, on the whole, sympathetic?"

"Certainly sympathetic, even exciting. I was going to say mysterious."

"Oh, mysterious; but you don't?"

"No."

Jallez showed more curiosity than he was willing to show. When he spoke, it was in the unexcited tone he knew so well how to assume:

"I must say, I should hardly have suspected mystery there."

Jerphanion avoided giving a direct answer. There was a hint of undisclosed riches in his silence; then:

"One gets the feeling," he said, "of being in touch with all sorts of things. Let me explain it this way: When you talk to me, even incidentally, of modern literature, I feel that you're in direct touch with what's going on, with the movements under the surface. You hint more than you say; I seem to hear overtones. You give off, as it were, an atmosphere in which an outsider like myself is a complete stranger, an atmosphere of meetings and talks, of the latest theories of the cafés. . . . You bring with you the mystery of strange countries which I shall never see except through the medium of your conversation, whose air I shall never breathe except in your descriptions. Well, imagine the same sort of thing, but set in a different world."

"What different world?"

"The world of politics and social problems, of groups, tendencies, and cliques. I get the impression that things are happening there, and I want to be in it."

Jerphanion gave himself a little private pat on the back. "I couldn't have made it clearer that compared with Clanricard I feel an outsider; but at the same time I've not lost too much prestige."

On the contrary, he maintained a fine sense of his own importance. He was like an explorer who has just found the way to a new continent and comes back with the news. There's considerable credit in merely being able to say: "There and there is unknown land." In the

same breath he establishes the existence of the unknown and reserves
it for his own further examination. It's to him that people will have
to refer for future details. So far from seeing his importance diminished by the fact of his present ignorance, he sees it increased by the
prospect of future discoveries.

What was troubling Jallez was a tiny attack of jealousy. No longer
would he be the only one to introduce Jerphanion to mysteries. His
friend's intellectual thirst would find other means of assuaging itself.

He asked with an assumption of indifference:

"When are you going to see him again?"

Jerphanion was surprised by the question. He felt suddenly ashamed
of his anxiety to see Clanricard again so quickly. It seemed to him to
involve a lack of reticence, to be an act of disloyalty to Jallez. He got
himself out of the difficulty with a lie:

"Oh, one of these days; I said I'd write."

5

JERPHANION DISCOVERS LAULERQUE

This time Jerphanion arrived too early. Across the vast spaces of the café, touched already by the first onset of emptiness, and apparently dominated by the watchful gaze of a dozen or so streetwalkers, he saw advancing towards him three people whose appearance, in such a place, had all the charm of the unexpected.

To right and to left walked two thin, serious-looking young men; between them, a young woman, smiling, sensitive, attractive. The young man to the left was Clanricard. His companion on the right, slightly shorter, had an alert, quick, almost nervous expression, and a face that was almost completely devoid of colour. Eyeglasses, balanced precariously on his nose, gave the impression of being some sort of mechanism designed for the rapid reception of messages. As he moved, his body, perhaps accidentally, had the appearance of being slightly twisted. The nearer they came, the prettier the young woman seemed to be. The three of them advanced through the midnight emptiness of the café at a devious and uncertain pace, ignoring, with an air of preoccupation, the disappointed glances of the prostitutes. Suddenly they saw Jerphanion and, making straight for him, surrounded his table.

"Let me introduce my friend Laulerque. . . . I may say that he didn't need much persuading. He was very anxious to meet you. Our friend Mademoiselle Mathilde Cazalis suggested that she should join us. She too is deeply interested in all these questions."

"I think too," added Laulerque, with a mischievous smile, "that she was moved by curiosity to meet a student of the central Training College."

The student of the central Training College was conscious of an agreeable sensation, although the serious part of his nature was vaguely disquieted. "She'll hamper our discussion and confuse my thoughts." He was a man who liked to devote himself entirely to one thing at a time, and tonight he was concerned with problems entirely different from those offered by two charming eyes and a pair of full, fresh lips. "Is it likely," he thought, "that she can be interested in all these questions, with a face like that?"

"From what Clanricard tells me," said Laulerque, "you've had a narrow escape. . . . You were within an ace of being swallowed up by the party."

"Would that have been so very serious?"

"No, it wouldn't have been serious at all, and that's the trouble. You would simply have gone to swell the ranks of an army the whole point of which is that it has been enlisted not to fight. And that being so, why join it? I don't imagine that you're ambitious for the sword of Monsieur Prudhomme or the uniform of the National Guard?"

"You're very hard on it."

"Hard? Not at all. As a matter of fact, I'm very kind. Monsieur Prudhomme never hurt a soul. Marxian Socialism, on the other hand, is criminal. Its self-appointed task is to brutalize the masses, to drug them for the shambles. But I won't elaborate the argument, out of deference to Clanricard and this lady here, who have heard it all before; besides, a man like you can see the point at once. What was it that persuaded you to join the party? The itch to do something, I suppose, the desire to serve. You have energy and enthusiasm—at least I presume so—and you believe in a goal. . . . The point is, what goal?"

Jerphanion was slightly nonplussed by this directness. He saw in the soft, moist eyes of Mathilde Cazalis a look of amused curiosity. Clearly she was wondering how he would react. She sat with her chin resting on her hand. She seemed to be offering him her mouth as something calm but desirable.

Laulerque was insistent:

"What *is* your idea of the goal?"

Jerphanion forced himself to make a deliberate answer.

"I believe that the goal is a complete change, as soon as possible, in the whole structure of Society; a change sufficiently radical to put an end to injustices which are no longer to be borne, and to absurdities which are an outrage to the intelligence—injustices and absurdities from the results of which Society itself is the first to suffer, and which, if they are not mended, will end in complete destruction and chaos."

"Right. For simplicity's sake, let's say that the goal is revolution."

"If you like to put it that way."

"Do you think that the Socialist Party is in a position to bring about this revolution within the next two or three years?"

"Unless it is helped by exceptional circumstances, no, certainly not —the time is too short. Besides, speaking personally, I should prefer an evolution, provided it is quick, to a revolution of the old type."

"Excellent! . . . Well, now, do you think that the Socialist Party is capable of preventing a European war from breaking out in the near future?"

Laulerque's questions followed one another with changes of subject as rapid as a boxer's openings. "I mustn't look too big a fool," thought Jerphanion.

"Yes," he replied, "I think it could do a good deal. But I must admit that I sometimes wonder whether a war is quite so pressing a danger as all that."

He noticed that Laulerque's eyes were bright, that he was blinking rapidly, drumming on the table with his fingers. He hastily added:

"Last year I did think it was pressing. I don't say that the danger has altogether vanished, but I have a feeling that nobody wants to be the first to begin—that, fundamentally, no government wants war; also, possibly, that from the material point of view no government is in a position to make war."

"It's more or less Sampeyre's opinion," Clanricard said quietly.

"Your illusions do you honour, my dear sir," Laulerque remarked.

"War, however, will break out within two or three years, unless something is done quickly to stop it; that's the first point. The second point is that the Socialist International (I'm not talking only of the French branch) is entirely incapable of preventing it."

Jerphanion would have liked to find an answer, if only not to disappoint Mathilde, whose raised eyebrows, pouting lips, and appealing eyes proclaimed a mood of painful expectation. But the only arguments which occurred to him on the spur of the moment were lacking in both force and relevance. Laulerque's self-confidence would have been entirely untouched by them. He preferred, therefore, to assume the expression of a man who is accustomed to weigh his words before speaking.

Laulerque continued:

"I needn't prove to you that with the prospect of a world war in two or three years—for it will be a world war; you have no illusions on that score?—everything else, your grand transformation of Society, becomes a pleasant little pastime. It's as though a man condemned to death should consult a doctor about his liver—unless, of course, you believe in the intervention of the Socialists, the workers, the social-democrats, and the rest of those placid gentlemen who fish in the waters of politics? If you do, I should like you to have heard the confidences which a certain Robert Michels, leader of the German revolutionary party, made us one evening. What do you say, Clanricard?"

"I must admit," Clanricard remarked, "that he wasn't very encouraging."

"Still," Jerphanion said after a pause, "you won't deny that here, in France, a man like Jaurès is fully conscious of the danger to which you refer. . . . You listened to your German; I listened to Jaurès, a year ago, not far from this very spot. No one could hold it against him that he doesn't keep his party, and the proletariat generally, keyed up to the danger of war: it's his chief preoccupation."

"True enough; Jaurès certainly isn't blind. He believes too much in the spread of reason, in parliamentary action, in the pressure that can be exerted by the masses, and relies too confidently on his preaching of the gospel in the market-place. All the same, it won't be his fault if the proletariat of Europe lets itself be dragged to disaster with its eyes shut. Unfortunately, the most he can do is to save the face of French Socialism."

"But if you don't believe in all that, what do you believe in?"

"I?—oh, perhaps in nothing; nothing that we can do."

"Come, my dear fellow," Clanricard protested, "you're contradicting yourself. I've heard you say a hundred times that there's always something we can do."

"Until the moment of the 17th Brumaire!" threw in Mathilde Cazalis, laughing.

Jerphanion was pleased to note in her voice a trace of the Southern intonation, which is so much fuller and warmer than that of the North, seeming to find delight in the feel of syllables, like a cat rubbing itself against the furniture. Although he did not regard himself as a Southerner, the recognition gave him, vaguely, a sense of being related to her and of having a particular claim on her.

Laulerque's expression, indeed, was far from confirming his words. For a man who no longer believed in anything, his eyes shone too brightly.

"I don't want to go into a lot of things which Clanricard and this lady are sick of hearing," he said in a bored tone.

After this preliminary disclaimer he proceeded, rather against his better judgment, to trace the course of his familiar theories. It was well that Jerphanion should realize the precise nature of his quarrel with the "philosophy of history," of his objection to the theory of historical fatalism and the slow, deceptive working of general tendencies; that he should understand his belief in free will and the initiative of the individual, his confidence in the power of a few to achieve results by means of secrecy and concerted action. But because he really did dislike repeating himself, he made a point of summarizing his arguments and retouching some of his formulas. In particular, he invented, on the spur of the moment, a neat little antithesis between "novelists' history" and "platform history."

"People are so sick of hearing about the power of individuals to determine history that they think of it now as something unreal, childish, a story-teller's dream. 'Oh, yes,' they say, 'that's how a novelist thinks of history!' What they want is the history of the public speaker, so they've had it till their digestions can't stand any more. Public speakers take naturally to that sort of thing. 'The inevitable march of time'—why, the words say themselves. There you have a ready-made phrase only waiting to be spoken. A period of history becomes at once a period of oratory—no wonder the words are the same! But the truth of history, the reality of history, isn't made for the platform; it has to be tracked and followed into too many corners and backwaters. It can't be reconstructed by a trick."

The student of the central Training College appreciated at its full value this symmetry of thought, which, as a matter of fact, had been carefully prepared for his benefit. But he did not make the mistake of snapping at the bait, of seizing on the words as an excuse for argument. It was clear that Laulerque had allowed himself the indulgence of an incidental embellishment, the flash of a momentary illumination. Perhaps he wanted to show that even an elementary teacher could have his moments of brilliance. But there was nothing about him of that foolish complacency which is the victim of its own eloquence and sacrifices the truth of an argument to felicities of phrase. On the contrary, he was obviously in the throes of a burning sincerity, obsessed by a great idea. If his eloquence was a shade too studied, it was probably because he wanted to tone down the violence of his thought, to give himself time to discover some formula simple enough and suggestive enough to capture the attention of his hearer.

Jerphanion was less sensitive than Jallez to the quality of those he was with. He couldn't, however, help realizing that he was in the presence of a quite unusual personality. He even admitted to himself that he had never met anyone quite like him. How find words for his impression? Clearly the man was a fanatic. There was in his greygreen eyes the sort of bright glitter that one would have expected to see had they been black, but of a quality that was reminiscent of

certain chemical substances. His skin was colourless, his mouth firmly
marked. A nervous tic seemed to keep his face in a state of perpetual
movement, twitching, quivering, so that the whole man gave a curious
impression of being continually alive. A fanatic chock-full of intelligence, not at all the crude visionary. But how reconcile the intelligence
with the fanaticism? . . . Obviously, by recognizing behind the
intelligence the presence of great will-power, of some directing force
which was never out of control, which continually issued its orders—
"You understand what to do? Well, do it."

Laulerque continued to develop his theory, interspersing the explanation with occasional sallies. He proclaimed the virtue of individual action directly applied, showing how events could be sharply
influenced, ridden on the curb, jerked out of their course. He described
the way in which it was possible to intervene in the development of a
situation with a stroke carefully timed and carefully placed, how an
act of free will could be forced like a tool between the joints of a
resistant material, how the application of quite a small amount of pressure, provided the point of attack be shrewdly chosen, though it may
show to the eye no more than the tiny spot of blood produced by a
needle-prick, will nevertheless exert a power out of all proportion to
its apparent strength.

"Is it all just fine words, belated romanticism?" Jerphanion asked
himself, but it was merely out of deference to his conscience that he
put the question. Listening to Laulerque it was not of fine phrases
that he was chiefly aware, but rather of a method of intellectual approach, of a certain precision and lucidity of mind, of a freedom from
all moral scruple which constituted in itself a sort of innocence. It
was as though he were watching a surgeon at work. "A new terror-
ism?" He conjured up before his mind's eye the figure of Robespierre,
partly because it is natural for a Frenchman to think of Robespierre
when he hears talk about dedicating to the service of humanity resolution undeterred by pity, and cruelty unsullied by personal desires,
partly because Laulerque's face reminded him of that spareness, that
purity of line, which makes so memorable the head of the lawyer

of Arras. But a fanatic like Robespierre moves in a world of abstractions, dreaming of a Supreme Being, of the happiness of France, of a righteous system of law and justice. Such a man averts his eyes that he may not see the bloodshed he has caused. His very crimes have about them something of theory. They are not deliberately willed as crimes. He deceives himself into believing that they follow inevitably from the principles which dictate his actions. He gives the necessary orders, but claims no merit for the deed, he holds himself to be nothing but the instrument of necessity. In a dry and academic speech he demands the heads of fifty victims without so much as looking at the Assembly which trembles at his words. What holds his gaze is a ghostly vision, an allegory of virtue, projected upon the wall before him, colourless, generalized, saved from insipidity only by the horror of its implications. A tyrant of this type, moving in its cloud of murdered witnesses, is apt to be a bore. Laulerque's method was different. It breathed an atmosphere of sharp reality and was based upon an acute awareness of people and circumstances. It was nothing if not individual. It carried with it—and to that extent was indeed romantic—a sense of adventure, a suggestion of plots, of bombs secreted beneath special trains, of five quick shots from an automatic, of sudden volleys in a palace corridor, of motor-cars leaping forward beneath a hail of police bullets. It offered the prospect of clandestine meetings, of journeys at daybreak, of cross-country flights, perhaps of beautiful plotters with mouths like Mathilde's, of parting kisses and whispered words—"Promise me that you will not die." It held the key of a world of youth, rich in violence and stratagems, of Stendhal's world adorned with the emblems of a vanished past: a dagger driven into a back from behind a lifted curtain, a tiny flask emptied quickly by ringed hands into a ruby goblet. Its general effect was to evoke less the public and headlong violence of the Revolution than the subtly contrived crimes of the Renaissance. It was full of a sort of fierce love of life.

"The kind of thing," thought Jerphanion, "to turn the head of a pretty woman." From time to time he stole a glance at Mathilde, only to see that she was not trembling, that she gave no sign of being excited, but smiled with an air of indulgence. Occasionally she looked at him as much as to say: "You mustn't mind him; he's like that."

Again the thought came to Jerphanion: "And a man like that is a Paris schoolmaster! Perhaps this very afternoon he was teaching the metric system and giving twenty lines to some brat for confusing the linear with the cubic metre. So much for those who say that routine destroys the soul! Well, that's a comforting thought!"

Chapter

6

A TOPSYTURVY WORLD

Laulerque was speaking now of secret societies.

For over a year, he said, he had been going deeply into the question, and was more than ever convinced that they held the clue of history. The disguises which they adopted were so various that it was sometimes difficult to recognize the essential identity of aim beneath them. The Church itself, though to the man in the street it seemed to be all open and above-board, was composed of a whole series of secret societies. The history of the Middle Ages was the history of the various Orders, religious and knightly. The history of the Renaissance was the history of parties and factions which spread their tentacles over Europe. The most active of them had kept alive the classic ideal of freedom of thought, the tradition of pagan naturalism, the Greek cult of reason and the individual. Within the frontiers of different countries they had contented themselves with pursuing limited and local objectives, assuming whatever disguises might be dictated by circumstances, but what united them all was the common ideal of overthrowing the temporal and spiritual despotism of the Roman Church. And how had the Church defended itself? By producing within its own body a new crop of secret societies, the old ones having, in course of time, lost both their vigour and their character of secrecy. Of this new crop the most important was the Jesuits. It was impossible to understand the history of monarchical Europe before the Revolution unless one viewed it from the centre of that formidable spider's web which had been created by the Society of Jesus. Even the Revolution itself could only be fully explained in the light of the preparatory work undertaken by the secret societies which had inherited the ideals of the Renaissance. Growing progressively bolder in their views, they had, for more than a century, deliberately set before themselves the violent destruction of the old world as soon as the opportunity presented itself, and the creation, from its ruins, of a new order of Society.

"Remember that formula which the initiates so constantly used to keep their determination fresh and vigorous: 'Tyranny must perish!' Remember those mysterious passwords which were circulated from one end of Europe to another and tacked on to the ends of letters filled with the innocent gossip of literary and social cliques, like the countersign which sentries repeat to one another to keep themselves awake. Have you ever asked yourself how, unless France had been prepared and ready mined, the explosion of the 14th of July could have been produced so swiftly and with such shattering effect? By what miracle that same 14th of July could have produced, within forty-eight hours, the first signs of similar explosions at different points all over the continent? Why it was that the armies of the Revolution were so warmly welcomed beyond the frontiers until the day when they were guilty of the crowning foolishness of trying to force on others their new discovery of loyalty to the tricolour, which had formed no part of the original plan? Even that piece of idiocy and breach of confidence couldn't destroy at once the results of the plan, a state of affairs which long benefited Napoleon. The situation was ambiguous, and he decided that it should remain so. In every town he conquered he found people who insisted on believing that the good work was going forward. 'The method,' they said to themselves, 'seems odd, but the work goes on. This fine fellow in top-boots has come to strike the final blow. He is the representative of the Revolution.' And indeed, at first, he regarded himself as a representative and drew his strength from that fact. But he soon betrayed his charge, becoming absorbed in trivial ambitions, seeking to provide for his family, to get himself accepted in the faubourg Saint-Germain of monarchist Europe, to marry, with all the pomp of organs and cathedral chimes, a titled little goose."

It was not the first time that Clanricard had heard these particular variations of Laulerque's theory, but they fitted so well into his present preoccupations, gave his mind so precisely the food it needed, that he willingly listened to them again. He was anxious, also, to see how Jerphanion would react to them. It is always pleasant to verify in a stranger the power of ideas with which one has become too familiar to judge of impartially. It was Jerphanion, however, who got the most lively and least qualified pleasure from Laulerque's words. Not that his reason didn't find objections at every turn; still, he felt in no hurry to give them utterance, preferring to enjoy at his ease the pleasure which comes from a new point of view provoking echoes in one's own mind, searching out the turns and twists of one's inner self, awaking old memories, reviving dead or slumbering thoughts. Pleasure of this kind has something in common with the sap that rises in a tree, giving life and energy. It warms the spirit, and brings once again into contact whole areas of our mind which have lost the habit of communication, so that they accept naturally, and with delight, an excuse for renewed co-operation, irrespective of the value of what promotes the movement. Time enough later to be critical, and to shatter this new, this delicious but fragile confection.

Though, therefore, for the sake of appearances, Jerphanion made an occasional interruption, he surrendered himself, without too acute a feeling of guilt, to the delight of seeing the world in a new way, controlled and manipulated by secret societies, a world in which events are ordered over immense distances along hidden threads of communication woven and plaited, attached and tangled in a web of delicious intricacy. History, until then nothing but an official façade shoddily whitewashed by the eloquence of many generations of professors, became suddenly a subject of passionate interest, something to dream about. The student, newly enfranchised, found that this history was a land in which he would never tire of wandering, dark lantern in hand, a world of secret passages, of staircases built in the thickness of walls, of false partitions responding to a spring, of trapdoors and cellars, subterranean shafts, and twisting tunnels. Everything about it was matter of surprise, adventure, thrills, and delight; a little childish, perhaps, but saved from futility by a profound sense of the ideal. These shadowy schemings which would do nothing more than provoke a smile if they were designed only, as in old-fashioned novelettes, to culminate in the marriage of a charming princess or the punishment of a traitor, became somehow the tortured birth-pangs of a new world, the struggle of Man through the ages to escape from the darkness of his prison.

But suddenly Jerphanion became once more aware that he was sitting in a huge, half-empty café on the Place Clichy, exposed to the glances of wandering night-birds and the eddying whispers of the street; that he and his companions were no more than four moderns lost in the Paris of 1910, elements in the brightly lit civilization of an age of machines and universal suffrage. How was it possible to imagine that such a rootless, superficial, obvious world could hide an undercurrent of intrigue? What room, in such conditions, could there be for grand and secret schemes? Had one, even, any certainty that its inhabitants dreamed, in their hearts, of any future goal? The ideals of such a world were no more than official programs stuck here and there on walls by permission of the police. Who would take the trouble to plan, like criminals, the details of great days to come? The only effect of such dreams as Laulerque's words evoked was to breed a sense of impotence and despair. The phrase "We Are So Much Alone" ran in letters of fire about the furniture, like the flickering sentences of a night sign.

Something that Jerphanion said gave the measure of his thoughts. Clanricard agreed with a nod of his head and a widening of his eyes. Mathilde reflected that men could find ways of tormenting themselves which women, similarly educated, would never dream of, or, if they did, would take in their stride. "They always seem," she thought, "to be carrying the weight of the whole world. Women are more modest. They only bother about the problems that touch them closely, and there is no lack of those. As soon as their emotions are involved, the affairs of the world seem nothing but shadows." She refused to have an opinion—or, rather, her mind oscillated between two opinions. At one moment it seemed to her that in such matters men were all rather simple, all more or less megalomaniacs, without the common sense of women, since they were not so conscious of their limitations; at another she saw in their attitude a proof that the masculine intellect was ruled by a certain nobility of outlook. Man was, as he had always been, the protector, ever on the watch for danger while the women and children led their lives of trivial care within the tents.

Even Laulerque began by agreeing. Like everybody else, he liked to think badly of the times in which he lived; but, he asserted, whatever else the present lacked, it certainly was not a great and urgent task.

"Urgent, yes," Jerphanion agreed, "great, yes—nobody sees that more clearly than I do—but not so urgent, all the same, as that which lay before the men of '89. The extent of the work which they had set themselves to do, the determination necessary to carry it out, was indeed staggering. If there was a conspiracy, as you say there was, then surely never have conspirators had a nobler aim to fire them, to keep them tense and purposeful through long years of waiting."

Often had Jerphanion clenched his teeth with enthusiasm at the thought of all the great changes that were waiting to be made in the modern world, but thinking of them now, he found them trivial in comparison with the great movement of that earlier day. He envied the men who had been alive in that century, not so much those who had made the revolution as those who had known the long fervour of faith and preparation.

"I don't agree with you," said Laulerque. "Obviously it's difficult to compare the two things, but we too have an old world to destroy, a new world to make, a world that needs principally to be rescued from two tyrannies which were almost unknown before, two tyrannies which have come into being since that last emancipation: militarism and capitalism. And there's another point: Those others you were talking of had time to play with; time was on their side. Each year their chances grew better, and the power of resistance of their enemy diminished. The enemy didn't even put up a fight. It was as though he became gradually hypnotized, waiting for the blow to fall. Events gathered speed of their own accord. That's not so now. Time works against us. A disaster is approaching to smash us and all our plans. If we don't succeed in stopping a world war within the next two or three years, everything we have done so far goes for nothing, and humanity will be forced once more on to its knees. That's the long and short of it. Before we can begin thinking of anything else, we've got to stop something terrific from happening. And what resources have we got for such a task? None of any weight compared with what's got to be stopped. We've got to act with unbelievable precision and speed.

"You've heard those stories in which a hunter suddenly sees a six-foot bear coming at him and realizes that he's only got one cartridge left. A few ounces with which to floor hundreds of pounds. If he waits a second too long, or if his aim is a hair's breadth out, he's a dead man. A dramatic situation, you'll admit, and enough to keep any number of conspirators tense and purposeful. Well, if there was, at this moment, any secret society worthy of the name, that would be its job."

Thereupon, as a result of something said by Laulerque, they began to talk of Freemasonry. But, to Clanricard's surprise, Laulerque, with a tolerant air, said:

"When all's said and done, if I were in your place, that's where I should look."

"But why not in your own?"

"Oh—chiefly because I'm headstrong. Besides, I've already flirted with Rothweil and given him the slip. It would bore me to begin again. . . . But I'm told that there are new and rejuvenating elements at work among the Masons. It's the only international body, except the Church, which has a chance of doing anything secretly. So far as concerns the dangers we were discussing, it's just possible that Masonry might be able to do something—it's just possible that it's actually doing something already. I don't know Monsieur Jerphanion well enough to advise him, but if you're asking for yourself, well,

I'll just tell you something that Darnould said the other day. . . . What's to prevent your knowing the truth about it? Go and have a word with Rothweil or Liguevin—Rothweil for preference. No one's got a right to complain of his isolation if he makes no effort to get out of it."

He glanced round the café, which, after filling up when the theatres finished, was once more empty. Three or four women still occupied the most prominent seats—not that they hoped for anything, but, obeying a sort of instinct, hoping to cheat fate by drinking this cup of ill-luck to the dregs.

Laulerque took out his watch, gave a little whistle as if he'd only just realized how late it was, and said casually:

"I think we might declare the meeting closed."

They went towards the door. A few flakes of snow, very hard and very small, were beginning to eddy in the raw air.

Laulerque said to Clanricard:

"Will you see Mathilde Cazalis home? I'm going to walk a little way with Monsieur Jerphanion. Good night, both of you."

Chapter

7

LAULERQUE'S GREAT SECRET

"Won't they think we've abandoned them a little soon?"

"Not a bit of it. Clanricard will be delighted at being left alone with his little Cazalis."

"They're on good terms?"

"On exceedingly good terms."

A moment later Laulerque qualified his words:

"Don't think I mean more than I do. She's a sensible young woman, and I'm pretty certain there's nothing definite between them. Perhaps one day they'll get married; meanwhile they seem to like being together. She's willing enough to accept admiration from anyone, but she likes it best from Clanricard; that's all."

Although he assured himself that it was no business of his, Jerphanion was glad to know that there was "nothing definite" between Clanricard and Mathilde.

Laulerque went on:

"She's pretty, don't you think? And there's nothing of the schoolmarm about her."

"She's a teacher?"

"Yes; she takes the infant class in the little Lycée Condorcet. It suits her very well. She likes to think that she holds advanced views, but at close quarters the Montmartre urchins smell a bit. So she spends her time telling fairy-stories to the children of the middle classes and thinking about the poor."

He broke off for a moment; then:

"I have an idea that if Clanricard doesn't hurry up, she'll slip between his fingers. Without noticing it, she'll grow accustomed to a different atmosphere, and then she'll meet some neat little professor with just enough Socialist leanings to quiet her conscience."

Jerphanion reflected that, leaving Mathilde Cazalis entirely out of the question, he really took too little trouble about his own appearance. Why should advanced views be incompatible with a certain quiet elegance? The two things combined might even breed a new harmony, an original sort of reputation. What a surprise young Bernard de Saint-Papoul would get, all the Saint-Papouls, including Jeanne, if, one of these days, they should see a new Jerphanion sit down to dinner with them, a Jerphanion whose tie, the cut of whose jacket, the smallest detail of whose get-up, should be a lesson in good taste, a discreet comment on the latest variations of fashion.

"Not that it would worry me," said Laulerque; "I'm inclined to think it's a mistake to expect too great a degree of heroism in women. . . . Where are we? I can perfectly well come as far as the Boulevards with you. Walking home doesn't bother me, and I don't care what time I get to bed. I'd like to have a little private talk with you. Clanricard's an excellent sort of chap, a lot above the average; still, there are things I'd rather not discuss with him. I've known him for years, and I've known you for exactly one evening, but that's got nothing to do with it. . . . You wonder whether I meant what I said when I advised him to try his luck with the Masons? You were a bit surprised?—Well, and why not? He's probably told you one or two things I've said about Masonry which didn't sound as though I was particularly enthusiastic? I've not changed my opinion, but I should like to qualify it. When all's said, one's got no right to condemn an institution like that except from the inside. Have you got any views about it?"

"None at all."

"It irritates me not to know more about it. I sometimes say to myself: 'After all, these brethren of the Three-Pointed Star did found the Third Republic, and got it out of more than one difficulty. All the things that we've seen gradually realized in the Constitution were all, twenty, fifty years ago, items on the agenda of their lodges. It's not altogether absurd, therefore, to assume that they look ahead, and it seems likely that a good many of their ideas coincide with mine.' Of course, I might join them and back out later, but the part of a renegade is not one that I like playing. I'm not by nature a turn-coat."

Laulerque looked at Jerphanion out of the corner of his eye as he walked, as though he were still waiting for his opinion.

"I don't say anything," Jerphanion remarked, "because, as a matter of fact, I've nothing to say. I don't mind admitting that I've thought more about Freemasonry this evening than I've ever done in my life."

"You don't know any Masons?"

"I probably do, without realizing it."

"Is there nothing of the sort at the College, no proselytizing?"

"I don't think so, I've never heard any talk about it. . . . You'll probably think me ridiculously simple. Naturally, like everybody else, I've read various attacks on Freemasonry, but of the fanci-ful kind. I used to think of it as a kind of bogy man to frighten Church people with—the sort of thing they liked to blame for bad dividends or a rainy summer. I put it in the same category with other figures of conventional villainy like priests and Jews. . . . I knew that it carried with it certain benefits, and had an idea that in certain professions one got on quicker if one was a Mason, but apart from that. . . . So, you see, I was a bit surprised when I found out the importance that you and your friends seem to attach to it."

"I'm afraid that some of their reasons won't bear looking into . . . but, yes, on the whole, we do give a good deal of thought to it. I can easily see Clanricard as a Mason. I think it would give him stability, and since a good many of their members must be adventurers or people on the look-out for nice little jobs under the government, they'd get their money's worth out of an enthusiastic and disinterested recruit like him. You're not tempted yourself?"

"Not in the least. Perhaps I'm absurdly prejudiced, but I can't help thinking of the whole thing as rather a joke."

(Jerphanion thought of Jallez's amazement if he heard that his study-companion was preparing to undergo Masonic initiation.)

Laulerque made no reply. They reached the Place de la Trinité and crossed it in silence. The snow, as thin and hard as ever, was swirling more thickly, but the stinging sensation of the dry little particles as they struck the faces of the walkers was not unpleasant. In all the whole extent of the square there were only two other wayfarers besides Jerphanion and Laulerque, widely separated and walking quickly. A cab was coming out of the rue de Châteaudun. Half the lamps had been extinguished, but the emptiness was faintly luminous, and the sleeping city seemed vaguely watchful. The suspended life of the neighbourhood gave no sense of peace, nor was its emptiness a genuine solitude. The feeling of being near the heart of a great city was persistent. The two men, walking slowly, could talk as intimately as they liked, but always with the consciousness of possible eavesdroppers. They were careful to modulate their voices, as they would not have been at the same hour in the rue de la Villette or in the neighbourhood of one of the central railway stations. When they approached a particularly dark or hidden doorway, when they passed a row of railings, a line of trees, they let their words die away, or left a sentence uncompleted. At the corners of streets they looked automatically to the left and right.

As they reached the chaussée d'Antin, Laulerque seemed to hesitate. He scrutinized the perspective of the street. It appeared to be almost completely empty, except for a couple of policemen patrolling the crossing by the rue de Provence. The ground floor of the houses made a band of darkness broken by many little irregularities.

"Oh! . . ." Laulerque muttered, as though he had just made a decision. "Yes . . ." and he made as though to go down the street, keeping carefully to the middle of the roadway.

"Are you afraid of being attacked?" Jerphanion asked. (Jallez had told him that it was always safer in suspicious neighbourhoods to keep to the middle of the road.)

"Oh no, not a bit; besides, there are two of us. . . . No. . . ."

He spoke with an absent-minded air, as though he were pursuing some train of thought. Then, lowering his voice to a whisper:

"Look here, I had the most extraordinary adventure the other day. I've not told a soul; you're the first person I've mentioned it to. I'd gone to—well, to a large bookshop belonging to a publisher of editions of the classics. I wanted to get a specimen copy of a book that they don't give away very freely. The clerk seemed uncertain, asked my name, and went to consult his chief. When he came back he said: 'Mr. So-and-so would like a word with you.' I was taken to a small office, where I found a middle-aged gentleman whose face was vaguely familiar. He waited until we were alone. 'You're the same Monsieur Laulerque whom I met at Monsieur Sampeyre's?—Yes, that's where it was; you recognize me?' Then he added rather oddly: 'I should like to have a talk with you. Might I come and see you some day soon, or would you rather come and see me?' I live in a pretty untidy sort of attic, so I said I could easily go to him. We fixed a day and I went. It was one evening last week. He received me in an elegant little flat, very nicely furnished, where he seemed to live alone. We talked. There were a lot of door-hangings and double curtains and thick fabrics. The whole place was soft and padded, so that our voices were as much deadened as though we had been packed in cotton-wool. He said that he'd heard me elaborating my views at Sampeyre's, that I naturally hadn't noticed him because I was very much excited, that he'd been exceedingly impressed and was interested in me. In proof of what he told me, he repeated one or two very acute observations he had made about my appearance, extraordinarily acute. Then, after a lot of verbal precautions, which I spare you, he said suddenly: 'I heard you say, sir, that you wished there existed a secret society "worthy of the name" ' (it's a phrase, as a matter of fact, I often use), 'working for the realization of certain ideals more or less identical with those you yourself set store by. You said that if such a society existed, you would make it your first duty to become a member; isn't that so? Well, it does exist. Its ideals are such as you described, and it has a very good chance of realizing them. Will you join it?' Well, you agree that was pretty staggering?"

"It certainly was. What sort of a fellow was he?"

"Rather nondescript, but certainly not the clerk type. There was an appearance of energy about him; he might have been an army officer. I answered as you would probably have done, that naturally I was interested, but that I couldn't say yes, even in principle, on the spur of the moment; that I must first know the precise objects of the society, its organization, the kind of people its members were, and be given some idea of what it had already done. He answered, perfectly calmly, that it was a rule of his society that new members should know only the person who introduced them. I opened my eyes a little at that and should probably have laughed if I hadn't been influenced by the quietness of his tone. He seemed to think it all as natural as teaching me the rules of a card game. He added that it was all a matter of individual confidence: that there was a noviciate of as long a period as one liked, during which the new recruit could study his introducer and be studied in turn. 'I'm prepared,' he said, 'to give you all the information you like to ask about myself.' Later the new member might be introduced to other members, even to the leaders, as circumstances might require; but, generally speaking, he would remain ignorant of the organization as a whole, of its real centre, its methods, and of the people who composed it. 'But in that case,' said I, 'members might meet one another in the ordinary course of their lives without knowing it? Isn't there some sign of mutual recognition?' 'No general sign,' he answered, 'but if, in the execution of some special task, it seems desirable that two or more members should know one another, they are given the means of doing so. It's all a question of convenience.' While he spoke, he took down several pamphlets from a shelf and laid them before me. The biggest of them was a Doctoral thesis in Science, dealing with some very obscure point in physics. There were also some off-prints bound in different coloured papers and two or three numbers of the *Revue Rose* with a cross in blue pencil on the Contents page. I didn't quite grasp what he was after. 'These,' he said, 'are a few of my works. If things had gone a bit differently, I should probably have been, at this moment, a professor at the Sorbonne. Not that I'm not very well off as I am; I'm freer.' 'Assume for a moment,' I said, 'that I took you at your word and was tempted to become a member; still, I don't like the idea of being made to do things blindly. I like to know what I'm doing, perhaps even to discuss my actions.' He gave me a little smile. 'To discuss? I understood you to say that you were fed up with all these parties which do nothing but discuss and chatter. I thought you wanted people who could make decisions and act. . . . Do you think, my dear sir, that action is possible unless certain orders are given silently and executed without discussion? What matters is being in agreement about the ends to be pursued.'

" 'Well, leaving that side of it for the moment, what sort of instructions should I receive?' 'The sort that you would like to carry out. Please realize that we take the likes and dislikes of each individual into consideration; we're not such fools as to make our members act against their inclinations. You, for example, have holiday periods each year, fairly numerous, fixed, and reasonably long. You might like to have some little mission abroad.' 'What kind of a mission?' 'Sometimes no more than to get in contact with somebody, to give him a letter or an oral report, and to bring back his answer. Should the need arise for some—some rather cruder and less intelligent instrument, well, we try to find one.' He added: 'I should make it clear at once that the rule among us, from highest to lowest, is complete disinterestedness. All expenses are paid, but it is understood that our work is done by people to whom there can attach no suspicion of personal interest, whose sole inspiration is devotion to a common cause. In certain circumstances we have to make use of people who will only work for money. In that case we pay them, but they are in no way part of the organization. They are our paid servants, and we employ them as little as possible.' At this point in the conversation I remarked that I had only the foggiest idea of what this common cause was. He answered me with a smile: 'It's the same as yours, my dear sir, the same as yours. That's another of our rules.

We avoid, as far as we can, approaching people whom it's necessary to convert. That's not our object. What we try to do is to find and bring together a little body of men who have developed, independently, certain definite views.' I was no further than when I started, but there was no way of getting him to explain himself in greater detail that evening. Nevertheless, the thing obsessed me to such a degree that I paid him another visit three days later. I hadn't even contemplated any final decision, but there were a few questions I wanted to ask him."

"I should think so!" said Jerphanion.

"Naturally, eh?" and Laulerque laughed gaily. "But before I go on, tell me what questions you would have asked him. I should be interested to know."

"First of all there's one I should have asked myself, concerning certain impressions which would have embarrassed me from the start."

"What impressions?"

"I can speak frankly?—I mean, you've not committed yourself?"

"Good Lord, no, I'm not such a fool. Go on."

"Well, in the first place, this employee in a bookshop, this sort of floorwalker, who is the agent, the important agent, the recruiting sergeant, of a powerful secret society—I don't know—but doesn't it all seem rather bogus?"

"You haven't met the fellow. More important still, you haven't met him in his own flat. That makes a difference."

". . . Then the artlessness of the whole business, the absence of the most elementary precautions. He didn't give you many details, I agree, but he told you the main idea. What is there to stop your going straight to the police? All they'd have to do would be to have him watched and shadowed, and they'd very soon find out who his colleagues were. One thing would lead to another, and they'd be at the centre of the organization in next to no time."

"Go on, go on."

"I don't know, but somehow the whole thing seems to me to be unconvincing."

"Then you'd be inclined to say straight off that it was all a hoax?"

"Not quite that, perhaps, but I should argue like this: Here's a decent, rather crack-brained fellow who finds life a bit flat and the routine of an office too drab, so he invents a little story. Perhaps he's managed to interest three or four other eccentrics in it too. Or else—"

"Go on, go on."

"Or else, taking a more serious view, I might ask myself whether, in fact, the whole thing wasn't simply an organization of espionage in the service of some foreign power."

"Oh, come!"

"That hadn't occurred to you?"

"No, I confess it hadn't; to a certain extent, as a matter of principle. Once one begins dreaming of espionage, one's like a jealous husband who gets a fixed idea that his wife is deceiving him. From that moment the least thing breeds suspicion. I've only got to read an article by Jaurès in favour of peace to imagine that Jaurès is in the pay of Germany. In the same way I might argue that Gurau's syndicalist campaign in the *Sanction* is being subsidized by Germany, or that he edged his way into the last Ministry for the sole purpose of watching German interests. I might say that Sampeyre is supplementing an insufficient pension with funds from the same quarter . . . certainly I might . . . and that he's been commissioned to establish a revolutionary cell in the teaching profession. Oh, once one starts that sort of thing—!"

"You can't deny that spies, and espionage services, with all their ramifications, do exist? Just because suspicion sometimes runs to ridiculous extremes, one can't say that it's never justified. . . ."

"True enough, but in that case the objection you made a moment ago, and which I confess I had made myself, argues against you. If my man is an espionage agent, he ran just as much risk as in the other case, by telling me what he did."

"But with this difference, that he made a false trail for the police. That's enough about that, though. What were your questions?"

"For the most part, the same as yours. I tried to make him understand, as politely as I could, that it gives one a bit of a shock to find a revolutionary organization, with a program of direct action, turning up in the disguise of a white-collar worker. He wasn't the least put out, but agreed that it was a most improbable business. 'But all the better,' he added, 'because another of our rules is to enlist our members, as far as possible, from among people whose appearance and social standing give no rise to suspicion. It is a source of great strength to us. We should be fools to look for followers among professional agitators and social outcasts. Folk like that, with no visible means of support, are just the sort that the police keep an eye on. Sooner or later they'd be bound to come under observation, even if they didn't anticipate the authorities by offering themselves as informers.' That was my opportunity. 'Talking of the police,' I said, 'your recruiting methods don't seem to me to be very prudent. For all you know, I might be the kind of chap who'd go and unbosom himself to the first cop he met.' He smiled. 'You argue badly, my dear sir, because it's you and not anybody else I'm talking to. But let us assume, for the sake of argument, that you do give me away. What then? What sort of proof have you?' He made a gesture towards his office files. 'Let them search as much as they like, open my letters, inquire into my affairs; I've nothing to fear. How are you to know that I haven't good friends at police headquarters who would throw information of that kind into the waste-paper-basket along with the dozens of letters they get every day from madmen or people with persecution mania? How do you know that I haven't ways of making practical jokers of that kind sorry that they tried it?' His tone altered; he looked me straight in the eyes. 'We're not talking about somebody else,' he said, 'we're talking about you. I may have been mistaken in thinking that you were ready to put your ideas into practice. Your appetite may be stronger than your stomach, but I'm quite certain of one thing, that when you leave this house you'd rather throw yourself in front of a train than give me away. Why? Because you know that I'm a man who is working for an ideal; you're convinced of that. Even if you don't want to work with me, even if you disapprove of me, still you respect me. Do you expect me to believe that a man like you, who'd hesitate about handing over a murderer to the police, would give me away? . . . Not a bit of it.'"

Laulerque stopped speaking and came to a standstill in the middle of the pavement beneath a lamp-post of the avenue de l'Opéra, whither their absent-minded wanderings had brought them. "You know," he said with sudden earnestness, "when he spoke like that there was something fine about him. I forgot all about the office worker. The effect was extraordinary."

But Jerphanion, with a young man's mania for discussion, retorted: "Still, it didn't prevent your telling me all about it this evening, and, for all you know, *I* might be a dirty little sneak."

Laulerque gave a start.

"Well, but even if you were, I've kept back certain details. . . . Besides, if you're the first person I've mentioned this to, it's because I, in my turn, am sure of you. . . . You see, I fall back on his argument. Fundamentally that idea of his is perfectly sound: it's fine and exciting and based on something that goes pretty deep into human nature, the idea that a chain of mutual confidence and loyalty can be built up link by link. Sceptics will tell you that you ought never to trust anyone, that you never know enough about your oldest friend, about your wife or your son, to be certain that they won't betray you. They're right, because that's exactly what does happen to them, and they deserve it. But don't you feel that nothing in the world could make you give this man away whom you've never even seen? Speaking for myself, I really believe that if you made use of what I've told you to set the police on his tracks, I should hunt you out and strangle you, just to avenge myself; no, not myself, but the idea of the loyalty that one man owes another. I'm not sure, but I believe I should."

They started walking again. Laulerque was in a mood of exaltation, which, owing to their continued precaution of keeping their
voices low, manifested itself almost entirely in his face. Jerphanion,
too, found the idea a fine one. In this deserted avenue they had established, the two of them, a law of honour for the whole species.
The light falling upon them from the high, nimbus-crowned lamps
gave to their testimony an air of undisputed solemnity. In future
years, when the disappointments of life might shake their faith in
human nature, they would see again in imagination, perhaps with a
shock of surprise, two long lines of street-lamps above a vista of
empty pavements and find in the memory a sense of comfort which
they might find it difficult to explain.

"But," said Jerphanion, "didn't you try to get more details about
the objects of this society? All that part of it has seemed to me, so
far, to be a bit vague."

"Yes, I did try, but he doled the explanation out to me drop by
drop. I gathered that in the beginning their organization, which
seems to be a fairly recent affair, had wide and rather abstract ideals,
with a general tendency towards the transformation, the unification,
of the human race—I'm making myself clear?—and especially the
unification of the white peoples. From the beginning they have
avoided democratic methods, although their intention has been the
greatest good of the greatest number. They have never believed in
the ability of the masses to realize their vague hopes of betterment.
They think, for instance, that Socialism may serve to keep alive an
attitude of readiness, of preparation, among the working population and, more generally, in society as a whole, but that, by itself,
and in the form of demagogic and parliamentary action which it
has everywhere adopted, it is incapable of leading to anything definite,
quite apart from the fact that its economic doctrine is in many ways
narrow and impracticable."

"More or less," Jerphanion interrupted, trying to avoid making his
words sound ungracious, "the same ideas you were expounding this
evening at the café?"

"Yes, but please don't think me a parrot. Never having been at our meetings at Sampeyre's, you may find the coincidence rather suspicious. But Clanricard will tell you that I've said all that, over and over again, for a long time past; it's one of my hobby-horses. But listen to what I'm going to tell you. They too are convinced, it appears, or have recently become convinced, that their more general schemes must be subordinated to the more urgent necessity of the immediate future—namely, the imperative duty of preventing a European war. Information which they have received from their members in the various countries—some of them in pretty high-up positions—makes them think that such a war will break out, at the latest, in two or three years, unless drastic measures are taken to stop it. (I confess that it was from him I got the idea of two or three years which I mentioned awhile back; personally, I should have put it at a bit longer.) Briefly, I take it that their immediate object is this: to prevent war by the use of the secret and direct means which I have already spoken of."

Jerphanion shook his head.

"I'm not quite clear . . ."

"Ah? Well, let me say this, that I've got a feeling that in addition to these—these special methods, they reserve to themselves the right to act also in a more roundabout, a less violent way, by using any means that may come to hand. He asked me whether I was a member of the Socialist Party or a Mason. I asked whether that would prevent my joining. 'Not at all,' he said, 'provided that loyalty to us takes precedence of any other loyalty, and that membership in any other organization is understood to be justified only if it is of benefit to the cause.' Well, there's nothing particularly stupid about that, is there? I confess that his words set my imagination working. Suppose Clanricard becomes a Mason, as he wants to do, that you overcome our various objections and indulge your whim of joining the Socialist Party, that I, because I'm more headlong than either of you, let myself become a member of their mysterious society. . . . Well, we could still remain in touch with one another, could exchange views and help to circulate certain slogans from one group to another. . . ."

Jerphanion thought: "Our friend's taking the bit between his teeth!"

Aloud he said:

"You forget that each of us will be only a tiny cog in these various organizations."

Laulerque, absorbed in his thoughts, did not hear. His face was twitching, he sniffed the air.

Jerphanion added, with a suspicion of friendly irony:

"Of all us three, it's you, I think, who are most anxious to take the plunge. Am I not right? It won't be long before your recruiting sergeant sees you again."

Chapter

8

A NIGHT WALK

Now Jerphanion was alone. Laulerque, as though a prey to sudden fatigue, had refused to go farther than the middle of the Pont des Arts. For a few moments they had leaned on the balustrade, watching the river. The flickering but fixed reflections, the calm depths, the abiding surface flowing between the ancient buildings of Paris, reminded them of the things that are changeless, of the long legacies of peace, of the strength of that royal indifference which the passing moment is powerless to disturb. "Life," it seemed to say, "is not only impatience and the violent frenzy of disaster."

Then Laulerque had said: "As soon as I've anything more to tell you, one way or the other, I'll drop you a line"—and they had parted.

Jerphanion knew that he was too excited to sleep before morning. He would lie awake listening to the sounds of the dormitory beneath the half-walls of the cubicles.

It would be better to continue his walk through Paris, to let his heart beat an accompaniment to his steps along the streets. Paris at night is the friend of lonely men, sympathetic to confidences, surprised at nothing. Its breezes make reply, its foggy vistas, lit by scattered lamps, whisper: "No one understands as I do; no one can keep a secret better. All thoughts are safe with me."

Never had Jerphanion felt himself less threatened by melancholy or boredom. His heart beat to a rhythm which was like the march-step of a patrol taking up its position for a raid at dawn. At each moment a fresh train of thought fanned his interest to a transient state of white-hot fervour. Intelligence illuminated his being, just as on a night of summer storms the lightning stabs and bites and pierces the darkness in every quarter of the heavens. Stupidity was far from him, and age.

The mood he felt, however, was far from being one of comfort. He was excited, irritated. Perhaps the chief cause of his suffering came from his having to admit the extreme complexity of a whole wide zone of reality into which he had really penetrated for the first time, which hitherto he had imagined to be pleasantly simple. This feeling was all the stronger since, as a rule, he liked simplicity. It satisfied the virility of his nature and the peasant element in his heritage, giving him the sense he needed of form in his thinking. But not being a fool, he refused to pretend that it was present when it was not.

How obvious everything had seemed when he had wandered through those appalling slums! The evil had been plain for all to see; the knowledge of what *ought* to be done had stood out so clearly illuminated by the radiance of his anger. The only problem then had been how to transform an outburst of emotion into the planned development of intention.

To see things at close quarters is to run a grave risk. No wonder that many people shut their eyes the nearer they get, and allow themselves to dream at the very moment when it is most necessary for them to see clearly.

No longer could he feel himself in the atmosphere of romantic charm which, an hour before, had been conjured up by Laulerque's words. He had lost the sense of that neatly ordered, topsyturvy world in which secret societies were like so many mole-runs, so many labyrinths of busy insects, through which the planned determination of a few minds burrowed with such marvellous rapidity. In such a world the liberty of man took its revenge on fate, building a body politic in which cause and effect escaped from the dismal law of necessity and everything was possible.

Why had the charm dissolved? Because now the time had come to look more closely at the details. Here, before him, was the entrance to one of the mole-runs, the starting-point of one of the labyrinths. Into one of these holes he would have to creep, and the only guide through these mysteries was to be the departmental manager of a business house! He tried to tell himself that actuality is always like that—unattractive, improbable, more or less absurd. (If chance had provided some other approach to the mysteries—Freemasonry, for example—wouldn't it have seemed just as improbable, just as absurd?) In any case, imagination had received a douche of cold water.

What ought he to think of Laulerque?

He was exciting; he was bursting with vitality. But it was not vitality that Jerphanion needed so much as clear guidance. He was like a traveller walking briskly towards an unknown country, but worried by the idea that he may be on the wrong road.

Was Laulerque the sort of man to rely on for guidance? He was neither ignorant nor a fool. There was no reason to suspect his honesty. In certain circumstances he might be ready to hold human life cheap, but the impression he gave was of a man with a high standard of morality. He might be a fanatic, but one couldn't just dismiss him as a visionary. His eyes were bright with enthusiasm, but they were also shrewd. For want of a better term he might be called a visionary realist, which was almost the same thing as calling him an adventurer, in the best sense of the word. Yes, he had the temperament of an adventurer.

Was he simple? One can't be an adventurer without a certain admixture of simplicity. "But perhaps," thought Jerphanion, "it's cheek on my part to think of simplicity in connexion with Laulerque. He knows by experience a lot of things which I take at second hand. Many ideas which are only just dawning in my mind he has already got beyond. It would be truer to say a constant freshness of outlook, a readiness to go off the deep end. Is his critical sense weak? Yes, there, I think, I've touched the spot. I can smell out the elementary teacher in him as I can in Clanricard, and it comes back to that. The difference between a man of his training and a man with a classical education, assuming the same social background for each, lies just there, in a less acute critical sense, which comes to the same thing as saying a lack of distinction."

Jerphanion saw again in imagination the face of Mathilde Cazalis, the expression of her eyes, the hint of kindly mockery in her smile. A woman, trained in the same school as these men, has probably no more critical sense than they have, but she has a natural fineness of apprehension, he thought, which takes its place, and for that reason she couldn't help seeing where a man like himself had the advantage of them. So much justice one must do to women. Their desire to improve themselves, even if it aims no higher than certain positive satisfactions of personal comfort, sharpens their sense of a natural hierarchy.

"There's no question of my trying to steal her away from Clanricard. That's the kind of thing I hate. There's something degrading in all this struggle of men to possess women, with its automatic technique. If a friend introduces me to the woman he loves, because he thinks her beautiful and desirable am I to fall in love with her as a matter of course? If I do it's no better than the reflex action of a frog. That sort of thing compromises the whole possibility of nobility and freedom in human relationships. It's as though Jallez had introduced me to his little Hélène and I had taken advantage of his absence to start serenading her. The idea makes me sick. Just imagine Jallez's face when he came back—for he'd see at once what had happened— the contempt with which he'd look at me. 'Ah, so that's the sort of man you are! I was mistaken in you.' Not that Clanricard is Jallez. He'd merely look miserable and hurt, and perhaps a little reproachful. 'I'm trying to put myself in your place,' his eyes would say as he looked at her; 'I know I don't deserve you, but I thought . . .'"

Whereupon, Jerphanion realized that even his scruples disguised an unpleasant self-satisfaction. "Enough of Mathilde Cazalis," he said to himself. "A fine sort of fellow I am, if the only result of a day like this is to fill my head with a lot of ridiculous nonsense about a pretty girl. I mustn't forget the two M's." (He alluded thus to a formula which he had recently adopted for his private use as a discipline to control his thoughts: *Memento magnitudinis,* "Be Mindful of Greatness." Sometimes he gave the phrase a Greek form: Μέμνησο μέγαν, which introduced again the two M's, and by its concision, combined with the uncommon language and the odd letters, gave it greater strength as a protection against worldly diversions and even against the ironic comments of his own intelligence. He had already proved the value of the formula. Applied at moments of unworthy thought, it roused him like cold water on the forehead.)

Once again the memory of the two M's brought him to his senses. Crossing the wide space at the end of the rue de Médicis, he said to himself: "Let me see precisely what point I've reached. Where did I start from? What was my point of origin? To determine that is one of the chief rules of life. There are certain days on which one realizes the truth for oneself with peculiar vividness, when, thanks to a moment of unusual clear-sightedness which is the outcome of a concentration of all one's faculties, one can see to the very end of the road one ought to tread. There are people who never forget such moments, who, in spite of temporary deviations, are never again at a loss for the true goal. What matters to them is starting right. They may oscillate, but it is always round a fixed axis. Strength of purpose like that is magnificent. They are the strong men. Others are sent wandering to left or right by the first accidental occurrence, are brought up short by the second, and lose their way. The zigzags of their course cross one another. Each casual happening sends them off on a new tack; each haphazard stopping-place is a new point of departure. Beware of the fate of the croquet ball! What, for me, was the true beginning? No need to split hairs; it was on that December afternoon when I walked through those appalling slums and 'felt' the fact of Revolution. That was the place and that was the incident. If I wanted to go further back still, I might place it on the occasion of a certain reverie on the College roof after Caulet had left me. But the axis is the same. It is well to realize that there are hours in one's life which, because of the enormous quantity of intellectual energy that they set free, are worth a whole train of years and have the right to determine those years to come, which, in fact, are their offspring.

"After that came Clanricard's article which Jallez showed me; my exchange of letters with Clanricard; then today. Have I lost my sense of direction? Is that initial drive still active, moulding events, forcing its way through them?"

Jerphanion had a feeling that he had strayed. From the idea of the necessity, the urgency, of Revolution, he had gone on to the quest of a "Church." Then had come the question, what Church? Ever since half past five he had been listening to talk about it. Alternately he had been advised and warned, had found himself repelled by this, attracted by that, and at each change of view he had wandered a little further from the true axis of his intention. He had let himself be amused, had been like a child listening to fairy-tales who cries: "More, more!" The question of joining the Socialist Party had been a step in the right direction, but how about Freemasonry? That had led him away at a considerable angle. Quite apart from the fact of his illogical prejudices, which, however ridiculous they might be, were not easy to overcome, it was as though he had been told that he had got to become a Mohammedan before he could go on, or accept the rite of circumcision. How about Laulerque's secret society? Even if it wasn't just a dream, it was no more than a by-road which would probably end in a wall.

"When one stands at what I call the *point of departure* of a certain line of action, one has a certain intuition of the immediate future. It may be worthless, but it is one's own, inseparable from one's determination to act in a certain way, and explaining it. What was it that I felt that afternoon? Was it the proximity of war, the tragic urgency of an attempt to prevent war? No, what I felt was 'Revolution,' there's no getting away from that."

The sound of his footsteps on the pavement of the rue Gay-Lussac was pleasant to him, and he took advantage of the happy lucidity of his mind to bring his ideas about war up to date. He still thought, as he had thought two hours ago, that the threat was not so close as some folk liked to imagine. It was quite likely that the various governments found it to their interest to play upon the fear of war, either to intimidate one another or to keep their various peoples in a state of obedience —a sort of year 1000. The terror of the year 1000, judiciously exploited, had not weakened the supremacy of the Church. The fear of war, by keeping the masses in a state of terrified anticipation, weakened their drive towards revolt. Besides, the armed preparedness which such a fear justified gave to governments the weapon they needed to over-awe an uprising.

What Jerphanion did not take into account was that his own fear of war had diminished in exact proportion as his memories of military service faded into the past. His hatred of militarism had lost its original fervour and had become merely a condemnation of the theory. He found himself now and then complacently entertaining thoughts which a little while ago he would have considered almost shameful. He found himself being pleasantly excited when he read in his newspaper that "our progress in aviation is advancing by giant strides," that the exploit of Latham, who, at Châlons, on the 7th of January, had risen to a height of three hundred feet, would cause consternation in the ranks of "our enemy of tomorrow," and that the army of "our Russian allies," which had been impaired in 1905, was once more a formidable weapon. A few days ago he had seen a battalion marching in service uniform down the boulevard Saint-Michel and had not been exempt from feeling, in common with the rest of the crowd, an agreeable tingling.

He went even further, for in his heart of hearts he sometimes wondered whether the lust of battle in a people isn't evidence of health and youth, which one should no more deplore than the lust of sex in individuals or the meat-eating tendencies of the human animal. The feelings which he had had this evening at the sight of Mathilde's limpid eyes and red lips had fitted, in an odd way, into these ideas of his. Jerphanion had not read much of Nietzsche, finding little to his taste in that author's angry emphasis which disguises so much pathological distress. But the fact remains that the voice of

Nietzsche sings from the grave a hymn to violence which the new century hears with too great a readiness, though each one of us pretends to take notice only of those tones in the singer's voice which flatter his own passions. Even the Revolutionaries, though they condemn war, admit the spirit of war to their dreams.

Jerphanion had never confided these transient feelings to Jallez, in the first place because they *were* transient and more or less involuntary, but secondly because he was afraid of Jallez's response. It was unlikely that he would be indignant; probable, even, that he would show every sign of understanding; but it was quite possible that they might, as a result, become ever so slightly estranged. There might come into his eyes a look which said: "If that's what you think, we no longer speak the same language. I don't think you're diseased, but, after all, each man has the microbes that suit him."

Jerphanion had reached the central corridor of the dormitory. He approached Jallez's cubicle. He longed to wake his friend, to tell him —what? Everything if he could, and if that were impossible, to set down for a moment at his side the heavy burden of anxiety which he had carried with him through the streets, as one camel might say to another: "Look what a load I've got, just feel it!"

In the darkness he looked at the curtain, at the half-partition. He tried to distinguish Jallez's breathing, but Jallez was one of those men who sleep inaudibly. His sleep was as little like that of an animal as sleep can be. He confessed that he dreamed a lot. Probably he was dreaming at this moment. Of what? Perhaps of things he had never spoken about.

Would he be angry at being waked? Possibly not, but there would be something his his look, something that said: "Was it really necessary?" and Jerphanion dreaded that sort of unspoken question.

But what he dreaded most of all was having to tell Jallez that in hiding from him the fact of tonight's meeting he had lied. That in fact he had lied he was willing to admit, since he could hardly do otherwise, but he was not proud of the fact. What he could not admit was the possibility of Jallez knowing it. And that feeling was more important than any other, because its effects would last longer. To-morrow morning Jallez would no longer be asleep. It would no longer be a question of waking him. But it would still be just as impossible as it was now to confess that he had lied to him. He would never be able to speak to Jallez of this evening that had been full and so disturbing, this evening that seemed made to be the subject of a long talk. Perhaps some day or other he might find a way of coming back to it. But "Meanwhile," he thought, "the punishment of a trivial sin is heavy."

Chapter

⑨

MEN ABOUT TOWN

For some moments Germaine Baader had been aware of a rubbing sensation that kept on being repeated down the whole length of her left leg. The contact would have been even more sensible had it not been deadened by the stuff of her dress. It was obvious that another leg was trying to stroke hers, and that the operation was being performed through the medium of a calf whose apparent thinness did not promise a high degree of attractiveness. Now and again a knee came into action, and occasionally even an ankle. The movement was a slow one, made without subtlety and apparently without hope, and might have been almost the result of a nervous tic. It had started suddenly. Germaine had been for a moment uncertain about its point of origin because her left-hand neighbour, Jacques Avoyer, had looked so innocent. The table was certainly narrow enough to have allowed Treilhard, who sat opposite, to reach her leg, but he would have had to be a remarkable acrobat to have produced that sensation of a contact alongside and parallel to her body. Besides, his whole attention was concentrated on talking. He interrupted a sentence with a splutter of laughter which disturbed the champagne standing in the glasses nearest to him with a fine spray. Avoyer nodded his head slowly. The stroking continued.

Treilhard was saying that he had it from the most reliable sources that the real reason for the delay in the production of *Chantecler,* about which all Paris was talking, lay in the fact that a new turn had developed in the course of the negotiations taking place between the Rostand family and two large hotels. Some months ago an agreement had been reached about the amount of the daily commission to be paid by the Majestic to the Rostands during their stay, but meanwhile a rival establishment had made a more attractive offer. Pressure, therefore, was being brought to bear on the Majestic to increase its figure.

"The management is jibbing on the ground that the Rostands have already given their word. It's even said that they've duly signed a form of receipt. The Rostands, in reply, say that they have no intention of repudiating their word, but that there's nothing to prevent them interrupting the rehearsals and going back to Cambo until spring. That would spell disaster for the hotel, because a whole crowd of Americans have taken rooms for a definite date and would be furious at any postponement."

The story was received with varying expressions of assent, though nobody went so far as to question its accuracy. In a party of this kind the truth of a statement is not of prime importance. The guests are there to tell what they know, and to hear what others know, about what is going on in Paris, regarding the little supper as a clearing-house of information even more than as an opportunity for entertainment. Such people impose upon themselves the periodic duty of bringing their knowledge up to date, less to gratify their own curiosity or sense of self-importance than to avoid the risk of being found wanting. Only so can they maintain their position and their reputation in a world upon which they depend utterly and in which a loss of prestige is quickly followed by serious material consequences. But the spirit in which information is received differs much from that of a learned assembly. It is true that statements are weighed and valued, but the weight attached to them has nothing to do with the degree of their authenticity. What is chiefly necessary is that they should have reference only to those occurrences most in the public eye, that they should be recognized as the current and fashionable view, but with the added attraction of being slightly original and highly spiced. If they repeat something already known it must only be in the sense of exaggerating it, and nothing is too improbable to be believed provided it is sufficiently "amusing."

Having established to her own satisfaction that the enterprising leg belonged to Avoyer, Germaine quickly withdrew her own. Avoyer, intent upon the business of nodding and perhaps victimized by the rhythm of his own movements, made no attempt to follow it, whereupon Germaine began to wonder how far concern for her own dignity, solicitude for her career, and the requirements of good manners would allow her to proceed with the withdrawal. She was, after all, the mistress of a Minister, so that even the necessity of extricating herself from the results of speculating in sugar (as a matter of fact, that little affair had all been satisfactorily settled) would no longer force her to tolerate the intimacies of a man like Riccoboni. But Avoyer, no matter how repulsive he might be—and in some ways he was more so than Riccoboni—was the dramatic critic of the *Sanction*, the friend, perhaps the instrument, of the oil-magnates, had a finger in several pies, and might be in a position to do her a good deal of damage. This little supper had been got up in her interest, largely by Avoyer's instrumentality. His influence might not be very great, but what there was he increased by giving it a wide field. Theatrical enterprises are fragile craft, and if he took it into his head to make some ill-natured comment about her to Henry Mareil, to Bérénine, to Marquis, or to M. Roger Sammécaud, the whole business might be wrecked. It wasn't worth taking such risks just to avoid an encroaching calf! Even Gurau, since he had become a Minister, was more careful than he used to be not to get on the wrong side of people, more concerned about the opinions of political nonentities. "The fellow may be a scoundrel, but I can't afford to be in his bad books!"—why, that was the sort of thing she heard now every day of her life.

She let her leg move once more towards the left, though not so far as it had been originally. This time it was only her knee that was really vulnerable, all else being withdrawn. Avoyer would understand that, though she did not resent his advances, she expected him to observe the normal reticences of polite society, and, in fact, he did content himself with pressing his knee against hers without attempting to caress it.

Henry Mareil was talking now. He was on Germaine's right, and shared the honours of a feast which had been organized as much for him as for her. He had an attractive, soft face, the only strong feature of which was the nose. His grey-green eyes were sensitive and slightly effeminate. He spoke deliberately in a quiet and kindly but rather weary voice. If anyone said anything while he was speaking, he gave way with a politeness which was a shade too excessive. He never laughed out loud, but frequently smiled. He made a point of looking people straight in the eyes, and it was while he was doing so that he most liked to smile, stressing, as it were, his affectionate concern, so that it was almost as though he said: "We were just made to understand each other."

"You know," he remarked in his quietest tones, and with a careful avoidance of that over-compassionate note which, in the circumstances, might have sounded ridiculous, "Rostand is really a tragic figure. He is a man of great talent who has been acclaimed as a man of genius. Not being a fool, he realizes the mistake. Since *Cyrano,* but especially since *L'Aiglon,* his life's really not been worth living. He says to himself: 'Somebody will notice; it's bound to come out.' Over-zealous friends would have us believe that he's in the position of a man who, having produced a series of astounding masterpieces, is now engaged in the impossible task of trying to do better than his best. But—" the quiet kindliness in Mareil's voice became more noticeable—"is that the sort of thing that happened to Hugo or to Wagner? No; what happened in their case was that one fine day they just *did* better their best. One wrote the *Légende des siècles* and the other *Tristan,* without making any fuss about it, simply because they both of them had stuff inside them that hadn't yet come out. Getting rid of it didn't make them ill; on the contrary, it eased them. Do you know that two or three years ago Rostand was within measurable distance of madness? Not the madness of megalomania, but the madness of a man who is frightened out of his wits, of a man who can't go on functioning. For months together he did nothing but roll on the ground, on the carpets, on sofas. . . ." Mareil's voice, as he described the scene, took on its silkiest quality. "There were terrible fits of sobbing," he went on, "and a complete refusal even to hear *Chantecler* mentioned. And then, suddenly, one day in came Madame Rostand with the manuscript rolled up in her hand, as an executioner might have come into the torture chamber carrying some familiar implement. Her wretched husband's cries were heart-rending: he literally howled for mercy. Just imagine the scene. . . . But in the end he took the manuscript. There he lay, face downwards on the sofa, mouthing the speech he had left half-finished. All the part of the play he had so far done seemed to him to be absolutely worthless. And nothing would come. For two hours, three hours, he lay like that, crying and longing to die. He buried his head in the cushions and tore at the stuff with his teeth. Finally the doctors got angry and insisted that his wife leave him in peace."

The company was listening with the most flattering signs of attention. Not a touch was missed, not an inflexion of the voice. Mareil was pleased at his success, the extent of which was made obvious by the few seconds' silence which fell on the table as he finished speaking.

"Still, he must have got better," Sammécaud shyly observed, "because one hears that the play is actually finished."

He was sitting at the end of the oval table, to Germaine's right, and with Mareil and Marquis on either side of him. He had himself insisted on occupying this retired position, though the company had been loudly informed, as they took their places, that everything was to be quite informal, except that Germaine would be asked to sit in the middle. Treilhard put himself opposite her, and the seat at her immediate right was naturally reserved for Mareil, who was the male guest of the evening. The other place of honour, to Treilhard's right, had been given to Mareil's mistress of the moment,

Suzanne Vignard, known as Suzette Vignal on the stage, where she exercised her limited talents in comedy parts. Avoyer had managed to worm his way into the chair at Germaine's immediate left, and Bérénine was at the opposite end of the table. There was a pleasant air of the casual about the whole arrangement.

Sammécaud's contributions to the conversation were few and cautious. He kept his eyes constantly fixed on Germaine.

"Yes," Mareil replied, "they say it's finished, and of course I sincerely hope they're right. It was essential that it should be finished, in view of the number of interests involved."

"You mean to say—"

"I mean to say nothing at all."

But there was no stopping Treilhard. He turned full on Sammécaud, and strong in the superiority of the man about town, at two o'clock in the morning, over the simple millionaire, said loudly:

"Why, the thing's an open secret. Everyone knows that *Chantecler* was finished by Madame Rostand. I've even heard that the son added a line here and there."

"The son! . . . Oh! Oh! . . . The son! It's a good thing dinner's nearly over!"

Avoyer roared with laughter and, under cover of his own guffaws, started again a very faint stroking movement against Germaine's knee. Treilhard looked important.

"Oh, dear me, the son!" Avoyer repeated, as though calling all to bear witness to the excellence of the joke.

"A little young, perhaps," Mareil murmured with a slight air of reserve. (As a matter of fact, he was no longer thinking at all about what he was saying, though he tried to disguise the fact.)

"This poor Chantecler!" cried Bérénine; "fate's not even sent him to the casserole, but only to the family stew!"

"You should say to the witches' cauldron in *Macbeth*. You know they're always playing Shakspere at Cambo."

"And how was it all finally arranged?" asked Sammécaud, in a tone of great deference.

"Arranged?—Faked, you mean, to look like a play?—Oh, the audience'll love it; nobody's going to put it under a microscope. I'm told, though, that it's easy to see which are Madame's speeches, because they're even more high-flown than her husband's."

"The cock makes the noise, but the hen lays the egg,"[1] Bérénine exclaimed.

The table was loud in applause.

"Did you hear that?"

"Damn good!"

"My dear chap, you simply must let me make a note of that for future use!"

Bérénine rapidly gauged, with the eye of an expert, the effect of his epigram upon the company. He was like a naval officer noting through his glasses a shell's precise point of impact and calculating its size from the volume of water displaced. It was not so much the actual applause that he went by as those subtler indications which are more flattering because less easily imitated, indications that cannot lie, such as a fleeting expression in the eyes or a quick movement of the body (somebody, in the grip of laughter, suddenly flings himself back in a chair; two neighbours turn towards each other, as though to share delight). He allowed himself the merest adumbration of a smile, first of all because good manners forbade him to laugh at his own witticisms, but chiefly because he was still in a condition of nervous tension. It was his habit to go to a party like this prepared to work, and work not like a labourer who has only dead matter to overcome, but like a primitive hunter or man of war, like a toreador, constantly alert against the ill nature of the living, always prepared to deal with the unforeseen situation, ever ready to anticipate the nature of a response which the occurrences of a moment may completely alter. Sometimes, but not very often, he came ready prepared with a few epigrams which he would have made during the day (he never got up till noon) on the most likely subjects of

[1] The French contains a play on the word "Chantecler," which it is quite impossible to reproduce in English.—TRANSLATOR'S NOTE.

conversation. These he would have ready for use, and the only problem would be so to arrange matters that they should seem to spring
naturally from the conversation. A certain amount could be done,
of course, by getting the talk to run in the right direction, and laying a little ground-bait in advance. But Bérénine's nature was essentially sociable. Loneliness depressed him. In the little bachelor flat
which he had carved for himself out of the middle of his mother's
apartment, he could never get down to anything, but hung about,
smoking, yawning, and idly turning the pages of books. Something
would give him an idea for an article, and he would jot down the
first two or three lines. But really to get on with it he needed the
noise and bustle of a newspaper office round him as he worked.
Writing came easiest to him when he had to do it on the hastily
cleared corner of a pal's table, with people coming and going all
round, and shaking hands with him over his shoulder, and talking
all the time: "Hello, m'lad!" "Hello, old man!" "How's things?"
"Shove those matches along!" "Didn't see you yesterday at the
Princess's," "Going to poor Adolphe's funeral tomorrow?"—and a
thousand and one odds and ends of words that buzzed like mosquitos
about the flame of his consciousness, exciting him and giving an
edge to his awareness. The same sort of things happened with his
conversational witticisms. Every time that he came into a roomful of
people, every time, more especially, that he went out to a dinner
or a supper, Bérénine kicked himself for not having put in that
half-hour of preparation which would have given him now such a
sense of support. But he was the kind of man who finds stimulus in
a sudden emergency. Faced by the necessity of acting, his intelligence
at once became wakeful and alert. In the very act of unfolding his
napkin he would set himself to accomplish, with a degree of skill
of which he was completely unaware, two perfectly distinct opera-
tions: on the one hand to follow the turns and twists of conversation so carefully as not to lose a word, on the other to compose, while
listening, two or three epigrams, two or three barbed comments with
which to shoot at this moving target. Naturally such witticisms would

have some connexion with the subjects under discussion, so that
although the conversation was to some extent distracting, in that
it demanded a degree of attention that might have been employed
in the labours of improvisation, it made up for this by the stimulus
it provided for his invention. Thanks entirely to the chatter, ideas
thronged in on him every minute, several times a minute. Most of
them, it is true, were stupid enough and hardly deserved to be called
ideas at all, being no more than odds and ends of memory or dead-
ends of conventional talk. For an idea to be an idea in any genuine
sense, the intelligence must be conscious of that particular kind of
sensation, unlike any other, which is the product of true invention
(no matter how trivial the matter, if invention has a part in it, the
sensation is unmistakable). But it would have been too much to
expect that the need for work should end there. It is rarely, indeed,
that a witticism springs fully grown from the brain, balanced and
pointed and formed. Occasionally there would come one of those
happy evenings of inspired intoxication, when the champagne acting
upon some peculiarly responsive state of the nerves would turn him
into one of those almost legendary figures of the table, unerringly
apt, infallibly quick, the hero of a new saga of the town. To those
of us who know such evenings, what ecstasy do they not bring, what
sense of being truly and at last alive! Epigrams bubble up so easily
that the brain is hardly aware of them until the tongue has already
given them shape. The sound of laughter, never failing, is at once
their echo and our reward. The women, with laughter seeming to
impart a roundness to their throats, give one soft and sidelong looks.
Success brings confidence, and each shrewd stroke leads on its own
successor. As the iron gets hotter, each blow of the hammer sends
up a higher plume of sparks.

But on ordinary days, when no such inspiration came to his help,
he had to submit to a tedious routine of work like any plodding
scholar or careful experimenter checking results. Then it was that
he had to hunt for synonyms, fabricate phrases, give to his words just
the carefully deliberate twist that would bring them down right-

side-up with the proper air of consummate mastery. And all the time he would be thinking glumly to himself: "How flat it'll be! But I haven't uttered a word since the soup; if I don't say something, they'll think I'm losing my touch"—conscious all the while of the slightly corpse-like taste of the chicken in aspic.

In just such a mood of discontent Bérénine now sat biting his lips. (His real name was Lerond. He had experimented with several pseudonyms, but finally settled on this one, which dated from the honeymoon of the Franco-Russian alliance.)

"I'm not up to scratch," he thought; "they're only laughing so as not to humiliate me." This evening's epigrams, he felt, lacked style. He dreamed of witticisms that should drive to the heart of a subject. In his moments of ambition he imagined other men about town chatting in theatre corridors, repeating something he had said, and agreeing that it had the true Bérénine touch, in the sense that it was not only amusing, but profound. For three minutes now he had been trying to work up something about *Chantecler,* about Rostand, about his family, and about the various hagglings in which they were said to be involved, which should be more than a mere pun, something which would be repeated tomorrow all over Paris, something which his colleagues on the smaller newspapers would steal. (To be the victim of such a theft is annoying, but it is also flattering. Sooner or later someone would say: "If Bérénine didn't say it, it's the sort of thing he would say—at his best.")

But the phrase would not come. Bérénine was miserable. He thought about his age, about his hair, which was going grey and getting thin, about the tooth he had just lost, which had come out so easily. He settled his monocle and emptied his glass. Why was it that there were evenings when the champagne, no matter how dry, failed to warm one? Relentless occasions when even the wine had a sobering effect? His thoughts turned to opium-smokers, to politicians who were said to give themselves an injection of morphine before making a speech.

But Treilhard was in the middle of a new story about *Chantecler,* telling how *L'Illustration,* having paid every penny of four hundred thousand francs for the right to publish the play, was bringing an action against an Italian paper for having pirated one of the chief scenes. "You know, I suppose, who sold it to the *Secolo?* Well, you needn't look far: Madame Rostand!—perhaps because she wrote it. . . . What a world!"

"How much did she get?"

Treilhard assumed the expression of a man deliberately weighing his words, careful to say nothing of which he isn't sure.

"A lot, naturally, but I'm not certain of the figure."

Suddenly Bérénine's voice rang through the room, pitched on the high, metallic note which he kept for his profoundest witticisms.

"It seems to me that this bird of yours is like every other cock. He may sing his hymn to the sun, but his feet are set pretty firmly on the dung-hill."

There were two or three half-hearted laughs. Here and there mouths opened rather more widely than was absolutely necessary, but the sounds that came from them were short and sharp, like the stroke of a wooden clapper. A few pairs of eyes were turned politely in Bérénine's direction. Avoyer began to rub Germaine's knee in a sudden access of daring. There was a pause in the conversation as though a group of well-bred people were making way for a gentleman in a hurry who had forgotten to apologize.

Bérénine suffered acutely. His annoyance was increased by the presence in his mind of the most agonizing doubt that can beset an artist who has missed his effect. "What's the matter with them? It was a good epigram, a damned good one. What do the fools expect?"

Chapter

10

GERMAINE'S ANXIETY. HENRY MAREIL, JEW AND AUTHOR

Germaine was no less preoccupied than Bérénine. This supper party, apparently so casual, might well mark a turning-point in her career. So far none of the guests had made any allusion to what had brought them together; it was quite possible that they might all leave the table without a word being said. Not that that would necessarily be a bad sign. It would be quite enough if Henry Mareil came up to her in the cloak-room while the attendant was bringing the wraps, and let drop a word or two: "It's really been a very great pleasure for me . . . very great. . . . When should I be least in the way if I came round to see you during the show? . . . You could spare twenty minutes for a quiet chat? . . . Splendid!" But if Mareil said good-night with a few words of conventional politeness, then she would know that all was lost.

Since Gurau had become a Minister, Germaine's ambition had shown signs of restlessness. Gurau, however, didn't take it very seriously. He seemed to think that his own advancement should be enough to satisfy both of them. After all, the allowance he made her, though still slightly irregular, had been definitely increased. When she refused to be put off he either avoided the issue or took refuge behind a joke. "You forget," he said, "that I'm only a wretched little Labour Minister; if I had Public Instruction it would be quite a different matter. . . . Besides, what if Doumergue refused you? . . . An engagement at the Comédie Française? It's too soon for that, or too late. It would be beneath your dignity to hang about there. The directors would vie with one another to keep you in the background. . . . In two or three years, perhaps. By that time I shall have changed my job; who knows? I may even be President of the Council. . . .

Even after the elections my influence will be greater. I'm certain of it. Meanwhile the important thing for you is to get a big reputation on the Boulevards, so that then, if you still insist on burying yourself, at least they won't be able to keep you down. What you want is that the public should say: 'If Germaine Baader's gone to the Comédie, we'll insist that they use her.' "

Perhaps, in arguing thus, Gurau was not altogether sincere. Germaine was well aware that what mattered most to him was to keep intact his reputation as a man of honour. No one much minded his being the lover of an actress. The knowledge that he was so gave him, in Paris, a certain reputation for worldly smartness, and his constituents in Touraine were not fanatically austere. At worst, the less important newspapers would say: "When the Minister of Labour has had enough of receiving delegations of scavengers and electricians, he is not averse to a pair of pretty arms which can help him to forget the problems of a minimum wage and the eight-hour day." But he did insist on being able to reply: "The Minister is not tied by the affections of the private man. He is proud of his mistress, but any position she holds is due entirely to her own abilities."

Germaine had found herself compelled, willy-nilly, to follow his advice and had decided that she must capture the attention of the theatre public by a startling success, or, better still, a series of startling successes. Meanwhile someone called M. Roger Sammécaud had very kindly offered to help her. Gurau introduced him during a dress rehearsal at Marquis's theatre. She thought him well-mannered and rather shy. During the weeks that followed he came two or three times to see her in her dressing-room. She enjoyed these visits, because they were so entirely different from those of the ordinary hard-bitten swains whose heavy feet she could usually hear a mile off. Sammécaud treated her as a woman of intelligence whose conversation was worth the tribute of attention. He listened. He seemed to think about what he heard. He hinted tactfully that, ignorant though he was of the theatre world, he had seen enough to realize that injustice was as prevalent there as elsewhere, and that reputations owed more to intrigue than to talent. Germaine was perfectly well aware that he belonged to a powerful ring of oil-magnates to whom the control of Gurau's paper, and of the theatre in which she herself was playing, was a mere trifle. Knowing this, she admired still more the unobtrusiveness of his manners. Never by so much as a single word did he lead her to suppose that he thought himself absolved by the consciousness of power from the necessity of being agreeable. Nothing appeals more to a woman who dislikes sacrificing her pride to her desire for success.

It was natural that Germaine should speak to him of her ambitions and of the limited extent to which she could rely on Gurau to help her.

"I shouldn't like to say that he was wrong," he said thoughtfully. "I respect him all the more for having scruples, even excessive scruples; it's better than seeing him scrambling in the gutter with the rest of them. He's a fine character, you know."

"Oh, but I do know it!" she replied.

"He has a great future, and he's got to be careful. It's essential for him to keep out of the mud of politics."

She realized, however, that Sammécaud was watching for an opportunity to play his own hand.

One day Avoyer paid a visit to her dressing-room, bald, short-sighted, important, and full of some mysterious errand. He took care to see that the door was shut. "I think," he said, making a gesture with his arms, "that I'm on to something pretty good for you. . . . Yes, naturally. But hush! . . . The least slip and everything will be spoiled. Pretty good, I repeat. A great friend of ours—you know whom I mean—has told me of your very natural ambitions—and let me say, by the bye, that you really should have told me about them before; you don't know what a good friend you have in me. To cut a long story short, I've got busy, *misterioso*. One can't be too careful even in my position. We live in a time of mad grabbing. It's not a question of just pushing to the front, the thing's become more like a stampede. Well, now, you know, I think, that I'm well in with everyone at the Porte-Saint-Martin, from the highest to the lowest. They tell me things there that they'd never tell anybody else. It wasn't from Hertz I got it, nor yet from Rostand, for a very good reason, as you'll see; nor even directly from Simone. But get it I did. It's this"— he lowered his voice to conspiratorial depths—"Simone is going to walk out on them! And she'll do it suddenly, a week or two before the dress rehearsal. But isn't she bound by her contract? you'll ask. Not so tightly as you think. . . . They've ended by getting on her nerves, the whole lot of 'em. They're vaguely uneasy because of things she's let drop, but they think it's nothing but a fit of ill temper that she'll get over, and they're quite unprepared. There's an understudy, of course, but no one who could create the part. In my opinion, there's only one actress in Paris who could take the risk of such a part if Simone lets them down—you! Temperament, age, voice, talent —you've got them all. What a Heaven-sent chance! I've already put down a little ground-bait—carefully, of course, so as not to let them get wind of anything serious. The night before last I said to Hertz and Coquelin: 'I suppose you know all about this flu epidemic? Not many people die of it, but I'm told that it means three or four weeks in bed, sometimes six or eight. Let's knock wood! Have you thought what you'd do if your Pheasant got the flu? It'd be nothing short of a disaster. We've got nobody else. Why?' I asked them. 'It's really flying in the face of destiny. Why? Because, I suppose you'll say, there *is* nobody.' We talked the whole thing over on the spot and ran through possible names. I dropped yours casually. I can't say they jumped at it; they made various objections: 'The name doesn't carry enough weight, wouldn't look well enough on the bills,' and so on, but the suggestion stuck."

Germaine interrupted him. "Rostand would never agree. He hardly knows me, though I did once say some lines of his at a matinée. He demands such a lot."

"I can bring pressure to bear on Rostand all right, on the whole Rostand clan. When I say *I* . . . you understand what I mean. . . . That particular royal family's always short of cash. I see you frowning, my dear, but you can rest assured that I shouldn't do anything crude—good heavens, no! But people will always listen to good advice when it's given by someone who can help them, or not help them, in other ways."

For a fortnight she lived on the prospect of this rich dish. But at the end of it Avoyer said: "Bad news for you, my dear. It was all arranged; if she went, you were to have the part. I had it all fixed. But she's not going, after all; it's been patched up. . . . You know what women are!"

Although she didn't cry easily, Germaine couldn't help bursting into tears.

This time it looked as though things were really more hopeful. Avoyer was still beating round, but Sammécaud had taken it into his head to run the affair himself.

The plan was to get Henry Mareil to promise Germaine the chief part in his next play, which was due for production at the end of the winter. She was tied for eight more months to her present engagement, but the question of Marquis's permission was little more than a matter of form.

Henry Mareil was one of a group, with Henry Bataille and Henry Bernstein, known as the "Three Henrys." He was ten years older than Bataille and fourteen years older than Bernstein. He had been slower in getting started (he had had a period of loafing, during which he had tried his hand at all sorts of things), and success had come to him by degrees. The public had got into the way of lumping him with the other two and of treating all three as leaders of the same generation. Sometimes Mareil, who hated the idea of growing old and was very anxious that women should like him both as an author and as a man, congratulated himself upon a confusion which took a good many years from his age. But at other times he found himself irritated by it. He would have preferred to see the difference between him and his namesakes more definitely stressed, could it have been done without unduly accentuating his age, and to observe, in the attitude of the other two, a tactful acknowledgment of his seniority. Bataille, if he did not show exactly respect, treated him with a shyness and a courtesy which seemed a very good substitute. But Bernstein's manners were as intolerable as his obvious hurry to win success. Every time that Mareil saw him in a passage at a dress rehearsal he was conscious of irritation, and avoided meeting him if he possibly could. But the other, with the uneasy, roving eyes of a man of prey, always marked him down before he could get away. He never waved to him nor gave him a smile, but it was as though he said in so many words: "I've seen you; it's no use your going away," and a moment later Mareil, uncomfortably conscious that a slight embarrassment had come between him and the casual acquaintance with whom he might be talking at the moment, would feel a light touch on the shoulder and, turning, would be aware of Bernstein topping him by a head and already letting his eyes wander away to some other part of the room. The tiny mouth, which belonged by rights to some organizer of prize-fights or some Frankfurt business man, would let fall a phrase which Mareil in his heart of hearts felt as a wound to his pride. One evening Bernstein had said nothing more than: "Are you at work on anything?" but the words reeked of patronage, incredulity, and sarcasm to such an extent that deep within himself Mareil read into the innocent phrase an intention that, put into words, meant: "No one ever speaks of you nowadays . . . one never hears of you . . . do you really have to work two years on a play which will only have half the success of the last?"

Mareil, who was not lacking in clear-sightedness where his own affairs were concerned, admitted sometimes to himself that his dislike of the other came from professional jealousy. "At thirty-three," he reflected, "he is as well known as I am at forty-seven, and he's probably made more money already than I have. What was I at his age?— a man with vague dramatic ambitions. But," he added, "it's only fair to admit that a success of Bataille's would not irritate me to nearly the same extent. One's feelings for a man are dictated by his character. The emotions that Bernstein rouses in me are bitter and ignoble.

I don't deny his ability, but I hate it. The crude cads he puts into his plays make one despair of human nature, just as his style makes one despair of the French language. One could be more vulgar than he is, or more pretentious, but to be more vulgar *and* more pretentious at the same time would be impossible. He has found the exact mixture. As to his methods of achieving success, well, even if everything they say about him isn't true. . . . In the old days even the greediest careerist observed a certain decency, a code of manners, which were part and parcel of the traditional elegance of the Boulevards. . . . A Jew like that breeds anti-Semites."

Henry Mareil was a Jew. His real name was Lucien Wormser, and his family, on both sides, came from Bésançon. His mother was a Cahen. His more distant origins were hidden in obscurity. Some of his ancestors came from the South. Rightly or wrongly he liked to think of them as belonging to the Sephardim; it pleased him to believe that they had preserved the purity of their race to a high degree. Any modification there might be had come from inter-marriage with the people of the Mediterranean basin to whom they had always been more or less related and whose faults and qualities were both marked by a certain charm. The Sephardim type, once it had become emancipated from the conditions of extreme poverty, achieved a considerable degree of physical beauty. It was impossible not to admit that they sprang from a fine stock.

He never forgot the emotion of which he had been conscious one day on the Meijerplein at Amsterdam. Across the huge square the Synagogue of the Sephardim and the Synagogue of the Ashkenazim faced each other. Mareil was not a learned man. He knew little of the history of the Dispersion and was not affected by the mysticism of his race. But on that particular occasion he had been deeply moved, surrendering himself to the emotion of the moment, giving to his heart a full liberty of choice. "You fair-haired Jews," he said to himself, "with your freckled faces and your eyes of blue or green or grey, I do not reject you. But you must allow me to prefer our brethren of the South who have kept their heritage less sullied. I envy them their dark skins, their deep and lustrous eyes, and that profile which in its purity shares with the Greeks of the classical period, with the Florentines of the Renaissance, with the Virgins of the French cathedrals, the distinction of being one of the most beautiful profiles in the world."

A little later, walking along the Kalverstraat, he looked at himself in the shop-windows. He could almost claim that profile for himself, though it was, perhaps, a shade too soft, a shade too effeminate. But his eyes were grey-green, and his skin too pallid to be called strictly brown. He looked at one reflection after another, and smiled with a slight sense of heaviness at his heart. It was no use pretending that he was altogether of the noble race. He was marked by some of the impurities of the Dispersion. But these he accepted as one accepts poor relations, with a silent sympathy that soothed the wound of which his pride was conscious.

Passing the French frontier on his way home from that tour, he had been so completely overcome by an access of love that the tears had sprung to his eyes.

For Mareil loved France passionately; how much he only realized as he grew older. At first he had accepted quite naturally, with the other children of his age, with his schoolfellows, the fact of being French. But little by little he had grown to wonder at it, not as at something strange, but as at a happy gift of fortune. In just such a way a young man of good family might wonder at his luck in finding the woman of his choice and ask himself perpetually whether he were worthy of her.

He was shy at voicing this sentiment of love, but that its existence should be doubted hurt him deeply, and still more so any expression of surprise that he should have it. "My feeling is all the truer because I am a Jew," he argued. "It is no inevitable, no organic, consequence of birth, but depends upon an act of conscious choice. It has the emotional quality of true love. My ancestors could have chosen not to settle in France or could have left it. I might have felt myself an exile, whereas in fact I adore France and never cease to see it as a beloved woman."

His nom-de-plume was a symbol of this sentiment. On a Sunday in April the young Lucien Wormser had gone walking in the outer suburbs. At that time he was employed in a bank in obedience to the wishes of his family, but was secretly engaged on a play which he meant to offer to the Odéon. In the course of his walk he had happened on the village of Mareil and noticed that it was called on the map Mareil-en-France, presumably to distinguish it from other places of the same name.

"Mareil-en-France!" What more beautiful name could he have found, what more lovely place on this day of fitful April sunshine? The landscape was in no way remarkable, but it breathed the air of the Île-de-France, and to the young man the Île-de-France was the epitome of his adopted home. Everything spoke to him of France— the changing sky, the clouds, the early green of the trees, the soft but bracing air; the church spires, the roofs, the little hills; the blue-enamelled street signs; the quiet town hall; the atmosphere of kindly republican welcome; the dowdy clothes of the people, their sensible and friendly eyes. All round him, like the concentric rings of a tree, spread the country-sides of France, cautious and hospitable. He could feel about him the lives of these people, shrewd and alert, richer in thinkers and lovers than in athletes; of these people who a hundred years ago had been moved by a great fury of desire to bring the reign of justice to all mankind. On that day the young Wormser had known an hour of exaltation that neither the April winds could chill nor the mud of the roads damp.

Since he was at an age when the human intelligence is, fortunately, more sensitive to the sublime than to the ridiculous, he had no misgivings about comparing this day's emotions to the famous spiritual revelations of history, such, for instance, as that recorded by Pascal. "I have *found* France, as he found God. The whole course of my life will be determined by the experiences through which I am passing at this moment." And, in fact, life became for him as a fire of sweet-scented woods burning upon an altar. His heart-beats, the rhythm of his breathing, the procession of his thoughts, fed slowly to that flame, shone there and crackled. "I have found my name as a writer. I shall call myself Lucien Mareil; or, rather, Henry Mareil, because Henri shares with Louis the glory of being the most French of all names; it is the name of the king whom most I love. In the future when I see my name in a newspaper or on a billboard, when a friend greets me: 'Henry Mareil . . . Mareil . . .' deep within my heart a voice will add, like a whisper hidden in a kiss: 'en France . . . Mareil-en-France.' No one can laugh at me, because no one will know. It will be my darling secret—Mareil-en-France." So shaken was he by emotion that his trembling lips shaped themselves to a kiss, and he longed to take the wind and the trees into his arms.

He pledged his future, saying: "I will be the most French of writers." There, on the spot, he began to compose the opening lines of a mystery play in poetic prose, a "Mystery of France" which should be a pendant to the famous *Mystery of Jesus,* but he lacked the lyric gift, that sensitive concentration of the spirit that can strike fire from the abstractions of thought. He gave up the idea of a mystery.

With that one exception, Henry Mareil managed pretty well to keep his promise, in the sense, that is, in which he had understood it. His conception of France and of the French genius was not of the highest, deriving, as it did, from the more casual and easy-going of its historic periods. Mareil realized perfectly well the existence of those Middle Ages which had flowered in great architecture and in the thought of philosophers and mystics. When he spoke of "the cathedrals" he assumed an expression of solemnity, and two or three times during his life he mentioned *The Imitation* in the hushed tones of one who knows what he is talking about. He could, on occasion, remember Rabelais and Pascal, and admired without qualification the masters of 1660. He was well aware of the truth of observation and psychological profundity to be found in their works, of their insight into the springs of passion, of the "happy turns" of their phrasing. But the austerity of their thought, their intellectual elegance, the nervous tension that inspired their style, gave him no particular thrill, though he would never have dared to confess that to him Racine, for instance, translated into prose, with the rhetoric replaced by concise and "nervous" dialogue, would gain much and lose little by the obliteration of an outmoded pomposity. It was with the spirit of the eighteenth century that he felt really at home, though not in its moods of philosophical discovery or reformist zeal, nor even in its moments of dryness and cynicism. He loved its effortless outbursts of spontaneity and easy sophistication, when it had merely to be itself to be exquisite. His ideal author was no single figure of the eighteenth century, but one who should combine certain of its qualities, a sort of mixture of Marivaux and the Abbé Prévost. Like Marivaux, he should be equipped with delicacy of intuition and grace of style, with ingenuity even, where ingenuity was in place, but for the trivial happenings of life he should be master of an easier vernacular, and in passages of full emotion capable of employing the language of real passion. At need he should have it in his power to lay his elegance aside and to evoke the flavour of bitten flesh, the atmosphere of love in the small hours, of exhausted passion and the violence of lust, which emerges for us, almost with the smell of dirty linen, from the effortless achievement of the author of *Manon*.

So far, therefore, from objecting to his reputation as an "author of the Boulevards," Mareil rejoiced in it, drawing it about him like some soft, delightful garment. In what sweeter or more intimate way could the eternal spirit of France proclaim that it had recognized him as its own? There was, of course, a bad and petty side to this world of the Boulevards. Its interests were too often circumscribed; it believed too easily that its little happenings could shake the world, ascribing to every new love-affair of an actress an importance equal to the possible results of the next English general election. But, after all, much the same could have been said, in an earlier day, of the life of the court. Its outlook had been just as limited, its atmosphere as full of gossip and frivolity. But, for all that, it had held within its tiny circle, distilled and rarefied, the essence of the French genius. The world of the Boulevards was the heir of the court, fulfilling in an age of democracy what once had been the function of the royal entourage, maintaining the right of the few to dictate the public taste. The very narrowness of its intellectual outlook was a condition of its power, since the fine flower of every civilization had endured only through the medium of such walled and self-sufficient cliques. Malicious tongues might object that the court had been composed of princes of the blood, of dukes, peers, and marquises, that it had collected round itself all the historic names of France, while the world of the Boulevards was nothing but a bohemia of journalists, dramatists, actresses, and fashionable idlers, but such an argument was only superficially true. What had given elegance to the court had been, not birth, but the fact that it occupied in the general map of Society a position peculiarly central, drenched in the full light of publicity, open to the gaze of a whole people. Why did the faubourg Saint-Germain occupy now so small a place in the life of the nation? There were still great names in France; but names alone, it was clear, could give but little light. Why, the very phrase: "the greatest names of France" meant less now than it once had done. How much would the Brissacs, the Castellanes, the Rohans, the d'Uzès, mean to the decent Paris middle classes of 1910? But Rostand, Sarah Bernhardt, perhaps even Henry Mareil—ah, that was a different matter!

Henry Mareil had suffered bitterly at the time of the Dreyfus affair. In the beginning he had been convinced of the captain's guilt and had been more indignant than a Gentile would have been at the crime that had been laid at the door of a Jew. He had been inclined to think the punishment too mild. When the movement for revision was started he shrugged his shoulders. "How typical of my co-religionists!" he thought. "How tactless, how indiscreet, just when the whole thing was being forgotten!" He had remained an anti-Dreyfusard right up to the eve of the Rennes trial. Perhaps his attitude concealed a certain fear of the world he lived in, but if it did, he was quite unaware of the fact. His conscience was clear and uncompromising. "Naturally," he reflected, "you are anxious to see a man of your own race cleared of suspicion, but that is all the more reason why you should insist more than others upon the necessity of proof. You are a Frenchman first and a Jew second. You are a Jew as another man is a provincial. If you came from Languedoc wouldn't you think it ridiculous to make all this fuss about admitting that another man from Languedoc might be a traitor? All this Dreyfus agitation is splitting France in two and diminishing her in the eyes of foreigners."

During the Rennes trial he refrained from taking sides. It was only towards the end of the Waldeck-Rousseau Ministry that he became convinced of Dreyfus's innocence. He took a subtle pleasure in saying: "Yes, I admit that I needed a lot of persuading."

Shortly afterwards, the propaganda of the Action Française was the cause of fresh bitterness to him. Its first effect was to make him regret the well-mannered monarchists of the Boulevard to whom the fact that a man was a republican was no worse than that he was badly dressed. It had, however, an added disadvantage in that it perpetuated the spirit of anti-Semitism by endowing it with a sort of official status. But what wounded him most deeply was its attitude of monopoly, its refusal to allow men like himself the right to all those feelings which lay nearest to his heart, its attempt to compromise such feelings by saddling them with a dogma which, even if he had not been a Jew, he could not have brought himself to adopt. He was embarrassed by certain phrases which he met with in the writings of Maurras or of the young enthusiasts who modelled their style on that of their master, because he realized that they expressed something of what he felt himself, by a certain shrill, nervous, intimate quality in their references to France, a use of radiant, quivering abstractions, an almost sensual revelling in the national tradition. "It's I who ought to be saying that," he exclaimed; "it's exactly what I thought, exactly the way in which I responded, when I used to walk in my adored country-side, ploughing through the April mud near the village whose name I took." He blamed himself for never

having written his "Mystery of France." "How proud I should have
been of it now! How much more at my ease I should have been with
these people!" Even the rigours of Maurras's attitude gave him a sort
of painful pleasure. "There's probably no one but he and I so absolutely French. We are two lovers of the same woman, and when one
of us makes some allusion to a hidden beauty, no one but the other
can understand—and the other wants to kill his rival."

One day he very nearly wrote an open letter to Maurras. He pondered the first sentences. If it achieved its purpose it would assure him
a fine intellectual position, but to do that it must achieve it completely. Because he wished his letter to move its readers, to speak to
the heart, he was afraid of giving himself away by the over-softness
of a style that had become too much accustomed to adopt the caressing cadences of love, too prone to fall into a brittle dryness when love
was laid aside. "It would look as though I were making advances.
He would reject them with a little grimace of disgust, or accept them
with indulgent contempt. And everyone would say: 'What cringing
creatures these Jews are! He went out of his way to ask for a snub!'"

He failed to write the letter as he had failed to write the mystery.

He felt uncomfortable about this evening's business. He knew
what was expected of him, and realized that there was a plot afoot.
Not that he was displeased, for he was far from being offended at
the thought that so many not undistinguished folk had got together
to persuade him, to overwhelm him with attentions, to influence his
decision. There was enough of the woman in him to like being
courted, besieged, imposed upon, and, like many women, he was
inclined to yield, not from weakness or laziness, but from a wish to
reward so much flattering attention. But as an author he was cautious
and circumspect. A natural and instinctive discretion warned him
when he was in danger of making a fool of himself. No one knew
better than he did the theatre and the cast which each of his plays
demanded. Capus had once acutely said of him that if, like every
other writer, he gave the leading role in his plays to the actress he had

been to bed with, he saw to it that she had an audition—before they went to bed! Nor had his affair with Suzette Vignal given the lie to the epigram, for he had offered her nothing but one small part, just about suited to her talents, and even then she had had to do everything she knew to make anything of it.

Mareil had very little experience of Germaine Baader. He had seen her play, but not often, and in plays which he did not care much about. He thought her intelligent, clever, and gifted with a certain amount of individuality. She was not too different from the character he had portrayed, but he was afraid that she might distort it in rather a tiresome way. What mattered to him was not the degree of such distortion, but its general use. "I wrote it," he thought, "with Réjane in my mind. I knew that for various reasons I shouldn't get Réjane, but it was Réjane's appearance and Réjane's voice that I worked to. That, therefore, should be the determining factor." In writing a woman's part, he always kept before him, in imagination, the figure of some living actress. It was a simple method of setting his inventive powers to work, though he never drove it to extremes. He always repudiated the idea that he was what he called a "dress-maker-author," one of those writers who modelled a character to the last inch on some leading lady, so that only if she played it, and on no other condition, could it come alive. One evening, after seeing Jane Hading, he had left the theatre intoxicated by the thought of her and on fire to write for her. On his way home in his cab the idea of a play began to form in his mind, situations, scraps of dialogue, expressive gestures. By the next day the whole scheme might have vanished, but if the play ever came to be written, it would be under the influence of his memory of her. But once the play was finished, Jane Hading—if Jane Hading was the actress in question—ceased suddenly, by some curious process of ingratitude, to be indispensable. "If I can have her, so much the better, but I shan't go out of my way to fix it. As a matter of fact, it would be interesting to see what somebody else could make of it." There was, in such curiosity to see what somebody else would make of it, a certain element of perversity, something that arose from the dilettante nature of the Jew in him, though he himself attributed it only to the most meritorious of motives. He liked to compare himself, in this matter, to Racine. "He, too, wrote for a definite actress, or, rather, he let his imagination be stirred by the idea of some actress. But once he had set to work, the disappearance of Champmeslé ceased to matter; the work remained." How did Racine (or Henry Mareil) differ from the "author-dressmakers"? In this way, that they copied the model slavishly, making use of every individual and superficial trait, even to tricks of movement, instead of using the "idea" to set the tone of the composition. "We," he decided, "use the model as a means of getting contact with human nature, of achieving the general without losing sight of the living individual."

He was accustomed, therefore, and even pleased, to see his characters realized in a way different from his original conception. In any case, there is bound to be a certain amount of distortion in the progress of a play from manuscript to production. It is one of the active conditions of the theatre, and the author who fails to accommodate himself to it is ignorant of the nature of his medium. For in the theatre accident plays an important part in every achievement, and the skill of the dramatist lies in discounting it as far as possible. The unforeseen points of a play, the profundities which it achieves in ways that were never intended, and which, for that very reason, are more striking than they would otherwise have been, all the uncalculated effects which make the greatest successes, are often due to a happy miscasting, to a delicate maladjustment between the character and its interpreter. But the author must know how to acknowledge and make use of such mistakes, like the adventurous jeweller who mounts a stone in a setting that was not made for it. To employ Germaine in Mareil's new play would certainly be a case of miscasting, but whether a happy or, at least, a "workable" miscasting remained to be seen.

Mareil was, moreover, a man of great subtlety, who could take into account every aspect of a problem. He did not forget that Germaine was Gurau's mistress, and Gurau was a man for whom he had a great respect and in whose future he believed. He was convinced that a word from Gurau would ensure him, in the next honours list, the decoration which he both deserved and desired. The need which he felt for recognition would probably be best satisfied in that way. He was afraid that the fact of his race would close the doors of the Academy to him or delay indefinitely the moment of their opening. He would, therefore, find compensation in the second best and make for himself a remarkable career in the Legion of Honour. "There is no reason," he thought, "why I shouldn't be a Grand Officer of the Order before I die."

He had, too, other matters to think of: what Porel, to whom he had more or less promised the play, would say when he heard of this choice; of Germaine's figure seen from the tenth row of the orchestra; of her voice; of the weight she would carry in the opinions of the four or five chief critics; of how her name would look on the bills; of the partners it would be best to give her; of how he could use Suzette Vignal without risking a scene. (It remained, too, to decide whether he should employ, for the rest of his cast, those whose talents were not sufficiently outstanding to eclipse Germaine, or whether it would be better to insist on a standard of general brilliance, in order to make it obvious that in giving her the chief part he had set himself to give a great artist the chance she deserved.) Suddenly the idea came to him: "Why, she must be a Jewess, with a name like that." He hadn't thought of that before and couldn't remember whether anyone had ever mentioned it to him. He would ask Bérénine later on. From the corner of his eye he studied Germaine's profile and colouring. Probably Jewish, he decided, judging by the setting of the eyes and the way in which, despite the fact that they were blue and clearly defined, they managed to impart to her face a sort of languorous quality; Jewish, but of the fair-haired type, the mixed blood of the Ashkenazim.

This sudden idea almost made him reconsider the whole question. Jewish women did not attract him, nor did he wish to have it thought that in pushing Germaine he was yielding to racial prejudices.

But at that moment Germaine, conscious of the direction of his gaze, looked straight at him with her really very beautiful eyes. She smiled, and her smile was the very best kind of smile. It did not disguise the nature of her hopes. It said quite frankly: "I do so want to please you; I am so anxious about your decision." But there was nothing fawning about it, nothing mean. It seemed to add: "I should be proud to work with you. I'm not a coward, and I know what it means to work."

Mareil was moved. "She can't be a fool," he said to himself, "if she realizes that to look at me like that is the best way to persuade me." Deeper within himself, and nearer the region of his heart, came another thought: "Brave little fair Jewess; your people in these northern lands have cured themselves of the laziness that still dogs us, your cousins of the Mediterranean."

When the cloak-room attendant brought out the ladies' wraps, Mareil, who had gone over the whole problem again, took his cigar out of his mouth and, leaning towards Germaine, said, almost precisely as she had foreseen:

"I should very much like to have a quiet talk with you. When should I disturb you least, after the first or the second act?"

Chapter

11

INTIMACIES IN A MOTOR-CAR

Sammécaud had offered to drop Germaine at her door on the Quai des Grands-Augustins. The car went by way of the boulevard de Sébastopol, which was crowded with market carts. The consequent slowness of their course was very satisfactory to the oil-magnate.

At the corner of the Grands Boulevards he took advantage of a sentence which he found himself uttering quite spontaneously—"I'm so delighted that things have turned out like this, really delighted"—to get hold of her hand. The same impulse seemed to have prompted both the gesture and the words, and it would have been ungenerous in a young woman to try to determine where the sincere congratulations of a good friend ended and a more purely selfish sentiment (almost as flattering in its way) began.

First of all Sammécaud's right hand lay on Germaine's left. Next he raised this gloved left hand and imprisoned it within both his own, meanwhile continuing to congratulate her upon the success of their little plot.

"I looked at Mareil carefully during supper. He was hesitating, and I'm sure that he came with the intention of giving a polite no. But you defeated him; that's the long and short of it."

"Do you think so?"

"I'm sure of it. He's a man who likes to be asked for favours, but when he gives his word, he keeps it."

"But he hasn't given his word; far from it. He's not tied himself in any way."

"Nonsense! I heard what he said when he left you, and particularly noted the tone of his voice. He's tied all right. The important point now is to prevent him taking a chance of any difficulty that may arise later and using it as an excuse to get out of the business. I'll keep a close watch on him, though; I'll find some way of being useful to him. . . . Avoyer told me that he has a pretty hard struggle to make ends meet."

"That surprises me. His plays are very successful."

"Certainly, but it's two years since the last was produced. He spends pretty freely, and I'm told he gambles a bit. Besides, his mistress must cost him a good deal. I'll find a way somehow. . . . Do you think he enjoys dining out?"

"I don't know. He's rather smart, isn't he? I should think he likes invitations."

"So should I, and—"

Sammécaud was about to add: "and being a Jew, he probably sets a good deal of store on getting into certain houses," but although he was not sure that Germaine was Jewish, he changed his mind and turned his sentence into: "and he probably thinks it good for his career. I can arrange to have him asked to some pretty useful houses, and in a way that will appeal to his vanity."

(Sammécaud started to plan a particularly brilliant little dinner in the rue Mozart, for which he would mobilize a force of titled guests, drawn from Marie's family—nobody like Bertrand or Duroure or Allory this time—no, certainly not like Allory. Mareil should be the lion of the evening, and the Countess should be told to see that he was the centre of conversation. He went further and planned an invitation for Mareil to La Noue: "Come, dear master, and do a fortnight's work in our little corner of the country. It's very simple, but very quiet. You want to revise your play before rehearsals begin; well, then . . ." La Noue, with its park, its rooms, its staircases, and its corridors.)

Germaine listened with only half her mind. She, too, was thinking about Mareil, but in a different way. All of a sudden he had become the man with whom she was going to work, for whom she was going to work, her boss, in the best sense of the term. In the theatre Marquis was called "the boss," but he didn't deserve the name. A theatrical director like Marquis wasn't really a boss, but a shopkeeper with shows for sale. She was merely part of his window display. When had he ever been seriously interested in her work? Somewhere about the fifteenth or twentieth rehearsal he came and sat in the auditorium and listened to a whole act without saying a word. Now and again he would make some sardonic joke. He loved to demoralize an author, remarking, for instance, without conviction: "Your third act's no good. I'd cut it, only I can't send people home to bed at half past ten." Now and again he would get excited and exclaim: "Marvellous! If the fools don't like that, I don't know what they want!" But it was the enthusiasm of a shopkeeper, of a middleman, delighted to put on the market some article which he had not made, but hoped to sell. The genuine boss was someone who took a passionate interest in an actress's work, co-operating with her in its production, using her for its realization. Antoine, to judge from what people said, was a real boss. Germaine had often dreamed of working under Antoine. But she told herself that she wouldn't get on with him, that the experiment would be disastrous, that it was better to let it remain a dream in which she could take refuge when her professional enthusiasm was starved of satisfaction, as a romantic but sensible wife contents herself with a dream of deceiving her husband.

For Germaine was in love with work, welcoming the idea of being ordered about by a real boss, not merely because it gave her pleasure to obey, but because she delighted in giving the work that was asked of her in full measure and overflowing, because she delighted in bringing a smile to a face that smiled with difficulty. She felt that in all her life as an actress nobody had yet asked enough work of her, nobody had found a way to get from her all the energy that was hers to give, that bubbled inexhaustibly within her, that gave her pleasure by the sheer force of its vitality. (It was in work that she felt herself most surely alive, most at peace with herself, in work that her pride, so often ill at ease, at last found satisfaction.)

She knew that Mareil made his people work hard, especially his leads, as he ought to do. He would take individuals apart, explain the tiniest details to them, and coach them. He had the reputation of being an exacting master, fussy, a grumbler. It was an unheard-of thing for him to say "Good" at the first go. He knew when an instinct was good, and could teach people how to follow their instinct, but he had no patience with blurred outlines. He was known as an excellent instructor, and his reading of his plays had become famous. Again and again Germaine said to herself: "How pleased he's going to be with my work! I'll get up at eight o'clock if necessary, I'll get my massage through quicker. I can easily put in an extra hour's work when I get back from the theatre. I won't let Gurau distract me by making love too often. It's a waste of time for him as well as for me. Mareil shall see how obedient and intelligent I can be. I'll understand everything he tells me, I'll astonish him. And what enthusiasm I'll show! When he says: 'Not too tired, my child?' I'll answer: 'What, me? I'm good for another two hours if you like,' even though I'm dropping with fatigue. But I shan't drop with fatigue. What shall I call him? Master? I'd rather call him boss: it would be nearer the truth, but I'm not sure that he'd like it."

She felt revive within her the spirit she had shown as a courageous schoolgirl. Her thoughts went back to the Lycée Fénelon, to a mistress who had known how to get everything she wanted from her just by taking for granted that she *could* get anything out of Germaine Baader, the little fair-haired girl with the blue eyes who sat in the second row.

The smell of the markets, a mixture of gutted fish and bruised cabbages, began to invade the car. Wagon wheels passed close beside the windows. But no market smell could disturb the hymn to work which Germaine was singing to herself with all the intensity of her nature.

The better to sing it, she clasped her hands upon her breast, or, rather, she clenched them, one within the other, like someone preparing for a supreme effort.

But Sammécaud was caressing her left hand and her arm. He brushed her ear with his moustache and murmured one of those phrases which have become so common in life and in fiction that it is difficult to say which first invented them.

Again Germaine said to herself: "Oh, *that* doesn't matter!"

Chapter

12

A SUBURBAN WALK

When Jallez and Jerphanion had passed the Clignancourt gate, they saw the avenue before them stretching out of sight. A misty sunshine filled it with a light that softened the features of its poverty. A huddle of hovels and small beer-shops spread up to the slopes of the ramparts. A lot of wheeled traffic was coming into Paris and had slowed down as it approached the city toll, long lines of wagons with slackened traces, and halted carts drawn by fat old white nags with hairy fetlocks, who stood musing between the shafts like old countrymen. Horses coming the other way, from Paris, seemed suddenly to change their gait, the drivers to crack their whips differently, as though stressing the fact that from now onwards they had to do with a different world.

Jallez and Jerphanion moved through a land that smelt of mussels and fried fish, whose grass looked like the stuffing of old mattresses, where the very house-windows seemed to be tired and the breeze that touched the bushes was sullied by the bubbling, greasy waste of factory boilers. But, for all that, the trees stepped bravely on to the horizon, and the sun, stronger than cold or fog, gave to all it touched a pallid life. Here and there a sheet of corrugated iron shone faintly blue, and old plaster took on a patina of gold.

"I suppose to a man like you, who's still got his peasant's nose, this must be a pretty filthy smell?" Jallez remarked.

"Not filthy exactly; odd, rather, and sad, like the sound of a distant phonograph in an empty bar."

"I should think it has much the same effect on you as, for instance, the unexpected smell of a cow-shed in the rue de la Goutte-d'Or has on me, the townsman, bringing a deep and satisfying sense of the poetry of the country-side, though it's nothing really but a whiff of dung."

Both of them felt oddly cheerful. In Jallez the mood was one almost of intoxication, being a product of many memories and sustained by causes deep-seated in his being. Jerphanion, though surrendering to the excitement of the moment, was surprised at himself. Whence came, he wondered, the power of such a place, and of this winter morning?

The avenue was not very wide, but it was long, losing itself in the blue January haze. The roadway, the leafless trees, the stream of carts, seemed to come together in a point, converging in a distance of light mist. There seemed no reason to think that this effect of dimness was due to anything but the illusion of perspective. The fog apparently had nothing to do with it. It was as though the atmosphere of these suburban spaces became thicker, more solid, in obedience to some law of its own being, marking thus its urgent onward pace, its power to charm, to fascinate, to draw the wanderer ever forward. The distance was haunted by vague thoughts of blue eyes, of promised happiness at the road's end, of a doorway opening on the future.

Jallez and Jerphanion felt in all their limbs the buoyant sense of adventure. Between the trees petty traders had spread their wares. Here a rutty lane struck off from the main avenue, bordered by single-storeyed huts; there a pale young face was smiling in front of the four glass jars displayed in a grocer's shop that badly needed painting. It was the fitful smile of one who, through long years, has grown used to outwitting the promptings of appetite. As the face turned to meet a stranger's gaze, the tired and shadowed eyes would open a little wider and the smile would vanish into some mysterious fastness, like a wild animal fleeing to its lair.

"Poverty," thought Jallez—"I feel, this morning, disinclined to say wretchedness—poverty, freedom from burdens, detachment. Possessions mean so little. The object of money is to circulate. The jars in the grocer's window are not really so inaccessible. One can earn two sous, one can earn twenty sous; the point is not to let the earning fill one's life. It is the January sun that lightens the weight of life. Already in January the days are lengthening, giving one a foretaste almost of spring's sweetness without the loss of a single hour of spring. It is the spring, the summer, the gentle season, that makes the riches of the poor, the only riches that they can be sure of never losing. Not for them is the promised pleasure spoilt by waiting. Weariness is forgotten in the sight of an avenue that dwindles to a distance lost in mist as sweet as smoke from a wood fire. From time to time the carters shout; the teams take the slow pace of the suburban roads. It is just cold enough for the warm body to find pleasure in the open air. One will never be poorer than these poor. One will always be able to start out some morning down such an avenue as this. All that one needs is shoe-leather."

Jallez thought about his future, while the sunshine and the distant haze, the smell of fried fish, the curve of the branches, and the smile seen on a dead-white face combined in his imagination to make an image that spread and spread until it took on the form of happiness, for ever turning in his brain like the fumes of drunkenness. "I will never let myself be caught," he told himself, "never let myself be trapped; by no career, by no promise of money. I will always be ready to set out as I do this morning. There is no other youth than this. I swear that when I am thirty I will still be young—or dead. The times we live in are brittle. I feel it. Who is there that does not feel it? If one listens one can hear them crack. No one knows when they will collapse, nor where the first signs of collapse will show. When that time comes, those alone will be happy whom no bonds hold. The wise man will be he who has kept contact with his fellows, for then he won't have so far to fall. I'm not going to pretend that these people here about me are my friends—one should fight shy of rhetoric—but at least we can reach one another without having to turn a world upside down in the process."

Jallez reflected that the happiness he felt was like a harmony in music. "I am like nothing that I see around me, no useless echo of a single person here, but all the same there is room for me. I could find my place here without any difficulty. There is nothing to prevent me, and a great deal to help. How good it is to set out like this with a friend to the end of the road, with all the day before us! What delight to think that life can bring me happiness so cheaply! For how long?—Ah, that's another story. We mustn't ask too much. The fullness of joy is enough. Let's not torment ourselves with thoughts of impermanence."

He marvelled that his joy could be so pure as well as so airy. If the torments of his life, its anxieties, and its pains, had not altogether vanished, they had withdrawn into the semblance of a cowed and distant host. No summoning cry came from them. In sober hues they stood there in the shadows, like some faint trimming of the stuff of life. Withdrawn and barely audible, they served for excitement rather than unrest. What mattered was to lose no fraction of the moment's pleasure, to live fully in each minute, to set each second singing, to give them all their orders for the day: "Heads up! You think you're being watched? Well, then, don't look back; it's not worth while."

Out loud he said, more than once:

"How happy I am, old man!"

Or:

"Don't you think it's fine? It's stunning, absolutely stunning!"

Then, since Jerphanion seemed to agree, but said nothing, he continued:

"Why is it so stunning? One can't help wondering. I don't care this morning what happens; it's amazing. If I flunk next year's exam, I shall become a pedlar and hawk things about suburban streets: photograph frames, perhaps, the sort that have little cardboard struts at the back and stand about on the furniture; or coloured picture postcards for courting couples—you know the kind, with embossed flowers and bits of verse:

> When I gaze in the soft melting depth of your eyes,
> It is God who enfolds me and bids me arise."

Jerphanion laughed. He particularly liked the second line.

Jallez stopped opposite a tinker's booth and declared again that he was happy. Jerphanion glanced at him out of the corner of his eye. He too was happy, but saw no point in challenging fate by announcing the fact quite so insistently.

Then Jallez became talkative, jumping from idea to idea, interrupting his friend. Certain mannerisms of speech which the other had never noticed before began to mark his talk. He kept on beginning sentences with the phrase: "Notice, my dear fellow, that—" and then, suddenly, seeing a little mongrel with a long, dirty tail, lifting its leg between the two halves of a large round pumpkin which a greengrocer had stood on the ground before his stall, he asked for news of the dog Macaire.

Chapter

13

THE DOG MACAIRE GIVES RISE TO A PROVERB

Though Jerphanion had often told Jallez about the dog Macaire, he had never been able to introduce them. One of the animal's exploits, of which the sight of the trickling pumpkin reminded them, had recently taken on the dignity of a proverb among their friends at the College. The incident had taken place a few days earlier in the drawing-room in the rue Vanneau while Jerphanion was waiting for his pupil. Mlle Bernardine, always ready for a little chat with the bearded student, had offered him a cup of tea. In the middle of their conversation the lady had been called from the room by a servant with some message, and he was left alone. After a few moments the door was gently pushed open, and Macaire appeared. As on a previous occasion, the dog approached and sniffed first at his feet, then at the bottom of his trousers, but this time with all the signs of friendliness which are due to an old acquaintance. What happened next, however, was without precedent. Macaire moved away from Jerphanion and began a leisurely perambulation of the huge carpet, zigzagging as he went, and marking his progress by a series of small drops, all of a size and equally spaced, on the floor behind him. It was done as though it were the most natural thing in the world—something that happened every day. He hardly hesitated in his progress, constricting his hinder parts with a barely visible movement and making no attempt to lift either of his back legs. When he had finished, he returned to the young man's feet and then left the room by the way he had entered it. A minute later Bernardine returned. She noticed the freshly deposited line of dots that lay in a decorative pattern, finely conceived if a little complicated, beginning and ending at the young man's feet. She seemed surprised, and was clearly just going to say: "Who did that?" when she checked herself, apparently unaware that this display of tact clearly threw the oddest suspicion on the waiting student. Jerphanion was on the point of clearing himself by accusing Macaire, but decided that to do so would be lacking in manners. He was seized by a desire to laugh. When one wears a full beard it is easy enough to hide a laugh by constricting the jaws, but one can only do so if one refrains from speaking.

When Jallez heard the story, he said at once: "I insist on your introducing me to this dog. But how is it to be managed? It won't be easy. I tell you what; get him to follow you one day, and I'll meet you at the corner of the street; I'll give him a piece of sugar, and we'll smuggle him off."

But it was easier said than done. Meanwhile, the two friends agreed that Macaire's manœuvre had been the expression of a subtle train of thought. The dog, they decided, was a master of sly malice. Clearly he had wanted to mystify the old lady and to amuse Jerphanion while involving him as an accomplice.

"He may have been trying to victimize you," Jallez suggested. "I'm just wondering to what extent he wanted to get you involved. . . . Fatally, I'm afraid. You couldn't help being suspected; the proof was there. You must admit that a dog like that leaves nothing to chance."

But Jerphanion refused to admit it, disliking the thought that Macaire would have played such a trick on him.

Pending an agreement on the facts, they adopted the phrase "to make water like Macaire," or, more discreetly, "to make the round of the carpet," when they wanted to describe any treacherous manœuvre whose consequences develop by delayed action at the expense of someone who is left to exculpate himself in the absence of the guilty party.

For instance, in the course of a conversation with another group of students, when someone who prided himself on a knowledge of parliamentary procedure entered upon a rather laborious description of Briand's recent attitude towards Clemenceau and other politicians, Jallez interrupted by saying quite casually: "Oh, yes, he's the kind of fellow who makes water like Macaire." To which the first speaker, who was from the provinces, and hated to be thought ignorant of Parisian slang, replied: "Exactly."

14

FIRST REFERENCE TO TELLIÈRE AND GENTILCŒUR. "THE PERFECT LIFE"

Thus it was that Jallez asked:

"How is Macaire? When are you going to bring him?"

He imagined Macaire, whom he had never seen, zigzagging along beside them, sniffing at the footprints of passers-by and lifting his leg against the rough rinds of pumpkins, with all the refinements of subtlety which he alone knew how to employ.

Then he abandoned this idea and started, with shining eyes, to look for others, as a man looks for friends in a crowd. He devoted himself to the cause of his happiness, not seeking stimulus for it, since it needed none, but ready to seize on every chance for it to show its power. He said to himself: "Now I'm going to think about this, now I'm going to say that, and while I say it, I shall feel more than ever that I am happy, that today is a day of days." The brilliance of each new idea gave the measure of his happiness, as the degree of incandescence of a substance held in a flame gives the measure of its heat. He felt that because his happiness was born of the sense of companionship, he must share it with his friend, that he must feed the fire of intimacy with even the most trivial adventures of his mind. "This is what I'm thinking, this is what amuses me; Jerphanion must think it too."

"You remember those two fellows I told you about, Tellière and Gentilcœur? Well, I've met them again."

"Tellière and—?"

"Gentilcœur. I've told you about them more than once."

"Oh, yes, I remember. . . . Keep your hair on!"

"I am keeping it on. Now, those two men belong to a very remarkable type. It's always difficult to achieve style in one's living, and still more difficult to maintain it, but particularly the kind of style I'm talking about. One needn't be a conjuror to become a dandy. All that's necessary is to have an eye for the niceties of a tie or an eyeglass. Of course there's a certain way of speaking, too, a special vocabulary, and a proper equipment of gestures—a manner of crooking the little finger, for example. I don't deny that one's got to work to get the effect; still, it's a profession like any other, and concerns nothing but the outer man. But with these men I'm talking about it's quite a different matter, a question of style that's almost on the heroic scale. Think, for instance, what prodigies of skill it would need to keep oneself one whole day in the state of mind in which we are at this moment!"

(Jallez looked anxiously about him, as though afraid of some threat.)

". . . Just think what it would mean to get one's daily life on to that level and keep it there. Morning to night, just think of it, the vast spaces of time that lie between any morning and any night, and of all the sobering, all the flattening, influences that are bound to assail one, between the moment when one scratches one's head on waking to the last sniff one gives before going to sleep. Think of the hundred and one accidents that occur to humble your pride and weaken your knees. No, men like that are an honour to the human race!"

Jerphanion thought that Jallez was getting rather too much excited.

"You mean the two fellows who decided to take everything as a joke?" he said flippantly.

"How you do cheapen things! It's not worthy of you."

Jerphanion felt slightly abashed.

"I don't know them, of course; I'm only talking at random."

"You should say rather that they've decided to take everything in a lyric mood, a mood, one might say, of high intoxication, not violently, like the Sei getrunken of Nietzsche's Zarathustra, but light, mercurial, a mood that is never divorced from intelligence and a sense of irony; the sort of mood that was known to Rabelais, to the Voltaire of Zadig and Candide, to the France of Jérôme Coignard."

"Hm, I don't quite see its practical application."

"You must have known at school those wonderful times when four or five in a class find that they have the same tastes, that they understand one another as it were instinctively, without the necessity of explanations. They improvise, they invent, setting themselves as an ideal the creation for their little group of a life that shall be unique and perfect. In such a life there can be no 'neutral' times, no minute that is not lived tensely to the full. Living thus, one never collapses on to oneself, never slackens, never gives the intelligence a day off. Joke follows on joke. One of the group, for instance, makes puns as naturally as he breathes, and the extraordinary thing is that such puns never bore one. Each of them seems to be a snap of the fingers in the face of respectability, a gesture of liberty, like a gust of wind that catches a woman's petticoats. The power of response in the others is never dulled. They are ready to laugh even before the pun is made. Even when they say: 'Oh, shut up, you fool!' it's with a sense of delight. Then there are the hoaxes played on the masters, each elaborately planned, the ragging of 'grinds' and toadies, the private language one uses, the special words one invents, so satisfying to those who know the secret, so apt for use at the moments when they are least expected. (And then, when one gets sick of them, one drops them, the great rule being never to run a good thing to death.) One invents myths and legends, fantasies that are suddenly made to live. One becomes the colonel, another the bald-headed banker, a third the archbishop with the varicose veins. From that moment the banker's habit of stroking his head while he looks mournfully at the open skylight is enough to throw one into a fit of ecstatic joy. . . . Does all that mean nothing to you?"

"Oh, yes, I see what you mean."

"Perhaps in the provinces schoolboys do less of that sort of thing?"

"Perhaps; but without supposing that, aren't you forgetting the moments of boredom?"

"Yes, I am forgetting them because they're too close. But boredom is only an element in school life, a diversion. For the moment I'm concerned with Tellière and Gentilcœur. . . . To go back to this question of the 'perfect life.' Speaking generally, I have the greatest sympathy with, the greatest admiration for, anybody who has tried at some time in the past to achieve that kind of thing. Man's natural pusillanimity inclines him to whine at life, to accept a ready-made existence, and the drabber it is, the more inevitable he tends to find it. Think of the daily life of most families, of the people who only feel comfortable when they are talking about illnesses and funerals and children's stomach-aches and the money they've lost. It's so easy to live a colourless existence—one's only got to let oneself go; while to decide, some fine morning, that one's going to enjoy oneself, or be brilliant, gracious, anything rather than a dim daily-breader, even if it be only for a time, even if one doesn't believe one can keep it up for more than a month or a week. . . . To live on the grand scale is simply a matter of intensity. Just to take up a challenge like that is to work in the cause of intensity, to move in the direction of greatness."

The increasing frequency of florists' and the shops of monument masons told them that they were approaching the neighbourhood of the cemetery of Saint-Ouen. As though by agreement Jallez and Jerphanion stopped in front of a row of little evergreen shrubs standing in pots, with, behind them, an array of sickly chrysanthemums, not entirely devoid of charm. Plated-metal receptacles of different shapes stood here and there, while in the recesses of the shop, islanded in spaces of cold light, separated one from another by warmer shadows, were various inscriptions commemorating, in general terms, the sentiments that bind humanity, the hopes with which mankind arms itself against death.

"What I find difficult to accept in these efforts after what you call the perfect life," said Jerphanion, "is the sense of effort, the compulsion of nature, the *forcing* oneself to do something."

Jallez thought for a moment, then:

"I understand that," he said, and was again lost in reverie. "God knows I love natural things. Nothing has estranged me from certain people more than their affectations. How complicated it all is! Obviously, the particular kind of style which a man tries to impose upon his life must correspond to something essential in himself, to something that is already active in some way or other. One can't imagine a lot of ugly women organizing a Decameron, any more than a set of pretentious gossips planning a life of bacchic ecstasy, however mercurial. Tellière and Gentilcœur have the gift. I imagine that they got to know each other at school, and that the memory of those early successes was the foundation upon which they built their creed and their undertaking. That alone is to have achieved something worth while. How long do most people remain capable of bacchic ecstasy? Tellière, I should say, is about thirty-eight; Gentilcœur hardly more than thirty-two or three, though if they were at school together, the difference must be less. . . . In any case, they are not young, but they're alive as no one past twenty is usually alive! What alertness it must have needed, how splendid a refusal to allow their vitality to be damped! Don't forget that hardening of the arteries begins at twenty-five!"

Jerphanion was struck by this last remark, which was made by his friend with impressive earnestness. He began to reckon the number of years (years indeed, perhaps months!) remaining to him before the hardening of the arteries should become a matter of personal concern. It occurred to him that it might be a good thing to hang up in the inner room of his consciousness, side by side with his *Memento magnitudinis*, another warning: "Remember that hardening of the arteries begins at twenty-five," and he would have translated the phrase at once into Latin and Greek had he not been prevented by certain difficulties of vocabulary.

Chapter

15

JEANNE, THE DRESSMAKER'S ASSISTANT. A WOMAN'S SHADOW

They had, however, left the shop of the monument mason some way behind, and Jallez was detailing to his friend the latest information he had been able to come by about the way in which Tellière and Gentilcœur arranged their lives.

Suddenly Jerphanion interposed:

"And the woman problem?"

"What about it?"

"Well, I mean it would be interesting to know their solution."

"Yes, I suppose it would."

"I imagine it would be one of the chief difficulties in that sort of experiment."

Jallez smiled.

"You're no fool, Jerphanion, my lad. Who ever would have thought that an old mountaineer would be so shrewd about things like that! They've certainly been seen with women, but I don't know how they deal with the ticklish part of the business. Obviously they can't just let things take their course. They must have some method."

He smiled again, stole a covert glance at Jerphanion, and hesitated. He decided that their present mood of elation dispensed him from observing the ordinary rules of discretion. He would take a risk.

"Do you mind my asking how *you* solve the woman problem?"

Jerphanion was not expecting so direct an attack. It was the first time that Jallez had ever asked him such a question. No confidences had followed the story of Hélène Sigeau.

He now seemed rather confused and, with his eyes fixed on the ground before him, began fingering his beard.

"My dear fellow, my solution isn't worth talking about. Nothing could be flatter."

It was obvious, however, in spite of his words, that he was not trying to hide anything. Jallez, who was usually extremely unwilling to ask people about their private lives, and even to listen to confidences when they were made unasked, was suddenly consumed by curiosity. Here was another miracle that happiness could accomplish. He began to dream of a world in which there should be no reservations.

Jerphanion went on:

"The question of a solution doesn't arise. My arrangements are of the most temporary and humble kind. For some time I had an affair with a charming little working girl."

"In Paris or in Lyons?"

"Here, in Paris. Oh, in Lyons I had one or two casual adventures of the same kind, and started a violent passion—you'll laugh—for a married woman who never noticed it, I think. . . ."

"As in Arvers's sonnet?"

"Yes, except that the husband wasn't a poet. He was a tailor."

"Did you go far with the other 'casual adventures'?"

"You mean, did they have any results? Well, yes, the ordinary ones."

Jallez made the mental comment, not without a sense of jealousy, that his friend's experience of love—of carnal love, at least—had begun a good deal earlier than his own, that it had already been more varied, and had led to no useless complications.

"Here in Paris I had this little piece called Jeanne."

"Jean—Jeanne. That's very nice."

"Wasn't it? She made the same remark the very first time we met."

Although Jallez was not particularly pleased by the coincidence, he passed it off with a laugh. It emboldened Jerphanion, however, to go into further detail.

"Yes, Jeanne was her name, and she was a dressmaker's assistant. She had a way of laughing at nothing, of telling me stories about the workroom, and talking of her uncle Eugène."

"You had your money's worth?"

"Yes, I used to think that I was like those tourists who after being shown Notre-Dame, the Louvre, the Obelisk, and the Eiffel Tower can't help the reflection that they're all exactly as they expected them to be."

Jallez was overcome by a return of modesty. Perhaps he was embarrassed by a sudden realization of the vulgarity of their conversation. As though to hide a sordid little incident behind a screen of generalities, he said:

"No doubt, as you are interested in social conditions, you took the opportunity to make a few indirect observations? I'm not joking. To be in love with a woman of a particular class is the best way of getting into touch with that class. The working people of Paris live in a world of their own, as we all do."

"Oh, I'd come in contact with it before. But my affair with Jeanne gave me an idea, or perhaps confirmed one I had already, that the working classes of Paris, and of anywhere else, for that matter, are extremely complicated and very hard to fathom. I don't say corrupt, although many people agree with Cato the Elder in considering complicated and corrupt as synonymous terms. To make a long story short, I left Jeanne because I suspected her of playing me false with a gentleman of about thirty-five who was giving her money—I use the word 'suspected' as a matter of courtesy. He wasn't really the sort of man she'd fall for—in fact she cared much less about him than about me, but all the same she let me go without any fuss. If she cried, it was only because she thought it was the right thing to do in the circumstances. She obviously thought it was better like that, and decided there was no point in regretting the past. As for the parents, well, they of course had known about it all (Jeanne was such a chatterer)—the mother as a result of detailed confidences, the father from various allusions and odds and ends of women's talk which he had caught while he seemed to be thinking of something else, sitting with his elbows on the table and grumbling, or smoking his pipe at the window, at the other end of the room. They had regarded the business with me as nothing more serious than a young girl's whim —'One's only young once'—though probably the mother had warned her against children and diseases. But when the other fellow appeared with his money, the whole family realized that there was something serious in the wind. I suppose it makes you want to say: 'What a crew! —the girl was only waiting for a chance to go gay, and the parents for the various advantages that would come to them from having a daughter in that line of life.' And since that particular family was nothing out of the ordinary, you'd be tempted to generalize and to say: 'What a world! What people!' But it's not so easy as all that— not that I wasn't pretty harsh in my judgment at the time. I felt bitter, and my bitterness gave me a pleasant sense of superiority. But imagine yourself in their shoes. They come of common-sense stock. For them, a romantic interlude with a student ranks as 'fun,' whereas to take up with someone who will keep you is—well, I won't go so far as saying that it's precisely virtuous, but at least it's one way of settling down. I've asked myself whether matters would have taken the turn they did if, instead of being myself, I'd been a young plumber of the neighbourhood."

"Why shouldn't they?"

"I've got an idea that my chief sin in the girl's eyes and her parents' was having no money. If I'd been a young plumber, that would have been natural and perhaps rather appealing. Probably in the long run she'd have deceived me just the same and gone off with someone else, but she wouldn't have had such a clear conscience."

"Probably because she'd have gone on hoping that the young plumber would marry her?"

"If not the young plumber, then somebody else of the same class. The young plumber would have benefited vicariously from the merits of the mechanic or the bus conductor or the carpenter who was to come along later and marry her. He would have enjoyed by proxy the marital rights, in their widest sense, of one of his mates. Drive the argument a little bit further, and one can frame, for the benefit of the sociologist, a theory of the collective husband."

"But you were not part of this collective husband?"

"No, the most I could manage to become, thanks to a moment's rashness which neither the girl nor her parents had foreseen, was a particular and accidental husband. And since, in my case, the collective husband wasn't in question, I had no right to the consideration reserved for his earliest manifestations—no right, that is, to the unselfishness and loyalty which a young girl like that shows in her affairs of the heart. It was inexcusable for me to be so poor and to be able to give her so few presents."

"One question, if you don't mind. Had she known anyone before you?"

"She'd certainly had flirtations."

"But—had she given herself to anyone?"

"I think so."

"You're not sure?"

"You find that comic?"

"Not at all," Jallez replied very seriously, "not at all."

"She made one or two vague references, and I didn't press for details. That sort of thing rather disgusts me, and I wasn't particularly anxious to know."

After a moment's pause Jallez asked, rather hesitatingly:

"You didn't find it possible—to know, without asking?"

"It's supposed to be easy enough. Perhaps it is in theory, but in practice it seems to me that there's room for doubt. Don't you think so?"

"Perhaps."

"Short of being an expert, and experts don't grow on every tree. Besides, in my case the doubt wasn't a matter of much importance. In other cases it might have been."

Jallez seemed to be extremely interested by the problem, and extremely averse from pursuing it.

"Well, then," he said, "you parted. How have you managed since?"

"Since?— Oh, nothing worth mentioning. Two or three wretched little adventures of the most sordid physical kind."

He felt himself trembling on the brink of another confidence. Like Jallez, he felt the day's joyful influence and was sensible of the atmosphere of frankness which seemed to be exhaled from their surroundings. The suburban avenue and its various incidents, dwindling away into a distance of light mist, had the effect of making him oblivious of his personal concerns and scornful of the little world of troubles which each of us carries with him as a load, clutching the key in an anxious hand. Every object was blankly presented to his gaze wherever he looked, softened by no veil of beauty—houses, factory chimneys, waste plots. No order anywhere, a mere casual agglomeration of bald facts, without any hint of mystery. And yet there was something in it all that could rouse his interest and his curiosity, so that he found himself constantly seeking some formula of unity, which as constantly escaped him. It was as though the very absence of mystery, realized on so large a scale, was, in the last analysis, itself mysterious.

But Jerphanion was better armed than Jallez against influences which had less precision for him than for his friend. "No," he decided, "I won't say anything about that."

"From what you tell me," said Jallez, "you don't seem, up to now, to have had much concern with what people think of as love on the grand scale. All these adventures of yours appear to have been pretty casual—that's to say, if one leaves out of account the affair of the married woman of Lyons. Is it that you're afraid of love, or has it just happened that way?"

Jerphanion got rather red.

"Chiefly, I suppose, it happened that way. But I've sometimes wondered whether for people like us, who think they've got a job to do in the world, the best solution of the woman problem isn't just a series of solutions of a casual kind. But in matters of that sort I haven't much confidence in theories or schemes. Don't you think that it all depends primarily on whom you meet or don't meet?"

"Yes, but also on how much you want to meet somebody, on where you look, and on what you think you'll find; for that's how one controls circumstances."

Jerphanion took a sudden decision and lowered his voice.

"As a matter of fact," he said, "quite lately I have met somebody. I don't say that at the moment it's a matter of love on the grand scale, and I hope it won't be; still, if I hadn't resisted— Now, I should never have dreamed of meeting this woman where I did meet her—quite the reverse—and she only corresponds very imperfectly with any idea I might vaguely have formed of the woman I might fall in love with. Let me add that even if I were ready for another little affair of the Jeanne type, I've no wish, at the moment, for sentimental complications."

Jallez listened, pondered, looked at Jerphanion's profile. Then: "You said you had to resist?"

"Myself, naturally. . . . " He started to laugh. "No one attacked me."

"And why did you resist yourself?"

"Because it was a question of—of the girl of a friend."

He spoke with some emotion. It was the matter of no more than a second for Jallez to examine two or three hypotheses. Was it conceivable that Jerphanion had met Juliette, about whom they had never spoken? Then he remembered that his friend had mentioned a young woman who was more or less engaged to Clanricard.

"Of an intimate friend?"

"Neither very intimate nor very old, but one I'm particularly anxious not to play a dirty trick on."

"I understand."

"What do you understand?"

"I repeat that I understand."

"So much the better. I needn't explain, then."

They exchanged a smile, and remained silent while they walked on about fifty yards. A truck full of crates kept level with them, moving at a slightly slower pace. The noise it made was an excuse for their silence.

Finally, however, they outdistanced it.

"Some day," said Jallez, "I'm going to ask your opinion about physical love."

"About physical love? That's an embarrassing subject."

"Do you think so?"

"I mean, there are so many ways of approaching it."

"Obviously. . . . One in particular, which may or may not be personal to me. I'm anxious to find out."

He walked on, his head bent, deep in thought. Jerphanion waited.

"It's true enough," Jallez continued, "that it occurs only as a result of certain spiritual dispositions. Think for a moment. . . . Oh, I know I'm a tiresome sort of chap; sometimes I get disgusted with myself. . . . Why do you look so surprised? I *am* thoroughly tiresome. I have a hateful facility for discovering subjects with which to torment myself, or, rather, I should say objects, so real do they seem. I go out of my way to make them assume an importance that prevents my just brushing them aside. You remember that famous evening when you found me with a lot of books about astronomy on the table? The evening we discussed Baudelaire. That's not the point now, but I mention it to remind you of the occasion. At that particular moment I was not passing through a very acute period—the word 'period' is especially apt. I want you to think of it as analogous to the 'periodicity' of an electric current. With me it's always a matter of various subjects of torment which follow one another, but overlap. The fact that one is dominant doesn't mean that the others vanish. . . . Well, for months now my life has been poisoned by an idea. Oh, nothing out of the ordinary, a perfectly commonplace idea. . . . But I see I'm going the wrong way about trying to explain it. Let me ask you a question instead. Doesn't it seem to you that there are days when merely to know, for example, the approximate dimensions of the stellar mass of which the sun forms a part, merely to have the simple idea of some quantity in time or space, of some fact of cosmic velocity, seems to deprive of all importance the things which must be considered important if life is to go on? I don't mean it romantically, but in a terrifyingly prosaic and positive sense, a sense as far removed from emotional complications as the rule of three. At such moments one realizes that to do anything one must endow it with at least a minimum degree of importance. Napoleon thought it important to dominate Europe. Hugo thought it important that people should speak of him three thousand years from now. Did they think it, or didn't they? To my mind there's no doubt about it. It was because of the intensity of their belief that they could concentrate such a mass of energy on attaining their ends. Now, put down on paper figures to represent the ambitions of Napoleon and Hugo and write beside them two or three astronomical quantities. That's the only argument needed. But from the moment one ceases to believe in the importance of 'ends,' one is left with only one reason for action: the necessity of forgetting one's own nothingness, as Pascal puts it, or, if you prefer it, a despairing dilettantism? You may add to that the sheer pleasure of acting, quite irrespective of any ends to be attained. That may be so, but I'm not sure that one can go on acting for long without making some such reflection as 'The end I'm attempting to achieve is an important end: however tired I feel today, I'm going to make an effort because an effort's worth while.' At such a moment, if your intelligence has got into the bad habit of whispering in your ear the average age of the red stars, it's all up with you; you might just as well spend the day in your arm-chair smoking cigarettes. And the worst of it is that if you did, you would have no sense of inferiority. No one's going to be able to bully you into acting by saying: 'Other people aren't such fools as to bother themselves about the age of the red stars. They've heard all about it as well as you; you're not the only person who's taken a degree, but it doesn't bother them'—just as though you were a sheep being taken from La Villette to the slaughter-house in a cart, but a sheep who knew what was waiting for you, and somebody said: 'What! you're depressed because you're going to be killed this afternoon? How ridiculous to meet trouble half-way! Look at your pals, they're not worrying.' Haven't you had moments like that?"

Jerphanion did not answer at once. He blinked, then he said:

"Naturally, I've had thoughts like that, but somehow they've never had much effect on me. Hearing you speak, I begin to wonder why. I must admit that if one really kept ideas like that in the forefront of one's mind and let them influence one, the reaction would be bound to be as you describe it. The only way out is not to keep them in the forefront of one's mind. Either one must be ignorant of them, like the coal-heaver at the corner, or one must accept them superficially as a schoolboy learns a list of the administrative districts of France. Well, then, it is simply that I'm frivolous-minded? Am I, too, just one of those people we were speaking of the other day, or, rather, you were speaking of, who just let ideas in at one ear and out at the other? Clearly, life's got to go on, and there's nothing one doesn't get used to. Think of the astronomer in the Observatory, who at this very moment, with his eye to the telescope, is eating his heart out because his colleague has just got the rise of two hundred francs that he ought to have had. A man like that is inoculated against the power of infinity, whereas I haven't got nearly such a good reason as he to minimize my own affairs. I know, of course, that there is a nobler answer to your problem."

"What?"

"Pascal's—that the real standards of value are spiritual and incapable of being dwarfed by your comparisons; that a fine poem, or an act of heroism, is something that is incommensurable with the volume of the nebulæ or the age of the red stars."

"Perhaps so, but strip Napoleon's ambition of the belief that the surface of Europe is something of value, or Hugo's that three thousand years of fame is important; what then? Do you really think, quite honestly, quite seriously, that a belief in nothing but spiritual values would produce much action? Do you think that those who are inspired by such values put as much into their work as those who believe also in material values? One can get a lot of pleasurable satisfaction out of ideas of that kind, but do they inspire one to 'produce'? You see what I mean by the word? I take it in its fullest sense, implying richness, courage, determination. By producing I mean covering the little bit of space within one's reach with solid objects that, in addition to giving the producer satisfaction, shall have value in themselves and the quality of lasting. To do a thing like that means making a great effort, means plodding on even when one's feeling lazy. It involves, too, the necessity of coming to terms with material things, and the idea that time and the spatial conditions of the world are things to be reckoned with. If one thinks them of no real importance one may perhaps write a short mystic poem, or a few epigrams; one may carve an exquisite statuette of ivory; one may even take part, with a disillusioned eye, in diplomatic conferences and amuse onself by shuffling the cards; but one's not going to build the Acropolis, or write the *Légende des Siècles,* or found an empire."

Suddenly becoming aware of the solemnity of his words, he burst out laughing, continuing, a moment later, in a tone of deliberate slyness: "I haven't forgotten that we were discussing physical love."

"So much the better; but what has physical love to do with what we were talking about?"

"I'm quite serious. I know from experience that there is such a thing as the torment of the infinite. Those who've never had the experience have every right to mock at it, but those who've been through it know that it's an agony like any other simple human agony, without any frills. True, it may be one of the contributory causes of the finest poetry, but it may also take the form simply of a sickness arising out of an absence of limits. It's not always a question of feeling dizzy on the heights, but often of not being able to hang on to the lower rungs of the ladder, of not being able to find somewhere to hide. The rungs give way, the walls vanish, carried away by the wind which blows to the ends of the universe, which has no end. Pascal spoke of a position midway between the two infinites, but one can only stay there a moment, the moment of tension that marks its discovery, like a climber who rests a few minutes on a ledge of rock. . . . Finally the need for some limit becomes an obsession, and that limit is just what physical love can give."

Jerphanion looked at Jallez with considerable surprise. His friend's words seemed to indicate that physical love was something that he had only recently found, a state of affairs that did not square with the ideas of his prowess which Jerphanion had entertained.

He said:

"Why just physical love? Why not love in general? I remember your saying one day that love shut us off from the rest of the world."

"Oh, I often seem to contradict myself. . . . Just now, whenever I think of love in a general way, whenever I try to set love in this universe swept and torn by the winds of the infinite, I see it in the form of two people standing on a canal bank."

"On a canal bank? What an extraordinary idea!"

"I don't know why—certainly not because of any symbolism. I mean a perfectly real sort of canal, here in Paris, or on the outskirts of Paris—the tow-path of the canal Saint-Martin, for instance, which is quite near here. I see them walking slowly, stopping, embracing each other. They stand close, face to face, and he holds her by the waist, looking intensely at her. She looks at nothing. Her eyes may be focused anywhere—on his shoulder or on the grey sky—but she looks at nothing; she is content to be entirely absorbed by his gaze. . . . Beneath their feet are the rough cobbles of the tow-path. The water is close at hand, with an empty boat and the dark tunnel of a bridge. The idea of this immeasurable universe whose limits the human spirit is for ever extending, breaking down, smashing. . . . And then this man's staring gaze and the face he is looking at so intently, all that takes on for me an oddly poignant quality. Worlds all around them rushing through space, nebulæ spinning in tight balls or strung out in long streamers, like wreaths of smoke in a storm, billions of miles, billions of years, a shower of burning cinders; and this little female creature, held motionless by his arms, watched by his eyes. It is a scene that touches the limit of improbability, something that it is impossible to justify. You see what I mean? What I get from all this is no sense of grandiose antithesis, no gesture of challenge in the face of the vast and absurd excesses of the universe; nothing like that, but a feeling of tenderness, of compassionate fear for those faces on the brink of the abyss. What I want to say to the man is: 'You are right. Hang on to your minute. Perhaps we shall never know what its place is in this maelstrom of the worlds. But never, since the first moment that man tried to imagine all that he loved as the centre of a vast spinning chaos of circumstance, has there been more reason for him to fix his gaze upon this tiny, tiny face balanced on the great circle of the abyss.' "

Jallez and Jerphanion were passing, at this very moment, a railway bridge. To their right the criss-cross of metal rose and fell beneath the mass of the curved framework, on which the heads of nuts looked like pimples on a reptile's hide.

"But I think of physical love as something different again. Suddenly one is really shut in. Here too there is a sense of the absolute, and the miraculous thing about it is that it is an absolute of solidity. It belongs to the same family of things as that whirling tempest of matter all around in which one can find no resting-place. Suddenly one is conscious of limits, so close, so solid, that one can gain assurance by touching them; a glowing cell whose walls keep the outer darkness at bay, closing one in, refracting its light on to the body within. . . ."

Jerphanion listened, and as he listened he tried to make application of what he heard. "To what actuality of his own does all this respond? What is the experience he is going through? I can't believe that he is only just discovering physical love, but perhaps something is happening to him which he finds more intoxicating, more complete than anything that happened before."

A little later they entered Saint-Denis by a bridge which crossed a canal filled with grimy barges and lined with factories. ("Perhaps," thought Jerphanion, "this is the very canal he was describing just now.")

"You've never been to Saint-Denis before?" Jallez asked him.

"Never."

"Well, then, just wait and see. Although it's so near Paris it's got all the atmosphere of some provincial town of the north. I think you'll like it. I don't mean only the Basilica; that you'll certainly like, because you like Notre-Dame. In a way it's an epitome of its school, a sort of 'typical Gothic cathedral,' sturdy and honest. If one didn't know beforehand about the kings who are buried there, the idea of kings wouldn't occur to one, or if it did, it would be the idea of a kingly office still in close touch with the people, something very far removed from Versailles. . . . There is a very pleasant street that runs straight through the centre of the town. It leads from that church there, the belfry of which you can see, to the Basilica, in a direct line from church to church. It is a busy, crowded street, the very type of the main street of a northern city. There's also rather a jolly Town Hall between the market and the Basilica. It must have been built—I don't know exactly when, but some time during the Second Empire, by an architect who meant it to resemble some old building. But he was lucky enough to employ a stone that weathered quickly, so that the façade, especially the upper storeys, has taken on an impressive appearance of great age."

They agreed that half the effect of architecture is due to the "deceptive action of time," and that there is no art, however vulgar or even stupid in its original state, which cannot be modified by age. They spoke of the Middle Ages, which both of them loved; about Villon, whose praises were sung by Jallez with the rather feverish passion to which he sometimes gave vent. He quoted some lines from the *Grand Testament,* among others:

> "And women's bodies, fair of show,
> So dainty, soft, and point-devise . . ." [1]

which led him to expatiate upon the wonderful way in which the vagabond poet could endow his sensuality with a refined and delicate melancholy. He went on to argue that those æsthetic philosophers are wrong who maintain that a man only thinks a woman beautiful because he desires to possess her, laying it down as an axiom that the

[1] This English version is taken from a translation of Villon by the late George Heyer (Oxford University Press, 1924). For permission to use it the present translator is indebted to Mr. Heyer's widow.—Translator's note.

idea of beauty is purely illusory, and nothing but a transference of the sexual instinct.

"I agree that he might desire her even if she weren't so beautiful (after all, a Hottentot desires a Hottentot), but my point is that he would still find her beautiful even if he didn't desire her at all. Of course it's odd that the most beautiful unit of animal life is the female of the human species. I admit the extraordinary and almost incredible coincidence, but it's no more extraordinary than its companion fact that the male of the species happens to be the most intelligent unit of animal life."

Jerphanion did not miss the opportunity to observe to himself that Jallez's ideas, however far they might diverge from their starting-point, always tended in the same direction, and he found it by no means unpleasant to follow his lead. Jallez next proceeded to glorify the beauties of the female body, by a series of discreet hints of so general a nature that all suggestion of coarseness was avoided. Nevertheless, it was no abstract type of beauty that his words evoked as he proceeded. As the smoke of a fire takes on definite shapes, his words began to suggest certain concrete contours, certain qualities of outline and colour. Vaguely Jerphanion began to see the form of a naked woman taking shape before his eyes. "His woman," he thought, and tried to see clearly the figure thus vaguely adumbrated.

The street grew wider as they advanced, until it opened into a square in front of the Basilica. On their left was the market, a hive of morning activity, filled with the gay liveliness of the food-stalls, the noise of bargaining, the smell inseparable from such places. Above them the façade of the Town Hall, particularly its upper part, did indeed look as though it were crumbling with the decay of centuries, and at the far end stood the Basilica, with an air of almost excessive repose. The idea of the naked woman, though still confined to the region of their imaginations, seemed, in a fleeting way, to superimpose itself upon the world of visible objects.

Jallez and Jerphanion walked towards the church. The two towers had the appearance of having grown at different speeds. Above the porches, like smoke or the shadow of a swallow, too indistinct for definition, Jallez's naked woman flitted, as though seeking its place in one of the niches.

A NEW GAME

An hour later Jallez and Jerphanion were seated opposite each other at an inn on the main road, a real country inn. Between them was a thick wooden table. Jallez was leaning back against the wall, facing the bar. Jerphanion was opposite the wall, which was adorned with two advertisements of liqueurs.

Beside them stood a bottle of white wine and two glasses. Each had before him a piece of squared paper provided by the landlord. They were absorbed in trying to make a fair copy in duplicate of a sort of diagram composed of three columns.

The left-hand column contained a series of questions, the middle column Jerphanion's answers, the right-hand column Jallez's.

The game had begun when they came out of the old cemetery of Saint-Denis, to which they had paid a passing visit after wandering about the town. Their talk had been of many things, and Jallez had alternately voiced and concealed his preoccupations. "What sort of death would you choose?" he had asked. "And at what age?" They debated the problem, finding it full of meat, each setting himself to formulate a mathematically accurate answer. The game thus well started fired them to continue. They devised other questions, some of them of a less serious kind, determining their answers with the same earnestness. Although they had made a rule that the replies must be perfectly spontaneous and arrived at independently, they criticized each other, raised objections, defended their choices, and egged each other on to an ever greater accuracy of definition, an ever more meticulous sincerity. "What! I'd never have expected you to say that!" or "Lucan? No, no, old man, you're exaggerating," or "You're not thinking! You say so today, but you won't tomorrow." In practice they made a good many concessions. The game was still going on when they entered the inn, and they agreed that it was essential that they should get the results down on paper.

This is what they wrote:

LIST OF PREFERENCES

(valid for the first quarter of 1910)

	Jerphanion	Jallez
Month	August	June (or October)
Age . . .	35	25
Age of death . .	89	70
Manner of death .	Old age (with such contributory cause as slight influenza)	Heart attack
Colour	Orange-red	Blue-grey
Woman's name . .	Mireille	Juliette
Public monument .	Parthenon (from photographs)	Cathedral of Chartres (from first-hand knowledge)
Picture	"Mona Lisa"	Rembrandt's "On the Road to Emmaus"
Musical composition .	"The Ride of the Valkyries"	Adagio of Beethoven's *Op.* 106
Play	*Polyeucte* or *Don Juan* (Molière's)	*The Tempest* or the First Part of *Faust*
Statue	"Victory of Samothrace"	Rodin's "John the Baptist," or the "Smiling Virgin of Reims"
Poems . . .	Hugo's *Le Satyre*	Six poems to be chosen from the *Fleurs du Mal*
Hero of fiction .	Pantagruel	Faust
Heroine of fiction .	Antigone	Yseult
Historical hero . .	Marcus Aurelius	Socrates
Artist	Leonardo da Vinci	Beethoven
Writer	Hugo	Hugo (in the strictly specialized sense of "writer")
Philosopher . . .	Spinoza	Plato
Individual . . .	Aristotle	Goethe

Reading over what they had written, they agreed that their list was incomplete and badly arranged, and that on more than one point there was a certain amount of ambiguity as a result of brevity.

No one, of course, was to see it but themselves, and Jallez put in a claim that his answers should be regarded as valid only for the day, the precise date of which he wanted to put at the beginning. Jerphanion, however, carried his point that validity should be held to extend to the whole of the present quarter.

Three carters at the bar were discussing the weather, which was fine, but would not last. They foretold rain for the morrow. One of them said that in the south-east of Paris it had been raining for several days without a break, and that in the neighbourhood of Lagny, from which he had come, the Marne was already in flood.

In front of the inn a horse belonging to one of the teams began to neigh loudly at regular intervals. Another was pawing at a crack between two cobbles, and seemed angry at not being able to tear up a tuft of yellowish grass.

Chapter

17

JERPHANION TRIES TO UNDERSTAND JALLEZ'S LOVE-AFFAIR

That evening, seated in their study, and profiting by the fact that Jallez was dining with friends, Jerphanion rapidly jotted down the following note:

NOTE

I'm writing this in order to get down on paper the various inferences which I made in the course of a walk with Jallez, so that I may be able later to compare them with any more definite information that I may get hold of.

I intend to make notes of this kind whenever the occasion seems to warrant the trouble. Primary object: exercising and verifying my powers of observation in the matter of character. Secondary object: collecting a quantity of human documents at first hand. Underlying motive: the amusement I expect to derive from it. Obvious danger: that I shall soon cease to be amused. Chief snag to be avoided: making notes about things that aren't worth it. On no account must I be lured into keeping an "intimate diary"—a thing that I detest. No hint of the literary touch about it. It must be strictly in the manner of a police report.

Jallez certainly is worth while. He is the most interesting man I have ever known intimately, and also the most complex. To understand *him* would be evidence of a quite remarkable degree of perspicacity.

What exactly is the problem? To reconstruct his experiences from what he told me today, and from what he only hinted at, his general behaviour, etc. . . . Perhaps some day he'll tell me of his own accord, but that's not very likely. He's not in the habit of making confidences except about things that happened so long ago that they've ceased to have any direct significance (Hélène Sigeau). If he does tell me, so much the better; then I shall be able to check up on my solution.

In other words, what I've got to do is to substitute for the vague impressions of which I'm always conscious when he's speaking, and with which it would be easy enough to be satisfied, precise hypotheses which will admit of verification when the time comes.

I will begin by putting down the things I'm certain of. First of all, something *is* happening to him; secondly, that something has got to do with love; thirdly, this love-affair is something to which he attaches very great importance; and fourthly, the fact of physical passion has for him now an unaccustomed significance, a significance which was not present in his earlier affairs. I don't think that up to here I've much distorted the facts.

Now let me get to closer grips with the problem.

The woman he's in love with is probably called Juliette. I thought his choice of the name in his list of preferences barely justified by any general reason of æsthetic taste. When I asked him about it, he was clearly embarrassed, saying that he was probably influenced by his memory of Shakspere's Juliet—an argument that rang false.

She is probably a young girl, of a social class in which discretion is the rule for young girls. The fact that there are exceptions doesn't disprove the rule. No parallel, therefore, between this girl and my dressmaker's assistant, Jeanne.

Can I place her more exactly? I have an idea that he sees her pretty often, and without much difficulty, and that their meetings are of considerable duration. I don't know much about young girls "in society," but I shouldn't think they are as free as all that. I can't imagine Jeanne de Saint-Papoul managing to meet a young man several times and spending several hours with him every week, still less (if the shade of Mlle Bernardine will permit the word) with a lover. The only other alternative is that she is a student, but there's no evidence for that. Say, then, for the sake of argument, a nice young girl of the middle class.

Another point: he seems to me to be rather surprised—I was going to say almost disappointed—at the amount of liberty she is mistress of. On one occasion he said: "If one hasn't got a sister, one thinks of young girls as being very severely watched, as they used to be. Fashions have changed without one noticing, and the conditions of life for young girls are now very much what they are for young boys"—a remark which confirms my supposition that she belongs to a social class in which girls are traditionally watched over.

In fact, as a result of knowing Jallez, she is no longer a "young girl," in the technical sense. I'm certain she is his mistress. There's nothing very odd in all this. What is odd is the importance that Jallez seems to be giving to the physical aspect of love. If he were someone else, I should think that he was discovering physical passion for the first time, but that's most unlikely of Jallez. His experience of that must go back a long way—further back, probably, than my own, and I should think it's been more varied. The only explanation is that this present affair has revealed new and profounder aspects of it to him. It's not very surprising that it should be so, that he's never been deeply in love with anyone since Hélène Sigeau. His other mistresses only touched his heart and his emotions superficially. This is the first time that he's possessed a woman whom he loves completely (or, perhaps, that he loves completely the woman he possesses). It's natural, therefore, that the whole question of physical love should have become transfigured for him, so that, being as he is, a man who feels nothing conventionally, to whom every experience is something real and individual, he has the illusion of discovering it for the first time. Although I've not nearly the same lyric gift as he has, I can well imagine what physical experience might become in the arms of a woman with whom I was passionately in love. It's also possible that the young girl in question is particularly skilled in the art of love. Why not?

In spite of myself, I can't help seeing her naked. Not that this idiosyncrasy gives me any pleasure—in fact, being his friend, it's rather embarrassing. But it's his fault—no question of that—for imposing on my imagination the picture of a naked woman. I remember how, as a result of what he said, I was obsessed by the idea as we were walking towards the Basilica. She seemed to be floating above the Gothic ornaments. What little Christian modesty I have left made me try to cover her with a few shreds of drapery and mix her in with the company of virgins and saints on the façade.

The image is clear enough in my mind. A body of medium size, not very small and not very slim. Not plump either, but very definitely feminine; rather dark-skinned, and with dark hair; not very remarkable hair (nothing he said or did gave me a very clear impression of her hair). I can't see her eyes, but I imagine them as dark, too.

I've got a pretty clear idea as well about her moral make-up. Not that I'm particularly interested in her character, but Jallez has now and again let drop certain opinions about women's nature in general, about the eternal feminine—cursory attempts, as it were, at a summing up. Now, I'm interested in what Jallez has to say on any subject, and I'm curious to see whether his present view of women is the result of his general reflections, his general knowledge of life, and his reading, or whether it is the universalizing of some actual experience. If it is the latter, then the value of his statements would be considerably modified.

He has often referred to the feminine heart as an "abyss." He used the word laughingly, because he has a dislike of emphatic formulas and made phrases. But there was something in his mind. It seemed to me that he was impressed by the contradictions and complexities of women. "They hide their true feelings, they lie, much more easily than we do—so easily that one wonders whether they don't find pleasure in it." Talking about their bodies, he quoted Villon; and about their minds, Schopenhauer and Vigny (the Vigny of Delilah, not the Vigny of Éloa). Although refusing to accept any general woman-hating theories, he seemed to find it natural to go to woman-hating authors where it was a matter of making observations rather than of drawing conclusions. I should say that he spoke of women's lies rather as a spectator than as a victim. Perhaps there is some connexion between this state of mind and the liberty of movement enjoyed by his young woman, since, obviously, she can't get free of her family without having some skill in lying.

I have an idea that he is thinking less than ever of marriage, and I'm glad of it, for general as well as particular reasons.

He has given me to understand that he walks about Paris a good deal with her, and I must admit that the idea makes me rather jealous and rather displeased. I find it difficult to explain why that should be so. Our walks together seem to have a unique quality about them which they ought to keep. They have the power of raising our existence to a level of serene delight. At such times we are united by a sort of high activity of the spirit, a sort of intense medium into which we can plunge and in which everything takes on a character of calm ecstasy. Such an experience is precious and difficult to maintain, like everything that demands for its realization a difficult combination of circumstances. If, for example, one day we took a girl friend with us on one of our walks, the whole thing would be different. It might be pleasant or amusing, but in a totally different and, I do honestly believe, an inferior way. In the same way it makes me uncomfortable to think of Jallez and his Juliette (if her name is Juliette) taking one of *our* walks together. Love is out of place in a rite of that kind. Either Jallez would try to recapture the mood of the walks he takes with me, and then it would be spoiled, or else he would try to create an entirely new mood. I feel that it is unworthy of him to think of one of his sentimental saunters on the same terms as one of our walks. By doing so he is guilty of a confusion of planes and of values, which he would severely condemn in another.

I make an exception of what he told me about their meetings in cemeteries. That was the one point he very nearly spoke to me about. He tried, of course, to maintain the impersonal note. "It seems to me," he said, "that there is no better place for lovers to meet than a cemetery like Père-Lachaise or Montmartre. . . . One waits in one of the paths close by some tomb that no one ever visits, and assumes the personality of one of the descendants of some family, say the Rennevaud-Dumazy, on whose mausoleum the last date visible through the encroaching moss is 1876. . . ." But he kept on hesitating, and then, suddenly, his talk fell into the mood of the past imperfect: "One day when I had been waiting for almost an hour—a thin rain was falling at the time . . ." instead of keeping to the present tense of his generalized description. Simultaneously, he abandoned the discreetly amused, sort of Jules Laforgue tone on which he had begun, and started to speak, I can swear, on a note of personal emotion.

When he left me to go to dinner with his friends, I began to think about these love trysts in the cemeteries of Paris. I understand now why he took me, the other day, to Père-Lachaise. We wandered about the paths, stopping here and there. He hardly spoke except, now and again, to say: "Isn't it all rather charming?" or: "Don't you agree that there's nothing sad about it, even though just now, save for the cypresses and yews, the trees are leafless, and only a few birds sing? Imagine what this grave is like in May, and this little mounting path, when there has been no rain for two days, and the trees are still bright with their early green."

I always think of him now as waiting in some such path for his lady. He walks up and down among the gravestones, reading the inscriptions, the record of "odd names," dates that "bring a lump into the throat." "Have you ever noticed," he said to me once, "how many odd names one finds in a cemetery, and how names that sound ordinary enough when spoken in the bustle of daily life become odd when one sees them written horizontally on a stone or has them forced on one's attention by the pediment of a mortuary chapel?" Suddenly he sees his beloved at the far end of the path, walking quickly between the graves like somebody who is late for an appointment, heralded by the shimmer of leaves and the songs of birds. I imagine her smiling, a little flushed, dressed in some light material, and carrying a closed umbrella or parasol. Probably the path is narrow, so that she has to walk rather carefully in order to keep to the gravel and avoid stepping on the slabs that belong to the dead. Perhaps, as she hurries, her skirt brushes a tombstone, or the end of her dangling umbrella touches an evergreen or a geranium. How, I wonder, do they meet? Do they smile a little differently because of the graves about them?

I've tried to imagine why he arranges these cemetery trysts, and what it is that makes him go on with them; because he does repeat them, anyhow occasionally. The thing fascinates him, obviously, since he makes each meeting last as long as possible. "A Paris cemetery is a very big place," he said to me, "with every sort of street and lane and cross-road. There are endless paths; there are slopes and little hills. One can wander there for hours without seeming to come back to the place from which one started."

He denies that he is deliberately courting any feeling of romance, arguing the most prosaic advantages. If one is afraid of meeting any-one, he says, one runs less risk in a cemetery than anywhere else. It may be that his lady, despite her apparent freedom, is nervous for fear someone may tell on her. For all her parents' willingness to wink at her story-telling, they might have to pay attention to information of that kind and change their attitude. It may be that Jallez himself doesn't want to be seen. He hates that kind of publicity. Besides, how-ever independent he may be of his relations, I'm pretty sure he wouldn't like to have to answer their questions about a matter like that, no matter how discreetly they were asked.

Let that be as it may, it doesn't alter the fact that his manner of talking about all this sort of thing stinks of poetry; so much so that I begin to feel the influence myself.

It's a kind of poetry that I have every reason to find unsympathetic, because it evokes a mood of morbid romanticism, which, as a matter of fact, is not natural to him.

How morbid is it? I must admit that there's nothing in his senti-ments, so far as he's confided them to me, that could be strictly called baudelairean, no attraction to the idea of death, no liking for decom-position or hankering after dancing skeletons, no craving for horror, no perverse ecstasy induced by the rank smell of corpses. There's nothing of that sort about him. At most, perhaps, there might be a touch of the moral atmosphere of Barrès's *Amori et dolori sacrum,* which he made me read this autumn, and parts of which I liked. There's this amount in common between his mania and Barrès's book, that both find a certain charm in the proximity of love and death, a sweetness in just touching the garment of the dead, a blindness of passion that is induced by their presence. Thoughts of the grave preach no sermon against kisses. The very fact that they tell us of peace and the end of all things, that they make most of our troubles seem foolish, and our planning empty, gives added worth to love, which is nothing if not an intoxication, nothing if it is not of the here and now. Such thoughts are the gift of wisdom, not of morbid sickness; of wisdom clear-sighted, born of the ageless knowledge of mankind, renewing itself as the year renews its seasons, no more to be repelled than the sweetness of the spring when first it snares our senses. One's only got to put oneself in his position. Let me imagine for a moment that I hold in my arms a young woman bright of eye and fair of face, that behind us lie those graves, such as I have seen them, adorned and bright with flowers. I see them above her head, which lies against my heart, behind her neck and her hair, a serried presence of stone and wrought ironwork, of roses and written names, of symbols of mortality. And over us and them the trees filled with birds. (Jallez's very words.) How well I can imagine the swooning sweetness of the moment that would seem as though it were an emanation of the very ground we stood on! We should feel as though we were the one fresh bloom among a faded company, and hear from those other, dead and draggled flowers a voice exhorting us: "Live to the uttermost!" I know that the flesh beneath my lips would seem more sacred then than ever. If at such a moment there should dawn in my mistress's eyes the light that told of passion reawakened and the surrender of desire, I should find in it a special innocence, since in no other place would desire seem less a selfish thing, less bounded in the single life.

But these walks in Père-Lachaise and the Montmartre cemetery have other charms as well for him. I can hear him say again: "How strong a sense one has in a cemetery of being in a *city*!" He has often insisted on this sensation of being in a city, stressing the multiplicity of the paths, the crowded presence of those little houses. I remember him saying how much easier to "read" they were than the houses of the living. The inscriptions interest and move him. He sees them as street-signs, though more eloquent than most, telling of fundamental things; "the street-signs of destiny." In them the passer-by can read the meeting-points of lives, the constant criss-cross of existence, the growth and death of families. What he loves to feel in these great cemeteries is a sort of transference of the city's life, a sort of "melancholy personification" of Paris.

I said to him once: "I should like to ask you a question, but I'm afraid you'll think it stupid."—"What is it?" he said.—"When you are in one of these cemeteries," I asked, "do you feel something more than what you've described, something that you can't just simply account for by your own feelings?"—"Explain."—"I mean, are you conscious of a presence that is not your own nor yet your companion's, nor yet that of anyone else who happens to be walking round the paths?" He smiled, admitting that he would be hard put to it to answer.

"You mean," he said at length, "something that comes directly from the dead men and the dead women about us? I'm not sure. . . . I don't very much want to say anything definite, but I'm coming more and more to think of the human soul as something that's capable of a great many different modes of existence. . . . A sort of meteorological idea of the soul."

He wouldn't say any more, and we were just then getting near the end of our walk, in the most crowded part of the boulevard de Sébastopol. It was difficult to carry on an intimate conversation because of the noise. Besides, we were very tired.

But I see I've been wandering from the point. I swore that I wouldn't indulge in literature, and that's just what I have done. I didn't set out with the intention of following Jallez into the by-ways of his thoughts and feelings. What I meant to do was reckon the chances for and against a set of perfectly definite hypotheses, and I hope that I shall soon have an opportunity to verify my guesses and see where I've won and where I've lost.

Before I finish I should like to put on record one particular point which I've noticed more than once today, and that is how far removed Jallez's preoccupations seem to be from those of Clanricard and Laulerque, and even from my own. One could almost say that he has no interest in what's actually going on round us, or at least not in the moral, social, and political problems that are exercising the rest of us. In certain respects he's in close enough touch with actualities, and even with most transient aspects of life. But it's rather as though for him there was no fundamental difference between the momentary and the eternal; as though on one side there was something that is at once present and eternal, and on the other something that religious people, and Jallez himself, would call scornfully "the temporal." I don't care; I'm not merely a dreamer. The present condition of society and of the human race is stifling and oppressive, especially for those of us who are young, who feel the approach of disasters for which we are not responsible, and who get no help from our elders, at least in the ordinary way of life.

I didn't dare talk to him about all this today, but I will as soon as possible. One question in particular I mean to put to him: "Don't you feel the need of some sort of Church? Do you feel you can do without one?" He will probably answer: "Yes, with the greatest ease." But I'm not sure that if he does, it won't be, at bottom, just an affectation of superiority.

Chapter

A LITTLE LIGHT ON ROTHWEIL.
BOATS IN THE STREET

On the 26th of January, Jerphanion received the
following letter from Clanricard:

"I've fixed things with Rothweil. He expects us the day after tomorrow, the 27th, at a quarter to five. Can you meet me at half past
four at the Café du Delta? That will give us time to get to him without hurrying. I only hope that between now and then the floods won't
have completely cut off your left bank from my right.

"Yours very sincerely,

"E. Cl."

By twenty minutes past four Rothweil was in his study, ready for
the visit of the two young men. Before coming up from the shop by
the private stairs, he had said to his chief assistant:

"I don't want to be disturbed. If the salesman from Limoges calls,
you see him. Tell him to leave his prices, and say I'll telephone him
tomorrow at his hotel if I can."

The assistant was used to receiving such instructions. He knew
that his employer very often had visitors of importance who had
nothing to do with the business of selling shoes, and that at such
times he mustn't be bothered. These visitors reached the first-floor flat
by way of the door that gave on to the public staircase.

Rothweil's study was a smallish room, lit by a single window looking on to the rue de Dunkerque. The furniture, Gothic in style, consisted of a large table, the corners of which were adorned with carved
gargoyle-like figures; a long bookcase which occupied almost the
whole of the back wall behind the table; a smaller bookcase, heavily
sculptured, between the corner of the same wall and the window; a

canopied seat; several chairs of vaguely Merovingian design, and an elbow-chair of no particular style, upholstered in tapestry. The seat reserved for the use of the master of the house was an arm-chair of roomy proportions.

The window was large, and, being situated at the far end of the room, which had greater length than breadth, provided an adequate amount of illumination. Four panels of ancient stained glass, however, had been hung in it, and although these imparted a pleasing quality to the impersonal and slightly stale light that drifted in from the rue de Dunkerque, they impeded the passage of a considerable proportion of it.

This light had no sooner made its way into the room than it became visible as a dusty, eddying haze. The eyes of an occupant were drawn first to the confused fragments of coloured glass and then, returning to the main area of the room, were conscious of the slow, lazy rotation of the motes that filled it.

There were several pictures on the walls and a considerable number of engravings, or reproductions of engravings, with recognizable subjects. Thus on either side of the fire-place hung David's "Oath of the Tennis-Court" and Prud'hon's "Justice and Truth Pursuing Crime," while a small alcove was adorned with "La Source" by Ingres. Over the mantelpiece, and facing the table, was another engraving representing an ancient palace or temple of vast proportions, standing on a rocky plateau with precipitous sides.

One of the pictures, which, despite its general faded appearance, retained traces of bright colour, showed an artificially composed landscape in which a company of charming figures, naked or partially naked, were executing a dance, and presumably represented a scene of "Fauns and Bacchantes." On the white marble chimney-piece stood a slim bronze figure of a youth in pensive attitude. Here and there, in the obscurer parts of the room, a few nudes of young men and women gave to the shadowy interior an air of furtive gaiety.

There was a pervasive smell, so subtle as not at first to be noticeable. But it was of so remarkable a quality that by degrees it attacked and held the attention. There was a suspicion, but no more, of tobacco in it, and it seemed difficult to account for it by the large number of leather-bound books which occupied the shelves. Further analysis determined the fact that it was at its strongest in the neighbourhood of the door, and visitors who knew something about the character of the house remembered the shoe-shop below.

Rothweil prepared himself to receive his visitors. Leaning back, the curve of his stomach touching the table, his elbows on the arms of his chair, his right cheek supported by the closed fingers of his hand, he gave himself to thought.

Suddenly he leaned forward, sniffed, took from a folder of green paper a note, of which he already knew the contents, and proceeded to read it again.

It ran as follows:

"Jerphanion (Jean) is at the present moment a second-year student at the College, where he boards. He is the son of a schoolmaster. His father works in the department of Haute-Loire. There is nothing particular to say about the father, who is probably a good republican. The son was educated at the Lycée in Lyons. He did not pass into the College particularly high, but has since proved himself to be among the soundest and most distinguished men of his year. He chose to major in literature, and took his degree easily (honourable mention, if I am not mistaken). He chose as the subject of his thesis 'Rousseau as Legislator,' treating it in a spirit of sympathetic understanding. He is on good terms with his fellow-pupils, but takes little part in their various activities. He seems to have little regular contact with any students, or groups of students, of the Sorbonne. Consequently there have been but few occasions on which he has given expression to his ideas or his tendencies in the presence of witnesses. His chief, and almost only, intimate is a man called Jallez, of his own year, very brilliant, but eccentric, who adopts an attitude of detachment from his fellows, certain of whom he regards with ill-disguised contempt, which he extends to their political convictions. Jallez seems to have great influence on J. J., whom he encourages, unfortunately, in an attitude of dilettante scepticism. Otherwise, J. J.'s personal opinions, so far as it is possible to discover them, seem to be frankly of the Left, with a tendency towards the extreme Left. Although he was brought up as a Catholic, he is a free-thinker where religion is concerned, and entirely untouched by that new snobbery of Catholicism which is so fashionable among certain members of the younger generation. Not long ago he very nearly joined the Socialist Party, but held back, for the time being at least, for reasons of which I am ignorant. He talks of Jaurès with respect and admiration, and has spoken on several occasions of the necessity and imminence of a social revolution of a more or less collectivist nature. Although not openly opposed to the Radical Party, he clearly shares the fairly general prejudice against the personalities of those at the head of the Third Republic.

"So far as moral qualities are concerned, J. J. seems to be energetic, capable of concentration, and reserved. He works easily and quickly. His private life calls for no particular comment.

"Summing up, I should say that J. J. would, in general, be a valuable recruit, who might one day render outstanding service. But it is essential to make quite certain of the seriousness and sincerity of his interest in the Order. It is possible that he is inspired by nothing more than curiosity, and if that is so, his friendship with Jallez might turn out to be rather dangerous. Without going so far as to suspect him of carrying out a hoax inspired by his friend, it would be wise to take special precautions in his case. It should be unnecessary to add that the normal tests of initiation should be dispensed with. It ought to be possible to discover the sincerity of his intentions without them, and, if my suspicions are correct, their employment would serve only to whet his curiosity, and provide fuel for his irony."

There was no signature.

In the same file were two short letters. One of these, signed "Ad.

Marjaurie.·.," was no more than a covering letter to the document already quoted. The other, adorned by an almost illegible signature, and bearing at the head of the page nothing but the date, ran as follows:

"Dear Friend,

"The young man of whom you write seems to be sound and serious, though marked by a certain quickness of temper inseparable from his age. I believe he has character and that he is ambitious. He goes out often and for longish periods, and the regularity of his work suffers from these interruptions. But his general behaviour gives no cause for serious suspicion, and he can work hard enough when he has to. His tastes and the direction of his thought accentuate, I should say, the tendencies of his heredity (his father is a schoolmaster). He belongs, or thinks he belongs, to the extreme Left; but up to now a sort of peasant shrewdness has prevented him from joining any party.

"Outside his regular work at the College, he acts as a tutor in an aristocratic family of liberal leanings, and seems to have shown tact in the exercise of his functions.

"In general, I can see nothing in him to contradict the views you have already formed. Any difficulties there might be would probably arise from the critical nature of his temperament and from the independence of his judgment, which is more than normally marked. Apart from the fact of his personal ambitions, I should say that he would be more open than others of the same standard of education to the influence of ideals and to the purely intellectual quality of the arguments addressed to him.

"Very sincerely yours."

Rothweil was deeply sunk in thought when the servant came to say that a lady was asking to see him.

"Who is it?"

"I don't know her name. She's been here once or twice before."

The servant, whose age and appearance were those of a housekeeper, spoke primly.

"All right, then. . . . But say I can only spare her a moment."

He rose to receive his visitor, who turned out to be a woman of about fifty, in no way out of the ordinary except, perhaps, that she was a little too heavily powdered and seemed to be dressed in her Sunday finery.

He spoke to her in a low voice, asking with rather anxious haste: "What has happened?"

"Nothing. . . . I only came to ask you to turn up earlier if you can, say at half past five."

"But why?"

"Because otherwise you won't have time. It isn't his fault. It was impossible to arrange it better."

"Half past five. . . . But that's much too early."

"A quarter to six, then, if you'd rather."

"A quarter to six! A quarter to six! All right, then. The floods won't stop my getting to you?"

"There's only a couple of inches under the archway. They've put down a plank gangway as far as the steps. You needn't even wet your feet if you're careful. At several places in the street it's as much as a yard or a yard and a half deep, and there's a boat doing ferry work with a sailor in charge."

"A jolly trip on a night like this!"

"It can't be helped."

"It's going to take a hell of a time! I shall have to start much sooner."

"Not so much. Allow an extra ten minutes."

Clanricard and Jerphanion were punctual to the dot. Rothweil explained that, owing to an unforeseen engagement, he was sorry he could spare them only a very short time. It would be best, therefore, to come to the point without beating about the bush.

There was, as a matter of fact, a considerable amount of beating about the bush, but it lasted a comparatively short while. Rothweil allowed the two young men to do the talking. He listened to them with close attention, and observed them carefully as they spoke. In particular he watched the face of the student, who seemed to find talking difficult. He behaved exactly as though the two young men had come merely to ask his advice.

"Let me imagine myself in your position," he said. "You are perhaps at what may be the most important period of your lives, the period at which one takes a definite line. I think I understand your feelings. You are conscious of a force working within you, and you don't want that force to be misdirected. You, Monsieur Clanricard, I know already—at least, I think I do. We have met often, and I believe sincerely that your instinct has directed you aright. Yes, your place is with us. We need men like you, convinced participators in our work, enthusiasts, future apostles—indeed we do. And you, I believe, will find among us peace for your spirit. . . . When conservative folk say that what a man needs is a religion, they are right. In its Latin sense, you know, the word 'religion' means that which binds us to others, brother to brother. . . . We must have a feeling of solidarity with others so that we may advance together towards a common ideal. . . . Yes, we want to feel ourselves rubbing shoulders with our friends. *Væ soli!* Woe to the man who stands alone! Why should we grant to the enemy the monopoly of so great an advantage, the moral strength which comes from a sense of brotherhood? You're right in thinking that a political party is not enough, that it doesn't give just that. There must be political parties, and there's no reason why you shouldn't belong to the one which reflects your ideals, but you need something more. I'm glad that you've reasoned all this out for yourself, and glad to see that what you want has brought you to us. . . . In fact, my dear Clanricard, it comes to this, that I am entirely at your service."

He paused a moment; then:

"So far as you are concerned, Monsieur Jerphanion, let me say that I am flattered to think that you have approached me—flattered and slightly embarrassed by the idea that a young man of your talents and your prospects should have thought of asking my advice in so

important a matter. .... I have not the honour of knowing you as
well as I know our friend Clanricard. .... Let me say in general
terms that I believe you to be set in the right direction. More than
that I cannot say on so short an acquaintance. There is a certain person for whom I have, from every point of view, the very highest regard. I consider him to be quite an exceptional individual, a noble
man. I should like you to talk to him. I can't pretend to foresee the
nature of your final decision, but this I will say, that whatever it may
be, it will be taken with full knowledge of our cause and for reasons
that will do you honour."

Rothweil spoke carefully and with moderation. The tone of his
voice was slightly nasal and asthmatic. Now and again, in a pause
between his sentences, he looked his interlocutor in the face, but he
spoke for the most part with lowered eyes. He had a trick of touching the links in his cuff, of picking a speck of dust from his sleeve,
of pulling down his waistcoat over his protuberant stomach. He did
not smile, and there was no trace of humour in his voice. Not that
he assumed an air of gravity, but that he seemed to maintain, without
effort, an unbroken attitude of seriousness.

He gave Jerphanion the address of the man of whom he had
spoken: M. Lengnau, 5 rue Guy-de-la-Brosse, and with it a short note
of introduction, adding, as he did so:

"It's only a couple of steps from your College—rather nearer the
Polytechnic."

To Clanricard he said:

"Come and see me again whenever you like."

A little later Rothweil was looking with astonishment at a sheet
of lightly rippled water, which, in the darkness, seemed to die away
at his feet like the margin of a lake in some sandy cove.

It washed about between the paving-stones with an alternate movement of ebb and flow. Farther on it seemed to be deeper. The street
looked like a dark canal between the banks of its houses. A few vague
and dingy reflections showed at intervals. The two nearest street-

lamps were still lit, but farther on, the only illumination came from windows. The shops were in darkness and obviously closed. The lower storeys of the houses appeared to be sunk progressively deeper and deeper in the flood, but it was difficult to see exactly where wall ended and water began. Some fifty yards ahead was a square, where the current of three streets joined and formed a wide pond, the centre of which was alive with the flickering play of reflected lights.

On the right-hand pavement a sort of gangway or bridge of planks had been laid for two or three yards close along the wall. A few people were standing about, some on this gangway, two others in the roadway, close to Rothweil, by the margin of the dark and rippling tide.

Someone said.

"I was this way an hour ago. Twenty more paving-stones, at least, have been covered since then."

A small boat was seen advancing from the square, crowded with people and lit by a flare. It stood out in the darkness as a confused mass, moving slowly, to an accompaniment of splashings, to which was added, now and again, the sound of a voice which gave an air of strangeness to the scene. The man in charge was standing upright in the bow, plunging a very long pole at an angle into the water. He had handed his lantern, a hurricane lamp, to one of the passengers, who held it at arm's length and was looking curiously at the water as though watching for fish.

Rothweil climbed into the boat with the others who were waiting. Muddy water flowed over the planks of the gangway. At first the keel of the boat grated against the paving-stones in a series of jerks that frightened the women. It was not cold, but the body had to combat a pervasive and unnatural dampness which lowered the spirits. There was a general feeling that the adventure would end in chronic rheumatism for all of them.

The passengers pointed out to the man in charge the houses where they wanted to be dropped. Rothweil's was among the first.

He set his feet rather nervously on the planks which had been laid into the entrance, a few inches only above the surface of the flood. A small oil-lamp was burning at the end of the passage. There was about the spreading water an air of insolence. It forced its way into the most hidden recesses like a mob taking possession of a conquered city.

The ceiling seemed to be so low that Rothweil walked down the corridor with his head bent. The planks shifted disquietingly beneath his feet. To reach the staircase it was necessary to jump sideways, and, being clumsy, he let his foot slip on to one of the steps which was already under water.

Chapter

19

THE TRAVEL DIARY OF
STEPHEN BARTLETT

Here I am again in this city. Seeing that I left it on Christmas Eve, I've been away more than a month. *C'est épatant* [1] how quickly a month passes. I'm annoyed at not getting my old room; I worked *des pieds et des mains* to get it, but so far without success. The landlady has promised it me for next Wednesday. Since the word of a Frenchman is worth about 75 per cent of the word of an Englishman (that's to say, it's about equivalent to the word of an Englishwoman), how much reliance can I place upon the word of a Frenchwoman? I imagine that 40 per cent is a reasonable figure.

My chief reason for disliking this room is the wall-paper, which is covered, in the most visible places, with loathsome stains. Besides, I had grown attached to the old one.

I find that there's a good deal of charm about Paris, although, coming out of the station, I was seized with the oddest desire to laugh. I controlled myself as far as possible before the porters, who might quite naturally have thought me lacking in respect for their native land. I can't imagine why I found everything so comic. It was quite a kindly feeling.

During my visit to London I gave the clearest possible evidence of my fondness for Paris. Lunching one day at the Garrick, I fell out with one of the worst dramatists of the United Kingdom (and probably of the world), who had asked me to sit at his table. He was foolish enough to maintain that there is no life in Paris, and that one can't enjoy oneself there. I remember, in particular, how angry he made me by saying that there was no movement in the streets. He had

---

[1] The words in italics were written in French in the original.

the temerity to declare that one is more crowded in the London tubes during the rush hours than in the Paris Métro, and that compared with Fleet Street the rue de Montmartre is a quiet country road. I made him eat his words, and witnesses of the scene have assured me that I did not behave like a phlegmatic Britisher!

I didn't get under way for the *Rive Gauche* without difficulty. The honourable editor of the *D. M.,* who has been born out of due time and would have made a good ebony-merchant a hundred years ago, informed me that my trip to France had produced all the results he expected from it, and that he could employ me more usefully in connexion with the general election. I wasn't quite clear what he was after, but he maintained, with some show of plausibility, that the present elections are more than usually important, and that for the time being the English newspaper-reader is more interested in them than in what is going on abroad. He commissioned me to write a series of articles on what everyone agrees is the main point at issue: the position of the great English landlords. He stressed the fact that these articles would link up, by a happy coincidence, with what I had contributed from the Continent. He asked me, with that addition of flattery to impudence of which he has the trick, to write them as only I knew how, "not in the violent and ignorant spirit of the party politician, but clearly and coolly, like an economist," and to introduce into them "the slightly amused tone of the impartial onlooker" which I had used with such effect in my studies of social classes in France and of "the various strata of purchasing-power." (I must admit that the arguments I borrowed from Ernest Torchecoul and fraudulently presented as my own, after the necessary adjustments, had an extraordinary success and won me the reputation of being a particularly bright investigator.)

I set to work, therefore, with the resignation of a convict. It was only after I had begun that I discovered, little by little, the infernal Machiavellism of the man. My foreign articles had been for him nothing but a method of using what was apparently an entertaining sideline as a preparation for the campaign which he was planning, and of which I was to be the passive instrument. Ernest Torchecoul had, in all innocence, been acting as the deus ex machina sent to serve the destructive purposes of the Lloyd George government. The more I had insisted, reflecting the ideas of Ernest Torchecoul, on the pathetic modesty of French incomes, the more I had touched the hearts of the English reading public by exhibiting the "strata of purchasing-power" as the outcome of humble savings, showing that the highest figure, which would entitle its owner in Paris to be called rich, represented a daily rate of expenditure of two pounds sterling, or about £800 a year, the more indignant would that same public become on learning through the medium of my "impartial" and "slightly amused" pen that the obscure Duke of Buccleuch (obscure for the man in the street) lived at the rate of £218,900 a year (roughly five and a half million francs); that the Duke of Sutherland owned 1,358,545 acres—or the equivalent of a French department—and that the accumulated incomes of no more than five of our great territorial peers amounted to 17,168,437 francs, a figure sufficient to account for about a thousand of the so-called "rich men" of Paris, reckoned on the basis of Torchecoul's figures. I had developed, under the tutelage of my friend Torchecoul, a taste for accuracy, and I reckoned the income of the Marquis of Lansdowne to the last penny, a computation more precise than the Marquis could have got from his agent, but for which he probably wouldn't thank me.

My devil of an editor had suggested as the general title of my series the striking phrase: "Is Feudalism Dead?" The "amused" onlooker gave free scope to his imagination by adding to the mathematical exactitude of his figures word pictures of the way in which the amounts were paid by the farmers, or descriptions of the scenes that took place at the coming of age of the heir; the long procession wending its way to the great house, with the musicians first and then the local clergy, followed by the tenant farmers with their families; the dutiful speech of the oldest retainer, and the patronizing benevolence of the young lord. So thoroughly feudal did I make these descriptions that my readers probably rubbed their eyes and began to wonder whether instead of the last number of the *D. M.* they hadn't got hold by mistake of some dusty novel by Sir Walter Scott from the circulating library. For the ordinary English city-dweller is entirely ignorant of these sights and customs, although they are often to be seen within twenty miles of his home. Nor does he realize—and it was my pleasure to enlighten him—that compared to our great city landlords, the mere territorial peers are paupers. He is ignorant of the fact that the Duke of Westminster does in fact own the whole quarter of London that bears his name (as though there were in Paris a Duc de la Madeleine in possession of all the district lying between the Rond-Point in the Champs-Élysées and the Opéra), and that with an income of three million pounds a year his lordship has every right to think of the Duke of Buccleuch as no better off than a miserable Scottish minister. Nor does he realize that if for twelve months in the year five of our poor country magnates have got to share out between them a mere seventeen million francs, the four great lords of London (Westminster, Norfolk, Bedford, and Portman) can spend, praise be to God, no less than two hundred and eighteen million, five hundred thousand, a state of affairs which ensures them more than a moderate competence, and gives us loyal subjects of the crown the satisfaction of knowing that these four rich Londoners weigh as much in the scale as twelve thousand so-called wealthy citizens of Paris.

Such revelations, however free from the "violent spirit of the party politician," could not but have the effect of creating a state of mind among ordinary decent folk that would be favourable for my employers' schemes.

I have just heard that out of the 640 Members returned up to last evening, 377 belong to the various government groups. I don't think that I'm exaggerating if I claim that of these, fifty at least owe their success to my articles and to the comments made upon them in the columns of other newspapers. In another five days, by which time all the results will be in, this total of fifty will probably have grown to eighty. It is fair to say, then, that the victory of two thirds of this number will have been due to Ernest Torchecoul, who thus becomes the deciding influence of about 10 per cent of the English election figures. If Mr. Lloyd George, who a little while back was tearing his hair in the agony of defeat, were not entirely lacking in any sense of gratitude, he would give M. Ernest Torchecoul the Order of the Garter, or at least a life pension, which M. Torchecoul would probably prefer, even if it didn't assure him of more than a thousandth part of Lord Portman's income.

In this connexion I should very much like to have the time to go into the mysterious question of the *D. M.*'s politics. No one believed, till now, that its fortunes were so closely involved with those of the Liberal Party, especially as it has always boasted a high-minded independence of outlook. I should like someone to explain the change that has taken place, though I wouldn't put anything beyond the capacities of the scuttler [1] disguised as a gentleman who directs its activities.

This gentleman reckoned on keeping my nose to the grindstone of his miserable job until the elections were over, but by the intervention of Providence the Paris floods came to my rescue. I had a good deal of difficulty in persuading him that what was happening in Paris was what I was particularly fitted to do justice to with my "brilliant gift for lightning sketches," and that it would be a crime to let me miss such a chance. Thank Heaven, the Seine rose a yard a day, and each telegram that came in from the Continent strengthened my argument. I was due to deliver one more article on the burning question: "Is Feudalism Dead?" and this I promised to write here. As a matter of fact, I posted it at the Gare du Nord at twelve o'clock last night.

Ernest Torchecoul was with me. I had been spending the evening with him, and showed him my article as well as the notes I had used for the rest of the series. Seated in a café opposite this economist with scurf all over his coat-collar, I derived considerable pleasure from the sight of him with a threepenny glass of beer standing before him on a sticky little iron table, turning pages in which the millions

---

[1] This English word appears in the French text.—TRANSLATOR'S NOTE.

of the Duke of Devonshire seemed to shrink from the indignities to which they were being exposed.

His comments interested me. He read much more into the facts than I had done, or, perhaps I should say, *took them more tragically.* He admitted that previously he had not realized the extreme importance of the English elections, but that now he saw how serious the situation was.

Speaking generally, I find myself constantly surprised at the way in which such things are looked at on the Continent. It would be more accurate to say "in Paris," since Paris has been the only field of my investigations. But I meet people in the cafés from every corner of Europe, and their remarks bear out my generalization.

They one and all seem to be expecting some vast kind of upheaval. Some of them want it, some fear it, others, like my friend Torchecoul, regard its approach in a spirit of philosophic detachment. But none of them seems to think that the present state of affairs can last. Their reasons for this belief are not always easy to follow. Sometimes they speak as though Labour or Socialism is making enormous strides everywhere and is undermining the fabric of the old world; in other words, that the poor are about to shake off violently the yoke of the rich. Sometimes they say that it is only natural, after so long a period of peace, to expect that sooner or later a war will break out between several of the great powers, arguing that we've been too near war on more than one occasion during the last few years to be able to avoid it much longer. If it comes, they say, it will cause a much greater dislocation of life than previous wars, because of the advances that have been made in the mechanism of fighting.

About the possible good or bad results of such an outbreak they do not agree. Several Frenchmen I have met maintain that war is desirable because France has allowed herself to be lulled to sleep by the long inactivity of peace. One of them gave vent to this extraordinary phrase: "France is bored." They say, too, that Germany has taken advantage of the peace to extend her domination in every direction, and that if her enemies allow her to go on as she is going, she will soon be mistress of Europe and even of Asia Minor. War, therefore, they think, would be better than the present state of affairs, because there is always a chance of winning it, and even if it were lost, defeat couldn't mean a worse condition of slavery than will result from a continuance of peace. I have an idea that they think they have a good chance of winning. They are convinced, in their hearts, that in a war against Germany, France would come out on top, with the help of her allies, among whom they count the British Empire. (I was surprised to find them so sincerely convinced of this. Not knowing many people in the Foreign Office, I had meant, during my stay in London, to ask the opinion of one or two friends on the *Observer* and *The Times*, but my days were so much occupied in reckoning the incomes of the Duke of Westminster & Co. that I completely forgot to do so.)

It seems to me that the whole question is complicated by national complacency. Many Frenchmen, though they wouldn't admit it, have never really got over the misfortunes of '70. In particular they can't bear to admit that they are no longer the leaders of Europe.

Besides, they argue, if France doesn't take the initiative, Germany will, and she'll naturally choose the best moment to attack. I don't follow the argument, because why should Germany bother to make war if, as they assert, she has only got to let a state of peace continue in order to dominate the whole of Europe? Still, it's true that Germany may fear an attempt by others to shake off this threatened hegemony, and may, for that reason, want to be first in the field.

And that, I believe, is the real truth of the situation. Each country is convinced that its neighbours have determined to start a war. If that is really true, Europe looks like becoming a shambles before I get my first grey hair.

Then there are others who are no less convinced of the imminence of war and rejoice in the prospect because they believe that it will be the occasion of that general upheaval which they are longing for, after which there will be no more inequality of wealth.

I noticed that my friend Ernest Torchecoul was smiling as he listened to these various arguments. I know that he has his own ideas about these things, as he has on the problem of Shakspere and the existence of Atlantis, but I've noticed that he is chary of prophesying. I rather think that he likes to be thought infallible.

He told me, however, after reading my article and looking at my notes, that he thought England was in a bad way. I couldn't help laughing. He looked at me with surprise and then said that on second thoughts the situation was probably less serious than it would have been elsewhere, owing to our natural slowness of intelligence. In any other country, he said, revelations like mine would have led to an outburst of public fury, and the Duke of Westminster would quickly have been hanged on the nearest lamp-post. The only result in England would be that Lloyd George would stay in power and find it easier than he would otherwise have done to make a slight addition to the Duke's income tax. The normal stupidity of the English, which had led in the past to the emergence as leaders of its few great men, provided a valuable factor of stability in the present uncertainty of the times. I believe that in his heart of hearts Ernest Torchecoul is a friend of social stability.

I want to note my impression that if we Englishmen like to talk about the weather and grouse over the rain that may fall tomorrow, the French love to talk about coming catastrophes. It is the reverse side of their temperament, which people like to think of as gay and careless. And in other respects they are gay and careless. For instance, they don't seem to me to bother much about their morals, or about the salvation of their souls in this world or the next. It would be a mistake, therefore, to *take too tragically* what, after all, is only an element in their intellectual make-up.

Let me come to the floods, which are responsible for my present visit. I find them perfectly delightful. I can think of nothing that could change in a more amusing way the appearance of a city one thought one knew, or give to each day a more dramatic sense of adventure. Each morning one opens the paper in a fever to see whether some new district is waterlogged, whether the torrent has burst up through the Métro and taken possession of the most unlikely places, whether in a few hours the supplies of light, milk, and bread won't have failed. The very paper, with its front page covered with large aquatic photographs, seems as though it were floating in a tub. All through the day one's interest is kept alive by the rumours one hears and by the sights one sees on one's walks. One goes to see for oneself whether some street which the evening before was dry and ordinary enough has been raised to the dignity of a canal and supports a proud fleet of boats. While I write this, I tell myself that the Seine is rising and that before I have finished this sentence the depth of water all over Paris will be perhaps half an inch more. Nor is this sort of excitement spoiled by any scruples of conscience, because up to now no lives have been lost. As to material damage, the general attitude seems to be grumpy rather than one of despair. Most people accept the discomfort in a spirit of fun. They realize that they'll probably never have another chance of living like the patricians of ancient Venice.

I write "Venice" because it turns up in every newspaper report. I use it myself so that my London readers shall not accuse me of a lack of poetic sensibility, or think that I've never been to Venice. I haven't, but the admission would injure my journalistic reputation.

Although I don't know Venice, I'm pretty sure that the present appearance of Paris is not in the least like it. I'd even go so far as to say that Paris has never seemed to me so northern. In the inundated districts I am conscious of a bodily sensation which surprises me and which I find it difficult to describe further than to say that it gives me a curious feeling of my own country. I have noticed that a certain coolness marked the conditions which I left behind me in London. Its absence was responsible for much of the charm I felt in being "abroad," for the exotic southern quality which I found in Paris. And now it has suddenly returned. Similarly with what the eyes see. I admit that the submerged quarters of Paris, with their houses half sunk in dirty water, the circulating boats filled with shopping housewives, and the boatmen shouting to each other as they try to keep their poles free of one another, give the place the genuine appearance of a city of canals. But the impression I get is of some northern port—for instance, of some of the most characteristic parts of Amsterdam.

Deep down, I'm rather disappointed. I feel myself shaken in the conviction I formed when I made the acquaintance of the Sacré-Cœur from the window of a railway train, thanks to the kind offices of a Frenchman who caught a cold as a result. I am beginning to ask myself whether the Sacré-Cœur is really, as I then thought it, a monument marking the starting-point of an avenue which leads to Venice and Constantinople. I dislike having to reconsider ideas on which I have already built an exciting fantasy.

On second thoughts, I think it would have been better to have the floods in September or October. It's quite likely that the lovely skies and sunsets of that season would have persuaded the rue Guénegaud to take on a really Venetian appearance, and that the avenue de l'Opéra, laced with skimming boats and dominated by the magnificent façade of its theatre, might have presented a passable substitute for the Grand Canal.

But I'm afraid it's too fanciful to hope that even after a rainy summer the Seine in October could reach the level of almost 34 m. 80, which is today's record, according to the special edition which the hotel boots has just brought me.

How ought I to translate this figure? I really don't know. Looking at the Appendix of Weights and Measures at the end of my *French Conversation for English Travellers*, I see that 34 m. 80 is equivalent to 115 feet. That seems to me a lot even for a Parisian river in the last stages of anarchy. Perhaps it includes the normal height above sea-level?

Never mind, I'll tell my English readers 115 feet. They'll compare it with the height of their own cottages, and get an almost sacred thrill out of it. Many of them, remembering my attacks on the great English landlords, will think that the days are upon us foretold in the book of Revelation.

20

MAURICE EZZELIN GETS AN ANONYMOUS LETTER

On his way back from lunch Maurice Ezzelin passed the little cubby-hole in which the office care-taker liked to doze in front of his gas fire. The man raised his head.

"There's a letter for you, Monsieur Ezzelin," he remarked. Never before had there been a letter for Maurice Ezzelin. The other's face almost assumed a smile as he held out a yellow envelope, which was made of the cheapest kind of paper and obviously contained very little.

"When did it come—this morning?" Ezzelin asked.

"No, just now—that is, about an hour ago."

Ezzelin waited until he was in his office before opening the letter. None of its other three occupants was there. He could read it at leisure.

"Dear Sir:

"The individual who writes this is not accustomed to sending anonymous letters, but no one likes to see a decent fellow like you being deceived by his wife; yours is laughing at you, the trouble with you is that you're too trusting, it's not my business to warn you, but I can give you all the proof you want whenever you like to ask for it; almost every day she meets a certain young man who can't be anything much, because he sees her at times when most men of his age are usually working; they visit hired rooms together and don't seem to mind much who sees them. I imagine that this sort of thing isn't much to your taste, and if you want further details you can have them by carrying your newspaper rolled up under your arm so that I can see it when you leave home next Wednesday morning; turn into some quiet street, and I'll fix a meeting; I can assure you that I'm not doing this for pleasure, nor because I want to break up a happy home; sincerely yours."

The letter was written on both sides of a single sheet of ruled paper, of the kind used in business houses. It was in an educated hand, probably a woman's, that seemed to have been slightly disguised. The spelling was better than the punctuation.

The sense of suffering which came to Maurice Ezzelin contained no element of surprise. During their short honeymoon he had been able to deceive himself about Juliette's feelings for him and had even persuaded himself that she was in love with him. Later, in the early days of their marriage, he had hoped that the aversion she displayed, occasionally, to his advances, would diminish, and that the general sweetness of her character would overcome the fits of melancholy and violent bitterness which now and then took possession of her. But towards the end of 1908 he had felt less confident of this happy result. The precise occasion of these doubts had been Christmas Eve in that year. He had wanted to take her to a restaurant, and when, at length, she had consented, it had been with a bad grace. He would never forget that miserable dinner at the Réveillon to which he had pinned such high hopes, the alternate hardness and misery of her face, the sudden violence of her glances, the sighs which she had uttered. He knew that she had married him after an unhappy love-affair with somebody else. "She's thinking of him," he told himself as he stared at the comfortless white table-cloth; "perhaps she's imagining herself with him."

Since that mournful Christmas he had had no doubts about her attitude to him. She did everything she could to repulse him, and if, by chance, she yielded, it was with an air of extreme suffering. She never said a word at meals and got through her household duties as quickly as possible, as though she were trying to put herself in the right with a master whom she loathed, and whose reproaches, in this comparatively unimportant field, she was intent on forestalling. She went out immediately after luncheon, often without waiting for him to start for his office, offering as excuse a meeting with her mother, some shopping to be done before the rush hours, or the necessity of profiting by a break in the rain. "I can only keep well if I do some walking every day," she said; "the doctors told my parents so; you know that as well as I do. It'll probably be raining in an hour's time, and then I'll come back." But in fact, when he came back himself about half past six, he usually found the house empty, even when it had been raining all the afternoon.

At seven, or a quarter past, sometimes not till half past, he would hear a faint sound from the direction of the front door. But there would be no sign of Juliette. She went straight to the kitchen to put their dinner on the stove, then shut herself for ten or fifteen minutes in her dressing-room. When finally she did appear, he would say casually: "I've been here quite a long time."

He confined himself always to such unprovocative remarks, refraining, sometimes, even from them, when he saw in Juliette's eyes a warning light which he had grown to dread as prefacing something more disturbing even than anger. He was one of those men who never, as long as they live, overcome their fear of women, of those, too, who feel that they can't help being always in the wrong, and that every circumstance of life makes them more so. He had put himself in the wrong by marrying Juliette without being certain that he could make her happy, by thinking that he was of sufficient stature to compensate her for the love that she had lost. Mme Vérand had more than once warned him, saying: "It's quite possible that she may think she has a grievance against you," and he blamed himself for not seeing it sooner. In a general way he recognized that Juliette was his superior. She might be less informed, but she had had a more liberal education. Her knowledge of music was considerable, whereas his enjoyment of it was ignorant and sketchy. Occasionally she read a page or two of some "literary" work, or copied out a poem into a notebook, while the only reading he did was confined to his newspaper or to volumes of popular science. He even thought of her as rich because she had had a small dowry when she married, though he might have argued that it did no more than serve as pin-money for her, not even benefiting him indirectly to the extent of flattering his marital pride, seeing that they hardly ever went out together. Many of his colleagues, whose wives had a job, were better off financially and enjoyed pleasanter company at home than he. But such arguments would have been distasteful to a man of his temperament. That he should dare to formulate them would have seemed to him but one more proof of his guilt.

He had every reason to suppose that she was deceiving him, but up to now nothing had occurred to convince him of it. He had always been able to say to himself: "Obviously she doesn't love me. . . . She's still thinking of that other man. . . . She tries to forget by going out with her mother, or even by herself. . . . She avoids me. . . . But I've no right to assume that she's deceiving me. . . . Besides, whom could she be deceiving me with? . . . She may be regretting her lost love to the extent of finding me intolerable, but that's no reason for thinking that she's running after someone else."

And now here was the anonymous letter. It changed everything. Juliette's mysterious behaviour was no longer something that could be kept deep down in his heart as a secret, hidden sorrow (something that a timid man could refuse to think about when the pain grew too intense). People didn't always, of course, act in good faith. They weren't above slander; besides, they might be wrong, might be suspicious without reason, seeing evil where no evil was. Still, there was a great difference between imagining a person guilty and seeing the guilt written in black and white by a stranger. It is harder to doubt the second than the first.

He was on the point of destroying the letter. It is generally agreed that an anonymous letter is contemptible. A noble nature destroys anonymous letters and throws them in the waste-paper-basket. But one can't know that they're anonymous unless one reads them, and once read, they can't easily be forgotten.

Other things, too, are generally agreed, but they're not always mutually consistent, and do little but complicate the situation. For instance, a jealous husband is not a pleasant character. A husband who allows a woman to marry him without loving him, and who fails to win his wife's affection after the event, finds it difficult to get much sympathy. The general view is that she is his "poor little wife," and if the poor little wife ends by finding consolation elsewhere, she is not condemned too harshly. On the other hand, a husband who condones his wife's infidelity is not let off so easily, the assumption being that he has kept his eyes shut from interested motives. "A husband's honour" is a phrase that appears constantly in the newspapers. Its implications are obvious. A moment comes when a husband *must see;* the difficulty is to know exactly when the moment is. When, precisely, does one cease to be a jealous husband who tortures his "poor little wife" and become a man defending his honour? At what point does a decent fellow who knows what's going on but avoids a scandal shade off into a collusive wretch who rightly incurs the world's scorn? Does an anonymous letter constitute such a point? In so far as it is anonymous it must be despised—so much is agreed— but are its contents also to be despised?—especially when the writer offers further information? Isn't the mere fact that it's been written a proof that the misfortune in question has ceased to be anyone's purely private affair and has become the subject of general speculation and talk? Doesn't its existence mean that if the husband's eyes continue to be shut, people will begin to wonder? Doesn't it serve the purpose, this anonymous letter, of a sort of public warning addressed to a man's honour, saying in so many words: "What are you going to do about it?"

Chapter

21

A DAMPNESS IN THE AIR: SMELLS

It had been dark now for nearly two hours. Winter was not yet past, but now and again a gust of still, warm air woke the street to life, to be followed by a moment of such perfect stillness as seemed beyond the power of another gust to break. A freshness hung above the pavements. A wanton wind frisked in passing skirts and found its way to inner secrecies, gathering warmth as it penetrated to far recesses of the body, though it chilled the flesh in passing with the sharp freshness of the evening. At such moments the body was aware of a light, lascivious touch, shamelessly seeking a welcome. It was as though, beneath the shelter of its clothes, the secret flesh were bare, as though, unseen by passing eyes, there in the public street the splendour of nakedness, fresh from the hidden intimacies of rooms, moved in a new triumph. The air's sweet briskness drove fatigue away, and feet, tired till then, drew vigour from the cold night breeze as from a bath. The whole body was renewed and braced. Tingling from the racing blood, the flesh was warm, though another's hand might have found it cold—firm but cold.

So thrilled, so freshened, Juliette would have needed little persuasion to induce her to return to the exhausting séances of love.

Again a slow warm gust of wind stirred the street about her. Her hair was heavy with the evening, as though, like a sponge, it had sucked up all its moisture. She could feel it against the nape of her neck. A few loosened strands played about her temples, giving to her head a sense of caressing fingers.

In the streets was a feeling of freshness, not known till now. The floods had brought to Paris a new delight. It seemed that the waters had left behind them as they retreated, deep in the earth, far beneath the houses, in the very walls themselves, a dampness that never ceased to permeate the air. And now and again, without warning, days would come when the city was filled with the smells of fields and woodlands after rain, with the sense of old damp farms nestling in some basin of the hills. The memory of disaster now withdrawn set in the heart a hunger for the spring and brought it, in imagination, nearer. Never had the hope of spring been so intense as it was this year.

"There was something he was never tired of saying in the old days (for now I'm afraid, as I never was then, of talking to him about the future): 'Take what the present offers. Learn to enjoy it. A day will come, perhaps, when you will realize that this moment in which now we live was the loveliest, the purest, of your life. You will be sorry that you did not recognize it when you had it, that you spoiled, if only a little, the fullness of its perfection. And then it will be too late.' He was right. I must fight against the mania that seizes me to regret the past. I'm always asking myself whether our first year together wasn't the most exquisite of all, whether he did not love me more in those days. But I mustn't. I won't ask too much of life. There are times when the situation seems intolerable, when I should like to be dead, when I say to myself: 'For anyone who's been mad enough to do what you have done, there can be no more happiness, there can be no future.' . . . But it's not true. I can prove it's not true. . . . It's no good thinking about what might have happened, no good saying that if I'd not committed this madness, if I'd waited, he would have come back, that he always meant to come back, that he would have loved me as he loves me now, that I should have been spared this nightmare. . . . If he'd come, I should have given myself to him as I have given myself since, but then he would have been the first, there would have been no one else. . . . Sooner or later we should have got married, when he had made up his mind that he wanted to get married. He's always said that he didn't, but knowing me would have made him change his mind . . . I would have been so gentle with him, I would have been everything to him. We could have gone about openly together, he could have introduced me to his friends. I'd never have let myself be a nuisance to him. . . . It's no use thinking of all that. . . . I ought to have waited a little longer, not to have given up hope. . . . If only he'd sent me a word to tell me how he was. . . . It's all too frightful. . . . No, no, it's not frightful at all; how can it be, when a moment ago I felt so happy? It's lovely, it's like a beautiful love-story . . . but can it last? I'm never free from terror. So far I've had luck, but it only needs such a little thing to smash it to pieces. Each time that Pierre comes to one of our meetings, I look at his eyes. If he seems gloomy, if his face doesn't light up, if he doesn't smile the moment he sees me, I'm terrified; my heart comes into my throat. . . .

"Would he leave me at once if he knew? I daren't guess the answer. Would he understand that I lied only because I loved him better than anything in the world, that when I first saw him again in that little square close to the Seine, where there is a ruin, I just hadn't the strength to say anything? . . . When he was suddenly there before my eyes again—Pierre, my own Pierre, whom I had thought lost for ever—how could I have said: 'How are you, Pierre?' and then, straight out, have said *that*? . . . I remember how, when I said: 'How are you, Pierre?' the strength of my emotion was such that I couldn't even open my lips. . . . Was I to tell him then and there to go away, to leave me desolate and deserted? Was I to lose him again, this time for ever? . . . I couldn't have done it. . . . And then, I thought that perhaps he knew, that he would let fall some hint that would tell me he knew. . . . It wasn't for me to make any sudden announcement. There would be time for explanations later, time to talk about all we had done—and suffered. . . . We mustn't spoil the first lovely moments. . . . He took my arm, first outside my cloak, then slipping his hand beneath it. A tug was hooting, just as he had described in his letter. . . . And then, later? . . . I kept on saying to myself that I must tell him . . . but when? . . . Should I have done it that first day, before we parted? But suppose he had never come back? Could I risk that, risk never seeing him again?

Nothing could happen worse than that. The one thing I must be certain of was seeing him again. I wasn't sure that he didn't know. I said to myself: 'Perhaps he didn't want to speak of it for fear of spoiling our first meeting. If I say anything, he will frown; perhaps he will think, as he once laughingly said to me, "Women have no tact." ' Later, then? But it became more and more difficult. The longer I waited, the more right he would have to say: 'How could you conceal it from me, how could you lie to me so long?' And then, when I was with him, I thought only of him, of us. If anything else came into my mind, I drove it out with loathing. For whole days, for whole nights I had been tormented by it. Wasn't that enough? When I was with Pierre, our love for each other was the only thing in the world that mattered; all else was as something that had never happened. There were moments of such happiness that I believe I should have killed anyone who threatened to take them from me.

"But a day came, last autumn, when we were walking in the cemetery of Montmartre, when I almost told him. I can see now the tombstones and the dead leaves. . . . It was a mild day. Pierre had been talking of all sorts of things in that way he had, when he was in a good mood, of seeming to understand everything. . . . I nearly spoke. The words came, sticking in my throat. 'O God!' I cried to myself, 'give me courage. It will be such a relief to tell him.' The gravestones white and grey were all about us; Pierre was smiling, looking now at me, now following the train of his thoughts into the distance. But I couldn't do it. It was as though I meant to kill myself and then, at the last moment, hadn't the courage. . . . There was Pierre, walking beside me, there was my happiness, our happiness, however incomplete it might be. How could I take it in my hands and break it? It was more than I could do to drive away, far away into the distance, my smiling Pierre, with his eyes so full of fondness. O God, who in my place could have done such a thing? But I did what I could, short of telling him, arranging things so that Pierre should feel no awkwardness, no surprise, so that he should imagine that when I was away from him I was still leading the life of a young girl in my parents' house. He is not naturally suspicious. He never lies to me, and so can never think of me as lying to him. But he is very sensitive, and that makes it very hard to prevent him wondering, despite himself. . . . Once or twice I got the impression that he found my replies ambiguous, that he suspected me of not telling the truth, but only about trivial things. . . . So long as I could keep that up, all would be well. . . . But then, there is the other man. Suppose he decided. . . . Oh, well, if he does, so much the worse for him. . . . Let him think what he likes. . . . If he gets restive he can. . . . All that matters is that Pierre. . . . But, O God, can it last, can it go on? . . . I promised myself not to think of the future, but how can I help it? Even if my happiness were perfect, I suppose I should always be frightened that it wouldn't last. But it's so far from being perfect—so tiny a scrap of happiness to be frightened about. . . . Oh, let that at least not vanish! Pierre, if you only knew, you would see that I ask very little of life."

Another gust of night air stirred the life of the street. Again a mild dampness seemed wafted from the depths of the Paris earth. But with it there came to Juliette's senses a smell of quite a different kind, a dampness from some other source that moved upwards between her breasts. It was of all smells the most sweetly intoxicating, the smell of a lover clinging to her in the embrace of their bodies, the physical sense of their union. The memory of the room she had left, of their lovers' hour, moved with her as she walked, like a column of smoke. Companioned thus, thus sweetly swooning, what thoughts could she spare for even the immediate future? Pierre was right, the present was all that mattered. What use in thinking about what would happen, about that home whose claims had already been denied, the home that awaited her returning, stealthy feet, about the stranger sitting there, patient behind his newspaper?

HUSBAND AND WIFE

Maurice Ezzelin held out the letter without rising.

"What's that?"

"Read it; you'll see."

Had he been looking at Juliette he would have seen the sudden tension in her face that marked her effort at self-control. But his head was turned away. He was hoping that nothing drastic would result from this daring act of his, that matters would settle themselves. How that could be he did not know. All he wanted was not to be involved in this sudden stroke of fate which it was no longer in his power to influence.

"Who gave you this letter?"

"It was delivered at the office."

"You've got the envelope?"

"No, I tore it up."

"That's a pity."

She smiled. She seemed almost calm, a little contemptuous. Ezzelin began to feel himself in the wrong.

"You mean to have this meeting?"

"What meeting?"

"Why, all this business about the rolled newspaper under your arm."

Juliette spoke calmly, on a note of faint irony. But her voice sounded strained. Her breath came sharply, and her eyes were sparkling.

He answered her uneasily:

"No . . . certainly not. . . . I haven't said I was going to."

"But please do."

"There's no suggestion of a meeting."

"I quite understand that. It'll all be quite casual, all between gentlemen."

"But I've told you I don't want to."

"If you hadn't wanted to you'd have destroyed the letter. Men of decent feeling, men who have self-respect and who respect their wives, destroy letters like this—anonymous letters!"

She spoke quickly, almost stridently, but without the least hesitation. Never had any words come so readily to her lips. Inwardly she was obsessed by desolating terror, but the surface level of her mind was clear enough. Her ideas were ranged and ready for action, from whatever quarter the attack might come.

"Don't shout!" he said. "You know how every word carries in this house. I could perfectly well have kept the letter from you and gone out with my paper under my arm to get whatever information there is to get. . . ."

"That would indeed have been delightful! Oh, you make me sick! You make me sick!"

She flung the words at him at the top of her voice, started to cry, and dropped into a little low arm-chair by the window. Seated there, her right cheek supported by her hand, she seemed to be staring through her tears at a fold of the double curtain. Ezzelin could see nothing of her but a tear-stained profile, set and bitter.

She spoke without changing her position. Her voice was harsh. It seemed hard to believe that so hard, so cynical a tone was indeed hers.

"Everyone said I was mad to marry you. . . . When I think what I gave up to do it. . . . I knew the sort of narrow existence I should drag out with you in your miserable job and no future. . . . Obviously I've no right to complain, since I was warned. So much the worse for me. . . . But when I think of all my friends who aren't a patch on me, either physically or in any other way, who hadn't a penny to bless themselves with. . . . Not one of them but has done better for herself. . . . But I did at least hope that you'd treat me with respect. You ought to be ashamed of yourself."

And that, in fact, was how he did feel. Sitting there with bowed head, he silently cursed the untimely zeal which had inspired the sender of the anonymous letter. But, for all his discomfort, he refused to cut in his own eyes the ridiculous figure of a husband persuaded by a wife's ready tongue to see black as white. He forced himself to ask in a low tone:

"Then you won't tell me whether it's true?"

"How do you mean, true?"

"That you've been, that you are, deceiving me . . . that there's someone you're in the habit of meeting . . . the—the young man mentioned in the letter?"

She looked at him with scorn and hatred:

"You're mad; you're completely mad."

It occurred to him that at least there was method in his madness.

"That's as may be," he said; "the fact remains that you're out a great deal, and that your attitude to me is extremely odd. . . . It's not difficult to see that you've no love whatever for me."

"That's not my fault!"

"Is it mine?"

"One can't force oneself to love a person any more than one can force oneself not to have regrets." Her voice rose. "If you're sick of me, why don't you let me go? What you want is to keep me boxed up all day in this flat, which I loathe, instead of letting me go out with my mother. How does my going out with my mother hurt you? Ask her, if you don't believe me. . . . In any case, I shall tell her what's happened, and my father, too. They shall both know how you treat me."

This time she burst into a passion of sobs. She spoke loud enough for all the neighbours to hear. They could hardly fail to know that the quiet little woman on the third floor was unhappy.

Maurice Ezzelin was terrified. He hovered round her, making appealing gestures with his hands.

"For Heaven's sake, be quiet!" he cried; "everyone will hear. What do you want me to do?"

She answered through her sobs:

"I—I—want you to tear up that letter, and—and to swear—"

"To swear what?"

"—not to go out—with your newspaper under your arm—and if anybody stops you—to—to have nothing to do with him."

"All right, I'll swear."

TWO OLD FRIENDS

Sammécaud stepped on the brake of his forty-horse-
power Bertrand and addressed himself to Champcenais in a tone of affectionate intimacy.

"Have you got five minutes to spare? Well, then, let's have a
drink." (He liked, now and then, to draw attention to the fact that he
moved in the best English circles and slipped automatically into English habits.) "It'll warm you. With this car one goes faster than one
intends. Coming down the avenue, I thought you looked a bit cold.
I should hate to think I'd let you catch a chill. . . . Besides, there are
one or two things I want to talk about."

He pulled into the pavement opposite Maxim's. They went in.
The bar was almost empty. A man was polishing some brass work.

"Splendid! Sit here, old man; you'll be out of the draught. Well,
now, tell me; you're satisfied with what you've seen of them? That
fellow, now—what's his name? I never can remember. . . ."

"Who?"

"The one who seems to be an Alsatian—the director. . . ."

"Scharbeck?"

"That's the man. He's the most troublesome of the lot, isn't he?"

"Not exactly troublesome—I should say he's got the clearest brain
of them all, and more ideas than most."

"Not than Haverkamp?"

"Oh, of course, not than Haverkamp. But then I don't regard
Haverkamp as one of them. . . . Scharbeck, naturally enough, was
a bit suspicious of me at first. . . . He'd rather have raised the extra
money among his friends—Lommérie and Company—but they feel

that they're deep enough in already. They'd have found it, but not with much enthusiasm. They're not quite sure of me; in fact, Haverkamp's about the only one who was really keen for me to go in with them."

"He knew I wanted you to?"

"Yes; besides, seeing things, as he does, on the grand scale, he naturally plumped for the solution which made the biggest show and promised most. I was ready to put down a million, with no questions asked. The others could only have managed half that amount, and even so they'd have done it with a bad grace. Then there's the question of who's going to hold the controlling stock."

"The question for Scharbeck?"

"For Haverkamp, too, but in rather a different sense. He realizes that things'll be easier to run with me on one side, and the rest on the other."

"You don't think they've made too many mistakes so far, wasted too much money?"

"No. Turpin's played the fool a bit. He put two of the villas— no, three—too near the edge of the hill, in order to get his 'picturesque effect'—you've no idea what he's like with his æsthetic pretensions, and what a talker!—with the result that they slipped down, or cracked, or something, I'm not quite sure what. He didn't survey the ground thoroughly enough and suddenly found he was building in a pocket of clay."

"You think he's a humbug?"

"No, but he's got his weak spots. Those villas of his, for instance, will have to be buttressed; nothing very serious, and in other ways I'm pretty sure he's saved us money. He's got a sense of style, too; one or two of his ideas are really amusing. He's just the man for a job like this, where one's got to work for a general effect and bluff the public a bit. His Casino's going to be really delightful."

"Are the other buildings done?"

"Not yet, but they're well on the way. The hotel and the pump-room will be ready to open in two months. What's holding up the Casino is this Enghien business. You really must get that settled within the next six weeks."

"So you think I can manage that?" Sammécaud shook his head and smiled. He was flattered. But it was a lot to ask him. "Have you any idea of the number of people I've got to get moving, the difficulties that must be overcome?"

"The hardest part's been done."

"There's only one thing I can do for you, just one."

"Perhaps, but it's the one essential thing."

"Let's assume that the miracle happens and that the law's passed before the Chambers adjourn. Even so, it is no good to you for the present season."

"That's where you're wrong. The foundations are ready, and a great part of the building well advanced. What Haverkamp doesn't want to make public at present is that we're thinking of having a Casino. Consequently we've got to be careful not to give the appearance of the place too definite a character. But the moment we're sure, we can go full steam ahead. Turpin's magician enough to get a presentable Casino ready by July, or by August at latest. . . . Remember, I said six weeks."

"Allowing that everything goes smoothly, I still don't think it can be done. We've got to reckon with parliamentary delays."

"The text's ready to the last comma. It can be passed in five minutes, during a morning session. Three weeks later it'll be through the Senate. The whole thing'll go as smoothly as posting a letter. It's become an affair of public morals. No one'll dare stop it. A lot of the smaller papers have already been drumming it into their readers that the opposition is in the pay of the Enghien company. Haverkamp's done wonders in that way. Besides, you must remember that there's a wave of rectitude sweeping the country just now."

"Aren't you afraid that as soon as you open your Casino the Enghien people will start an outcry? 'That's a bit too easy,' they'll say; 'you've got to toe the line with the rest of us!'"

"By that time the law will have been passed, and a law like that can't be amended every week. Besides, we've got a perfectly good argument. 'While you were about it,' we can say, 'why didn't you set the prohibited limit at three hundred or at five hundred kilometres? Do you want to turn the whole of France into a huge convent? Do you want to tell the world that amusement's forbidden in France? We've had quite enough of wet blankets!' Trust the smaller newspapers to run that as another stunt; Haverkamp'll see to that."

Sammécaud burst into a guffaw.

"You make me laugh! You've got a pretty good nerve, I must say! . . . But what I don't see is how you're going to get the government to rush the bill through like that, as though the place were on fire. 'It must take its course,' they'll say; 'what's the hurry?'"

"What the government's got to be made to see is that if the business is allowed to hang over until after the season, it'll look like a joke, and a not altogether disinterested joke at that. I don't suppose Briand wants it to be thought that he's in the pay of the Enghien people."

"If I'm not mistaken, what you want me to do is to persuade Gurau to put the spurs to Briand. That's all very nice, but what sort of a tale am I going to tell Gurau?"

"Aren't you sufficiently intimate with him to be perfectly frank?"

"You're mad!"

"I think you're making too much of it. You're like one of those over-refined men who are always wrapping up their advances to little ladies in endless hints and precautions, while the little ladies, all the while, are saying to themselves: 'What's he waiting for?'"

Sammécaud smiled.

"Maybe; but you forget that some women are honest, and that they will only cease to be honest on condition that they can deceive themselves."

He had spoken without intending a double meaning. But suddenly he felt uncomfortable and looked hurriedly at Champcenais.

"I certainly wouldn't risk it with Gurau," he said.

"There's one way left. Haverkamp has been preparing the ground.

Have you read his last little article in the *Sanction*?"

"No; I can't say I make Haverkamp's prose my daily food."

". . . It's amusing enough now and again. . . . But the point is that he's had the cheek to attack the intention of the law, not violently, but in unmistakable terms."

"Well, what about it?"

"What about it? Don't you see that that gives you just the opportunity you want? You go to Gurau and you say: 'Do you know it's being said that the Enghien people have bought the *Sanction*? The best answer to that is to persuade Briand to rush the law through.' "

"And you think he'll be innocent enough to believe me?"

"Isn't it the case of the little lady? You don't expect her to believe, but only to seem to believe."

Sammécaud thought for a moment or two; then he smiled.

"What are you thinking about?" asked Champcenais.

"Nothing. . . . Something rather funny. . . . I heard that Haverkamp had become a Freemason—quite recently."

"Do you think it so odd for a man like him to be a Freemason?"

"Not at all . . . what makes me laugh is the idea that he combines Freemasonry with being the confidential agent of the Catholic gang, of Lommérie, Lathus, and that lot. . . . Ha ha!"

"Perhaps it puts him in a better position to look after their interests. . . . If he's working for the passage of this law through Parliament, don't you think that his Masonic connexions are a help?"

"Undoubtedly! Perhaps that's why he became one!"

Both laughed. Champcenais went on:

"Gurau knows more or less what's going on at Celle?"

"He may have read Haverkamp's publicity stuff, but he probably didn't pay much attention to it. He's not the sort of man to be always shoving his nose into other people's business, and he's not suspicious."

"And he doesn't know the role I'm playing in the business?"

"I don't think so."

"Well, what about it?"

"I'll see what I can do. You know, my dear fellow, that I'd do anything I could to please you."

Sammécaud felt himself thinking of Champcenais with warm affection.

Chapter

24

THE MIND OF A MINISTER AT ELEVEN A.M.

Though the room was vast as a banquet-hall, he was sitting quite alone in the middle of it. The windows, the height of the ceiling, the distance of the walls from the seated figure, the way daylight entered from every side, the size and configuration of the doors, even the angle at which a sunbeam touched the floor, the very joints of the parquet, all had about them an air of pomp and palaces. Since childhood such things had always been connected in his mind with the idea of worldly power, with the idea of something so far beyond him as to be barely human, so completely unattainable as not even to form an object of desire. (They belonged to a world somewhere high up, entirely cut off from the world of daily life, a world the existence of which one couldn't help believing in, because there were proofs and signs of its reality, but which belonged to a supernatural order, like those clouds peopled by saints and angels which floated, in old pictures, above the actual world of labourers and merchants.)

It was only fair to recognize the part that fate had played in all this. When he was just the son of the Town Clerk of Tours, when, at the end of his fifth term at the Lycée, the whiskered magistrate, who was known as "Uncle Sourdeval," had expressed a doubt to his parents whether it was worth while going on with his education (how miserable, how heart-broken his mother had looked as she hid her disappointment behind a mask of silence!), what would he have said, what would any of them have said, if some magician could have shown him, in years to come, sitting in the middle of this Ministerial office?

One ought, he thought, to be grateful for one's luck, to force oneself to enjoy success, even when feeling sulky and dispirited. Moods have a way of making one unfair, of turning one, too often, into a spoilt child, so that one doesn't see the wood for the trees. There are worries here as elsewhere. No sooner has one become a Minister than one realizes that a Minister's day, like the day of any ordinary man, is full of worries, is broken up and parcelled out into a whole series of worries, most of which are petty—petty fears, petty annoyances, such as the sudden terror of not being up to one's job, the suspicion that one has been let down. Small humiliations, even, play their part in it (one may have used the wrong tone of voice, the wrong words, in speaking to a subordinate, or in receiving a visitor; a colleague may have treated one rather too cavalierly, or some insignificant politician whom one was trying to get rid of may start an interview on a note of insufferable familiarity and end it with threats). One realizes, too, pretty soon that a Minister's troubles haven't even the merit of saving one from the various worries of every day, be they great or small. (Germaine had been behaving oddly of late; the tailor had ruined that new suit; just what was the meaning of that pain in the back that started a week ago and wouldn't stop?) Should any or all of these things make one forget the essential fact that one is *here* in this great, light room, and that millions of fellow human beings would gladly accept one's worries if only they could be in one's place?

Gurau opened a drawer, took from it a small square looking-glass, propped it against a paper-weight, and gazed at his reflection. It had been a red-letter day in the history of his appearance. This very morning he had shaved off his moustache. For a whole month he had been regularly diminishing its extent, so that the ultimate change should be less noticeable, and now the last trace of it had vanished. Long ago Germaine had expressed a wish to see him clean-shaven. Would she be pleased now that she had got what she wanted? She must have known it was coming, since she had seen the intermediate stages, but it wouldn't be less of a surprise for all that. It is amazing what a difference there is between a tiny moustache and no moustache at all. The lips, suddenly revealed, are like those of a stranger.

It is as though the mouth suddenly "sees the light of day" in the sense that the phrase is used of a new-born baby. "I never knew my mouth was so distinguished, so interesting-looking." The whole face seems to have undergone a sympathetic change. Even the expression of the eyes is altered. "Mine look larger, more dominant, more attractive. They're the kind of eyes that make a man attractive to women. I'll look in on Germaine about midnight, on my way home from dinner. She's not expecting me; she'll probably be in bed, since she's not on in the last act, but that can't be helped. It'll amuse her. I shall be in evening dress, with this new face of mine. It'll be fun. . . . And what'll Briand say when he sees me? I expect he'll have a good laugh. Or perhaps he'll be so preoccupied with the problem of old-age pensions that he'll just stare vaguely at me and take no notice."

Gurau put the looking-glass back into his drawer. The idea of old-age pensions gave him an uncomfortable shock. Why? Because he considered that Briand was treating him too much as a negligible quantity, that he was behaving too much as though that particular measure was his own private affair. Obviously, quite apart from the favourable results he expected from it at the elections of the 24th of April, he was anxious to have his name connected with it. He was worried by the contempt of his old Socialist colleagues. He wanted to show that the "social traitor" had only seemed to be betraying the cause of the people in order the better to serve it. Let others preach an imaginary Utopia, he at least would give the workers something definite. It was all very well to bring the trade-union leaders and the Syndicalists to heel, but he knew that it was equally important to get the support of the rank and file whom they claimed to control. "It's a clever move, but where do I come in?" So far, Briand had been managing the whole business, just as though the Minister of Labour didn't exist at all. Was it an intentional slight, or merely thoughtlessness? Each time that Briand had condescended to speak about the projected bill it had only been because Gurau had forced himself on his attention, had nudged, as it were, the President of the Council with his elbow. There had been inter-departmental conferences, of course, but so far none of those serious discussions, none of that working together that the veriest tiro would have thought to be indispensable.

But Gurau had as much right as Briand to concern himself with a reform of this kind, as many, if not more, reasons to keep his fingers on the pulse of the situation, to present himself to the working-class voter as the champion of working-class interests. "Briand's an odd fellow. What's his real motive? What's he getting at? Is it that he's just an opportunist?—No, that's not quite fair. He has his serious moments, I was almost going to say his moments of conviction. . . . The odds are that he's never really thought about it. . . . Is it simply that he's in love with power? . . . Not quite; it amuses him to govern, but he's not so intense about it as some people. He probably thinks that among all the boring jobs one has to do in the course of a lifetime, the job of being Prime Minister is one of the least boring, and when he's old he'll resign himself to being President of the Republic in the same sort of casual, comfortable way that he does everything else.

"Anyhow, I'm not going to let this dilettante who doesn't really believe in anything steal my thunder in this matter of old-age pensions. After all, I *do* believe in things, and I see further than he does. . . ."

Since Briand hadn't condescended to consult the man most qualified to advise, it would be perfectly fair to play a trick on him. How about saying suddenly: "This scheme of yours has been badly presented. The working-class leaders will throw the gift back in your teeth, and, speaking for myself, I don't feel inclined to force it on them"—ending up with: "I've no responsibility in the matter, and I'd rather resign"? That's what he would say, but he would let it be clearly seen that what he meant was: "If you want me to risk my reputation in this business, you'd better change your attitude." For all his air of detachment, Briand would be annoyed. It was necessary for him to get the pension bill through before the elections. Gurau's resignation would give the opposition a good argument and would bring to nothing all Briand's preliminary work in committee and in the lobbies. The news would make a fine show in the papers, especially in the Syndicalist press. "Gurau resigns because he refuses to be party to what he regards as a trick on the working classes."

It might turn out to be the best move he had made for a long time, and the best insurance against the future.

He stretched out his hand to the telephone, turning over in his mind, as he did so, the opening sentences of his intended conversation.

"Get me the President of the Council; I want to speak to him personally."

And then:

"My dear President, forgive my troubling you, but I must see you this afternoon."

At this moment the door-keeper entered with a card.

Roger Sammécaud

Gurau made a face. "What's he want to come bothering me about?" But he knew that the oil-magnate was not in the habit of paying aimless visits. At half past eleven he had an appointment with M. Albert de Mun "of the Académie Française." There were ten minutes to spare: "Quite long enough for me to get rid of Sammécaud."

"Ask the gentleman to come in."

His hand still lay beside the telephone. He hesitated; then:

"I'll ring up presently, before I see de Mun," he decided.

Chapter

25

CONTINUATION AND CONCLUSION
OF A MINISTER'S DAY

"All right—if it's really so urgent!"—and Briand had made an appointment for six o'clock.

Just before leaving to see the President of the Council, Gurau, who had signed his letters earlier than usual, set himself to tidy up the odds and ends of papers that littered his desk. He gathered together several notes which he had taken during his interview with de Mun. He had got into the habit of taking notes when he had a visitor, sometimes because the question under discussion really interested him, sometimes to give the impression that he was a Minister who took his work seriously (often for both reasons simultaneously). He wrote in pencil, on little squares of yellowish paper which he cut up for himself.

In the presence of this influential orator and member of the Académie Française he had begun by playing his favourite part. But little by little a genuine interest in what the other was saying began to take possession of him. Now, as he re-read the notes he had made, Gurau felt again the particular emotion of which he had been conscious while the Catholic deputy was speaking.

The man's attitude had been, so to speak, the perfection of correctitude, but there had been something more in it than that, a touch of formality, a quality almost of simplicity, a hint of being on his best Sunday behaviour. The impression he had made upon Gurau was that of a gentleman who had come to discuss his daughter's marriage settlement, or of a colonel paying a call in mufti. His moustache was pointed and well curled, and there was a tiny mole on his chin. It was his eyes and the general expression of his face which gave the effect of simplicity. Gurau found it difficult to imagine any but conventional phrases issuing from those too eloquent lips, difficult to believe that he would be tempted to listen with more attention than politeness demanded.

But there had come a moment during the interview when he had ceased suddenly to be the amused host of a rather typical visitor and had become an interested listener. He was being told things he had never suspected; pictures began forming themselves before his mind's eye; he was conscious of feeling emotion, indignation, a sense of guilt, of asking himself questions that touched his self-respect. Each time he looked up it was to see the face almost of a stranger, the mustachioed face of a fine fellow who was speaking with all the earnestness he could command in an effort to convince his hearer, and whose rather simple eyes brimmed with a consciousness of tragedy which he seemed to be feeling as his own.

"Obviously," Gurau reflected, "we had no idea that the state of affairs among these home workers was so bad. . . . Take the figures he quoted me: 43 per cent work from ten to twelve hours a day, and not a few do sixteen and sometimes nineteen hours—that's to say, nineteen hours out of the twenty-four!—in addition to the other things they've got to attend to, like looking after the house. Then there's a child, perhaps, who's got to be rocked or fed between bouts at the sewing-machine, and an old mother, as likely as not, who's beyond taking care of herself. It's enough to make one cry! Where did I put that other note I made about their earnings? Ah, here it is: 'As a general rule daily earnings amount to 1 fr. 60 or 2 fr. 60. . . .' Three sous an hour. What do the unions think about it?—They don't; so far as they're concerned, the thing doesn't exist. All these years they've been busy building up their organization, strengthening the pyramidal edifice of a proletarian aristocracy. Somehow, it's never occurred to one to look at it all from this point of view: the only thing we've bothered our heads about has been *organized* labour. The Third Estate of '89 thought of itself as constituting the 'People'; and the trade-union movement of today is doing much the same thing—neither more nor less sincerely. They don't seem to have the slightest idea that outside their membership, in the vast swamp that surrounds their working-class fortress, exists this enormous swarming mass of petty traders. In the eyes of this half-starved, disfranchised class such things as the minimum wage and the right to strike are the privileges of their masters. They compose a sort of Fifth Estate, despised and, what's worse, exploited by their neighbours of the Fourth. Old de Mun, talking away in that soft voice of his, said something quite casually that sent shivers down my spine! Who is it that these miserable slaves work for, tear their guts out for, nineteen hours a day at three sous an hour? For the women of the rich middle classes? For the great ladies of the faubourg Saint-Germain? Not a bit of it! When one works for the rich, whether at emptying chamber-pots, making dresses, or sewing underclothing, one gets well paid for it. What the slave at three sous an hour is doing is to make pink lace chemises, chintz dresses, and feathered hats for the wives and daughters of plumbers, or Sunday cravats and waistcoats for mechanics. Working people demand luxury, and it's got to approximate as nearly as possible to the luxury of the rich—with this difference, that it's got to be cheap. But can't the middleman, the shopkeeper, do something to improve things? Why shouldn't he pay more for his labour? Out of the question! He might as well shut up shop straight away. His customers know what they want and they mean to get it. No, three sous an hour or nothing."

Gurau chewed the bitter cud of this thoughts with a certain sense of pleasure. For a man of ability who has lived for a long time under the domination of fixed ideas, there is, often, a feeling of relief to be derived from seeing those ideas in an unfavourable light. No matter that he had sworn for years by the gods of trade unionism that he had staked his credit as a journalist and his future as a politician on the victory of organized labour: the spirit of contradiction would never allow itself to be entirely silenced. And side by side with the spirit of contradiction stood one more powerful still, the deathless Mephistopheles, the spirit of denial. And it whispered in his ear: "And so you really think that there's a magic formula for cleansing the world of injustice! Poor fool!—your efforts amount to no more than substituting one injustice for another."

There was, too, a pleasing sense of superiority to be got from such thoughts. Ironic melancholy might weight his heart with sorrow, but at the same time it gave him a gratifying feeling of being above all parties and superior to all enthusiasms. He felt himself made free of a land where none dwelt but a favoured few with keen, disillusioned minds. Not that he couldn't, when he wanted, get as closely in touch as anyone with the believers, the earnest, the enthusiastic, for with them he needed but to speak as man to man, using the language of a common humanity. After all, to whom did even Jaurès speak more intimately? And this very morning the Count Albert de Mun, member of the Académie Française, had exchanged confidential glances with him and had parted from him almost as though they had been two lifelong friends. Why, even Sammécaud—

Because, even though Gurau let his mind dwell as little as possible on what Sammécaud had said, he couldn't altogether forget it. He had a curious feeling at the back of his mind that there was some connexion between what Sammécaud and Briand each expected of him. For the moment he didn't bother to analyse more closely the nature of the connexion, relying upon the quickness of his intelligence to make clear the resemblance later.

For some odd reason, the emotion which the visit of Albert de Mun had caused him, and which he now remembered as he looked at the little pieces of yellowish paper, seemed to have put him in a favourable state of mind for crossing swords with the elderly, bantering, subtle, and sceptical Briand.

He was less concerned to discover the reason for this odd psychological fact than to profit by it.

Gurau left the President of the Council about a quarter past seven. Briand saw him to the door and parted from him on a note of badinage.

"And now I suppose you're off to one of your smart dinner-parties, eh? You haven't much time to dress—not that that matters to a man of your experience. . . . Jaurès, now! That's a very different story! Do you know it was I who explained to him that the tab at the bottom of a boiled shirt front was meant to button on to the pants to prevent the shirt from riding up? . . . It had never occurred to him. His shirts were always riding up, with the result, since he sweats a great deal, that their fronts were always a mass of creases. Ah, well, when a man's an idealist! . . ."

As soon as Briand was alone he rolled a cigarette, went to the window, and stared meditatively into the night.

"What exactly is he playing at? It's odd. . . . No doubt I've ignored him a bit too much over this pensions business; it was stupid of me. But what's biting him in this Enghien affair? Is he afraid that people are going to suggest things? . . . He must have become very sensitive all of a sudden—he wasn't so touchy when it was a question of oil. . . . A curious chap. At one moment it really seemed as though he was issuing an ultimatum. I know perfectly well that sooner or later he'll leave me in the lurch. What he wants is my job; I've no illusions about that, but it doesn't suit my interests to let him go just yet. As for Enghien, that's neither here nor there; I'm not going to see my bill knocked on the head for the sake of saving a few gaming-tables."

Gurau walked down the boulevard Saint-Michel, where he had been dining. He turned on to the Quai des Grands-Augustins just as the lamplighter was beginning to put out the street-lamps.

He was pleased with his evening. The party had been a brilliant one, and he had shown up well. "They've got to admit that for a Minister of the Republic I'm fairly presentable."

He kept to the pavement that runs in front of the houses. When he reached the block where Germaine lived he stopped and raised his eyes. "Hullo! Not in bed yet? I'm pretty sure she's not expecting me!"

He hesitated a moment then crossed the road to get a better view of the fourth-floor window which he knew so well. It made a solitary patch of light in the darkness, and looked suddenly larger than usual, somehow out of its due place, as though he had never seen it before.

"She can't have drawn the curtains. It looks almost as though the sitting-room were lit up too. Probably one of the little corner lights is on, or perhaps it's just that she hasn't closed the communicating door."

Despite himself, he began to be uneasy. He almost felt guilty at having come. But he put the thought from him: "It's just as well I did, whatever's going on." Odds and ends of thought began tumbling about his brain with lightning speed, plunging him alternately into moods of anger and apathy. "I'm more in love with her than I thought I was," he said to himself. He was conscious of that sensation, as of anticipating events, which seizes us at certain moments of tragedy. It was as though, by giving time a sharp jolt, he had managed to get ahead of the actual moment. "I'm sure that in a minute I shall see her shadow," he thought, "and there will be a second shadow with it."

A moment later everything happened exactly as he had foreseen. The fact was hardly more real than the imagination of it had been. At most it was as though one aspect of reality had suddenly become another, ceasing to be something of which he was assured by his own senses, to become something that had been pointed out to him by another. "Look up there," such another might have said, "or am I dreaming?" and, "No," he would have replied, "you're not dreaming." But at half past twelve at night the river-bank is deserted. There was no sign of anybody else. Even the lamplighter had disappeared, extinguished, perhaps, like one of his own lamps.

Gurau had no idea to whom the second shadow could belong. An inner voice said: "If you want to know, go up." But he paid no attention to the advice. Some other consideration seemed to drive it from his mind. He felt it more in accord with destiny—with his own private destiny—to tear his eyes from the attraction of that illuminated window. Looking instead at the parapet which vanished in the direction of Notre-Dame, he allowed his spirit to be flooded by a pain that was at once proud and cowardly.

A change in the light that came from above made him raise his head again. Someone had drawn the double curtains. He smiled, clenching his teeth and grinding them a little. Then, with sudden decision, he set off briskly towards Notre-Dame. "I'll see, as I used to see, the flying buttresses in the darkness. I will think of my painted window."

He suffered deeply, but with a strange medley of emotions. A part of him seemed to have died, but vaguely, half apprehended, he seemed to hear the murmur of some crowd coming nearer and nearer, to be conscious of a song that heralded a new birth, promising salvation in the future.

A cool breeze blew down the river towards him, bringing a sense of freshness such as he had never known before. Automatically he passed his hand across his face and was surprised at the nakedness of his lips.

Chapter

26

"I HAVE TAKEN THE PLUNGE"

In response to an express letter Jerphanion set out one Tuesday evening at half past eight, to meet Laulerque at the Café du Delta.

"I must apologize for summoning you like this without warning," Laulerque said, "but I'll explain. Your affairs have been constantly in my mind. What have you decided?"

"Since that visit to Rothweil which I told you about, I've seen Clanricard only once. The next day he went to see Rothweil again; he's probably told you about it?"

"He has, and I've an idea that something's doing. There was a sort of bashfulness about his way of speaking; obviously, he'd rather have said nothing. He was almost like a young girl in love."

"Perhaps Mademoiselle Cazalis is getting jealous."

"I wouldn't put it beyond him to neglect her a bit in the ardour of his conversion. Now's your chance!" Laulerque added, laughing. Then:

"I always thought he'd bite. But what about you?"

"Well, I've been carrying that letter of introduction to Lengnau about in my pocket. I wasn't quite comfortable about it. You see, I didn't want to get into touch with a man like that without knowing a bit more about him, and about Masonry. The things I wanted to find out about it were the sort that I couldn't ask him and didn't dare ask Rothweil—quite prosaic details, some of them, but which seem to me not unimportant. Haven't you got the same sort of curiosity? For instance, what exactly is a Lodge? What sort of a place is it? There must be somewhere where they meet?"

"Naturally."

"What's the procedure? What does one have to do when one's admitted? What happens at their meetings? I know, of course, that they discuss certain questions, but aren't there also ceremonies of some kind?"

"I believe there are."

"A sort of ritual. . . . One hears all kinds of things about the tests that newcomers have to undergo. Do you know at all what they are?"

"No."

"One doesn't want to be exposed to too humiliating or grotesque a hocus-pocus. At any rate, one would like to know something about it beforehand, but naturally one can't have any experience of that side of the business before one's admitted?"

"Obviously not."

"Not even secretly, if one took precautions?"

"I imagine it's quite impossible."

"Couldn't one get someone who's already been initiated to talk about it?"

Laulerque smiled; then:

"They're sworn to secrecy, you know. They can reveal nothing, not even details of fact, without betraying their oath. I wouldn't count on that."

"Well, then?" Jerphanion asked with an air of disappointment.

Laulerque started to laugh, and added, on a note of triumph:

"As a matter of fact, I know a fellow who's just washed his hands of it."

"What, of Freemasonry?"

"Yes."

"Would he talk?"

"He might."

"That's fine! When can I meet him?"

"Wait a moment—you don't mind his being a sort of renegade?"

"Good God, no! If I was thinking of entering a monastery and wanted to know what I should have to do, what sort of life I should have to live—in fact, the whole bag of tricks—I should think myself lucky to be able to talk to an unfrocked monk. One takes one's chance where one finds it."

"Good! The man I was speaking of will be here in twenty minutes. I made an appointment with him, but I wanted to have a few words with you before he came. He's an engraver, a man of some education who knows a thing or two. He's read a lot in a desultory sort of way, a bit vulgar to look at, but you mustn't judge him by his manners. He's an independent sort of chap, rather a rough diamond, and a bit restless. But I think he's honest. I don't know him intimately. I've not told him your name. How shall I introduce you?"

Jerphanion was excited.

"I don't know," he stammered; "let's see—how about Monsieur Richard, a student of literature? . . . But there's one thing that's bothering me."

"What's that?"

"Well, yesterday I decided at last to send that letter to Lengnau. He'll ask me to go and see him."

"What of it?"

Jerphanion thought for a moment. Then:

"Oh, nothing—but suppose that, as a result of talking to your engraver, I find myself with a distaste for Masonry?"

"That won't prevent your going to see Lengnau. At least you'll have heard both sides of the question."

"That's true. . . ."

For some moments they were silent, thinking their thoughts. Jerphanion looked impatiently at the clock. Suddenly he asked:

"And you?"

"Well?"

"What have you decided?"

"It's finished; I've taken the plunge."

Instinctively Jerphanion looked round to see that nobody could overhear them. Then, lowering his voice:

"What?" he asked, "in the direction you spoke to me about?"

Scarcely opening his lips, Laulerque replied:

"Yes—I've undertaken a mission."

"You're not joking?"

"I couldn't tell you before. From now on, I oughtn't to breathe a word of it to anyone."

"But . . . I'm not asking you any questions."

"You're the only person who knows. . . . You're not like other people."

Laulerque stared hard at Jerphanion, as though he were recapitulating all the conclusions he had come to about him and were putting them to the test of a solemn scrutiny. Jerphanion felt himself blushing. Laulerque continued:

"I've got the highest possible opinion of you. . . . Besides, I'm not going to go into details. . . ."

"They've sworn you to secrecy?"

Laulerque raised his hand.

"That goes without saying. . . . In future I shall have to hold my tongue even with you. I shall feel the loss, and it won't be because I don't trust you; but when one submits oneself to a discipline one's got to take it seriously. . . . This is probably the last time that I shall ever talk to a friend about all this, and it pleases me to think that you're the one."

"He's a fine fellow," Jerphanion thought. He was moved both by the confidences that Laulerque had made and by the idea of the vague dangers that he imagined his friend to be on the point of encountering. He said:

"Please understand that I don't want to persuade you to tell me anything. But I'm a bit anxious about you. It all seems to me to have happened so suddenly. It's a terribly serious thing. . . ."

He stopped, waiting to see whether Laulerque would confide still further in him.

The other half-closed his eyes, leaned forward, and murmured:

"The mission I told you of will be during my next Easter holiday. I'm going abroad . . . to Holland."

He smiled. Jerphanion asked, with a worried look:

"But at least you know what they're asking you to do?"

"Not with any certainty."

Laulerque kept on smiling.

"I admire you!" Jerphanion exclaimed, and sighed.

"Oh, in itself it's a perfectly simple business. There's someone I've got to meet, an envelope I've got to deliver, another one I've got to bring back. Perhaps there'll be nothing but blank paper in the envelope; perhaps they just want to test me. You don't think they'd give a beginner anything very terrible to do?"

"I don't imagine they'll tell you straight off to go and dynamite a train. But even carrying papers in an envelope, papers you know nothing about, can be pretty serious. You'll have to pass the frontier. . . ."

"Actually, I shall have to pass two. . . ."

"Doesn't that make you think?"

Laulerque shrugged his shoulders and made a grimace.

Jerphanion pressed his point:

"I can understand taking a responsibility, however heavy; what I could never bring myself to do would be to take it blindfold."

"It's the whole basis on which secret societies are built. You refuse to accept it? . . ."

"More or less. . . ."

"All right, then; but in joining a secret group, no matter how little secret it may be, you will be collaborating, in spite of yourself, and without knowing it, in actions which you will have no part in judging. You will be taking responsibilities which you know nothing of. What are the real objects of the Masonic movement? What part will you have in the deliberations of its secret leaders—assuming that its leaders are secret?"

Jerphanion did not reply at once. He thought for a while, and then said:

"That is a point, certainly, and it makes me think; but to some extent it's a question of degree. I've never gathered that the Lodge can force its ordinary members to do anything it wills. A member,

I imagine, is always free to refuse. If the leaders make use of him to serve their mysterious ends, it's only in a very general, a very vague, way. So far as personal responsibility is concerned, he only undertakes, surely, what he wants to undertake?"

"Possibly; but in that case it would be too placid for me; I should get no excitement out of it."

Jerphanion pressed his point: "You really have thought seriously about what you're letting yourself in for? How if, one of these days, the gentleman in Holland or elsewhere, to whom you're sent with a message, gives you a package containing, not odds and ends of paper, but a bomb, with instructions to place it somewhere . . . ?"

"Well?"

"You'll obey?"

Laulerque smiled, and his eyes shone.

"Why not?"

Jerphanion lowered his eyes. He was abashed by the thought that, compared with this Laulerque, he must seem a simple countryman, a poor little bourgeois seeking peace at any price. He tried to excuse himself by saying: "A lot of his talk is pure bravado, pure exhibitionism," but when he looked again at the thin face opposite his own, he couldn't deny the reality of that burning, inner flame. He concluded his attempt at argument by saying almost piteously:

"I just can't understand your state of mind."

Suddenly, as though wishing to change the conversation, Laulerque said:

"I went to see my doctor again the other day."

"Why, did you feel ill?"

"Not particularly, but I hadn't been for more than a year, and I gather that I'm the sort of man who ought to see his doctor every three months at least."

Jerphanion was conscious of a slight shock. He looked at Laulerque, at the eyes behind their glasses, at his thin face, his neck, at his chest beneath the covering of clothes, trying to keep from his gaze as much as possible any suspicion of anxious curiosity. When he spoke he forced himself to adopt a light tone.

"You don't look as though you needed to. Surely you're strong enough?"

Laulerque smiled, leaned forward on the table, and said, turning his face sideways:

"I don't give much for the sort of stuff doctors tell you. Mine," he added, with sudden bitterness, "is a fool, a mere animal. One is nothing to him but stomach, liver, or lungs. He doesn't recognize the existence of anything else. I wonder, sometimes, the effect he has on his more imaginative patients."

Jerphanion was deeply moved. His brain teemed with a confusion of thoughts in which a sense of brotherly concern predominated. He would have liked to "say something"—something to the point, something tactful. He felt extremely shy and quite incapable of making any sensible remark. Even to say nothing appeared to him a form of gaucherie.

Laulerque rescued him from his embarrassment.

"I don't know why I'm telling you this," he said; "probably it's because I caught sight of someone who reminded me of him."

At this moment a newcomer entered the café.

"Here's my man!" Laulerque exclaimed.

Jerphanion thought: "In an hour, perhaps, I shall know everything there is to know about Freemasonry. . . . It would be too good to be true!"

The idea gave him a sort of mental spasm as delicious and at the same time as intolerable as a passionate spasm of the flesh. He was conscious even of the same sort of restlessness as seizes one in the onset of desire.

Chapter

27

THE MYSTERIES OF FREEMASONRY

"Yes, I chucked it up; I wasn't turned out. It's not easy to get turned out. I just stopped going, and now I regard myself as completely free. Not that I say things against them in public—oh no; anything I tell you must be strictly between ourselves; not because I'm frightened—I've got my job, you see, and that makes me independent—but because I don't want to be thought a skunk."

"Were you a Mason for a long time?"

"About two years. For eighteen months I went regularly, though from the first I realized that it wasn't my sort of show at all. But you know how it is, one's foolish; one thinks one's too deeply involved to get out; one says to oneself: 'Some of the details are grotesque, and there are aspects that I dislike, an atmosphere that I find repugnant, but I shall probably get used to it all'—and that's where one's wrong."

Jerphanion thought to himself: "This is the second genuine Freemason I've ever met."

Ardansseaux, the engraver, was a small, fat man, with protuberant eyes. The top of his head was completely bald, set in a fuzzy circle of hair. He seemed to have a constant irritation in his throat, and when he spoke, each of his phrases played, as it were, an obstacle race with impeding coughs, like someone picking his way carefully along a stony path. His coughs were accompanied by a good deal of spluttering. He emptied half his glass in two gulps.

"You believed in it when you joined?" Jerphanion asked.

"Of course I did. I've always had a passion for ideas, but I like thinking for myself, with a book on my knee. But at the time I became a Mason I'd just had a pretty bad jolt. My wife, whom I idolized, had run away. She took our child with her. And then one day a friend spoke to me about Masonry, and I said to myself: 'Try it, old man, perhaps it'll take the place of home.' "

"He too," thought Jerphanion . . . "and I? . . . We're both unhappy, but my unhappiness is perhaps a little less narrow than his, more general." He couldn't, however, help seeing Ardansseaux in a new light. This fat little man had found in love a source of terrible suffering, and instead of consoling himself by playing cards in a café, had sought relief in the alleviations of philosophic companionship.

Jerphanion's interest, however, was not in the unfortunate lover, but in the eyewitness of Masonic mysteries. But he didn't want to betray too impatient a curiosity. He said, therefore, with as detached an air as possible:

"Once you'd joined, what was it that you particularly disliked?"

"Pretty well the whole show."

"Really?"

"Yes. In the first place, I'm a bit of an artist: appearances matter to me. You should just see the place where we used to have our meetings! They call it their temple—I imagine it's pretty much the same whatever Lodge you belong to. Well, you can't imagine anything more ridiculous. I'm no friend of priests, and I think all dogma's absurd, but take me to Notre-Dame or Saint-Merri some Sunday when there's plenty of music, and I can appreciate it."

"What's a Masonic temple like,"

"What's it like?"

"Yes."

Ardansseaux raised his head. He looked towards the ceiling, and his eyes seemed to be more protuberant than ever. He opened and shut them slowly in an apparent effort to concentrate on some illusive image.

"A temple?" he repeated, "a temple? . . . Oh, it's an ugly sort of a place . . . it's . . . well, it's hard to describe. You've got to see the colours and the decoration for yourself. . . . I remember once I went into a little Protestant church, an evangelical sort of a place . . .

but, no, that won't really give you the idea. . . . Try to imagine . . . no, that's not it either. . . . I was going to say that it was more like a big café in a provincial town—you know the sort of thing, with pillars and thingumbobs all over . . . or a Turkish bath, except that there's no swimming-pool . . . or a swell whore-house . . . not really, you know, but simply regarded from the point of view of general effect, of atmosphere, looked at structurally, if you understand me, as an example of the bizarre."

Jerphanion and Laulerque exchanged glances. Jerphanion's seemed to say: "Do you think this is the sort of fellow to give me the definite ideas I'm after? . . ." He saw the secrets of Masonry, which he thought he'd been on the point of fathoming, which never before had he been so anxious to master, receding maliciously into a fog of vagueness.

Ardansseaux brought back his gaze to his two companions. He seemed conscious of their disappointment.

"I'm no good without a bit of paper and pencil to explain my meaning. . . ."

He rummaged in one of his pockets, brought out an old envelope, found a bit of drawing-pencil in his waistcoat, and began to sketch on the envelope a sort of plan, keeping up a flow of comment as he did so. The lines made by the pencil were thick and black, and the details of his drawing suffered in consequence. Now and again he scribbled a word in the margin, indicating by a line the detail to which it referred.

"Here are the four walls—all this part is what they call the Orient; it's raised, and arranged more or less in a semicircle, with steps and a balustrade. This is the throne of the Worshipful Master, with an altar in front of it, and the altar of the Oaths. This little square is the pedestal of the Worshipful Master—I've shown the shape of it roughly. Here, on either side, are columns—five, or six, I don't remember the exact number—built into the wall. . . . In some temples the columns may be arranged differently, I don't know anything about that. On either side of the entrance, here, are two more columns, bigger than the others, covered with bronze, with some arrangement of light which can be made to illuminate them internally at will. . . . There are heaps of little tricks like that, they love them. Most of what they do reminds one of the effects in a children's pantomime: 'What's going to happen next, Papa?—I'm frightened, Papa, let's go home'—I could give you any number of instances. It's one of the things that got on my nerves from the start."

"What's in this open space here—chairs?"

"Eh?"

"Is that where the members of the Lodge sit during the meeting?"

"Wait a moment. . . . In the first place, it's not called a meeting, but a session. . . . No, they don't sit in the way you think they do, that'd be too simple. . . . No . . . along each side there are benches, facing one another . . . the middle part is empty except for the emblem of the Lodge, which is set horizontally, like that. It's made of canvas, painted. In some temples I believe it's a sort of blackboard with figures on it in chalk, like you have in schools, but I can't say for certain. The benches on this side are called the Column of the South. . . . It's symbolic, and not to be confused with the other columns, the real ones I mean, the pillars. . . . The benches opposite are called the Column of the North . . . naturally. Thus you have North, East (the Orient, they call it), South. . . . That leaves the West. . . . On the West is the entrance to the Sanctuary."

"The Sanctuary's outside, then?"

"Yes, but don't muddle me. In my Lodge the Apprentices and the Brethren sat here, on the North side, with the Apprentices in front. The Masters sat on the South. In some Lodges I believe the Brethren sit here, on the same side as the Masters. It probably depends on how many there are of each—anyhow, it's a detail. Now, here—I've no more room. . . . On the dais I've forgotten to indicate the table of the Speaker and the table of the Secretary. Then here there's the table of the Brother Almoner and the seat of the Junior Deacon, and another on this side which is—let me think—yes, the Senior Warden's—no, I can't remember. . . ."

"It all seems very complicated."

"You've said it! Complicated, I should think it is! . . . No, what a fool I am! The Senior and the Junior Wardens sit here in front of the two illuminated pillars, with the Brother Tyler by the door, between the two Deacons. . . . You can take my word for its being complicated! And then there's a whole lot of gadgets I haven't mentioned, but which you've got to know by heart before you can be a good Mason: the letters on the pillars, the inscriptions, the emblems. One mustn't confuse the insignia, either. One says to oneself: 'That brother with the thing hanging round his neck is surely the Senior Deacon,' but you're wrong, for the Senior Deacon is the one with the ruler and the sword. This one who has only a plumb-line is the Junior Warden. It's like that the whole time; you'd think they'd muddled it all up on purpose to impress people, especially newcomers, and to keep them fussing about trivialities. Most of the time the brethren are sweating with nervousness lest they forget the way the novices ought to walk, lest in their excitement they may start off with the left foot, or lest they confuse the South and North when the Worshipful Master cries: 'Brothers who adorn the column of the South.' And so it goes on, because one's got to remember which are the right gestures, too, so as not to strike one's thigh when one ought to strike one's forearm, and not to cry: 'Hail! hail!' a minute before the others. Then they make one take up such an oblique posture that it's impossible to keep an eye on one's neighbour and imitate him. In a small gathering like that the slightest blunder is noticed. You know that they're thinking you a blockhead, with the result you're in such a constant state of tension that it never enters your head to protest. It's like being on parade the whole time."

Ardansseaux laughed and broke into a fit of coughing.

"That," he said, "is what they call free thought."

Jerphanion fingered his beard, frowned, pursed his lips, and nodded.

"Is it really as bad as that?" he asked; "so tied up with formalities? Aren't you talking of things that are more or less obsolete now?"

"Not a bit of it."

"Then, according to you, it's more complicated and more formal even than a church service? In church the priest and his assistants have certain ritual actions to perform, but at least the faithful are left alone. All they've got to do is to get up or sit down at the right moments, and—"

"Much more complicated—I've not gone to church much since I took my first Communion, but I remember what happens pretty well. In the Lodges it's all super-complicated. Even when you think all the mumbo-jumbo's finished and that they're going to discuss some point on the agenda—and presumably you've only joined because you're interested in ideas—it all starts again. If you want to speak, you've got to get up, clap your hands, and stretch out your arms towards the Warden of your column. A lot of inspiration you get that way! It explains why everything has such a bogus air, if you know what I mean. You get the impression that even the arguments have been rehearsed, that everything that's said has been got by heart. They can't do anything naturally or call anything by its right name. You might imagine that before opening the session the Grand Master would say quite simply: 'Just see that the door's locked, so that we shan't be interrupted.' Not a hope! What he does is to put on his most sepulchral voice and say: 'Brother Senior Warden, what is the first duty of the Wardens of the Lodge?' While he speaks, everyone is standing at attention. The answer is: 'O Worshipful Master, his first duty is to see that the Lodge is duly covered, and that all the brethren who occupy the columns are truly Masons.' Then the Senior Deacon starts fooling about in the corridors, and the Wardens stalk down the columns squinting at the members, like a lot of children playing at robbers. . . . And so it goes on. They don't talk about reading the minutes of the last meeting, but 'rehearsing what was traced upon the tablets at the last session.' And then their banquets! I went to two or three of them. The odds are that the fool next you tries to put you out of your stride by pretending that he's been at the game longer than you have. He starts talking about the Veil of the Platform or asks whether he has not Spread your Standard instead of his own—although all he means is the table-cloth and the napkins. It's just the same with the rites of initiation; they're just about the limit!"

"One hears a lot about them," said Jerphanion, in his most winning voice, trying to modify his curiosity as much as possible.

"They don't like one to speak about them, you know."

"About them or about everything?"

"About them particularly. . . . Besides, it'd take a long time to explain it all, and be rather a bore."

The young student had the impression that Ardansseaux was trying to shirk the issue. "It's odd," he thought, "after telling us so much."

But Ardansseaux seemed aware that his sudden change of attitude might appear rather baffling. He made a sharp gesture with his left arm and moved his head and shoulders like a man who is shaking off an access of fear.

"Oh, I'm not such a fool as to mind their threats. . . . If I was frightened I shouldn't have spoken about them as I have done. Besides, you won't tell anyone, will you?"

Jerphanion and Laulerque reassured him.

Ardansseaux seemed to be thinking; then:

"Where I went wrong," he said, "was in ever letting myself be a party to all that nonsense; I ought to have realized that I'd taken the wrong road. Not that I hadn't some excuse. In spite of everything, you see, one's a bit stunned by it all, and the more interested one is, the less one pays attention to what's going on. I only began to criticize it all later, when I'd been present at the reception of others. There's something rather deplorable, you must admit, in seeing these poor fools with their eyes blindfolded, their left arms and the whole of their left breast naked, as though a doctor were going to give them an injection, the trousers of their right legs rolled up above the knee, and limping because they've had one of their shoes taken away. It's more like a display of hypnotism in a booth at the fair. And then there's the Three Journeys, and the Perils: the brothers making noises like animals, and the sham thunder off stage! It varies, I believe, in the different Lodges, and according to whether they think you're a coward or not. But it's always the same kind of stupidity. For instance, they spin the wretched chap round like a top, or let him run his nose into the wall, or make him walk the treadmill like a squirrel; but the pick of the bunch is the magic lantern."

"What's that?"

"A sort of fireworks arrangement that they blow into while they point a sword at the victim's chest—a cardboard sword, of course. The whole business is a sort of mixture of an art-students' ball, a popular melodrama and an amusement park, with this exception, that you're surrounded by a lot of old bar-room bums in their Sunday best, like you see in drawings by Huard or Abel Faivre, and that they're all doing their best to take the show seriously. Even when they're playing practical jokes they keep on saying, in spite of themselves, that it's all symbolic and hides a profound philosophic truth. And those are the sort of chaps who say that priests are a lot of play-actors, and that the ceremonies of the Catholic Church are nothing but mumbo-jumbo."

"Isn't there some business too about coffins and last wills and testaments?"

"Oh, yes—the Mirror room, with black walls and skeletons and skulls and terrifying inscriptions—yes, that's how you begin. That's before you get to the amusement-park part—more like the Hell-Fire Café, but still, all on the level of a country peep-show."

He paused, gulped his drink, and went on in a different voice:

"I've already described the kind of people you meet at these ceremonies, and that explains the whole business. Of course there are different types. My Lodge wasn't such a swell crowd as you'd meet in the more fashionable districts, but even in mine you only got a lot of dolled-up bar-room bums. Or, rather, that's what the majority were. In addition, you'd find a smattering of dentists and petty officials, a few lawyers and doctors, but mostly briefless lawyers and doctors without patients, the kind of fellows who wear big beards and affect solemn airs and love to talk in sepulchral tones about 'Brethren who adorn the Column of the South. . . .' But it's pretty obvious what they're all after. And then, of course, there are the ones who think they may get something out of it all, and those whose heads are full of vague ideas, like myself, who get sick of sitting all day with their noses glued to a desk. But that sort soon get bored with it and don't go on long. There are a few, too, who've just never grown up, and get a kick out of dark rooms and skeletons and oaths and secret passwords—a lot of children, really, with a taste for words with a special meaning which give them a pleasant feeling of being in on some secret business, especially when the words they use seem to refer to some mysterious truth which appeals to their imagination. For them everything refers to the Temple and its construction. They talk of nothing but trowels and plumb-lines and T-squares, of adorning Columns and roofing the Temple, of Brother Tyler and Brother Deacon. That's the whole game, so far as they're concerned —to say everything they want to say without using any but the language of building, and to have a sort of communal activity which appears to refer to the building trade. In that way they can manage to go on telling themselves fairy-tales. It's the kind of thing we all did when we were kids. I remember when I used to play at being a cabby or an engineer or at fighting battles with my friends. And even when I was older—I used to go to a drawing-school, I remember, a very interesting and go-ahead place . . ."

Ardansseaux directed towards the top of the mirror opposite a melancholy stare which was apparently fixed upon the ghosts of his dead youth.

Jerphanion thought: "In a moment he'll be saying how good it was to be young, and how little one realized it. But for me the good time is the here and now, the present moment. What matters is to be aware of the present, as Jallez is always saying, to concentrate on it." The thought gave him a passing and delicious thrill, but he was prevented from indulging it because of another idea that was tormenting him. What Ardansseaux had just said about playing at initiation recalled a conversation he had recently had with someone. Probably it had been with Jallez, but when, and what had it been about? Nothing irritated him more than memories which just escaped his consciousness.

Ardansseaux went on:

"The fellows at this drawing-school had made up a sort of story about the Raft of the Medusa,[1] in which they were the shipwrecked sailors, and everything had to be made to fit into the story. For example, they pretended that the stumps of charcoal were fish-hooks, I never knew quite why. One of them would shout across the room to another: 'I've broken my hook,' and anything said on the spur of the moment had to be made to conform to their particular vocabulary. But in their case the rules were made for the fun of the thing, as in all games, and part of the joke was to see the amazement on the faces of the newcomers. . . ."

"I've got it!" Jerphanion thought: "the Perfect Life—that day we walked out beyond the Clignancourt gate." He was conscious of a feeling of relief, and smiled at the engraver, nodding his head in agreement.

"Well, it's the same with the Masons. They, too, make rules for themselves, and create difficulties, just for the fun of the thing. They're just a lot of fellows who get together now and then to play a complicated game. The rest of the time they've got their jobs, their troubles, their ordinary lives, where there's not much opportunity for playing games. For them the Lodge meetings are a holiday. But just because in their daily lives they're serious folk with a position to keep up and no time for fun—you've only got to see them to realize that— they'd never dare, ordinarily, to meet for a game, even in the privacy of four walls with all the doors shut. They'd be ashamed to

[1] The "Raft of the Medusa" is a famous picture by the French artist J. L. A. T. Géricault (1791-1824). It was inspired by stories of the survivors of the wreck of the *Medusa*, which took place off the African coast.—TRANSLATOR'S NOTE.

do such a thing at their age. So they've got to have some sort of grand excuse. Therefore all their mummery's got to be symbolic. Everything's a symbol, everything's got to be made to stand for ideas, ideas that they all more or less share and as a result of which they became Masons, but magnified, glorified. From that moment the T-square, the plumb-line, the dais, the way the apprentices walk, the gesture of horror before the corpse of Hiram, even the treadmill and the magic lantern, take on a sort of sublimity. Not the most miserable little bar-room bum of the lot but tells himself he is working at Rebuilding the Temple, and gets the last ounce of magic out of the words. He feels that it is something into which he's got to be initiated, that it's not something that just anyone can do. If those fellows at the drawing-school had been able to kid themselves like that about the Raft of the Medusa, they'd have been more excited about their game even than they were. And there's another thing. Among the brethren there are always one or two who've got, so to speak, a nostalgia for religion, either because the ceremonies of the Church moved them when they were young or because they're temperamentally inclined that way. Well, they find that they needn't any longer regret the loss of these things, that Masonry too has its mysteries, only instead of being mysteries for a lot of old women or conservative great ladies—dreams about One God in Three Persons or the Immaculate Conception—they're the sort of mysteries that free-thinking republicans needn't be ashamed of. Besides, at church they were nothing but faithful members of a flock who had nothing to do but listen with their mouths open and watch the priest perform his ritual, while now they are, as it were, priest and congregation at once. And they're told that all the great philosophers and writers who have done battle through the ages for the emancipation of the human spirit, who have written in verse or in prose, whether the great speeches of Hugo or anything else, have been mixed up with these mysteries to which their work in some sort refers. They're told that all these men have borrowed from the Masonic idea . . . that all the great figures of history, including Napoleon, were initiates who had been made free of the secrets of Masonry; that they, too, had worked for the Rebuilding of the Temple. So you can see how flattering it is for the poor bar-room loafer to reflect that he, too, when he goes through his little ritual, is engaged on the same task."

"But what seems to me really interesting," said Jerphanion, who had found the engraver's last words suggestive and akin to some of Laulerque's more exciting theories—"yes, really interesting—is this: that behind all the façade of ceremonies, or, if you prefer, of pretences, there really is a doctrine, more or less secret, with a very long tradition behind it, which has already influenced history." He looked at Laulerque. "I can't imagine anything more thrilling than to know what that doctrine is."

But the engraver shrugged his shoulders.

"Nothing but a lot of claptrap and eye-wash. I thought that too at first, and it helped me to put up with all the nonsense. But except for certain empty phrases which you can read in books, it never came to anything. Of course they've got to make people believe something like that just to keep them keen, and also to defend the movement against the kind of criticism that represents the Masons as nothing but a band of unscrupulous adventurers well organized, and determined to get their way by any means in their power. 'What!' they say, 'a lot of blackguards?—Oh, that's where you're wrong; why, we're a society of philosophers, and if you don't believe it, just look at what we do.'"

Again Jerphanion glanced at Laulerque as though to say: "Help me to question him, to find the really essential question."

But in Laulerque's grimace he seemed to read his answer: "Oh, I think he's shot his bolt; you won't get much more out of him. I've done my part of the business, which was to bring you together; it's up to you to make him talk."

Nevertheless, Jerphanion asked a further question:

"You spoke, just now, of a strong organization which has certain objectives."

"That's what their enemies say. . . ."

"Yes, I understand that. But let us drop, for a moment, the language of innuendo and say that the Masonic movement has certain ends in view—a statement which it seems to me can hardly be denied, whether those ends really correspond to its doctrine or whether the doctrine is merely a red herring, an alibi. What, in your opinion, are those ends? Are they what everyone more or less believes them to be, nothing more esoteric than the defence of free thought against religion, and the maintenance of the Republic, or is there something else which no one speaks about?"

Ardansseaux gave signs of extreme embarrassment.

"It's all very obscure," he said; "one can say nothing for certain, one can only guess."

"Guess?—but in what way?"

"I don't know."

"All right: but the mere fact that you say one can only guess means that during your career as a Mason you got the impression that there was more in what they were doing than merely putting a lot of promising fellows through a series of ridiculous exercises. You said too that they were disciplined, but if so, it must be for some purpose. What is that purpose?"

"Well, there are certain watchwords that they put about—for instance, when it's a question of supporting this or that candidate at elections, or of urging some cause, or of fighting against something. Everyone's supposed to do what he can, how he can."

"I quite understand that. But are there no schemes on a larger scale, more secret schemes?"

"How can one tell? I asked myself just the same question after I'd joined. 'What do you count for,' I said, 'in all this, you and all the other brethren? You're nothing but a lot of poor fools who get ordered about. One's told that all the Lodges are equal, and that there's no hierarchy outside the three grades that are represented in each of them, the Apprentices, the Companions, and the Masters; that once you've become a Master there'll be no one above you. But that's all my eye. They're not even consistent, because they themselves admit that there are higher ranks and Grand Councils. But in addition to what they admit it may well be that there are other ranks that they don't talk about, higher and more secret leaders. I can assure you one doesn't get to know much in a wretched local Lodge. One's just a puppet."

"But you must have said to yourself," Jerphanion urged, thinking of himself, seeing himself as a member of a Lodge, rubbing shoulders with bar-room loafers and broken-down doctors, and impatient to get out of the ruck, "you must have thought that with a little perseverance, and after you'd proved your worth and your enthusiasm, you'd get higher, that you'd worm your way into the little group that controls things, into the higher ranks of the general staff?"

Ardansseaux shook his head from right to left and made a face. Jerphanion insisted:

"Why not?"

"It's not as easy as all that!"

"How is it done, then?"

"My idea is that though they pretend to recruit the leaders from the ranks in the Lodges by a system of regular promotion, it's really all a put-up job."

"Well, but how do they recruit them?"

Laulerque made a sign to Jerphanion as though to say: "You're wasting your time." But Jerphanion was as obstinate as one of the peasants of his native village.

"Oh," said the other, "if you knew that, you'd know everything. But look at it this way—in the army an ordinary man who re-enlists as a sergeant is supposed to be able to reach any rank provided he distinguishes himself and passes his examinations and goes through his courses. And of course there *are* officers who have risen from the ranks. But how many generals do you know who started like that?"

"But at least one knows where the generals come from. According to you, the leaders of the Masonic movement are all drawn from a sort of Saint-Cyr or Military Polytechnic. But where is it? There doesn't seem to me to be anything corresponding to such institutions."

Ardansseaux half-closed his eyes, raised his right hand with slow deliberation, and looked important. Then he leaned forward on the table with a little movement of the head as much as to say: "Come a little nearer: I've something even more confidential to tell you!"

The others leaned forward too.

"When one becomes a Mason," he murmured, "one says to oneself that one is at last going to find out all about the famous mysteries. And what does one discover?—nothing, except that there *are* mysteries whose existence even one didn't suspect when one joined the Lodge, and that however much of a Mason one may become, those mysteries will remain mysteries, so far as oneself is concerned, for ever."

He puffed out his chest, obviously enjoying the effect his words had produced. Then he leaned forward once more:

". . . If one does find anything out, it's by pure luck, and nothing comes of it. I'll give you one small example to explain what I mean. Suppose you meet somebody who's high up in the Masonic movement—as you very likely might—just ask him, quite innocently, this one question: 'What are the secret Lodges one sometimes hears about?' "

"And what will he answer?"

"Wait and see! It's more than probable that he'll pretend not to understand what you mean, or he may put on an air of injured rectitude and tell you not to believe all the ridiculous and childish things you hear from enemies of the movement, or he may make a joke of the whole thing, and say: 'Good Heavens! *that* old story! If such things ever existed it was hundreds of years ago!'— Just you wait and see!"

"And what *is* the answer?"

Ardansseaux looked suddenly very knowing. He stared at the ceiling, and his face assumed the expression of one whose mind was full of pleasant thoughts. But all he said was:

"It's no business of mine."

Obviously it was no good pressing the question.

"Or ask him this"—he went on, and hesitated again. "No, on second thoughts, one can't ask that particular question unless one's a Mason already. . . . If ever you do become one—you probably won't, but *if* you do, well, try to get into touch with me again, and I'll tell you what it is you're to ask."

Suddenly the engraver became gloomy. He seemed preoccupied and stared at Jerphanion.

"Of course," he said, "I have your word of honour that should you even become a Mason you won't breathe a word of this conversation? You'll never mention my name?"

"I give you my word of honour."

As they walked together down the rue Rochechouart, Laulerque said:

"Well, what was your impression?"

"Of your man?"

"Of him first of all."

"He's no fool. He's got a kink of some kind, and he floundered about a good deal at first, but once he got warmed up he told us some interesting things."

"And of the main question?"

"Of Freemasonry? It's all very complicated. It attracts me and repels me. At first I thought that repulsion would win the day—the atmosphere of the Lodges seemed so childish. . . . But before he finished I found myself wondering whether it was quite so simple as all that. What did you think?"

"Much what you did. . . . Shall you go and see Lengnau?"

"Possibly. Would you?"

"Certainly I should."

What Jerphanion did not admit was the state of unsatisfied curiosity in which their conversation with the engraver had left him. He felt like a man who, having started casually to scratch a sore place, goes on so long that at last he produces a condition of irritation that is worse than the itch he set out to allay. The various details about Masonry which Jerphanion had just learned, which an hour ago he would have given anything in the world to come by, no matter how, seemed now to him almost worthless. He was half inclined to believe that he had always known them. The real mysteries, the only mysteries that he felt now he had ever wanted to fathom, were still unattained. With each step he took towards them they withdrew further, and he began to fear that this process of withdrawal would continue indefinitely. But it was too late now to give up the pursuit. He told himself that his visit to Lengnau would be only another disappointment; but nothing would make him give it up.

Dissembling as much as possible his real feelings, he said:

"When you get down to it, these famous secrets of theirs are like optical illusions that only deceive one at a distance. If I decide to go and see Lengnau, it'll be because I like to go through with things once I've started. But I can't do anything until I've got his answer."

Chapter

28

JERPHANION HAS A VISIT FROM MAURICE EZZELIN

Jerphanion was walking slowly along the ground-floor corridor. He stopped to look through one of the dirty windows at what is known as "Ernest's Fountain," which, beneath the falling rain, presented an appearance of the deepest gloom. The cause of his slow progress and of his eventual halt was a struggle of conscience. That very morning he had received from Lengnau a letter asking him to call the next day. "Am I," he wondered, "to go on leaving Jallez in ignorance of what is happening? Obviously I'm not obliged to account to him for my movements, and I'm pretty sure he doesn't tell me everything he's doing; still, I feel rather mean about it."

He had made vague references to his friend about his recent meetings with Clanricard and Laulerque and had alluded to certain "interesting conversations" which he had had about secret societies and Freemasonry. But it hadn't gone further than that, and he had got the impression that Jallez was only half attending to what he said.

"I'll tell him this evening that an opportunity has come my way of getting to know Lengnau, whom I've already mentioned to him incidentally. If he questions me I can decide how much I'll tell him; if he doesn't bother, I'll leave it at that. Then if he accuses me later of acting on the sly, I can say: 'My dear chap, I did tell you, but you didn't seem very interested, and I was afraid of boring you.'"

At that very moment he saw the porter, Louvois, coming towards him, without his hat and wearing his frock-coat trimmed with braid. The man was called Louvois, not because it was his name, but because his predecessor had been called Colbert. He had a refined face and walked with the slow, dignified pace of an old court official.

Louvois approached Jerphanion and saluted. He seemed to have something on his mind.

"Have you seen Monsieur Jallez, sir?"

"He went out some time ago. He had a lecture at one o'clock."

"That's what I thought."

Louvois scratched his cheek, moving his finger-nail upwards against the grain of his beard. He gazed at the fountain with a worried look.

"Does somebody want him?"

"Yes, somebody does."

"Well, tell him he's not here."

"Yes, sir."

But his "yes" seemed spoken only for reasons of courtesy. He continued to look at the fountain.

"Unless," said Jerphanion, "you think it's something important or urgent. In that case you might try to get hold of him at the Sorbonne. I'll go if you like."

Louvois, as though relieved by the suggestion, turned his gaze to Jerphanion. He came a step nearer and, lowering his voice, said:

"A gentleman's asking for him, but he looks a bit odd."

"Ah!"

"Perhaps it's only my fancy; but when I asked him to give me his name he said: 'My name won't mean anything to Monsieur Jallez'; and when I said I thought I'd seen Monsieur Jallez go out, he seemed annoyed. He said: 'If I thought he wouldn't be very long, I'd rather wait.' And then there's his manner, sir. . . . It's not exactly that he's excited, but somehow—well, he's not like one of the ordinary visitors."

"You'd like me to see him?"

"Well, I did think something of the sort, sir. . . . You're Monsieur Jallez's best friend. . . . I thought for a moment that he might be some relation up from the country, something of that sort . . . but in that case he wouldn't have said that his name would mean nothing to Monsieur Jallez."

"Obviously. . . . Look here, I'll see him. You go first and tell the fellow that Monsieur Jallez's best friend's coming to speak to him. . . . You didn't tell him anything about Monsieur Jallez?"

"Oh, no, sir; don't you worry yourself on that score. People don't get things out of me as easily as all that. When he asked me whether Monsieur Jallez would be away long—" Louvois finished his sentence by slowly extending his arms and raising his eyebrows. . . . "I'll be getting along, sir."

Louvois turned back towards his lodge.

Jerphanion, who had a lively imagination, ran through all the dangers that might be threatening his friend. The most natural supposition was that this was the young girl's father. He overtook Louvois.

"What should you say his age was?"

"Oh, about thirty or thirty-five, sir."

"Not more than that? You're certain?"

"No, not more, sir."

That particular hypothesis crumbled.

During the three minutes that he waited to give time for the setting of the scene, Jerphanion worked himself into a state of pleasing excitement.

Temperamentally, he enjoyed getting mixed up in other people's affairs. It was a form of indiscretion, but since, in most cases, he let his good sense control the inclination, it was rarely indulged. If, too, in so far as it was indiscreet, this tendency of his betrayed a certain lack of sensibility, it was also a form of courage and was not altogether devoid of generous qualities. Jerphanion was the last man to make himself scarce when his friends were in trouble.

Even if he had had time to think that this visitor might be a madman with a revolver in his pocket, the only question he would have asked himself would have been: "Shall I be helping Jallez best by talking to the fellow and trying to calm him, or had I better get hold of the police while Louvois holds him in conversation?" To have taken the line that it was none of his business would have seemed to him a piece of cowardice not even to be considered.

Jerphanion saw a nondescript sort of man of middle height standing between the pillars of the entry. He was dressed neatly in a rough-textured dark grey overcoat and held a derby hat in his hand. He seemed to be, as Louvois had said, about thirty. Every now and then he took a few paces forward and then stopped. He had light hair, a pasty complexion, and a large nose. There were two deep creases on either side of his mouth. His double collar was made of celluloid. At first sight there seemed nothing in his face to cause anyone anxiety.

Jerphanion cleared his throat and moved forward. The visitor had turned towards him.

Jerphanion saw two pale blue eyes which were without life or depth. Their lids were the colour of porridge and had rather red rims. The man's expression seemed to be sullen rather than angry. He looked at Jerphanion almost defiantly, giving the impression of a timid person who frowns in order to reassure himself. Still, everyone knows that timid men may often become dangerous.

"You are the gentleman who was asking for Monsieur Jallez?"

"Yes, I wanted to see him."

"Unfortunately, he's out, as you've already been told, and he won't be in until late. It's quite possible that he won't come back to dinner."

As the visitor listened to him he compressed his lips and shook his head. He blinked rapidly and looked about him.

"Obviously not a man of the world," thought Jerphanion. He kept a careful eye on the man's movements, accusing himself, as he did so, of having too active an imagination.

"I suppose it wouldn't be possible to go and find him?" the other asked in a voice which trembled slightly. He spoke like a Parisian, but with a slightly common intonation. Apart from that his voice was colourless.

"I'm afraid not; the lectures are not public, and no stranger is admitted. And I'm afraid," he added briskly, "that when he comes out of this particular lecture, he may go straight off to another equally impossible for strangers to attend, either in the library of the Sorbonne or in some other library, I don't know which. Even if I wanted to find him for some reason of my own, I shouldn't know where to look."

"Ah!"

The man scrutinized Jerphanion with his faded blue eyes as though to determine the proportion of lies to truth in what he had just said. Then he lowered his gaze, shook his head, and seemed to be plunged in thought.

Jerphanion continued with quiet reasonableness:

"Of course, if the matter were urgent or of very great importance to Monsieur Jallez, I would make an effort to find him, even if it meant wasting my time, and I can assure you that I haven't many spare minutes just now."

The visitor looked up again. He said:

"You are his best friend?"

Jerphanion modestly indicated that he thought he could say he was.

"You know something about his private affairs?"

"Yes, I think so—more or less."

"Ah—if I was sure—"

"Of what?"

"I know that this isn't the sort of thing—still—"

The stranger with the dim blue eyes seemed to be fishing for encouragement, to be looking for some excuse to confide his trouble.

"If," Jerphanion hinted, "you have some message for him which I could deliver, please consider me at your service."

Before replying, the other let his eyes wander over the pillars of the entry and the porter's lodge. Perhaps the place seemed to him unsuitable for confidences.

For a moment Jerphanion played with the idea of asking him into their study, but the idea was distasteful to him. He disliked the thought of seeing him in Jallez's chair. Besides, the privacy of their room was not something to be shared with any stranger. He looked at the weather; the rain had almost stopped. "Anyhow," he thought, "a few drops won't hurt a man like that."

"If you'll wait a moment, sir, I'll go and get my hat and overcoat. We could take a stroll in the garden—that's to say, if you're not afraid of the cold. No one will interrupt us there."

The stranger assured him that he was not at all afraid of the cold. But he gave an anticipatory cough or two.

As soon as they had reached the gravel path which ran between the shrubs, the visitor looked at him unhappily out of the corner of his eye and said abruptly:

"Since your friend confides his private affairs to you, he has probably mentioned his intimacy with a certain young woman?"

"I seem to remember his talking about something of the sort."

"Well, the woman in question is—my wife."

"Good heavens!— Are you sure?"

Jerphanion's expression, the tone of his voice, the way in which he stopped short in his walk, all gave evidence of the genuineness of his surprise.

He thought for a moment or two, then:

"I need hardly tell you, sir, that my friend Jallez is under no obligation to tell me what he does, but I can assure you that though he certainly is intimate with a young woman, it cannot possibly be your wife, for the very good reason that the young woman is not married."

"Ah!"

The other had also come to a stop. He looked fixedly at Jerphanion a moment before adding:

"It looks, then, as though it were some other woman?"

His face seemed to show a faint gleam.

"Do you happen to know her name?" he asked.

"I'm afraid I don't."

"Not even her Christian name?"

"He's never told me."

"Ah . . . my wife is called Juliette."

"Juliette?"

Jerphanion found it difficult to keep his surprise within decent bounds.

"You've heard him use the name?" the other demanded.

"No, not particularly."

They started to walk again.

"What made you suspect my friend Jallez?" Jerphanion asked.

"I think I'd better explain everything. I was married at the beginning of August 1908. I arranged the date so that it would coincide with my holidays—I get a fortnight, but what with the August bank holiday and the three extra days one's entitled to when one gets married, we managed to make it up to three weeks. We went to a pretty little place just outside Paris, and things were more or less all right. I ought to tell you that when I married my wife I knew that she had recently had a very unhappy love-affair. But when a woman's as young as she was, all she wants is to forget things like that. Most young girls have had some little romance—quite innocent, of course, but some kind of emotional adventure—and it's up to the man to know how to deal with it. During our engagement she had written me the most affectionate, sometimes even passionate, letters. One phrase I remember especially; it was: 'I long to lie all night in your arms.' Well, when a woman doesn't like a young man, she doesn't write to him like that, does she? I couldn't be accused, as some men can, of having married her against her will. Everything was all right at first. She had her moods, of course, you know what women are . . . and she certainly was very variable—in a good temper one day, in a bad one the next. . . . But I'm not nervous by temperament, and when she was sulky sometimes for three days together, sighing in corners, looking out of the window, refusing to let me come near her, and all that, it didn't bother me much, even though I suspected that her old love-affair had something to do with it. I told myself that it would gradually pass, especially if we had children. But I knew perfectly well that she didn't want to have children, that she was terrified of the possibility. Now, what I want you to realize is that sud-

denly, starting from one particular day, everything got worse. I shall
never forget the occasion, it was one evening at the Réveillon. It may
be that up till then I had been living in a fool's paradise, that I had
refused to look things in the face, but from that moment it was no
good pretending any more. She no longer loved me—in fact, she
could hardly bear the sight of me. If I had been like some men we
should have had terrible scenes. . . . She took to going out a great
deal alone. I won't pretend I wasn't suspicious, but I had nothing
certain to go on. And then the other day—I'll cut the story short because the details wouldn't interest you—well, the other day I got
definite proof that she had been seeing a young man regularly for
some time past, and I found out that the young man was the very one
she had been so intimate with before our marriage. I discovered his
name, and a lot of other details."

"When you married her did you know who he was?"

"No, all I'd been told was that he was a man of education, who
was going through some pretty stiff course and would probably make
a career for himself; nothing more than that. I didn't want to seem
too inquisitive, I'm not that kind of man, and I didn't want to think
about him."

"Did your wife admit that this was the man she was seeing again?"

"No. . . . Women find it difficult to confess that sort of thing, particularly a woman like my wife; she'd rather have been torn in
pieces."

"But in that case are you sure that you're not wrong? It's possible
that whoever told you about her may have given you false information."

"I'm perfectly sure."

A thin rain was still falling, wetting their clothes and pricking their
faces. The stranger's overcoat looked as though it were covered with
a sort of moist scurf. The damp gravel, the dark-leaved shrubs heavy
with raindrops, reminded Jerphanion of those cemeteries which had
seen the progress of that love which was now so ominously threatened. To the right, through the thin winter trees, he could see the

fronts of houses and rows of melancholy windows.

He carefully considered the question he was about to ask. At length:

"Excuse me, sir," he said, "but I must know precisely how we stand. What exactly was your intention in coming to see my friend?"

The visitor in the wet overcoat frowned. The two creases on either side of his mouth trembled slightly. Then he raised his eyebrows and made an indefinite gesture with his right hand.

"That would have depended," he said.

"Perhaps you wanted to ask him first of all whether what you had been told was true?"

"Oh, no, because I'm quite certain it was."

"Certain? Allow me to say, sir, that I don't see how you can be certain. An accusation of that sort is a very serious matter. In the first place, do you know what he looks like?"

"No."

"Well, then, even if you'd met your wife in the company of a young man, what proof have you that he would be my friend Jallez?"

The visitor said nothing.

"Besides, it probably wasn't you at all who did see them, and even assuming that it was the young man in question, how do you know they didn't meet by accident—you've told me that they knew one another very intimately at one time—and just walked together for a while?"

"I have evidence. There's no possibility of a mistake. I've had them followed."

The man lowered his voice:

"They've been seen going into a hotel together."

"And you would have told him all that?"

The other hesitated:

"—Yes," he said.

Jerphanion said nothing. He pulled at his beard and kept his eyes staring at the ground as he walked.

"What are you thinking?" asked the man, who was covered with fine raindrops.

"I was just wondering what his answer would have been. It's difficult to guess. I know nothing about the facts of the case, you understand, but let us assume for the sake of argument that he had not denied them, or had denied them unconvincingly, just for the sake of appearances or out of politeness. . . ."

The stranger's face darkened. The creases beside his mouth began to tremble again.

"If I'd thought he was laughing at me," he said, "I don't know what mightn't have happened."

"Why should he have laughed at you?"

"I'm not an educated chap like him: I've not got the kind of job he'll have."

The man in the wet overcoat spoke without bitterness and without envy. He seemed merely to be stating a fact which, however unfortunate, must be accepted.

"It's not at all the sort of thing he'd do," Jerphanion said.

"If he hadn't laughed at me, well—I should have waited to see what would happen. I should have asked him what he meant, what he thought the end of it all would be. One doesn't break up a home like that. One doesn't desert a young woman and make her miserable and then wait until she has married someone else to turn up again and steal her. Doesn't that seem to you a cad's trick?"

Jerphanion had only the vaguest idea of what had happened. It was horrible to him to hear his friend accused in this way, but how could he undertake his defence before he even knew how much of the charge he would be ready to admit?

"This is a poor sort of fellow," he reflected, "but he seems honest, and he appears to be quite sure of what he says. But I'm sure that Jallez wouldn't have told me a deliberate lie. What's it all about, then?"

He stopped, faced the stranger, and looked at him, fingering his beard the while.

"You may think that what I'm going to say is fantastic," he remarked, "but do you know, it has just occurred to me that quite possibly my friend Jallez doesn't even suspect your existence."

The other's expression was one of utter amazement.

"He doesn't understand what I mean," thought Jerphanion; "I shouldn't have used the word 'suspect.'"

"In fact," he went on, "I'm wondering at this moment whether he knows that you exist."

"That I exist? But how can he help knowing?"

"I fully realize that if he is on the terms you have told me of with your wife, my theory must seem to you ridiculous. . . . Still, I've got the impression that it may be so."

The stranger pondered the suggestion.

"It's quite possible," he said, "that he's never seen me, and that therefore he doesn't know what kind of man I am—no doubt they've got other things to talk about—but he knows perfectly well that I exist, that there *is* a husband."

Jerphanion said nothing, and the other continued:

"What you mean, I suppose, is that if he had known me personally, he wouldn't have behaved as he has done. . . . That is quite possible."

Jerphanion fought back a smile.

"—And I admit that in so far as that may be so my feeling against him is less violent."

Jerphanion no longer wished to smile. In some vague way he felt moved.

His companion continued, chewing, as it were, the cud of this new suggestion.

"I am perfectly well aware," he said, "that women don't draw the line at telling a few lies—but that, surely, is going a bit far! Do you mean to say that she would have hidden the fact that she was married? You forget that they knew each other intimately in the old days and that he must have had plenty of opportunity to hear her spoken of by others. With someone else she might have taken such a risk, but not with him. Besides, why should she have done it? Oh, no," he added with an air of greater conviction, "she couldn't have kept it up with him as long as this. When a woman's married, her lover knows perfectly well that she is not free to do as she likes, that she has to go home at certain fixed hours. . . ."

"But that's even truer of a young girl."

Some new thought seemed suddenly to be troubling the stranger.

"I *have* noticed," he said in a lower tone, "that once or twice when she came in she wasn't wearing her wedding-ring—she had put it in her hand-bag. She explained that she had taken it off to wash her hands. Oh, a little thing like that wouldn't put her out of countenance!"

He stood beneath the fine rain, deep in thought. The impression of his words was mingled, for Jerphanion, with the smell of wood and damp clothes.

"What I should like to know," he added on a different note, "is whether they were lovers before her marriage. I'm pretty sure they weren't, but one can never be certain."

He harked back to his preoccupation of a moment before: "Of course," he said, "if you're right, it alters everything."

Then:

"Are you going to mention my visit to your friend?"

"I don't know—I haven't thought about it. What do you think I ought to do?"

"It might be better. If you do, shall you tell him everything we've said?"

Jerphanion hesitated a moment before replying:

"You'd rather I did?" he asked.

He had been rehearsing that conversation with his friend, seeing in imagination Jallez's silent face, the tightening about his eyes and lips which would mean: "What have you been meddling with?" But when, rightly or wrongly, one has got mixed up in a friend's affairs, one doesn't undo the indiscretion by keeping silent. "Whatever he thinks," he told himself, "I have been a help."

He forced himself to adopt an air of experience which was far from natural to him. The mere fact that he found the attitude difficult invested it with a sort of interest.

"I needn't tell you, sir," he said, weighing his words carefully and stroking his beard, "that the situation is a very delicate one, nor need I remind you that much of it is still very obscure. . . . I have, in a sense, been the unwilling auditor of your confidences; I ask you now to trust me still further. I will try to do what is best in the circumstances. . . . My friend Jallez is a man of great goodness of heart; however he may have acted, I am quite certain that he would not be indifferent to the pain he has made you suffer. Will you promise to do nothing without seeing me again first?— Does your wife know that you have come here?"

"Oh, dear, no!" said the stranger in a tone almost of terror.

"Well, don't say anything to her until we have decided what to do —it would only make matters worse. I know that what I am asking won't be easy in your present, very natural, condition of excitement, but I want you to bear in mind that the whole thing may still be a mistake. I won't keep you waiting longer than I can help. Where can we meet?"

The man opened his overcoat, which was covered with fine rain, felt in the inside pocket of his jacket, brought out a letter-case adorned with a monogram in some silver-coloured metal, perhaps real silver, and took from it a visiting-card which was too large for elegance, rather thick, and slightly dirty. On it was printed, in light-faced type:

Maurice Ezzelin
17 rue d'Alésia

He offered it to Jerphanion with a look that was partly trusting, partly anxious, a look that seemed to say: "Are you, too, going to deceive me?"

"Write me a letter," he said, "as soon as you have spoken to him. The concierge will see that I get it. There will be no risk. If there's anything you'd rather tell me by word of mouth, arrange some meeting-place, if possible after six o'clock in the evening, but whatever the time I'll arrange things somehow."

Jerphanion's thoughts seemed to take up the echo—"arrange things somehow."

As though this thought spread waves of meaning in his mind, the young student was conscious of a feeling so complicated that he was not even sure whether it gave him pleasure or pain. There was sweetness in it, licence, pity, and something that brought a faint whiff of disgust. It was as though the normal certainty of his moral sense were suddenly shaken, reminding him of those summer days when the body seems to hang doubtfully between sensations of comfort and unease. He felt himself brought suddenly in contact with human depths the existence of which he had not hitherto suspected. But they were vague and ill-defined, neither wicked nor terrible, opening no vista into the torments of the soul, lit rather by some gleam of kindliness, of brotherhood, of compassion, making him suddenly aware of something lying behind all human life which could move him to unexpected feeling, of a link that binds all men, however little they will admit it. But this sense of man's dependence on man brought with it an awareness of promiscuity and degradation, as though warning him that there are surrenders and interchanges which can ill bear a close scrutiny, like those images of semi-wakefulness over which the conscious judgment seems to have no control. At such moments the feet seem set upon a slippery slope. A woman may be at once your wife and another's, and the fact that one recognizes in her another's ownership is not altogether distasteful. The wife of Maurice Ezzelin, 17 rue d'Alésia, was probably the mistress of Pierre Jallez, nor was it at all certain that in a fortnight's time she would have ceased to be either—that she wouldn't still be both. Jerphanion thought of Mathilde Cazalis and of Clanricard. He saw Mathilde's face with its provocative eyes and its inviting lips; Clanricard's face radiant with the light of faith, intent to serve, expressive of all that man respects under the name of sincerity. He saw the two faces together, side by side, each with all that it had of promise or denial for his own desires, and about them both the implication that dwelt in their proximity. In fancy he saw Clanricard's face draw near to Maurice Ezzelin's—in some such way as the ghost of the naked woman had seemed to float upon the façade of the Basilica—become superimposed upon it, substituted for it.

The thought displeased him. He disliked such tricks of the imagination.

Gingerly he took Maurice Ezzelin's card—the card that was a little too large, that was already slightly wet in the falling rain.

Chapter

29

HOW IS HE TO BE TOLD?

For over an hour Jerphanion had been saying to himself: "I'm going to tell him: I must—of that there can be no question."

Never had he looked so closely at his friend. He was trying to discover what was essential in his face, what was merely temporary; the clues to character, the passing shades of mood. But he failed to draw any definite conclusion from his scrutiny. It was as though he were seeking some point of least resistance, but he searched without method and had no great hopes of succeeding.

He saw two eyes that were blue with the colour of summer mornings. They shone with a light that was peculiarly their own, a fitful light that came and went, or, rather, that turned in upon itself as though to illuminate the darkness that lay within. And while he watched he tried over in his mind some opening phrase that he might use, such as: "You'll never guess what an odd visitor I had today!" What would be the best moment to risk it? Should he say it now or wait for some more opportune occasion? When those eyes of morning blue turned towards him he felt encouraged, but not to the extent of risking an intrusion into the secrets of the spirit that looked through them. "Tell me," they seemed to say, "what you have been reading, what you have been thinking. Talk to me about a poem, or about something that's been happening in the great world. If you like, talk to me about yourself; but when it comes to talking about me—well, no one does that unless I'm agreeable." When their light was withdrawn or, rather, turned in upon itself, their owner's presence was less daunting, but if his friend should take advantage of such a moment, saying, for example: "Forgive me, Jallez, but there's something I want to tell you which I think you ought to know . . ." it would, wouldn't it? be rather like pursuing someone into a secret fastness where, obviously, he wants to be alone.

Why was it that the expression of Jallez's mouth failed to ease one's anxieties as that of Maurice Ezzelin's had done? Even when it smiled there was about it a frightening hint of subtlety. Frightening? What was there to be frightened of? How came it that some people made one feel awkward, and how, too, was it possible that Jallez and Maurice Ezzelin could be in love with the same woman, that the same woman could, if not exactly choose both of them with the same degree of ardour, at least accept them both?

But that wasn't the question. Such odds and ends of curiosity were nothing but subterfuges, cowardly excuses for avoiding the difficulty.—"Do you know, old chap, I was walking along the corridor when Louvois came up to me and—"

What he needed was an opening, some word, some phrase which would serve as a point of departure. If only, Jerphanion felt, he could get going, the rest would be easy. The first minute of a conversation counts more than all the talk that is to follow, the first second even more so.

Probably the best solution would be to say, quite simply: "Early this afternoon—not long after you'd gone out—I was thinking over all this business of Lengnau and the Freemasons which I've told you about, when I came across Louvois, who was looking for you. It seemed that someone was asking for you. . . ."

But it's only possible to say things "quite simply" if one speaks without worrying about them first, if they come quite naturally in the course of conversation. Once begin, so to speak, walking round and round your interlocutor looking for a weak spot, as you might do before scaling a fort, and the whole thing ceases to be spontaneous. Nothing is simple any longer. The awkward silences, the forced chatter, the attempt to find some subject by which one may lead up to the point, the "By the way . . ." which one drags in so that it sounds wrong from the very start, like the first note of a nervous singer, only make matters worse.

By nine o'clock that night, when they were seated together in their study, Jerphanion had still said nothing, and the difficulty of speaking had increased. "If I say it now," he thought, "he just won't believe me. Instead of seeming to have met Ezzelin by chance and to have listened to him against my will, I shall give the impression that I've been nosing about in Jallez's private affairs. It will be as though I had said: 'You've been trying to hide things from me. I've gone to a lot of trouble to find out, and perhaps I've forced the issue; well, I can't help it if I have, you may as well realize that I know everything.'"

At half past nine he thought he'd got an inspiration. After a pause which he made as long as possible to give the necessary weight to his words, he began to speak, quite calmly, like a man who has waited deliberately, from motives of caution, before making a statement:

"I want to ask your advice, old man, on a case of conscience. Suppose that you had found out quite accidentally something that affected me very nearly. You have no definite proof of its accuracy, but you believe, on the whole, that what you have heard is true, and that I know nothing whatever about it. You feel uncomfortable about telling me, both because of the casual way in which you have come by your knowledge, and because you're afraid you may hurt me. Your embarrassment is increased by the fact that you're not certain of your information, and not sure that you're doing the right thing by talking to me about it."

"What a ridiculous fuss and mystification I'm making," he thought as he spoke.

Jallez, however, was paying close attention to his words, showing by an occasional movement that he was taking in each point and setting it duly before his mind. He gave no sign that he realized the existence of any personal application in what was being said, but seemed to be quite clear about the general case that his friend was laying down.

Jerphanion finished and waited in silence for the answer. He was the more anxious of the two.

For a while Jallez said nothing. A few scarcely perceptible movements of his face gave evidence of the intensity of his thought. He frowned, not in annoyance, but as a man frowns who is concentrating on a problem. Now and again he moved his tongue in his mouth, pressing it first against one cheek and then against the other, then letting it protrude between his teeth, and compressing his nostrils the while. He turned away his head, lowering his eyes, and smiling as though he were on the defensive. More than once he seemed on the point of asking a question.

Finally he spoke.

"Thanks, old chap; it was very nicely done."

There was no trace of irony in his voice.

"When I came in," he began, speaking slowly and pausing between his phrases, "Louvois told me of a visitor. . . . It all seems to have been rather odd. . . . I'm not sure that I fully understand what it's all about. I shall be clearer about it later. . . . Meanwhile, I'm sorry that you had all that trouble. . . . You must have had to listen to a lot of rather sordid conversation. . . . You won't have forgotten it by tomorrow? Good! Perhaps I'll ask you to tell me about it then. But not tonight, if you don't mind. . . . You've been very decent."

It was with difficulty that he disguised the reality of his concern. But Jerphanion was no longer looking at him. "What on earth," he was thinking, "did that fool Ezzelin say to Louvois?" His only wish was to get out of the study for a moment and to put a few questions to Louvois if he could catch him before he went to bed.

"Look here, Louvois, there's something I want to know. When

Monsieur Jallez came in, did you tell him that a stranger had been asking for him?"

"I thought I ought to."

"You were quite right. But do you remember what you said? I want to know for reasons of my own."

Jerphanion asked the question in a confidential tone, which he made as friendly as possible. Louvois abandoned his slightly affronted air.

"What I said was," he replied—"yes, I remember now—what I said was, half as a joke, in a manner of speaking: 'That husband of your little friend,' I said, 'didn't look any too happy, especially when he turned up first.' Then I said, still joking-like, if you understand me, sir: 'When you get mixed up with married women,' I said, 'you've got to expect a bit of trouble.' I'm only telling you roughly how it was. And then I told him that the chap seemed easier in his mind when he went away, and that that meant you'd known how to handle him. . . . Oh, yes, and then I gave him his name, which I'd written down on a piece of paper. Monsieur Jallez didn't seem to recognize it, which seemed odd."

"But how did you know it was the husband of—of his little friend?"

"Why, he told me."

"Told you, who?—the man who came here?"

"Yes, after you'd been talking to him."

Jerphanion looked reproachful.

"You questioned him?"

"Not me!—He out with it himself. It was on the tip of my tongue to tell him that the young gentleman's affairs were no business of mine, but he kept me chatting here a good quarter of an hour."

"He—he went into details?"

"Details! Details isn't the word for it!"

"How extraordinary of him! Do you think he told you all this just to do Monsieur Jallez a bad turn?"

"Oh, no—just because he wanted to get it off his chest. You know, sir, like the folk that'll tell all about themselves to the hairdresser or the bus conductor."

Jerphanion could not get over his surprise. Indeed, he was more than surprised, he was almost disappointed. He had thought better of Maurice Ezzelin. But what annoyed him most was the idea that for hours he had been carrying about with him something that everyone knew already, as though it had been a bomb.

"When you said all this to Monsieur Jallez," he asked, "how did he seem to take it?"

"He asked me one or two questions, but as though they didn't much matter. You know the sort of gentleman he is, sir; not the sort as says much."

Chapter

30

MIONNET BECOMES IMPORTANT

The same week was a period of great activity for Mionnet. On Monday he had an appointment at a quarter to twelve with the Comte de Mézan in the rue Le Peletier. The Count received him in the offices of the *Northern and Eastern Bank*, where he appeared to be entirely at home. He gave the Abbé no explanation of his right to be there, but merely said:

"I thought that a central place like this would be convenient for you. We shall be less interrupted than we should be at home. I hope you've no engagement for the early part of the afternoon? Good! Then I trust you'll do me the honour of lunching with me somewhere near by—quite informally—no women."

In this way their meeting was at once placed on a footing of easy friendliness. It had been led up to a few days earlier by a conversation they had had while dining with the Saint-Papouls in the rue Vaneau.

Mézan offered the Abbé a cigarette and began to talk. What he said was substantially as follows:

"You know, of course, all about our friend Saint-Papoul's present preoccupation? The matter is becoming urgent, because the important date is not far off. I don't mean his daughter's marriage, though that's not far off either; I mean the elections. Whether he was wise to run is another matter. The life of a hunting squire has always seemed to me to suit him admirably, but perhaps it's beginning to bore him. After all, a man still in the prime of life needs some emotional outlet, and politics are as good an excuse as any other, don't you agree? I'm sure the Countess does. Besides, there are material reasons to be considered. Things are a bit tight with him, and will be until he comes into his father-in-law's property. I've tried to get him one or two directorships, but the objection's always the same, that he represents nothing. He has received no decoration, and he left the Army as a mere sergeant. That doesn't mean anything. If, however, he became a deputy, I could be more of a help to him, and, looked at from that point of view, his political ambitions seem to me to be perfectly legitimate. But the trouble is that politics are a new game to him. He's quite fairly quick-witted and he gets on well with people. There's no reason why he shouldn't cut a decent figure in Parliament, though I doubt whether he'll make much of a career. Still, he'll get to know useful people and he'll pull his weight. You know the saying, that there's something to be got out of most men and most situations. Well, then, since he's decided to run, it seems to me that he'd better be elected. It won't be an altogether easy matter, though the difficulties are not insuperable. The hardest task will be to reconcile the various elements of his constituency. He's standing as a Republican of the Left, with a definitely Left program, including an income tax and certain measures of social reform. He's carefully avoided any declaration on the matter of the laws against religion, but he is in favour of a policy of toleration and reconciliation. In fact, Briand's line, pure and simple. There couldn't be a more orthodox government candidate.

"Now, the trouble is that he's being opposed by a certain Doctor Bonnefous, or Bonnafous. The points in favour of the doctor are that he's a commoner, that he lives all the time in the country, and that by reason of his profession he's of more use there than the Marquis. I should think, too, that he's a Freemason. So far as his program's concerned, he can hardly be more Left than the Marquis, except that he doesn't mind openly approving of the recent persecution and spoliation of the clergy. If the doctor had succeeded in getting himself adopted by the Radical Party, the Marquis would be in a bad way, but he hasn't, and that's where we're one up. The party headquarters in Paris have refused to declare themselves. It seems that Briand himself has been taking an interest in the matter.

The Marquis, professing the views he does, is a candidate after his own heart. It's no good pretending, however, that most of the Left votes won't go to Bonnefous, as well as those of the Protestant section —and there are a good many Huguenots in that part of the world. There is a risk that the Catholic vote may be split between two or three candidates who stand no chance and don't deserve to. Things being as they are, it is to the interest of the Church that the Marquis should be elected. I won't bore you with the details of all he's doing, and getting done, to strengthen his weak points. He's got a good agent, a man called Crovelli or Crovetti—I've got an awful memory for proper names—some sort of a Corsican, I think. Anyhow, in return for a few thousand francs, this fellow will work the ground for him. To win over the Protestant vote they've managed to unearth some old Calvinist great-aunt, and a whole lot of dyed-in-the-wool heretic relations. It's the Catholics he's most worried about, and that's where I can't do much to help. It so happens that, though my family came originally from the south, my business connexions are all in the north. And this is where you come in.

"One of your colleagues at the Catholic Institute is the Abbé Cabirol. You are on excellent terms with him; I know that he thinks highly of you. For many years now he has been a Professor at the Seminary of Périgueux, where his influence is very great. He has trained dozens and dozens of priests in that part of the country, and he keeps up with a great number of them. A word from him would do a lot. He needn't go into details; all that's wanted is that he should say: 'Make your flock vote for Monsieur de Saint-Papoul, or at least, don't prevent them voting for him.' That'll be quite enough. One can't, of course, ask a man like the Abbé Cabirol to act in that way without justifying the request, and it's for you to put the position to him. Give him the impression that you speak not as a personal friend of Saint-Papoul, but as a priest who has the true interests of the Church at heart. Anything that I can do to help as a friend of the family, I'll do, such as vouching for the excellence of the Marquis's sentiments and those of his intimates, and giving a guarantee that, despite the program forced on him by circumstances, he's a good churchman at heart. And that's just the sort of assurance that the Catholics down there need. The Marquis didn't like to ask you himself, but he would be enormously grateful for anything you could do. As I said just now, he'll find his own little niche in Parliament just waiting to be filled. There are not many men with his peculiar qualifications. He'll be extremely useful as a liaison officer between certain groups, and as a means of maintaining certain contacts. He may not have much initiative, but he's no fool, and he'll do his job well. For instance, I can't imagine anyone better suited, when he's got into his stride, to act as a sort of clearing-house for various views on matters of ecclesiastical preferment, such as appointments to vacant bishoprics, and suchlike. I'm sure you're not so innocent as to think that the separation of Church and State means that such discussions will remain for ever in abeyance?—You can take my word for it that such is not the case.

"And that reminds me that I want to talk to you about another scheme of his which seems to me, I must confess, rather childish. He's anxious, you see, to leave nothing to chance, and he has been wondering whether he couldn't make use of Monsieur Jerphanion in his campaign, by using him as a link with certain elements of the Left. I don't suggest that he'd go so far as actually to flirt with the Freemasons—that would be a bit too much of a good thing—but short of that, he thinks the young man might be useful to him. Now, I rather think that his ideas about the Training College people are a bit wide of the mark, and that's why I thought that you, who've seen them at close range, might . . ."

Mionnet agreed that the Marquis's ideas on this point seemed to him rather fantastic. Then he thought for a moment, smiled, hesitated, smiled again, and said finally that if M. de Saint-Papoul really wanted to make use of Jerphanion in his electoral campaign, there *was* a way in which he might do so to good effect.

"How do you mean?"

"Unless, of course, this fellow Crovetti considers it part of his duties to provide the speeches. I shouldn't think that's likely, and in any case they wouldn't be very good ones. If I were Monsieur de Saint-Papoul I should get Monsieur Jerphanion to write them, or at least the most important ones. I should get him to supply me with a whole series of speeches to cover all the necessary electioneering points. I don't know Monsieur Jerphanion, but I'm sure that if he were given a few hints, he could make a good job of it."

"That's a grand idea! I'll talk to Saint-Papoul about it. Between ourselves, I don't think public speaking's much in his line, and he'll be delighted to think that he's getting some return for the money which he's spending on his son's education—he's always grumbling at the expense. Of course, he may have to give the fellow a bit extra, but he won't mind that. He loves killing two birds with one stone!"

Towards the end of luncheon—which had taken place at the Grand Hotel—the Count said casually.

"I believe you're going to see Monsignor Lebaigue some time this week. . . . You seem surprised that I should know, but really it's perfectly simple. I am a great friend of the Duchesse de Migennes, and Monsignor Lebaigue, also an old friend of hers—in fact, he is the nephew of her mother's steward—has spoken to her about your work. I gather that it is of the very greatest interest, and, by the by, I'm not at all sure that it wasn't a master-stroke on your part, though an unintentional one, to confine your views to an official memorandum, instead of publishing them as a magazine article, even in a Catholic paper, as most men in your position would have done. The Archbishop, I may tell you, is extremely sensible of the propriety of your conduct. Now, I may be wrong, of course, but I see no reason why you shouldn't tell Monsignor Lebaigue, if you get an opportunity, of Saint-Papoul's candidature and of the plans we have been discussing to help it along. Monsignor Lebaigue knows what my views are, but it's quite possible that he may be a bit prejudiced against me, and, in any case, an expression of interest coming from so different a quarter and from a man like you might keep his interest in the matter alive."

The next day Mionnet sounded the Abbé Cabirol. His cleverness when dealing with matters of this kind lay in going straight to the point without any beating about the bush.

"The Comte de Mézan wants me to ask you a favour," etc.

The Abbé Cabirol listened to what he had to say and then burst out laughing. Mionnet showed polite surprise.

"I'm not laughing at your poor old Marquis de Saint-Papoul, whom I've vaguely heard of," he said, "but at the idea of Mézan. Do you know him? Do you know who he is?"

Mionnet made no reply, and he continued:

"Do you know, I mean, that he's closely connected with the Company?"

"Oh, I know he has their interests at heart."

"But, my dear chap, he's a member."

"Metaphorically speaking, perhaps."

"Metaphorically be hanged! . . . The Saint-Papouls know all about it. . . . I'm amazed that you shouldn't. . . ."

Cabirol explained that M. de Mézan was a regular member of the Order of Jesuits, that he had secretly professed the first three vows, but that later he might have been granted a special dispensation; that probably he had been allowed a certain degree of latitude on condition that he took the fourth vow, which the Order held to be the most important of all. ("It's not easy, as you may imagine," said Cabirol, "to get to the bottom of all their manœuvring, but I don't suppose they bother much about the dear Count's chastity and poverty—which are not subjects, in any case, about which they're fanatical—so long as he remains faithful *usque ad mortem*. And I should think that with the secrets he knows that's pretty necessary!") In fact, although in the ostensible hierarchy of the Order he didn't occupy the same place as the Fathers themselves—he had not undergone their long training nor was he bound by their obligations, however elastic those obligations might be—he was, all the same, one of the big noises of the Company.

"I can assure you that throughout the north—in certain matters, that is—his opinion counts for more with them than that of the Provincial."

He gave Mionnet a shrewd glance.

"Compared with a fellow like that, we, my dear chap, are nothing in the eyes of the Church."

He spoke with a suspicion of bitterness.

Mionnet protested that he had always understood that the existence of these "secret" Jesuits was just a fairy-tale.

Cabirol shrugged. A moment later he dropped his seriousness and began to speak of Mézan's little ways, of his famous tie-pin.

"Why on earth has he put you up to talking to me?"

"Probably," replied Mionnet, with his air of guileless common sense, "just because he's keen to see the Marquis elected, both because he's a friend and because he's a Catholic."

"I'm sure it's that."

Cabirol pondered his words, pursed his lips in a comic grimace, and scratched his bullet head, which was covered with a thin thatch of short brown hair.

"I don't suppose he's really trying to compromise me. . . . But if his object's what you think it is, he could have managed it without me. . . . Well, I'll think about it. . . . His candidate or another, it doesn't much matter. There may be something to choose between a Marquis under Jesuit patronage and a saw-bones in the pay of the Freemasons, but I confess I don't quite see what it is!"

On Thursday he was received by Monsignor Lebaigue in the little office which he occupied in the Archbishop's Palace. The walls were hung with dark red silk brocade, the lower part of which was stained and darkened.

Before Monsignor Lebaigue lay a note-book bound in green

247

cardboard, consisting of forty-eight pages which Mionnet had com-
piled at the beginning of December. While he spoke he played with
the edges of this book, flicking the pages with his fingers, which were
remarkably short and had bitten nails.

Before reaching this august presence the manuscript had already
passed through many hands, some of which Mionnet imagined to be
unknown to him.

He had submitted it in the first place to the Abbé Polleteron, his
old Professor of Theology at the Seminary, who in later years, in view
of his pupil's age and importance, had come to occupy the place more
of a friend than a master.

"I should like you to read it if you have an hour or two to spare.
I have embodied in it a few simple and practical ideas. If you think it
not entirely without merit, show it to anyone you think might be
interested."

The Abbé Polleteron had read it and had given it to one of his most
intimate friends, the Bishop *in partibus* (or, to abide by the Papal
decision of 1882, the titular Bishop) of Cybistra, who at this time fulfilled certain temporary and ill-defined, though presumably important, functions in the Archbishop's household.

"Read it, if you have a moment, and see that it's read by the right
people. It's of the greatest possible interest. You will find in it a complete program of action capable of immediate application."

Mionnet had called his essay: "A Short View of the Duties of a
Parish Priest in Paris." In the first few pages he summarized, in
politic phraseology, the general difficulties confronting the Church.
These he considered to be of various kinds, arguing that, to some
extent, they strengthened one another. The influence of rationalism,
and a false wish to dress up religion to meet contemporary taste, had
given rise to what in fact was a new heresy. Thanks to the vigilance
of Rome, the danger had been averted, but it was still in many quarters a troublesome element to be reckoned with. The worst danger
was that the best type of parish priest, the men of real integrity and
enthusiasm, had got into the habit of troubling themselves with mat-

ters which interfered with their prime and proper duties. There was
no need for the parish priest to concern himself daily with fundamental questions of faith, nor to embark on metaphysical discussions, no
matter how excellent his motives. These were matters that could
safely be left in hands better qualified to deal with them. The duty
of the parish priest was to shepherd his flock through the paths and
brambles of daily life, where action is of more importance than
philosophy. Another point was that discussions about matters of
theory had tended to divert attention from a fact of the greatest significance—the growing estrangement of the proletarian masses from
all questions of religion. The attempt to breathe new life into dogma
had done no more than to enlist the interest of a dozen or two refined
enthusiasts—if indeed it had done as much. Meanwhile, all unnoticed, millions of men and women were absenting themselves from
the Church of their fathers, for reasons that had nothing whatever
to do with the exegetical labours of the latest German commentators.

Some thought that the best means of countering this disaffection
was to carry the war into the country of those who had won the
popular favour, to fight them on their own ground, and to use the
weapons that they had chosen. Experience, however, by no means
supported this view. The soutane had not regained the respect it had
lost, by being seen in the hurly-burly of public functions. Arguments
with political leaders about the way their followers ought to vote
had often no other result than to increase an already existing animus
against religion, and to plant more firmly than ever in the popular
mind the idea that the Church was the traditional enemy, which
never intervened in political struggles except to assist, more or less
indirectly, the forces of exploitation and to thwart the people's legitimate struggle for their rights and for the betterment of their lot. Nor
could so deep-seated a distrust be dissipated merely by appropriating
one or two of the less inflammatory points of the extreme party program and by borrowing the vocabulary of political reform. In France,
and especially in Paris, the "people" are quick-witted, constantly on
the defensive, suspicious of traps, and only too ready to remember

with detestation those occasions in the past, irrespective of all questions of faith, when the Church has taken a hand in the politics of the city.

Besides, quite apart from its inefficacy, such a tactical program involved other drawbacks, not the least of which was the fact that it resulted in priests becoming members of political groups whose creeds they had to profess, thereby running the risk of alienating those members of their flocks who professed a different loyalty. Caught up in the machinery of these various movements, they had to render obedience to lay leaders, and therefore to choose between the hierarchy of the Church and that of their political organization, with the result that they found themselves in an intolerable situation.

In the course of this first part of his work Mionnet took the opportunity of enunciating a few home truths about modernism, Christian Socialism, and the *Sillon*. His tone, as was usual with him, remained throughout calm and unexcited. On the surface he merely stated facts in a simple, familiar style, but careful readers could discern beneath the apparently limpid and shallow prose, with its deceptive resemblance to fresh running water, depths of subtle implication and attack.

His strictures were introduced cleverly in small doses and were directed more against ideas and methods than people. Modernism was blandly buried without any unnecessary fuss and discussion, and the author's attitude to the few remaining scallywags of the modernist camp was one of kindly pity, as of a man who sympathizes with the efforts of those who are trying hard to get cured of some not very pleasant disease and had better be left to complete their convalescence in privacy. Towards the Christian Socialists, and the priests who, like the Abbé Garnier, had shown themselves to be politically active, he adopted a tone of gentle raillery, treating them, in his argument, as foolish and inexperienced busybodies. Only when he came to deal with the *Sillon* did a note of asperity creep into his style.

No reader of his essay could help noticing, even though he might not give much weight to it, the pervasive, the perhaps unintentional, air of superiority which marked it. In matters of theory this parish priest might manifest the most self-effacing modesty, but when it came to appraising facts, he spoke with the assurance of a Bishop. The confidence of his style, the certainty of his allusions, the clear definition of his ideas, all bore witness to the pen of a leader.

And this impression was strengthened by what followed. Having cleared the ground, Mionnet proceeded, without beating about the bush, to the constructive part of his program.

In a great modern city like Paris, he pointed out, the duty of a parish priest is perfectly clear. He has got to reconquer his public, to bring back into the Church those who have strayed from it, and, in particular, the working-class families.

To what extent should he rely for this purpose on the power of sermons, his own, those of his assistant clergy, or those of special preachers and "missionaries" visiting his parish from outside? Such weapons, he concluded, must not be neglected, but it is a mistake to expect too much of them; or, rather, it is no good pretending that such spiritual seed can grow except where the ground has first been prepared by work of quite a different kind.

The necessary preliminary of success is the patient and systematic organization of the human element, and such organization must be, in its nature and its means, strictly social in character, though it must avoid any use of sociological jargon.

It should take the form of developing and co-ordinating where they already exist, in creating where they do not, forms of activity designed to exercise a hold over the members of a parish by providing them with definite advantages. The ideal should be to get a firm hold of every working man from the moment of his birth, never to lose sight of him until he grew up, and then to get hold of him again in the persons of his children. Each should feel that his parish was a second home to which he was bound by interest, by the need of support and advice, and by the claims of decent amusement. Round the parish church should be grouped a whole system of day nurseries, dispensaries, benevolent societies, gymnastic and athletic organizations, clubs, and suchlike bodies, so that the normal life of a Christian would be spent in continual contact and daily friendship with his priest. The mother in need of special care during her periods of nursing, the young man in search of music, of amateur theatricals, of a chance of playing football, the father of a family bothered by having to write an official letter, wanting advice on how to apply for a job, or seeking assistance in some trivial matter of the law, should all turn as a matter of course to their Abbé, or to one or other of the several Abbés who might be attached to their parish. The Church ought to concern itself with every detail in the lives of its children, holding nothing too unimportant for its attention, ignoring no aspect of existence which could bear the light of day. "I see no reason," Mionnet wrote, "why the parish hall of the future should not include a dance hall. Surely it is better for young men and young women to get to know one another in a decent Christian atmosphere than to pick one another up Heaven knows where? Their future lives as married couples will be all the happier for such a start."

He paid tribute to attempts of the kind which had been already tried, making no claim for himself as the inventor of anything new. In the course of his argument he quoted various parish activities, benevolent societies, and athletic clubs in the Paris diocese which could be regarded as examples of what he meant, respectfully applauding the efforts of the Assumptionists, who, according to him, had so far been alone in their recognition of the need of some sort of systematic action along these lines. It was clear that he knew all there was to know in this particular field. And here again he assumed, without any parade of ostentation, an air of superior knowledge, surveying the scene with an eye which could truly be described as "Episcopal" in the strict etymological sense of the term. "Episcopal," in fact, was the word that came naturally to the reader's mind.

What had so far been done, however, he regarded as no more than a beginning. Too many existing institutions were partial or isolated. Too many parishes were without them. Too few priests realized their importance as the necessary centre of their labours and the condition of their moral influence; not nearly enough were taking such work as the standard by which they should model their conduct.

Where, however, most of these activities failed was in addressing themselves to those who were already more or less regular church-goers, in contenting themselves with enlisting those who came to church, instead of forcing the Church on the attention of those who did not.

What was needed was some organization which would cover the whole of Paris and its suburbs with a continuous network of social activities, sufficiently elastic to meet various requirements, but so closely woven that no district could escape. An attempt must be made to draw into such a network the whole working population of Paris, no matter how suspicious it might be at the outset, or even actively hostile in theory to "priests and all their doings."

The welcome to be extended must be designed on the most liberal lines. In particular, it was important to avoid giving the impression that every service must be immediately repaid by blind obedience to the clergy. There must be nothing of the recruiting sergeant about their methods. The line to take was: "You come to us because by doing so you get some advantage or amusement. Don't bother about anything else. It's enough for us to see you happy and to know that you and yours are benefiting by decent, healthy surroundings."

The chief thing was to get an atmosphere of confidence well established. Talk would be the best propaganda, the sort of talk that would naturally be put about by mothers of families and by young people. Of course it would be necessary to see that the habit of certain ceremonies, such as baptism and the first Communion, was insisted upon in working-class districts where such things had fallen into disuse, and that advantage was taken of appealing to people whom certain circumstances and certain periods of life might make susceptible. For instance, a woman who never set foot in a church would bring her baby to be christened, and that was the time to tell her of the existence of a day nursery or a dispensary. She would be the readier to listen because she would be entering on a period of endless worry, when the smallest spot on a child's face fills a mother with the fear of smallpox or chicken-pox, or the tiniest hoarseness sets her thinking of whooping-cough. Similarly, young people are on the constant look-out for amusement and for the chance of making friends, and the wish to take part in theatricals or to belong to a cycling club will be stronger than any prejudice that might be aroused by their surroundings, especially if the priest is careful to avoid unduly waking their suspicions.

Finally, Mionnet drew a portrait of the type of parish priest he hoped to see develop in increasing numbers. "Obviously," he wrote, "one can't expect every priest to model himself on such lines. Many will find that their vocation leads them in quite different directions. But it will be a long time before we have too many of the kind of man I envisage.

"I see him as active, quick-witted, gay, and easy of approach, always ready to get up a game and to join in it himself. The older boys will think of him as a friend, the younger as an elder brother more resourceful, more full of life, than themselves. No one will be afraid to pluck him by the sleeve or to shout: 'Come here, Abbé, we want you!' He will be the sort of man who can talk familiarly to his boys with a hand on their shoulder, who can say with perfect good humour: 'Here, now, no swearing! Swearing's not going to help you to hit the ball.' He will know how to have a smile for the workman who votes 'red,' and who comes to see him as he's sitting down to supper, because his son has told him that the Abbé is a 'decent chap' who's 'thoroughly in the know.' He will go to bed late and get up early, but for all that he'll be the kind of man who gets a good night's sleep. He'll have simple meals and not take long over them. He'll be better at arranging a picnic than at discussing a menu with his cook. He won't have much opportunity to develop a paunch, but neither will he be tempted to become melancholic or to indulge in morbid struggles of conscience. Let us admit that he won't take much interest in metaphysical speculations. His faith will be of the good honest sort that won't need much looking after. Boredom will be almost unknown to him. How should he be bored? His chief trouble will be finding enough time to do all he's got to do.

"And how about those whose chief concern in religion is mysticism? What will they make of all this? There's nothing for them to worry about. Every man's got his own job to do. Convents are the places for those who conduct long and moving dialogues with God, and there is room in the world for aged scholars whose concern it is to strengthen the defences of dogma against the attacks of heretics and atheists. The secular clergy of great modern cities have other work to do. Their duty is to help the multitude of lost souls, to shepherd the wandering flocks, to bring new lives into the fold. It is for them to be concerned with the humblest as well as the highest needs of their people, and thus to bind them to the Church by the real bonds of gratitude and affection."

"This little essay of yours is very remarkable," said the prelate with the short fingers. (Every now and then, when he was thinking most deeply, he raised his hand to his mouth and began to bite his thumbnail.) "His Eminence himself has deigned to read it, on my recommendation, and has expressed his very great interest. It certainly is very remarkable, very original. Regarded from some points of view, your theories are quite new. You probably have no idea how extremely opportune they are."

He rapped the cover of the manuscript.

"It goes a great deal further than you think. It contains, potentially, the matter of a whole revolution. I don't say that others before you haven't concerned themselves with these matters, but you are the first who has defined the issue so clearly and at such length. . . . This new type of priest that you have described. . . . What an attractive life it offers to our young men! Excellent, excellent. . . ."

Turning his head, he set himself to examine Mionnet with considerable attention, though he attempted to disguise his interest beneath a casual air. He had long known of his visitor's existence, but had never until now met him in person.

"Knowing, as we did, your reputation," he said, "we naturally foresaw that you would have something interesting to suggest, but I must confess that we scarcely anticipated that it would be in this direction. To that extent we have been surprised—most agreeably so. Unless I am wrong, you do not touch on such subjects in your lecture course at the Institute?"

"Indeed, no, Monsignor. As a matter of fact, my subject this year is Ecclesiastical Eloquence since the Counter-Reformation."

Monsignor Lebaigue burst out laughing.

"Is that so! . . . And you are attached to Saint-Thomas, are you not? . . . I don't suppose you get much chance there, either, of applying your theories?"

"No. . . ."

"Not that it isn't a parish church, but the parish is that of the faubourg Saint-Germain," the prelate said with a twinkle. "Besides, the kind of activity that you envisage is only possible where the priest in charge—well—I don't mean that it mightn't be a very good thing even there . . . but it would need, as you pointed out, a man of considerable tact to put it through. . . ."

Mionnet smiled discreetly at this reference to Sichler. His host continued on a note that had become slightly interrogative:

"So far your name had never been considered in connexion with one of the large outlying parishes, but there's no saying that a vacancy mightn't occur. . . ."

Mionnet declared his readiness to accept any post in which his superior might think he would be useful, but he managed to convey the impression that his gifts did not really lie in that direction, that it was not as priest in charge of a working-class district where he would have to superintend the details of parish work that he could be of most value to the Church. He had had, unfortunately, no experience of that sort of thing and could put forward no claim to recognition along those lines. The only merit he could boast was that he had given more thought than most to the need for the co-ordination of such work, to the desirability of a general program, to the wisdom of setting up some sort of staff for its control and administration. In fact, he made it clear that an executive post was not the sort of thing he had envisaged for himself.

The prelate was careful to let him see not only that he fully understood this point of view, but that he found nothing of which to disapprove in an ambition that knew so clearly what it was after.

"It certainly is unfortunate," he said, after a moment's thought, "that we have nothing like . . . nothing corresponding to a central organization which could concern itself with the working out of some program along the lines you have suggested. I am quite sure that our enemies, whether in the world of official politics or in the various groups, secret or not, make full use of such a machinery of planning and supervision. Nothing will ever get done unless we concentrate initiative into some central organization which can stimulate effort elsewhere. . . . That is exactly the kind of work for a man like you."

He got up. His attitude, his expression seemed to say: "It's a pity, but it's unlikely that a chance of that sort will present itself for a long time to come." Beneath the official tone, however, Mionnet thought he could fairly detect a more intimate assurance: "If not that, then something else, eh? The point is that we should know your worth. You've not got much doubt of it yourself, have you? Well, don't be impatient."

It was only on his way downstairs that Mionnet suddenly realized that he had quite forgotten to mention the matter of Saint-Papoul's election. He did not waste time in wondering to what extent the omission had been wholly involuntary, but he felt, all the same, slightly uncomfortable about it and reassured himself by reflecting that he would make up for his lapse by redoubling his efforts with Cabirol. "If Mézan asks any questions," he thought, "I can find some excuse."

Chapter

LENGNAU

"What time do you make it?"

"Ten thirty-five."

"I must be off. I don't know how long I shall be with Lengnau, but I doubt whether I shall be back for dinner. I don't want to feel rushed."

He paused a moment before adding:

"I suppose you wouldn't care to feed somewhere near there? You may know of some little place. . . ."

Jallez raised his head, letting the worried lines of his face relax.

"I don't see why not. I've got something to do in town early this afternoon."

The suggestion seemed to tempt him. His blue eyes were turned towards the window. He appeared, as he so often did, to be gazing at someone far off whom only he could see. On such occasions Jerphanion felt as shy of him as he had on the day of their first meeting.

"Where does your chap live?"

"Behind the Jardin des Plantes; rue Guy-de-la-Brosse."

"You've no idea when you will be free?"

"I imagine he can't keep me much after half past twelve. Besides, if I know you're waiting for me, I'll manage to get away. One can always make an excuse."

Jallez looked down and seemed to be thinking.

"I know a little bar on the Quai de la Tournelle, which is more or less in my direction, but half past twelve's a bit late."

"If I walk quickly, how long will it take me to get to this bar of yours from where my chap lives?"

"About ten minutes."

"Well, then, I promise to get away about five past twelve, in any case not later than ten past, so that I shall be with you certainly by twenty past. Will that do? It'll be nice talking to you at once, before my memory of this interview shall have gone stale. If one waits too long before discussing a thing like that, it's apt to die on one; one's mind works on it too much first. But in this way I shall be able to get your reaction almost as though you'd been there with me."

The grey-haired woman with the black shawl might have been either a servant or a relation. The room into which she showed the young man was large for Paris, and well lighted. Two windows, set well apart from each other, gave on to a view which must have been chiefly composed of sky and roofs. It was, however, difficult to get a clear sight of it through the crumpled lace curtains which hung unevenly before them in heavy folds.

The appearance of the room was striking. The whitewashed walls were almost entirely covered, including the space above the fire-place, with shelves of plain unpainted wood, of which the knots and grain-ing stood out red on the lighter ground of its surface. Here and there dabs and patches of putty made spots of alien colour. The shelves were packed with books which had been arranged, where possible, in double rows. In many places leaflets and copies of magazines and newspapers had been forced sideways between tops of the books and the shelf above. The middle of the room was dominated by a very large table placed rather nearer to the windows, and made, like the shelves, of plain wood, though of rather better quality, probably beech. There were five or six wicker chairs, one of which, larger than the rest, was furnished with arms. The whole impression was one of rather self-conscious monastic simplicity. A well-worn dressing-gown of dark red flannel lay across one of the chairs. On the projecting corner of the marble mantelpiece which the book-shelves left free stood a tobacco-jar of glazed pottery, two cherrywood pipes with long, thin stems, an opened bottle of mineral water, and a glass. A terrestrial globe was placed on a low table between the windows.

Jerphanion went over in his mind all that Laulerque and Clanricard had told him about Lengnau. He was not, they had said, the Pope of Freemasonry, nor even one of its high priests, since he avoided any direct exercise of power, but he might be described as one of its leading spiritual authorities, perhaps as *the* leading authority.

"Which means," he thought, keeping his eye on the inner door, through which, presumably, this man would enter, "that Masonry does have its spiritual authorities. Behind all the crowd of dentists, broken-down doctors, and bar-keepers, behind the local shopkeepers with their fat necks, paunches, and flabby legs and the Brother Overseer observing them with a watchful eye (brethren who adorn the Column of the South), behind all that there is, it seems, some sort of man of intellect capable of keeping his end up in discussion with, say, one of the modern writers, or with one of those University philosophers of whom we think so highly, like Brunschwig, Chartier, or Lévy-Bruhl; the sort of man Jallez wouldn't want to laugh at. It's difficult to imagine such a man in such a connexion. What impression does this room give, or try to give, with its wooden shelves, the dressing-gown left lying about, the bottle of mineral water? And how about the books?—Martines de Pasqually: *Treatise on the Reintegration of Being;* Matter: *St. Martin, the Unknown Philosopher;* Mesmer: *The Secret Revealed;* Monnier (Jean-Joseph): *On the Influence Attributed to Philosophers and Freemasons;* Mynsicht (Hadrian von): *Aureum Seculum Redivivum; Mysteries of the Secret Societies*—without any author's name. A highly specialized collection, or perhaps I've happened to strike a particular shelf devoted to such works, or it may be that I'm a victim of one of those tricks that a purely alphabetical arrangement sometimes plays. . . . Is love unknown in this man's life? Perhaps when I've seen him such a question will seem ridiculous. He may be some grubby old fellow with cotton-wool in his ears and dandruff on his coat-collar. . . . What part does sex play in the Masonic universe? . . . Rothweil had one or two attractive nudes on his walls. . . . And then what about those odd allusions of Ardansseaux, the way his eyes gleamed suddenly? . . ."

The man who came into the room was taller than Jerphanion by half a head, and well built. His hair, which was completely grey, but very thick, was arranged with a bushy shock well forward over his forehead. His face gave the impression of being large or, rather, of being long. The features were broadly sketched in, and its complexion varied between the extremes of grey and pink. He had a large grey moustache twisted into points, and seemed not to have shaved since the evening before. His eyes, beneath strongly marked brows, were of a very light, indeterminate grey. They gave the impression of being slightly faded, though not through weariness, and were, in their way, extremely handsome. They shone with a definite light of their own, quite different from Jallez's, more abstract, and probably less at the mercy of emotional moods. There was a hint of pride and nobility in his glance.

He wore a grey suit which, though far from being new, retained, by reason of its cut and the quality of the cloth, a definite air of elegance, and a shirt with a turnover collar which looked as though it were made of flannel. His dark green knitted tie was loosely fastened. An old pair of indoor slippers made of soft brown leather covered his large feet without disguising their irregularities. His walk was that of a young man.

Jerphanion's general impression was of a handsome, rather untidy man with the air of a thinker. He appeared to be entirely at his ease and rather aloof in his manner.

While he greeted his guest and waved him to a chair, his eye fell on the dressing-gown which had been left lying about. He picked it up and walked over to hang it up on a peg which was placed between the right-hand window and the corner of the room.

When he spoke, his voice was rather high, the intonation slow and slightly remote. Its note of self-assurance might have been repellent but for a mingled tone of caution and courtesy.

"And now, my dear sir, what exactly is your position?"

He made Jerphanion confirm certain details which he seemed to know already, listening patiently and occasionally asking a question, which, so far from interrupting the young man's narrative, had the effect of helping it along. "You're a student of letters, are you not?" . . . "You mean to take up teaching as a profession?" . . .

A silence fell between them. Lengnau crossed his legs, clasped his hands, which were long and well formed, on his knee, and looked at Jerphanion.

"Do you mind my asking what it was that gave you the idea of becoming a Mason?"

Jerphanion explained the need he had felt for a "Church," his hesitations, his meeting with Clanricard. (His words came haltingly; he was annoyed with himself, and astonished to find how difficult it was to describe the mental states which he had experienced so nearly.)

"I think I understand what it was that you found lacking in a political party, whether Socialist or another," said Lengnau, "but what was it that attracted you especially to the Masons?"

"The idea that Masonry is something different from, more than, a party; that it makes greater demands on the individual and employs more of his faculties. Also, I think, the belief that it acts more secretly and more directly; that it is, primarily, a secret society. . . ."

Even while he spoke, the young man felt that he was being too definite, that he was almost compromising himself. He hastened, therefore, to add that his feelings about Masonry were still contradictory, and managed to give the impression that they were almost equally balanced between attraction and repulsion.

Lengnau uncrossed his legs, stretched them, threw himself back in his chair, and put his hands in his trouser pockets. He stared with his large, colourless, and shrewd eyes at the junction of wall and floor at the opposite end of the room. His great feet, with the modelling showing so clearly through the slippers, were thrust out before him in a way that gave an air of insolence to his pose.

"Of course," he said, "you have already heard a lot of talk about Masonry?"

"More or less. . . . The fact that I was interested meant that for

some time past my curiosity has been on the stretch. . . . Certain
accidental occurrences have helped me, and I think I know a certain
amount, though naturally I have been cautious about believing all
I have been told."

(He spoke this time in a way that pleased him, charging his tone
with concealed implications. Jallez, he thought, couldn't have done
it better. Lengnau would see at once that he had to do with someone
who was by no means a simple and innocent beginner.)

"To what did all this information you speak of refer? To the
general organization of the Order?"

"No, it referred in particular to the way the Lodges are conducted,
to the atmosphere that one finds there and the sort of people one
meets . . . also to the formalities of admission."

The tone of his voice gave evidence of repugnance. Lengnau smiled
with an air of constraint, but he did not reply at once. Jerphanion
went on:

"Let me repeat, sir, that I don't insist on the reliability of my in-
formant. . . . I ask no better than to correct my impressions."

Lengnau thrust his hands still deeper into his pockets, leaned his
head forward, nodded slightly, and half-closed his eyes.

"Oh, they're probably accurate enough, so far as the material details
are concerned. They're not as secret as all that. From time to time
attacks flare up in leaflets and newspaper articles, and it's always
possible to find some renegade to 'unmask,' as he puts it, the Masonic
mysteries. The fool public is stuffed with descriptions. Customs are
quoted, formulas, names of ceremonies and offices, which to those
who are not Masons must seem sufficiently ridiculous. . . . You were
born a Catholic?"

"Yes."

"And probably educated as one? Well, then, you know it's not
difficult to make fun of Catholic ceremonies. It's been done more
than once, but it's a foolish employment. If Catholicism can be attacked, it's not through its ceremonies, which are magnificent"—
raising his eyes he stared into the distance—"which are," he added,

"inimitable. No, what can be legitimately attacked is their meaning, the content of such ceremonies, the teaching which lies behind the symbols . . . in short, the doctrine, the metaphysic, of Catholicism. Everyone is at liberty to attack or to admire the essentials of a creed; what is absurd is to laugh at the forms. . . . You know the sort of crude jokes I mean, about the priest administering the sanctified bread like a dentist pulling out teeth. Ugh! that sort of thing's vile, and disgraces the cause of anti-clericalism! I know of nothing in the world more beautiful or more deeply moving than the sacrament of the Eucharist. . . . If I reject it I do so because of the meaning that lies concealed within. There is in every rite a concealed meaning, and the whole problem for each of us is to know whether we accept or reject it, whether it gives us or not the answer we are seeking."

He turned his gaze back to Jerphanion and sat looking at him in silence. Then:

"If you had found your answer in the religion of your childhood, you wouldn't be here. Am I not right?" he asked.

He turned away his head, drew in his legs a little, seemed to think for a moment, and then began to talk again in the tone of one who enters on some explanation to an intimate friend.

"I don't share the opinion of those who think that one ought to differentiate in matters of religion, holding, with the disciples of St. John, that on one side there is the pure faith of the spirit—it has long been the custom of the Lodges to swear on St. John's Gospel—a religion without forms, accessible only to the chosen few, and that all the rest, the ceremonies and the symbols, are meant only for the crowd which without such things could never be brought to understand the truth. . . . It is a convenient theory, and very fashionable. If any particular piece of ritual sticks in your throat, you put it aside as belonging to the sort of play-acting which may be necessary, but which you discount in the secrecy of your inner self. Such an attitude implies a scorn of the common man which I do not share, and a misconception of the power of ritual. No one could speak with greater bitterness than did Pascal about the power exercised by material symbols, by appearances, over the imagination of the mob, but that did not prevent him from admitting in his own case the help to be derived from forms and ceremonies, and he certainly did not think of himself as one of the uninstructed. But Pascal saw only one side of the question. . . . You said something just now which struck me very forcibly, about the need of a Church which you and those of your generation feel so strongly. There is no such thing as a Church of the spirit. If you thought that spiritual communion was enough, you would try to attain it in solitude by the way of contemplation. You would feel no need of a Church, for what is a Church if not a group organized by ceremonies?"

He looked again at Jerphanion and waited. The young man was profoundly affected by his words, but felt incapable of making any answer. Lengnau got up and walked several times up and down the room with his hands in his pockets.

"One could talk for ever about the intrinsic value of ceremonies," he said, "and the point is not a very important one. The rites performed in St. Peter's at Rome are probably more beautiful than those of the primitive Church, which were, no doubt, poor, crude, and rather ridiculous, but that does not mean that they are richer in spiritual significance. Indeed, a day came when men decided that they were less rich—hence the Reformation."

He came to a stop before Jerphanion and passed his hand across his head. A loose hair seemed to be tickling his neck, and he took some time trying to find it. He carefully examined his fingers once or twice without tracing it. When at last it was discovered, he tried to shake it off on to the floor, but had difficulty in doing so. Jerphanion watched him with as much attention as he had given to his disquisition on ritual. It may be that his comprehension of the argument was quickened by the purely human sympathy which this business of the hair woke in him.

"What one has got to realize," said Lengnau, "is that the rites of the Catholic Church may seem beautiful to one, meaningless to another. . . . The central fact to which they all refer is the idea of sacrifice, and unless one takes account of that, any criticism or mockery of them is merely childish. What is represented is the sacrifice of the Christian God, but this theory of sacrifice is extended to include mankind and the world. A sin has been committed and it must be redeemed; salvation must be won through suffering, and this salvation is at once an end to be attained and an act of destruction, for it involves the disappearance of the world as we know it. I'm not trying to teach you anything; Christian pessimism is something that we have always known, but it is important to realize it. The Masonic rites, on the other hand, all turn on the idea of construction. If you grasp that, you grasp everything."

Construction: what a lovely word! For a moment Jerphanion held it poised in his mind. A critical, an impatient curiosity might have asked: "Construction of what?" But about such a word there spreads a fine and lovely aura which, to a certain extent, is its own justification. It seems to contain the impulse of some solemn rhythm, to adumbrate something the splendour of which resides in the moment of its utterance, in the apparent universality of its sweep.

Lengnau continued:

"The various details of dress and procedure which you've heard about and possibly thought ridiculous, the terminology, the formulas, the titles of offices, and the decoration of the rooms, are all, you must understand, merely the outward form of a sort of religious drama, taking the word in the sense given to it by the ancients, a drama of Construction as the Mass is a drama of Sacrifice. The fact that the Mass may be said in a barn by a priest smelling of snuff, with a cracked voice and a lot of dirty choir-boys, doesn't affect the fundamental nature of the ceremony. . . . A sacred drama contains, too, the characteristic of repetition; the representation of the same mystery is repeated again and again. Another way of defining a Church is to describe it as a collection of people participating at certain fixed intervals in the symbolic representation of an identical mystery."

"I understand that," Jerphanion managed at last to say; "I know what the sacrifice of the Mass symbolizes, who is sacrificed and what.

But when you speak of Construction, I'm not sure what it is that's being constructed."

Before replying, Lengnau, who was standing against one of the bookcases, made a wide and slow gesture with his right arm, spreading out his fingers as though in an attempt to embrace all the books that the room contained. He began a phrase, then stopped, clasped his hands, pressed them together, and looked at the ground.

"There is a point," he said, "of which no doubt you are perfectly well aware, though you may not have considered it very closely. . . . If you try to see with a fresh eye the movement of humanity during the last two, three, or even four centuries, you must, surely, have been struck by an element of something new. . . . We don't notice it because we are used to it, and also because we are ourselves involved in the movement. But think, for a moment, of the various forward thrusts that have become manifest in different parts of the world, the ideals of which men have become conscious and of which they were never conscious before, the demands they have been moved to make, the needs they have come to feel. Constant use has dulled the meaning of certain words so that we have become indifferent to their significance, careless in their use. . . . Take, for example, the words *progress, liberty, emancipation, democracy, human brotherhood.* . . . We are inclined to give too much importance to definite historical events, thinking of them as exceptional incidents, seeing them in distorted perspective, concentrating our attention on the particular form given to them by the circumstances of the time, obsessed by the violence which accompanied them and which we think of now as indefensible . . . the Revolution of '89 . . . the thunderclap of '48 which burst over Europe. . . . What we don't sufficiently realize is that all these things were only part of a general tendency universally at work over a period of centuries. Believe me, if one could get far enough away to get a clear view of this combined effort of mankind ever since the end of the Middle Ages, undistorted by rhetoric, one would be amazed and profoundly moved. . . . One would become aware of a whole series of facts which, considered even in isolation,

would seem strange and remarkable. . . . Serfs becoming free men
. . . heretics no longer being burned . . . nobles surrendering their
privileges . . . white men fighting one another that black slaves
might be freed from a life of shame . . . rich men questioning their
rights and apologizing for their wealth . . . great military empires
proclaiming the necessity of peace and the union of mankind. . . .
Don't think that I ignore the many set-backs that there have been or
the disasters which have occurred, nor that I discount the malice of
knaves and the lies of hypocrites. But I should be blind if I did not
see how all these remarkable changes have been working to one end."

His voice had risen as he spoke, his eyes were shining, he was almost
trembling. His outstretched, open hands seemed to be proffering a
gift of refreshing fruit. Jerphanion felt the contagion of his mood.
"Taken by and large," he hastened to assure himself, "what he says is
true. Any criticism of detail would sound cheap. Only a fool would
want to be smart at his expense." The odd thing was that the element
of staleness, of commonplace, of outworn idealism which Lengnau's
speech contained seemed to increase its power of persuasion. It was
as though the power of thinking, with the maximum of reality and
vitality, thoughts which are as old as the world and of which the
ordinary man has grown tired, appeared suddenly as the essence of
strength.

"Well, then," Lengnau continued in a calmer voice, "if you can
realize that, you can realize what it is that the Masons mean by the
Construction of the Temple. I don't say that everything so far
achieved along these lines has been the work of the Masons. It hasn't,
but they've had a part in all of it, and it's the Masons who have
contributed the plan, the fixity of purpose, the element of unity,
without which these labourers in the cause would have remained
scattered and have been too easily discouraged. That has been so
from very far back. I have studied the origins of the movement" (he
indicated again the shelves of books); "they go back far into the
Middle Ages, not into the Middle Ages of the self-tormented ascetics,
but certainly to the period of the craftsmen and the master builders

who raised the cathedrals. At the very time that they were building monuments dedicated to the religion of sacrifice, to the religion of the end of the world, moved by a sort of revenge on the part of the spirit of Construction, they laid the foundations among themselves of those secret societies from which the Order was later to spring, the Order whose avowed object was to be the Construction of the World. Don't forget either that in more modern times men as great and as different as Goethe, Saint-Simon, Auguste Comte, Hugo—I'm sure you're not one of those silly young men who laugh at Hugo?—wouldn't have been what they were, and wouldn't have done what they did, had it not been for the presence of Masonry in the background, even when, individually, they were not themselves Masons. Consider, for instance, the ideal of humanism or of democracy, including even Socialism. One must admit that so long as it is confined within the limits of its official program, seen merely from the point of view of its ostensible intention, it's a pretty humdrum affair compared with a great religious ideal. It lacks driving force, vision, and as soon as it becomes detached from fact, from immediate and material achievement, tends to become a mere matter of meaningless talk, the kind of thing that we've become accustomed to laugh at when we hear it in political speeches, a hodge-podge of abstractions suited for elementary-schoolmasters and usually delivered with a strong southern accent . . . 'our unfailing loyalty to the ideas of joostice and of progress.' . . ." (Lengnau gave an excellent rendering of the intonation of the southwest, and his face assumed a quite unexpected air of gaiety.) "Nor must we forget that once you reduce these famous principles to the level of their own inherent claims, you are opening the way to discussion, to a bandying of pros and cons. . . . Take universal suffrage, for example. Once I begin to argue about it in isolation from other facts, I'm perfectly within my rights if I champion a form of government based on the hierarchic or aristocratic principle. . . . But if it becomes clear that this limited secular ideal is only one stage of a plan, one phase in the achievement of the Great Work, the whole thing is put on a different footing. We are at once conscious of the profound truths embodied in these things, of the way in which they inter-connect, of the necessity that drives them forward. Objections of detail, trivial absurdities, all vanish."

He stopped and looked once more at Jerphanion, as though aware that the silent question in the young man's eyes was still unanswered.

"You're about to say"—he sat down, leaned forward, and rested his two hands on his knees—"you're about to say that all this doesn't explain what the Great Work, what the Construction of the Temple, is?"

He lowered his voice and spoke slowly on a low, intense note.

"If you were anyone else I should say: 'First become one of us. As a Mason you will come gradually to understand our objects and to realize the splendour of our aim . . . in proportion to your worthi-ness as a member.' But to a man like you I can speak freely. Well, the Great Work which for centuries has been the object of Masonry is no less than the complete unity of mankind." He repeated with slow emphasis: "Complete, in every sense, and in every direction, even the purely mystical." He accompanied the phrase with a movement of the arm towards those very book-shelves at Jerphanion's back which the young man had already examined. "We have always been in touch with the mystics, with occultism, and we are so still. A single chain leads from the Cabbala to ourselves. . . . The complete unity of mankind," he repeated: "surely you can feel the weight, the density, of those words?"

He ceased speaking for a moment, but his eyes never left his visitor's face. The young man found himself suddenly remembering certain explanations which Laulerque had given him of the objects of the society which he had joined as a result of his meeting with the mys-terious bookseller. "Surely," he thought, "they're not the same people, but if not, what are they?—perhaps a sort of storm detachment of Masons—or is the similarity of aims nothing but a coincidence, merely the effect of certain ideas that happen to be in the air? Still, whatever the connexion, why don't they work together? Are there differences of opinion which I know nothing of, or is it simply that they employ different methods? . . . Perhaps Laulerque's lot see more clearly what he calls the comparative urgency of ends and are more acutely aware of impending dangers."

"Does that seem to you just a phrase like any other?" Lengnau asked, "or are you conscious, deep down in yourself, as you hear it, of something fine, something definite, something new? . . . Do you feel as though a curtain had suddenly been drawn revealing a great truth?"

Jerphanion replied that he had certainly felt the presence of a great and fine idea, and that, contrary to what he might have expected, it seemed to take definite form in his mind, instead of remaining vague.

"I said," Lengnau continued, "in every direction, including the purely mystical, and I can't insist too strongly on the fact that this Unity is much more than a simple organization for political or material ends, more even than a merely rational concept. . . . It surpasses and transcends any such obvious organization, though it includes it, drawing it after itself as a fisherman draws his line. . . ."

Ideas crowded suddenly into Jerphanion's mind. He thought of Auguste Comte, of the Supreme Being, of a passage of Hegel, of an eloquent phrase of Renan's, of certain mysterious hymns of Hugo's. . . . "He was right when he said that there was something in common between all those men. They, and others like them, looked forward to the accomplishment of some ideal future. There is a tradition of prophecy. . . ."

"We were speaking just now of the Masonic ceremonies," Lengnau went on. "Now, those ceremonies are not merely a symbolic presentation of the Construction of the Temple, for they can be regarded in a sense as containing a sort of mystical technique of unity. . . . I have worked out the idea in a leaflet which I will lend you later. . . . They are, as it were, an exercise in communion, involving not only the virtues of apprenticeship, but containing also a power of diffusion, a definitely formative influence. . . . We believe that the ideal of Unity can be contagious; you should bring your mind to bear on that thought."

His voice had risen little by little as he spoke. Once again he lowered it. He laughed.

"You are now in a position," he said, "to understand the part played in all this by the purely secular program of the republicans . . . it is an episode, and nothing more. It is clear, is it not, that the pretended audacity of such a program looks pretty small by the side of—"

He broke off, shrugged his shoulders, and passed his fine hand through his grey hair.

". . . There's no secret in what I'm telling you, no plan, more or less concealed, that can only be executed after a period of delay. Far from it. Once get the principle clear, and all you've got to do is to think it out, just as you would think out the corollaries that flow from a theorem in geometry. . . ."

His voice seemed to betray some internal agitation; it was clear that his mind was seeking some lucid phrase that would explain his meaning.

"Look at it in this way. Many of our politicians are convinced Masons, but their work keeps them with their noses to the grindstone of passing events. They have lost the habit of entertaining the long view. . . . Let us say, for the sake of argument, that they have thrown in their lot with the Radicals. Well, they are becoming increasingly aware of the growth, still further to the Left, of a Socialist Party with very advanced views about, for instance, internationalism. They are beginning to feel uncomfortable. They don't want to get the reputation of being reactionary, but they feel that in accepting this extreme international point of view they are in danger of being stampeded. They are conscious of a certain sensation of giddiness and are afraid of being swept from the Left to the ultra-Left as a result of their dislike of being thought less enthusiastic than the next man, or simply by a sort of mechanical process of follow-my-leader. In their heart of hearts they would like to sit back and relax as soon as the secular and democratic program showed signs of being well on the way to realization. They are patriots with a Jacobin tinge. They have never forgiven Germany, and they distrust the English. The limit of their natural wishes is to see a good anti-clerical republic securely entrenched behind its frontiers, benevolent towards its own people and not necessarily at odds with its neighbours, and provided with a strong army commanded by free-thinking generals. You know Rothweil, don't you? There's a man who has not altogether lost the sense of an ultimate ideal, but so far as practical politics are concerned . . . well, I've seen the tears come into his eyes when he's been speaking about Alsace-Lorraine. . . . Now, a man like you must realize that assuming the objects of the Masonic movements to be what they are, the whole conception of frontiers, of countries, of nations, becomes meaningless. The very existence of Masonry is built upon the assumption that the development of patriotism which has taken place all over Europe in the course of the last hundred years, together with the recrudescence of nationalities which has been its logical result, is nothing but a temporary setback in the general progress of mankind. So far as this one point is concerned, we not only accept the extreme Socialist view, we go beyond it. In our eyes it is nothing but a temporary and relatively mild expression of that straining towards the Great Work which we have set ourselves through the centuries to achieve, in conjunction with ideals of a far vaster and profounder significance. The right view for us to take is that Socialism is one of the instruments with which historical development has provided us. The Socialists themselves may not realize this, but that doesn't matter. We have got to make use of the anti-patriotism which they profess just as we made use, earlier, of the spirit of anti-clericalism. . . . Do I frighten you?"

"Indeed no," the young man answered. "I'm only trying to understand you, to follow your argument. I'm grateful to you for speaking to me like this."

Lengnau got up and began to walk about the room with his hands in his pockets. "I'm showing more than ordinary confidence in you," he said. "If you were a fool or a knave you could turn what I'm saying into every kind of monstrous misinterpretation! But you see now that the secret of Masonry is not something that can be explained in two words. I don't mind telling you that although you have not yet been initiated you know a great deal more than many who have. . . . In short" (he fondled with his hand the globe by which he happened to be standing), "I sometimes ask myself whether mankind as we know it today, having freed itself of its old idols, hasn't created new ones which will have to be overthrown in their turn, whether the watchword of the twentieth century won't have to be a new sort of 'Down with Tyranny!'"

He gave an odd laugh as he added:

"And that will give our enemies a new excuse for saying that we only destroy."

He stopped and leaned forward, fixing his gaze vaguely before him.

"It is the irony of our fate that we, the builders of the world, should have been regarded through the ages as the evil geniuses of destruction."

Then, turning towards the young man:

"I don't mind betting, my dear sir, that even you are not entirely guiltless, even now, of such a thought."

He raised his head and looked towards the landscape that could be seen indistinctly through the curtains.

"No one could admire the Catholic Church more than I do. . . . Before we came on the scene it was the only body of men concerned with building, and in a sense we are its children. . . . It is not our fault that a time came when the Church seemed suddenly to be the great rock that barred the road of progress. Ah, if only she could have had a change of spirit, if only she could have been renewed by our leaven! . . . If only she had had the vigour, the youthfulness that would have made her more and more catholic, more and more universal. . . . After all, what is our Great Work if not a striving after complete catholicism?"

He smiled, changing his tone:

"But I'm dreaming. It's not only a question of an old institution that has got beyond the power of assimilating new ideas or being transformed by them. There's a fundamental cleavage. . . . Remember what we were saying just now about Christian pessimism and the condemnation of life. . . . To the Catholic all that is good lies in the past—the earthly paradise, the fall, the redemption—while for us it is the future that counts. The Christian God is old and angry, He thinks only of revenge and punishment, sitting up above, with a thunderbolt in His hand, and waiting for the moment to crush us and our works to dust: *solvet sæculum in favilla.* What could He have in common with our God, who is young, who is yet to be, whom we think of as an architect? His face may be full of care, but He has shining eyes, and in His hands are His plans and His compass. His feet are planted solidly on the earth in the midst of His growing walls. The air about Him is thick with the dust of plaster, and round Him throng the busy apprentices, the companions, the master builders."

Once more he smiled. His voice took on a tone of amusement. "You probably don't know, or you may have read it somewhere without paying much attention to what you read, that some of our enemies seriously accuse us of being the disciples of the Devil. Oh, yes, in their eyes our young architect bears an uncomfortable resemblance to that beautiful angel Lucifer, the Prince of this World, whose great sin was that he taught men to have faith in themselves and endowed them with the pride of knowledge, the hope of happiness here on earth. . . . It's funny, isn't it?"

Jerphanion reflected that the charge of worshipping the Devil, of being the tool of Satan, did not seem to cause his host any uneasiness.

Lengnau continued:

"Sooner or later the question was bound to arise, who was to rule, the Church or ourselves. . . . Personally I don't believe that the Church is any longer the main enemy—in fact, I by no means despair of an ultimate alliance. One of two things must happen, either the utter destruction of the enemy, and—" he lowered his voice, "—for my part I no longer believe in the possibility of that—or an alliance more or less openly admitted. . . . After all, we and they are the only champions left of the Universal . . . and also of the Spiritual, for Socialism is hopelessly involved in materialism. . . . The metaphysical difficulties could be solved. . . . Why should not their God accept our young architect? All we ask is that He should leave this world to him and keep the other for Himself. . . . Don't you agree?"

"Aren't you rather suggesting that he should consent to be a God in exile?"

"Perhaps, but covered with honours. Haven't we already seen the God of the Bible abdicate in favour of Christ? . . . Well, we shall see. . . . You know, of course, the famous dream, that one day a pope may arise who will be one of us?"

He added gaily, with the air of one who clinches an argument:

"There are already Freemason bishops."

In the silence that followed, Jerphanion wondered what time it was and thought of his appointment with Jallez. He got up to go. But it occurred to him that the memory of the rare intellectual feast which he would take with him might be spoiled by his regret at not having extracted an answer to the main problem which had brought him there.

"I am enormously grateful for this interview," he said. "You have opened my eyes to all sorts of possibilities. I shall have a lot to think of. There is one thing, however, I am still not quite clear about. . . ." (He sought encouragement in the image of Laulerque, conjuring up a picture of his leanness, his fire, his sense of reality, his ironic self-possession. He thought also of Jallez, whom he was so soon to meet.) "What I mean is, I'm not quite clear about how Masonry can take action against certain contemporary scandals, certain immediate dangers. I realize that the Great Work implies the gradual removal of injustice from the body of Society, and the destruction of national frontiers. . . . But all that's in the future . . . in the very distant future. . . ."

"Naturally the complete removal of injustice is a matter for the future, and a future so distant that we can only reckon it in astronomical terms, but the great thing is that we are always moving towards it. Every day we are getting nearer. Take, for instance, the question of old-age pensions; it was owing to the Lodges that we got them. It will take a hundred years to settle the problem of frontiers, perhaps less."

"But suppose a European war breaks out in two or three years?"

Lengnau smiled in an odd way and spread his arms wide.

"Well," he said, "what of it?"

The two men were standing facing each other close to the door which opened on to the corridor. Jerphanion looked at Lengnau, who had just said: "Well, what of it?" The man's face was still calm and dominating. The curious smile that lit it seemed to express superior irony even more than the consciousness of revelation. Somehow, Jerphanion felt, one couldn't even laugh at him. It was all terribly baffling.

The young man looked at the unpainted shelves, at the white-washed walls, at the bottle of mineral water. He was aware of a very odd feeling in the pit of his stomach, composed partly of disappointment and bewilderment, partly of a sense that he was out of touch with something, partly of a feeling that he had been thrown back upon himself, and that he was uncertain of himself. A horrible feeling of tumbling down a hole.

Their further conversation was of no importance.

Through the window could be seen the two little tables on the café terrace, the opposite pavement, raised by a few steps above the level of the street, the stone parapet, and Notre-Dame behind the bare winter branches. From time to time there passed a horse-drawn carriage, a hand-cart, a red snub-nosed taxi, or a rattling motor-truck, but for long periods the roadway, the parapet, and the church formed a silent scene of late winter. At such time the sense of the city's life seemed concentrated in the silent figures of a few lonely pedestrians.

Jerphanion described his visit. He talked a great deal, and though he drank a lot, he forgot to eat. He was a prey to the excitement that takes hold of a man when he tries to re-create for another's information some experience that he has just been through. At such times the mind selects, even while it remembers, accentuating the details of the scene, slurring over the moments of uncertainty, the discontinuity of conversation, the slightly confused passages of indeterminate thought. The narrator is inclined to take sides, to become a special pleader. In his eyes the listener is a bored spectator, difficult to rouse to any show of interest, who has to be thrilled and won. He must be persuaded, above all, that the recounted experience was important, since for the speaker it has the profound significance of something that has become part of his being. Thus it was that the person of Lengnau assumed the proportions of a giant. The words he had spoken took on overtones and depths of importance, and the whole interview, seen in perspective, was enriched with accumulated detail and added commentary. Jallez listened without interrupting. He seemed to be following the recital with attention. From time to time, even, it was as though he made to his friend a silent appeal: "Whatever you do, don't leave me to myself; keep me interested: don't abandon me too soon to my thoughts."

Eased of his exaltation, Jerphanion was struck by a moment's compunction.

"Sure I'm not boring you, old man? Here I am unloading my affairs on to you as though they were of prime importance, as though you had nothing else to bother about."

"Not a bit of it."

"Yes, I am: do you know, it's suddenly struck me that I must be behaving like one of those fellows you really dislike, who only get excited about theories and abstract ideas—political theories too, which are the worst kind of all. . . . They talk and talk, and quite forget to live."

"What are you getting at?"

"Confess that you don't like them! You were very severe once, I remember, on the subject of philosophers."

"We were talking about professionals, specialists. . . ."

"You don't care two hoots about that side of life. . . . You'd give all Lengnau's ideas, which I've just been telling you and embroidering with my own comments, for a single verse of that miserable Moréas whom you were so busy tearing to pieces the other day, or for a mood of poetic sensibility. . . ."

Jerphanion paused, and then added on a note of affectionate intimacy: "Even for a mood of unhappiness."

Jallez looked down at his plate, on which a view of the exhibition of '89 fought a losing battle with the scattered scraps of cheese.

"You're wrong, you really are," he said, with a slight change of tone. "I've no taste whatever for unhappiness, or none to speak of. I'd willingly become a Freemason or a Buddhist or anything if I thought that by so doing I could lose the sense of my own personality. I was profoundly impressed by what you told me the other day about your friend Laulerque. I understand his state of mind so well. I can easily imagine myself becoming a terrorist just to escape the haunting fear of death."

"But that's a terrible admission of scepticism. Do you mean that the great doctrines of the world, the great causes that have moved mankind, are good for nothing except to save us from boredom and despair?"

"That's often what they are good for. . . . But you're right. It's foolish to generalize; I was speaking only for myself."

His voice underwent a quick change:

"As a matter of fact, I was listening very carefully; I could repeat everything you said. If I didn't seem to respond, it was because I didn't know what advice to give you. You've heard both sides, and both are probably true, the ridiculous mumbo-jumbo, the orgy of broken-down doctors which your engraver described, as well as Lengnau's fine ideals. But I think you should realize that you'll meet more broken-down doctors in the Lodges than men like Lengnau."

"That's true of any collection of people."

"Possibly, but when he came out with that 'Well, what of it?'

which seems, quite naturally, to have disconcerted you, I think that, in your place, I should have asked one specific question."

"What?"

"I should have said: 'It seems to me that the prospect of the distant future consoles you rather too easily for the threat of immediate disasters. . . . What I am looking for is the chance of joining forces with men of fixed convictions, men of energy, men closely united in a common purpose to work, by the most direct means possible to them, for the cure of certain evils and the prevention of certain dangers. By the word "Church" I mean unity and enthusiasm raised to a higher power than normal, and not the chatter of theologians. Vast dreams of betterment have their charms, no doubt, but not when the enemy is at the gates. I am no lover of Byzantine subtlety. What interests me in Masonry is the idea of a secret society, of a mysterious league of action, not its activities as a school of free thought. . . .'"

"That's exactly what I told myself, but too late, when I was already on my way here—an *esprit d'escalier,* I believe it's called. At the moment I had no thought for anything but the discomfort his words had caused me."

"Didn't you talk to him at all about the dirty side of the movement —all the political bribery it's set its hand to, the spoliation of Church property, and the hubbub there is in the Lodges each time that one of the brethren is caught with his hand in the till?"

"I didn't have a chance; that sort of thing was so foreign to the spirit of our conversation, so far removed from what we were discussing, and so relatively unimportant. It would have made me feel mean to bring up things like that, mean and petty."

"You could have led up to it indirectly. You could have asked, for instance, about the precise division of functions in the movement. Admittedly there are men like Lengnau, but there are also the broken-down doctors. Who is it, ultimately, that gives the orders? Who is it that really counts? Are all the little opportunists, the big-scale gamblers, the nondescript scamps, merely there to be made use of, unknown to themselves, for the realization of noble ends envisaged and determined by others? Is there an aristocracy of Masons who lead the main body in pursuit of the Great Work? Are all the mean little parasites of the movement nothing but fuel to make the wheels go round? Or is all this talk of a Great Work nothing but an excuse, a screen, to hide a deliberately organized gang of profiteers and gamblers who are bent on nothing but the attainment of power and place? If you'd rather confine the question to an individual case, what precisely is Lengnau's function? How important is he? Is it his job to inspire the leaders or to provide eye-wash for fools?"

"Really, I couldn't have asked him all that. But in your heart of hearts, what sort of answer are *you* inclined to make?"

"How can I know? I must say I'm not too happy about that 'Well, what of it?' of his."

"You think that throws light on what you've been saying?"

"Yes, I do. It's not the kind of thing a leader would say, or one who inspires leaders. . . . It's the kind of thing one would expect from an astrologer. If you'd rather, I'll put it this way: either it's the remark of a man who lives with his head in the clouds, or it's a piece of sheer stupidity."

Jerphanion frowned and scratched his head. Then, suddenly, with an air of being partly serious, he said loudly:

"You make me sick!"

Jallez gave a jump.

"What do you mean, I make you sick?"

"Just that, you make me sick!"

"One doesn't abuse people without telling them why."

"You've already stopped me once—from joining the party."

"*I* stopped you? I like that! I never lifted a finger to stop you. If you're not old enough to take responsibility for your own acts, go and pick a quarrel with your friend Laulerque. I suppose you'll say next that I'm stopping you from becoming a Mason. Do you want to become one?"

"That's not the point."

"Isn't it?"

"No, the point is that when I came here, I felt I was coming to talk things over with a man of exceptional ability, the sort of man one doesn't meet every day. I had just had a profoundly moving experience. . . ."

"In which you include, of course, that admirable phrase: 'Well, what of it?' "

"I only told you that because I wanted to be perfectly honest. Every big experience, every big man, has a weak point somewhere. You go and make a mountain out of a mole-hill!"

Jallez seemed to be annoyed. Perhaps he had other reasons for his bitterness.

"The trouble with you," he said sharply, "is that you're not only a shrewd peasant by nature, but you add to that the craftiness of a country priest. You want to make people believe that you're longing to devote yourself to great causes, while all the time you won't do anything that involves a risk; and then you accuse others of damping your generous enthusiasms. I shall call you 'he-who-wants-but-doesn't-dare'!"

Jerphanion reddened. The phrase "wants-but-doesn't-dare" reminded him of Clanricard. "How lucky," he thought, "that I didn't talk to Jallez about Mathilde and my scruples! What an argument that would have given him!"

Now that Jallez was started, he showed no signs of stopping.

"Write to Rothweil," he said, "just to please me, or to Lengnau, whichever you prefer, and tell them you've seen the light. You'll make a magnificent Brother. I can see you with an apron on your stomach and a lot of dangling thingumbobs. You've already got the chief thing that's wanted, a beard."

Jerphanion bit his lip and looked at his friend in silence. Then:

"If you heard someone talking like that about serious things, *you'd* be annoyed," he said. "You never think anything's serious except what happens to interest you."

The sharpness went out of his voice as he continued:

"Do you know that all the time Lengnau was talking to me about this drive that's been going on through the centuries, this conspiracy for the Unity of man, this Plan, I was thinking of you. Yes, I was thinking: 'This would seem grand to Jallez, he'd recognize in all this the marks of greatness which he loves to welcome wherever he meets them!' It's a terrible thought—yes, terrible—that really fine men can misunderstand one another so hopelessly. That's why everything goes wrong, and the rotters come out on top."

Jallez turned away his head.

"If I give you the impression that I was blind to the greatness of what you have told me," he said, "I was wrong. But I thought that in your case it was a matter not of admiring this movement, but of actually becoming part of it. . . . Do you really want to do that? If you do, then don't ask anyone's advice . . . unless you're the kind of man who can say a thing to himself and yet resent it when the same thing is said by somebody else, even when he's given the impression that he wants it said. . . . Forgive me, old man. I'm in a bad mood today. Twenty past one already? I must go."

Chapter

32

THE BREATH OF THE PIT

"Well, that's that! All this business of Freemasonry gets on my nerves, and his other manias which never come to anything. It's the common side of him coming out, almost a sort of dishonesty; and he's frightened of me. As a result of all this talk I shall be late. The little square with its ruins; stone piled on stone; the song that stones can sing; these quays along the Seine, how calm a sense of exaltation they can give! And the river! —amazing to think that it can swell to such a size, that it can inundate these streets. But sooner or later it finds its own level again. That's the way with every kind of excess—to reach a point of crisis and then to subside—a superficial thought, perhaps, but it helps one to endure life's changes. The square with a ruin in it—the place where I found her again, that Christmas Eve, after losing her for so long, where perhaps today I'm fated to lose her again. The whirligig of time! I'll take her to a hotel somewhere between the canal and the Gare de Lyon. Do I really want her still?"

He wasn't sure. He didn't feel particularly in the mood to make love, though he realized that the idea of making love is perfectly compatible with an attitude of contempt, of disgust, and even of anger. What mattered to him at the moment was to have Juliette there before him so that he could study her at leisure, observe her. He was consumed with impatience to know, yet capable of waiting patiently to attain his knowledge. Gradually, inevitably, she would be compelled to confess. By degrees the truth would be forced from her.

He had thought at first of taking her for one of their walks in a cemetery, but a room would be better. Concealment is less easy indoors. Within the intimacy of four walls her lies would be less proof against the attack of his questions. Better to let this meeting seem like all the others; better to observe the usual rites, including those of the body.

"She's lied to me. She's made me guilty of a lie, of one of the worst lies it's possible to be guilty of, of the lie I'd least anticipated: of adultery. If what I've been told is true, I'm steeped in adultery." The thought made him angry; it hurt him to think that he had been involved, unknowingly, in adultery. He didn't pose as a plaster saint; it was not impossible that he should find himself in the position of seducing somebody else's wife, though as a rule he had a pretty low opinion of that kind of prowess, but if such a thing should happen, he must at least be allowed to take responsibility for his actions.

"If I hadn't happened to go out early the day that poor wretch came to see me, if he had found me instead of Jerphanion . . . I'm not thinking so much of the fact that I should have felt a fool, hearing it all, like that, from the husband, nor that my air of surprise would have seemed to him a miserable little bit of play-acting . . . it's a more human aspect of the situation that obsesses me now, the thought of suddenly finding myself face to face with a chap on whom I've just inflicted about the worst wrong that one man can be guilty of to another, with a chap whose grievance hasn't got even the saving grace of violence, but who simply and without comment displays the fact of his pain and of my injustice. . . . At least I could have given him my word of honour that . . . But should I have given it? Wouldn't self-love have stood in the way—the fear that he mightn't believe me, even an element of what certain people like to call gallantry? . . . the sort of people who think it smart in such circumstances to be taken for a sad dog, whose code of behaviour is on a par with that of duellists or gamblers—morality with an eyeglass."

He hated to think that the first woman he had ever completely loved should have been stolen from somebody else. The idea seemed to reach back and dirty in retrospect all his discovery of passion. Well, that's what came of avoiding so carefully all the grubby little adventures which satisfied the other young men of his age; that's what came of thinking over and over again this problem of love before admitting it to the intimacy of his heart! But something else there was which caused him even acuter suffering, an instinct, perhaps, of the animal in him, of the primitive man. Who can say? Why should it not be that certain values in life are comprehensible only through instinct? May there not be a wisdom of life older than the wisdom of cities, deeper than reason can plumb?

He had believed in the virginity of his woman, gloried in it in obedience to the unwritten laws of mankind, and more than most he had deserved virginity, since he had brought to her what no unwritten laws demanded—his own. He had been fooled, and he felt the humiliation of not having seen through the trick. But there was more in it than that. True, he remembered a certain feeling of surprise that first day, a suspicion that had occurred to him, but which he had silenced out of loyalty towards his beloved, and because he had a hatred of undisciplined thoughts; besides, it's never easy to be sure in such matters even when one's had long practice in love. (That certainly was the opinion of his friend the "crafty peasant," which he had voiced as they walked one day in the northern suburbs.) But it was not for this reason that a sense of bitterness assailed him. A noble soul is hurt by the discovery of deception, not because it wounds self-love, but because it involves the loss of an ideal. A human being, chosen tenderly and with love as the medium through which belief in human nature is to be asserted, gives the lie to that assertion. That's what matters, and what matters most of all is not having been fooled, but seeing something precious, something crowned and glorious, suddenly brought low.

"Can she really have done this thing to me? Why should she do it? Urged by what perverse taste for deception? What was there to stop her from telling me the truth that Christmas Eve—more than a year, almost eighteen months, ago—when we found each other again? The fact that I had left her should have made it easy, should have given her the excuse she needed. 'You went away, so I acted as I pleased. I'm not accountable to you.' She needn't have met me, or, if she wanted to see me again and felt she couldn't blurt everything out at once, why couldn't she have written me a line first, giving me some hint that would have prepared me, would have prepared both of us, for her confession? I don't understand it, any more than I understand how she could bring herself to get married. When did she do that? Not that it matters, but it certainly can't have been before we parted; that would be beyond belief. But between the time of our parting and that Christmas Eve, so short a time had elapsed. That day, then, in her dark cape, she was already a young married woman? A young married woman! I don't begin to understand. It's not likely that she was forced into marriage: her parents were always under her thumb, and when she liked she could be as obstinate as a mule. No, a few months, a few weeks, were all she needed to console herself for our parting—a parting which, she has told me so often since, plunged her into despair. In that short time she could meet somebody else, get engaged, get married, get sufficiently sick of her husband to meet me again without a qualm, and, a few days later, grant me everything I asked as though it were the most natural thing in the world. I did nothing to bring pressure on her; I merely said, quite simply, quite openly, that if we were going to see each other often, it seemed to me absurd that we should not be lovers; that I hadn't the courage to start all over again that long process of abstention which once we had observed, but which I no longer believed in. I told her that I could promise nothing, that, as a matter of fact, for purely personal reasons, I felt less attracted than ever by the idea of marriage. I never tried to appeal to her pity. I told her she was perfectly free, I warned her. I even went out of my way to impress upon her the fact that my planning, my intentions, were purely selfish. . . . I don't understand. . . . And then how about all that's happened since? To think that for fifteen months she managed to keep up this almost daily game; to think that she's never given herself away; never, by so much as a word or an action, hinted at the truth; that in the moments of our greatest intimacy, when everything seemed to be so frank between us, she never felt driven to cry out: 'Oh, Pierre, Pierre, I can't go on!' It's amazing, it's the kind of thing I mean when I talk of hell!"

He had reasoned so surely that he could no longer think of anything as true, or as true enough to exclude its apparent opposite. Ezzelin's visit to the College had actually taken place; Louvois and Jerphanion had certainly not conspired to invent it. There was no room for doubt. But Jallez still hoped for some miraculous intervention which might prove reality at fault.

Suddenly he asked himself a question: "Will she come? Jerphanion told me, of course, that the fellow promised not to mention his visit to her. But was he able to keep his promise? And if she knows that I have found out, will she be brave enough to come?"

He saw before him the "little square with a ruin in it." It was a very different day from that other. The light was sharper, more full of life, making the world seem happier, emerging already from the darkness of winter. To the left, on the square's outer edge, he saw the outline of a young woman who was almost motionless. He wasn't yet sure whether it was Juliette. With each step he took he thought he recognized her a little more certainly, but still he hesitated. It was as though the agony that turned and twisted in his breast like a nest of ants, like a mass of worms, was preventing him from getting any association into his ideas, stopping the details of his vision from forming into proof and certainty:

"It is her hat . . . her cloak . . . her way of holding herself." . . . And then, suddenly, a thought dawned in his mind: "Juliette Ezzelin. . . . Her name will be Juliette Ezzelin!" It seemed to him that the whole amazing improbability of the situation was concentrated in that single fact. The square came nearer; he could see each stone of the ruins, the smallest shrubs. He recognized a certain hat of hers that threw a deep shade on her eyes; a black plush coat she had that reached half-way down her skirt. He recognized her figure, the curve of her shoulder.

"Juliette Ezzelin? Juliette Ezzelin?"

A crowd of emotions swept together into his mind: anger, irony, a noble scorn, a desire to kill her, a desire to drive far away this woman who belonged to him, a desire to walk by her side without looking at her.

They had been together for an hour; for forty minutes of it they had been in this room.

At first they had walked the streets almost in silence. Pierre had tried to stay calm, but his face had had an odd look. Several times she had asked:

"What's wrong with you today?"

He had answered with forced cheerfulness:

"Nothing special, really nothing. . . ."

She said no more until they reached the next corner, smiling a little nervously, looking at him out of the corner of her eye. But then she returned to the attack:

"I know you so well. . . . You're hiding something from me. Is it something wrong I've done?"

He thought to himself: "I could say straight out: 'Why didn't you tell me you were married?' Another man wouldn't hesitate." But he still hoped that she would tell him of her own free will. He didn't want to deprive her of this last chance of redeeming her lies, or take from her this opportunity for one poor act of grace.

He thought also: "How often she must have suffered with a secret like that on her heart! . . . Each time that I was a little gloomy, that I failed to smile, that I was less tender than usual with her. . . . How could she stick it?" He was amazed at the extent of this profound and foolish courage.

For a while she pretended to sulk, but all the time she was looking at him. As a rule he was alive to her least whim and mood, but now he obviously regarded this fit of sulks as a feeble weapon which he could brush aside, the moment he wanted to, with a flick of the wrist.

Then she tried being tenderly reproachful. "You don't love me any more, is that it? You're tired of me? You used to seem so happy when we met . . . when you used to take me to some room."

Never had she complained more sweetly or put such a note of tenderness into her sorrow. He listened to her in silence, half smiling. It gave him no pleasure to see another's suffering, but he thought it fair that she should suffer a little. Besides, he did not wish to surrender the position of quite exceptional advantage which he occupied at present. He had suspected for a long time that Juliette was clever in her own way, and he was inclined to believe now that, if she wanted, she could be a hundred times cleverer than he. "Once the battle is really joined, what tricks won't she produce for her own protection, what means won't she find for making me look a fool, for forcing me, in my turn, to stand on the defensive?" He took full advantage, therefore, without any feeling of guilt, of these few moments in which she scented danger but, not knowing its nature, could do no more than hang her head like a coaxing child, while in the secrecy of her heart she gathered her forces.

And now she was in the bed, lying naked on her back, her body twisted a little, her legs half-bent. She had drawn the sheet over her. It lay slantingly across her, showing more of one breast than of the other. Her head, pressed backwards, made a deep dent in the pillow. She lay with her right arm behind her head in an attitude of misery. He could see the dark tuft of hair in her armpit.

She was staring straight before her. There was a strained look in her eyes, fierce, almost hard. She had shed no tears, but her expression made him think of tears, of a flood of tears pressing from within against the mask of her face.

The words she spoke seemed curiously incompatible with her expression. Her voice was clear and relatively calm. More than anything else it was the voice of one who reasons quietly. There was scarcely any trace in it of irritation or of irony. She spoke as a woman might speak who was trying to soothe a lover obsessed by persecution mania, on whom the only effect of his unjust charges might ultimately be to produce a state of nervous strain.

"I tell you again, you're mad. . . . I don't see even that I've got to justify myself, since I don't understand what exactly it is that you're getting at. If only you'd tell me who could have put such an idea into your head. . . . There are plenty of evil-minded people. . . . Perhaps you got an anonymous letter? . . . It's extraordinary how silly an intelligent man can be; really, it's enough to make one cry. . . . If you were a grocer, I could understand an anonymous letter affecting you like that. . . . But you, a man of your education! . . . I can't tell you how disappointed I am."

He too, lying naked beside her, forced himself to remain calm. But the effort made him seem like a slow agent of the torture.

"There's no question," he said, "of an anonymous letter. How I found out doesn't matter."

"You won't tell me how you found out?—how you pretend you found out?"

"I tell you again, that's a mere detail. You shall know later. It seems to me that it's you who ought to do the explaining, and the explanation I want is of *what* I found out."

"If you won't tell me where you got this fairy-tale, I'll tell *you*! You just invented the whole thing!"

He started to reply, but stopped himself, overcome with amazement. The slow, heavy sound of a wagon came to them from the street, the horse's steps one after another, the iron shoes striking the ground with a noise that was at once hard and muffled. Jallez, hearing, in a mood that was akin to a lucid interval of drunkenness, found himself delighting in the sound's power to move and calm him with its mingling of softness and metallic strength. He was conscious of a rush of indignation, of anger, that threatened to turn him dizzy, and set himself to resist it. He tried to force his reason to argue against itself. "Remember that you're dealing with a woman. You look at things from too masculine a point of view, too logically. You don't know enough about women; you don't know how to deal with them. Here you are, trying to reduce her by dint of argument, to force her to confess by proving to her that her attitude is absurd. It's easy for her to laugh at that kind of thing. What's putting you out is the reasonable attitude she's adopting on her side. She's not listening to *your* arguments. All you're doing is to make her angry, and you'll end by making yourself angry too. Give it up."

He looked at the woman's body which the sheet revealed and hid, at those lines and shapes which to a man are so inexhaustibly wonderful. He saw the colour of her skin, smelled its scent. He thought of his own nakedness, not with shame, but aware of the degree of weakness it implied in him at such a moment. He forced himself to admit that merely to be right is nothing. He remained silent.

But she went on:

"Besides, it's easy enough for you to convince yourself that you're wrong. Go to my home and ask. Question my mother's concierge."

She spoke almost calmly: only in certain inflexions of her voice was there a trace of strangeness.

Once again Pierre was so astonished that he crossed his arms and said nothing. He looked at her. "Is she mad? What's her game? Is she playing for time, for an hour, for a day? But what good will it do her? Does she think I shall get tired of questioning her? Doesn't it occur to her that even if I get tired today, the craving to know will take hold of me again?"

He felt suddenly frightened, horrified, as though he were suddenly in contact with, intimately involved in, that obscure region of the universe where falsehood, crime, and madness mingle and breed. He said again to himself that it was as much good trying to penetrate into such a corner of hell by the exercise of his reason as it would be to take a candle into some underground shaft where neither flame nor lungs can withstand the poisonous gases.

He leaned over and kissed her high on the forehead.

"My poor darling," he murmured.

Her face twitched, but she said nothing.

He continued in a low voice, speaking as gently as he could:

"I am trying to put myself in your place. . . . Obviously, I don't know everything, and unless I can get some idea of what's been

happening— Surely, I should understand better than anyone? . . .
I am your best friend. Be sure of one thing, my sweet, that I'm not
in the slightest degree angry with you. Don't tell me anything now;
you're in no state for explanations. . . . Let's leave it at that. . . .
You know that I know. . . . Perhaps, thinking it all over tonight,
you'll see that you were wrong to let me go away in the state of mind
that's been forced upon me, that it would have been better to— Well,
you'll see how you feel. . . ."

As he spoke the words "go away," she turned and suddenly looked
at him. But almost immediately she again averted her eyes.

"Tonight," she said in a whisper, "tonight I may have killed
myself."

Two hours later Juliette clung to Pierre in the dusk, weeping. She
choked, she groaned, at moments she almost cried aloud. Her face
was swollen. For the twentieth time she stammered out: "You won't
leave me? You won't leave me? I only did it because I was terrified
of losing you. . . . Say you believe me, Pierre, say you believe me!"

He had a profound sense of pity. He, too, was utterly exhausted.
Life had never seemed to him so miserable. He dreamed of solitude
somewhere, God alone knew where; of some little mountain valley,
some barren heath, some deep forest. He thought of monks, belonging to some strange religion, returning from their work with their
spades on their shoulders. . . . Soon now they would be in their
chapel, singing a hymn. "O world, is it thus you punish me for
having left you?"—with some such words as those their psalm might
open.

He stroked her face, and his eyes looked out above her body into
the room, as though at some future coming slowly to birth in the
dusk. His eyes, brighter than ever, but now a little haggard, asked
a question. But he could see nothing clearly.

THE LONELY

TWO DOCUMENTS

The issue of the *Temps* for the 15th of April 1910 contained the following article which filled its second and third columns:

"A RIFT IN THE LUTE

"Coming, as it does, on the eve of the Parliamentary elections, and following hard on the heels of the imprudent old-age pensions bill, a bill of which we had reason to believe that he was ill-advised enough to be proud, the resignation of M. Gurau from the Ministry of Labour, which, under any circumstances, would have been an event of importance in Parliamentary circles, takes on peculiar significance and deserves, we think, very particular attention.

"Not that his letter of resignation, which has been already published in the press, nor the paragraph issued by the Havas Agency, which seems to be the work of the same pen, throws much light on the incident. It is not in the nature of such documents, nor their intention, to admit the reader to the inner workings of their author's mind. Was it not M. Clemenceau, who, apropos of a member of his party, once jokingly said: 'When I want to know why he took a certain course of action, I read his announcement to the press. Among all possible reasons, those which he gives in print are undoubtedly false. What the true ones were, I discover by a process of elimination.' We shall not make use, in the present case, of so irreverent a method of induction, not but that the attractive and complex personality of the ex-Minister of Labour is of a kind to justify, we might almost say encourage, a certain subtlety of interpretation. We feel, however, that we are within our rights when we suggest that perhaps M. Gurau has not revealed the secret springs of his thought when he declares, as he does in the note of the Havas Agency, that since he has been compelled by his opponents at Tours to prepare for an election campaign of great bitterness, he does not wish to take the field armed with the advantages, if only the moral advantages, that attach to him in virtue of his position as an active Minister; that therefore he has been at pains to procure himself complete liberty of action. It had not occurred to us that the delightful district of Touraine gives birth to party passions of such acerbity that intending candidates feel themselves forced to take preliminary measures of so exceptional a nature. Still, *experto credamus Roberto*.

"We can get a little more light on the incident if we glance at the issues of the *Sanction* which have been published during the present half-year. Not that the resignation of M. Gurau, whose position of importance on the staff of that paper is well known, was either very plainly announced or actually discussed in its columns. Our contemporary has shown remarkable discretion. But even the most hasty reader of the *Sanction* cannot but have noticed that, for some months past, M. Briand's social policy has not been receiving very enthusiastic support, and that in particular the old-age pensions bill—that bill which has had the strange experience of being supported by M. Jaurès, opposed by M. Jules Guesde, and passed by an almost unanimous vote of both Chambers, neither of which really wanted it and both of which secretly thought it impracticable—that this bill, we say, has been the object, in the pages of the *Sanction,* less of praise than of criticism (criticism, it is scarcely necessary to add, based on quite other arguments than our own). Every objection raised to the measure in Syndicalist circles was blandly reproduced, and we were treated to the alluring spectacle of a paper which is known to be entirely sympathetic to a certain Minister making covert attacks upon a bill which that same Minister has officially to defend. Under the guise of pointing out the difficulties which the government in power would find in their attempt to give effect to the proposed law, M. Gurau's friends, condemned by reason of his Cabinet rank to temporary silence, have missed no chance of inflicting a series of pin-pricks on M. Briand and of denigrating his activities and the general trend of his policy, as things illusory and dangerous.

"Are we to suppose that the sensational speech delivered last Sunday at Saint-Chamond by the President of the Council was intended to stress, rather than to minimize, a potential divergence of opinion within the government? However that may be, it is clear that the rift between the two Ministers has widened, and we shall be much surprised if M. Gurau—who doubtless will soon be returning to his old occupation of journalism—does not take advantage of the situation to set his name to a series of slogans which will be greedily snapped up and used, as soon as the elections are over, by the opponents of the national union.

"Dare we say that for our part we are not sorry for what has occurred? The personal policy of M. Gurau, and the more or less long-term ambitions which he may entertain, present a separate problem, to which we shall have occasion to return. They do not demand immediate consideration. The lesson to be learned from the present situation is for us, and for others, obvious enough. It stresses a very real danger. M. Briand may have broken irreparably with his old political associates, to whose violent attacks he is more and more exposed, but that does not alter the fact that he is only too anxious to deal tactfully with them and to offer them security for the future. Officially he is holding out the olive-branch to the Centre and even to the Right, however superficial, however suspect his attempts at reconciliation may seem to some of us to be, but there can be no doubt that he is simultaneously making tacit promises, to call them by no worse a name, to members of the extreme Left. Let us hope that he will realize in time that his blandishments may be ill returned, and that his desire to win over, at any price, the open or secret enemies of the social order may result in embarrassment to himself. It will be well if the electors, more far-seeing than Macbeth, realize in time that beneath the pleasant branches of a reform movement, more or less coloured with Syndicalism, the army of Revolution advances."

Jerphanion had been commissioned to compose for M. de Saint-Papoul a manifesto to be entitled "People of Bergerac, we must come into the open!" which was to conclude with the following quotation from the Saint-Chamond speech, printed in large capitals: "The Republic belongs to no party."

He was working on it when he received the following letter.

"My Dear Friend:

"What had to happen has happened. Today I underwent the rites of initiation. I would willingly have waited still longer before taking this step, had I had any hope that we might take it together, but I have a feeling that you have already decided, for the time being at any rate, against committing yourself. It was from a wish to be tactful, therefore, that I did not press you further in the matter, on the occasion of our last meeting, though I had already received my summons to the fateful session.

"I do not think that I shall be betraying my oath of secrecy if I communicate to you a few of my impressions of today's ceremony. We have so often discussed these things that I cannot bring myself to regard you as a stranger where they are concerned. We even promised, you may remember, that the first of us to enter the Order should confide in the other. I know that such a promise cannot be completely fulfilled, since it is incompatible with sincere membership, but fortunately my conscience is clear. I run no risk of being false to my oath, because, as a matter of fact, I have nothing to reveal to you that you did not know already. I do want you to realize, however—and in saying this I am infringing no Masonic secret, since what I am about to say is negative only—that certain details which you found particularly distasteful were not quite fairly represented. For instance, I have every reason to suppose that the sham execution and other stories of the same sort are purely legendary. What really interests you is the moral aspect of the movement. I should be deceiving you if I pretended that I was conscious of no embarrassment. I certainly was at first, especially when I found myself alone in the Hall of Mirrors. I admit that the scheme of decoration is slightly ridiculous, and that the questions which are put to one, as well as the wording of the oath, are rather schoolboyish. One must not forget, however, that all institutions, of whatever kind they be, all ritual ceremonies, must be designed to appeal to the capacities and satisfy the demands of *average* people. It is too much to hope that one will always have to do with those of exceptional intelligence.

"Speaking generally, I can say that I managed to accept these preliminary formalities at their face value, without losing sight of the great ideal to which they have made me a party. To sum up, I can honestly say that though the prospect of taking this step has caused me much nervous uncertainty, I am not sorry now of the decision that I made. La Fontaine says that the over-sensitive are unhappy. That is true in the domain of art, but truer still in matters of action.

"Let me know when you have an evening to spare. I have given your messages of goodwill to Mlle Mathilde Cazalis.

"Yours affectionately,

"ED. CLANRICARD."

SUMMARY

Jerphanion goes to a bar in the boulevard Sébastopol, where he has arranged to meet Clanricard. They exchange views about their own generation and about the way in which its demands and ideals differ from those of their elders. They discuss such questions as Church and anti-Church, Freemasonry, Sampeyre, the Third Republic. Clanricard mentions the ideas of Laulerque and suggests a meeting. This meeting takes place the same evening in a café in the Place Clichy after Jerphanion has dined at the College and had a brief talk with Jallez. Mathilde Cazalis is present at it. Laulerque elaborates his views on Socialism, on the threat of a European war, and on the position of the individual in history. He develops an odd theory of a world controlled by secret societies and discusses the question whether one should become a Mason. Laulerque walks home with Jerphanion and tells him in confidence of an interview he has had with a mysterious bookseller who turns out to be the agent of an international secret society. Jerphanion finishes the walk alone and decides not to wake Jallez in order to tell him of his evening's experience.

Germaine Baader, Sammécaud, Treilhard, Marquis, Avoyer, the dramatist Henry Mareil, his mistress Suzette Vignal, and the journalist Bérénine, all meet at supper in a smart restaurant. They exchange gossip (*Chantecler,* the Rostands, etc.), and Bérénine makes several epigrams. The object of the meeting is to persuade Mareil to offer the lead in his next play to Germaine. Mareil's career and psychology are described. Sammécaud takes Germaine back in his car and embarks on certain intimacies which she absent-mindedly permits.

Jallez and Jerphanion take a long walk in the suburbs, starting from the Clignancourt gate. They talk of many things: of the dog Macaire, of Tellière and Gentilcœur and the perfect life, of Jeanne the dressmaker's assistant and the morality of the lower classes, of physical love and the terrors of infinity. They go through Saint-Denis, look at its monuments, and evoke the image of a woman's body. We find them again at a country inn, making out a list of their special preferences. The same evening Jerphanion jots down his various suppositions about Jallez's love-affair and analyses his friend's liking for cemeteries.

Jerphanion and Clanricard pay a visit to Rothweil to discuss the possibility of their becoming Masons. Before seeing them Rothweil has an interview with a woman whom he appears to know intimately. He approves of the young men's intention. After they have gone he leaves for a meeting at the other end of Paris, which is now under flood.—Stephen Bartlett's travel diary: the part he has been playing in the English elections; his impressions of the Paris floods.—Maurice Ezzelin gets an anonymous letter which tells him of his wife's relations with a young man. Juliette returns from a meeting with Pierre, and he shows her the letter. A domestic scene follows.—Sammécaud and Champcenais drop into a bar, where they discuss Champcenais's part in the Celle development scheme and the possibility of making use of Gurau.—Gurau's pleasant reflections in his office at the Ministry. Sammécaud is announced, and he arranges to see him before an interview he has arranged with the Comte de Mun. At the end of the afternoon he reads over the notes he has taken of de Mun's conversation. He goes to see Briand with the intention of doing what Sammécaud has asked him. After dining out it occurs to him to pay Germaine a visit, but just as he is about to go up to her flat, he sees a man's shadow against her window.

Laulerque asks Jerphanion to meet him at a café and tells him that he has become a member of the secret society about which he has already told him. He introduces him to a certain Ardannseaux, a renegade Freemason, who gives Jerphanion all sorts of details about the inner life of the Order.

THE LONELY

At the College, during Jallez's absence, Jerphanion receives Maurice Ezzelin and listens to his grievances. After a great deal of hesitation he mentions the affair to Jallez, who evades the subject.

Mionnet has an interview with the Comte de Mézan, who tries to interest him in favour of Saint-Papoul's election campaign. He talks to the Abbé Cabirol, and later goes to see Monseigneur Lebaigue, who congratulates him on his paper: "A Short View. . . ."

Jerphanion, at the suggestion of Rothweil, pays a call on Lengnau, who explains to him the profound idealism and noble aims of Masonry. Jerphanion leaves with mixed feelings and discusses the interview with Jallez, whom he has arranged to meet at a little restaurant. They have a bitter disagreement. Pierre meets Juliette, and they go together to a hotel bedroom, where they have a miserable explanation.

An article in the *Temps* about Gurau's resignation, and a letter from Clanricard in which he tells Jerphanion that he has become a Mason.

BOOK EIGHT:
PROVINCIAL INTERLUDE

Chapter

THE ELECTION AT BERGERAC

At the elections of 1910 the first count in the second parliamentary district of Bergerac, which took place on the 24th of April, resulted as follows (the figures quoted are those published in the *Temps* of the 26th; the ensuing revision by the municipal authorities made very little difference):

	Votes recorded: 13,822
Number of registered voters: 15,401.	
Doctor Bonnefoux. Radical-Socialist	6,145
de Saint-Papoul. Republican of the Left	5,513
d'Enjalbal de Nizes. Conservative	1,032
Gouzennes. International Labour	612
Touch. Farmers' Union	321
Giordano. Anti-Masonic Republican	191

On the 25th, Saint-Papoul's principal supporters were summoned to an important council of war. The meeting was held in a first-floor room of the Café de l'Univers in the Place du Palais at Bergerac, where the party's committee rooms had been established.

Those present were: the Marquis de Saint-Papoul; M. Hector Crivelli, the expert in charge of the campaign; Messieurs Pauthes and Pelfigues, the mayors of two of the largest communes; M. Ratier, Town Councillor of the Canton of Villamblard; M. Soulard the undertaker, president of the Republican Club; M. Roques, proprietor of *L'Animateur,* a local paper active in support of the Marquis's interests and entrusted with the printing of the bills and other literature needed in the campaign.

Each of these gentlemen had a glass of absinthe before him, with the single exception of the Marquis, who had ordered a bottle of

Vichy water. He was suffering from a complete breakdown of the digestive system. In spite of all his resolutions to the contrary and of all his efforts to abstain, he had found himself compelled during the past fortnight to absorb a vast quantity of wines, apéritifs, and even of spirits. Excessive sobriety would have served him ill with his constituents. Votes are given more readily to a man who can carry his liquor. It would take ten years of physical exercise to make up for two such weeks of excess. He was conscious of a burning sensation throughout the length and breadth of his body, of a feeling that something was gnawing at his vitals and eructating in his belly, of a contraction of his muscles and of fire within. The feeling began at the back of his mouth and ended at his buttocks, with an area of concentration somewhere between his ribs and his navel. How on earth would he be able to summon up sufficient courage to swallow, between now and the 8th of May, another couple of hundred glasses, even if they contained nothing more violent than Vichy or even than plain water? Experience shows that once a certain point of digestive chaos has been reached, even water from the tap acts on the stomach like corrosive fluid. Nor can complete abstinence avert the evil. It is as though the bodily organs, trained to endure punishment at certain fixed intervals, resort to self-torment if it fails of recurrence. So acute a state of bodily discomfort did not tend to make the Marquis take an optimistic view of his chances.

In addition to everything else, the weather was atrociously hot. Two of the gentlemen had taken off their coats. The rest, with the exception of the Marquis, had been content to unbutton their waistcoats and loosen their belts, with the result that their shirts bellied out and showed the tags at their base projecting like little tongues. Now and then one or other of the company would take hold of this tag, which lay so conveniently to the hand, and would give it a series of short tugs while he spoke, thus inducing a slight draught.

They all spoke in the accent of the south-west. The Marquis had found himself using it more and more as the campaign progressed, and Crivelli, who was a Corsican from Marseilles, found no great difficulty in adopting it, which he did from an instinctive motive of politeness. It had only been necessary for him to speak in a lower register than usual, to keep his voice well centred on his chest, and to avoid certain nasal peculiarities and contortions of the throat. The general conversation was thus a flow of quick, full sounds, clearly and firmly articulated. The various voices, though sounding each at a different pitch, combined pleasantly, though now and again, as the discussion grew heated, the general harmony of tone was broken by an occasional queer, shrill contribution from Crivelli, who forgot, in the excitement of the moment, to keep a careful watch on his speech.

The meeting was engaged in reviewing the situation. Opinion in general held that it was encouraging but critical, though individuals differed in the degree in which they leaned one way or the other. Hector Crivelli represented the party of extreme confidence; the Marquis, its opposite. He said little, frowned frequently, and from time to time laid an anxious hand upon his stomach.

The figures published on the previous day were examined in detail. The fact that Dr. Bonnefoux had a lead of 632 could not be denied, nor could the company help admitting that merely to top the poll at the first count was bound to help. Several hundred doubtful or nervous voters would be sure to rally to the apparent winner and give him their second choices.

A careful reckoning of the figures, however, showed that the doctor, assuming that he could rely on swinging the poll so far given to the Labour candidate, couldn't possibly go above 6,757 as his total. There remained a margin of 7,057, or three hundred more than the doctor's possible reserve. The question was whether the Marquis could manage to get hold of them.

Certain aspects of the published figures demanded careful attention.

In the first place, the total number of voters was remarkable. Almost fourteen thousand out of less than fifteen thousand five hundred registered had gone to the poll (89 per cent), a higher percentage than any attained in the district in living memory. Such a result was in itself sufficient evidence of the bitterness of the struggle. It was scarcely to be expected that many new voters could be routed out for the second ballot. The number of abstentions could doubtless be accounted for by bedridden old men, village idiots, and folk who had long ago decided to have nothing to do with politics. Hector Crivelli, however, urged that a last effort be made to comb out the constituency, arguing that by dint of spending a little more money the Marquis could still rake together two or three hundred fresh supporters. After all, bedridden old men could be got to the poll in cars, and even a village idiot could be furnished with a political conscience for an hour or two.

The next point to be considered was the comparatively high number of votes polled by the Vicomte d'Enjalbal de Nizes, and by this Socialist fellow, Gouzennes. The figures had come as a double surprise, for no one had imagined that the Labour candidate could rely on more than three hundred names, and the Marquis's friends had been convinced that though the supporters of the extreme Right might conceivably number something in the neighbourhood of a thousand, they would probably be frittered away among the various candidates. But now, at a blow, the Vicomte d'Enjalbal, a petty aristocrat of Sarlat who had a house in Bergerac, and this Gouzennes, who was a country schoolmaster, had both emerged as adversaries to be reckoned with.

It remained to forecast the probable trend of events and to decide upon the best plan of campaign in the circumstances.

M. Ratier, the Town Councillor, was of the opinion that they had been wrong in regarding Dr. Castaing, the retiring member, as a negligible quantity. This old man of eighty-two, who had represented the district since the earliest days of the Republic, had announced at the time of the last elections that he would not again sit for the constituency. Time had obliterated any political colour he might originally have professed, and he had grown accustomed to being returned by a poll of eight or ten thousand, without any serious opponent in the field. He had frequently been elected unopposed.

"We were unwise and frivolous!" said Town Councillor Ratier, tugging at the tab of his shirt. He spoke in a resonant and remarkably flexible voice, articulating his sentences so that each syllable had the effect of a little bouncing ball. "I realize, of course, that Dr. Castaing stated explicitly his intention of remaining neutral, wishing, as he said, to end his days in happy agreement with all his neighbours, but that was no reason for us to neglect him. It was up to us to rouse in him a sense of civic duty, despite his age. We ought to have made him see that his whole life had been a lesson in toleration, a repudiation of destructive party strife, and to have urged him, on that account, to support, however discreetly, a candidate who stood for republican mildness and conciliation."

According to Ratier, the only thing to do was, at all costs, to get Dr. Castaing to write a short letter of approval, which Roques could then set up in type and display throughout the district. There was no need for the Grand Old Man to come out openly as a supporter of the Marquis. All he need do was to warn the electors against a policy of dissension, and perhaps to quote that sentence from Briand's speech, already famous, about the Republic being the preserve of no single party.

"I should like to stress the fact," continued Ratier, emphasizing each syllable, "that his being a doctor like Bonnefoux is in our favour. Like all colleagues, they heartily dislike each other."

He offered to approach Castaing himself. It was agreed that he should do so within the next twenty-four hours.

It would be as well also to put in a little work with the minor candidates of the Right, and Hector Crivelli undertook to deal with Giordano.

"He's nothing but an adventurer; I know the type. He's hard up, and I can buy his votes at ten francs a time. All you've got to do is to open, in my name, an account of twenty-five hundred francs; if I can get out for less, say for eighteen hundred or two thousand, so much the better."

(Malicious gossip had it that Giordano was nothing but a creature of Crivelli's, who had been persuaded to stand only to give colour to this modest financial operation.)

Touch, who represented the agrarian interest, was generally regarded as little better than a half-wit whose head had been turned by the example of Marcellin Albert. He preached to the peasants a hodge-podge of mystical Christianity and natural rights, with an eloquence which concealed the half-frenzied nature of his gospel. If he could be influenced, it would be only through the instrumentality of the Church, and here a word from the Abbé Cabirol might prove decisive.

The Marquis was quite definitely frightened of M. d'Enjalbal de Nizes. "I really believe the man's got a grudge against me," he said; "he's a little puffed-up nobody whom I've ignored, or seemed to ignore. . . . Frankly, I have never asked him to any of our parties at the château, or offered him a day's shooting, and I should hate to have to eat humble pie to him."

After considerable discussion it was agreed that here too the Church would furnish the most likely weapon. Perhaps Cabirol could be induced to use his influence in this case as well as with Touch, or perhaps some other means of approach could be found. The Marquis mentioned Monsignor Lebaigue. The others agreed that the petty landowner of Sarlat could scarcely ignore a hint dropped by the Archbishop of Paris (His Eminence would, of course, be left to choose his own methods) to the effect that the spectacle of two great gentlemen and good Catholics playing into the enemy's hands would produce the worst possible impression in high Church circles, not only in Périgord, but very much farther afield.

To sum up: So far as the opposition of the Right was concerned, there was every reason to hope that:

Giordano would retire in favour of the Marquis; that Touch would withdraw unconditionally, with, perhaps, a few opprobrious references to "a lot of atheistical and party swine"; that the Vicomte would retire to an accompaniment of veiled hints, the general upshot of which would be to urge upon his supporters, without any actual reference to the Marquis, the duty of behaving like true Catholics and true Frenchmen, that is to say, of preventing at all costs a victory for the Masons and the champions of the International. To make certain of the last of these events it might be necessary to let the Vicomte understand that he would be among the most welcome guests at the château and at the Marquis's shooting parties.

The case of Gouzennes was made the object of a hasty survey. Was it likely that this leader of the Revolutionary party would retire in favour of Bonnefoux? And, if so, how far would his followers be guided by his instructions? The question was left undecided.

Finally there was the Prefect to consider. (They were already sure of the Assistant Prefect, but he could do little without his chief.) The attitude of this official was doubtful. The instructions issued by Briand in his capacity as Minister of the Interior, which office he held jointly with that of President of the Council, had been definitely in favour of the Marquis. But the Prefect was a Mason. Officially he had given Saint-Papoul a certain amount of rather lukewarm support, but it could hardly be doubted that he was secretly siding with Bonnefoux. It was imperative that the Ministry should take disciplinary action, and that Briand should have the courage to say openly: "Monsieur de Saint-Papoul represents precisely my own policy. I attach great importance to his success."

Certain immediate steps were necessary before this plan of action could be set in motion. So far as Dr. Castaing was concerned, everything was settled, and Crivelli had undertaken to see to Giordano. The Marquis's share was to get at once into communication with the Comte de Mézan, through him to open up negotiations with the Abbé Mionnet, by means of the latter to set Cabirol once more in action, and, if possible, awaken the Archbishop to a realization of the position. In doing so he should not be afraid to assure Mionnet of some durable and quite exceptional mark of his gratitude and esteem. "Tell him he shall have a bishop's mitre as soon as he's old enough; that you pledge yourself to see that he's not overlooked."

But what was to be done about Briand? What strings could be pulled there? The assembled gentlemen ran over the various sources of influence they might be able to tap. Crivelli had friends who were on "the most intimate possible terms" with Briand. But his way of mentioning them and the sound of their names did not encourage the party to enlist their services. The Marquis suddenly remembered that he was distantly related to Admiral Bouey de Lapeyrère, Minister of the Navy. But on what terms was the Admiral with Briand? Was the chance worth risking? He asked for the general opinion, but showed his own lack of enthusiasm in the project by the pessimistic way in which he spoke of it and the gloomy expression of his face.

But the man from Marseilles was all for trying. "Have a shot!" he cried.

M. Soulard, president of the club, offered to do his best with Ruard, the Minister of Agriculture. "He's from the Haute-Garonne," he said, "and so is my wife. Her family and his are intimate. I can but try."

M. Pelfigues was of the opinion that no stone should be left unturned, and Crivelli agreed with him.

"Do you know what I should do in your place, Marquis?" he remarked: "I should write to this fellow Jerphanion, who's done so well for us up to now, and tell him to come along as fast as he can. He's pretty good with his pen, and the odds are that we shall want a speech or two at short notice, and a few knock-out slogans to scatter broadcast. If we wait to give him instructions by letter, it'll be so much time wasted."

Pelfigues, Pauthes, Ratier, and Soulard all agreed that Jerphanion was pretty good with his pen, a fact which the Marquis could scarcely deny. He disliked, however, this public reference to the young student's collaboration in the campaign, although he realized that it was no secret. He frowned, therefore, still more heavily, and objected that Jerphanion was kept in Paris by his work and that the authorities of the College would probably refuse him leave of absence. Roques supported the objection, hinting, rather bitterly, that there were those on the spot who could make just as good a showing on paper.

"What do you bet," cried the Corsican, turning to Saint-Papoul and ignoring the other, "that I get him here the day after tomorrow, and let him go again by Sunday night? Four days won't be too much for him, and that's all I want. I'll get him to run us up a nice little supply of ready-to-wear speeches in that time, and two last-minute manifestoes. We shall want those—one to be the kind of thing that everyone expects, the other a surprise."

As it was already nearly one o'clock and there was still a good deal to discuss, the company agreed to lunch together. They said "loonch" in the local manner. Those of them who lived in Bergerac objected that they hadn't told their wives that they wouldn't be home, but it was pointed out to them that during an election, as in war-time, wives ought to realize that husbands weren't their own masters. Besides, it was so late that the good ladies would probably have sat down already.

The argument ended by a mass movement from the Café de l'Univers to the Hôtel de Londres et des Voyageurs, which was well known for its cooking and its cellar.

Chapter

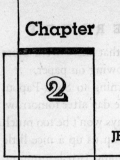

JERPHANION'S LETTER TO JALLEZ

My dear old fellow:

I had such a rush to get my train the other evening that there was no time to say good-bye or explain matters to you. But I've no doubt you caught on to what had happened, O man of nimble wits, and in any case it's a grand story, and superbly degrading! Dupuy played up splendidly. He gave me four days, and I got the impression that I could extend them to six. My excuse was brilliant. I told him that as I was dealing with La Boétie in my diploma thesis, I thought it would be a good thing to make a few investigations on the spot in the libraries and archives of Aquitaine. Don't give me away.

I meant to write to you as soon as I got here, but I was caught up in a whirl of business, so don't growl at me. The first object I ran into was Crivelli, the formidable Corsican robber who acts as agent to my noble master (not martyr). He's a marvel, and carries out his loathsome duties with perfect elegance. He has developed a manner which is a cross between that of a park-keeper, a fencing-master, and an ironmonger. He has a slight limp, which he says is the result of a fall from his horse when he was an officer-cadet at Saumur, which is as it may be. He's taken a liking to me and treats me as a colleague, spiriting me away into corners and holding me mysteriously by the arm. He regards the Marquis and his committee as so many customers for whom we've got to deliver the goods, so that the sooner we understand one another the better, which doesn't mean to say that we haven't got to do our best for them. I suspect a good deal of underhand business which I've not yet got the hang of.

The Marquis is a scream. He's a changed man, running round and shouting, and speaking patois with the best, and he doesn't seem to mind being tapped on the stomach by every purple-faced ragamuffin in the place. I'd even go so far, if I knew enough about the subject, as to say that he's becoming slovenly in his dress.

The question of where I was to live has been a hard nut to crack. The Marquis, probably as a result of being scolded by his wife, who's naturally mean, wanted to stow me away in the family château, which is a good fifteen miles away. By doing that he could have reduced my daily keep to about fifty centimes. But Crivelli went up in smoke: "Ah've got t' 'ave t'yoong chap under me hand!" So, to cut a long story short, here I am at the Hôtel du Centre, at special commercial rates, which work out at eight francs a day. I've got a room like a passage, all length and height, with double curtains dating from the time of my grandmother, which look as though they'd been hung as the result of a death-sentence and died in the most appalling convulsions. The bed sags, the victim of ten years of travelling salesmen's enormous bottoms, but it's soft enough, because travelling salesmen won't put up with hard beds. The red eider-down looks as though it's been used to polish a good number of toe-caps. The general effect promises fleas, but I owe it to the spirit of Truth—our common mistress—to say that so far not a single flea has shown its face.

To sum up, I'm in clover. I sleep until half past eight and don't get up till I've yawned dozens of times and given myself an extra snooze. I eat masses of excellent food. In this part of the world pigeons, chickens, foie-gras, and salmon trout are regarded as Spartan fare, and the landlady is surprised that I don't complain. Truffles are rather more common as flavouring than onions in the College kitchen (God forgive me for mentioning so sickening a subject!). I drink Sauterne and Saint-Émilion with every meal. I work during the morning, from ten to half past eleven. I hold a council of war with Crivelli, the ex-cadet of Saumur, over our midday drinks. After lunch I take a long time off in the interests of digestion, and my brain only begins to work again about four. Between times I go down to Roques's printing office to see the proofs of some handbill full of violence and insults, composed in my best manner, and coach the Marquis in his evening's speech. He pretends to regard what I have written for him as a mere sketch, put together according to his instructions, which he will elaborate himself. For instance, yesterday he said to me: "Let them have it good and hot," or "Give the Catholics something to smile at," or "Go easy now; most of the voters in this particular parish are Protestants." He's careful to save his face by slipping in a phrase or two of his own. I'm amazed by his memory. I read out what I've written, once, then he re-reads it and stuffs it into his pocket. He may take another squint at it later, but he can't always be certain of getting the chance, because he's hardly ever left alone. His brain's fresh, I suppose, because he's used it so little.

Yesterday afternoon I went with him to a neighbouring village. His audience was composed of about three dozen fellows with cropped heads and heavy moustaches. There were none of the interruptions and catcalls you might have expected, but a general atmosphere of profound thought. He stammered a bit, but not too much. He deliberately turns my sentences upside down and has a passion for introducing so many "whiches," "whats," "becauses," and "althoughs" that he makes my periods into a hodge-podge of qualifications and subordinate clauses which seem as though they'll never end. But probably I'm the only person who notices it.

The natives are very amusing. Up to now my idea of the south has been purely conventional, because although my own native soil is geographically so close, it is spiritually a world away.

The first thing that surprises me is to find what natural speakers they all are. Though they're barely literate, they have an extraordinary gift for making well-balanced and sounding phrases. They produce past definites and imperfect subjunctives as thick as the truffles of their native land, and with scarcely any grammatical mistakes. They hardly ever pause or hesitate or make use of vague locutions. At times one could almost swear that they had learned their speeches by heart. The Marquis is much less eloquent than most of his listeners. But one wonders whether words *mean* anything to them, and one's tempted to say no. But I'm not so sure. I'm inclined to think that, taken separately, the words don't convey much to them, but that they do get a sort of general impression, the tone, as it were, of what's said, rather as one does in music, but it's a kind of music in which the various notes, E flat or G sharp, have a sort of sonority of their own. You should hear what they make of such phrases as "The indefeasible rights of the rural proletariat" or "Freedom slowly broadening down," etc.

I love their bursts of high spirits, which alternate with moods of solemn and even gloomy concentration, for they're very emotional. Under all this spate of meaningless phraseology there's a bottom of sound common sense and scepticism. They've got a wonderful gift of seeing the subtleties and contradictions of life.

Only one thing spoils my pleasure—the thought that you're not here to share it. What fun we'd have together! What winks we'd exchange! What impressions we'd laugh over in the evening privacy of our rooms! We'd have adjoining rooms, and at two a.m. I'd knock on the wall. How sickening it is that simple little things like that never seem to work out properly! And all the while time's passing. When we're forty and respectable, with children (you won't have any, perhaps, but I shall) and our little savings, and who knows how many miles—geographic or spiritual—between us, it'll be too late to share an adventure of this sort. It's a sad thought, my friend, very sad. More and more do I realize the impossibility of recapturing the chances that we let slip. And something tells me that in time to come what we shall most regret in our past lives will be just the little things like that, which we shall have achieved or missed. (Always remember that hardening of the arteries sets in at twenty-five!)

Yes, I should have enjoyed having you mixed up in my dirty work, or knowing that you were watching me at it. Do you know that yesterday, when I got back from the village I've told you of, Crivelli, the chief of our robber band, made me go and interview a wretched schoolmaster, a decent fellow called Gouzennes, who stood as Socialist candidate in the first ballot and polled 700 votes. It was uncertain whether he'd withdraw or not. Naturally it wasn't to be expected that he'd retire in favour of the Marquis, nor was there much risk of his officially supporting the opposition. The danger was that he'd retire with a general cry of "Down with reaction!" and that, as a result, three-quarters of his votes would go to Dr. Bonnefoux, the Radical-Socialist and Freemason. I was as wily as a serpent. First of all I said quite calmly that I'd been instructed by Saint-Papoul's committee to approach him with a view to his retirement in favour of the Marquis, who was a sincere friend of the people. He jumped as though he'd been shot. In the first place, he said, it was nothing to do with him; it was for the party to decide, adding that it was pretty cheeky to ask him to help the candidate of reaction.

Then I began to flatter him. "Everyone knows," said I, "that the party thinks very highly of you, that you can twist the people of the Dordogne round your little finger. The party will decide what you tell it to decide." Next I became confidential. "So far as my personal feelings go," said I, "I don't give a hoot for the Marquis. I happen to be his secretary, but I don't share his politics. My sympathies are with the extreme Left; in certain ways I go even further than the party. I'm being frank with you. Setting politics aside, I can say that the Marquis is a decent enough chap, with liberal ideas. Personal considerations apart, I feel far more kindly disposed towards him than I do towards a dirty bourgeois hypocrite like Bonnefoux, who is a secret enemy of the working class and who stands for a party whose real object is to wreck the Revolution. Be that as it may, I fully understand your feelings. Do you know what I'd do in your place? Naturally, you won't go repeating what I'm going to say—well, if it was me, I'd take my chance at the second ballot and let the candidates of the bourgeoisie go hang! Let them fight their own battles. The great point is that the active forces of revolution should feel their strength and get a sense of solidarity. They must get into the habit of standing apart and strengthening the element of class-consciousness at the expense of mere electioneering tactics."

He seemed to believe me, and there is a rumour going round this morning that, authorized by his Federation, he will make a fine gesture of leading a forlorn hope, and will stick to his candidature. I played every mean trick I could think of to persuade him. I even— I can't keep the truth from you—used the College, Jaurès's College, as a weapon. Nor did I spare my poor old father: I found that references to his position as a schoolmaster were decidedly useful. In fact, I stopped at nothing.

Setting it all down in cold blood like this, I can measure the depths of degradation to which I fell, and I tremble at the thought. You will despise me, old chap, I know, and I ask myself now why I did it. It's all so complicated. What appealed to me in the first place was the idea of succeeding in a job with which I'd been entrusted, even though success meant no personal advantage: the kick that my egotism got from showing these creatures that I could do better than they expected, that I was no end of a fellow. Then there was all the fun of playing a part in the twofold sense of influencing events and being a somebody, the ironic, half-bitter amusement to be derived from taking hold of the puppet-strings and finding that, after all, it was easy enough to make the figures dance. And then, you see, I excused myself for yielding to these various temptations by the thought that nothing of any importance was at stake. In arguing that from the Socialist point of view Saint-Papoul was as good as the doctor, I was fighting my patron's battle without injuring the true cause. By persuading Gouzennes not to withdraw, I did the Marquis a good turn, it is true, but at the same time I may have been working for the ultimate success of the Revolution, the forces of which, after all, do run the risk of becoming demoralized, do weaken their power of attracting recruits, if they're always to be asked, for reasons of vote-catching, to act as the allies of others and keep their own flag furled in a corner.

The thought of you had something to do with it, too. You won't believe it, but it's a fact. I said to myself: "When he calls his pal

Jerphanion a 'cunning old peasant,' what he really means is that he's a bit of an oaf who's got his head stuffed with abstract ideas, but knows nothing about men (or about women either); who's ignorant of psychology, a simple soul about as unlike a character from Stendhal as it's possible to be. Well, I'll just show him." I don't suppose I have shown you, but that's neither here nor there.

And there was one more reason—I'm not trying to be subtle for the sake of being subtle—and that was that I seemed to see in this business a splendid chance of hardening myself against the possible lessons of experience. I've got, you see, a sort of idea that my future may lie in the sphere of action. Now, one of the curses of the active life, the chief reason that the spirit of man wears itself out and cheapens itself by a long course of action, is the fact that one's for ever being tempted to compromise, to intrigue, to make oneself party to heart-breaking manœuvres. And the mere recognition that they are heart-breaking is no protection against eventual degradation, because the human stomach can get used, by degrees, to any food, however bad. In order, therefore, to inoculate myself against the allurements of action, I decided to make a big enough meal of cynicism and political lying to disgust any decent man for the rest of his natural life. I could make the experiment without any risk of defilement, because the real me wasn't being involved at all. It wasn't Jean Jerphanion who was doing all this, but some nameless secretary of the Marquis de Saint-Papoul. I was merely a *corpus vile* for purposes of demonstration.

Well, that's my explanation, and I've no doubt you'll pooh-pooh it. Nor am I altogether sure that you'll be wrong. I have a feeling that your life is better worth living than mine—I don't mean that ironically; I'm not so entirely lost to decent feeling as that—and that you're strong enough, unlike me, to live it without feeling the need of a confidant.

Good-bye for the present, old fellow. Write me a line soon if you can bring yourself to forgive my long silence. Let me know what's happening to you. There are times, you know, when I really want to show you that I *do* sympathize and to give you—you don't mind my saying this?—a word of comfort. Only you're such a reticent old devil.

Your really devoted, but rather foul

JEAN JERPHANION

PS.—There's one thing I must tell you, though I've hesitated a long time before plucking up enough courage to do so. The day I came away I got a letter from our friend M. E. I read it in the train. It seems that, in return for his promise to do nothing, I undertook to have it all out with you, and talk things over. I take it that he's feeling ill-used. He doesn't actually say that I'm letting him down, but I think he wants a little encouragement and looks to me to provide it. It's all rather embarrassing. Forgive me if I'm touching a sore spot.

J. J.

Chapter

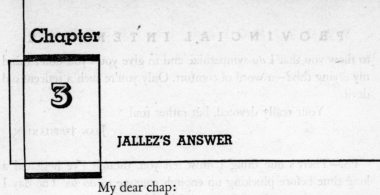

3

JALLEZ'S ANSWER

My dear chap:

I was much amused by your letter. I can see you're not bored, and I must confess that in other circumstances I should have enjoyed sharing the adventure. Not that I should have approached the job with anything like the degree of competence or shrewdness that you are showing. You appear to be behaving like a past master of intrigue. Reading your letter I find myself thinking of Talleyrand, of Metternich, of the Duc de Morny, and other gentlemen of that stock. But I shouldn't have disturbed you by inopportune qualms of conscience. I should have watched your activities with admiring eyes, ready, whenever you might have needed me, to serve under your orders. I believe you are right in treating politics as the art of using any convenient means to reach a goal that's not, in itself, much to boast of.

Here there's no news. You're wrong to accuse me of being reticent. It's not being reticent to feel shy of bothering other people with my affairs, especially when they're not really of any importance. Besides, you've seen for yourself that my reticences—if that's the word for them—don't do me much good, and that chance always manages to come along to assuage your curiosity.

Things are neither better nor much worse. They drag along, maybe to some sort of solution, though they've not yet reached it. I regret such a state of affairs for the sake of the person whose interests you have at heart; sometimes I regret it for personal reasons.

What you tell me of the natives in your part of the country seems to throw light on several obscure features in the psychology of the dog Macaire. Do you agree? Make careful note of your observations;

the problem is certainly worth the trouble.

I envy you this short but fruitful immersion in the life of the provinces. I don't really know anything at all about them, except what I saw, as it were, out of the corner of my eye when I was doing my military service—and one doesn't see much that way! I've got a sort of taste for provincial existence (sometimes a distaste, almost a sense of horror). It's not only that things *look* different. A whole new set of stresses comes into play. I should like to know it at first hand. You've known it already, and it's not fair that this second chance should come your way. But you have all the luck: health, strength, love, money. You're so rich now that I don't believe you'll know what to do with all your wealth. But I've no doubt that somewhere in Périgord you'll find some rascally banker, used to fleecing priests and old women, who'll relieve a practising Socialist like you of these various accumulations.

Good-bye. I've not got the energy to write more, because it's a heavy, sultry day, and I'm feeling a bit below par. Besides, I've got nothing really to tell you. Please write to me, though, at enormous length; spare no details. In that way you'll bring a little grist to this disused old mill.

Yours,

P. J.

Chapter

4

THE SECOND BALLOT

At half past eleven on the evening of the 8th of May the Marquis de Saint-Papoul with 6,499 votes was leading by 139 from Dr. Bonnefoux with 6,360. Figures were yet to come in from one of the outlying districts where, it was said, the ballot-boxes had been upset. But this district had only 103 names on the register, of which no more than 85 had polled at the first ballot. There could, therefore, be no further doubt of the Marquis's victory.

The "provisional" results were not published until the morning of the 9th. The figures were as follows:

Total votes recorded: 13,364

de Saint-Papoul. Republican of the Left	6,536 Elected
Doctor Bonnefoux. Radical-Socialist	6,406
Gouzennes. International Labour	380
d'Enjalbal de Nizes. Conservative	25
Various	17

An analysis of the figures of the two ballots made it clear that the narrow victory was due in the main to the withdrawal of d'Enjalbal and the renewed contest by Gouzennes, the Labour candidate, although in both cases a certain number of voters had failed to obey instructions. Doctor Castaing had refused to take any action. Of the thousand extra votes cast for M. de Saint-Papoul it was clear that 400 had swung over from Touch and Giordano, and a further 600 from d'Enjalbal. A large number of the Vicomte's supporters had refused to back the Marquis, whose ideas were a little too much enlightened. On the other hand, about half the Socialist vote had gone to stiffen the Republican total.

In any case, it was clear that the double intervention of Mionnet and Jerphanion had turned the scale.

The victory of the Marquis and his gallant allies was celebrated more than once. At midnight on Sunday fifty of his supporters "quaffed the festive bowl" at the Café de l'Univers, and Crivelli sent to M. Jean Jerphanion, 45 rue d'Ulm, a telegram worded as follows: "Victory certain gratitude valuable collaboration raise glasses to your health." (The concluding phrase read, on arrival: "raise *gasses* to your health.") The Marquis had at first objected that the celebration was premature and might bring him bad luck, and Crivelli had had to demonstrate at least ten times, pencil in hand, the simple truth that by no possible means could 103 outstanding votes materially affect a majority of 139. But the Marquis distrusted figures, and if he was finally convinced, it was by the enthusiasm of his friends rather than by the exactitude of mathematical proof. So many people, he felt, could hardly all be wrong. He therefore gave an order for champagne, stammered a toast (Jerphanion having forgotten to prepare one), and drank two glasses, the devastating effects of which went unnoticed in his growing sense of triumphant happiness.

Next day, when the result had been officially announced, he gave a dinner to twenty-four guests at the Hôtel de Londres et des Voyageurs. Those present included the members of the council of war which had been held on the 25th of April, as well as the local notabilities who had formed Saint-Papoul's Committee or who had been active in support of his candidature. There were about ten mayors, district and town councillors, and a number of "important figures" of the constituency. The secretary of the local prefecture, who had been invited in his private capacity as a friend, tactfully voiced the congratulations of his official superiors.

M. de Saint-Papoul considered that he had done all that could be expected of him (there would, of course, have to be printed a manifesto of gratitude, the text of which Jerphanion was asked, in a second telegram, to provide), but Crivelli took him aside and made it clear that his chief supporters would be pleasantly impressed by an invitation to an intimate party in the family château. The Marquis tried to raise objections of a practical nature, but realized that he would have to give way. He suggested, therefore, a luncheon party to be held the following Sunday. Crivelli, however, gave him to understand that to be a real success the affair ought to take the form of a dinner, followed by an invitation to spend the night at the château, where there were plenty of guest-rooms, a rich breakfast with coffee or chocolate, rolls and butter, and, finally, a farewell luncheon. He need, Crivelli thought, ask only about ten persons, and produced a list of guests with his own name bringing up the rear. The Marquis was a little unnerved, not so much by the fear of what it would cost as by the thought of the trouble it would involve; less by the threat of personal discomfort than by his foreknowledge of what his wife would say when she heard of this projected orgy of country politicians. "They'll break my plates," she would cry, "be sick all over my rooms, and dirty my bed-linen. There's no reason to do a thing like that. Fancy putting yourself on that sort of footing with them!" He felt, however, that his reputation as a great gentleman with democratic leanings was at stake, as well as his career as a deputy and his chances of re-election in the future. Besides, he knew his neighbours well enough to assume that, flattered by being treated by him as equals, they would all be on their best behaviour.

"If it's got to be done," he reflected, "let's get it over quickly!" The excuse of short notice would make it possible to do things fairly simply. Besides, he was in a hurry to get back to Paris.

He arranged, therefore, that the party should take place on the following Wednesday and Thursday.

Chapter

5

A GENTLEMAN AT HOME:
THE LIFE OF A SQUIRE

Opening his eyes, on the Thursday morning, after a short and restless night, M. de Saint-Papoul became aware that his room was full of daylight. He looked at his watch, which lay on his night-table beside a little round box containing bicarbonate of soda, and a glass of water. "Twenty-five past four. I can't have slept for more than two hours."

He took stock of his physical sensations, wondering whether he was likely to doze off again, and decided that it was improbable. He felt excited; the light bothered him; his brain was active, and his heart beat heavily. But his chief sensation was one of happiness. The fact that he was tired didn't bother him. "I've slept badly," he thought, "but there are lots of people who never sleep at all and live to a green old age. I ate a great deal and drank too much, but the human system recovers its strength best when it's not being constantly watched, as is proved by the fact that I've got no burning sensation in my stomach at this moment and can scarcely feel any constriction round my middle, and very little suspicion of wind. I am a deputy. To know that I have been elected is extraordinarily pleasant, but it's nothing to the pleasures to come, greetings, bows, 'Monsieur le Deputé,' the policeman, the bailiff, the station-master . . . and, at the end of it all, Parliament itself, where the destinies of France are decided. I shall have as much right to be there as I have to be in my home, with my own seat, my own desk. I shall walk bareheaded in the corridors, Ministers will take me by the arm and give me the latest tip about what's going on. There are some pleasures in life which are done with as soon as they're enjoyed, others that are rich in consequences both great and small. Marquis and deputy. Soon I shall be the best-known man of the district. Reputation and power will both be mine. It's something to have rank without influence, or influence without rank; but to have both—that indeed is success!"

He took a sudden decision:

"I'll get up, dress, go down to the stable, and saddle Zephyr—entirely by myself, without getting anybody else up; why not?—and go for a ride of three or four hours."

He sat up with a single movement, jumped out of bed as briskly (he told himself with pleasure) as a young man, ran to the door on his bare feet, opened it, and listened. Not a sound. The country worthies enjoyed untroubled slumber. No noise of retching came to him, no sour and vinous smell of troubled stomachs; not even those distant sounds of doors opening and shutting, of water running, which give evidence of restless sleepers.

"A decent lot of fellows! On the whole they behaved very well. I expect one or two have been sick in their beds or on the floor—we shall know all about that later and I'll get Blanche to do the necessary washing without saying anything to my wife. I wonder whether wine stains can be got out of blankets and carpets easily, especially when they contain a certain amount of stomach acidity?—Well, it's no good meeting trouble half-way. I'd willingly sacrifice a bed-mat or two to be elected."

While engaged with such thoughts he was hurriedly washing himself.

"I'll shave when I get back. It'll be five or ten minutes past by the time I'm off. . . . I shall have time for a ride of three hours or so without hurrying. . . . I'll go round by the woods and then up the Tremblade valley. . . . It won't be hot. After that, we'll see. I can easily be back by eight or half past. They'll none of them be up. And even if anyone does notice my absence, I shall have done nothing contrary to the laws of hospitality. A man can do as he likes with this time of the day. Besides, an early ride like this will fit splendidly into the picture. 'Our new deputy is a man of incredible energy. After carrying through an election campaign which would have sent anyone else to bed, does he think of resting? Far from it! he gets up at five o'clock and goes for a gallop in the forest.' Rather a change from old Doctor Castaing. . . . That reminds me: it wouldn't surprise me to discover that Josephine had been having a little mild fun—or perhaps not so mild—with one or other of our friends; or possibly with two or three at quarter-hour intervals. Not that I mind; it's all in the way of hospitality. She's a pretty little piece, and a credit to the house. Still, I shouldn't like to think that any of my guests had caught anything from her. I don't think it's likely, but one never knows with a free and easy girl like that. . . ."

He had taken down his riding-clothes from the left-hand corner of the wardrobe which was built into the wall. They had not been brushed for some time. The breeches were beginning to get worn. With all the expenses of an electoral campaign, all the bills waiting to be settled, all the unexpected expenses and liberalities which would be bound to arise, it was not the moment to think about new clothes. "Still, Mézan did throw out a hint of one or two directorships, and meanwhile it'll be hard if Papa-in-law doesn't do something handsome next quarter. . . . Anyhow, I don't mind. Money spent on buying such pleasure as I'm enjoying now is well spent. . . . Then there's the car I shall have to buy. . . . How useful it would have been during the campaign!"

He visualized last night's dinner: the great dining-room with its fine painted beams and its candelabra. The service, perhaps, had left something to be desired: Blanche had been dressed anyhow, and Casimir had had a stain on his shirt-front which would have sent the Marquise into a fit if she had been there. She would have seen nothing but the stain. But there had been about the scene an atmosphere of intimate grandeur. It was as though he had said to his guests: "I am treating you as old friends." There had been masses of food, and the wine had been beyond all criticism (with the exception of one bottle which had been slightly corked). Expressions of appreciation had burst spontaneously from every side, despite the reticence which the company had set itself to practise in the interests of good breeding.

Great care had been taken to avoid the smacking of lips. Several of those present had been clearly embarrassed by the demands of polite behaviour. Should they, for instance, empty their glasses every time the butler offered them more wine? Or if not, how much should they drink? And how fast? Which was the greater risk, to look like a greedy winebibber or seem to lack appreciation of an admirable vintage?

Thinking it all over, the Marquis found himself the prey to an astonishment which led him to question a good many of his customary ideas. Yesterday evening had not been very different, so far as material details went, from what he had anticipated, but the general impression he had retained of it was, to some extent, unexpected. Ever since his childhood he had had to deal with people in the social class to which his guests belonged, but never before had he had occasion to receive a whole group of them under his own roof, so that their atmosphere filled the house, to behave to them as though they had been people of his own world, as though he were receiving, for example, a party of neighbouring landowners for a shoot, or to look forward to a future in which such intimacy with them would be part of the normal conduct of life.

He had anticipated an impression of greater coarseness, and, in particular, had expected to suffer from the contact much more than he had done. "A dirty job," he had said to himself, "which I can't get out of," and had prepared himself for the ordeal by damping down his susceptibilities and setting his teeth.

But as a matter of fact he hadn't suffered at all. Of course, he had laid himself out to be pleasant, and they had been on their best behaviour; still, even allowing for that, it was wonderful how decently everything had gone off, except for one or two little details of good manners which didn't really matter in the least. The local squires could learn a good deal from these guests of his about how to behave at shooting luncheons, or at any meal, for that matter, at which ladies were not present! The Marquis de Lescous, for example, belched and farted after a meal like a fireman; and as for the conversation!—why, yesterday evening there hadn't been a tenth of the crude talk he was accustomed to listen to when he was alone with a party of so-called gentlemen. The conversation had turned on politics and on other interesting subjects which most of these little country squires wouldn't have begun to understand. His future son-in-law, Lavardac, wouldn't know what you meant if you asked him to explain the difference between direct and indirect taxation. He would just look superior, and he would be wrong. Those were just the sort of people who started shrieking like a lot of parrots at any new law which they thought affected them. The world of today needn't bother about what they thought, because in fact they didn't think at all. Take Ratier, for instance: he might be a little pompous and have rather an accent, but if it came to serious conversation, Lavardac couldn't keep up his end with him for a moment. . . . One can't go through life getting out of everything with an elegant gesture.

In short, he discovered rather unexpectedly in himself a fund of respect for commoners, petty tradespeople, and the lower classes and found that he could get on with them very well indeed. It was delightful to have had to make so little effort. "The whole thing went perfectly naturally," he assured himself. "I'm sure they felt it, and that they were grateful to me." It pleased him to find in himself the stuff of a sincere democrat. "No one'll be able to pretend that I'm just an ambitious fellow playing a game."

Helped by lack of sleep and by the quality of youth and adventure in the light of early morning, he found himself, as he tied his tie and brushed his hair, thinking thoughts that were rather disturbing, but rather exciting. It was as though he were listening to somebody who was speaking in paradoxes. "When all's said and done, mere birth is nothing. What counts is a man's personal worth. If I didn't happen to be intelligent, if I hadn't a gift for speaking. . . . Of course, if one bears a very famous name, if one's a Rohan, a Montmorency, a La Rochefoucauld, it's as though a piece of French history were walking the streets or coming into a room. But what about the others, about you or me? The whole thing just becomes a farce. We should think it pretty ridiculous if, in two or three hundred years' time, people gave themselves airs and thought themselves made of different flesh and blood from other men just because their ancestors happened to have been police sergeants or registrars under President Fallières. . . . There's more than one grand family that derives its title of nobility from an ancestor who was something like that, or even less, under Louis XIV. I don't pretend to be much of an expert at genealogy, but I bet there are descendants today of some apothecary ennobled by Louis who don't think their family tree a joke! Or perhaps they trace their lineage to the loins of Jupiter, or to some spot a little higher up, where he may have had it injected with an enema. . . ."

He took a path through the woods, where large stones, some rounded, others rough and sharp, lay in a loose and yellow soil.

The track mounted and twisted between banks. Zephyr climbed with a fine, brave action. First he would strike the earth sharply with his hoof as though seeking firm foothold; then, having found what he sought, he would hoist himself up with a strong thrust of his loins that could be felt the whole length of his body, right through to his chest, and this movement would be accompanied by a swishing of his tail and a fine tossing of his head.

Zephyr was a chestnut half-breed. He had once been an Army horse, but had been discarded prematurely for some unexplained reason. The Marquis deliberately allowed it to be understood that what had occurred had been due to no fault in the animal, and that when one's a friend of a horse-dealer who himself is the friend of a vet, one sometimes gets the chance of a remarkable bargain.

Zephyr stood high on the ground and had a long head. His action was rather clumsy. His movements were exaggerated, so that he seemed always to be putting more effort into the surmounting of a difficulty than the difficulty itself warranted. It was laughable to see him striving and wriggling to get up a not very steep slope. But the rider on his back felt all this commotion of the body between his legs as something curiously appealing. It was as though the horse were saying in so many words that no task was too great, that no command would be questioned, no labour shirked. He never made an effort to spare himself, never held back, or showed any petty caution; only the will to give always of his best, and confidence supreme. "Is that what you want me to do, master? Don't worry, I will do my best to please you." And thereupon he set himself to do rather more than he need have done, rather more than could be done with elegance. He climbed as fast as another would have done, he never stumbled; he was conscientious and reassuring, but he certainly was not one of those, whether men or animals, who get the reputation of doing things without an effort.

M. de Saint-Papoul was very fond of him, and treated him with the utmost consideration. Before he started out on his ride this morning, he stroked his muzzle, scratched his mane, and spoke to him. "Do you like the idea, Zephyr, old man?—Eh?—You'd like to go?—You won't be bored?—We'll go for a ride in the woods, eh?—It's a lovely day.—You shall have a good rest when you get back."

The Marquis never went out without his crop, because its presence in his hand was indispensable to his idea of himself as a rider of elegance and was necessary to his moral comfort. (If he forgot it by accident, he always went back for it.) But it was merely a decorative adjunct. He never used it except to transmit to Zephyr a few messages of affection or intelligence. These messages were of various kinds, and he liked to think that each had a particular meaning. Zephyr, however, interpreted them by a much simpler code, according to circumstances; as, for instance, a hint to keep his eyes open or an appeal to exert himself. Perhaps, however, through the course of years they had acquired for the horse certain subtle shades of meaning.

Sometimes, for instance, the Marquis would stroke Zephyr's neck, slowly and obliquely, with the handle of his crop; at other times he would administer a series of light, sharp taps, in quick succession, upon his right flank; or, again, holding the crop at arm's length, he would lean over the horse's withers and tap the upper part of his shoulder. In each case it was the rhythm of the movement, rather than the place on which the touch was administered, that gave the sense of the message. The slow stroking meant: "Go on like that; you're a dear old horse, and I'm very fond of you; I know that you're doing your best." The sharp taps meant: "Don't go to sleep; get ready; watch out." There were other varieties which were administered just for fun.

In addition to these applications of the crop, the Marquis, of course, employed the normal language of riders, pressing with his thighs, gripping with his knees and calves, using his heels. As these, however, were without spurs, there was nothing in the movement more forcible than an appeal. Finally, he frequently patted the horse's neck, and sent a whole variety of messages to him through the medium of the reins.

The Marquis never used spurs even on the most important occasions. He hated those cruel implements and boasted that he never needed them. He regarded them as the symbol of a barbarous epoch in the history of riding when obedience was obtained by the infliction of pain, even after a horse had been broken in and it was only necessary to transmit an order that was perfectly well understood. And, in fact, it was never difficult to make Zephyr break into a gallop, stretch himself, or take a jump. It may be that M. de Saint-Papoul was enjoying the fruit of that earlier, rougher training in the Army riding-school which his horse had undergone, and that the gentle pressure of his heels served to recall in Zephyr's memory the terrifying rowels of other days and the sudden bursts of energy to which they had goaded him. The matter is not one of great importance.

The Marquis was pleased to think of himself as a good horseman. Not that he enjoyed the idea of riding in the abstract. The exercise was inextricably mixed in his mind with the places in which he took it, the scenes to which it introduced him, the points to which he journeyed thus, and the weather that he enjoyed. It formed in his consciousness a sort of totality of impressions made up of jumping ditches and of galloping, but also of the trees, the undulating prospects, the smells caught, and the passing animals seen, which served as a background to it.

The path which he followed this morning was one of his favourite rides. It led from the château up a gentle slope between two rows of plane-trees, then crossed a brook, and continued its upward course for about half an hour, through woods, with here and there a short descent. At one point it skirted a rocky ledge whence, through a clearing in the trees, it commanded a view of the château perched on its hill and flanked by lawns and greenery. The vineyard on the opposite slope was, from here, invisible.

Next came a stage of ups and downs during which the eye was conscious, even from the vantage-point of high ground, of nothing but a sea of foliage. It was easy, at this point in the ride, to cross unaware the limits of the estate and then, by first bearing slightly to the left and again more definitely to the right, to reach the edge of the wood. From that point the path debouched into a plain, parched in its upper stretches and covered with scrub, but becoming richer as one descended. This was the beginning of the Tremblade valley.

The solitude here was delicious. As one advanced, the flow of water increased in volume. At first it bubbled up from the spongy soil with a pleasant sound, then formed into tiny rills which, in their turn, united into a single stream. It was delightful to trot on the meadow grass and to pass, from time to time, a ruined hut with, here and there, a herd of cattle. Only some way farther on, round a bend in the valley, did the first farm appear. If one wanted to keep the sense of loneliness, one could do so by taking, to the right, a footpath of trampled grass which gradually turned to an earthen track and finally, rising abruptly, became wild and stony. This steep ascent gave Zephyr a fine opportunity of showing his sureness of foot and of making a grand display of thrusting with his loins. At the summit was an expanse of ferns and young oak-trees no bigger than under-brush, covering a sort of plateau closed in by a near horizon where often a gentle breeze fanned the wayfarer and turned his thoughts to poetry. The view was closely bounded, but the wind spoke of high, open spaces. At the plateau's end was a ravine, crossing which, one came to another valley and, following this, within half a mile, to a softly carpeted bend in the hills. On one side lay the plain, on the other a region of vines and of fields where grew wheat, corn, and tobacco. If one was in a hurry to return, one could do so from here by a good, well-shaded, dirt road which, several times interrupted, led back by way of the two biggest farms of the estate, with their pigs, geese, and chickens, by the ruins of the old village of Saint-Papoul, reaching the château at last after skirting the vineyard.

While he helped Zephyr to climb, the Marquis had an eye for the slopes about him, noting the outcrop of blue-grey rock in the furrows and the bearded tangle of roots. Higher up were the little trees in all their bravery of young green. How lovely the light of early morning seemed, welling up beyond the tree-tops! It tipped their summits with sunlight, while he himself moved in a shadowy world of fresh and fragrant smells. The air was full of the song of finches, warblers, and robins. A magpie flew, chattering, from tree to tree. In a bush a dove cooed gently.

He came to a place where the path descended. The slope was gradual and the ground, despite its broken character, firm. Zephyr broke into a jog-trot. Beneath his hoofs the earth gave way a little, but not enough to cause nervousness in the rider, whose body reacted to the sensation of sliding by little movements of resistance which communicated themselves to the bridle. It is rather pleasant to be shaken up a bit, since it gives one the illusion of being young, of not having grown soft, of being still capable of deriving pleasure from an experience which exposes the body to rough usage. Seen thus in perspective, the physical exercises of the bathroom in the rue Vaneau appeared as a joyless and ridiculous substitute. How much more effective in every way this riding was! One ought to have an hour's exercise on horseback every morning, but it was not easy to manage in Paris. Getting to the Bois was a tiresome business, and then there was all the fuss about wearing the right clothes which came to complicate the pleasure of riding and turned it into something artificial.

On the top of the next rise the path divided. The foliage of the tree-tops looked like a sheaf held in a fork. This countryside, he thought, was full of charm. No need to have been born there to appreciate its shy appeal. There was no monotony about its views—not that it offered far-spreading prospects or wild solitudes; but its air of intimacy had more of mystery about it than that of the Île de France, for example.

Curious what an impression of expectancy one got from this rise and fall of the ground, from these half-hidden roadways out in the hillsides, from this wilderness of tiny peaks and wooded valleys, interspersed with stretches of ferns and neglected pastures. It was as though the whole countryside were waiting for something strange to happen, but pleasantly strange—abductions of fair damsels, duels followed by reconciliation, lost princes found disguised as beggars.

Saltus. The word formed itself suddenly in the Marquis's mind. He had probably never given it a thought since his student days. Once, long ago, at college, one of the Fathers had gone to a great deal of trouble to explain to his pupils the meaning of the Latin word *saltus*. The Marquis was not sure that he had fully understood it at the time, nor that he now remembered what had been said. But it occurred to him that what now lay before and around his feet— this mixture of undulating woodland, of clearings and meadowland, these sudden freaks and frolics of the ground, this intimate closeness of the view—was exactly what the ancients had meant by the word *saltus*, including in it the sense of southern sunlight and the illusion of romantic quests that emerged, for him, from the secrecy of these rolling hills. The thought enchanted him. He would have given a lot to find on the tip of his tongue some verse of Horace or of Virgil that was graced by the music of that word *saltus*. "I ought to have thought of it," he reflected, "when Monsieur Jerphanion was here."

To ride on horseback through this *saltus*. The thought seemed to concentrate for him the various aspects of the morning's expedition, all that it contained of ease and of fatigue, of laziness and of effort, of discomfort and of feudal pride. It meant the jerking of the animal beneath him, which he could foresee and to which he could adapt his body by a responsive movement that was as natural as breathing, no matter how often it was repeated. It meant the path that grew more rocky and sandy as he advanced, the ferns, the brambles, the bushes, the clumps of thicker woodland, the rise and fall of the track, the valley bottoms which made him shiver with sudden cold, the sun that struck warm upon him as he emerged on to higher ground, scrambling along the face of a rocky slope; the copses already hot and odorous; a dropping or a rising course. It meant the horse that carried him with such simple loyalty, asking no better than to share the trail with him. Now and again he would caress its neck or whisper endearments in its ear, conscious of a certain pleasurable emotion in thus listening to his own voice speaking in solitude to one who, though not human, was still his friend. He loved his horse. He hoped that it still had years of life ahead. Horses, fortunately, are long-lived, not like those poor dogs who leave you after a few years just when you have grown fond of them.

In just such a way had he ridden when he was young, when he was still a child. He had been born in this country, this *saltus,* he was its lord. Lord in a small way, perhaps, and yet not, for that matter, so small. It's not the richness of the soil that matters, nor yet the price that is paid for it. A city business man who has made a fortune may buy a fine estate which will bring him a handsome return for his money. The value of a family estate is reckoned otherwise. Not for whims of fashion is it bought or sold; its worth has nothing to do with its price; not for money paid has a man become its lord. Poverty and many acres may well go together.

Poverty? Was it poor, this estate of his? Perhaps. Large it certainly was; not so large as it once had been, for little by little its outer bounds had been whittled away. But the heart of it had been preserved, thanks to those ancestors of his who had not failed in their duty. There were many landlords who had come to ruin, who had sold their birthright for ready money which they had invested elsewhere—and likely as not lost—or quite simply to avoid the cost of maintenance and the trouble of disputes with their tenants.

"How well I remember," he thought, "the walks I used to take with my father! He taught me how to ride. He didn't like spurs, but he wore them. His mare Fauvette was a black half-breed. I wonder whether he was already planning a rich marriage for me when we rode together during my last holidays when I was eighteen and still at college? The estate was a heavy responsibility, and he knew that I shouldn't have a penny. He was a shrewd man, avoiding excess in all things, except when he lost his temper. He was terribly hot-tempered, but he was careful never to make an important decision when he was roused, not even to dismiss a servant. Rage with him was simply a means of relieving himself, nothing more. . . . It wasn't such a bad idea of his to find me a rich wife of good family and reasonable looks. The plebeian origins of the grocer had already been partly refined. The sieve had been shaken, and the money dropped through, while the vulgarity of its source was caught and held. . . . It needed a man of my father's tact and sanity to adjust the exact proportions. We understood each other perfectly, and when it came to this marriage scheme of his, he knew exactly how to prepare my mind for it. He took his responsibilities much more seriously, if it comes to that, than I take mine. It's no good ignoring the fact. I've let things take their own course in this matter of Jeanne's engagement to young Lavardac. Not that it's anything to be ashamed of, but my pretty little Jeanne deserved a better fate. . . . With all that swarm of brothers and sisters, the fellow'll have less than a million when he comes into his estate, counting everything, and he's already half-bald. . . . And she's made of fine stuff; attractive too, with those tormented eyes of hers. I can just see her married to some great man of letters, the sort who ends as a member of the Academy, or to someone in the diplomatic service. What a charming wife she'd have made for an ambassador! No good thinking of that now; it's too late. I'll try to arrange matters for Bernard in good time. Raymond's a born old bachelor. My only fear is lest he may suddenly rush off, without a word to anyone, and marry his washerwoman; and not even a young pink-cheeked one, at that, but some old hag who will turn out to have been his mistress for ten years without anyone knowing. . . . Still, it's no good meeting trouble half-way. . . . My father arranged things a long way ahead. Of course, I'd dreamed of a love-match, and, after all, I wasn't so very far from getting one either. I was delighted with Clémence, and she satisfied me for a long time. She had beautiful eyes—still has—and a charming mouth. Those who knew who she was might, perhaps, have detected a slight lack of breeding: she was just a shade too much like the handsome daughter of a Toulouse shopkeeper, but taking all in all, she was a good sort, and she's been an excellent wife to me, devoted to the children, though not quite so strict as she might have been. There's been rather too much of the hen with her chicks about her. She always was over-demonstrative and lacking in discipline. No tradition, that's the trouble—manners of a good middle-class family. I could never forget her mother—the grocer's daughter; the strain was always peeping out. But two things about her were superb when I married her: her breasts and her haunches! Unfortunately she put on weight as she grew older and had children, but, my God, in those early days! If she'd had the slightest touch of sensuality, if she'd shown any desire to respond, I really believe I'd have worn myself to a shadow in those first few months! Paulette, now, is a very different proposition, although compared with her I'm almost an old man. The frenzy she gets into, and makes me get into! Of course she does it because she knows I like it, but it's not all put on. I've had enough experience with such girls to know when they're pretending. There are days when Paulette loves to carry passion to the point of complete exhaustion—one's only got to look at her to see that—whereas I don't believe Clémence has ever reached even the stage of wanting more. It's extraordinary how temperamentally different women can be. One must make allowances, I know, for the fact that in our class, and especially in those days, there were prejudices and traditions of modesty which prevented a young woman from learning the art of love from her husband unless she was more than normally loose, but when the first weeks of marriage pass without the husband daring to go the limit to waken a response, then good-bye to all hope of happiness. There's nothing for it, from the woman's point of view, but to wait five or ten years until some lover comes along to show her what's what, unless in the meantime she's become absorbed in her children and spoiled for anything else. They're ready to do anything with a lover, to learn anything from him, once they've taken the plunge. I never really made the most of Clémence when she was young and fresh, as I ought to have done, no matter how passive she seemed to be. What a fool I was! There are ways and means; I could have done it quite simply, quite naturally, but I didn't, for fear of shocking her. Even the Church allows that sort of thing, I believe. When I think of the pleasure Paulette gives me, who's as thin as a lath, I can just imagine what it might have been like, those first years of our marriage, with that gorgeous rump of hers! My father wasn't squeamish, but he never mentioned things like that to me. I remember how he cross-examined me on the eve of my marriage and advised me not to take it too seriously when it came to satisfying my private tastes. 'The great thing,' he said, 'is to see that the interests and the honour of the family don't suffer, without, at the same time, turning oneself into a matrimonial drudge. . . . There are always compensations to be found elsewhere.' If he could see me now, he'd be proud of his son. He was never really keen about the Republic, but he was sane enough not to let his dislike of it go to extremes, like some of these fools. I remember his talking to me about them, saying: 'They've always grumbled, under Napoleon III, under Louis-Philippe. They probably grumbled under the Restoration because the fellows who'd bought confiscated property weren't made to cough up quickly enough. They probably grumbled under Louis XV because the King didn't ride the Parliaments with a sufficiently high hand.' He'd be as pleased as Punch to see me a deputy, although he'd pretend to be laughing at me. He'd be proud of my little dressmaker, too. He'd approve of my taste, and chuck her under the chin. . . . I should think old father-in-law Montech'll be pleased at the result of the election; he's just the sort of man who would, and I hope he'll show it. He can't say that his daughter only married a name. Not that he's had much to complain of; the title of Marquise in exchange for a pretty measly dowry (reality scarcely ever does come up to expectation) wasn't too bad. . . . But now! . . . His telegram of congratulations wasn't as enthusiastic as it might have been, but I suppose he's not quite sure of himself; anyhow, when I answer it, I'll say that my pleasure's been a bit damped by the thought of all the hideous expense. It's not long to the next quarter; let's hope he can take a hint. It's one thing to marry an heiress, but quite another when her old father hangs on to ninety. As things have turned out, it doesn't seem to me that I've had the best of the bargain!"

A turn in the path reminded him of one of last year's shooting parties, of his friends the petty local squires of Périgord, of the gamekeepers, the beaters, the dogs; and the thought brought in its train an endless vista of such memories stretching back into the past; meals at various houses or in country inns, and all the pleasant turmoil of their arrival. Days of hunting, he remembered, too, with women taking part, and other quieter and more formal parties, given to mark some family occasion.

The movement of his horse conjured up in his mind a picture of the life lived by these small landowners, a life that was in part his own. The thought of its easy abundance, of long days in the open air, filled him suddenly with pleasure. Limited perhaps it might be by the daily routine, bound by the sequence of the seasons, but in all other ways how free! A life of natural pleasures, rich in contentment and happy rivalries. He regretted that he had not made more of his opportunities. "In Paris," he thought, "when one's got to be careful, as we have, and to live in a narrow circle, life's meaner than it is here. There's so little to touch one's emotions." Now that he was a deputy, he would be kept more than ever in Paris, though of course his life there would have more meaning, more importance, than it had had hitherto. On the other hand, it would entail frequent visits to his constituency. "I shall spend most of my time in the train. Luckily there are ways of making oneself comfortable; one can take a sleeper, and I'm strong. . . ." He wondered how it would all turn out. "Perhaps life will be just as pleasant in another way, but it'll be a different sort of life." There might yet be room for his country-gentleman's existence; still, what he could keep of it wouldn't be as jolly as it had been in the past.

He savoured the movement of his horse, the colour of the high morning light, the sense of himself as a proud but benevolent lord of lands. A passing peasant touched his hat, and he acknowledged the salute nonchalantly with his crop. As a deputy he would have to adopt other manners, other pleasures, other ways of taking exercise. A good republican doesn't ride. A deputy of the Left can have a day's shooting now and then, but not in the same way as a Marquis, nor with the same friends. There was something in the way that the woods, the undergrowth, the vineyards, spread before his returning gaze that spoke of farewell.

As he urged Zephyr up the last slope that led to the château, M. de Saint-Papoul said to himself:

"They must be up by now. I'll be very nice to them. At luncheon I'll have up some of the old brandy."

Chapter

6

LAULERQUE'S WHITSUN

As he came out of the station at Amsterdam, Laulerque was surprised to find how light it still was. "I know," he thought, "that it's already the 15th of May, but in Paris the twilight would be much more advanced. It's extraordinary what a difference a few degrees of latitude more or less will make as one gets on towards midsummer." It pleased him to find that a fact which he had learned from books was thus verified in experience.

"I'll find my way," he decided, "without asking." He didn't even want to take from his pocket the little square card on which Mascot, manager of the bookshop D—, had sketched a rough plan of the environs of the station and marked the way he should take to the hotel. In the course of the journey Laulerque had examined this plan so often that he had fixed it in his memory.

"This is the square—the *Stationsplein*—and over there, just opposite, is the sort of jetty he mentioned and the boulevard which leads from it. My hotel is on the right-hand side, after the third turning beyond the harbour basin. It's all quite simple."

He tried to recognize the salient features of his itinerary without letting his movements give him away as a stranger. He avoided stopping, hesitating in his walk, holding his head too high, looking to the right and left, or presenting to the passers-by, to the neighbourhood generally, too questioning and uncertain a gaze.

"Always keep in practice," Mascot had said, "even when, as on this occasion, there's no particular need for caution."

The golden rule was to avoid attracting attention, not only in order to baffle any eventual watch that might be kept on him, but to prevent his appearance from stamping itself on the memories of casual pedestrians. It was therefore necessary to behave as much like a native of the place as possible, or at least like one who was perfectly familiar with it. A quick pace, a preoccupied air, the head slightly bent, such were the likeliest means of remaining unnoticed.

Unfortunately, to behave in this way was to lose much of the pleasure of travel. It is very difficult to enjoy one's first view of a city in which one has just arrived, to appreciate the lay-out of a square, the close or distant view of public monuments, the colour of the sky, of the roofs, of the house-fronts, if one's got to walk like a travelling salesman on his way home, his mind filled with trivial concerns, his eyes on the pavement before him, and a little suitcase in his hand. So directly, too, is the mind influenced by the conduct of the body that one very soon finds oneself thinking that, after all, one arrival is very much like another, and that going from the station to one's hotel is the same everywhere. The unusual is never so exciting as one likes to think it's going to be. There's not a city in the world where the house-roofs don't serve to carry away the rain-water, or the chimneys to make a draught for the fires. The fact that the roofs happen to be rather steeper and the chimneys more prominent is neither here nor there.

"Why couldn't they arrange this meeting at Dordrecht? I rather like Dordrecht. I managed to get a few walks in there. Tomorrow I'll look round the town. Perhaps they avoid having several meetings running in the same place. . . . I wonder whether the old-timers take all these precautions, and how much eye-wash there is in it all, and I wonder, too, who it is I'm really working for. It's an odd business altogether."

He was conscious of a feeling of fatigue beneath his shoulder-blades, as though two equally balanced weights were suspended there, and of a twitching sensation in his chest. But these vague symptoms did not worry him now as they usually did. "After ten hours in the train," he thought, "I'm naturally tired. If I didn't happen to know that I was more or less a sick man, should I guess it from my present state? I know lots of people who are always complaining of exhaustion, but who look strong enough. . . . Besides, I'm not as tired as all that! Anyhow, I've sworn I won't think about it. This great thingummy here must be the Stock Exchange. It's not bad. I rather like the colour—pity I can't examine it at my leisure. Perhaps I shall be able to see it from the window of my room. From this point I've got to count three streets. How narrow the houses are! I like these strong colours."

He saw a very narrow doorway, a corridor that looked like the entrance to a trap, and, at its far end, a very steep staircase leading into the recesses of the house.

He climbed about twenty steps, taking his time over each of them and holding on to the banisters. To his left he saw the reception desk. A conventionally dressed man with a large round head was standing behind the grille. He glanced at Laulerque, bowed slightly, and while the latter was thinking out a sentence, spoke to him in French.

"Good evening, sir. You would like a room?"

"If you please."

"Single?"

"Yes."

"Number 18."

He held out a form for Laulerque to fill out.

"What price is the room?"

"Two florins, including breakfast."

Laulerque filled out the form, as Mascot had told him to, in the name of M. Legras, 33, born at Rennes (Ille-et-Vilaine), travelling salesman, with a permanent address in Paris. Then a servant girl with carroty hair and a freckled face showed him to his room, which was on the floor above.

The room was very narrow, but of considerable length. The furniture consisted of a single bed of dark wood, a low wardrobe without a mirror, made of very black oak, a wash-stand, a very small table, a bedside table, and a single chair. Everything in the hotel seemed to be exceedingly small.

He washed his hands and his face, combed his hair, and sat down. The chair was not very comfortable. He changed his position once or twice, then, becoming conscious again of his fatigue, felt that he would like to lie down on the bed. Since the red woollen coverlet looked very clean, as did everything else in the room, and since he wanted to keep his boots on, he lay down obliquely with his feet hanging over the edge. He had great difficulty in finding a comfortable position for his head. The pillow was small and very hard.

He kept the light burning so that he should not go to sleep, but closed his eyes. In a sort of half-dream the noises of the street came to him thin and muffled. Carriages passed slowly with a sound that was quite different from the echoing quality to which he was accustomed in Paris. For minutes together he could hear nothing that resembled a motor horn, but there was a frequent tinkling of bells.

He had been there for about a quarter of an hour when a knock came on the door. He sat up quickly, passed his hands over his hair to smooth his ruffled locks, took up his eyeglasses, which he had put on the bed-table, rather cautiously opened the door, and saw the same maid with the carroty hair. She assumed an unhappy expression and said something in what he assumed was Dutch. She repeated it several times, and then burst out laughing at her inability to make herself understood. She conveyed by signs, however, that someone below was asking for Laulerque. Using signs in his turn, he tried to explain that he knew what she meant and that she might show the visitor up, adding at a venture: "Ja, ja, aufsteigen, hier, ja, hier."

The maid, nodding her head as though to indicate that she understood, took her departure. He thought: "Mascot told me not to go out and to take no steps. Somebody, he said, would visit me in my room. . . . Well, they've not lost much time." He repeated to himself the word that the visitor would use to make himself known, and his own reply. Both were names of places. "What are they going to give me to do this time?" he wondered. He felt excited.

There was another knock on the door, which he half-opened. The maid stood aside to make way for a young woman, or, rather, a young girl, simply dressed and wearing a small hat without a veil.

Laulerque rather hesitatingly closed the door. He looked his visitor over in a way that betrayed his uncertainty. She, on her side, watched him with an amused smile; then, still fixing him with her gaze and scarcely moving her lips, she murmured, almost as though she were pronouncing an affectionate greeting:

"Teterchen."

She smiled again, as though saying in so many words: "Are you surprised? That's it right enough."

He was, in fact, so much astonished that for a moment he said nothing. Then he pulled himself sharply together, made a slight sound of clearing his throat, and murmured quietly, returning her smile:

"Szeged."

She took from her hand-bag a thick, white envelope of ordinary size, on which was written the address: "MM. Ephrussi Bros., rue de Jeûneurs, Paris." There was no street number.

"I was told to give you this."

He offered her the only chair; she sat down. He took the envelope and looked at it absent-mindedly, reflected that it seemed rather heavy, then, after wondering for a moment where to put it, slipped it for the time being into the left inside pocket of his jacket.

The young woman reassured him.

"There's no risk," she said. "It sometimes happens that the French customs officials search travellers to see whether they've got any tobacco or lace, or, if they're coming from Holland, jewels. But they've only got to touch that envelope to see there's nothing in it but paper. As to its contents, I imagine either that it's written in code so as to read like a commercial letter to Ephrussi Brothers, or else that the visible text means nothing of importance and that there is invisible writing beneath it. Naturally, you won't pay any attention to the address. That's only put in in case you happen to be questioned by the police. You know all about that."

Her French was very correct, but she spoke with a distinct and not unpleasant accent which Laulerque failed to identify. She was of medium height, neither very pretty nor very fresh-complexioned. He noticed in particular that her lips were brown rather than red. Her appearance, however, was not unattractive. She gave the impression of vitality and frankness. Now and again he seemed to detect in her face a fleeting gentleness that reminded him of a young boy.

"Have you only just arrived?" she asked.

"I got here about half an hour ago."

"You've been here before?"

"No, this is the first time."

"Did you have dinner on the train?"

"I certainly did not. I drank some coffee at the Dutch frontier. I'm beginning to be hungry."

A sudden idea made him smile, but he didn't dare to put it into words. He knew that when two members of the society met on business they were supposed to be together only so long as was strictly necessary, and that it was forbidden them to enter into any personal relationship. He thought too: "They've probably sent this young woman in order to test me."

She went on:

"Your luck's gone. They've got an absurd custom here of dining at five o'clock or half past. You'll find it difficult to get anything at a restaurant. The only alternative is a tea-shop or something like that, and I'm not sure that, being a holiday, most of them won't be closed. You've no idea of the stupidities one's got to put up with if one lives in this country."

Laulerque replied that he didn't mind what he had nor where he had it. Could she tell him somewhere to go, or at least whereabouts he might find something?

"I'll show you, if you like," she said.

He thought it incumbent upon him to appear doubtful.

"There wouldn't be any harm in it?"

"What harm could there be?"

"Well, being seen together, for instance."

"I'm the only one who could be affected by that, supposing, what's most unlikely, that we meet someone I know. But the truth's the last thing they would suspect. Anyhow, it doesn't matter."

"And how about the rules of the society?" He spoke laughingly, so as not to seem too much like a keen and innocent young greenhorn. "Shan't we be cheating? Perhaps you'll denounce me for yielding to a young woman's attractions."

She shrugged her shoulders and looked at him as one friend might look at another.

"That's likely, isn't it?"

Then she got up.

"Come on. I don't know whether the place I'm thinking of will be open. They've got a wonderful choice of sandwiches, cheese, ham, shrimp paste, everything you can think of."

She helped him to read the bill of fare, translating certain words. "Have that; you'll see, you'll like it. Don't you think that their bread is excellent?"

She would take nothing but a cup of tea to keep him company.

"I dined at home, before coming to the hotel."

She spoke of the people she lived with, to whom she had alluded once or twice.

"They are diamond merchants, rich of course, but only relatively so compared with others. I'm the children's governess. Their house is very lovely and very well arranged. Dutch houses are wonderful: they, and the painting of the old Dutch masters, are the only things I like about the country. I teach French and German; I've got a nerve, haven't I?—not but what I speak German pretty well, better than I do French."

"But your French is excellent."

She protested, shaking her head and pouting. None of her features was beyond criticism, but there was a certain charm in the expression of her face; it was as though illumined by some inner life of the spirit.

"Don't be frightened that I'm disobeying the rules nor that I'm making you disobey them. I don't want to know your real name, and you shan't know mine."

"Not even your Christian name?"

"There's no need. . . . General conversation's not forbidden. . . . I come from far away in the south. Do you know Agram?"

"Agram? Isn't that in Austria-Hungary?"

"Yes, in Croatia. Locally it's known also as Zagreb. It's a pretty town, with fine buildings, much gayer than the towns about here."

"Is it a small town?"

"Certainly not, it's large. There's nothing like it in the whole of Holland; nothing, I mean, that gives such an impression of being a great centre. It's like one of the finest German cities. It has a corso which is very beautiful and full of life. You know the kind of thing I mean, a boulevard with trees and grass and cafés. In the late afternoon everyone meets there, young men and young women. . . ."

She stopped speaking, and a sad expression came into her eyes. Turning away her head, she rested her chin on her hand and bit the corner of her lip. Laulerque wondered whether she was going to cry. She sighed.

"How wretched it all is!" she said.

"What's wretched?"—he asked the question as gently as he could.

"Oh, nothing . . . only that sometimes life seems to go so wrong. Things are so easy for some people, and one doesn't know why."

Seated before this face which, despite the irregularity of its features, was so attractive, Laulerque tried to imagine the principal boulevard of some big provincial town, but not in France; idle crowds moving up and down, young men and women sauntering. He saw one of the young women—the one whose face now confronted his—walking this boulevard years before, watched her meeting each day the same young man and exchanging glances with him. One day they would stop and exchange a few words, half tenderly, half in mockery, just as those around them were doing. Another day they would arrange to meet in some less crowded place. He seemed to see them in those other places too—in gardens, but it was the corso of Agram with its crowd, its cafés, its greenery, that seemed always the true setting for their love. It was the thought of this corso, of the movement of the crowd on its grass, that made her want to cry now. That corso would have been the centre of her life if it had developed in accordance with the ordinary, simple rules of existence. Happiness should have ripened there for her, incident following incident, like grapes on a vine. No one can be sure of escaping unhappiness: when great disasters strike the world their effects are felt by all alike. But until they strike, it is madness to refuse the happiness which ordinary things can bring, to refuse to be, if such a thing is possible, a young woman walking up and down the corso of Agram on her lover's arm. Exile. A little table covered with a cloth of coloured checks. The counter, seen through a mist of thoughts, piled with saucers and rolls of shiny bread. An unknown companion opposite, never, perhaps, to be seen again. A strange house where children wait, children whom one must not allow oneself to love, just as, when one falls asleep in a railway car, one must not let one's head slip on to one's neighbour's shoulder. Now and again, cloaked in the profoundest secrecy, some ambiguous mission which must be carried blindly through, perhaps for the sake of an ideal, perhaps just for the thrill it gives, but always in ignorance of the risks (even of death, perhaps) that it may bring in its train.

Laulerque found unexpected questions forming themselves in his mind. The first, which came again and again to his consciousness, began with the words: "How about myself? . . ." and a second: "Is all heroism nothing but a substitute?" But these questions were not as dangerous for him as they might have been for others. Except on very rare occasions, he could always send unwelcome queries to the right-about.

She had directed their walk along the Sophiaplein to show him the canals.

"Already the moon is beautiful. You don't dislike moonlight, do you? In this quarter of the town there are lovely canals with old black houses, and roofs like this" (she sketched an inverted V with her finger). "It's not as good as Venice, but it's good enough for us, isn't it? No one but lovers should go to Venice."

"You've been there?"

"To Venice? Never. I've often heard people speak of it. Venice, you know, is quite close to Agram. In my country almost all young married couples go there. Lots of my friends have been. Some of them thought of me and sent me picture postcards."

A moment later she added:

"Friends, I mean, of my own age."

The figure of the young woman was lit simultaneously by the light of a street-lamp on the opposite bank and by the moon. She was smiling now. Laulerque tried to distinguish the elements of despair hidden behind her smile, but all he could see was the beauty, the appeal, that the moonlight gave her features. "How fine and brave of her," he reflected, "to smile like that when her thoughts must make her want to cry!" She lifted her face in such a way that the light from the summer sky which silhouetted the black gable ends of the houses shone in her eyes. They burned with a sort of melancholy exaltation. The pupils dilated until they seemed to him to be of the deepest black (he thought, however, that he had noticed that her eyes were dark green). From the water there came a strange emanation which changed for him the whole quality of the night. Chill there was in it, and a hint of brine and sewage, the sound of weary ripples and the frightening sense of deep water. But the breeze that reached him was soft, lulling him more sweetly than the breath of streets, murmuring a welcome in the shadowy corners.

Dreams came to him, but not as day-dreams come, for they had in them something of the permitted indulgence of sleep when the spirit lays aside responsibilities. The thought occurred to him that always in the picture he had painted for himself of the heroic life there had been a place for a woman. Not for a woman who could make him momentarily forget the labours and perils of the day, and who knew them not, but for a woman who should take her part in them. She should be not the warrior's relaxation, but the companion of his toils, polishing his weapons, keeping watch, taking secret messages. "Why shouldn't I fall in love with her? Isn't she 'mine,' the one whom destiny has brought to me in a way so strange as to be worth noting? She is not very beautiful, or, rather, she was not an hour or two ago, but now I delight in her. I see that she is of those who take beauty from their surroundings, who can become transfigured. Besides, a fighting woman should not have the beauty of a doll. . . . And, that our love may be really free, really heroic, nothing shall compel us to change the manner of our lives. She shall remain here, I there. From time to time we shall meet; at the same moment we shall exchange kisses and the messages of danger. Why shouldn't it be so?"

But up to now they had said nothing to each other of this danger, of this life of heroism, of the reasons and the ends that must be held to justify it. Their silence, certainly, had been dictated by discipline, but a faith that is inarticulate runs the risk of being doubted, if not in the matter of its zeal, which can be recognized by certain signs, at least in that of its inspiration. Eyes that flash with the same enthusiasm may hide quite different thoughts. Laulerque at times had an uneasy feeling of cross-purposes at work. "After all, what guarantee have I that she thinks the same thoughts as I do, that she believes herself to be fighting for the same cause? . . . What a hideous thought! . . . Making people go here, there, and everywhere, giving to each the excuse, firing each with the fanaticism, of his own peculiar mania! Extraordinary, but not absolutely impossible. The most subtle, the most cynical puppet-show that the world has ever seen, helped by all this business of mystery, and used in the service of God knows what interests. . . . And all that would go on until one day two marionettes, through disobedience or through love, might take it into their heads to confide in each other the enthusiasm that fired them."

It seemed to him that the best way of assuring the explanation he wanted would be to put into words all that he had been thinking, giving it the form of a joking hypothesis.

"Do you know what just came into my head? . . ."

She listened smiling, but said nothing. He continued:

"Suppose that you and I became friends, very great friends. There's nothing to forbid that, is there? Then we might, I suppose, talk of the weather, but never of our—activities, of our ideas?"

She smiled.

"There's no reason why we should become great friends. . . . Perhaps we shall never see each other again. . . . I may never have another envelope to give you. . . ."

"But I may quite easily be sent to Holland again. . . . Well, once I've done my business, surely I should have the right, if I had time, to send you a word, to meet you again just for my own pleasure?"

"No, I think not. Wouldn't that be a breach of discipline? Besides, you won't have my address; and you mustn't try to find it out."

"She's making fun of me," he thought, "but she's half serious all the same. She clings to these obstacles; she likes to feel herself a prisoner. I shall get nothing from her unless I respect the rules of the game."

"So be it. I know less about discipline than you do. I'm new to all this. I'll abide by what you say."

"Even if I decide that tonight is to be the last meeting of our lives?"

"I should still hope that you might be given the mission of meeting some unknown, and that the unknown might turn out to be me."

As they walked he had very discreetly taken her arm. He held the back of it only, without pressing it, but every now and then giving it a slight touch as he might have done had he been walking with a friend of his own sex. She appeared not to notice anything.

He continued:

"You haven't answered me. Suppose we could see each other again without infringing any of the rules . . . that we could become friends, exchange thoughts on all sorts of subjects. . . . Should we never feel the need of being sure that we were each of us working for the same cause? Is that the one thought that we should never confide?"

She looked at him.

"Do you trust those who sent you here?"

"Yes."

"Well, then? . . . If you came without trusting them you would be mad."

He felt that it would be stupid to insist. He slid his hand forward until it held her forearm. He pressed it slightly. She started nervously, but did not free herself. They passed a bridge and came to another canal.

"After all," thought Laulerque, "I mustn't expect too much. My luck's not been so bad." He looked at the moonlight, at the flat expanse of shimmering water, at their two shadows, at her profile beside him.

A few minutes later, and of her own accord, she said:

"Here in Holland no one believes that a war will break out, perhaps because they're proud of being the home of the Hague Tribunal, but also because the majority of them are pacifists in their hearts and can't imagine that anyone could really want war. I know many people in my own country who want war, and they're not all on the same side by any means. You've no idea of the state of confusion that exists there. Here everything seems so comparatively simple. Even in my own family I have cousins who are members of secret societies. It isn't exactly war that they're after so much as the destruction of the dual monarchy and the liberation of the southern Slavs. But they argue that it would be easier to attain all that as a result of the confusion that war would bring. And on the other side there are the people in Vienna who want war in order to crush the internal enemies of the dual monarchy."

Laulerque was just going to say: "Do you think we shall succeed in stopping that? That we're numerous enough, powerful enough?"

—but she stopped him with these surprising words:

"If things had turned out differently for me, I might have been conspiring with my cousins."

He had tried to make her go back with him to his room in the Hotel Damrak, but she had shrugged her shoulders as though at the absurd suggestion of a child.

She even said:

"It's after midnight. I'm never out after midnight. You'll be responsible for their thinking very badly of me. I must go back at once."

She let him kiss her cheek. When his lips touched her, she squeezed his hand violently. He tried for more, but she refused to give him her lips, not as though she were angry, but with an air of determination which was completely free of coquetry.

They parted on the Dam, where she found a cab. She would not let him go with her to her house, and she gave the address to the coachman in a low voice. Laulerque managed to hear indistinctly a word which ended in "park."

But at the moment of leaving him she took a little note-book from her bag, hurriedly wrote a few words on one of the pages which she tore out and gave to him.

"If you want to send me news of yourself, you can write to me in this name, Poste Restante, Amsterdam. I will call in there next week."

He read, written in a severe and angular hand, the words:

Margaret-Désideria.

Chapter

7

MIONNET'S STAR IN THE ASCENDANT

On the 25th of June the Abbé Mionnet's mail contained a request that he would go and see Monsignor Lebaigue at four o'clock the day following.

The prelate received him after keeping him waiting for only a few minutes.

"Ah, there you are! Excellent. You didn't think I should be communicating with you so soon? When I'm interested in anyone, however. . . . Unfortunately, I fear you must be prepared for a disappointment. . . . What I have to speak to you about isn't what you think, far from it; but life's like that. You make a hit with the violin, you attract attention, but when a vacancy comes it's for a trombone! What I'm offering you now is a trombonist's part. You can think it over at leisure; we shan't hurry you; you can have at least a week in which to make up your mind. For the moment, if you'd like me to, I'll give you a rough idea of the general situation, without dotting any i's. If you find yourself opposed to the suggestion in principle, there'll be no point in going further in the matter. If, on the other hand, you are not, generally speaking, hostile, you can come and see me again in two or three days. I'm anxious that you should have plenty of time for reflection. We in the Church are not in love with rash decisions; I, particularly, dislike them. If you agree to come and see me again, I will go into details—details which, needless to say, you will keep to yourself, whatever line you take eventually. Then you shall have another two or three days to turn it all over in your mind, and at the beginning of July you will give us a definite yes or no. Is that all clear?"

Mionnet smiled and bowed.

"One more thing: once you have decided, you must be ready to move at a moment's notice. You won't, I imagine, have much difficulty in getting free of the Catholic Institute? Doubtless your course of lectures and the examinations will soon be over? If need be I can have a word with Baudrillart."

He coughed, bit all round his thumb-nail, and continued as follows:

"Well, the situation is this: We're having trouble in one of our dioceses. When I say 'we,' I'm not being quite accurate, because the business doesn't really concern the Paris authorities directly. Rome, however, has asked us to lend a hand in the matter. To cut a long story short, a delicate situation has arisen of a kind that can't be dealt with by the usual means. Let me explain in rather greater detail. The occupant of the see is not old—far from it—but he recently had a severe illness, a thing that may happen to anybody. It is said that he will make a perfect recovery, that he is half cured already. That may or may not be so. What really embarrasses us is that he was guilty of certain foolish acts before he fell ill, acts which may have been responsible for his attack. . . . I know what you're thinking, but I can assure you it's nothing of that sort. I won't go so far as to say that his morals are beyond reproach, because I know nothing about them, but they have nothing to do with his present embarrassments. Several possible courses have already been under consideration. We might ask him to resign, but that's not a thing that we like doing. In the circumstances, it would merely underline the scandal, and there is still time to minimize its effects; perhaps, even, to discount them altogether. It would be possible, of course, to leave him where he is with instructions to take no action, and to hand over the actual administration of the diocese to a vicar-general. The trouble about that is that the Vicar-General—there's only one; there might of course be two, but, in fact, there is only one—is more or less tarred with the same brush, and at the moment is in rather a hang-dog mood, despite the fact that he's a protonotary apostolic. Why not, you'll say, appoint a coadjutor? Well, in the first place, that's another of the things that, as you know, we don't much like doing, for various reasons; besides, it wouldn't really meet the case. No, the best course, we think, would be to set up a temporary commission with as little fuss as possible and entrust it to a man of energy and tact who has no connexion with the locality . . . a man not very high up in the hierarchy, so that his presence won't offend or give rise to scandal. He must, however, be someone who . . . you understand me? Someone who can exert personal authority, who has a sure touch and can take in a situation at a glance. I warn you, it's rather a dirty business. You'll have to handle all sorts of people, clerical and lay, men and women, and you must expect more kicks than bouquets. And when everything's been put straight—as by God's grace we hope it will be— you must be prepared to fade away as though nothing had happened. It's a sort of Jesuit job; you know their motto?—'Give help where help's most needed.' Well, that's the thing in a nutshell. It means tucking up your habit and going hard at it. The prospect doesn't frighten you? . . . If you succeed, I can make no promises; I have no authority to do so; besides, you're so young. But you'll have had a chance to show your mettle such as doesn't fall to everybody's lot. . . . It's an opportunity."

Mionnet, after first expressing his sense of the honour done him and of his own unworthiness, asked to be corrected if he had attached more importance than was right to the proposed task. Was it, to a certain extent, and without any overt declaration, a matter of substituting for a bishop who was getting remiss in his work, of taking over, in fact, a part of his authority and of his responsibilities, of making decisions and issuing orders in his place? If that was so, the difficulty—apart from the extent and the novelty of the work— would be to compel the obedience, in the absence of any official title, of those who would be his superiors in the hierarchy, to ensure even their toleration of his presence. Was he, however, wrong perhaps in thus interpreting the situation and was nothing more intended than a visit of inspection with limited powers and within a strictly limited sphere?

"Both," replied Monsignor Lebaigue. "Naturally, there's a whole department of routine diocesan work with which I hope that you'll not have to concern yourself—unless, that is, you find everything at sixes and sevens—all that part of a bishop's work, for instance, which has to do with his public appearances and which concerns only the outward dignities of his office. I needn't insist on that. You won't be asked to bless the crowd. It is probable that your first duty will be to intervene in a perfectly definite situation. But one thing leads to another. A diocese in which things of the sort I'm talking about have been allowed to develop is a house which is being badly run. You'll have to peer into all kinds of corners, and you'll have authority to do so. You need have no doubts on that point. Your arrival will be expected. The people on the spot will clearly understand that though the man who's been sent to them may not have stripes on his sleeve, higher authority is behind him, and that what he says goes. That'll be made perfectly plain. I warned you that it would be a dirty job, and I promised you plenty of kicks, because, human nature being what it is, you won't be received with unmixed pleasure. You'll have to be constantly on your guard against traps. Besides, in addition to the clergy who will be amenable to the argument of authority, you'll find that you are up against a lay element with which you'll have to deal in other ways."

Monsignor Lebaigue gave Mionnet a shrewd look and added, with a little burst of laughter:

"Oh, as an apprenticeship, you could ask nothing better!"

Mionnet said that he would think it over and consider how far he regarded himself as competent to undertake such work; that in general he considered himself as being entirely at the disposition of his superiors to be used in any work to which they might think it advisable to call him; that one needn't be a Jesuit to admire their motto and to adopt it for one's own guidance. In short, he concluded, the only thing that might make him hesitate would be the magnitude of the proposed task and the sense of his own incapacity.

A further interview was arranged for the next day but one.

This time, Monsignor Lebaigue rose from his chair to greet him. "Well, have you made your decision?"

"Almost, Monsignor. That's to say, unless when I hear the details which you were good enough to promise me, I find that it involves unsuspected difficulties."

"Good; then lend me your ears. You've not guessed the diocese in question? Well, it's M—. Knowing that, you realize that it's not in the jurisdiction of Paris. I ought to tell you that the Metropolitan, the Archbishop of B—, is a very old friend of His Eminence Monsignor Amette, whose opinion he is fond of asking. He is, moreover, a man not remarkable for courage, whose qualities of heart are greater than his intelligence and strength of character. It is a pity that the expression 'pious donkey' has already been used in connexion with somebody else whose memory"—Monsignor Lebaigue was here shaken by a fit of laughter—"we hold in particular veneration. I may say, in confidence, that that explains how it is that matters at M— have been allowed to get into their present state. A metropolitan worthy of the name would have put us on our guard before now. He's certainly had enough warning. But"—he laughed again—"he is not the sort of man who remains wakeful for long. He quickly lapses into somnolence. . . . Besides, he has a horror of scandals, of dealing with people, of everything like that. . . . No doubt he thought that things would come right while he took his nap. . . . But things haven't come right. If now Rome makes representations to us instead of trying to arrange things with the people on the spot, it's because Rome thinks that an emissary sent from a distance will find fewer obstacles and will be able to act with a greater sense of detachment. . . . Let us be fair, though. The idea of a special mission, tactfully handled so as to avoid any obvious upset, came in the first place from the Archbishop of B—. Fear of scandal sometimes makes a man inventive. . . ."

He stretched his hand towards a bundle of files which lay on his left, and took them up one by one.

"There's one thing which I forgot to mention the day before

yesterday, but I don't think it'll bother you much, and that is the length of time the business'll take. It's difficult to be precise on that point. It may last three months, it may last two years. It will entirely depend on the results you can attain and on the measures which you will consider it necessary to take. If the situation is grave enough to necessitate an amputation, there will be no point in letting things drag on. If, however, the patient can be cured without an operation —I refer to the diocese—you will have to wait. . . . You've already spoken to Monsignor Baudrillart?"

"Not yet, Monsignor. I didn't consider that I had any authority to do so."

"You don't think he'll make a fuss? . . . Well, we'll see about that later."

He found the file for which he was looking and opened it.

"Ah, the diocese contains about 367,000 souls, almost all of whom are Catholics, at least by birth. A fair size, you see: 43 rural deaneries, 256 parishes. . . . You notice that I'm going into the matter as though I were making you a formal proposal. . . ."

He looked at Mionnet.

". . . Gives you an anticipatory taste of what's to come, eh?"

Mionnet could not help blushing. Monsignor Lebaigue went on, after vigorously rubbing one of his nostrils:

"One Vicar-General—there were two at one time. I don't know why there's only one now. . . . He is a protonotary apostolic, as I think I told you. . . . A complete chapter, to wit: one Canon who acts as secretary to the Bishop, a diocesan Director of Education, a diocesan Director of Social Work, who is also a Canon and can't have much to do, and a third Canon who combines the office of chaplin of the Sacré-Cœur with the duties of editing the *Religious Weekly*. Those are the people with whom you'll have direct dealings. But the only one in whom you can have real confidence, on whom you can rely for information, and from whom you can find out how the land lies without the risk of walking into a trap is the editor of the *Religious Weekly*, a fellow called Delhostal. . . . But now let's come to the point. You should know that the present crisis has to do with the tramways. That's not exactly what you were expecting, eh? I won't go into details, partly because I've not mastered them myself, partly because it's your job to find them out, but I can give you a rough idea of what's been happening. Our good friend the Bishop, Monsignor Sérasquier, is pretty well off; he is also a bit of a megalomaniac and has always had a weakness for dabbling in matters of finance. Well, it so happens that he got himself rather too deeply involved in the organization of a local company for the running of an electric street-car service. The business involved, over and above the mere provision of track, such things as the harnessing of water-power and the building of factories—the idea was to combine the tramway concern with a wider enterprise for supplying electric light to several of the neighbouring villages. . . . The prime movers in the business were certain local notables who had the reputation of being honest, but you know as well as I do that it only needs the presence on the board of one adventurer, even of one irresponsible individual, one slightly dubious character, to change the whole complexion of affairs. The Bishop was as much entitled as anybody else to lose his money, if he wanted to, but where he went wrong was in letting it be generally understood that the authorities of the diocese were behind the undertaking. You know what happens in these provincial towns. It's quite enough for a few somebodies to say with a certain inflexion: 'Monsignor is greatly interested,' or 'The Bishop has made a point of recommending the tramway company; all the canons have taken shares'; to have the same effect as though the matter had been printed in capitals and exhibited on every billboard. My own opinion is that Monsignor Sérasquier, having tied up rather too much money in the business, got uneasy and wanted to spread the shares as widely as possible in order to cover his own commitments. . . . However that may be, things began to go wrong. Expenses turned out to be heavier than the estimates allowed for, the contractors got cold feet, and, in short, whether or no there was a certain amount of ill will involved, work on the scheme has come to a standstill. Everything is planned, and there's no open talk of liquidation or bankruptcy, but thousands of people are beginning to feel the pinch; they're getting panicky and starting to kick up a row. They make no bones about holding the Bishop responsible, and declare that if he hadn't vouched for the undertaking, they'd never have touched it. There's a nice little scandal getting under way. One of the noisiest critics is, it seems, a certain stock-breeder, who's gone so far as to threaten that he'll get the shareholders to institute proceedings for fraud. He's a popular sort of fellow thereabouts, who knows a lot of people and can bring a good deal of influence to bear. It'll be easy for him to get plenty of support for these proceedings, and even if they come to nothing, the moral effect of the business will be, as you can well understand, deplorable. I've been told, too, of a certain great lady, or almost great lady, who runs a salon at M—. So far she's made no threats, but I understand that her influence will count for a good deal. At this point things become very complicated, and I shall probably get it all mixed up. You'll have to make a very careful inquiry. The man I've told you about called Delhostal, the only one of the Chapter who's not got shares, will help you. The husband of the great lady I've mentioned will probably do all he knows to discredit the tramway company, because he was preparing to launch one of his own and is furious at having the ground cut from under his feet; it's said, also, that he has a personal dislike of the Bishop. But I'm told that it might be possible to get round him through his wife, and that in that case he could arrange everything satisfactorily, either by coming into the affair himself or by using his influence with the contractors. It's even said that he's behind the noisiest section of the critics of the scheme, that he's got an interest, for example, in a big cement and raw-material business, which is one of the most important of the creditors and was the first to shut off supplies. Furthermore, I have reason to believe that the lady has the ear of the Prefect, and in a case of this kind the Prefect's got to be reckoned with. The company, you see, has had to get a departmental concession, and it appears that, if the Prefect turned nasty, there's a clause in the contract which would enable him to withdraw the concession. If that happened, the fat would be in the fire."

Monsignor Lebaigue paused a moment before continuing in a different tone:

"I won't go into the—the more intimate details of the affair. I've no doubt you'll hear all about them when you get there, and I don't know how far they're to be believed. It's all very complicated, and because it's complicated it's annoying. The whole thing will need extremely delicate handling. It's not merely a question of a quarrel between friends and enemies of the Church; if it were only that, it would be too simple, and, in a sense, easier. Far from it. I'm not saying that the enemies of the Church aren't on the look-out, and that they won't do their best to exploit the scandal if a scandal develops, but the discontented elements, those who consider that they have been victimized, include a number of excellent Catholics, and they're by no means the least embittered. It's they, in particular, who are making such a hullabaloo about the Bishop's part in the business and who are the loudest in their demand for his head. (The infidels are quite cynical on the point; his head or someone else's, they don't care.) They've already made representations to the Archbishop of B—, who'd be glad enough to take their part if it wasn't for the fact that by doing so he'd be broadcasting the fault and handing our enemies a weapon to use against us. What you've got to do is, in some way or other, to settle things, to get tempers back to normal, and to arrange the affairs of the diocese, if necessary, at the cost of the removal of certain individuals, a removal which would be carried out tactfully and by degrees. In saying this I wish you to understand that I make no exceptions—not even of the individual chiefly responsible. But all that is something that can only be considered after the storm has calmed down, when public attention will be no longer on the alert. You understand the general idea?"

Mionnet assured him that he thought he did, but that, all the same, he was rather appalled at the amount of energy, cleverness, and even of practical knowledge that it seemed to be expected he would be able to bring to the task. It wouldn't be a question only of understanding the inner workings of a diocese. He would have to master the details of corporation law, the technicalities of electric supply. He would have to be able to tackle financiers and industrialists on their own ground.

"Let us not exaggerate!" cried Monsignor Lebaigue. "No one is asking you to discuss estimates with the contractors or to find the money yourself with which to put the business on its feet again. You can perfectly well begin without knowing the first word about finance or electricity. Your work will be purely psychological—to enlist sympathy and to transform ill will into good will, or, at least, into a spirit of neutrality; to pour oil on troubled waters and to make the good Catholics realize the damage they risk doing to their religion. You may also have to administer a salutary shock to the powers that be. For all this you need nothing but character and intelligence, but those two qualities are essential. Once you let yourself be thwarted or outmanoeuvred, all will be lost."

Monsignor Lebaigue had got up. He looked hard at Mionnet as though he were judging the contents of a cask, and his expression said as plainly as though he had put the thought into words: "Hang it all, if you succeed, so much the better for you. If you fail—well, if you fail, it means that we have been mistaken in you; and that's that."

But what he actually said was:

"I will give you another forty-eight hours in which to make up your mind."

Chapter

THE RED NOTE-BOOK

Mionnet, entering his study, looked gloomily at his two suit-cases, his small trunk, and the various parcels and odds and ends which he had not yet been able to pack. His table was still covered with litter. He hesitated a moment and looked at his watch. "If I don't get my writing done this evening," he thought, "there'll be no time tomorrow. Once I get there, I shall be too busy. . . . It'd be a pity not to finish it."

The decision taken, he cleared a space on the table. Then, lifting the tray from his trunk, he took from the bottom, where it was hidden under a pile of linen, a japanned tin box secured by two secret locks. This box he opened. It contained two books of about the same size as itself, which lay one on top of the other. Both were handsomely bound, one in green leather, the other in dark red.

He took the red book, shut the box again, sat down at the table, laid the book in front of him, and turned its pages. The paper was of good quality, strong and glossy. The first sixty or so pages were covered with careful script divided into what appeared to be chapters, the shortest of which occupied two or three pages, the longer as many as ten. At the head of each, in the middle of the line, was written a number in roman figures, but the arrangement of these numbers appeared to have nothing to do with numerical sequence. Thus, IX came after XVII, and XVII was repeated at least twice. The text was set in the form of a dialogue, but every alternate reply was regularly prefaced by the letter M followed by a dash, and these sentences were, on an average, very short, and were, in many cases, replaced by a line of dots. The other replies, most of which were much longer, were introduced, just as regularly, by the letter P. In several instances the

beginning of a chapter was composed of several lines of dots, sometimes interspersed with text, sometimes not.

Mionnet turned the pages, glanced at what he had written, smiled,
and turned some more. In this way he proceeded until he reached the
first blank page. Then, flattening the book with his hand, he prepared
to write.

In the middle of the line he inscribed a large XIV, at the side of
which he put a small 1 in brackets. Then at the bottom of the page
he added, in the form of a note:

"(1) See pages" . . .

He hurriedly turned back until he found two chapters already
numbered XIV, noticed the numbers of their respective pages, which
were 4 and 29, and inserted these figures in his note. With two fingers
of his left hand he continued to keep the book open at these two
places.

Turning back to the chapters in question, he hurriedly ran through
them, sat for a moment concentrating his thoughts, and then began
once more to write.

He stopped frequently, as though hesitating over the turn of a
phrase. When he did this, his attitude became characteristic. He
leaned his head slightly forward, closed his eyes, wrinkled his forehead, and supported it on the five fingers of his left hand, keeping
them close together and touching the precise middle of his brow.
Now and again he turned his head slightly, rather as though he were
trying to hear some scarcely perceptible sound.

It was obvious that during these pauses he was concerned not with
questions of composition or criticism, but with memory. He was
trying to find some word that he had actually heard rather than a
word apt to his purpose, a sequence of phrases dictated by memory
rather than a suitable arrangement of ideas. He followed the same
principle when he scratched out anything that he had written, though
as far as possible he avoided having to do so. Before setting down a
sentence he waited a moment to make sure that he had remembered
it correctly, and if he later changed his mind, he tried to make the

correction by means of a pen-knife. He clearly wanted the book to preserve a clean and pleasing appearance.

After about an hour and a half's concentrated and careful work, he had written the following.

. . . .
. . . .

Breath very strong. The garlic difficult to put up with; it appeared to be mixed with a smell of wine.

. . . .

Got muddled during the saying of the *Confession*. Not yet quite clear about her circumstances.

. . . .

P.—I really must say, Father, how much ashamed I am at having insisted, as I did, on seeing you this evening. It must have been very inconvenient for you, with everything upside down and your packing to do. It's not the eve of a feast-day, and I don't mean to take communion. But you're going away, and Heaven knows when you'll come back, when I shall see you again. I wanted to congratulate you. Yes, indeed, Monsieur de A— has spoken to me about it. He said it is very remarkable at your age; that actually what they're doing is to give you a bishop's appointment, and that if you do well, there's nothing you mayn't look forward to. I repeat exactly what he said; make what use of it you like. So, you see, I didn't want to let you go without confessing once more to you. I'm really very much upset. I grow attached to my confessors, and I've no idea whom to go to in your place. Are there any of your colleagues you can recommend? —someone of about your own age? I don't like old men, they never listen, and they're not interested in one's affairs. They become indifferent, probably as a result of hearing too many people. Not that I expect to find anyone who will listen to me as you do. There'll be nobody at Saint-B— when you've gone. Between ourselves, your priest in charge is always thinking about something else. One might disclose the most appalling torments of conscience, but it would make no difference, his head would still be in the clouds. I've tried every kind of confessor, some of them with a big reputation. I'm quite sure that I don't want an old man. What's the name of the other visiting priest here, the rather reddish one? . . .

M.—. . . . .

P.—What a name! I'm quite sure I shouldn't like him. Of course he's young, but he looks after himself so badly. He's the kind of man who doesn't wash, you can take my word for it. I expect his feet smell, to say nothing of anything else. One needn't be dirty to be devout. Besides, they say that red-headed men have a peculiar smell, worse than most people. The very idea of being in a confessional with him on the other side of the screen is intolerable. It's close enough as it is for the time of year. Not that I want somebody who's all perfumed like the Abbé C—. Far from it. Meeting him at the Comtesse D— de E—'s, I can laugh it off, but in a constricted space like this I believe it would turn me faint. You must tell me, Father, if I'm getting off the point and making you waste your time. Alas, I shan't have many more opportunities of wasting it! I'm not forgetting what it is I want to say. I always feel at home with you. I don't mind admitting it frankly, because, other things being equal, you're not at all the kind of man who could give me evil thoughts, if I can say so without offending you. But I feel I can tell you everything. You see, I do so believe that if one's to find grace, it's important not to be put off by impressions, and what I've got to tell you is very, very difficult. I can't see myself mentioning it to a confessor whom I didn't know already. But I suppose that, from the point of view of conscience, I ought to, oughtn't I? It's a piece of luck that you were able to hear me today, on the eve of your departure. Must I confess my ordinary sins first, Father?

M.—As you like, my child.

P.—Perhaps it would be better, in one way, since if I leave them till later, I may forget them; besides, they will give me courage. Well, then, Father, I have been guilty—I'm sure I shall leave a lot of things out, because I haven't prepared this part of my confession. But if I remember anything later, I suppose I can always mention it next time to my new confessor?

M.—Certainly.

P.—But it won't prevent your absolution being generally effective, will it?

M.—Oh no.

P.—Well, then, I'm not quite sure, but—oh yes, I've several times been guilty of gluttony; I broke my fast twice, once on Whitsun eve, and another time as well, but I'm not quite sure when. I've made hasty judgments about various people. I remember saying, for example, that the Comte de A— was a dirty Jesuit. That's rather awful, isn't it?—because I was guilty not only of disrespect to religion, but to its ministers. Do you think the Count ought to be regarded as a minister of religion? . . .

M.—I don't think so.

P.—If I died suddenly after saying a thing like that, should I die in a state of mortal sin?

M.—I think not.

P.—I've quarrelled on more than one occasion with my sister-in-law. I've been guilty, Father, of a lack of charity towards her. I told her that the amount of noble blood she had wasn't worth talking about; I told her she was miserly, and that her meanness stunk of the back shop, and a lot of things like that.

M.—Had she provoked you?

P.—No—or rather, yes. She made fun of something I said, she laughed at me with my nephews behind my back. I'm guilty of having said that she'd turned my brother into a dirty climber, that he was ready to become a Jew or a Freemason if it would help him to succeed, and that I hoped that Monsieur F— de G—, who's a real gentleman, would put a spoke in his wheel. But I kissed my sister-in-law afterwards, and I burned candles for my brother's election. I'm guilty of having had doubts about the existence of God and about the truths of religion. I'm guilty of having often envied unbelievers because of the wicked lives they can live. . . .

M.—In this world; but do you envy the fate that's in store for them?

P.—Oh, no, of course not. But when I thought that, I had doubts about the future life. . . . I am guilty of having several times been lacking in respect for the saints. I can't help it; the stories about them are sometimes so comic.

M.—Wouldn't it be better to give up your daily reading, if the profit you derive from it is so mixed, or to substitute for it some other form of reading which would not have the same disadvantages?

P.—But it interests me. Am I committing a mortal sin?

M.—If it's only the imperfection of their mortal state that affects you like this, if you are guilty of no hostility, no essential impiety . . .

P.—Oh, dear, I wonder why I'm bothering about all that, when I think of what I'm going to tell you in a moment!

M.—I am listening, my child.

P.—Do you know Monsieur H—? It's stupid of me to ask, but I'm so bothered. Of course you know him. Oh, where am I to begin? I want you to know that I've been interested in that young man ever since he started coming to the house. I saw at once that he was intelligent, informed, and comparatively well-bred, considering what he sprang from, and that he knows his place. I liked talking to him. I don't have many opportunities of talking to people. I live a lonely life, a very lonely life. Those who see me now and then don't probably realize how lonely. My little J— is the only company I have, but now that she's grown up I see less of her. Besides, she'll be going away soon. You know all about that? You're going away too. My little J— is going to be married in a few weeks, and then she'll leave me for good. Of course there's a difference; I know the two things aren't comparable. But it all means the same, that I don't have a very gay life. I've always sacrificed myself for my brother. You'd think, wouldn't you, that he'd take some notice of me as a result? But he doesn't. He makes me wild. He's always laughing at my little fads, as though he hadn't any of his own!—what with his exercises, which I can hear through the wall, and the wretched little whore he keeps.

I've never breathed a word about that to my sister-in-law. He's not bad at heart, but he's an egotist. He thinks it perfectly natural that I should ruin my life to help him, just as was done in noble families before the Revolution. You see, then, that it wasn't so very wicked of me to find a little pleasure in this young man's society. There was nothing wrong in what I did. We talked about serious subjects—not only about serious subjects, but that was only when other things cropped up, naturally. Besides, I've not seen such an awful lot of him. I've counted the times. I've had, perhaps, three or four real conversations with him. It's my dreams that are beginning to worry me. I've always dreamed a lot, but as a rule my dreams were quite illogical, nightmares—you know the sort of things, about robbers, and being chased, and falling over precipices. Oh dear, it can't be so very bad to dream of someone one meets almost every day. You don't think, do you, that one ought to get too much worried over qualms of conscience?

M.—. . . . .

P.—That's what I always thought. But you see, to begin with, I started to dream of him naked.

M.—. . . . .

P.—I mean *he* was naked, completely naked. And in my dream it was I who took his clothes off. I don't mean that I dreamed about undressing him in detail. You see, I never have undressed a man altogether—at least I don't remember having done so. I've helped my brother take off his hunting-clothes—the upper ones—and I undressed my nephews when they were children, but only when they were quite small. . . . Perhaps once, when J— was ill; but I'm sure he kept his shirt on. But all that was entirely different; even the impression it made on me was different. You see, even in my dream I knew that I was doing something wrong. When a thing like that is only in one's dreams is it a sin?

M.—. . . . .

P.—Of course. . . . I can't say that next morning I thought about it "with pleasure," as you put it. But I didn't refuse to think about it.

Perhaps I'm not sure whether I thought about it with pleasure. I said to myself: "Here's a pretty state of affairs! Who'd have said I should dream things like that!" I blamed myself. But all the same I saw myself again undoing his buttons, and, do what I might, I couldn't help the thought sending me into raptures. That's quite definitely a sin of the imagination, isn't it?

M.—...

P.—What I want to know is, have we any influence on our dreams? When I went to bed the next night, I seemed to hear a little voice saying deep down inside me: "If only I could dream as I did last night!"

M.—You did not pray that this temptation should be taken from you?

P.—I said my prayers as I always do. But I didn't make any particular request. You see, my thoughts were elsewhere.

M.—So the dream came again. But tell me, has anything worse happened since?

P.—The only thing that happened was that when I next met Monsieur H— I was very uncomfortable. I didn't dare look at him, just as though we'd really been guilty of some wickedness. I had an idea that if I looked at him I should see him actually without any clothes on. But, Father, please don't think that I didn't struggle. I did. Perhaps I ought to have come and seen you at once, but I didn't dare. The whole thing was so stupid. But you would have given me good advice, while, as it was, with no one to rely on but myself, I became discouraged. It's all terrible. The Devil had the last word.

M.—...

P.—I ended by not caring. I allowed evil thoughts to come as they would. As I told you, I made myself ill with struggling. I thought to myself: "Why shouldn't you give yourself a little treat? After all, they're only thoughts, and they give you pleasure. There's plenty of people who don't stop at thoughts!" Clearly, it was the Devil prompting me; I know that. But I couldn't stop it. I was on a slippery slope, wasn't I?

M.—..

P.—Particularly touches, Father; I thought about the way I had touched him all over his body; but I always knew that the thought was impure. And then at other times I imagined myself holding him close against me when we were both naked.

M.—You have gone on seeing him?

P.—Naturally; he has even stayed to dinner once or twice. My brother has always gone out of his way to be polite to him, because of the various ways in which he's been useful. He still needs his help from time to time.

M.—Has your attitude towards him always been perfectly correct?

P.—If he'd paid any attention to me, he would almost certainly have noticed something. But he's not within a mile of suspecting—at least, I don't think he is. Women are at a great disadvantage in these matters. When my brother wants his little tart he always manages to let her know. I'm not in his confidence, but I hardly imagine that it's she who runs after him. And my brother's a married man, and so much the more to blame. But it doesn't prevent his being considered a good Christian, and I don't suppose that if he happens to go to confession, the priest refuses him absolution—especially now that he's a deputy.

M.—..

P.—I've taken no resolution. But tell me, Father, apart from the question of impure thoughts—and, as a matter of fact, I could get rid of them if I had the least glimmer of hope—apart from that, would you say that this could be called guilty passion?

M.—..

P.—If he proposed to me, I should certainly not refuse him.

M.—..

P.—Of course, because even if he wanted to, he'd be kept from doing so by this ridiculous prejudice about age, although I'd have you note that the opposite sort of thing is happening every day. The Comte de K— has just married a girl of twenty-three. But I want you to understand that I don't say for a moment that he'd dream of proposing; I'm not quite blind! All I say is that I'm not really to be blamed, since if it only depended on me, I'd be ready to say yes tomorrow.

M.—. . . . .

P.—I am only too anxious to keep my love pure. Anything else that there may be in it comes from the Devil, as I've told you. I've always thought that sort of thing disgusting, and I see no reason to change my mind now. All I want is to see him as often as possible, to talk to him, to watch him. I've suggested to my brother that he might invite him for the holidays.

M.—. . . . .

P.—Do you think I did wrong? But I've told you that it's the only way I know of ridding myself of impure thoughts. Without that I should never have the strength of will. I should relapse. I don't ask much: to watch his comings and goings from a distance, to breathe the same air. I will look after his things, his linen.

M.—. . . . .

P.—I swear that if necessary I'll see to it that he notices nothing. I shan't pester him. Don't forget, Father, that I have been brought up in the great world. I've never had the reputation of being either a fool or thoughtless. He will think it's all just affection. After all, Father, if I hadn't been so used to scrutinizing my motives, to analysing myself, as they say, mightn't I, too, have thought of it as merely affection? There are the dreams, of course; but a lot of people never remember their dreams and attach no importance to them. Tell me, Father, in order to get absolution, I needn't, need I, give you all the details of certain things that I imagined in my dreams, and even when I was awake?

M.—. . . . .

P.—I find it so painful to tell you of these aberrations, really I do, I have to assure myself again and again that the secrecy of the confessional is absolute. It is, isn't it?

M.—. . . . .

P.—I know. . . . . Forgive me, Father, if I seem . . . . I am so upset.

And now, as we are talking about the difficulty one finds in speaking about certain things at confession, although one knows perfectly well that in a case of that kind the priest is as secret as the grave . . . I want to take the opportunity to rid myself of something. It's a burden I've carried for a very long while, a burden of such a kind that I wonder sometimes whether all my communions up to now haven't been sacrilegious.

M.—. . . . .

P.—You see, each time, my conscience told me that I ought to speak of it to my confessor—when I say each time, I'm exaggerating a little, because there were times, luckily for me, when I didn't think about it; my conscience kept on saying that though I was not the person primarily responsible, I ought to confess what had happened. Well, I never have mentioned it, at first because I was a young girl and shy, later because—really I don't know; say, if you like, from a sense of decency or as a result of cowardice and disgust.

M.—. . . . .

P.—Well, then: I was sixteen at the time, or rather I was in my sixteenth year. It all happened in the summer at our family château. We had a manservant who did all sorts of odd jobs, half a sort of stable-boy, half a valet. My own room was in one of the wings, close to a tower. No one lived in the tower, which was used to store lumber. On the same floor as my room, there was a room in the tower which was used for keeping boxes and trunks in, things dating from various times, some of which were no longer used at all—I expect they're there still. I don't know for certain, because I've always avoided going back there. Well, this storeroom had narrow windows, one of which, as a result of the tower's shape, looked straight into mine. Now, you must understand that this man used to make all sorts of excuses to go into the tower whenever he thought that I was in my room. He used to go as near as possible to the window which looked on to mine, without ever standing right close up to it. In that position he could be seen by nobody but me, but to me he was completely visible as a result of the way in which the windows of the tower were set. I'm sure you'll never guess the awful thing he used to do, turned full towards me.

M.—I think I can guess.

P.—Are you sure you can, Father? You've heard people talk about that kind of thing? You think others have had a similar experience?

M.—Unfortunately, yes.

P.—Well, if they've talked about it, they're braver than I am.

M.—Was this—incident often repeated?

P.—Very often indeed at that time; almost every day, I should think.

M.—About the same time?

P.—Yes.

M.—And when would that be?

P.—Between three and four in the afternoon—certainly before tea. I am sure of that, because I can remember feeling sick in the drawing-room when I went down to tea.

M.—But were you obliged to be in your room always at that time?

P.—No.

M.—Well, then?

P.—Whatever you may think, Father, I swear to you that I was horrified by what I saw, sickened, frightened. Even now to think about it gives me a feeling of terror. The whole thing disgusted me with human nature, and especially with men. I could never have believed that they would be so bestial.

M.—You weren't compelled to look? Even without leaving the room it must have been possible to find some corner which wasn't in view of the tower? In any case you could have turned your head away, kept your eyes fixed on your work or on some book?

P.—I can't explain it—that's really why I've reproached myself so often for never speaking of this at confession. I knew that I had behaved badly.

M.—And it never occurred to you to complain to your mother?

P.—In the first place, I don't know how I could have spoken to her about such a thing, but the chief reason was that the man made me extremely frightened. I felt certain that if he were dismissed he would come back and murder me some night.

M.—Looking back with your later knowledge, do you think that the excuse was a reasonable one?

P.—It seems to me that it was natural for me to be frightened.

M.—Are you sure that your refusal to tell your mother was not in any way the result of a fear that to do so would bring about the cessation of an exhibition which took place every day, and from which you did not avert your eyes?

P.—Oh no, Father, I am certain it wasn't. I'm not trying to make myself out more innocent than I was, as you see, but that's no reason why I should make myself out worse.

M.—I'm not trying to make you out worse. Your curiosity, at the age you then were, was perfectly natural. And what the man did was natural too.

P.—What are you saying, Father?

M.—I'm merely reminding you that if one listens to the calls of nature, she is capable of leading one into every sort of aberration. You yourself said something of the same kind a little while back. To live according to nature is to live in a constant state of mortal sin. Christian virtue consists in not living according to nature.

P.—But, Father, tell me, was it, so far as I was concerned, a mortal sin?

M.—It contained elements of mortal sin.

P.—Then has every confession I have made since been incomplete, because I omitted to speak of it? Has every communion been sacrilegious?

M.—Probably, in the course of the various confessions you have made since then, you have from time to time accused yourself of harbouring evil, unhealthy, and impure thoughts, without particularizing them?

P.—Certainly, Father.

M.—Well, then, although it would have been better to particularize, this incident has been included in your repentance, and in the

absolution which you have received. In any case, you have repaired
the omission today.

P.—Oh, how happy that makes me! What a weight you have taken
off my mind by saying that! I am sure, too, that I can go on seeing
Monsieur H— and thinking of him without there being any harm
in it.

M.—. . . . .

P.—It will be so much easier for me to rid my mind of impure
thoughts now that I know that they are natural! I want to say to
God—I may, mayn't I?—"Dear God, since nothing is too difficult for
You, You can bring a miracle to pass and make him decide one day
to unite himself to me in Christian purity. Meanwhile, You won't
blame me, will You, for taking an interest in him? Because You
wouldn't blame a young girl who's engaged to be married for thinking of the young man she loves, or for trying to see him as often as
possible."

. . . .

Having made this last line of dots, Mionnet seemed to be considering whether there was anything else of importance to add. But after
looking at his watch and at the condition of his luggage, he came to
a quick decision and wrote beneath the line of dots the date: "11 July
1910."

He did, however, take from the inside pocket of his cassock a small
note-book, which, after a hurried examination, he opened at a page
marked in the top left-hand corner with the numeral XIV.

This page contained the following information written in very
small script:

"Bernardine de Saint-Papoul. Eldest sister of the Marquis of the
same name. 55–58 years old (?). Unmarried, and probably a virgin.
Gave up part of her fortune to her brother, with whom she lives.
Constitution strong. Education limited. Intelligence, in certain respects, above the average. Mental quirks."

He read this twice through, nodding his head, pouting with his lips, smiling, and picking the inside of his nostril with his thumb-nail, like a man who is trying to find some formula. But, his glance falling again on his watch, he gave vent to a scarcely audible "zut!" closed the note-book, shut the red volume with a resounding smack, laid it in the metal box with its green companion, and put the box back into its hiding-place.

Then he began to occupy himself with his packing.

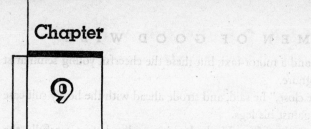

Chapter

9

FIRST TASTE OF PROVINCIAL LIFE

Mionnet arrived at the station of M— at 10.10. He had passed the night in the train; he was tired; above all, he was dirty, and the sensation caused him discomfort. He put the two suit-cases on the ground and looked up and down the platform to see whether anybody had come to meet him.

In a moment or two he saw coming towards him a young priest who seemed to bear the marks of the seminarist. His upper lip was badly shaved, and he had two sore places on his chin; otherwise his appearance was pleasant.

He took off his hat, bowed, and said: "The Abbé Mionnet?" in rather a thick, singsong accent. He stooped over the bags with the obvious intention of taking possession of them, but Mionnet allowed him to lift only one of them—the heavier.

"Have you any large luggage?"

"One trunk."

"If you'll give me your ticket I'll send somebody to get it."

He showed Mionnet the way to the exit. When he smiled he showed his gums; he wore his hat rather on the back of his head, and gave a general impression of extreme cheerfulness.

The station square seemed very ugly to Mionnet, small in extent and irregular in shape. The far side was occupied by two hotels, one of three storeys, the other of four (the Terminus and the Universe). He was surprised to see flags flying from the station entrance, and poles carrying armorial shields set up round the open space to the left. Then he remembered that the next day would be the 14th of July.

Arriving travellers had a choice between the hotel buses, several horse-cabs, and a motor-taxi, but these the cheerful young seminarist seemed to ignore.

"It's quite close," he said, and strode ahead with the heavy suit-case knocking against his legs.

Mionnet made a face. He had not considered very carefully the manner of his arrival, but he had assumed that, in the ordinary course of events, he would be met by one of the canons, and that he would find a carriage waiting for him at the station. It seemed to him that the importance of his mission had been underrated by the people on the spot. If this was typical of what he was to expect, he would have to teach them a lesson.

They went down street after street for what seemed to Mionnet an interminable distance. From time to time the young priest made an effort at lively conversation. He began by introducing himself:

"I'm the Abbé Delhostal's assistant on the *Weekly*. I left the seminary last year; I come of a local family; my name's Bouère."

"I beg your pardon?"

"Bouère."

He added brightly:

"When I was doing my military service, one of the company commanders was called Mionet. Would that be a relation?—though of course," he continued, "he spelt it with only one N. You spell it with two, don't you?"

He next proceeded to point out to his companion some of the local sights.

"That building over there's the old prison. They've got a new one now at the other side of the town, on the hill, quite close to the police station, much better situated. There's a nice square in that direction, with a public garden. The Church School's not far off."

He went on:

"I'm taking you to the pension where you'll be staying."

"Where I shall be staying?" thought Mionnet; "what's he talking about?" He showed by his expression that he expected further details.

"Yes," the other continued, "it's the pension where the Abbé Delhostal takes his meals. I do, too. But he doesn't live there. He has rooms of his own. You'll be in a little annexe opposite; it's very comfortable."

They had left the newer portion of the town and were now in an older, more crowded quarter, with narrow, winding streets which were not without charm. There were hardly any shops. The houses seemed to be of a middle-class residential kind. Their architecture, though undistinguished, gave an impression of solid comfort. Mionnet began to find his bag very heavy.

They reached a small square, paved round its outer edge, with a centre of trodden earth which boasted three miserable trees.

"Here we are. . . . If you'll wait a minute I'll go and get the key."

Mionnet had lost no time in putting down his bag. The young Bouère had done the same and was now ringing the bell of a little two-storey house of reddish-grey stone, with a slate roof.

He came back with the key and indicated another house of about the same size, but whiter, which stood at a corner made by a narrow street and the square, almost exactly opposite the house at which he had first stopped.

"You'll be much better off here, much quieter. The owner of the pension bought this house for next to nothing. It faces east; you'll find it very cheerful."

"The landlord doesn't seem to have put himself out much," thought Mionnet. "This is an odd sort of a town!"

They climbed one flight. The atmosphere of the staircase was close, though not unpleasantly so. There was a pervasive smell of scrubbed wood, linen-cupboards, and genuine beeswax.

"I can't remember whether it's to the right or left," said the young priest.

He tried the key in the left-hand door, which opened. Two rooms were disclosed leading out of one another. The first, which had only a single window, combined the functions of office and sitting-room. The second, which had two windows and was situated at the corner of the house, was the bedroom. Everything seemed very clean; the general effect was of plain, light colours. There were some low armchairs upholstered in white cotton material with a pattern of pink flowers, double curtains of pale green rep lined with faded pink silk, and a double iron bedstead with brass knobs and a white cotton coverlet. Photographs stood on every piece of furniture, the bedroom mantelpiece (the sitting-room had no fire-place), and were hung on the walls. Particularly noticeable were two enlargements of a man and a woman, both of middle age. In addition there were two or three sacred images and two little views of Fontainebleau painted in green and blue on sections of tree-trunks. The floor of the sitting-room was of oak blocks, that of the bedroom, for some unexplained reason, of carefully reddened tiles only partially covered with rugs. Mionnet looked round to see what facilities there might be for washing and writing. In the corner of the bedroom, between the windows, he saw a high, old-fashioned wash-stand, with drawers and cupboards. The top and the shelf were of marble, the basin and other fittings of blue and white china. In the sitting-room there was a small round table and a tiny desk.

"Do you think," he asked, "that it would be possible to get hold of another table?"

"Oh, I'm sure it would."

Mionnet completed his examination and made sure that there was nothing to be seen but the two rooms. He asked a question.

"I don't know where the lavatories are," said the seminarist, "but there's certain to be some; they're probably on the landing."

"What does one do about water? Are there taps in the lavatories?"

"Probably," the other replied with optimistic nonchalance. A moment later he added: "Naturally, you haven't said Mass yet? You must be hungry. Have you got a dispensation from Rome to cover journeys? I'm told it's quite easy to get. Anyhow, I've arranged things at the Cathedral; you can say Mass in the Chapel of Saint Joseph. I said you'd be there at a quarter to eleven, because that'll leave you time to get a bite afterwards. But it's already half past, by the right time."

"And I shall take at least a quarter of an hour to clean myself up a bit."

"Really? On a week day? Well, it's only about five minutes away. All you've got to do is to ask for the sacristan. . . . The Abbé Delhostal is coming here at twelve o'clock to take you out to lunch—that is, unless he fetches you from the Cathedral."

He made as though to leave the room, but changed his mind.

"On second thoughts, you may find it rather difficult to find the Cathedral, even though it is so close, and the sacristan. I'll wait."

Mionnet made it quite plain that he didn't want him to wait in the room. The other understood.

"I'll go out into the square. Don't bother about me, but don't be too long."

Left alone, Mionnet set himself as quickly as possible, and almost at the same time, to do a variety of things. He began to unpack, he looked for the lavatories, which he found at the end of the passage, he washed his face and had a hurried shave. He noticed, with a feeling of bitterness, that the water lathered badly, so that the soap turned into an unmanageable paste which dried as soon as he applied it. He had to rinse his face five or six times before he felt clean.

His preoccupation with the water, however, did not prevent him from pondering certain points of annoyance.

He was irritated at not yet having got hold of his trunk. "The poor fool'll probably forget all about it. If they'd sent a carriage it would all have been so much easier." It seemed to him ridiculous that the bedroom shouldn't have a wooden floor. "And they boast of provincial good sense and comfort. It's all very well in the summer, but what's going to happen if I'm here all winter? My feet'll get frozen on these tiles. I shall have to jump from rug to rug as though they were stepping-stones across a stream." He had just noticed that the only fire-place was in the bedroom, and that it was fitted with a slow-combustion stove. "Contrary to all good sense," he thought; "I shall be asphyxiated at night, and I shall shiver by day when I'm working in the other room. Lucky that the tiles aren't there." What chiefly worried him, however, was the question of money. "Do they mean me to live here at my own expense?" It was a point he had not discussed before he left Paris, and it had not been possible to raise it during his visit to the Archbishop. "As a matter of fact, I had a sort of vague idea that they'd put me up at the palace, that they'd look after all that part of the business. I never dreamed they'd stick me into a family pension." The arrangement might have very serious material consequences. "I agreed to two hundred and twenty-five francs a month, because I thought that at the very worst I should only have to feed myself."

This unpleasant surprise added the last straw to the general impression of his arrival. They certainly were treating him without ceremony. "Money apart, it would have been more suitable to put me up at the palace, or in some building belonging to it, even if it had been less comfortable. I only hope they can arrange some sort of office for me. If need be, I shall put in a claim for one; otherwise I shall be nothing but a wretched little assistant priest sent to take up some obscure post. They could hardly have done less if they'd tried."

The result of his cogitations was that he set himself to revise and develop the rules which he had already laid down for his conduct. "I thought I should be starting with a certain admitted prestige, so that I could adopt at once an attitude of politeness combined with firmness and discretion, the attitude of a man whose least frown would not have passed unnoticed. Had that been so, I could have taken my time about avoiding mistakes and steering clear of traps. But things have turned out very differently. Either because they don't realize the situation or because they pretend not to, they're treating me as very small beer. The sooner I disillusion them on that point, the better. They must be left in no doubt of my importance. For instance, I wonder whether I was sufficiently aloof with that young fool there. I ought to have taken a cab: it would have been a mark of respect due to my position—even if I'd had to pay for it myself. It would have struck the right note."

The "young fool" was resignedly pacing the square, casting now and then an imploring glance towards Mionnet's windows. "Not so bad," thought that gentleman. "He looks like a little priest in a farce serenading his mistress, and about to get a chamber-pot emptied on his head for his trouble."

The thought came at the right moment to restore Mionnet's good humour. After all, he thought, the clean, simple rooms weren't so bad. The position and outlook of the windows made them look bright, and they seemed to be pretty quiet. "Quieter than I should have been opposite, with the other lodgers coming in and out the whole time; quieter than I should have been at the palace, where I should always have had somebody's eye on me." As for the heating arrangements, well, the winter was a long way off; there'd be plenty of time to fix things.

He washed his hands once more, with a final curse for the messy soap, and went down.

"I see you're wondering what those are: they're fish-cakes made of pike. You must be hungry, if you've had nothing since yesterday evening. You needn't be nervous about eating them; the cooking is excellent here, and you can tell from the smell that the fish is as fresh as anything. Are you fond of fishing?"

The Abbé Delhostal, one of the canons, was a rather large man somewhere in his fifties, well proportioned and healthy-looking. Owing to the breadth of his chest, he did not give the impression of being fat. His complexion was reddish, his expression open, his eye brown and bold.

"I told them to keep this room for us," he said; "we can talk more freely here. Let me warn you that the white wine's a bit dry."

The chief dining-room, which could be seen at the end of a short passage, was about twice as big, and was occupied by five or six guests who were taking their meal there.

"I usually eat here with my secretary. But he's found a cheaper pension and has abandoned us. There's sometimes a magistrate at the table behind us; otherwise, nobody. I'm not really afraid of committing myself with the other guests, but one's got to be careful. . . . Unfortunately, they don't heat this room in winter, and it's rather cold."

A moment later he said:

"You've not seen anybody yet?"

"Nobody except the young Abbé who met me. . . . Is he your secretary?"

"He's not very bright, but he's not a bad lad. I'd rather have him than some little Nosy Parker they might give me in his place who'd always be telling tales. . . . You've come straight from Paris? Did you look up the Archbishop of B— on the way?"

"Yes, I did; I went from Paris to see him last Saturday. Just a flying visit, there and back."

"What did he say to you?"

Mionnet did not reply, which would have been true, that his visit had been purely formal, and that the Archbishop had merely offered him vague words of encouragement. He thought it more in keeping with the tactics he meant to pursue to say, in rather a reserved tone:

"I thought that Monsignor seemed to be worried by the situation. I don't mind admitting that I was rather frightened by the importance he seems to attach to my mission."

Delhostal did not answer. He gave himself a plentiful helping of the fat, golden ham omelet which had just been brought.

"The food's not so refined as you'd get in a Paris restaurant," he said, "but the ingredients are first class."

He swallowed a few mouthfuls and drank a glass of red wine.

"Of course you've not seen Monsignor Sérasquier yet? You'd better go early this afternoon. You can explain that as soon as you got here you had to say Mass, and that when that was done it was too late to pay a visit—that you were afraid of interrupting him at luncheon."

"Is he so punctilious?"

"Rather; but it's not that. I don't want him to think that I made a point of seeing you first."

He picked his teeth, apparently plunged in thought; then, gazing out of the window, he continued, musingly, in level tones:

"He's not a bad old thing at heart. He must have had style once; he still has, as you'll see. He's been born out of due time. He says so himself, but it's true, for all that. He was very young when he was made a bishop, and had a great future. But his ideas were too big. He's never been able to get used to the fact that since the separation of Church and State the spiritual lords have had to draw in their horns. . . . It's not easy to maintain in improvised surroundings the pomp that was so naturally observed in the old official palaces. Besides, the income's pretty small now, and he's got the lesser clergy to keep. I needn't tell you that those who enter the Church in the hope of making a fine episcopal career have chosen a bad moment in the world's history. . . . He was too sure of himself, and too fond of the ladies; that's to say, he was, until his accident. But even before that he was getting on."

He modified his statement:

"What I mean is that he was too uncompromising—not sufficiently ready to condescend. He took too high a line—for instance, there was the affair of Madame de Quingey—you've heard about her?"

"Is she the 'great lady' who has so much influence?"

"Oh, 'great lady's' rather excessive, though I suppose that in a country place like this she might be called that. She's certainly influential, very much so. He oughtn't to have treated her as he did, as though she'd been a decent little nobody or some timid creature of no importance. . . . And he's paid for his foolishness."

His conversation was interrupted by the appearance of a chicken.

"Do you like the drumstick? It's delicious, provided the bird's not too thin or too old. They've rather a way here of leaving their fowls too long. . . . It's the same with the peas and the beans. They grow splendidly, but they always pick them about forty-eight hours too late. What was I saying?—Oh, yes, that he blundered pretty badly over her. Not that I want to be melodramatic about it. I don't, for a moment, insinuate that she plotted against him out of revenge. She knows nothing of business; she's all for sentiment, and, like him, she's as proud as sin. But I do think she was pleased when she saw him playing with fire and burning himself pretty badly, and knew that he regretted the time when he could have relied upon her."

Despite his curiosity and his sense of astonishment, and although he realized that his companion, who was perfectly ready to be indiscreet in this the first moment of warm intimacy, might become more reserved as a result of longer acquaintance, Mionnet did not dare go to the length of putting direct questions. He did not wish to betray either the extent or the imperfection of his own knowledge. He confined himself, therefore, to making a few harmless remarks and to smiling a good deal.

"As for the Vicar-General," the Canon suddenly declared, "he's" —there was a momentary pause, then: "I'd better warn you," he said; "he's a dirty skunk!"

With a vigorous jab of his knife he cut through the joint of a wing.

"But for him, nothing would ever have happened, or at any rate things wouldn't have got to the state they're in now. He hates the Monsignor, because the Monsignor is by far the bigger man. He hates me because he thinks that I prevented his becoming bishop. It's a lie, of course; I wouldn't have cared if he'd become a cardinal so long as he cleared out of here. He's as false as they make 'em, a worm, a toady. He toadied himself into becoming protonotary apostolic, and much good may it do him!"

He poured out a glass of wine, drank it, and seemed to calm down.

"I told you," he went on more quietly, with an almost jovial air, "that a good many of my colleagues dislike me. They accuse me of spying on them. They went so far as to say that I was responsible for several of the Montagnini notes.[1] Can you beat it? When you know

---

[1] When, in 1905, relations between the French Government and the Vatican were broken, the Papal Nuncio left for Rome, leaving behind him, as Chargé d'Affaires, a certain Monsignor Montagnini, one of the councillors of the Nunciature. A number of notes passed between him and the Vatican, and copies of these, as well as of

me better you'll realize that's the last sort of thing I could be accused of doing. I'm much more likely to make enemies by my frankness. What is true is that at one time I had to intervene on behalf of certain members of the laity hereabouts, all of them very honourable men and all of them now dead, who had been slandered in the Montagnini notes, because I thought it probable that Rome would believe them to have been guilty of certain abominable actions. Between ourselves, they were mistaken. I saw some of the notes, and very amusing they were. I copied them for my own entertainment, suppressing the names, and I'll show them to you some time. But fancy thinking that I'd denounce my colleagues! Such a thought would never enter my head! It's not my fault that the Archbishop thinks highly of me and regards me as almost the only reliable person here. When he asked me what I thought of this tramway business, I said what I'd already said twenty times to the victims themselves—that one can't make as many mistakes as that without being sorry for them in the end. . . . As a matter of fact, I could have had this job of yours if I'd been willing to take it. But it's better as it is. You come from outside, you know nothing of anybody here, you've not been mixed up in the business in any way. You're sent here by authority and you obey. But suppose I'd taken it on. They'd have said at once that I'd arranged the whole thing just to have the glory of saving the diocese and damning my enemies."

A little later their conversation took a more intimate turn, Delhostal offering his guest some fatherly advice.

"You're a Parisian, aren't you?—at least, you were educated in Paris? Have you ever lived in the provinces? It's a totally different thing, I can assure you. You've got to be careful, especially in your position, of women. Perhaps they're not so stupid in Paris; probably not, because they've got other distractions. Anyhow, it's all much easier there. But in a place like this!—people don't believe it when

---

letters written by him to members of the French hierarchy, were kept in his office. Finally Montagnini was expelled, his office broken into, and a selection of his papers published as the "Dossier Montagnini."—Translator's note.

they're told, but I can assure you it's true. There are women here who literally run after anything in a cassock. They're mad about us—provided we don't repulse them too violently. The women of the upper middle classes and of the grade just a little bit lower are the worst. Just as there are women who run after officers, so there are women who run after priests. I don't say you can count them by hundreds, but you don't need hundreds to get twelve miserable sinners into trouble, because of course they aim high. They don't, as a rule, bother about the small fry. I don't mind telling you, I avoid 'em like the plague."

With the arrival of coffee and liqueurs he went even further. His tone became more confidential, though in no way mysterious, or at any rate not sufficiently mysterious to make what he was saying sound dubious. The deep, throaty tone of his voice, and the smile with which he accompanied his words, merely served to evoke a picture of all those pleasant and normal activities of life which good manners have agreed to keep more or less secret, but which never harmed a soul.

"I realize," he said, "that at your age it's difficult to live like a Trappist. Of course you can take a trip now and then to Paris, but it means a pretty long journey. If you find yourself in need, let me know. I'll give you some introductions. It's not a thing I'd do for everybody" (he swallowed a mouthful of coffee), "for various reasons. . . . But I think I can give you something pleasant to remember; very pleasant."

Chapter

10

A PRINCE OF THE CHURCH

When the Separation between Church and State took place, the headquarters of the Bishopric of M—, which had hitherto been situated in a fine seventeenth-century building close to the Cathedral (since turned into the Museum of Fine Art), were transferred to a very lovely, if medium-sized house which had been built about the middle of the eighteenth century, when it had been designed as the residence of a notability of the local Parliament. The main building was approached through a fine gateway comprising a small lodge now occupied by a concierge and across a paved courtyard. At the back it looked on to a garden which, though small in extent, contained some noble and well-grown trees.

The windows of His Lordship's study, into which Mionnet was immediately shown, gave on to this garden.

Monsignor Sérasquier, who had risen at his entrance and now advanced two steps towards the door in welcome, proffered him his ring to kiss and waved him to a chair. He then resumed his seat in an arm-chair which was set at the right of the large desk and so placed that the prelate faced the garden and presented his left profile to his guest.

He gave, at first sight, an impression of great dignity with which was mingled a certain quality of disdain. He was slightly above the middle height, and not unduly stout. The most remarkable things about him were his face, the carriage of his head, and his hair. The face was large, with a long, straight nose, a high forehead, and a finely chiselled, sensitive mouth. The chin, however, was rather weak. A thick shock of silver hair brushed back surmounted the head, which its owner had a peculiar habit of tossing with a backward movement.

This characteristic gesture was accompanied by a fluttering of the long, bluish eyelids, which now and again seemed to veil the Bishop's glance as though in an effort to distract it from the trivialities of his surroundings. The man's general air of nobility seemed to be neither affected nor acquired, but it was certainly self-conscious.

His Lordship began the interview by asking Mionnet about his journey and about the preparations made to receive him. He deliberately set himself to mention such things as the "10.10 train" and "the little square at the foot of the rue du Bailliage," as though to draw attention to the fact that his faculties were in no way diminished.

There were traces of hesitation in his speech, he stammered slightly, and the deliberate care with which he articulated was faintly noticeable. But Mionnet, had he not already been warned, would probably not have interpreted these tricks as symptoms of a recent illness.

On the other hand, a sudden movement revealed the right corner of the Bishop's mouth, which had not been presented to the visitor at the moment of his entrance. It was distorted—not much, but sufficiently to give an air of distress to the otherwise nobly featured face.

The voice was still musical, though it contained certain rather unpleasant notes. The impression it gave was that it would have been charming if only the desire to charm had been as definite as the desire to dominate.

The Bishop's attitude to his guest seemed, at first sight, to be a mixture of rather patronizing familiarity and of mistrust, even of fear. At moments it took on an aggressive quality which was modified by an odd air of equality. It was as though he were constantly implying, though not saying: "I shouldn't speak like this to others, because they wouldn't understand me."

At first he made no direct allusion either to the actual situation or to the part in it which Mionnet had been called upon to play. He confined himself to a series of general statements, which he enunciated in a tone that was obviously intended to be detached and even jovial.

"The fact is, I've been a thorn in their sides for a long time past.

They've never liked me. Oh, I can see their point of view. I'm not at all the right man for them, nor, if it comes to that, for the times in which we live. Everything today seems to me to be on such a mean scale."

He let his eyes wander towards the ceiling, which was at least twelve feet high, and then towards the extremities of the huge room which lay to either side of him. It was as though he were once more drawing attention to the miserable insufficiency of the surroundings in which he was compelled to live.

"I have the impression always of having to deal with a set of wretched little clerks huddled over their ledgers and fussing about trivialities. People in Paris have a way of taking a condescending attitude towards the provinces, not realizing that in certain old-fashioned ways our life here still retains a certain amplitude, a certain largeness of vision. I should never have found any difficulties in dealing with provincial conditions if difficulties had not been deliberately put in my way, and if I had been given a free hand. Not that I should ever have felt really at home in a town like this. It is true, of course, that one is less conscious here of the general flat mediocrity of modern life, but, for all that, the pettiness of everything is dreadful. A noble spirit stifles here."

He seemed to be possessed by a feverish desire to talk of himself. "I ought to have been a Renaissance pope. . . ."

His outburst was accompanied by a smile, but at the same time he looked rather anxiously at his visitor out of the corner of his eye.

"It's probably in my blood. I am descended directly from the elder branch of the Comtes de Sérasquier. The Sérasquiers were one of the great families of Provence, as great as the Mirabeaux and the Castellanes. I've never used my title. My grandfather, who was ruined during the emigration, gave it up. My father revived the family fortunes as a manufacturer. He was a follower of Saint-Simon. . . . He made a particular kind of paper which is still famous—there is, today, a brand known as sérasquier paper. He always refused to claim his title, though he told his sons that as his heirs they would have a right to it. My brother, who was the eldest of the family, predeceased him, at Tonkin. He was a lieutenant of marines. I never bothered about it. . . . These tatters of the past have always seemed to me faintly ridiculous, because they correspond to no reality in the modern democratic State."

He forced himself to smile again, as he added:

"And then, you see, when I entered the Church, I fully intended to become a cardinal, and etiquette forbids a cardinal to make use of any title, to display even a princely coronet in his arms. He is held to be higher than any prince."

He turned casually towards Mionnet and looked at him for a moment or two in silence. His eyelids fluttered.

"You were a student at the Training College?" he asked sharply.

"Yes, Monsignor."

"Like Baudrillart. . . . You'll find that useful. Oh, yes, you will. The mere fact that they've sent so young a man as you on a mission like this shows that they've got their eye on you. You'll win your spurs by taking my scalp. You will go back with it at your belt."

"Oh, Monsignor!"

"I'm only joking. . . . You went to B—? You saw the Archbishop?"

"Yes, Monsignor."

"What did he say about me?"

"Oh, Monsignor, His Eminence could only speak of you with the highest consideration. As a matter of fact, he said nothing to me except of the most general nature."

"He wouldn't; his attitude in all this business has been throughout more or less correct. All the same, he doesn't like me. He's weak, a man of straw. I always get the impression that he's afraid of falling back into the gutter from which he came. His father was a commission salesman."

Monsignor Sérasquier began to show signs of fatigue. Mionnet, watching him carefully, wondered whether he ought to go. But it was not for him to take the initiative, and the prelate seemed in no way anxious to bring the interview to an end. He panted a little, appeared to be revolving something in his mind, glanced rather furtively at Mionnet, and got up. At the same time he made a gesture with his left hand which was intended to keep his visitor from moving. He began to walk up and down the room with short steps, his hands behind him, his head thrown back. He may have been anxious to overcome his own feeling of weakness or to distract the other's attention from it. As he walked he continued to talk, pausing now and again between his sentences. He skirted the bookcase which stood against the wall, and moved behind his table, on which, now and again, he rested his hand for a moment. But his actions as well as his speech were embarrassed by his anxiety to show as little as possible of the right side of his face, and, when that became impossible, to divert his visitor's attention from the twitching that agitated the corner of his mouth. This determination forced him to adopt attitudes, to elaborate movements, and to space his phrases, in a way which, otherwise, would have been hard to explain. His speech, as a result, lacked continuity, and certain words, spoken from too great a distance or with his back turned, were difficult to hear.

"I have always been very independent. . . . I don't care a rap for them, you understand? . . . What can they do to me? I've got means of my own. . . . I've lost more money than any of them in this business. . . . I only went into it to give them a lead. They begged me to interest myself in it, just as they might have asked me to head a subscription list for the victims of some disaster, some flood. . . . But I've got enough left to live comfortably. There's nothing much they could do. They might, I suppose, ask me to resign for reasons of health, but in that case they'd have to offer me the title of Archbishop *in partibus,* Thessalonica, or something like that. . . . And what then? I should go and settle down in a pleasant villa at Nice. No, they won't do that; they'll try something else. . . . My strong point, you see, has always been that I'm invulnerable from the point of view of orthodoxy. I've always taken the lead in hunting down modernism in my diocese, even when it was fashionable. I made one or two examples at the Great Seminary. You've never dabbled in modernism, I hope?"

"Oh, no, Monsignor. I've a particular dislike for that brand of heresy."

"Good. If you take my advice, you'll stick to that; it's wiser. My own sympathies have always been Gallican, though within limits, understand me. I follow the tradition of Bossuet. At the time of the Separation I was careful to avoid forcing matters to the point of a complete break. I acted as the great bishops of the past would have acted. That's to say, I made it clear to the temporal powers that we should defend every foot of the way, and I fought to get every possible concession out of them. But I was careful not to let Rome exploit the situation to the extent of destroying our liberties and going off with the Church of France in her pocket. . . . It's no good being too narrow-minded and ignoring the lessons of history like those fanatical monks who have poisoned us with their propaganda. I don't pretend that Waldeck-Rousseau or that fellow Combes belongs to a particularly attractive type, or that they're even very reliable. But the Church has had to fight kings before now. The Republic's not the first government that's had the idea of enriching itself by confiscation or of ridding itself of the thousands of monks who've been getting so thick. The great Churchmen of France have known how to resist kings just so far as resistance has been possible, without handing themselves over, bound hand and foot, to the Pope. . . . I wasn't the only one whose mind worked that way. . . . Most of the bishops wanted a compromise; but Rome wanted war, and it only needed a few of her lackeys in our ranks to make the position intolerable. If we could have got round a table, we should have been able to extract a great many more concessions than we have. You've no idea what we could have saved, or won back little by little. I should have been in my palace at this very moment instead of in this barn. But our people pretended not to be able to see that the Government couldn't go back on its word. It was committed to an anti-clerical policy, that's true enough, but it was our business to see that it did as little as possible in that way, short of running our heads up against it. I was more active than most, and they've never forgiven me at Rome, and the people in Paris are fools enough to be at the beck and call of Rome in everything."

He stopped, and directed a sidelong look at Mionnet.

"Perhaps you're an ultramontane? Are the young inclined that way?"

Mionnet gave a non-committal reply which seemed to satisfy the Bishop.

"I'll tell you something else," he went on; "we'll talk more about it another day. For the moment the Vatican has got us, the Church of France, where it wants us. But this isn't the end: the battle's going on, with a difference. I've got a lot of diplomatic friends in Rome, and in the other capitals of Europe too. A whole lot of my relations are scattered up and down the embassies, and I can tell you, the Vatican is plotting against France. Remember what I've told you. If ever you get a chance of going to Rome and staying there for a bit, I'll put you in touch with certain people who'll open your eyes. Ever since Rampolla went, France has become the enemy. Merry del Val hates us."

He was again overcome by fatigue and had to sit down. Mionnet got up quietly from his chair with the expression of a man who is waiting for permission to withdraw.

"Come and see me again tomorrow at eleven," said the Bishop. "There are many things we've got to discuss. I want you always to deal directly with me. You understand? I'll help you. I must find a little corner here in the palace for you where you can be private. No doubt you've already arranged to meet my Vicar-General?"

"Not yet, Monsignor. I was going to call on him this afternoon."

"Ah. . . . Well, arrange to leave your card on him when you'll be sure of not finding him. Go between five and half past. There's a chapter meeting then. I'd rather you didn't see him until I've explained the whole situation to you. You've seen nobody else?"

"No, Monsignor, except, naturally, Monsieur Delhostal, the Canon, who was good enough to look after me when I arrived and see me to my rooms."

"Ah, yes, of course. Did he have a lot to tell you?"

"Oh, no, Monsignor; he talked a little about the place and the people; just general conversation, and the local food; he told me a good deal about that."

"That doesn't surprise me!" said Monsignor.

Before dinner Mionnet unpacked his trunk, which had at last arrived, and arranged his belongings.

After dinner he put in some hard work with the directory to the departments of France, which he had commissioned the Abbé Bouère to get for him.

While at the Training College, he had absorbed the tradition of Fustel de Coulanges and the lessons of Vidal de La Blache, with the result that he now had the greatest respect for year-books, time-tables, and, in particular, for the directory—in fact for every kind of simple statistical material. With him, however, this interest in informative documents did not go to the fanatical extreme that it does with some people. He would only try to reconstruct the contours of the modern world from the information contained in the directory if he could not do so by any other means. He had, however, noticed that the facts about the departments of France and their chief cities were given in that work with a solid and admirable brevity. Therefore he read with great care all that he could find about M— and its neighbourhood, noting down the most important details.

Two passages, in particular, delighted him:

"In our survey of the department certain industries have not been mentioned. The reader, however, will notice that there is no lack of those which are concerned with the comforts of existence."

And:

"The climate is bracing and healthy. The prevailing winds are those of the west and south-west. The dampness which is common during the bad seasons of the year appears to be responsible for the rheumatic complaints which are frequent in the district."

Chapter

11

TORRID JULY

All this while Paris was experiencing that change in the weather which heralds the approach of the dog-days.

When the end of June is past, the days cease to grow longer, and show the first signs of drawing in. But such early symptoms of the year's increasing age are scarcely noticed, nor do they make for sadness. The season of fine weather is fairly launched, and, as the days advance in serried ranks, no one begrudges the deepening fringe of twilight that they draw after them, provided they show their high midsummer pomps. What they lose in length they gain in strength and ripeness. So it is with the fruits of the earth, for even when their time of growth is ended, the faces that they show lose not a whit of cheerfulness. Nature works still, refining upon her labours, lavishing the last fine touch of richness. Not until later will the year's end begin to gather, making itself felt by sudden strokes that drive deep into its being. All at once, in the mists of early morning, in the cold dusk of a rainy day, the autumn is upon us. With a sadness that is half compact of gentle tolerance, we see before us the vista of the dwindling days, stretching like a tunnel filled with eddying winds and darkening clouds to the final term of Christmas.

With the early days of July the heat, till then restrained or limited to momentary sallies and retreats, shows a safe and swollen strength. The restless winds of June vanish in one final storm, to be succeeded by more leisurely and ampler exhalations. From the northern plains huge layers of air advance upon Paris, not to descend until, in a momentary detour, they have passed above the Ardennes and the Vosges. At first brisk and fresh, with an almost pungent dryness, carrying the sharp and gritty flavour of the wines that grow in those eastern valleys, they thicken and get hotter as they come.

Paris mornings are coloured then like steel. The vanishing vistas of the avenues look like a sword-blade, and on the surrounding heights the silhouette of houses shows against a sky that is more than ever subtle in its shades. The horizon quivers. The hill-tops of Belleville and the Butte-Montmartre, with their roofs and house-fronts, seem more than ever real and crowded. The impression comes not from any detailed vision of their shapes—for they, on the contrary, are veiled in haze—but because of the sense they give of the life within, the air of crackling movement which they offer. The sky above them, grey in the main, but faintly blue and lightly shot with pink, seems deeper in substance, yet, at the same time, more impenetrable, as though it were compact of so vibrant a density that even thoughts, winging their way into that distance, would find it hard to gain a passage. The summits of the city's distant heights and the lower stretches of the sky, seen down the perspective of a street, join in a sort of midway no-man's-land, in which the quivering light looks less like the effect of atmosphere than the swarming movement of some half-descried activity. It resembles the combustion of innumerable atoms, the hot ashes at the base of a conflagration, the throbbing of a wall of flame held in behind a grate of steel.

But in Paris this pristine and unadulterated heat rarely lasts for long. Gusty winds rise from the network of its valleys, and breezes from the sea, never long absent, serve to modify or check the movements of the inland air. From its sweating streets the city distils a moist and heavy contribution of its own. The encircling hills which serve in winter to blunt the biting winds form in July a cauldron in which the summer heats ferment and gather strength.

When the first clearness of the early day is past, clouds gather in the sky. Sometimes they are no more than a soft and spreading haze, thinned here and there and ravelled out, so that it offers no more impediment to the sun than is sufficient to soften and diffuse its beams. The effect of such weather is not so much to veil all light as to destroy all shadow. The pleasant bands of deeper tone which stretch at other times across the fronts of houses or in the angles of buildings entirely vanish. Coolness becomes an object of search. From street to street there is no movement in the air. Swarming humanity goes unventilated. It matters not at all that the city is hollow and honeycombed. It is like a man taking a midday nap with his head beneath a blanket. The heat of bodies and of armpits lies heavy over all.

Sometimes, however, the clouds take shape. Patches of darkness appear in the sky, and these, as they increase in size, begin to draw together. Between them are narrow luminous stretches so white and dazzling that they hurt the eyes and resemble gutters filled with a flow of molten metal poured from some electric furnace. Muffled thunder echoes round this splintered dome, not so much heard as felt in the head like the throbbings of neuralgia. But the gathering storm comes to nothing. A few warm drops speckle the pavements and intensify the general dampness of the atmosphere, while the passer-by mops them from his heated forehead.

Paris, in the grip of just such a July, was suffering as though no similar experience had ever come her way. Women shopping in the great central stores withdrew, as far as possible, into the dim recesses of distant departments, in the innocent hope of finding there the coolness and shade of some grotto where dwelt an envied race. They forgot that in proportion as they got farther from the outer doors—exchanging, incidentally, the light of day for that of electric lamps—the air, with whatever limited power of circulation it still retained, would cease to follow them, and that they would find themselves imprisoned in an atmosphere like that of a public lavatory, redolent with the smell of scented soap or stifling with the dusty closeness of dress materials. Stacks of ribbon and the odour of glue from innumerable cardboard boxes made it more than ever difficult to breathe. The shop-girls followed their movements with wondering glances, as though they were watching some self-imposed penance. In workshops and offices, ground floors and basements, could be

seen faces suffused and red, or livid with exhaustion. Skins shone like
the bottoms of cooking-stoves. Everyone looked either over-excited
or in the last stages of collapse. Those who still had the energy to
chatter talked of the little seaside place on the north coast where they
were just off to spend a week, of some stream where they were going
fishing, some favourite forest, some mountain meadow, some river,
some place of coolness. If they didn't talk of such things, they thought
about them.

In front of the cafés men with their straw hats or panamas pushed
back from their foreheads drank iced beer. No sooner had they
finished their drink than they discovered that "beer doesn't quench"
and that "the really sensible man drinks something hot." They made
the remark to their next-door neighbour—and immediately ordered
something cold. Actually they were thoroughly enjoying themselves.
Life for them had the same sort of savour as when some physical
feat has been successfully accomplished. They treated their thirst as
they would have treated a mistress, careful to satisfy its demands
without destroying them altogether.

Another favourite remark was: "It's cooler in the subway than in
the streets," despite the fact that the peculiar smell of the air emerging from the subway stations was, as it always was, a mixture of sour
and sweet, a reek of hot steel and oil. The cab-horses wore pointed
straw hats with two red-bordered holes for their ears. The man in
charge of the municipal watering-cart, with its hose running on little
wheels, had made of his daily task a game of skill executed in the
open air, the point of which was to play accurately on the root of a
tree, just to touch the pavement with a thin jet of water thrown from
as long a range as possible, or to dissolve with a single quick douche
a complete pile of dung.

It was the end of the school year. Classes were being held with
every window wide open. For the last hour of the afternoon the
teacher would take from his brief-case a book of unusual appearance
and proceed to read aloud a passage from some modern author.
Elsewhere, however, in long, narrow rooms, young boys and girls,

each at a separate table, and each feeling slightly sick, were busy finishing a piece of composition which had been started that morning. Their watches lay beside them, and the floor beneath the tables was covered with the crumbs of the sandwiches they had gobbled down without letting go of their pens.

The squares were full of children, whose shrill cries were intensified by the heat, and whose chief pleasure seemed to be dragging their feet in the sand and raising great clouds of dust. Women with blouses so embarrassingly open that they disclosed the division of their breasts chatted together of colic and nursing, of summer dresses and the intimacies of married life.

Every evening the park of the Buttes-Chaumont and the unfinished park of the Butte-Montmartre were crammed with people who gave the impression of being there to see a show in some huge theatre. They waited for the coolness that would come with nightfall, tracking down the least breeze that showed signs of setting the still air in motion. They listened to the rumble of trains in the flat country to the north; they stared before them. Those in the Buttes-Chaumont, according to their various positions in the park, saw, above the vast arena of trees, the vague stretch of the outer suburbs dotted with golden points of light, the silhouette of the Sacré-Cœur distinct on its hillside, or, through a break in the near horizon, the glowing perspective of Paris. Those in the Butte-Montmartre could gaze on the whole sweep of Paris, seeming vaster than ever in the darkness, more than ever like a sea set with innumerable specks of fire. Here and there they recognized a line of lights, a patch of brightness, or named a stretch of blackness in the scene.

The inhabitants of every district set out, in this way, as soon as evening fell, to seek some open space in which they might relax. The west end streamed towards the Bois in its carriages and cars. The east end set out, equipped with slippers and folding chairs, for the grass plots of Vincennes. Others sought the river-banks and quays, the docks whence coal and plaster, stone and steel are loaded, free of trucks at this hour, where they could sit on the planks. Many found their way to the stretches of green that cover the twenty-odd miles of fortification, swarming at such times with humanity.

In the central markets dawn came so quickly that it surprised those supping late before they could fortify their spirits with drink against the cold melancholy of its onset. On the boulevard Macdonald hooligans who could not sleep for the heat, and feared boredom worse than the police, organized a series of gang battles. Their womenfolk, seated on the grass, watched in silent fear their warring champions, too much terrified even to swear save when a spent bullet whistled past their heads. Perverts ogled one another on the boulevard Rochechouart or pursued their intimacies in the dark thickets of the Bois. Eccentrics, with a crust of bread wrapped in a newspaper, weighed, with scrupulous exactitude, the merits of competing urinals.

The merry-making of the 14th, falling in the middle of such a month, was symptomatic of much in the life of Paris. Tradition associated it with revolution and the spirit of nationalism, and something of its origin still hung about it. It was observed only by the proletariat and the lower middle classes. The smart world laughed at it. The proletariat had probably no idea that it was celebrating the memory of a rising in which, long ago, it had pulled the chestnuts out of the fire for the benefit of the Gentlemen of the Third Estate. But it took advantage of the occasion to assure itself that Paris was still its own peculiar hunting-ground. It promenaded the streets in its shirt-sleeves as far as the centre of the city and the outlying districts, like a landowner who once a year makes a survey of his property. Seeing these wandering crowds, one was once more made aware that, in addition to the floating, half-starved population of the newer suburbs, there is also a settled class which looks on the capital as its own by ancient right, ready to maintain it when occasion calls, but liking, now and then, to play with the illusion that the pleasures of the streets are its sole monopoly. Children let off fire-crackers in the open street, the most populous squares were blocked by dancing couples, deaf to the protests of congested carriage folk. What right has anybody to be in a hurry on such an evening? Let them

wander afoot like their fellows. Haste could be justified by nothing—
save perhaps by the desire of seeing the fireworks. Those who were
knowing in such things, scornful of local displays, with a reasoned
preference for the exhibitions in the Tuileries Gardens or at the
Point du Jour, had made their plans in good time, and the difficulty
of getting punctually to their chosen vantage-points through the
packed streets played no little part in the evening's pleasures.

The military parade struck the nationalist note. In addition to
satisfying the craving felt by the crowds of middle-class spectators,
diversified by a sprinkling of old workmen and artisans, for those
large-scale spectacles and mob emotions which a republic supplies
so sparingly, it pandered to the jingo feelings that are the invariable
concomitant of uneventful lives.

Children who, caught unawares in the moving crowds, had
watched the march of cuirassiers and guns, trembling with excitement at the sound of bugles, now dispersed to look for their little
friends on some piece of open ground, there to indulge in prisoners'
base, drop-the-handkerchief, and sack races. They begged their
mothers to ransack cupboards for their oldest clothes so that they
might try their luck at climbing the greased pole for a bottle of sweet
wine. Their fathers, in shirt-sleeves, sat drinking in wicker chairs
before the little wine-shops. Their conversation was of gardening
or the incidents of their daily work. They discussed the latest blunders
of the Government, chatting like neighbours in some small country
town. For one afternoon the various districts of the city became once
again the villages they once had been. Local patriotism developed
in the market-place, striving to make itself felt even in the upper
floors of the newest tenements.

Sampeyre had played with the idea of spending the 14th of July
well out of the city, somewhere near Mont-Valérien or Saint-Cloud.
But he had been kept late at his lectures, had eaten his midday meal
at home, and later contented himself with a stroll through Montmartre. He had no particular goal. He knew the style and manner of

the holiday too well to expect to find anything new about it. He did not even take with him on his walk that hope which comes to all of us at times, of finding in some special spot a mood which may sweeten our progress with an accompaniment of pleasant thoughts.

But, for all that, he dreamed and remembered. Climbing the boulevard Barbès, between the rue Ordener and the rue Custine, he was overcome suddenly by the recollection of an early love-affair. It was long since he had thought of it save in those fleeting moments which bring to the human spirit faint and scarce-heeded hints of things past. Time and time again he had paced this tiny stretch of the boulevard without encountering a single ghost, and now in a moment they were all about him. He saw, without any effort to do so, every detail of that vanished time; saw himself walking with his beloved, holding her left arm, heard the words she spoke, the answers that he made. He could catch the very accents of her voice, the sound of her laughter. Had he walked there with her some long-dead 14th of July? Perhaps, but he could not remember. There was a pain in his heart, a lump in his throat. The emotion that he felt was in some respects sweet, but there was pain in it as well. It touched him at so many points, released such springs of sadness. It raised questions in his mind that involved the whole course of his life, setting him to question all that he had done in his search for happiness. He reflected that feelings such as these that now revisited him from the past were among the sweetest life can offer, feelings for which no later happenings can ever bring a substitute. Had he, perhaps, in those far-off days, set too little store by them? In the arrogance of youth he had held them as of little worth compared with the grand schemes of existence, deserving less serious consideration. He had been so sure that even if he came to regret them life would hold many others of a like sort. "But that's not true," he reflected. "There are people one never meets again, triumphs that never come twice."

Suddenly he was conscious of a terrible loneliness. As he reached the Place du Château-Rouge, gay with bunting, this sense of isolation became so acute that he turned giddy.

But he knew how to banish thoughts when they became too use-lessly cruel. He crossed several streets. Walking aimlessly, he found himself in one of the old squares of Montmartre, where the people of the neighbourhood had come together to drink and talk. In front of the cafés he saw fathers of families chatting to one another, while their children wrangled and shouted round the greased pole.

His thoughts turned to what he saw. He brooded on the truths of democracy. Smiling, he tried to set his mind to run in familiar channels; without effort, he imagined the conversation of these working-men. "What are they talking about?" In the first place, probably, about their personal concerns. Maybe they were repeating some joke, with exaggerated gestures of laughter. But sooner or later their talk would turn to politics. They would criticize and condemn; now and again they would approve. Compare what was happening here with what would be happening in some country ruled by a stronger discipline. There the people too would speak of their private lives, there too they would make jokes. But there would be no word of politics, no discussion of the Government. But would that mean that their minds were empty of such things? To some extent, per-haps, for thought, like everything else, grows rusty with disuse, and they would have accepted once for all the rule of adamant which forbade all talk of what is most important in life. As a result, their conversation would be deliberately trivial. Everything that mattered would be close prisoned in their minds. What they spoke of would be the preoccupations of children. The first great truth of democracy is this: that it makes possible a life in which men can discuss the things that matter, everything that matters, secure in their right to behave like adults instead of having to pretend to be children still. "These fellows here," he thought, "are doubtless talking a lot of nonsense. They are ignorant of much, they are easily credulous, they have the prejudices of their class. Each one of them alone would give disastrous advice to any government. But all this chatter, this ex-change of opinions through the length and breadth of a country, combines into the dominant note of a single voice, which, continu-

ally modified, provided it is not unfairly side-tracked, ends by attaining a sort of wisdom. And experience shows that such collective
wisdom is no whit inferior to that of kings, of ministers, of men
more duly qualified to govern. . . . That, too, is democracy. That
is the message of all these coloured lights."

Beneath these democratic coloured lights the people of Paris found
it all the easier to feel themselves at home, realized afresh, and with
no sense of inferiority, that they were the good old stay-at-homes, the
true citizens of their city, because for "the rest," for the rich and the
fairly rich, for civil servants and office workers with fixed salaries
and definite holidays, for all who were not "the people," this was
the moment of migration. Nor for them alone, but for the swarm of
pseudo-Parisians, shopkeepers, workmen, officials, linked to the life
of the city by the conditions of their labour and the habits of their
lives, but marked off from it by their origins, provincials from near
or far who had come to Paris to make good in some small business
or employment, but with a fixed intention not to die there. Meanwhile, until they could return for good to the land of their birth, they
would take every opportunity of going back to see that it still was
there. They crowded the third-class cars of the trains that were
taking the rich to the holiday towns of Europe. But at the time of
which we are writing, the true, native folk of Paris had not yet
learned to follow their example. At most they made use of a few
excursion trains, of two-day tickets, due to expire quickly, which gave
the citizen the comfortable feeling that if he wandered far afield, he
was securely fastened to the end of a string which would pull him
back again.

Cabs with luggage-racks, two-horse carriages, family omnibuses,
were everywhere; taxis with a trunk beside the driver and a wicker
basket on the running-board. While the dances of the 14th were
getting ready, all the west end of Paris, all that part of the city to the
left of the poverty line, was tumbling over itself to get away. The heat

and the glare of summer broke up this swarming hive of humanity. A last spasm of exhaustion scattered its debris over the countryside.

At the city gates a stream of cars, already numerous, waited in long lines before the toll-office to declare the amount of gas in their tanks: "The receipt will hold good for the return journey." Huge limousines with trunks on their roofs seemed, with their long noses, to be smelling out the strange new roads into which they were about to adventure. On the edges of the sidewalks gasoline was being offered for sale in blue, two-gallon tins piled one on top of the other. Every three hundred yards or so a halted motorist was busily engaged in patching a tire or blowing down a carburettor.

A few days earlier Germaine Baader, running into an old school-friend of the Lycée Fénelon, had asked her to dinner.

"Just the two of us. . . . After dinner, if you like, we can look at the fireworks from the window; they'll be quite close. We've got a whole heap of things to talk about."

And in fact they talked so much, leaning on their elbows by the window of the little drawing-room, that not even the loveliest cascades made by the rockets against the plum-coloured darkness succeeded in interrupting them. The whole of that night's spectacle, buildings, sky, and fire, was nothing to them but a gentle, caressing background to their conversation, seen out of the corners of their eyes.

"You knew, of course, that I'd had an affair with Gurau?—You can't think how lovely it is to be able to talk to you like this, as I did in the old days. We were always such good friends, you and I, we always understood each other so well. Do you remember the time when I helped you with your physics lesson, and you coached me in recitation?— It's funny, isn't it, to think of those days? It was natural that you should know I had become Gurau's mistress. No one could accuse me of having been actuated by ambition. In those days he was nothing but a simple deputy, and he hadn't a penny. I won't say that I ever had a real passion for him, but I liked him, and his conversation amused me.

"I don't suffer fools gladly. Knocking about the theatre, as I do, one meets a lot of nice fellows, but most of them are terribly uneducated. One can't always be making love, and I get bored with a man when I've got nothing to say to him, and really, a lot of dull chat about one's work isn't worth while; it's no better than shop-girls' gossip. . . . I don't like feeling that a man's too much my superior, but neither, on the other hand, do I like feeling that he's not up to my level: the charm's broken, either way. And then, in the theatre, the good-looking ones get so vain. It's not their fault, because all the girls just fall for them. Besides, they get into the habit of treating women in a sort of offhand, jolly way that I hate. I've never been able to get used to it. They get familiar, and they're always kissing one and mauling one about in passages, not because they really care two pins about one, but just because it's the thing to do, a sort of way of showing how maty they are. And if it does go further— Oh, I don't know, but somehow all the promiscuity seems to take the bloom off their kisses. One sees them carrying on in just the same way with all the others. . . .

"But Gurau was different—very aloof, very distinguished, and I liked his looks. Don't you think he's rather like an aristocrat of the old days? . . . I behaved very well. He gave me hardly anything, and I was often really hard up. Another woman would have left him long ago, but I'm not a bohemian, I like an orderly life. Nevertheless, I had to speculate a bit, just to make money, and I got into a pretty tight corner more than once. . . . I very nearly landed in the ditch. But he couldn't give me money, because he hadn't any to give. It was only after he became a Minister that I began to think he was making rather too much of his poverty. He still kept me short, though of course he did let me have a bit more, but not half, not a quarter of what I needed in my position. Everyone knew that I was his mistress, and people expected to see me with jewels and furs. . . . It didn't do him any good, I can tell you, because he got the reputation of being mean. When I told him so, he said: 'Not at all. They know I'm an honest man, and that no minister's salary is enough to let him

keep a woman on a scale of two hundred thousand francs a year.'
Not that I ever dreamed of asking him for such a sum, or suggested
that he should turn thief or sell himself. But I couldn't stand his constantly posing as the Honest Man, his way of setting himself up as
a model. For two pins he'd have told everybody that he lived on
lentils and had only two cheap ready-made suits in his wardrobe. I
don't know how other men manage, but they certainly look as
though it wasn't so difficult to have a little money. I'm perfectly certain that a minister can find heaps of ways of adding to his income
without ceasing to be perfectly honest. There's his newspaper, for
instance. The whole thing centres on him; he put it on its feet and
made a success of it, and he's as proud as Punch of the fact; he's told
me all about it a dozen times. But d'you think he's ever insisted on
getting a decent salary? Not he! They couldn't refuse him, but he
doesn't even ask for a fee as editor, and although his name doesn't
appear as editor, he really runs the whole thing. He merely gets paid
for his articles, and even so, at his old rate. But that's not all. What
do you think he did as soon as he became a Minister?—gave back to
the paper all the money he made by writing for it. Yes, he let them
pay him, gave them a receipt, and then handed it all back as a contribution towards publicity. I found, too, that he pays out a lot of
his salary as a Minister in subscriptions to various committees. It all
looks very fine at long range, but it doesn't bear a closer inspection.
It's all part of the game he's playing. He's his own audience, but
he's also his own victim. When I found out what he was doing with
the money he made from his articles—we were talking about money
and I'd said I couldn't understand how he had so little, that I suspected him of spending it in ways he didn't tell me about, pretending
to be jealous, and finally pressed him so hard that he had to confess
the truth—I said some pretty hard things. It all seemed to me so
stupid, such sham generosity, although I know perfectly well that
he'd have done just the same if he'd had a wife and children to
support. At first he tried to argue with me, but he soon gave that up
and just looked at me, with such a sad expression that I gave way.

I realized that in the matter of money he'd always be mean. . . . It isn't as though I'm extravagant, because compared with some women—with Sorel, for example—I'm not. Nevertheless, I gave way and remained faithful to him. There are plenty of women, I can assure you, who'd have argued that if he couldn't afford to give what he ought to give, or didn't want to, they'd stick to him because they were fond of him, but at the same time get their money from other sources. But I'm not that sort.

"Still, I did think that when he became a Minister he'd use what little influence he had to help me. There are heaps of ways in which he could have done that. But not only did it never occur to him, but when I mentioned it to him, he made excuses. Yes, my dear, there was I, the mistress of one of the most prominent ministers, and getting no more out of it than if I'd had a street-sweeper for a lover; and all because he wanted to pose as an Honest Man! When a man's an egoist—and almost all men are—when he doesn't want to bother about you or make some little sacrifice for you, you'll find he's always clever enough to trot out his principles or his ideals. Anything's good enough as an excuse. . . . Well, what was bound to happen sooner or later did happen. I wanted to get away from Marquis—I was wasting my time with him, and I had an idea that I'd like to try my luck with the Comédie Française. Gurau could have helped me there, but he said—and, as a matter of fact, I believe he was right—that I ought first of all to make a popular success, because otherwise I should just fritter away my time at the Comédie in small parts. That may have been true, but if I'd relied on him to help me make a success, to get me the smallest chance, I might still be relying.

"Well, just about then I got to know, through him—which shows that I acted in perfect innocence, I never saw anybody—a certain friend of his who has an interest in *The Sanction,* a very distinguished and very rich gentleman called Sammécaud, Roger Sammécaud—not that I imagine the name conveys anything to you—who's one of the biggest industrial magnates in France, and extremely cultivated and refined. This Monsieur Roger Sammécaud began to take a lot of trouble about me, in the nicest possible way. He hadn't, up to then, had anything to do with theatres, but it wasn't long before he knew all there was to know, and saw just how he could manage the business. It was through him that I got in touch with Mareil and was offered the leading part in his play. It was extraordinary how, from that moment, everything turned up trumps for me. It was almost too good to be true, and I'm inclined to believe that it was really in my destiny—the older I grow, the more I believe in destiny! . . . Well, little by little Monsieur Sammécaud began to make love to me. . . . He really had fallen for me, quite heavily. He made certain suggestions. I could still officially be Gurau's mistress, on the surface everything would go on as usual. Naturally Monsieur Sammécaud would rather have had me to himself, but he realized the position I was in. He was the first to say to me: 'You owe something to your career, and sooner or later he may be useful to you.' I don't suppose he ever really meant to have a regular affair with me, because he's married, with a family, and lives in a world of strict conventions. Well, to cut a long story short, we both of us avoided making difficulties for ourselves. It suited me admirably. He made me a magnificent monthly allowance—I don't mind telling you the exact sum, though I don't suppose it'll seem much to you, because you probably think that a woman in my position . . . but the fact is that I've been so little spoiled up to now—it was two thousand francs a month, twenty-four thousand a year. Not too bad, eh? And he was such a gentleman that he sent me the first month's instalment before he'd ever been to bed with me. He'd had nothing but a few kisses—rather long, but still only kisses. I can assure you you don't often find men in his world who behave like that.

"Of course, I didn't mean to keep him dangling longer than I could help, but just imagine what happened—the most extraordinary piece of bad luck, the kind of thing one reads in a book or sees on the stage and finds quite unnatural. The very first time I let him come here—and I thought I'd been so careful too—it was very late, after half past eleven. He'd called for me at the theatre, and my servant had gone to bed. I knew that Gurau had gone to a big dinner-party which he wouldn't have missed for the world (at bottom he's very vain and very snobbish). I had no reason to think he'd come to see me afterwards, because he knew that I was tired after the theatre and liked going to bed quietly, and he wouldn't have wanted to wake me up; besides, it's not the kind of thing he does. Well, would you believe that when he started to come home, about midnight, it suddenly occurred to him to pay me a surprise visit, just, it turned out, to show me what he looked like, because he'd shaved off his moustache that morning! I do honestly believe that he was quite without suspicion, but, you see, I had forgotten, when I made my arrangements, that the people he was dining with lived on the boulevard Saint-Michel, so that it was very little out of his way to look me up. But the worst of the whole thing was—and it's always the same where my luck's concerned, *such* coincidences that who *wouldn't* believe in destiny? —well, the worst of it was that neither Monsieur Sammécaud nor I thought of closing the shutters when we came in, or even of drawing the curtains. My maid had left them because she knows that I like sitting by the open window for five minutes or so before I go to bed. I was thinking of something else, I suppose, as was natural in the circumstances, and anyhow it's not usual for people to be hanging about across the street at that hour. As a matter of fact, we didn't do anything so very awful at first, and as soon as matters got going, I signed to him to draw the curtains, which he did. But meanwhile Gurau had arrived beneath my windows and had been surprised to see them lit up as though I was entertaining. He stood there on the pavement, and it appears that at one moment he saw our two shadows. . . . He very nearly came up, but he didn't, and went away instead. I said just now that it was particularly bad luck my not having drawn the curtains, but in one way it wasn't, because if I had he certainly would have come up, and if he had—well, I couldn't have opened the door. Brrr, I can just imagine what it would have been like, listening to his knocking. . . . As it was, I knew nothing about it all at the time. You're probably wondering how I ever did know? Quite simply—he told me. Naturally, there was a scene, though I never let him know that the man was Monsieur Roger Sammécaud— you'll keep that to yourself, dear, won't you? Not that it matters so much now; still, they see a good deal of each other and have a lot of interests in common, and I shouldn't like to make trouble between them; if he knew, the consequences might be serious. As it was, I made up some story about a friend at the theatre who had come back with me against my will and had over-persuaded me. I never pretended that I was innocent, although it would have been easy enough to make out that there'd been nothing worse than a little talk and a few kisses, which I could have proved by the very fact that the curtains had been left undrawn. A lot of women *would* have taken that line, and it usually succeeds. But I hate that sort of lie, it seems so stupid.

"Well, to make a long story short, we parted. You may be sure *I* didn't try to keep him. After all, I had found a successor, and the situation was about as simple as it could be. But as a matter of fact things didn't turn out at all like that. Monsieur Roger Sammécaud took the incident very seriously. 'If we go on seeing each other,' he said, 'Gurau's bound, sooner or later, to find out that I'm the lover for whom you've thrown him over, and I really can't subject him to an outrage of that kind. Gurau's my friend; I have the greatest admiration for him. We've got a lot of important work to do together. I ought probably never to have deceived him as I did, but after all I'm only human, and your beauty must be my excuse. . . . You see, I reckoned on his never knowing: and you didn't tell me that you meant to leave him for good. What's happened has changed everything.' If anyone else had spoken like that I might have thought it all just humbug, but I really do believe he meant it. He has very romantic ideas about conduct. He pressed me most urgently to make it up with Gurau. He behaved beautifully and gave me such a lovely brooch—I'm afraid it was an expensive night for him. But he didn't

stop there: he gave me to understand that if I found that I was suffering, from lack of money, for anything he had done, I'd only got
to tell him.

"I very nearly did ask Gurau to forgive me, though it would have
gone terribly against the grain to do so, but just then another affair
began to take shape. You must admit that not many women have an
experience like that; it would have been natural enough if my head
had been a bit turned. Think of it—the mistress of one of the fore-
most Ministers and of one of the richest manufacturers in the country
at the same time!—and that's what I was, for twenty-four hours. Not
that I regret anything. In the first place, Gurau hasn't remained a
Minister long, and he's even had to fight hard at Tours to get himself
re-elected, and then, it never does any good to spoil one's life with regrets. Another woman might have managed things better; I'm not
really a good plotter, if you understand what I mean. I'm intelligent,
all right, though perhaps you'll think me rather fatuous to say such
a thing about myself, but, after all, Mareil's told me so—intelligent,
but not *knowing,* not even very clever . . . and it's not my way to
indulge in petty spite. Perhaps I ought to have arranged our trysts
away from my own house; it would have been less risky, but it's too
late to think about that.

"You probably want to know whether I'm happy now. The answer is yes, very. I believe this is the first time that I've ever really
loved anybody. Mareil's a grand man, though I don't know how I
can explain exactly why he is. To begin with, no one has ever made
me work as he does, what I call working. It's sheer pleasure. He's
terribly exacting, but he's never unfair and he's never rough; he
never says wounding things. It's exactly as though he were supporting one with his hands. Every time I leave him I feel that I'm worth
rather more than I was when I arrived, and I love that. Then, quite
apart from work, I find him much more interesting than Gurau ever
was, though I can't tell you quite why. Gurau could talk about a lot
of things—it's more the *way* of talking, the tone. . . . With Gurau
the *things* we talked about always had to be interesting, and I always

had a feeling that I was making an effort. With Mareil, on the other hand, just to hear him say that it's raining, or that he met a knife-grinder on his way to my flat, gives me an extraordinary feeling of happiness. Everything he says becomes somehow strange and exciting. And then it's wonderful the way he listens to me. He _makes_ me more intelligent. Does he love me? you'll ask; yes, I'm sure he does. He never hesitated a moment about giving up his mistress, Vignal, and it was entirely on my account that he put off his first night until the beginning of next season, so that he could be sure of my being precisely as he wanted me. In bed I think he finds me a little lacking in ardour, a little inexperienced. You see, he's very sensual, and not at all—not at all simple—you know what I mean. But he's teaching me a lot, and all that will come by degrees, like everything else. . . . We're going on working at the play during the holidays. The general rehearsals begin about the 20th of August. I don't know whether we shall get away to the country before then, rural life isn't quite in his line. But he's promised to take me on one or two short motor trips for two or three days. He drives his car himself, and I believe he's very good at it."

About six o'clock in the evening of the last Saturday in July, seated in the bows of a skiff where the Seine becomes particularly wide between the Austerlitz Bridge and the bridge at Bercy, Jallez said to Jerphanion:

"I don't know yet whether I shall get away at all, nor, if I do, where I shall go, so you'd better write to me at the avenue de la République; letters'll be forwarded. When do you go to the Saint-Papouls'?"

"At the beginning of September; till then I shall be with my parents. Jeanne de Saint-Papoul's wedding is fixed, I think, for the 10th or 12th of September."

"And you'll be there. Try to behave, and don't forget to write me a detailed account. What a marvellous vacation you're going to have!"

"Perhaps you will, too."

"No, I shan't."

"Things still going wrong?"

"I'm annoyed with myself, and I've got a bad conscience. I think I'm behaving badly. On the other hand, I don't see what I could do to make things better. Some evenings I get devilish low, and I hate your going away. Although we never talked about all that, it helped me having you here."

"Still, you can write."

"There are some things one can't write. . . . I spend most of my time fighting somebody else's battles; it's one of my weaknesses, and a particularly fatal one when one's dealing with women, because it's a thing they never do, or hardly ever. Another of my weaknesses is that I'm terribly conscious, not so much of the past, taking the word in a general sense, as of what might be called the 'community of existence.' The Germans have probably got a word for what I mean, something like 'Zusammenerlebt.' Everybody feels it at times, I know, but with me it's especially strong, almost devastating. It comes over me, at times, when I'm walking along a street and turn round to find that a dog's been following me perhaps for a quarter of an hour without my realizing it. He looks at me, and suddenly, no matter how much I struggle against the feeling, I can't help seeing in his eyes an appeal to just that 'community of existence.' It's a feeling, obviously, as old as the world, one of the things that binds humanity together; but different people feel it differently. I'm inclined to think that it has nothing to do with any positive sense of affection. It's altogether different from any feeling of *attachment,* in so far as such a feeling is part of my active creation. In any case, it has nothing to do with my desire for security, with any wish I may have to avoid changing my habits, any desire to see round me the faces I have always seen. It's not a selfish emotion—unfortunately! Funny, isn't it? You wouldn't think I was a particularly social sort of chap, would you? It may be for that very reason that I'm conscious of the emotion. Instinctively I react against the dangers of this wish for a 'community of existence.' I sometimes wonder whether, meeting some old College companion ten years hence, or somebody like Marjaurie, I shall be conscious of the emotion. I should be surprised if I were. When one meets somebody for the first time, one's aware at once, or not aware, of a sense of contact. With some people one develops from the outset a 'community of existence,' which may or may not be pleasant; with others, no matter how long one may know them, that special relationship never develops. . . . Oh, I suppose all this is just a matter of hiding from reality behind a cloud of words. What I really want to know is why I don't put an end to a state of affairs which my reason tells me, again and again, that I ought to end. Sometimes I make up my mind to do it, and even compose in my mind the letter which will finally cut the knot. And then, suddenly, I happen to pass a shop that I have looked at with her, or which vaguely resembles one that I've looked at with her, and then, old man, I feel exactly as though I'd been ripped up with a knife, so that all my good resolutions come tumbling out. Making allowance for certain differences, I believe you'd feel much the same."

"D'you really think so? You flatter me, old chap."

"No, I don't. The feeling I'm talking about's got nothing to do with whether I'm fond of a person or like being with them, still less with whether I respect them."

They went down the river to the bridge at Charenton, and then along the bank of the Marne towards Alfortville. The riverside taverns were beginning to fill up. The sound of concertinas came to them. Lovers sat beneath the arbours or wandered hand in hand. Others passed them in boats, talking and shouting.

A little way off, an empty château watched the houses of the outer suburbs creeping nearer and nearer.

Chapter

12

STRIGELIUS WRITES TO HIS SISTER

My dearest little Sister:

I oughtn't to write to you this evening, because I'm in one of my bad moods. I feel terribly tired, but I've not got the intellectual satisfaction of knowing that I'm going to be ill, and that even if I get worse, I shall at least know where I am. It's probably the result of a hot, airless, stinking summer in Paris. Every year it's the same thing (winter's just as bad. The truth is I can't stick this climate). To make matters worse, I've had a stiff neck, which started before dinner, and it's ten o'clock now. Even writing to my dearest little sister hurts me, and I've got to keep my head in one position like an ox with its neck in a yoke. What I hate most about it is that it makes me feel invalidish. How did I get the beastly thing? I can't remember sitting in a draught. I washed my hair this morning; perhaps it's that. Things have come to a pretty pass, haven't they, if I can't wash my hair in July without getting a stiff neck which'll go on for three days?

And I'm only thirty-seven! Yes, I *am* thirty-seven. No one knows that better than you, because you had the nerve to congratulate me on the fact six weeks ago—it's already six weeks! I've been thinking a good deal about my age recently, for a lot of reasons. But now I've got to think about it from the point of view of physical weakness. (If you could see the position of my head, you would find the words *"from the point of view"* extraordinarily apt!) Nothing gives one this sort of obsession like a crick in the neck, or indeed anything that hinders one's liberty of movement. It makes one think about slowing down and breaking up, of final impotence (much worse than the lack of decision that goes by the same name); in short, of old age.

PROVINCIAL INTERLUDE

My dearest sister, I'm not joking. I'm brooding a lot on the fact of old age, not on the prospect of it in the future, but on my sense of it at this very moment. I really am getting old horribly quickly, and in more than one way. I was never much to look at, but now I'm becoming definitely ugly. You wouldn't believe how deep my wrinkles have got, and when I look closely at my skin when I shave, I realize that most of it is rough, pimply, blotched, veined, and spongy. I'm losing my hair. I don't like using a comb, because when I've finished, it looks as hairy and horrible as a Medusa's head. I've got to fight a pitched battle with lethargy before I can make the slightest effort, and when I've made it, I feel worn out. I have to avoid excess of every kind. If I happen to dine out—a rare occurrence—and eat and drink more than I usually do, I pay for it by three days of absurd little ailments.

It's suddenly occurred to me that it's not very nice of me to whine to my dearest sister about a subject like this, because as soon as one starts talking about age, the melancholy is terribly catching. But my dearest sister is still quite young, protected against the miseries I've mentioned by an almost incredible number of years. (Nearly ten years appears to me, *in this connexion,* an almost incredible number, though in other ways I confess the gap between us seems small enough. What odd rules this geometry of mine has!)

You can be certain that I lose no occasion of persuading myself, against all evidence, that I am still young and tender. Unfortunately the proof doesn't always work. I was quite cheered the day before yesterday by reading a paragraph in some solid newspaper or other which referred to the "young general," mentioning a gentleman who is at least fifty-four. It came over me suddenly that I must be quite a boy. But on second thoughts I realized that I was not a general.

This, my dearest sister, is one of those Parent Truths which, like the Mothers in the Second Part of Faust, can only be looked at in the strictest secrecy. I would confess it to no one except my little sister, and if she passed on to anyone in the world this confidence of mine, I should fight tooth and nail to deny it. I'm not joking.

What is this truth which I find it so hard to accept? It is this. In my heart of hearts I know that glory is nothing, and success still less. I am prepared to demonstrate how weak, how incredibly short a thing it is compared to the grandeur which the most superficial contemplation of the physical universe reveals to us (and, in a way, it's all physical, even glory, in the sense that it involves quantity and duration); prepared too to show, detail by detail, the miserable little manœuvres by means of which glory and success are usually attained.

Nor, in this respect, does my practice fall short of my theory, since not even the most malicious enemy could accuse me of humiliating myself, or even of stirring a finger, to attract either glory or success.

And yet—yes, here's the point; if, at this moment, past thirty-seven as I am, I could claim even the tiniest beginning of glory, if I could catch a glimpse of the faintest, least certain flicker of dawn—as one does, dear sister, of spring some days in February—even if, leaving glory aside, I could claim to be known, in however uncertain and temporary a fashion, for whatever ignoble reasons, if I could enjoy the material emoluments that go with success, if I could read my name in the papers and know that people were talking about me—everything would suddenly be different; I should regard the problem of my age from a new angle, and the crick in my neck would take on an entirely new significance.

I'm afraid this must shock you, my dearest sister; it probably does worse than that—shatters your illusions. I have never, never spoken to you like this before. You are used to thinking of me as a virtuous, almost as a heroic figure. You find it difficult to think of me in any other way. The idea you have of me has always seemed to be my explanation, my excuse, defending me from comparison with others—in one word, glorifying me. It must be mortifying for you to see me tearing the halo from my head and treading it underfoot (though it won't be any the worse for that unless it's only made of cardboard).

I should also, no doubt, shock those of my friends (the word is hardly merited), of my rather precious friends, who have every reason to agree with me, though they'd rather be torn in pieces than admit it, even to themselves. Where I myself am concerned, I have lost all sense of decency. I want to know the truth about myself. Its bitterness gives a not unpleasant savour to my thoughts. Other luxuries being denied me, I enjoy giving myself the luxury of a secret cynicism, a luxury that is all too rare. But when I say "secret," my dear sister, I include you in the term. You know that you are the one consolation I have in the world. I should hate to indulge in thoughts to which you were a stranger.

It's all very disconcerting (because we're talking of the human heart, which is a poor enough bit of mechanism, no better than a ninety-eight-cent watch). Don't think for a moment that I've changed my opinions or altered my *scale of values,* as the pretentious followers of Nietzsche (there's redundancy for you!) like to phrase it. I still believe that in this world, where nothing's worth much, where there's no particular reason to boast of one thing more than another, certain accumulations of words or signs do represent combinations so rare that the chances against their ever evolving, even in the course of hundreds of thousands of centuries, are almost incalculable. A bad sonnet written by a civil servant is, in itself, extraordinary enough when one views it, as one should do, in a perspective which embraces the age of the earth and the birth and death of stellar systems. Think of the innumerable worlds that may have come to be and disappeared again, of the endless nebulæ that may have perished in convulsions through trillions of years after accomplishing their dreary destinies, without producing a single sonnet (while nickel, gold, platinum, and probably radium can be found without difficulty in the smallest meteorite which happens to hurtle towards us through space). When one thinks, too, that this sonnet or this poem, no matter what its form, is, furthermore, the work of some great spirit; that the author, by dint of some curious magic, has put into it not only a harmony, a sequence, a repetition, of delicious sounds, marriages of words, methods of expression swifter and more powerful than were dreamed of before he wrote, but also reflections, either direct or allusive, upon the rest of the universe, concentrated formulæ of thought which contain, with unparalleled aptness, a whole tradition of noble human aspirations completed by the small crown of his own personal contribution; then surely one is justified in thinking oneself in the presence of a product, of a fine flower, with which nothing else in the universe can compare. I would say the same, or almost the same, for similar or dissimilar reasons, of other great works of the human spirit—a picture, a system of philosophy, a law of mathematics or of physics. I don't say with Mallarmé that the world has been created to bloom in a lovely book, because, unfortunately, I suspect the world to have been created for no reason at all. But *experience* does seem to show that the Master's formula wasn't so wrong after all.

I will go further: though nobody admires the beautiful book or even reads it, though the great discovery in philosophy or physics may be regarded by the human species as a negligible error, they still remain beautiful and great. It's surely obvious that if Newton's law had never been recognized or even known by anybody but its author, its universal validity, its value, would be not a whit the less.

You see, then, that I'm not denying my beliefs. But if I were a woman and empress of all the Indies, the fact of being empress of all the Indies wouldn't console me for having a club-foot or a crooked nose. In the same way, even if I knew I had written the most wonderful poem in the world, the knowledge wouldn't console me for being the only person in the world to know it. But the comparison's imperfect, because the empress in question would find in the fact of being empress certain direct compensations for the disappointments suffered by her womanly vanity (what a monstrous sentence that is!). What I mean is that although she mightn't be fêted and flattered as a woman, she would at least be fêted and flattered as an empress, and that, granted in her a certain degree of adaptability, she might derive as much *human* satisfaction from the one state of affairs as from the other. Whereas merely to know that one had written the finest poem in the world wouldn't be any substitute, *humanly* speaking, for the vulgar satisfaction, whether of vanity or any other quality, which mankind seems to stand in need of.

At this point common sense intervenes again with this annoying reflection: "Since no one can ever be sure that he has written the finest poem in the world, or even, to put it on a less exalted plane, a very good poem; and since, on the other hand, he can be quite sure that no one ever talks about it, the result very naturally is that he ends by believing that it is utterly worthless." Yes, it does really seem very difficult to deny that the writer, the artist, the scholar, the imaginative worker of any kind, must, if he is continually neglected, be forced to the conclusion that he is a failure—what Father, you remember, used to call, with that rather funny, rather common way he had of throwing his head back and clicking his tongue against his teeth, "a dried fruit."

Oh, my darling sister, that memory of our father makes me want to hug you. We understood one another so well even then. You were quite a small girl, and I a great lout of a boy, but when certain things were said at the family table, we used to exchange glances. I can see now the way your little mouth, so precociously subtle and clever, used to smother a laugh.

But to return to what I was saying. So far as I am concerned, the attitude of the world points to the hypothesis that I am a "dried fruit." I have published all the best of what I have written, so that I've not even got the comfort of being able to say: "Ah, but just you wait till *that* comes out!" I know I've produced very little, but Hérédia needed only a few sonnets to make him famous. As a matter of fact, a small output, when it's not accompanied with staggering results, only serves to confirm the dried-fruit theory. It's obvious that that's the case with me. I could count on my fingers the people who've read everything I've written—and the feat wouldn't make too great a call on their attention. And this few—happy, perhaps, but still few —have scarcely been what you'd call thrilled. The only man (I don't count you, darling) who's ever told me I was a great poet is Paul Fort. But, then, I've heard him say the same thing to others who I'm pretty sure are not. What bothers me—and this is a point I want to underline—is that people like me. I don't antagonize, I don't irritate; consequently I am forbidden the comfort of saying that the whole world of my contemporaries is blind to my merits or filled with hatred for me. If only I could deceive myself in that way, I could at least put it down to the fact of being a misunderstood genius. But I can't. There are several hundred persons—of just the type which ought either to rave about me or to inveigh against me—who regard me (so I am told) as a nice, "interesting" chap, much like the two or three thousand other interesting chaps you'd run up against in cultivated Parisian circles.

Notwithstanding which (come close, dear sister, and let me whisper this enormity in your ear), I still regard myself as rather remarkable. I don't say genius, partly because I've never been able to define genius in any really satisfactory way, partly because the word implies a sort of demoniac possession which I consider to be foreign to the highest manifestations of the human spirit. But once I start looking round for people whom I could regard as my superiors, I don't, frankly, find any. In a way it irritates me that this should be so, because if I could find such persons, in any appreciable number, the whole question would be solved. But to take only my special department of letters, no matter with how detached an eye I consider what I have produced and compare it with the work of my far more famous colleagues, I can't see that mine is in any way inferior; in fact, I am forced to admit that in many ways it is better. In many cases the comparison is devastating (for them). What seems to me decisive on this point is that I know no one I couldn't *make rings round*. Or let me put it this way: take every item of cleverness, of excellence, of invention, even of inspiration, in my colleagues; there's not one I couldn't, if I so wished, reproduce—or equal, because I'm not talking of copying. But the opposite is not true. Let them put their stakes on the table, I'll double them, and still have a pocketful of cleverness, excellence, invention, and even of inspiration, of which they've no conception.

I've said my "colleagues," but you know that actually I don't give two pins for specialization, which is applicable only to second-rate minds—that is to say, minds which are essentially superficial. Outside my special field I still have the greatest difficulty in finding anyone I couldn't make rings round, anyone of whom I couldn't say: "If I took the trouble to learn the technique of his job, to amass the necessary knowledge and acquire the particular language involved, I could do all that he's done, and a good deal more."

Of course, I may be mad. It's a perfectly possible hypothesis. I may have created in my mind a consistent system of insanity in which everything has to yield to my idea of my own greatness. Such things do happen, and when they do they're not always so tragic as people make out. I realize, therefore, that my state of mind is an equation which may be solved in a variety of ways. One is the assumption that I am mad, but I must confess that I don't really feel inclined to accept that explanation. Madness seems to me to be rather like dreaming. It's perfectly possible for people who have any gift of introspection to dream and yet not be able to rid themselves of their dream or to wake themselves from it. But that doesn't mean that they don't know they are dreaming. In the same way, I am sure that if I was mad, I should find it as difficult as anybody else to wake from my madness, but I should know that I was mad. Dear sister, I can hear your happy cry: "Since you've finally persuaded yourself of what I always said, that you're a great man, there can't be the slightest doubt about it. Everything's all right, we've only got to wait."

But that, my dear, is where we differ. Being still only a clever little girl, you believe that greatness *must* be recognized. But I don't agree. Not that I wish to take up a romantic attitude towards the matter. I certainly do not believe that a great man is bound to live under a curse. He may be recognized; but then, again, he may not. All I say is that there is no law in the matter. And my reason for saying that is that I don't believe that there is, anywhere in nature, a "law" in the strict meaning of the word, not even when one is dealing with cases of simple phenomena involving an infinite number of instances. Still less, then, is it likely that there should be a law—even an approximate law—for a sphere in which the phenomena are very complex and the number of instances strictly limited.

It's simply a matter of each individual case and of the calculation of chances. Leaving aside any question of the intensity of genius (excuse the word; I use it for convenience), men of the type of Hugo, Balzac, Wagner have many chances—provided they don't die too young—of being recognized, both by reason of the *size* of their output and because they attack their public from many different angles. My case, you'll agree, is not quite the same.

One's also got to consider the relation of an artist to the period in which he lives—a matter involving a greater degree of chance than people will usually admit. On one side you have the artist's tendencies and preferences—his taste, let us say; on the other, the taste of his contemporaries. So far as my work is concerned, the present age fills me with disquiet. Neither its good taste nor its bad is any use to me. Its great men are Rostand in verse, France in prose. I don't despise either of them. But you must admit it's unlikely that the general gaze, turning, like the beam of a lighthouse, in the directions that they have made popular, will stop to take notice of me. Take the case of Barrès. Apart from the fact that he did everything he could to concentrate the beam upon himself, he was, in essentials, right in the path of the light that fell full upon Pierre Loti—rather beyond him, to be sure, and slightly more to the left; still, so placed that the light caught him. It's the same with Gide. He's not yet shining with the reflected rays, I know, but he's produced a lot, and its appeal is various. Besides—and this is a point to be noted—the lens catches him from a variety of angles. His final master-stroke has been to found the *Nouvelle Revue Française*. I'm not sure that even he sees just how great a master-stroke that is (you must remember his Norman heredity).

I'm afraid I'm boring you with all this chat, but it's a subject I never tire of talking about. I'm probably the least successful man in France, but I know more about the conditions of success than anyone. I never cease brooding and meditating upon it, not upon its laws

—because, as Carmen said of love, it hasn't any—but upon its habits and its usages. Perhaps one of these days I shall write a great work, despite myself, to be called *Success,* with, as subtitle, *Its Conditions and the Means of its Attainment.* The author's name will be Strigelius. The signature would seem so impudent that I've no doubt many people would believe it to be a pseudonym adopted by some fashionable author with which to father on the world the *obiter dicta* which he didn't want to publish under his own name. It'd be funny, wouldn't it? Almost like one of Villiers's tales.

One of its chapters would be called "Ages." (Please note that my thoughts on success are at once extremely disinterested, because I have devoted a great deal of time to studying something that has no connexion with me and never will, and extremely egotistical, because, however far they diverge, they always refer to my own particular case, and any disguise they may assume is sewn with white thread for all to see.) I have deeply considered the ages of great men: (1) the age at which they *began* their work; (2) the age at which they began to *make it public;* (3) the age at which it reached its maximum of *actual value;* (4) the age at which they began to be *successful;* (5) the age at which such success reached its highest point (the maximum *relative value*). I have given much thought to the interconnexion of these different aspects. There are cases, as you can see for yourself, where 4 and 5, sometimes even 2 (Saint-Simon, Chénier), take on the form of *posthumous* success. I must evolve a special system of numbers —italics, for instance—to show that the age I'm speaking of is the age of somebody who is dead. Thus, I should write that the actual age of Rimbaud is *56,* of Mallarmé *63,* of Baudelaire *89* (nothing very much, if one takes a long view), and of Alexander the Great *2266* (worth noting, that last!). You will notice that I am not confining myself to people in the same sphere of activity, so that the problem becomes more extensive and certain phrases need explanation. For example, in the case of Napoleon or Alexander, what exactly do we understand by the expressions *began their work* and *began to make their work public?* Obviously, for men of action, *work* and the *making public of their work* are apt to be identical activities, and success often follows hard on the heels of this *making public* (in the same way that a check to their proceedings tends to be immediate and incapable of rectification). If the work in question happens to be a battle, success—in other words, victory—is decided in a single day, and failure can be reversed only by posterity. (Looked at in this way, the situation yields certain truths that are not always fully realized—such, for instance, as that the actor, the public performer, although he may call himself an artist, is really more akin to the man of action than to the poet or composer; or as this, that the author, as soon as he begins to write for the stage, begins to approximate to the man of action.)

I'm wandering from the point, dear sister—just talking for my own amusement, but I don't suppose it's very amusing for you. I never get tired of chatting to you. It's twenty minutes after midnight by my clock (what a pretty, sad little chime it has!). Thérèse is asleep, and so are the children. It may be just as late when you read my letter, because the Paris post arrives in the morning, doesn't it? And when one has a husband, a child, and a house to look after, one can only find time for a big brother's essays when night brings a let-up from the day's duties and gives one the privilege of solitude.

You ask whether we will come to you during the holidays. It's sweet of you to be so insistent, but I can't make up my mind. In the first place, speaking selfishly, I want to use this wretched fortnight of leisure (perhaps I can spin it out to three weeks) for work of my own. If I came to you it wouldn't be very easy. It's bad enough here with the children, but with you we should be living more than ever, if that's possible, in one another's pockets. And there are other reasons. The journey, when there are so many of us, costs a lot, and I'm pretty short, as usual. Oh, we're not paupers; we can just scrape along, and, in a way, that's worse. (There are times when I envy Verlaine's poverty, with its freedom from all responsibilities, its floating with the tide, its power to induce a sort of lyric mood by reason of its very desperation.) In your house—I may as well say it, since I'm in a mood for confidences—I should be conscious of an atmosphere, of human relationships, in which there would be a certain tinge of bitterness. Please understand me, my dear, dear sister: I'd give anything in the world for a fortnight alone with you. Oh God, how heavenly that would be! What endless talks we would have! It would be the old days come again, but with strange, poignant overtones made of our experiences. . . . But that's impossible. You have a husband, a fine fellow of whom I'm very fond, but I find his presence disturbing, depressing. All the time I'm with him I find myself thinking of the engineer (it is an engineer, isn't it?) in the *Jardin de Bérénice*. . . . Then again, you say that my brother is not going touring or mountaineering in the Alps this year, but is staying at home to superintend the work on the villa which his admirable industry has enabled him to build. That's just more than I can stand. I don't mind his scorn at a distance; I can even stand being with him for one hour each year. But to run the risk of seeing him almost every day, of listening to his allusions, his reflections, however general they may be, however well meant, of seeing the airs he gives himself, of feeling that that typical bourgeois regards me as a poor devil who, though he has not yet brought dishonour on the family, spoils the look of things by being such a piece of "dried fruit"—that really is more than I can stand. Is that another surprise for you, dear sister, another cause of disillusion? You've always deceived yourself about my "character": I've got so much less than you think I have. I've got enough to stop me doing work unworthy of myself, to resist the lure of money or vanity, but I'm lacking in energy. I know perfectly well that though I'm not naturally prolific, I could produce more than I do. For instance, I'm aware that without commercializing myself, I could, in addition to what I consider my real work, write a few simpler and more popular books which would increase my reputation and attract a wider public, but I'm stopped by laziness and by a feeling that it's not worth while (that battle-cry of the idle!). I ought to have lived in the reign of Louis XIV. If I had, perhaps one fine day Boileau might have gone to the King and said point-blank: "Sire, do you know who is the greatest poet in your kingdom?" "No, who is he?" "Sire, Strigelius." "Who do you say?" "Strigelius, Sire; s, t, r, i, g, etc. . . . . Your Majesty must commission at once an ode, a tragedy, and a ballet." Unfortunately, I can't see Émile Faguet bursting in on old President Fallières with a remark like that.

And, since that can't happen, I find myself falling back on the specious nobility of silence. I will confess to you, dearest of sisters, a favourite and dangerous dream in which I sometimes indulge. I imagine a man who knows, beyond all possibility of doubt, that he is the greatest figure of his age, not only capable of writing the finest poem or the most beautiful symphony, but able also to solve, better than anyone else, the social problems of his time, to devise for France the most perfect system of alliances. He is so sure of it that the knowledge alone satisfies him. He refuses to make anyone else a party to his schemes, because, in the first place, to specialize, to canalize his abilities, means that he will have to impose limits on himself, but also because he distrusts himself: *margaritam ante porcos;* he lacks the aggressive spirit, he would hate to be misunderstood; finally, because this secret colloquy, this monologue in the throne-room, appeals to him as something magnificent and sweetly pleasant.

You can understand, can't you, the history of such a man? First he makes his work public without expecting or receiving recognition; next, he writes for his own private satisfaction without troubling to publish; finally, he ceases even to write.

But I want you to know, my dear sister, that I fully realize the fallacy that lies behind this proud privacy. Nothing that remains potential only can ever be fully great. I know from experience that a poem is born only at the moment that one decides to externalize it in writing, at the moment when one comes to grips with the material, with the difficulty of language. No great poem can be said to exist so long as it is merely in the mind. In the same way—despite Renan— there never was, never could have been, in the pocket of a second-lieutenant the plan that would have won the campaign of '70. No mere plan can ever win a war. At most there can be a hypothesis from which action can start, a general intention sufficient to determine the particular way in which the facts are to be approached. There must always be, in addition, a man who constantly acts and reacts according to circumstances, some of which are foreseen, some unforeseen. I know, too, from experience, that if I remain for any length of time without actually writing, my "great thoughts" get into the habit not only of remaining imperfect and confused—that is to say, of not being great thoughts at all—but also of falling short of reality, of never coming to the point of birth. For to bring a thing to birth is a form of taking trouble, and to say "What's the use?" is to embark on a course which may have fatal results.

At such moments I am aware that my "great thoughts" tend to shade off into a preoccupation with the gas-bill which Thérèse has mentioned the night before, or to vanish in the wake of a thousand futile trivialities. Do you know, I made myself wretched for a whole week because the cook had left her greasy finger-marks on a piece of new wallpaper which I had put up at great expense in our study-dining-room, and that during that time I spent endless hours and a great deal of ingenuity, at the cost of much mental misery and nervous exhaustion, simply in deciding how best I could remove the stains without spoiling the surface of the paper?

Now I really will leave off. Calm your fears! It's ten past one. . . . It's such a pleasure for me to talk to you. Give everyone my love. If you insist, we will send you two of the children, the least intolerable; you can choose which two you prefer. (It's unfair that the poor little wretches should suffocate in Paris just because I'm over-sensitive.)

Write to me soon. I send you my love. So does Thérèse, so do the children; but I especially.

Yours ever,

Marc

1.40 a.m.

PS.—I went to bed, but I've got up again to add this:

(1) You know how impatient I shall be to get your answer. I've spoken of very serious things, and I've stripped myself naked in the process. I don't want you to think too badly of me.

(2) I didn't forget to hunt up particulars of the man called Albertinus Strigelius, and I found out a lot of odd things which I'll write about later. But I still don't see how we can be connected with this olibrius. How is it that our wiseacre brother doesn't show some interest in the problem?

Chapter

13

MIONNET TAKES STOCK

Although Mionnet had been settled at M— for more than two weeks, it was borne in upon him that he was still unknown to a great many people in the place, and that only a very small minority realized the significance of his presence there. That this should be so surprised him. He had always imagined that everything was known in a provincial town as soon as it happened, and that unless one took very especial pains, it was impossible to ensure a secret being kept.

It is true, of course, that his experience was rather out of the ordinary. Had it been a layman, instead of the Abbé Mionnet, who had come on a similar mission to M—, his arrival would, in the first place, have been announced in the local newspapers. Furthermore, the functionaries concerned would have spoken freely to all and sundry about the matter, and even if they had not, their wives would very soon have spread the news.

But in his case nothing of the sort had happened. The authorities of the Church are not in the habit of airing their private troubles in public or of communicating them to the press. If they discuss such business at all, they do so only in the strict intimacy of their own circles and with a degree of reserve which is unknown to laymen. There is little risk of their mutual confidences ever reaching a larger public. The absence of family life deprives them of the sounding-board that, for others, is provided by a home.

If Mionnet found his self-conceit slightly affronted by this condition of silence, he realized the advantages that accrued from it. Whatever steps he took could be taken in privacy. When he set himself to gather information or to get into touch with the enemy, he found himself, it is true, confronted by people who, though they might be carefully on their guard, were not more so than is usual in provincial society. The result was that he had more time than he had expected in which to take his bearings, and far greater freedom of movement.

He could, therefore, allow himself to wait on circumstances, and set himself to approach the problem simultaneously from a variety of angles.

He had made no definite plans, knowing that to do so would be to take up a purely arbitrary position. Once on the spot, he realized that the time needed to evolve the necessary strategy would be better employed in assembling the many possible sources of information and opportunities of action. Speed was of the first importance.

He therefore took his part in conversations, and listened to confidences and complaints, with an open-mindedness which made an admirable impression. Those who knew what he had come for thought of him as a man who had not yet drawn his conclusions, and, on that account, were more free than they would have been with their information. Those who only vaguely suspected, or actually did not know, the meaning of his presence were not put on their guard.

To be thus tactful in no way oppressed him; it chimed well with his character and gave him considerable amusement. He liked to see things clearly, but hated those systematic pedants who always work according to a program, classifying everything in advance and foreseeing everything, only to find themselves at the mercy of facts the subtle shades of which escape their owlish spectacles, so that they approach them only in the mood of those who seek the proof of their *a priori* assumptions. He showed no application in working with abstractions. Improvisation was his delight.

Consequently, he was content at first to feel his way, and the ideas which he formed as a result of this method were by no means of equal value.

He showed himself more than willing to take part in the interviews with Monsignor Sérasquier which the latter seemed to desire, and listened to him with attention. Monsignor tired himself out, became confused, and on more than one occasion hopelessly contradicted himself; but Mionnet showed such respect, such obliging deference in his presence, such willingness to share his point of view, however incoherent it might be, that the Bishop came to regard him finally as precisely the ally he had always wanted and whose activities he could direct.

From these various colloquies something, though not much, did eventually emerge. Monsignor was incapable of any clear explanation where matters of money were concerned. He was hazy about the nature of water-power. He spoke of "electric cables" and "electric current" with a worried air. When he quoted figures, he was guilty of errors which might involve any amount from 1 to 10. (At such times Mionnet would nod his head slightly, as though to say: "That's near enough.") But the moment he had to deal with questions of psychology, individual or collective, he was more in his element. His judgment of people, ecclesiastic and lay alike, was remarkably shrewd and practical. Listening to him, Mionnet more than once reflected: "When I see so-and-so, I'll remember that." In the course of their conversations he sketched, without seeming to do so deliberately, a complete sociological map of the district, adding, here and there, little finishing touches, qualifications, and subtleties. What the Bishop provided was a survey of the old-fashioned, casual kind, in which Stephen Bartlett would have found nothing of Ernest Torchecoul's intoxicating precision. Economic facts were not ignored, but they were presented in terms that translated them into human characteristics and manners.

He would say, for instance: "A very large section of the local middle classes live well below their income, but that doesn't mean that there are not some who live above it. There is no love lost between these two groups, and if you get one of them interested in anything, you automatically antagonize the other." A day or two later he went into greater detail. "Those who live below their incomes belong to the old-established bourgeoisie. There are families here who have been in the same houses since the time of Louis XV. My own landlord is just such a type, which doesn't, however, mean that he isn't delighted to make what he can out of me. He can't help it, but he'd never admit the fact. He accepts the chance which has come his way as an honourable excuse for a good investment. I pay a tiny rent, but he behaves as though he were giving me the house for nothing. In a way, of course, he is, but, all the same, it pays him." Another time he said: "The members of this old-established bourgeoisie pretend that they take no direct part in business. Lack of capital would prevent them playing any large part financially, and they would find it humiliating to occupy any subordinate position. But, mark you, as soon as word gets about that there's money to be made, they slink off to their bankers to see whether they can pick up a few stocks. If the results are disappointing, they're the first to make an outcry. They have no sense of responsibility and would be surprised if you told them they had been speculating. Their attitude is that somebody has stolen their money." A moment later Monsignor added, without seeming to stress any connexion between the two ideas: "They're people, as a rule, who are pretty closely connected with the local administration."

Nor was he less illuminating about the poorer classes. "There are a great many agricultural labourers," he said, "who until recently have never had any liquid capital. . . . Naturally, they are no more anxious than their better-off neighbours to risk it. Their tendency, as a rule, is to buy land. But though the large estates go pretty cheap, smaller plots are pretty expensive. They are only interested in land if they can work it themselves. If they've already got enough to do with what they have, or if the question of distance arises, they abandon the idea of buying. The idea of employing servants appals them, and sub-leasing to farmers doesn't pay. The result is that they are more frequently tempted than you'd think by the chance of investing their money in some local industry . . . provided they're offered a big enough return. . . ." Again: "The whole question is complicated by the fact that the people hereabouts, especially in the rural districts, though they're good Catholics, vote radical. It's a curious situation. They go to Mass, but they don't like priests, or, rather, they expect their priests to mind their own business. Monks are their abomination. Yes, it's curious, but very typical of the old French character. Only those who are ignorant of history find it surprising. It should have been given due consideration at the time of the Separation. . . . But Rome knows nothing of French history. . . ." At this point Monsignor wandered away from the tramway question, but Mionnet waited patiently for him to return to it.

The Bishop made no reference to Mme de Quingey in the course of these conversations, nor did he mention the live-stock dealer. Mionnet was more than once on the point of speaking about the latter, but hesitated to do so.

As he listened to his superior, his private thoughts were busy. "He's by no means a negligible quantity," he reflected. "He's often silly, and illness has weakened him, but he's thought a lot about these things. He's not the kind of man who just repeats what he's been told. When all's said and done, he is, or has been, a man of some distinction."

He evolved a general theory from these observations of his. He realized, not for the first time, with considerable interest, that when individuals occupy leading positions in society, it is pretty obvious why they do so. It is not always that they deserve to be where they are, and very rarely that they seem to be the best men for the job. But almost always there is some quality of character or intelligence which marks them out from the general run, even though they are often lacking in moral distinction. It is just here that the ideas of the very young are most wrong. When one is twenty, one likes to think, on the strength of one or two instances, that all people in high places are fools. But that is only a very imperfect theory.

Mionnet soon realized, furthermore, that, judging from what he had so far seen, Monsignor Sérasquier was the only one of the whole gang who deserved to be treated with consideration. He had been kinder than any of them to the newcomer. "I hold his fate in my two hands," Mionnet reflected, "and the fate of a good many others as well" (the thought made him smile with a certain access of pride). "Well, if he goes on behaving as decently as he has done so far, if my impression of him remains favourable, I should like to do what I can to save him."

But this feeling of kindliness in no way committed him to acquiesce in the Bishop's version of the situation, and no matter how poor an opinion he might have of others whom he interrogated, he didn't hesitate to make a note of their evidence when it seemed to him to promise well.

His daily conversations with the Canon Delhostal at meal-times did not, to be sure, concern themselves always with the matter in hand, but nevertheless in the course of them he managed to make himself master of many useful details. They were not his only means of approach to the problem, since he arranged three or four meetings with one of the other canons, Manguy, Vicar-General and protonotary apostolic, a thin, short-sighted man, with a soft, polite voice and a nondescript appearance. Their first meeting was very short, and the Canon confined himself, on that occasion, to trivialities.

"Ah, so he's fixed you up at old Mother Roubier's; I hope you are comfortable. Are the daughters at home?"

In this way Mionnet learned that his landlady, Mme Roubier, had two young grown-up daughters, who were often away, and about whom Delhostal had not breathed a word.

At one of their later interviews he managed to find out what the Vicar-General thought of the business in hand. Canon Manguy launched out into a panegyric about Monsignor Sérasquier, though he confined himself to that gentleman's past. "You've no idea," he said, "what a wonderful man he used to be. It is indeed a pity that you never knew him then." He praised his generosity, and his sense of modern needs; he referred with approval to his prestige. "If only he'd been careful to keep his methods above suspicion, none of these complications need ever have arisen."

The Canon, it appeared, regarded the tramway enterprise as, in itself, a perfectly reasonable undertaking, and quite likely to succeed. The trouble, according to him, was that certain undesirable and inefficient people had come to be mixed up with it.

"Monsignor was losing his mental vigour even before this recent accident of his. He allowed the sort of people to get control whom he would never have tolerated in the old days, and winked at the state of affairs which resulted."

The talk turned on Canon Delhostal. The Vicar-General smiled resignedly.

"I expect he's been blackening all of us, hasn't he? He has many fine qualities, but he always likes thinking the worst of people. . . . His attitude towards Monsignor Sérasquier has not been of the pleasantest, though the Bishop has always treated him well. He has a lot of influence, and he's none too scrupulous about the means he employs to attain his ends. Your presence here must gall him considerably, especially now that he realizes how able you are. I don't think he'll put up with it for long."

Mionnet was on the point of answering with annoyance that the length of his stay would not depend on the attitude either of Delhostal or of anybody else at M—, but it occurred to him that the Vicar-General was counting on his taking that line, and that in exaggerating his colleague's power of interference he had sought to enlist the newcomer's sense of importance against him. He contented himself, therefore, with a smile which implied that the other needn't bother his head about him. He asked the Canon for the names of those laymen who were most hostile to the Bishop and whom it was most necessary to disarm.

But his interlocutor avoided giving details.

"You know how it is," he said: "so long as there's a feeling of confidence abroad, people are very patient and very easily handled. But as soon as they get panicky, there's the devil to pay."

Mionnet mentioned Mme de Quingey, the cement-factory to which Monsignor Lebaigue had referred, and the excitable cattle-dealer, whose name he had recently found out to be Firmin Gambaroux.

Canon Manguy, however, remained on the defensive:

"I don't know that the lady has much say in the matter, though her husband has, of course. He's a man with an interest in a good many local enterprises and he would have liked—he still would like—to get his finger in that particular pie. He's very well in with the building contractor about whom you were speaking."

A moment later he added:

"I'm not sure that Monsignor would altogether like you to go too far along that particular path. As to old Gambaroux, I expect I've heard the same sort of stories that you have. But I know nothing about him. I don't think, if I were you, that I'd seem to attach too much importance to him."

Mionnet established relations with all the other canons except two. He also had a talk with the senior priest at Saint-Martin's. Nor was he above sounding his landlady, Mme Roubier, about the business of the tramways. Mme Roubier sighed and seemed to be embarrassed. Her views on the matter appeared to be vague. What did emerge, however, was that the scandal had taken a strong hold of public opinion.

In the course of his investigations Mionnet found out the name of the lawyer who had drawn up the company's charter, and of the bank which had issued most of the stock. The lawyer was called Beauvoir. The bank concerned was the Sermaize Bank, and seemed to have a good name. Its manager was a certain M. Gravisset, much respected in the neighbourhood.

After carefully pondering the wisdom of approaching these two individuals, Mionnet decided to pay a visit to each of them.

Beauvoir was perfectly affable, but before he would answer the Abbé's questions he was curious to know by what authority he asked them.

After a moment's hesitation Mionnet admitted to the lawyer, under cover of professional secrecy, that he had been commissioned by the

Archbishop to make an inquiry. Maître Beauvoir bowed and asked whether his visitor could show any official authorization. He apologized for having to be so careful, but pointed out that the matter was a serious one and that the professional secrecy to which the other had referred would be interpreted in the strictest possible sense.

Mionnet had, of course, no written authority to show. He made it clear that he was asking for no breach of confidence, but only for confirmation of certain matters which were public knowledge. He had hoped that, at the same time, he might have been favoured with a general view of a delicate situation by a man fully competent to give it, and, if necessary, with a word of advice.

Maître Beauvoir replied that Mionnet had a legal right, like anybody else, to obtain, at his own expense, a copy of all the documents relative to the formation of the company, or, simpler still, could consult the originals at the Registrar's office or in the presence of a magistrate. Beyond that he had nothing to say.

The attitude of M. Gravisset, the manager of the bank, was more human. He explained the exact extent to which he had been involved, referred to the mistakes which, in his opinion, had been made, and, without presuming to give advice, managed to hint at a few suggestions. His views, in the main, agreed with those of Canon Delhostal, with whom Mionnet had several further meetings and whom he soon came to regard as his chief or, at least, as his most valuable source of information.

But there was one point which neither Delhostal, Gravisset, nor anybody else, including the Bishop, could help him to clarify, but which seemed to him to be of capital importance. How far had the enemy pushed his attack? Had legal action been taken? And if so, by whom and on what grounds? Had proceedings actually started?

Odd though it might seem, no one would venture to answer these questions with either a definite yes or a definite no. What was odder still was that no one seemed seriously to have considered the point. Mionnet found it hard to believe. He thought at first that those of whom he asked the questions were avoiding giving a reply, either because of some silly idea that they might compromise themselves or because of a shamefaced reticence. But finally he had to admit that the ignorance of his interlocutors was sincere, and he was amazed at the extent to which the frivolity of sober-minded people could go, at the degree of laziness they would permit themselves in matters which might affect them so nearly. But was mere carelessness an adequate explanation? Was there not also here an unconscious avoidance of that detailed knowledge which might conflict with the romantic attitude to life; knowledge that, fundamentally, could satisfy the emotions less than the almost mythical dangers to which the imagination can give rise?

At all costs he must put an end to this rather absurd state of uncertainty. He thought that the best means of doing this would be to go straight to the District Attorney.

The District Attorney was away taking a cure at Vichy. Mionnet was received by his deputy, M. Girard, a young man about his own age, of frank appearance. Mionnet played his cards cleverly. Without involving himself in indiscreet confidences, he made it quite clear why he was at M—, hinting that he would gladly have refused so difficult a task, but that he had to obey his superiors (he indicated that these were the highest ecclesiastical authorities of France), and that, having come, he wished to perform his task as competently as possible, as much in the interests of the general public as in those of the Church. The deputy at once felt himself in sympathy with this man of his own generation, spoke quite openly, and went straight to the point. An additional reason for his confidence was that he recognized a resemblance between the careers in which they were each in the position of learner. He felt that he wanted to help him, almost to act as his guide.

He put himself at his visitor's disposition and told him all he knew of the affair. He had not, personally, had much to do with it, but had heard a good deal of talk. No official complaint had yet been made, nor were proceedings actually pending, but it was probable that both would develop. The District Attorney had had a good many visits from individuals who would probably subscribe to a legal claim, and had received a good many letters, both signed and anonymous, though such documents were not, of course, in form, legal complaints. He had listened to his visitors and made notes of their grievances. He had, however, while not bringing any pressure to bear, asked them to consider carefully the gravity of having recourse to law in so serious a matter. He felt friendly, within limits, towards the Bishop, but was not particularly sympathetic in his attitude to the Church. He was, however, a tactful and moderate man, who thought that nobody would stand to benefit from a scandal of this sort. The deputy agreed with him, but doubted whether it would be possible to avoid proceedings. He shared his chief's opinion that the whole business had been marked more by foolishness than dishonesty. Nobody doubted Monsignor Sérasquier's good faith in the main. Should legal action be taken, however, a certain amount of mud would stick to the Bishop even though he might not be directly involved. Mionnet, therefore, need have no fear that he would find the judicial authorities hostile to his mission.

Girard gave Mionnet some general advice, promised to go into the whole affair, and particularly to consider what practical solution he might be able to suggest for the liquidation of the whole affair without leaving too sore a feeling of resentment in the minds of the victims—for unfortunately there had been victims—who ought to be persuaded to hold their hands or at least to observe a benevolent neutrality. He admitted that it wouldn't be easy. "Folks round here," he said, "are slow to move, but once they've got under way it's difficult to stop them."

They agreed to meet again the next day, and chatted awhile before they parted. They discovered that they had both been educated in Paris; that one had been just finishing his studies at the Lycée Henri IV while the other was a pupil at Louis-le-Grand. Girard said that he had very nearly gone on to the Central Training College, and when he found that Mionnet was actually a graduate of that institution and had taken his degree in history, he looked at him with new interest, as at one of those important converts whose life is shrouded in mystery but full of so rare a quality that even unbelievers find themselves attracted. He admired more than ever now the Abbé's simplicity, his gay and open manners. They said good-bye to each other almost in the tone of boon companions, and as Girard shook the Abbé's hand he repeated that he was completely at his service, that the other need have no compunction about asking his help in case of necessity, and that should he himself get wind of any sudden development he would at once send word to Mionnet's lodging.

"Ah, so you're at Madame Roubier's. She's got two pretty daughters; very decent girls, I believe."

After his second interview with Girard, Mionnet found himself able to arrange the various bits of information he had collected into some sort of order and to make a general survey of the situation. The results at which he arrived were as follows:

Two years earlier, Monsignor Sérasquier, who, despite his incapacity to understand figures, liked to dabble in industrial and financial speculation, had given his moral and material support to a project for forming a company to supply the department with electric cars. The enterprise was well planned and had a good chance of success. The prime mover in the affair, however, a certain Charles Latteignant, had, for reasons of health, handed over the supervision of the business, a year later, to his nephew Charles Robert Latteignant, a conceited young man who had never completed his education. This youth made a great show of being an engineer, talked endlessly about "modern methods" and "instruments of precision," and spent most of his time leading a gay life and dazzling women by his technical pretensions. On the ground that the company's equipment should be of the very latest, he chose the most expensive and least proved materials, and made with his contractors a series of supplementary agreements in which, as a result of the unusual difficulties with which he was confronting them, he allowed himself to be grossly overcharged, and consented to the inclusion of several dangerous clauses.

The estimated cost of the undertaking was considerably exceeded, and the work seriously delayed. Despite the fact that repeated appeals for additional capital were issued, the company's funds became increasingly compromised. The contractors and sub-contractors, in a sudden access of nervousness, or worked upon by malicious influences, insisted with more than customary obstinacy upon immediate payment, and, since they succeeded only in getting a certain amount on account, shut off their supplies. All work had been suspended for the last three months. At any moment the creditors might insist on appointing a receiver, and if they did not do so at once, it certainly was for no reason of magnanimity on their part. Nor was this the only danger, since the civil authorities had a perfect right to withdraw the concession which had been granted to the company.

The direst threat of all, however, came from the crowd of small investors, and it was they who were behind the threatened claim and the proceedings for false pretences. Even if it was found that legally there was no case to be made out, the intention to bring one would, in fact, cause a scandal which would involve the Bishop and spread beyond the confines of the diocese.

To whom, and in what degree, must responsibility be imputed? Monsignor Sérasquier had certainly been guilty of imprudence and excessive optimism. It had been wrong of him, in the first place, to become involved too openly and too personally in an affair of this kind, and later, not to have opposed the appointment of Charles Robert Latteignant. The gravest charge against him, however, was that he had redoubled his support of the enterprise at the very moment when it was on the point of failing, a fact of which he must have been perfectly well aware. There was plenty of evidence for all these blunders, for his part in the affair had, unfortunately, blazed an obvious trail.

The role played by Manguy, the Vicar-General, was not so easy to determine. He was said to be a friend of Charles Robert Latteignant's, and rumour went so far as to declare that at one period he had been in receipt of secret commissions. This, however, could not be proved. What was certain was that he had given the Bishop very bad advice, and that as soon as things began to go wrong, he had been clever enough to make himself scarce. He had very nearly managed to get himself regarded as one of the victims, leaving Monsignor to bear the full weight of public odium. It was difficult to believe that he had been altogether displeased at the turn things had taken. True, he had suffered a certain amount of inconvenience, but this had been compensated by the embarrassment caused to his superior by the scandal. Mionnet realized, even at this early stage of the inquiry, that one of the pleasantest results of his mission would be to put a flea in the ear of the protonotary apostolic.

The other canons had been little more than supers to these principals. They were of no importance. He would make a note of their names, but it was clear that they would be of no assistance in furthering his investigations.

What part had Mme de Quingey played in all this? It seemed certain that there had been an intrigue of several years' standing between her and the Bishop. Naturally, it had never been publicly acknowledged, but the lady had made little effort to deny it and seemed to be proud of the connexion. Monsignor had broken with her some time before his recent illness, some said because he was tired of her, others because he had found another charmer.

Was it true, as the more romantic spirits in M— maintained, that she had revenged herself by instigating her husband to attack the tramway company? It did not seem very likely. M. Hubert de Quingey had no need of additional reasons to make him desire the collapse of an undertaking the promoters of which had had the bad taste not to seek his collaboration. On the assumption that he would rejoice in the opportunity of getting back at the Bishop, it was more natural, and more consonant with good morals, to assume that his grudge against him had sprung not from the fact that he had given up an intrigue with his wife so much as that there had been something to give up.

Still, it was reasonable to suppose that had no rupture occurred,

Mme de Quingey would at least have made some attempt to pacify her husband. This she could easily have done. A considerable part of the family fortune was hers, and M. de Quingey could have taken certain steps only with her consent.

The story of some connivance between M. de Quingey and the contractor who was chiefly responsible for the present state of hostilities was at least plausible. But it would be difficult to approach the one while ignoring the other.

It would be just as dangerous and rather more difficult to come to terms with the cattle-dealer. So far from showing himself shy of supporting a collective claim against the company, that gentleman, probably in common with the other section of the enemy forces, seemed to be waiting for nothing so eagerly as the bankruptcy of the whole concern. He was busying himself throughout the district in collecting signatures, and openly boasted of the very considerable number he had already amassed. The odd thing was that he was reputed to be a fairly good Catholic.

What was best to do in the circumstances?

If the company were allowed to stew in its own juice, it would be difficult to ensure any general spirit of resignation. It was not likely that the victims, whether real or pretended, would respond to an appeal for Christian charity.

The other alternative was to put the enterprise on its feet again; but how could this be done? It might be achieved by enlisting tactfully, and on the ground that the interests of religion were at stake, a certain amount of capital from outside, but to ensure the success of such a measure it would be necessary to reconstitute the board of directors. Or it might be possible to raise the amount of new money required without going beyond the confines of the diocese, which meant entering into negotiations with M. de Quingey. Should this course be adopted, it would be essential to assure at least the benevolent neutrality of Mme de Quingey.

An attempt to recapitalize the company, especially if it were done with local funds, would pacify the contractors and induce them to listen to reason (all the more since probably a good many of them would have an interest in the new flotation), and in such a case the present stockholders would undoubtedly be more docile even if they had to sacrifice a certain proportion of their money. Finally, the judicial authorities, whose support was indispensable, would have every reason to discountenance legal proceedings.

But it was no use ignoring the fact that the support of M. de Quingey would have to be bought pretty dearly. So far as he and his friends were concerned, it would be a matter of buying up the business for a song. If this were done, the building contractor would be satisfied. But how about the cattle-dealer? One of the first things to be done was to get in touch with him and to find out exactly what it was he meant to do. But Mionnet had no idea how the necessary contact could be made.

These various steps, the ultimate success of which was extremely problematical, must be taken at once, but meanwhile public opinion demanded satisfaction of a different kind. Several of the higher Church functionaries might have to be disgraced. To admit openly, in this way, that certain blunders had been committed would be less embarrassing than attempting to cover them up.

Apart from the main current of his reflections, and for more purely personal reasons, Mionnet began to wonder what exactly he thought of Delhostal. In almost every case the conclusions he had drawn from his investigations had agreed with the hints given him by Monsignor Lebaigue before he left Paris. It was obvious that the latter had got his information, whether directly or not, from the editor of the *Weekly*. There was every reason, therefore, to suppose that this comfortable Canon was a shrewd observer and a clever man. But he was also an informer. There could be little doubt that he had been mixed up in the Montagnini affair, and that more recently he had been sending confidential reports to certain high functionaries— probably not always the same ones—on the conduct of his colleagues, of the Bishop, of the lesser clergy, even of certain laymen who were known to be sympathetic to the Church. What was his reason for doing so? Self-interest? Possibly, but possibly also jealousy and a desire for vengeance. Most probably, however, he had been influenced by reasons of disinterested pleasure. The human race is rich in informers, but the society in which they move is not always favourable to their activities. It sometimes happens that a prevailing tone of moral good taste shrinks from their methods, and when that is so, governments are shamed into discontinuing the use of civil spies. They are harried by constituted authority and by various professional organizations, with the result that their activities are rendered nugatory. At such times they are the victims of a long closed-season. But let anything out of the ordinary occur—a revolution, a war, a period of oppression, a dictatorship—and the informers raise their heads again like grass after rain.

Mionnet was not unaware that this summary survey of the situation might be full of mistakes. His training as a historian had convinced him that truth in any matter involving human activity is the most difficult of all things to attain. But he held it also as sure that action is only possible on the basis of a certain simplification. Therefore he wasted no time in looking too far ahead.

He had promised Monsignor Lebaigue to keep him informed of the progress of events. Since he found it neither possible nor desirable to commit everything he had to say to writing, he made a hurried trip to Paris, travelling third-class, and returning two days later. His intention was to let the Bishop have his first impressions (or as many of them as he thought it wise to impart), to submit the rough sketch of his intended solution, and to ask for a free hand. He also intended to hint at the disciplinary steps which might have to be taken.

The interview went off well. Monsignor Lebaigue was flattered to learn that his forecast of the situation had, in the main, proved accurate. He spoke with approval of Delhostal, and congratulated Mionnet on the diligence which he had shown. He expressed himself as being in perfect agreement with the suggested line of action and in favour of a conciliatory attitude towards the probable enemy. He thought it best, however, to move slowly, to give as little away as possible, to make promises only where promises could not be avoided, and to keep a line of retreat open. He admitted that he was coming to see that disciplinary action might have to be taken. He realized fully the important part played by the cattle-dealer in the general situation.

Before withdrawing, Mionnet found it possible to mention the question of his lodgings and his fear that he might have to pay for them himself.

"Don't bother your head about that," said Monsignor Lebaigue. "Your keep is their concern; I'll drop them a line about it. I'll arrange it somehow."

Chapter

14

FARMERS

At the upper end of the market-place at Chamboriges, in the large empty space between the fountain and the ironmonger's shop of the elder Malicorne, Firmin Gambaroux was giving parting instructions, in his usual loud voice, to his assistant, Prosper Chanac, who was standing in the driving-seat with the reins already in his hand.

"You've got it all clear?—the station at Saint-Georges-du-Monteil. Don't go by Andrieu; you've got too heavy a load for the grade; go by Chanteuges. It's almost a mile longer, so you ought to be there about half past three. See that the papers are filled out. I'm sharing a truck to Paris with Richaud, of Genelard. I shall have lunch here, and start about a quarter or half past two, but I shall go the short way by Andrieu, so that I ought to be there almost as soon as you."

Prosper Chanac, without answering, jerked at the reins, clicked his tongue once or twice at the horses, cried: "Git up, Pépin," and removed a quid from his cheek to his pocket, in order to free his mouth for the necessary encouragement of his steeds. The latticed market-cart moved off with its burden of eleven calves packed close together, their spines contorted in the narrow space, their feet a confused medley, their noses bumping against one another's rumps. The two horses, Pépin, a spotted black, and Brouillard, a dappled grey, pulled out of the pot-holes in the market-place and reached the main road in a series of jerks so violent that it seemed as though the wooden superstructure would shake to pieces.

Gambaroux, arms akimbo, followed it with his eyes, uttering a few curses from force of habit. Then, with his big round felt hat pushed well to the back of his head, his full, freshly shaven face, and his black smock protruding over his stomach, he crossed the square and went to look for his friends at the Café Mayres. The hardest part of his day's work was finished. Later, between four and five, there would be an anxious hour at the station of Saint-Georges. The station-master was a fool, but it was easy enough to get on with Richaud of Genelard. He only hoped that the parcel Richaud had to deliver at Jéoncels wouldn't make him too late. Once they'd got the cattle off, they could go and drink a bottle at Mother Caffu's, opposite the station.

As soon as he opened the door of the Café Mayres, he saw his friends already seated at one of the tables against the farther wall. Lhermitain, from Chaufailles, was there, Boyer Jean, from Valouze, Tétard, from Chanteuges, and young Provotais, from Maisons-Dieu —four farmers whom he was in the habit of meeting at every market in the department and with whom he'd soon be eating his dinner at Mother Parampuyre's—more usually known as Old Ma Pock-Face. Richaud, from Genelard, who usually made one of the party, was not there, having already started on his journey to Jéoncels.

Tétard had not yet finished settling up with his customers. He held in his hand a fat purse stuffed with gold coins. In front of him stood a little old peasant who was speaking in a shrill voice and making exaggerated gestures with his right arm, which he kept raising above his head. Tétard was smiling good-naturedly and explaining something which the peasant seemed not to understand.

Firmin Gambaroux, from Estivareilles, looked at the four farmers with pleasure. They were friends rather than competitors. Not that one or other of them hadn't been known to snatch a bargain from under his nose. Lhermitain, from Chaufailles, in particular, a man not altogether devoid of malice, had once or twice offended in this way, and Boyer Jean, who was a rather affected bumpkin, had at times been rather familiar with some woman whom he knew Tétard or Provotais or even Gambaroux himself had their eyes on. But such things were peccadillos which didn't count in comparison with the services that the members of the group did one another, or with the good humour which never left them when they were together.

Gambaroux hesitated a moment before ordering his drink. He looked appraisingly at his friends' glasses. At length he decided to follow the example of Lhermitain from Chaufailles and take a Picon-vermouth.

Gambaroux had been up since five. He had been astir earlier than usual. Chamboriges is a long way from Estivareilles, and though Roussette was a good trotter, the road was hilly and he had to reckon almost three hours for the journey. The hill at Barrettes, alone, which was over a mile long, would take twenty minutes. Prosper Chanac, even with the wagon empty, could hardly expect to do the distance in less than double the time, having to be careful not to exhaust the horses in view of the afternoon's trip with a full load from Chamboriges to the station of Saint-Georges. He had to start, therefore, about five o'clock. On this particular morning Gambaroux had been anxious to see the wagon off, so that he could have a look at Pépin, who had had a fit of colic the evening before.

Having seen Prosper off, Gambaroux decided to fill the time until his own departure by making up the books. Before doing so, however, he got himself a snack without disturbing his wife, who, as a rule, didn't get up until half past six. His early breakfast was, as always, composed of a thick slice of sausage, bread, and a piece of bacon. To this he added, later, a piece of cheese to help him finish up the bread, but so small a piece as hardly to be worth mentioning. The meal was washed down by a pint of red wine. When he ate in this casual way, Gambaroux never bothered about a plate, but held the bread with the meat or the cheese on it in his left hand, using his right to manipulate his sharp-pointed knife. He drank from a plain, fluted tumbler.

His accounts were not very complicated, but they took time because of the necessity of remembering omissions. Each time that he busied himself with them, Firmin thought with envy of his father, who had managed to combine the roles of innkeeper and baker without ever using pencil or paper.

He hated figures; so much so that he found no particular pleasure in reckoning up his recent gains, calculating those to come, or planning ways and means to increase his profits. Unlike some people, he had no passion for business.

Nor did he like getting up early. When he had two market-days in neighbouring towns, it was his habit to sleep on the road instead of returning to Estivareilles. Monday night, for instance, he usually spent away from home. But Saint-Just, where he had to be on Wednesday, is at the opposite end of the department from Chamboriges. As a matter of fact, there were often other reasons for these "nights out," or perhaps the situation could be better explained by saying that the "other reasons" conveniently produced themselves on the occasion of these belated evenings and served to pass them very pleasantly.

When he had finished his accounts he harnessed his mare Roussette to the box-cart with the help of Antoine Voudes, his only other servant. Before starting, he banished the slight trace of melancholy produced in him by such early rising with a small glass of plum brandy, a drink which he considered to be the least heavy and the most productive of good humour at this particular time of the day.

He set off at ten minutes past seven, looking very gay in his black smock and grey-striped trousers. A folded woolen blanket served to mitigate the hardness of the driving-seat, though it was, perhaps, a little too hot for the time of year.

His two-days' beard pricked him uncomfortably. He decided that he would get a shave when the market was over, while the salesmen were busy with their animals round the public scales. He never shaved himself, partly from laziness, partly because he considered that to do so was a mark of poverty. How would the barbers live if the cattle-dealers began saving their four sous?

These early hours were the pleasantest part of his day. The air was fresh and the troubles of business still to come. Except when he slept on the road, he always started off like this from Estivareilles, but always in a different direction. Monday, Beauvoisin; Tuesday, Volaison; Wednesday, Saint-Just; Thursday, Chamboriges . . . Estivareilles being very conveniently situated almost in the middle of the department. Gambaroux had once played with the idea of settling at M—, but decided that there would have been no point in doing so. Estivareilles was a pleasant, almost rural little town, well supplied with running water. He could be comfortable there, and he had a fondness for his native fields.

At eight minutes past eight he was at the bottom of the hill at Barrettes; at twenty-five past he had reached the top. There was a fine view and an inn called the Pine Tree. Gambaroux went in, according to habit, while Roussette, who had been going well, got her wind at the door. Here he had his first drink of white wine that morning, a half-pint, which he swallowed in a couple of draughts separated by an interval of two or three minutes. Then he lit his first pipe.

As a rule the first glass of white wine and the first pipe raised Gambaroux's spirits above the general level of happy contentment of which, up to then, he had been conscious. His lungs expanded. He breathed as though he were tasting the air. He looked to right and left with shining eyes. His mind was filled with cheerful, rather sly thoughts. If there was anyone to talk to, he voiced them; if not, he kept them to himself. Back in his cart, he took up the reins with an increased feeling of certainty; he leaned forward towards his mare and tickled her flanks with his whip.

He reached the first houses of Chamboriges as ten o'clock was striking. He always stabled his horse at the Viallon-Burebat inn, although he took his breakfast elsewhere, at Mother Parampuyre's. That good lady, however, had no stable, so he got off cheaply by tipping the waiter at Viallon-Burebat and drinking something in the bar without even sitting down. This morning he chose a small glass of local brandy.

That done, he hurried off to the market, which was only about a hundred yards away. He walked rapidly across the square, greeted as he went by various peasants whom he knew by face and sometimes by name. Several of them came in from their villages, in patched smocks, every other month to sell a calf or a heifer; others put in an appearance only once or twice a year.

When some of them shouted: "Come and see me, Monsieur Gambaroux, I've got a nice little heifer for you," he waved airily to them with his hand or cracked a passing joke, but he never stopped. He was in a hurry to join his farmer friends at the Café Mayres. Nevertheless, it was a good opportunity to nose about in the crowd and take a hurried look at the best of the stock. Lhermitain had probably been before him, but that had meant being there earlier, getting up earlier. It wasn't worth it. Life wasn't long enough.

The other farmers, who'd driven many miles already that morning and sharpened their appetites, had ordered a ham omelet of twelve eggs. There was still a piece left for Gambaroux. "Another plate and a glass! Hurry!" cried Boyer, who came from Valouze. There was a quart of red wine on the table, which the members of the group drank hurriedly. This meeting before business began was not a time for eating and drinking, but for fixing prices. Lhermitain as a rule took the lead. He was the biggest farmer of the lot, and the only one who kept in touch with the current trend of the market. He had newspapers sent to him from Lyons, and sometimes even telegrams from La Villette.

The question of prices, however, was not a very absorbing one. The variations were small and, as a rule, pretty regular, depending as they did, primarily, on the season and the weather. A dry spell brought them down, because the peasants were afraid of running short of feed and therefore got rid of their young stock as quickly as possible. From May to September of a hot summer was a time of low prices, but they usually rose a bit at harvest. This was due to the fact that the peasants were too busy in the fields to find time to leave their villages, so that the markets at such times were small, or, in the language of the trade, "lean." This, however, was compensated by a noticeably low run of prices at the first market when harvest was over.

It didn't, as a matter of fact, much matter about having the latest news from Lyons and Paris. One could buy just as well if one took as a basis the average price fetched by stock the week previously. The difference at the end of the year would be infinitesimal, and business had been done like that from time immemorial. Lhermitain's inside information did, however, make it possible to snatch a little extra profit. If one got wind, in this way, of a rise, one insisted on sticking to the prices that had obtained the week before, and the peasants, who had no idea of what had happened, were perfectly contented. If there had been a drop, one passed it on. Between ten and eleven o'clock the peasants would make a bit of a fuss and would threaten to withdraw their animals. Some of them would be as good as their word, but most of them, who had made up their minds to sell or who had to, could do nothing if Firmin Gambaroux from Estivareilles, Lhermitain from Chaufailles, Boyer Jean from Valouze, Tétard from Chanteuges, young Provotais from Maisons-Dieu, and Richaud from Genelard walked up and down between the stalls, all saying with perfect good humour but unshakable obstinacy: "I said nine sous a pound, and I won't give a penny more."

Like most of his friends, Gambaroux was only interested in animals for slaughter. The sale of breeding-stock took place, for the most part, between the peasants themselves. Provotais, however, did a little in that line.

For purposes of slaughter, Gambaroux concentrated for the most part on calves, unlike Tétard, who was chiefly interested in cows. Now and again the former bought a cow if the bargain seemed peculiarly tempting, but he didn't go far afield for his market, contenting himself with selling it to the butcher at M—.

Business was done between ten and half past eleven. For most of the farmers, with the possible exception of young Provotais, who was a bit querulous, and certainly for Firmin Gambaroux, it was a time of high good humour.

The last glass of red wine with which he washed down the ham omelet put him on good terms with life. He got up without hurrying himself, his stomach projecting comfortably beneath the full folds of his smock. His body felt heavy, but the sensation was warm and comfortable; his blood circulated briskly. Things had a luminous, sparkling appearance. He liked the faces he saw about him. He wanted to joke with his neighbours and poke them in the ribs, to ask them what news they had. He wanted to see happy looks about him, to hear hearty laughter, instead of being confronted with resigned expressions or greeted with the forced gaiety of tactful neighbours. He felt capable of anything. Despite a certain mistiness of outline in the objects that met his view, a certain excess of light, he found that he could hear and see with great precision. Never before had he noticed so accurately the difference between one thin and shabby-coated calf and another that was well-fed and glossy. Never before had he been able to judge better the quality of the meat beneath the hide. It didn't need any complex calculation to tell that. All round him were people shouting and plucking him by the sleeve: "Make it another penny, Monsieur Gambaroux, you won't find another animal like that anywhere in the market." They stretched open hands towards him: "Call it a bargain, Monsieur Gambaroux! Nine sous and a half and it's a deal!" But no matter how much he would have liked to slap his hand down on the bargain, he refused to close. He needed all his wits to see the enormous difference, the bottomless depths, between nine sous and nine sous and a half. Detailed accounts could be left until later when an hour and a half's drive in the open air had sharpened his appetite again. His man Prosper, who was good at figures, would help him. It was all, he felt, a fine bustling, noisy game, played in an atmosphere of heat and sweat and dung and sunshine, a game without risk. What danger could there be for Firmin Gambaroux of Estivareilles? What could threaten him, not only today, but tomorrow and on all the days to come, here or elsewhere? Nothing in all the world could diminish by a jot the certainty of his gaze or sow within that massive body the tiniest seed of doubt.

Chapter

15

THE PRIVATE THOUGHTS OF A FARMER

No, nothing! The longer he thought, the more certain did he feel. It was fine to be a farmer, for a farmer's business was not the sort to worry a man or keep him awake half the night. It was like one of those properties one used to buy in the good old times—planking one's money down once and for all and then sitting back to enjoy it. When a peasant sees a farmer driving along a country road, he may envy him, but if he does so, it is without bitterness. "If I'd had the money," he thinks, "that's just what I should have liked to be." Firmin Gambaroux had become a farmer because one fine day his mother had been able to give him the twenty thousand francs he needed to set up for himself, and she'd been able to give him so much because, although she was a widow with six children, her husband had been a baker and an innkeeper for thirty years, and after his death she had kept the inn. She had not been able to do the same for the other five, but it's enough for a woman's pride to have been in the position to make her eldest son a farmer.

With a fine job like that, what's a man got to worry about? Health? It was a point of faith with Gambaroux that his health was perfect—not only excellent, but perfect.

He had never been to a doctor since the days of his military service. Vets were the only doctors he'd bothered about. Not but what, if he'd been as fussy as some people, he'd have felt out of sorts and a bit anxious at times. But a wise man realizes that the organs don't do their work without occasional friction and a jolt here and there, any more than the best cart always goes without creaking. The more life a body has, the more likely it is to be conscious of its little imperfections. Sometimes of an afternoon, as he was driving home, Gambaroux would be aware of a distended stomach—as though that were a thing to be frightened of! Plenty of folk would be only too glad to be able to say as much! His gargantuan belches were the measure of his gratitude. True, his belly was a bit swollen and his arse sometimes felt a bit hot, but who would bother his head about details like that? Only a lot of old women seated over their knitting! Provided one can stand a lot of heavy food and a decent amount of drink, with an extra glass or two when one's feeling a bit down, one is pleasantly padded against the minor ailments of life.

Family troubles? For the moment, at least, Gambaroux hadn't got any, and had no reason to suppose he would have. His wife had three children to look after, who were busy growing as children of their age ought to. They were no more troublesome than the average, and no more often ill. She wasn't particularly amiable, to be sure, but a farmer who leaves the house at dawn, doesn't come back till dusk, and spends one or two nights away from home can put up more easily than most with his wife's grumbles. While he was driving about the district, his servant Antoine Voudes was pretty good at looking after the bit of farmland he had reserved for cultivation, one or two meadows, a few fields of oats, a few acres of alfalfa, enough to feed his three horses and the cow he kept to give them milk. There were a few ill-natured stories to the effect that Antoine, who was neither old nor ugly, managed to console his mistress for her husband's frequent absences, and these had come to Gambaroux's ears, but he didn't want to know anything about that so long as there was no public scandal. He was an easy-tempered man. After all, didn't he sleep almost every Monday night, when the weather was bad, with a young woman of Beauvoisin whose husband was away half the year working in the mines? And when he was at home, didn't Firmin console himself with another woman of the same village, a certain Rosalie, wife of a railroad worker, whose favours he enjoyed at least two Mondays a month? (Their meetings took place at the home of Rosalie's mother, who lent them a room for the purpose, which was better than her own house, where there was always the risk of being caught.) In other parts of the district he knew of two or three agreeable young women who were always ready for a visit when he felt in the mood for a bit of fun. The youngest of them was the sister of an innkeeper at Jumianges. He was really quite fond of her. She was one of his Friday girls.

Gambaroux was not particularly lecherous. He readily admitted that it was best to keep to regular habits if one could and that family life was the ideal to be aimed at. But for a man who is always on the move the laws of conduct are bound to be a bit elastic, and a well-nourished body is apt to be troubled by sudden cravings. The life of a farmer is a thing apart. What in others might be considered dissipation, fits naturally into the more generous contours of his existence.

It would be difficult to discover any point in his life about which Gambaroux could be said to have a legitimate grievance, anything that might be said to constitute a threat to his comfort or a problem for his mind. He was happy in his business, his health, his food, his drink, his women. There was, of course, the question of death to be considered; for everyone's got to die some time, even farmers, and it did occasionally chance that, seated of an afternoon on the driving-seat of his farmer's cart, he would let his mind turn to the idea of death. Maybe it was the sound of some tolling bell that set his thoughts in that direction, or the memory of some piece of news picked up that morning at the market—"Old so-and-so, from Mazergues; you knew him, didn't you? It can't be more than three weeks since I bought a cow off him, and now he's gone"—but whatever the cause, the idea of death got between his ribs as nothing else could do. A vision rose before his eyes of the interior of a church, and in his ears sounded the special chants appointed for the interment of the dead. . . . Roussette there before him, ambling so gently on, was already getting old, and the nearest inn at which he could drown his gloom in a cheering glass was still four miles away. "Yes," he thought, "we've all got to come to it sooner or later, and I shall die as my father died before me." But the thought, even as he gave it form, became a branch to which he could cling. He began to feel cheerful again. He would die, there was no getting away from that, but as his father had died, still young and vigorous, struck down suddenly by an apoplexy, without suffering, without even the knowledge that death was at hand. He would be spared the gradual loss of power, the slow decline. One day he would be dining as usual with his farmer friends, having his fun with some young girl, and the next— Oh, he would be missed, of course; a man who vanishes suddenly like that in the flower of his strength is always missed, but Antoine Voudes would soon console his wife, and the children would be laughing as usual three days later, as is the way of children. With his friends the farmer's memory would die more slowly. As they sat together at their meals they would speak of him: "Firmin Gambaroux. Ah, there was a man for you!" Meanwhile the important thing was to taste to the full every single day that remained of life. "Gee up, Roussette!"—Boyer Jean, from Valouze, must be at least a mile ahead. If he could catch up with him between here and the bridge, they would crack a bottle together at Grégoire's inn. The sight of Boyer emptying his glass, with his hat tilted jauntily over one ear, was enough to blow away all these ideas of death.

And what about the tramways? Thinking about them to himself, Gambaroux was inclined to shrug his shoulders and treat the whole thing as a joke. Not but what, even for a farmer, two thousand francs was a considerable sum. Reckoning his average daily rate of profit at a hundred, two thousand represented three weeks' work. With a sum like that he could keep the house at Estivareilles and everything in it going for a whole year—wife, children, Antoine Voudes, horses, cattle. Besides, it's infuriating to be beaten by a pack of blackguards. It was one thing to spend two thousand francs deliberately when one wanted a bit of fun, but quite another to lose them when one thought one was making a good investment. When a thing like that happened, one kicked oneself for a fool. Still, one would be an even greater fool to let two thousand francs spoil one's pleasure, unless one had a streak of meanness in one's make-up like young Provotais.

When the question of the tramways came up in a roomful of people, Gambaroux poured oil on the flames. He would bang the table with his fist and roar out that he wouldn't stand it, that he'd make the thieves cough up, that he'd get at their accomplices, no matter in what high places they might happen to be, that no one should say that a whole department could be fleeced with impunity by a lot of sharpers, even if some of them did go about in cassocks. Or he would wink knowingly and make a gesture with his right hand that said as plainly as words could do: "Wait and see—say nothing—rely on me!" Or perhaps he would take his interlocutor aside into a corner, set him down at a distant table, and bring out from the interior of his smock a folded packet of papers already a bit thumbed and dog-eared. These he would spread out, displaying the top page covered with fine, neat writing: "To the District Attorney," and then show the six pages of text which followed it, drafted, at his instructions, by the schoolmaster of Arcomieu, who had no love for the Church. Finally he would turn to the string of signatures which completed the document, set out with details of address and occupation in two columns, as in official registers, and would say: "Just write your name here."

Gambaroux neither liked nor disliked the ministers of the Church. On Sundays he went to Mass, or at least, in company with a lot of other men, hung about the church porch at Estivareilles for twenty minutes or so, when the doors were open during the ceremony. He was perfectly ready to show respect to any priest who upheld the dignity of his cloth. He had no wish to demand of them in their private lives virtues which he knew he would himself have been incapable of observing in their place. People said that the Bishop had an eye for a pretty woman. Well, so long as there was no open scandal, it didn't very much matter (except to the Bishop himself, if all that was hinted about his recent illness was true). No doubt, like everybody else, he liked his food and knew what it was to feel the urgencies of the flesh of an afternoon. But it was a very different thing when a Bishop, a Vicar-General, and the canons of the Cathedral made themselves the sponsors of a tramway company and acted almost as though they were its publicity agents. When men like that took a hand in the business, their recommendation was so authoritative that it could hardly be wondered at that the best of Catholics should be a bit put out when they discovered that all this fine patronage was no more than a screen for fraud. Charles Robert Latteignant was like many a younger son of good family, a man without ability and devoid of scruples. He'd be lucky if he got out of the affair with two or three months in jail. But Latteignant's misdoings alone would not have been enough to goad Gambaroux into all this feverish activity. No, what made the trouble worth while was the chance of teaching the proud Bishop, the Vicar-General, and the rest of them a lesson; of making it clear to the clergy that it wasn't their business to meddle in stocks; that when it came to barefaced robbery, it was quite enough to have to do with a pack of bankers.

Perhaps, in his heart of hearts, he was sick of the whole business, but he had taken too public a stand in the matter to be able to withdraw at this stage. Without quite knowing how it had happened, he had become the spokesman of the defrauded small investors, their hope. The word had gone round the department: "Firmin Gambaroux of Estivareilles has taken it up; he won't let go until we've got our rights. He's getting everybody to sign. He's seen the District Attorney. If you've lost money, go and have a talk with Firmin Gambaroux next Tuesday at market. He'll add your name to the list. Yes, you can make your mark if you can't write."

Gambaroux was in no hurry to finish. He realized that this was the pleasantest part of his task. Later, it wouldn't be such fun, when it actually came to setting the wheels of Justice in motion.

Chapter

ENEMIES

On this particular day, just as Gambaroux was sitting down with his four friends to dinner at old Ma Pock-Face's, he noticed a tall young ecclesiastic, well shaved and well dressed, a sort of young parish priest, who was eating at a table in a far corner. He did not know him.

The sight put him in a bad humour, and he deliberately turned the conversation, more than once, to the affair of the tramways. He spoke loudly of his list of names, which was lengthening daily, of his approaching interview with the District Attorney, of the punishment that was coming to the guilty parties.

The young priest gave no sign. Since he had begun his meal before the farmers and ate considerably less than they did, he finished first. But instead of leaving the room, he settled down to read his paper.

The farmers got up. Gambaroux was the last to leave the room, and just as he reached the door, Mme Parampuyre drew him aside.

"A word with you, Monsieur Gambaroux," she said, and began whispering to him with a very mysterious expression on her face.

"There's an Abbé here who wants to speak to you—the one who was eating at that table in the corner."

Firmin turned his head. But before he could make up his mind what to say, he saw the priest coming towards him with a smile on his lips, and his hat in his hand.

"I believe I have the honour of addressing Monsieur Firmin Gambaroux?"

"At your service."

Gambaroux followed the other's example and took off his hat very politely. He always felt embarrassed when addressing educated persons.

The Abbé looked him straight in the eyes and continued in a tone of great frankness:

"I came in this morning by bus from Chamboriges on purpose to see you. I should be glad if you could spare me a few moments."

Gambaroux's first feeling was one of pleased self-importance.

"Why, certainly, sir," he said. Then, rather awkwardly, he took a step towards the door and shouted to the other farmers:

"Don't wait for me, I've got something to do here."

He came back and glanced round the room.

"Where would you like to talk? Have you got a lot to say?"

"I should think I have! But I don't want to take up more of your time than I can help."

"Look here," said Gambaroux affably, "I'll give you all the time you need, but the only thing is, I've got to be at the station at Saint-Georges-du-Monteil to see about getting my animals off. How are you going back to M—?"

"By the evening bus, I imagine."

"I was just going to say—we could chat for a moment or two here, and then I could take you with me to the station. In that way we could go on talking at our ease. You can get a train at Saint-Georges which will get you to M— in thirty-five minutes. Only my cart's not very comfortable, and the worst of it is that I've got to put a calf in behind, because there wasn't room for him in the big wagon. . . . I'm ashamed to have nothing better to offer you."

Mionnet assured him that it would be a pleasure to drive with him through a stretch of country which he did not know, but believed on hearsay to be very picturesque.

"Have you had coffee, sir? Then you must have a liqueur with me. . . . No, I insist. We needn't start for twenty minutes. We'll give ourselves plenty of time, because when one's talking one doesn't want to drive too fast."

Chapter

17

A COUNTRY DRIVE

An hour later Gambaroux, the reins lying loosely in his hands, was thoughtfully contemplating Roussette's rump, while he pondered his thoughts in a pause between two phrases. His companion, not wishing to hurry him, let his eyes wander over the landscape. The calf, though his feet were bound, could every now and then be heard bumping against the woodwork of the cart.

The facts with which the farmer had been made acquainted took, at the end of an hour, the following shape in his mind:

A young Abbé, seemingly young for the important position which he occupied—and his distinction was obvious at first sight—had come from Paris expressly charged with a sort of mission to Firmin Gambaroux. The highest dignitaries of the French hierarchy had heard that Gambaroux was dissatisfied, and the knowledge worried them. It was clear that a man of such weight and moderation, and so good a Catholic, must have some good reason for abandoning his usual habits. Not only must everything possible be done to satisfy him, but his advice must be sought and followed. He knew the inner truth of the affair; he was in closer touch than anybody with the state of local opinion. Before deciding on any course of action, the authorities wished to know to what extent it would seem opportune or ill-advised to Firmin Gambaroux of Estivareilles, not so much as an individual, but as the mouthpiece of public opinion.

It cannot but be seen that Gambaroux's reverie lacked nothing of grandeur. The meal which he had taken at Ma Parampuyre's formed an admirable foundation for the idea he had since come to entertain of his own importance and of the importance of the role he was called upon to play. It should be added that he regarded this Abbé Mionnet, who now sat beside him on the driving-seat, with no unfriendly eye.

He hastened to make it clear that two thousand francs was nothing to him, speaking personally, but that he had undertaken the task of championing the lesser fry. It was the part played in all this business by the Bishop that seemed to him so intolerable. Examples must be made, even in the interests of the Church itself.

Mionnet's answering glance seemed to say: "At whom should we strike? Who are to be the victims?" and reading such words in his expression, Gambaroux found his own anger weakening. He was the kind of man who will storm and rage at an employee who has been caught in a dishonest act, but who, when the moment comes to dismiss him, remembers that the fellow has children dependent on him, and that he may be difficult to replace.

Urged almost imperceptibly by his neighbour, he admitted that, after all, the Bishop might not be the chief culprit, and that even if he were as guilty as his fellows, there were, in such cases, considerations to be weighed which might be of even greater importance. Everybody wasn't as clear-sighted as Firmin Gambaroux, and people mightn't always realize that in proceeding against the man one intended no irreverence to the office which he held. Disrespect was already too rife in the modern world.

The result of his further reflection was to make it seem that his sword of justice was now pointed rather at the breast of the Vicar-General. He suggested, with the air of a man who lays great stress on his proposal, that the disgrace of Canon Manguy would do much to satisfy public opinion. Mionnet listened to this advice with the air of a man who, while not rejecting the suggested course, yet deeply weighs the sacrifice involved.

In general, the two men seemed to be agreed that the law must not be invoked in the matter. It appeared that Gambaroux had never seriously intended that it should be. His vocal activities, his six pages of deposition, and his list of signatures had been really nothing but a means of shaking the ecclesiastical authorities out of their lethargy ("And I agree," admitted Mionnet, "that they take some moving, at times")—a means which had not been altogether inoperative, since results were already beginning to show.

Turning to the other aspects of the business, Gambaroux expressed himself convinced of the advisability of refloating the company rather than of letting it become bankrupt. He didn't much like M. de Quingey (a sentiment which relieved Mionnet of his fear that the two men might be hand in glove), but he realized that it would be difficult to do without him, unless it was decided to raise money outside the confines of the department—a line of action which he definitely favoured.

After a more than usually long pause for private thought, the farmer asked:

"If they decide to come in, how much do you think that Monsieur de Quingey and his friends will raise?"

"I've no idea. I want to have nothing to do with the negotiations. They're not my business, nor am I competent to deal with such things. . . . My job is to create, if I can, an atmosphere in which they can have freedom to develop."

"Oh, of course. . . . But obviously they won't stir a finger unless they think it a good bargain. I shall be surprised if they offer more than four or five hundred thousand francs."

Mionnet made a gesture of complete ignorance. Whereupon, after another interval of reflection, the farmer indicated that if M. de Quingey and his friends didn't want to shoulder the whole risk, he thought he might be able to raise a hundred thousand francs among his friends as additional backing. But such participation would, of course, be conditional upon their receiving a fair share of the profits.

Mionnet was careful to conceal any surprise he might feel at this new attitude on the part of his companion. He merely asked, in a conversational tone, whether, should occasion arise, he might make use, if necessary without mentioning names, of what had just been said.

"Why, of course."

On either side of the road the fields, bare after harvest, stretched away to the lower slopes of the wooded hills. One of the most noticeable features of this countryside was the frequent occurrence of short and shallow valleys. They lay to the right of the road, and though the amount of ground comprised in each was small, it managed to assume the mysterious quality of a self-sufficient site to which the downward and converging sweep of the neighbouring hillsides gave an air of crowded life. Mionnet was very sensitive to the appearance of natural features, and his eyes were quick to grasp the character of these valleys, delighted to find how constantly the structural theme was repeated in the scene before him.

This charming side-issue of their drive, however, in no way prevented him from being fully conscious of his companion's presence, and in particular of the curiously massive impression that it gave him. From the very first moments of their drive he had been struck by the physical influences which seemed to radiate from Gambaroux's body. "Physical" was the word that occurred to him, because the features that drew his attention to it were very definitely solid. The man's eyes might glitter, and his face might shine, but what chiefly gave the general effect was the warmth and smell of his breath. It wasn't necessary for Mionnet to know what was going on inside his head to be aware, there beside him, of a sort of shaggy manifestation of well-being that had almost more in common with a wild animal than with a man.

Suddenly, prompted perhaps by a look in the farmer's eyes or by the intonation of his voice, he said to himself: "There's nothing very mysterious about it; the man's drunk."

For about a minute he was satisfied with his inference; it seemed to explain everything. But then he started to criticize, not the rashness of the conclusion so much as the false simplicity of the idea. "Drunk?—a mere figure of speech. He's not incoherent; what he says is, fundamentally, a perfectly accurate expression of what he is thinking and of what he hopes. Perhaps, in the technical sense, he is drunk, but then he is lucky enough to have a profession which can quite easily be pursued in a continual state of drunkenness, provided it's not fighting drunkenness. Such a life has many advantages. In the first place it ensures that intensity of apprehension which is the essential presupposition of all happiness, and then it gives the power of handling circumstances with that admixture of dash which the ordinary man lacks in his normal state. He has developed the habit of being able to reason when drunk, not very elaborately, perhaps, but sensibly, and, at times, with a considerable amount of ingenuity. The solution which he has just suggested will probably turn out excellently for him. A sober man would never have thought of it, or, if he had, would never have spoken of it so frankly."

Perhaps Mionnet was surprised at his success, and a little disquieted by it. In analysing it thus, he may have been seeking to reassure himself. One of the pleasures of his life, in addition to reading directories and observing the details of landscapes, was appraising the worth in cash of the various individuals with whom he was brought in contact. The figure quoted by Gambaroux seemed to him to be unexpectedly high.

Chapter

18

MORE HASTE, LESS SPEED

Mionnet was careful to tell himself that the battle was by no means over. The success of the first skirmish had so far turned his head that he believed himself capable of taking all the remaining positions with the same ease.

He had managed to arrange several meetings with Charles Robert Latteignant and the two senior directors of the ill-fated company, nor had he failed to frighten them with his tales of Gambaroux (about whom he was none too easy himself) and of his friend the District Attorney's deputy, whom he represented as very angry and quite prepared to set the law in motion. His own nervousness in regard to the farmer was finally set at rest, but he refrained from passing on to the others the relief that he felt. He had promised Gambaroux that, for the time being, the knowledge of their provisional agreement should remain confidential, and that outwardly the farmer's attitude should appear to be unchanged.

The first real stumbling-block in the way of his plans came from the Quingeys. He had tried to make contact with them and to arrange an introduction either to the husband or to the wife. But the time of year presented difficulties. Mme de Quingey had arranged to spend August and possibly even the beginning of September at a small château in the mountains, not far from M—. In order to make her acquaintance Mionnet would have had to arrange a special meeting, and any such manœuvre would have stressed too baldly the nature of his intentions. Later, after her return to M—, it would be easy to get the Abbé invited casually to one of the little parties which she gave almost every week.

M. de Quingey was no easier of access than his wife. At the

moment he was touring Switzerland with friends. On his return he would join his wife at the small château already mentioned, and by that time the shooting-season would be in full swing. What with the time spent on his estates and visits paid to friends, it would be October before he put in an appearance again at M—.

Mionnet realized that he would have to be patient. That he might not be suspected by his superiors of relaxing his efforts, he addressed to Monsignor Lebaigue a long report, in which he made great play with the results he had already obtained in his dealings with Gambaroux. He went into the matter in considerable detail, but, thanks to the conversations which he had already had with the Bishop, he found it possible so to convey his meaning by hints and indirect references that, should his paper go astray, its contents would mean little or nothing to any reader who was not already informed of his intentions.

After some hesitation he ventured to say, in his covering letter, which was composed in a tone of greater intimacy, that these last days of August had been productive, for him, as for many good Catholics, of much quiet satisfaction. (He alluded to the final condemnation of the *Sillon* which the Pope had communicated in his letter to the French hierarchy.) He added that the same period had been richly satisfying in other matters recently under consideration at Rome. (This time the reference was to the decree issued on the 8th of August by the *Committee for the Regulation of the Sacraments,* which laid down the age of seven as proper in all countries for the admission of children to the First Communion.)

If the matter of the tramways was proceeding more slowly than he could have wished, he did not forget that it by no means exhausted the terms of reference of his official mission. As Monsignor Lebaigue had pointed out to him, a diocese in which such a situation could arise was a household in which much must be amiss. It was his duty to explore its every nook and cranny. Without seeming too obviously to pry, Mionnet managed to find opportunities for inquiring into the various organizations that existed in the diocese or were indirectly connected with it. Several hours of each week were thus taken up in the accumulation of relevant facts and the necessary recording of them in written notes.

Despite the wish that he had expressed on his arrival, and the vague promises made him by Monsignor Sérasquier, he had not yet managed to get the use of a private office in the Bishop's palace. Since, however, the Director of Public Charities occupied his room only at intervals, Mionnet got permission to make use of it on certain days for the transaction of work and the reception of visitors. He used the privilege sparingly, for though its concession was flattering to his sense of importance, he realized that it might hamper the freedom of his movements.

His time was soon to be occupied with other matters.

MADAME ROUBIER'S DAUGHTERS

One day, when Delhostal and Mionnet sat down to their midday meal in the little private dining-room of the pension, the hors-d'œuvre were brought, not by the maid whom Mionnet already knew, but by a slim and handsome young woman whose elegant appearance was rather out of keeping with so menial a task.

"This is the first time you've seen her," said the Canon as soon as she had left the room. "It's Émilienne, Madame Roubier's eldest daughter. We're pretty sure to see her sister, who must have come back too. She's more of a blond type, and her name's Clotilde."

They did, in fact, catch a glimpse of Clotilde, but not at close quarters, for she seemed to be busy in the main dining-room.

She was smaller than her sister, plumper, and fairer. Seen at a distance her good looks gave the impression of being of a more ordinary type. Mionnet decided that, making allowance for this difference, both the sisters fully deserved their reputation.

"There was a certain amount of coming and going in the annexe this morning," he said; "do they live there?"

"They may."

Émilienne came back. She was certainly very pleasant to look at, with her chestnut hair, oval face, regular features, and bright brown eyes. She was smiling and polite, but quite definitely aloof in her attitude. From the way in which she behaved to Delhostal it would have been difficult to realize that she had ever seen him before. One would have been tempted to think of her as some well-bred young woman of fashion helping at a charity tea.

The Canon, for his part, behaved towards her with a certain coldness. He helped himself to the dish she proffered, and without raising his eyes, asked, without any very great show of interest:

"I trust you had a pleasant vacation?"

"Very pleasant, thank you, sir."

No more was said; she again left the room.

"Where she spent it is quite another question," the Canon muttered. "They're an odd pair, she and her sister. . . . Have I told you about them?"

"No, never."

"Really? I thought—"

He paused a moment; then:

"When you look at their mother," he said, "you wouldn't think she could have produced two such girls, would you? It's all very mysterious, and I know no more about it than anybody else."

He considered awhile before continuing:

"It didn't occur to me that they'd be put in the annexe, but I don't know why they shouldn't be."

Mionnet ventured a remark:

"Does their behaviour give rise to talk?"

"There may be a certain amount of guessing, but nothing definite. Ah, my dear friend, it's easy enough to say that everyone knows everything, but there are some things that are not known, even in provincial towns."

He gave a guffaw of laughter.

"Luckily!" he added.

He became serious again. Leaning towards Mionnet, his mouth full and his fork raised to lend force to his sententious comment, he murmured in a tone at once embarrassed and confidential:

"I'm quite certain—absolutely certain—that these girls are up to mischief, here at home, and elsewhere as well. I've got no proof, no one's ever told me anything definite. That in itself shows that they're no fools. I'm convinced"—he looked searchingly at Mionnet—"that they're as cunning as they make 'em, and that you'd better be pretty careful how you go."

The conversation then appeared to take another direction.

"You've only been to Paris once since you came here?"

"Yes, only once."

A dish of string-beans had just been brought, and Delhostal took the opportunity to renew his complaint at the way the local people left the picking of their green vegetables until too late.

"It's all the worse," he said, "because they grow marvellously; even in the gardens of the upper town. The soil's absolutely first-rate."

He proceeded to develop a theory which Mionnet found plausible enough, that vegetables and fruit displayed, better than anything else, the properties of soil.

"Talking of the upper town and its gardens reminds me that I must show it to you some day. There's a convent there directed by a woman of great distinction. You're fond of music, aren't you? Well, if you like Gregorian chants, you'll be surprised at what they can do with very small resources."

In the course of several earlier conversations the Canon had already referred more than once to his duties as chaplain. So far Mionnet had refrained from asking a question which he had been often on the point of formulating. Now at last he spoke. It had a bearing on the investigation he was making into the various aspects of religious life in the diocese.

"There's something I've never been quite clear about. How comes it, since these women have managed to get back—a fact in itself surprising enough—"

"Do you blame them?"

"Certainly not; but how long have they been back?"

"A year and a half."

"That seems pretty soon, but I suppose an exception was made in their case."

"Neither the Prefect nor the local deputies are violently anti-clerical, you see. . . . But it wasn't nearly as simple as you suppose."

"I can understand that. . . . But what I was going to ask was, since they *have* come back, why haven't they reopened their school?"

"Because they couldn't."

"But in that case—I don't want to be offensive—why did they return?"

"In the first place, let me point out that only eight of them have returned—a pretty small army—and that their object in coming was to spy out the land. They saw at once that there could be no question of reopening the school. To do so would have been to ask for trouble. It would take me at least two hours to explain the details of the situation. I'll tell you all about it some day, if you're interested. To make a long story short, the school *has* been started again, but with a lay teaching staff, the members of which are friendly towards us, though not in any way dependent upon the clerical organization."

"I've already heard something about that."

"Not even financially dependent. The building belongs to a foreigner. It's all very complicated. One of the Sisters has been able to get her foot in there, but only by dint of renouncing her vows. She acts as a sort of go-between."

"What about the rest, the seven others?"

"You mean why haven't they gone away again? You're as intransigent as Combes himself. . . ."

"Don't misunderstand me. . . ."

"I was only joking. . . ." The Canon lowered his voice: "The concatenation of circumstances was very odd. This particular seven —or eight, I should say—always formed a closely united group, even in the days when the community was flourishing. They revolved round the Superior and remained together even after the sisterhood was broken up. At one time they lived abroad, and it was then that the foreign gentleman I have already told you of became interested in them. . . . The reason they've not gone away again is, in the first place, that they wanted to see what would happen to the new school, for the school is what chiefly interests them, and they never altogether abandoned hope. . . . The political wind already shows signs of becoming tempered. . . . But further, an exceptionally lucky chance came their way. There happened to be in the upper town a

very small convent, quite an intimate affair, standing in a large garden. It had been occupied, before the persecution, by a very obscure Order, which was started locally about sixty years ago. It never had more than five or six houses scattered about in France and Austria, and was called the Sisterhood of the Tabernacle. It was a contemplative Order for rich women who wanted to retire from the world and live a life of piety uncomplicated by austerities. This little convent was in the market. It suited the owners admirably to let it to the fugitives, and there they settled with as little fuss as possible. They live a very retired existence and see nobody. They wear their habits only within the privacy of its walls. When they come out, which they very rarely do, they put on ordinary clothes."

"But what do they do with themselves, if they can't teach?"

The Canon smiled.

"They have their music, as I said, and their prayers. They read, and they wait. Most of them have private means. They come of good families, and nearly all of them are young. Their relations would be only too glad to have them back, but they're happier where they are. The Superior is a woman of great distinction and great charm. . . . Naturally I took up again my old position as their chaplain, though in the eyes of the lay world my title is merely a survival from days that are dead and gone. . . . Not many people realize who it is that have come back. I'm not even chaplain to the new school; it was thought wiser that I shouldn't be. . . ."

During the afternoon Mionnet chanced on two occasions to run into the Roubier girls near his lodgings. The first time they were together and seemed to be laughing at some joke. The second time Mlle Émilienne was alone. She greeted the Abbé pleasantly, and said:

"If there's anything you want, sir, you must let me know. Mother sometimes forgets to ask. If you'll make a little list, I'll see to it."

20

WALKS ROUND M— OR THE
PLEASURES OF TOPOGRAPHY

The last days of August had been wet and sultry, but September opened with a period of delicious weather.

There were still a few showers, but they fell, for the most part, in the very early hours and lasted but a short time. The mornings were limpid. There was a sense of gaiety in the air, a purity in the atmosphere, that tempted the visitor to indulge in casual wanderings. Clouds gathered later, but they were white and sunlit, and in the wide spaces between them the sky was of a pale and brilliant blue. The air was fresh and sparkling, with just sufficient dampness to make it soft, just sufficient breeze to produce a pleasant sense of instability. Sometimes, towards midday, the sky became completely overcast, though never gloomy, and it was at such times that the showers broke. But in the afternoon the weather cleared up again. The streets, the sky, the houses, gave more than ever the impression of cleanness, and towards evening the clouds were touched with pink and gold by the declining sun.

This period of mildness coincided with a time of comparative leisure in Mionnet's life, and he took advantage of the combination to indulge in a series of walks. Their objective was M— and its nearer environs, but they were saunters rather than definite expeditions, without even the limited intention of getting to know the town methodically. If he embarked upon them with any plan, it was only to the extent of saying to himself: "Now's my chance to get the real flavour of provincial life. Not only is the weather pleasant, but the conditions of my life are peculiarly favourable. If I ever come back here again, it may be that I shall have duties which will

make liberty of movement difficult, and if my present visit lasts for a few more months I shall be too well known by that time to be altogether free. Not that that would stop my going for walks, but I should be noticed, I should have to be continually answering questions and exchanging greetings." For the time being, indeed, no one paid much attention to him. Most people thought of him merely as a priest taking a holiday, and since they did not expect to see him again, they took no trouble to remember his face.

At first his chosen route was almost always in the same direction —that is to say, away from the station, which, with the district that surrounded it, he loathed for many reasons. What precisely these were he did not bother to inquire. No doubt the ugliness of the buildings in that part of the town had something to do with his feeling, and the air of rather dismal modernity that marked them. (The streets were narrow, though not so narrow as those of the older districts, and straight, but irritatingly short. The overhead wires that served the ridiculous street-cars, and the noise made by the cars, were additional disadvantages.) There was nothing to redeem the dead level of the site, and for some unexplained reason the quality of the light entirely devoid of interest. Moreover, the neighbourhood was inextricably bound up in his mind with the vision of Bouère carrying his suit-case.

Sometimes he went through the centre of the old town, keeping to the two busy thoroughfares which met there, but for the most part he skirted it by following a succession of twisting streets, quiet and of a modestly residential character, lying now in shadow, now in sunlight, where, above the roofs, the thin trace of telegraph wires and the flight of birds made patterns against the sky.

Walking thus through ways that differed one from another only by the relative degree of solitude that filled them, he would come at last to one of the older quarters. At this point a street called the faubourg Saint-Charles led from the town so gradually that the eye scarcely noticed where the houses ceased and the country began (the city toll-office was farther on, invisible until the walker reached it).

The buildings here were of two or three storeys, the street itself about thirty feet broad. Very soon he came to occasional houses of a single storey, and these, as he advanced, began to predominate. The side-walks were narrow, raised high above the roadway, laid with large, ill-fitting paving-stones. Many trades were represented in the shops, some catering for the essential needs of the population, but seemingly unmarked by the stress and strain of daily competition, others offering special goods, and a few concerned with what might be called "heavy commerce." Finally, there were one or two which dealt in goods involving a certain degree of craftsmanship or in the materials needed by craftsmen for their work. Here a tinsmith displayed his wares, there a tanner: cabinet-makers, farriers, cobblers, saddlers and harness-makers, coopers, dealers in cloth, tarpaulins, and rope, manu-facturers of agricultural machinery and twine, all worked cheek by jowl. Many of the workshops were open to the public street and over-flowed on to the pavement. This suburban thoroughfare sloped gently downwards, then rose again and swept in a broad curve, still between houses, towards the right.

Before this curve was reached, it lay almost due north and south. When Mionnet passed down it at the beginning of his walk—that is to say, about two o'clock in the afternoon—the sun was directly be-hind him, so that the left-hand pavement was deep in shadow and the rest of the street brightly lit. The walls of the houses half-way up the slope shone white or yellow or pink according to the weather. The full force of the wind, which during this particular season blew from the west or south-west, was broken by the intervening bulk of the town. It came from his left and therefore helped rather than hindered his progress.

Mionnet never went as far as the open country, which began just beyond the highest point of the rise. It had no attraction for him. Midway in the curve of the street he had discovered on the left-hand side a narrow alley which continued the general line of direction he had till then been following, and climbed the hill at a steep angle. This alley, which, by reason of its direction and the severity of its grade, received, at this time of the day, the full rays of the sun, started from the wall of a house that was drenched by the afternoon glare. At its far end could be seen a patch of sky no bigger than a man's hand—of that northern sky the radiance of which seems superimposed upon an inner quality that is both dark and cold—and it had a peculiar charm for a man like Mionnet, who was keenly sensitive to the atmosphere of places.

At the lower end of this alley the houses were small and huddled close together. As it rose, however, these were succeeded by others, more widely spaced, and separated by garden walls. Beyond the crest was a level, unpaved road, almost a country lane, running between walls like those at the upper end of the alley. Other similar lanes joined it at intervals, and the general aspect of the scene was of a plateau dotted with country houses the roofs and upper storeys of which were occasionally visible above the garden walls or at the far ends of accidental vistas. Since, however, the gardens were large and thickly planted with trees, a pedestrian could walk for minutes together without being aware of anything but neat walls and heavy foliage.

Towards the north this plateau rose to a wooded height behind which lay the road into which the faubourg Saint-Charles led after its steep climb from the valley. In the other direction it merged into the upper town. Little by little the gardens grew smaller; the houses were older and less completely concealed. A fountain stood at a cross-roads where one branched off towards the new cemetery, and from here on the streets were paved, the houses stood flush with the sidewalk, and scattered shops were visible once more.

During these last weeks of September, Mionnet found it very pleasant to walk in this half-countrified region of long walls and large gardens. For all its rustic air, the sense of the city was never far distant and seemed to give to the thick greenery an added charm. The houses, of which now and then he caught a glimpse, instead of seeming buried in their trees, isolated and melancholy, gave the impression of comfortable retirement, of privileged tranquillity. There was about the place, too, a feeling of height in relation to the country that immediately adjoined it, a sense, except towards the north, that the roads led straight to an unencumbered view of sky or to a broad landscape of distant horizons.

As he approached the cross-roads by the fountain, he could see, at the end of a grass-grown alley, across an intervening barrier of low walls, the top of the Cathedral towers, which caught the sun upon their flanks and seemed, by reason of the heat haze that enveloped them, more distant than they were.

He descended the steep and winding streets of the old town, between old houses now occupied by workmen or respectable trades-men. The sharp differences of level produced not a few odd effects. Many of the house-doors were approached by flights of steps built parallel to the direction of the hill. The sidewalks were frequently cut by steps and raised high above the level of the road. The road itself, where the slope became abrupt, was furnished with projecting cobbles, which, though they were few and far between, gave some hold to the hoofs of ascending horses. The workshops of craftsmen in a small way of business were half-underground. But narrow though the streets were, the fact that they were on a slope, the general direction in which they faced, their frequent turns and twists, and the stepped arrangement of the roofs, admitted plenty of light.

By descending thus through the old town and bearing to the left, one came to the heart of the city and the Cathedral. Usually Mionnet kept more to the right. By doing so he reached eventually a sort of open space, very irregularly shaped, which was really nothing but the broadening-out of one of the old thoroughfares of M—. This wide section of the street was of considerable length, and marked the site of one of the old city gates. No trace of this gate remained, but the place had a very definite character of its own. It was the most "con-cave" portion of the town and seemed to draw to itself the whole life of the surrounding districts, serving as a meeting-point for a network of streets and alleys. Its very shape seemed designed to concentrate, as in the bed of a river, all the movement of the neighbourhood.

This side of the town was bounded by a small river which cut across the far end of the wide street. A bridge crossed it and led into the open country, which, however, did not begin at once upon the farther bank. Instead, there was an ancient suburb composed of a handful of low houses which were strung out along the road. They extended as far as a gentle hill planted with fine trees, beyond which lay an undulating country of small woods and open fields, not so high in general elevation as the plateau from which Mionnet had just returned.

He did not cross the bridge. It pleased him each time he came this way to renew the impression of being at *the most concave point* in all the town. There were several inns there, probably of very long standing, and he would gladly have gone into one of them had it not been for his clerical clothes. Occasionally a few carts and traps were seen drawn up before their doors. There was a sense of solitude about the huge hollow space, and the light that filled it gave him an odd pleasure the exact nature of which he found it hard to define. The sun left it early by reason of the high ground that surrounded it on almost every side, and its whole extent was permeated by a sort of limpid twilight, chilly, but suggestive of wide spaces, which gave to it a foretaste of fine winter weather, a character that was essentially of the north.

Sometimes Mionnet took the direct way back into the town, keeping to the street which, branching leftwards, continued the line of this long, wide place and climbed by degrees towards the city's heart. Sometimes, on the other hand, he took one of the smaller streets that started from the opposite side. This secondary route led, by gentler grades than those which marked the streets of the old town, between houses a century or more old, in front of which were sometimes tiny gardens. In this way he reached a sort of promenade planted with several rows of lime-trees, dotted with benches, and surmounted by a short length of the old town wall. Where the old fortification curved outwards in a bastion, the promenade had been widened to form a view-point over the surrounding country, and from the parapet the little river could be seen winding along some sixty feet below, separated from the old masonry by clumps of alders and stunted willows.

Even when he took the longer way, Mionnet always got home before dusk.

Almost every day he met one or other of Mme Roubier's daughters in the passages of the annexe; usually Émilienne. The two young women always chose this time of the day to tidy their own rooms and to see that the house generally was neat and orderly.

One day he found his door half-open and, entering, noticed Mlle Émilienne at the far end of the room, apparently occupied in doing something to his dressing-table. He had several times come on one or other of the maids similarly employed, so that he was not particularly surprised. He greeted the girl from a distance, politely but with a preoccupied air, hung his hat on a peg, and sat down at the desk in his little sitting-room.

Mlle Roubier's pleasant voice called to him from the farther room, fresh and rather abrupt, as usual:

"I wish you'd come here a moment and see if you like the way I've arranged this."

He went through the doorway, making a slight bow and murmuring: "Mademoiselle." He advanced to the middle of the floor.

"I've found you a bigger looking-glass," said the young woman, "and I've hung it here. I think you'll have a better light for shaving by. And I've brought you this enamelled jug because you complained of not having enough water. . . ."

She opened the cupboard of the wash-stand.

". . . A bigger slop-pail too. Oh, and this . . ."

"This" was a small article of an extremely intimate nature which Mionnet had modestly avoided mentioning in the list of wants which he had made a few days earlier on the advice of Mlle Roubier and given to her mother.

"It was the most troublesome of the lot," she went on, smiling with perfect self-possession. "We bought one at the bazaar, but when we got it home I didn't think you'd like it; so I kept it for myself, and I've given you mine."

(She spoke of it as though it had been a lamp or an inkstand.)

It occurred to Mionnet that perhaps he ought to have protested against such a sacrifice, and that he should have asked to see the other utensil so as to have been able to say that it was perfectly all right for his needs. But he realized, too, that a show of politeness in such a connexion might have looked like a piece of elaborate gallantry in the worst possible taste. He chose, therefore, to hide his embarrassment in a profusion of excuses and general expressions of gratitude.

He accompanied Mlle Émilienne back to the landing and bowed again several times. She was wearing a light-coloured dress of white foulard with a pattern in brown, red, and blue. She was scented, and the outlines of her body were plainly visible. The bright, simple colours of the house imparted to her a quality of country elegance, all modesty and good manners.

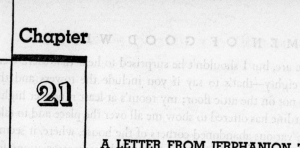

Chapter

21

A LETTER FROM JERPHANION TO JALLEZ

From Our Château of Saint-Papoul
this 11th day of September, 1910

My dear Baron:

Don't bite my head off; I know, I know. My last letter was dated August 22nd or 23rd and went to you from the Haute-Loire, although I promised faithfully to write to you as soon as I got here. It's not that I haven't thought about you, but I've been up to the eyes in a thousand and one trivialities—what we used to call *nugas* in our Latin compositions—and I didn't want to seem to be getting out of the difficulty by merely sending you twenty lines or so without substance.

I am writing to you, my dear Baron, in a room about two and a half times the size of our common study. It is in a corner of the top floor, and has two huge windows looking north and west. The first of these commands a view of the wooded heights of the estate towards the north, the second a smiling vista of lawns, trees, undulating fields and meadows which stretch to the horizon. When I lean out, I can see to the left a corner of the vineyard the products of which I am now in the habit of consuming.

The château is even more staggering than I had expected. In the first place, it is admirably situated on a little hill which rises out of a wooded valley, and gets the sun from morning to evening, as well as a series of wide and varied views. There are five towers, two of which are enormous, an extremely feudal entrance gate complete with drawbridge, and a fine courtyard. I must admit that the inside is neither furnished nor kept up on the scale of Versailles. It's so big that it would swallow a fortune. I don't know exactly how many rooms there are, but I shouldn't be surprised to hear that there were seventy or eighty—that's to say if you include the towers and the attics. (I'm not on the attic floor; my room's at least nine feet high.) Mlle Bernardine has offered to show me all over the place and to take me into the various abandoned corners of the house, where, it seems, she used to play as a girl and which have pleasant associations for her. I shall probably go with her when I have time.

The inhabited portion, or rather portions, consist, I believe, of about twenty or twenty-five rooms, of which the most important are really magnificent, especially the dining-room, which has the most wonderful beams and fifteenth-century windows, which I think you'd like. The drawing-room is huge (about as big as the dining-hall at the College), but, in my opinion, has been spoiled architecturally by being restored and filled—so far as my imperfect knowledge allows me to judge—with a lot of hideous furniture.

You know, my dear Baron, that I have been invited here in a purely social and friendly capacity, but I am not forbidden, during my stay, to put a few very discreet questions to the young Bernard on the subject of his holiday work; nor to sit in consultation with the Marquis when his political duties involve the exercise of his gifts as a writer or a speaker. As a matter of fact, he's not bothered much about that sort of thing for some time past. The preparations for Jeanne's marriage, and the general upheaval that they involve, drove every other consideration out of his head three or four days after my arrival (I got here on the evening of Friday the 2nd).

I have not had, therefore, much opportunity to observe—as you would have liked me to—the details of my lord's daily life (and that's one of the reasons I didn't write to you before). It seems to me fairly placid. Until the 6th the château was inhabited only by the family of the Saint-Papouls, who arrived from Paris with a full equipment of servants. The details of this family are already known to you. There was, in addition, a certain Vicomte Jean de Jerphanion, a young gentleman of great distinction, and the resident staff, the extent of which I am not in a position to give, not because it is so large, but because it seems to me that a good many of the servants divide their duties between the château and the farm.

Etiquette has so far been marked by extreme simplicity. I have been in the habit of getting up (the habit persists) about eight o'clock. It has been my custom to cast a friendly glance (I still cast) at the two Périgordian landscapes presented by my windows. Étienne has so far always brought my chocolate in person and brushed my clothes. (I find it impossible to reconstruct the state of mind which has led to my drinking chocolate here.) Between half past nine and eleven I have got into the way of establishing successive and more or less accidental contacts with various members of the family. There were days when I saw M. de Saint-Papoul returning from a morning ride or from a little solitary shooting. The season began with a great flourish a few days before I got here. A lot of people were asked from neighbouring châteaux, and novelty was introduced, it appears, into the scene by an attempt on the Marquis's part to include among his guests several local commoners, who had helped him win his election, and whom he now wished to reward and to retain for future use. The experiment, it seems, was not a success, or so Mlle Bernardine says; but, then, she never approved of it. I'd have given a good deal to be there and seen some of my old Bergerac friends! Ever since then the Marquis has confined himself to going off for two or three hours of a morning and walking over the estate with his gun and a favourite keeper called Laurent. These little outings have so far alternated with his horseback riding, but the hullabaloo caused by the marriage has put a temporary stop to these habits.

It is when our good friend Saint-Papoul plays the part of groom or hunter that I find him most Saint-Pathetic (don't be afraid, it's only the heat!). When he appears in either of those characters he becomes real, the representative of a definite type, the embodiment of a certain way of life.

He would take advantage of these casual meetings to open his letters in my presence and unwrap the papers, and we would exchange a few weighty words about the dangers that seem to be threatening the State. It looks as though this holiday time will sound the knell (notice my habit of fine phrases) of the policy of compromise which we have espoused. October will probably bring some nasty surprises. The Socialist agitation is gathering way, and the Left is breaking away from Briand. But we shall cling to power as long as we possibly can.

Midday has so far been the hour of lunch, the great beamed dining-room its scene. The meal is announced by prolonged ringing of a bell, and it takes at least ten or fifteen minutes for the company to assemble from the vast recesses of the house. M. de Saint-Papoul, who is a very punctual man, reproves the laggards. The table is so huge, and the atmosphere of the room so solemn, that I have the impression of meeting, not to eat, but to sign, say, the Treaty of Westphalia. The food, however, which is plentiful and rich, soon modifies the sense of grandeur, and is helped in doing so by the cackle of hens from the farmyard. The peaceful and familiar sound has a way of obliterating social differences which brings balm to my peasant soul.

The rest of the day has, up to now, been of a piece with these quiet beginnings. The Vicomte de Jerphanion was accompanied hither by his faithful bicycle and more than once has bestrid it with a simplicity of manner which is no small part of that young man's charm. Thus mounted, he has wandered as far afield as Bergerac, as Périgueux, and even, at times, as Eyzies. Tea is served at five o'clock in the great drawing-room or on the terrace for those who happen to be there to take it. (At such moments the Vicomte was more than likely to be sipping a grenadine or a kirsch in some local ale-house.) Dinner is at a quarter past seven, and nobody dresses for it. The rest of the evening is spent in the drawing-room. These after-dinner hours are not exciting. There is little conversation and no music. The Vicomte has played several games of chequers against various adversaries, and has usually won. A desire was expressed to teach him bridge. So far he has not shown himself very bright at it.

You see what a tranquil existence I am leading. There have been no visitors, unless they came at tea-time when I was wandering about the countryside. If they did, I don't suppose I missed much. Mme de Saint-Papoul has been out once or twice in the car with her daughter to pay calls on her neighbours. (They are proud of the car, which is a recent acquisition, and take every opportunity of displaying it. It is a large Panhard limousine.) On Sunday mornings, the Marquis, in his capacity as deputy, receives a few of his constituents, but secretly and by stealth.

I have written much of this in the past tense because since the 6th our way of life has been modified. The approach of the wedding has brought many unwonted additions to the population of the château. The change was announced by much excited coming and going of servants in the corridors; by Étienne's grumbling and air of harassed preoccupation when he brought me my chocolate; by agitated conversations between Mlle Bernardine and the Marquise; by the noise of beds being taken to pieces and put together again, and of furniture being moved from one room to another; by the smell of beeswax; by the rattling of pails and buckets; and by a general air of nervous strain at meal-times. The various arrivals have been carefully spaced out. I missed the earliest, partly because I wasn't warned, partly because I was shy. I was afraid of having to be introduced. I didn't like the idea of being involved in the chatter of greetings and the first exchange of news. But I very soon realized that I was missing something, and that, by dint of taking a few elementary precautions, I could witness these various disembarkations without becoming personally involved. I arranged things so that I should receive secret information either from Mlle Bernardine or from Étienne of the probable hour of arrival, or else I deduced it from such infallible signs as the departure of the limousine for one of the neighbouring railway stations, Mussidan, Périgueux, or Bergerac. That done, I had only to lie hidden, if necessary, in the pleasantly mediæval corridor close to my own room, from which I could look straight down into the courtyard, or in the pathway separated by shrubbery from the carriage drive which leads up to the château.

Some of the guests, as I have already said, come by train, finishing their journey in the Saint-Papoul car; others arrive under their own steam. To particularize, a couple of cars have so far put in an appearance, one of which seems to be of enormous size and weight. It broke down on the hill up to the château, and both passengers and baggage had to be landed with much fuss and improvisation of means. This accident enabled me to get a first-rate view of the proceedings. Three parties came in horse carriages of varying patterns, one of which, a most curious equipage, looked exactly like the travelling-coaches which one sees in old pictures. In order to get here it was dragged across the department by two great horses simply bursting with health and strength. I had a good look at it in the stable. The inside is very comfortable, very resplendent, and smells of a vanished age, an age which must have been delightful for those who happened to be born in easy circumstances.

For all my precautions, a moment comes when I have to be introduced, but that ceremony usually takes place just before dinner in an atmosphere of general conversation. I hear a vague murmur— "our cousins the So-and-So's" or "the Vicomtesse Thingumbob or Such-and-Such" (Bitch-and-Bitch would be more appropriate to the sporting character of the neighbourhood). Since the newcomers have to be introduced to one another as well, or are busy being polite if they happen to be old friends, the ordeal of our dear Vicomte J. de J. is soon over.

Who are all these people? Well, first of all, M. de Montech, father of the Marquise, and his wife, the grocer's daughter (whom I think I have already mentioned). She is of vast size, and moves with difficulty. The Marquise shows her much affection, though she quarrels with her from morning to night. (Their quarrels, I hasten to add, are conducted with extreme good breeding. You realize, of course, that the Vicomte J. de J. would leave at the first hint of vulgarity.) Then there is a young M. de Montech, a lieutenant in the army, who is, I believe, grandson to the former gentleman, and yet another de Montech (the place is thick with them), a silly old man whom the Marquise addresses as "Uncle." It appears that he was a militant legitimist about the time that Sarah Bernhardt was still a virgin, but he must have thought a good deal about things since then, since he told me frankly that "history never repeats itself," that Charles Maurras and Léon Daudet are "a couple of young blackguards," and that he entirely approves his nephew's politics. In addition to these there is a family of cousins on the Marquis's side, consisting of two young girls and a young cub of eighteen who gives himself airs. The father and mother of the bridegroom are here, both very tall, stiffer and more formal than the Saint-Papouls. They have come from Bordeaux with an unmarried daughter, and were joined at the château by a married daughter accompanied by her husband, who is so stupid as to be unnatural, and by a bachelor son. (The Comte and Comtesse de Lavardac are distant cousins of the Marquis.) Then there are half a dozen or so of people whose names I barely know, and still less the precise relationship they bear to the Saint-Papouls. The bridegroom, Robert de Lavardac, put in an appearance after everybody else, yesterday evening, Saturday, the very day before the civil ceremony was billed to take place. Was his late arrival due to press of business, or was it planned in accordance with some obscure rule of etiquette of which I am ignorant? Is it feared that he might take advantage of the secret passages and staircases of the château to pay nightly visits to his destined bride and so anticipate the blessing of the Church? I know not.

He certainly is not much to look at: dark-haired, pasty, narrow-shouldered, slightly bald, and not nearly so tall as either of his parents. At moments he looks slightly terror-struck, but at other times he seems gay enough, pleasant, and self-possessed. His speech is "distinguished," but rather mincing. He was coached by the Holy Fathers for Saint-Cyr, failed on medical grounds (so it's said), and then enlisted in a Dragoon regiment, with the idea of going on to take the officers' course at Saumur when his chest should have got stronger. It is to be assumed that he was still an inch or two too short, or that he changed his mind, because we still have the delightful privilege of seeing him a civilian like ourselves. Mlle Bernardine, from whom I get all this, and who is at times almost too willing to keep me informed, assures me that young Robert has no occupation except that of helping his father to run the family estate near Bordeaux, which contains some very famous vineyards. Mlle Bernardine dislikes him and pretends to be nervous about what will happen to the young couple. It seems that Pa Lavardac has promised to provide board and lodging and to give his son a handsome allowance, which will be referred to as a salary. But the old lady is mistrustful. She says that the money won't be paid regularly and that they'll have to live on Jeanne's settlement. You know that, ordinarily, such things don't interest me, but I just wanted to dazzle you by exhibiting my skill as an investigator. Would you believe it, my dear fellow, I've actually found out not only the amount of the said dowry, but the way in which it is made up. I have every reason to believe that (1) Jeanne is being given a small estate of about a hundred acres which her father owns in another part of Périgord; (2) that Grandpa Montech has disgorged a hundred and fifty thousand francs in ready cash; (3) that he has also made arrangements by which at his death a part of his fortune will go direct to Jeanne. Well, but Mlle Bernardine maintains that the estate brings in next to nothing, and that since it's probable that old Lavardac will default on his part of the bargain, the young couple will have no more than their board and lodging and about ten thousand francs a year until old Montech decides to quit. Faced with the prospect of such appalling poverty, I showed proper concern. I must confess, however, that I had to make a considerable effort to do so when I remembered that, given the happiest possible concatenation of circumstances—that is to say, assuming that we pass our finals, that we get appointments in Paris, that we reach the top of the tree before we die—we shall make a maximum income of nine thousand, on which we may well have to educate six children apiece. Still, I imagined that these people would have been safeguarded throughout their lives from the necessity of reckoning such niggardly sums.

You realize, of course, that such an invasion has considerably modified the atmosphere of the house. The passages are as thronged as those of a big hotel. (The guests have brought several servants each.) The table gets longer at each meal, and the huge spaces of the dining-room begin to take on an appearance of reasonable adequacy. I live in the expectation of seeing somebody get up to say a few heart-felt words when the dessert is brought.

Now that all these people are concentrated in one place, the general effect is to emphasize the provincial character of the company, to underline its particularly south-western complexion. Not that they talk patois, but that the territorial aspect is strengthened. There is plenty of good-humour, and no class aggressiveness. When conversation happens to turn on some minor member of the clan, the tone is intimate, the sense of family apparent. They know nothing of the working population and seem to be nervous of it. They regard its members as countrymen who have gone wrong, partly through their own fault, partly by force of circumstance, and they think of them quite naturally as being drunkards, wife-beaters, and as living in the constant hope of violence and loot.

So far as any standard of general culture is concerned, any glimmering of intellectual life, any knowledge of the world at large or any inkling of its probable tendencies, they are quite appalling. You can't imagine the narrowness and self-sufficiency of their outlook. I get the impression—and it's pretty awful, I can tell you—that M. de Saint-Papoul has to be careful *not to talk above their heads!* Grandpa Montech is the most disappointing of the lot, because to have got where he has he must have had a certain amount of intelligence and drive. Not that he's a fool. He's quite sensible at times, quite shrewd, and not without humour, but only in matters that concern him closely. As soon as he touches on any question that is the least bit general, he argues like a perfect fool. His old buffoon of a brother is rather more inconsequent and less of a fool.

As a result of all this, the Vicomte Jean de Jerphanion spends most of every meal biting his tongue to prevent himself from giving vent to ineptitudes. At such moments he would dearly like to exchange comforting shrugs across the table with his old friend the Baron Jallez (scion of an old family of Portuguese Jews which settled in the south-west and was ennobled under the Second Empire as the result of accumulating great wealth by fraudulent means).

Tomorrow the civil marriage will take place before the Mayor of Saint-Jean, and this will be followed on Tuesday by the benediction of the Church. This latter ceremony has given rise to much discussion. The women want it to take place in the chapel of the château, which, though considerably dilapidated and probably no longer sanctified, could, with a very little trouble, be smartened up with a bit of paint and blessed anew by a priest. The Marquis, however, thinks that such a course would smell a little too strongly of the *ancien régime* and has voted, as a good democrat, for the parish church. And he's probably right.

The occasion will bring down on our devoted heads a flock of additional guests from every point of the compass, like the flies in the *Iliad*. Since the dining-room won't be big enough, lunch is to be served in the drawing-room, which is now being turned upside-down for the purpose. (The small morning-room adjoining is already almost entirely filled by the wedding presents, the details of which I will spare you.) There will be a feast for the village people, served in a gaily coloured marquee which at this very moment is being erected in the courtyard. The only trouble is that there won't be many villagers. There was once a village of Saint-Papoul quite close to the château, but there's nothing there now but ruins and weeds, the inhabitants having decamped many years ago. (If only they could have foreseen what was to happen! . . .) As a result, we shall have to make do with a few farmers, reinforced by some volunteers pressed into service from the neighbourhood and marshalled across the fields in procession behind a couple of fiddlers. This has led to another dispute, between the Marquise and Mlle Bernardine, the question being whether "the poor" ought to be invited. I'm talking, you understand, of the local and professional paupers, picturesquely patched like harlequins, halt, and reasonably dirty. Mlle Bernardine maintains that to include them would be a Christian act, but the Marquise argues that it would bring an atmosphere of squalor into the scene. Mlle Bernardine had the nerve to ask me to decide between them (relying on my reputation as a Socialist). I decided in favour of the Marquise, on the ground that I had a sociologist's mistrust of that sort of poverty.

While we're on the subject of Mlle Bernardine, you may as well know that she's hanging on to my coat-tails. I can't get rid of her. When I first came she was full of solicitude about my room and my comfort generally, which was admirable. But now it's rather too much of a good thing. If she manages to get me into a corner, she sticks to me like a leech. Of course she's been a very useful source of information on many points, but I must say that as soon as I've found out what I want to know, I like to wash my hands of her. I only wish I had your skill in such matters!

She's an extraordinary old girl, as ignorant as a kitchen-maid, and cracked into the bargain. But at the same time she's intelligent; I was almost tempted to say: intellectual; that's to say, as far as a nitwit can be intelligent, and as far as anyone so completely uneducated can naturally get her mind working on intellectual lines. I wish I'd made a note of some of the questions she's asked me, questions of incredible profundity which seem to have been the outcome of some deep astuteness in her funny old brain.

I sometimes wonder whether perhaps she's got some idea of converting me—or of letting me *deconvert* her. Sometimes she'll pause in her ridiculous and boring talk, to sigh and raise her eyes, as though imploring the help of Heaven before plunging into the morass of incredulity. At such moments I want to throw her out of one of the fifteenth-century windows.

I also have to put up with Étienne's confidences. The fellow's passing through a violent Socialist phase—odd though that sounds. Where, I wonder, did he pick up the poison? What he complains of is not the economic condition of his calling (it would need a pretty good nerve to do that!), but its deprivation of rights and status.

(That's not the word he used, but it's what he means.) He's got other, more definite grievances, which probably account for his theories. For instance, he's shown himself incapable of learning to drive the car (he's nervous and apt to lose his head), with the result that a chauffeur has been engaged, and now that he's no longer a coachman, his wages have been very slightly reduced. *Very* slightly, I must admit; but *he* won't admit it, and he's furious. He hates the chauffeur and bitterly regrets not having voted for a Socialist last May.

That's all my news, dear Baron, or almost all. I've just spent an hour trimming my beard so as to look presentable for tomorrow and the next day. I'm expecting to be called upon at Tuesday's dinner to sing the "Wagoner's Wife." If she is as successful as I fully expect her to be, I shall give "The Village Pump" as an encore.

". . . The sun peeps o'er yon western hill."

I must spend the afternoon practising the incidental noises, which are usually my weak point.

Aristocratically yours,

JEAN DE JERPHANION

PS.—I like the view of Saint-Malo you sent. You seem to have spent your vacation in a magnificent bit of country. And now you're going to saunter about Paris with your nostrils full of the delicious autumn smells. I refuse to be sorry for you.

By the bye, I've got a grand story about Macaire, who's been spending his holidays here. But it's rather long, and I've got to get this letter off by the chauffeur, who's going in to Mussidan to meet two more brothers of the bridegroom. Remind me to tell you later.

Chapter

22

JERPHANION'S LETTER TO
MATHILDE CAZALIS

Having finished his letter to Jallez, Jerphanion saw
that he still had more than half an hour before the
car would get back with the additional members of the Lavardac
family and before the bell would ring for dinner. It occurred to him
that it was a good moment to compose on the subject of Mlle Bernardine, on Jeanne de Saint-Papoul, or on both a Note that should
be as penetrating, as observant, as brilliant in its skill, and as flattering for its author as the similar composition which, six months earlier,
had had Jallez as its subject.

Unfortunately, that analysis of Jallez, which was intended to be
the first of a series, had remained solitary within its cardboard wrap-
per. The knowledge that this was so irritated Jerphanion. He disliked
having to admit that he had failed to carry out any plan that he had
embarked upon. The word "intention" had become a buzzing fly
which he constantly heard circling round him, and the sound of
which he had grown to hate.

But on second thoughts he decided that half an hour was too short
a time; that his ideas about Jeanne were not fully formed and were
bound to develop during the next two days; that the prospect of a
tête-à-tête with the ghost of Mlle Bernardine was depressing. His
interviews with her in the flesh were quite enough.

He fell back on another "intention" which he had been turning
over in his brain and in his heart since the beginning of his holiday,
and composed the following letter, which, short though it was, gave
him a great deal of trouble to complete to his satisfaction in the half-
hour at his disposal:

Mademoiselle Mathilde Cazalis
   c/o M. Alphonse Cazalis
     Barjac
      (Gard)

11 September 1910
Château de Saint-Papoul
near Villamblard
(Dordogne)

DEAR MADEMOISELLE MATHILDE:

You may remember that I asked you for your address during the holidays so that I could send you a postcard or two. I have sent you none, but I very nearly did better—or worse; that is to say, I nearly paid a call on you on my way from the Haute-Loire to Périgord. Perhaps you haven't realized that we are almost neighbours?

I was afraid that I mightn't be welcome, or that I might compromise you. What would Barjac have said about such a visit?

You are often in my mind, perhaps a little too often from the point of view of strict good sense. If I haven't written to you before this, the reason has been that I was vaguely afraid of writing. I realize that what I am writing now is taking a dangerous turn. Perhaps I had better stop.

The enclosed postcard shows you the château in which I am stopping. You can write to me here—that is to say, if it wouldn't be too great a bore—up to next Friday. I leave on Saturday morning for Velay. I shall go the whole way by bicycle, though I've not yet made up my mind what route to take.

Believe me, Mademoiselle Mathilde, yours sincerely,

JEAN JERPHANION

Chapter

23

JEANNE'S WEDDING NIGHT: THE GROWTH OF AN IDEA

It had been arranged, for various reasons, that, the ceremony concluded, the young couple should spend the whole of Wednesday at the château, where the festivities would still be in full swing. Early on Thursday the car would take them to Souillac so that they might catch the Toulouse express. They would thus be able to get to Barcelona the same evening. After a short stay there they would start on a brief tour of Spain, going by way of Saragossa, Madrid, and Burgos. Finally, they would spend about a week at Saint-Sebastian, returning thence to France, and naturally taking the château of Lavardac on the way, where they would arrive before the end of the wine harvest, while the air was still heavy with the scent of the gathered grapes.

A little before eleven o'clock on Tuesday night the young bride and bridegroom left the great drawing-room while the dancing was still at its height. They were joined in the dining-room, whither they had gone to take a little refreshment at the buffet, by the Marquise. "You can go off to bed, if you like," she murmured; "of course you can—nobody need notice. . . . I wish you a happy night, dear children."

She looked tenderly at her daughter and pursed her lips into the gesture of a kiss. She longed to take her in her arms and to go with her the first few steps of the way, but feared lest so dramatic a farewell might be in bad taste.

In spite of her precautions, however, it was not long before the young people's absence was noticed. The news spread discreetly through the room, though its reception was marked by no more definite signs than a glance here, a smile there, and a question asked in seeming innocence: "Where is Jeanne?" This absence of the chief actors gave a sudden meaning to the whole party. It set free a thousand thoughts, all concentrated upon, all making fond play with, the same central fact, though for some the stark reality was swathed in veils of soft romance, while others itemized the event with varying degrees of detailed elaboration, hungrily stripping it of all disguise, setting it in the full glare of lewd imaginings (many, to "see" the better, danced with half-closed eyes), caressing it in thought with lingering insistence, as a cat will rub its fur against the furniture.

Jeanne was very tired. The excitement which had kept her going all afternoon had fallen flat. She was tired in her body, tired of eating, tired of people. For the last few days she had been too much on the move and too long on her feet; she had had too much food, had seen too many new faces. Worst of all, she had felt the hot light of public notice focused upon her. Wherever she went she had been looked at. At first the experience had intoxicated her, but she had soon grown surfeited. Her vanity was not great enough to keep the threat of a headache indefinitely at bay. For no consideration in the world, however, would she have changed places with anybody, nor would she have consented to postpone what now she knew to be inevitable. She was afraid that Robert, noticing her fatigue, might leave her alone from a foolish scruple of delicacy.

There was no trace of sensuality in her impatience. It was due chiefly to a desire to free herself from a state of painful expectation, but there was also in it a certain amount of intellectual curiosity: "I'm going to have *that* experience. I'm going to know what it is that other women know!" This curiosity was sharpened by several other considerations of a more intimate and more complex nature, such as: "Now at last I've got the chance of learning, without doing wrong, the most important thing in life, about which I could only have found out up to now at the cost of doing wrong." Finally, without giving definite form to the thought, she realized that she was about to verify a certain hypothesis upon which she had recently been brooding.

In the course of the last two days things had been happening to her, and within her, of so unusual a nature that her attention had been pricked into wakefulness. In the first place, she had asked herself, on more than one occasion, and as though the question had forced itself into words without any deliberate formulation on her part: "Do I love him? Do I love him enough to be happy in the idea of what is happening to me, of what seems to be earning me the congratulations of so many people?" She found herself watching Robert at every moment of the day without letting him see that she was doing so, observing his gestures, his attitudes, listening to the least word he uttered. And this she did, not with the sense of being a critic standing severely apart, but conscious of an uneasy community of interest with him, as though she feared for him the judgment of another, not realizing that this other was herself.

Towards the end of the second day she managed to free herself from this particular form of torture, or rather its importance for her suddenly became less. What now obsessed her, and now seemed urgent, was not the question whether she could possibly spend her entire life with a man called Robert de Lavardac, but the far more imminent problem—exactly what degree of shuddering distaste would be produced in her by the mere fact, uncomplicated by any further consideration, of lying all night long, in the completest intimacy, beside a man, sharing the warmth, and exposed to all the accidental contacts, of his hairy body.

It seemed suddenly to Jeanne that she was being asked to go counter to every standard of that civilization in which she had been so carefully bred. Civilization teaches us to keep from touching others and to avoid being touched by them; to defend the integrity of our bodies and our skins; to eschew promiscuity, the sharing of goods, the confusion of individuals; to think of contact as a weaker form of contagion.

Though as a rule she was careless of what was happening around her, she could not but notice the amount of talk that was going on, nor help guessing that she was its object. She saw Mme de Lavardac and her mother drawn together in mysterious intimacies, as though they were intent on resolving some problem of extreme delicacy, after which the Countess would go and look for her husband and take him aside into the small morning-room. A little later, hunting for Robert, she would see him talking with his father or listening to him with obvious embarrassment. When he rejoined her, she would ask him: "What were you talking about so seriously?"—a question to which he seemed to find it very difficult to reply. Finally, these odd manœuvres, the full extent of which she was not at all sure that she knew, came to a head when Mme de Saint-Papoul said: "I want you to listen to me, darling; there's something I must talk to you about," which had been preliminary to a secluded interview in the Marquise's bedroom.

There, behind closed doors, Mme de Saint-Papoul had embarked upon a long explanation which had been complicated by the speaker's wish to be explicit while not overstepping the bounds of decency. The substance of her lecture had been as follows:

"This isn't the first chat we have had together, and you know already that to be a young girl is one thing and to be a married woman is another. . . . I won't go over that again, nor will I talk about the rights that marriage gives to the man of your choice. . . . One marries in order to have children, and I hope you'll have a great many—that is, you're sure to have some; but you're very young, and there's plenty of time. There's the question of health to be considered. . . . You must make the most of your youth. If you don't take certain precautions there's always the danger that you'll have children before you mean to, or you may have them at a bad time of year—at the beginning of winter, for example. . . . Some think that these precautions are the husband's affair, but sometimes men don't know about these things, or dislike them, or forget. In any case, it's safer if the wife knows what ought to be done. Although I *am* your mother, I find it very difficult to speak to you of these matters, though

I wish my own mother had given me a word of warning. Not that I should have had fewer children, but I should have chosen the times of their birth with greater care, and that would have been better for them as well as for me. . . . But women of her generation never thought of such things, or, if they did, they hadn't the courage to talk about them. . . . In my day, one learned them by chance, and too late."

This beginning was followed, not exactly by a practical demonstration, but by very detailed instructions which Mme de Saint-Papoul, adopting a parental innocence of tone and employing very careful euphemisms, strove to make resemble as far as possible the lessons in the care of the body which she had given to Jeanne when she was a small girl. Jeanne, however, had experienced a shock. So would any young woman in her position, but though, like her, she might have suffered from a sense of shattered illusions, she would not have misunderstood the intention with which the advice was given. Not that, probably, Jeanne misunderstood it consciously or in the strict sense of the word, but, deep down, she ranked her mother's revelation with the mythical description of carnal intercourse the first hints of which had been deposited in her mind some two years earlier. In other words, she gave but half her attention to what her mother was telling her about children and the power of making conception a deliberate act, while she brooded bitterly upon the thought of bodily defilement.

Jeanne, therefore, went through her marriage night much (if the two things may be compared) as a scientist conducting a decisive experiment by which he hopes to verify some favourite hypothesis; or as a man, reading a newspaper of a political complexion other than his own, follows the misdeeds of the Opposition against which his own favourite sheet has already warned him. She was out for confirmation rather than discovery. Given the different moral backgrounds of the two young people, it was not likely that the result of the experience would be to reverse Jeanne's attitude, still less to awake in her a bodily response capable of making her suddenly forget her preconceived ideas on the subject.

Robert was rather nervous. He wished above all things to behave properly and not to make a fool of himself. Jeanne was conscious of no particular physical repulsion. Indeed, realizing that the *idea* of loving her cousin which she had long entertained had of late increased, she persuaded herself without difficulty that what she felt for him would easily develop into a pleasant wifely affection. She was not, however, sufficiently in love with him to surrender passionately to his approaches. On the other hand, she saw no reason to be unduly shy. She was aware of no feeling of attraction or excitement, and expected no gradual growth of desire. Her only thought was: "Why delay the inevitable?" She made no attempt to resist him when he removed the exquisite night-dress which had been the gift of her mother-in-law. She accepted with a good grace, even with a sort of gratitude, the gentle kisses and caresses which he lavished upon her, rather as a patient might feel gratitude to a surgeon for his reassuring conversation while he is busy preparing and sterilizing his instruments. But she felt that Robert was making rather too much of the introductory phase. She wanted to say: "Please go straight to the point; I know what to expect, and I'll be brave."

The difficulties and discomfort attendant upon the process of achieving an entry were less than she had feared they would be, and not, in themselves, worth bothering about. She was not a physical coward. Her nervous system was entirely under the control of her will. It seemed to her so natural that the act of defilement should be preceded by a certain amount of bodily pain that she was not tempted to exaggerate the pain itself.

But from this moment she allowed her whole consciousness to be flooded by the thoughts, the intuitions, the imaginings (more numerous and more complicated than she could take account of) which clustered for her about the magic phrase: "What a man does to a woman, *in* a woman, is to deposit his excrement." Jeanne made ready to receive this excrement. The man's position, his movements, the sort of animal concentration which she could see increasingly in his eyes, all gave weight to the idea and touched Jeanne's attitude of expectancy with a dramatic intensity. "I'm going to be the recipient of his excrement; I'm going to submit, in duty bound, to the worst of all outrages. It's my duty to submit without the slightest resistance or the least movement of defence." It was, she told herself, the law of her destiny, nor was it very surprising, when she came to think of it. Everyone in the world was subject to the law of sin and to the law of redemption through humility. Had not man been taught to be humble before his persecutors, to turn the other cheek?—spat upon, trampled, mocked with a sponge soaked in bitter drink. The cup must be emptied to the dregs. "I'll shut my eyes. In another minute perhaps I shall be just that and no more, just the receptacle of his excrement. . . . Then I'll wash myself as my mother told me to. So be it. . . . But first I want to focus my mind on the awful thing that's going to happen to me. . . . Oh, which *is* happening to me . . . which is happening inside me, now, at this very moment, now!"

She stopped breathing. From head to feet she was conscious of nothing but the sensation of this unspeakable horror. It flooded her body from the tips of her toes to the roots of her hair. No shame could ever be like this shame, not a detail of which was spared her. Nothing could ever cleanse her again of this filth; her whole body felt soiled and sticky with it. Then she began to breathe again. She felt broken, emptied. Never, in all her life, had she felt so utterly sacrificed, or so deeply soothed.

Chapter

24

NEW PLASTER:
AN EVENING AT CELLE-LES-EAUX

Mareil had solemnly promised Germaine that the rehearsal should be over by four o'clock, so that they could start off at once in the car which was waiting in front of the theatre. They would sleep at Chartres, then next day, which was Sunday, they would go on by Blois and Vendôme, lunching at Blois and seeing the château. From there they would go up the south bank of the Loire, stopping at Chambord and sleeping at Orléans. On Monday, by getting up very early, they could manage to be back in Paris during the morning, or at latest by one o'clock, returning not by the main road, which was impracticable, but by a charming route which would take them by Malesherbes and Fontainebleau.

Germaine had gone through the rehearsal in a half-dazed state. Her heart had been beating with a sense of excitement such as she had not felt since the days of her childhood when some great treat was in store. The plan of this trip seemed to her something marvellous, incredible. Although Mareil had already taken her on three similar expeditions during the holidays, she couldn't really believe that so many things, so many landscapes, villages, cities, châteaux, forests, so much going uphill and downhill, could be compressed into less than two days. "This evening we shall be in the country, we shall have *got ourselves* to the country. All tomorrow we shall wander about the country, and we shall sleep in some huge old bed. And yet we shall be lunching on Monday in Paris almost at our usual time." Difficult though it was to believe, she *did* believe, because in matters of this kind Mareil was extremely meticulous, and hated to have his plans upset.

Meticulous, once he'd got off: but it was the very devil to make him realize, in the middle of a rehearsal, that it was time to start. At such moments his passion for motoring was completely dominated by his passion for the theatre, and while a rehearsal was in progress, Germaine in the "boss's" eyes was nothing but a subordinate, an obedient pupil. She wouldn't have dreamed of using her authority as his mistress. Like a child, she kept her eyes glued on him to catch the hoped-for look in his face, to see his hand steal towards the little pocket where he kept his watch. When, towards a quarter to five, he spoke of running through a longish and difficult scene which Germaine had to play with two others, she plucked up courage to speak. Assuming a mildly reproachful air, and looking him straight in the eyes, she said:

"Do you think we've got time to do it properly?"

He smiled, seemed to rouse himself, and made that blissful movement of his hand towards his waistcoat pocket.

"Gracious! Nearly five o'clock; yes, you're right."

As soon as they had passed the Châtillon gate, where he had declared the amount of gasoline in his tank, and stopped a hundred yards farther on to fill up, he said with a worried air:

"I've been thinking. It'll be dark in little more than an hour. It's fifty-six miles to Chartres, and if we average twenty-two, that means two and a half hours, or rather more. I don't like driving as long as that at night."

Germaine looked terribly disappointed. He smiled, and went on in his most persuasive voice:

"I know it's my fault, darling. When I get worked up like that I forget the time. But don't worry. I swear we'll manage our trip. Tomorrow was to have been a short day, and it'll mostly be on the level. I planned to have left Chartres at half past nine. You wouldn't mind starting at eight, would you?—especially as I've shown you Chartres. We'll just have a look at the Cathedral from the car, as we pass."

He was a past master at making excuses and taking the sting out of a disappointment.

Germaine put her head on his shoulder and kissed him low down on the cheek. Their thick clothes made such movements difficult. "We look like two sacks of charcoal stuck on legs," she said; "whenever we get out and there's a looking-glass to be had, it makes me laugh."

As a matter of fact, she was very proud of her appearance. The padded silhouette of the motorist was recognizable at a distance as the mark of a still limited caste. It stood for wealth, or, at least, for easy circumstances, for up-to-date tastes, for an adventurous spirit. In the course of the centuries the feminine form has more than once been the victim of such odd disguises, but the sense of social privilege thus attained, then, as now, made compensation for the loss of outward elegance. The huge goggles, which threatened to spoil a pretty face, were the only serious blot on the get-up. But really modern cars like Mareil's—a twelve horse-power Bertrand, new from the works in March—had wind-shields. For the well-equipped and smart motorist, goggles now were only an additional safeguard for use on very dusty days or in a high wind, a sort of emergency fitting, worn becomingly above the edge of the woollen helmet or the visor of the cap, like two blisters proudly displayed.

Mareil took the road by the Châtillon gate, which at that time was one of the quietest ways out of Paris, where the outer suburbs become almost at once completely rural. The surface was not too badly worn, and two rows of old trees lined the way, trees which had long lived as neighbours and leaned all in the same direction as the result of the prevailing winds and of the angle at which they caught the light. The houses hereabouts were of an indeterminate age, without any particular beauty, but long grown native to the site, the outward sign of civilized and deep-rooted lives. Even Châtillon itself looked like a provincial market town, a town of the Île-de-France. A long, winding and rather sad-looking road, known of old to Mareil, led upwards between the walls of middle-class properties to a plateau which was suddenly the heart of the country. The light seemed thinner. It came from a point low down in the sky and struck in level beams straight in the faces of the advancing travellers. There was a pleasant nip in the air, and a very faint mist rose from the earth. A litter of yellowing leaves covered the little cobbles of the road as far as the eye could reach, looking like thousands of birds made bold by the loneliness. Among them, here and there, real birds took flight at the car's approach, dipping in wheeling companies with a sound audible above the purr of the engine and bringing a sweet sense of autumn to the scene.

The sound of the engine, too, was pleasant. The car was in one of its good moods. Mareil could tell its temper by a dozen different signs. He had no gift for mechanics and was hopeless in a break-down. But he had a curious and subtle feeling for his car. He knew nothing of causes, but the symptoms never escaped him. The slightest change in the rhythm of the explosions, in the pulsations, the tappings, the clickings, to which he was accustomed, caused him the most intense disquiet. But when, as today, all went well, he breathed more freely and was happy in his thoughts.

They began to run down into Bièvres. A wide view spread before their eyes, a valley stretching into the distance between woods and fields. Rolling uplands looked almost like the foothills of a mountain range. The whole character of the country seemed suddenly to change: in the evening light it was as clear as some corner of Morvan or La Creuse. Mareil turned to Germaine.

"I've got an idea," he said. "It would have been delightful to sleep in some village inn, but I've thought of something else which might be fun. You've seen all these advertisements of Celle-les-Eaux, haven't you? I believe it opened last month. It's on our way; we could get there in an hour. The hotels are naturally the very last word and absolutely brand-new. Besides, I expect they've kept the prices down to attract business. Paris seems so far away; don't you think it might be rather amusing? It would be like arriving at Vichy or Royat or Plombières."

Mareil loved to turn life into a game. He would have liked nothing less than actually to have found himself this evening in a great holiday resort packed with people. He had just had a very tiring week in Paris and longed to escape for two days from noise and chatter. But this new little watering-place, within reach of the city, nestling in a corner of the suburbs, was only half-real. It was a toy, a fantastic folly. "One could almost hold it in one's hand," he thought. "We shall be about the only people there. The hotel managers will fall over each other to make us welcome. It'll be great fun."

Although he had no gift for business—his early career in a bank had left him with nothing but a vague memory of the silliness of routine—he by no means disliked seeing its workings at close quarters. The activity of financiers gave him considerable pleasure: he liked the blatant clamour of modern publicity, willingly submitted to its deceptive lures, and loved to indulge his imagination with vague thoughts of the birth and development of great enterprises. He fully realized this weakness and was fond of saying to himself that it was his Jewish blood seeking satisfaction, though probably his imagination rather than his race was responsible for this particular characteristic.

They reached Celle-les-Eaux a good half-hour before dark and so were able to see the whole of it, partly driving and partly on foot. Mareil's enthusiasm was undiminished. In the first place, he thought the country "marvellous." "Look at the view. . . . It's all so fresh, so really the country. There's everything one wants—woods, plain, fields. . . . Look at the way that little valley snuggles down under the hill, or two hills, rather, with the houses showing through the trees. It's like a dream landscape. . . . Did you notice, just now, that quaint village away to the left, with its towers?—straight out of the Middle Ages. . . . Remind me to look up its name on the map. . . . The whole thing's just too marvellous."

"The whole thing," if it had been two hundred miles from Paris, would have seemed to him pleasantly normal, but the fact that Paris was almost within reach sharpened his sense of amazement in what he had discovered, and invested it with an added rarity. A mediæval manor eighteen miles from the city is more excitingly mediæval, a charming valley moves the soul to deeper rapture. Besides, it was always a peculiar pleasure for Mareil to find still one more beauty in the heart of his beloved Île-de-France.

After a moment's hesitation he announced that the buildings didn't "worry him at all." He even decided that they had been most "happily thought out" and that they were "thoroughly amusing." The more he saw of the place, the more credit he gave to Turpin and to Haverkamp—not that he mentioned these names, which were unknown to him.

"It really is quite extraordinarily good," he said. "I imagine that big white contraption is the Casino—very good proportions, fine, spare lines . . . extremely restful, with a delightfully unexpected silhouette. . . . The big building over there, with the balconies and all those funny little clustering roofs, must be the hotel, the chief hotel. . . . No, I agree, it's not in the same style, but one doesn't build a watering-place with a uniform façade like the Place Vendôme—the very reverse: one tries to get variety, an effect of surprise. The whole place is so largely planned, nothing mean or squalid about it. I'm sure, just from seeing it like this, that it's one of the finest hotels in France. . . . What do you say to spending the night there? Wasn't it a good idea of mine to come here? The promoters must be pretty sure of the medical value of the waters to build on this scale—they're no fools. People don't spread themselves like this for nothing. . . . Oh, no. . . . One can't advertise as much as they have done unless there's something to advertise. It's just the same as in the theatre. You may shout about masterpieces till you're black in the face, and spend a hundred thousand francs on publicity, but if the play's bad, you won't get audiences to come and see it. Sometimes, of course, a manager may quite sincerely make a mistake about a manuscript; there's no scientific certainty in the choice of a play; whereas in the case of a mineral water one presumably has a very careful analysis made—more than one, probably—before risking a lot of money in exploiting it. There are quite a lot of people here already."

He went into ecstasies over a half-finished lawn, and the still un-completed edging of a path. Despite his volubility, he was not blind to the actual dimensions of what he saw, and realized that the impres-sion of prosperity which gave him such pleasure was produced by the appearance of four persons at the same moment in a narrow path. But this mixture in him of common sense and willing subjection to illusion not only satisfied the general bias of his temperament towards playing—in the sense in which children play games—but excited, in particular, his sense of the theatre. In this artificial little township he felt in the same receptive state of mind as the spectator of a stage pageant, who asks no better than to be deceived and who admires most the "set" which manages to achieve the best results with the greatest economy of means. To know, in such a case, with exactly how little material the effect is obtained, so far from spoiling one's pleasure, is an added delight. The mind submits willingly to the de-ception practised upon it, and half the fun comes from realizing how well it's all been done.

In the course of their tour of inspection they came to the original part of the village. "The old La Celle!" Mareil cried delightedly. The idea that there was an "old La Celle" which was being left high and dry by the life that was emigrating to its "new West Side," but which, all the same, was being gradually modernized—"look at that café on the corner, and that confectionery-shop, and this neat little hotel; you see they're doing their best, they want to be in the mode"—seemed to him endlessly amusing. He played on this theme of his so many unexpected variations that Germaine, who was nat-urally rather prosaic and solemn and unapt to respond to such a rapid play of fantasy, ended by finding it all as laughable as he did, joining in the game herself, and contributing one or two observations of her own on the dull, respectable look of the old village and of the people they saw there.

They took a room with a private bath at the Thermal Palace. The entrance hall of the hotel was vast, with a reception desk and a porter. There were attendants and elevator-boys; huge, endless corridors, white ceiling-lamps, and rounded cornices. The decoration and furniture were in the style of the Salon d'Automne. . . . Here and there the lintel of a door was soiled with a dab of plaster, and fragments of it lay about in corners like little piles of sugared almonds. Occasional smears of enamel marked the nickel faucets. One or two of the doors were ill-fitting, and some of their panels had split. An occasional ceiling was marked with a crack in the plaster. But the general effect of all these minor blemishes was to stress the impression of brand-new luxury, bombarding the mind of the visitor with these evidences of prestige achieved by the latest thing in hotels.

"Twelve francs isn't dear," Mareil said to Germaine.

He was full of admiration for the site, which on one side gave a full view of the open country and on the other overlooked the mineral spring, so that there was direct access from the hotel to the bathing-establishment.

"I tell you what, darling," he added; "tomorrow morning, before they bring us our breakfast, I'm going to slip into the pump-room and drink a big glass of water, just to be in the picture. It'll be fun to think that I've 'done' my season at La Celle; besides, who knows, it might do me good."

They took their apéritifs on the terrace of the Casino, where, although the evening was cool, several lightly dressed visitors had collected. Unfortunately, most of them, not excluding the women, were rather fat, puffy, and middle-aged. A small orchestra of five played "Poet and Peasant," the "Scènes Alsaciennes," a "Fantaisie sur Paillasse," the "Marche Lorraine," and a "Réverie du Soir" for 'cello, by J. Tronchoux.

They dined at the Thermal Palace, in a huge dining-room. Of the thirty tables which it contained, about ten were occupied. But so cleverly had the various groups been arranged and spaced that the general effect was of select intimacy rather than of emptiness. Mareil paid a tribute, in the secrecy of his heart, to the success of this brilliant piece of stage-management. Where it was a question of making the most of a "thin" house, his experience as dramatist made him sensitive.

The head waiter, whose time was hanging rather heavy on his hands, took them personally under his wing. Perhaps the rosette in Mareil's buttonhole attracted him. (It was quite new, barely six weeks old, having figured in the July Honours List.) He was full of chit-chat:

"Things are going pretty well. . . . After all, we didn't open until the 15th of August, and the Casino's only been going since the 1st of September. Besides, it's been a poor season everywhere."

Mareil agreed that, all things considered, La Celle had begun its career brilliantly. The success, he added, was fully deserved.

"Oh, well, we've done our best," said the head waiter. "The place is being run by men of great ability. The director of this hotel is a Swiss; quite a young man, but he knows the ropes. I've got an excellent staff; I took a good deal of trouble getting it together. The waiters are all young fellows with their future to make, and for that reason they're willing to take low salaries to begin with. Take the hall porter, for instance. He was getting twenty thousand francs a year in hotels of the second rank, in summer at Aix-les-Bains and in winter at Nice. Naturally, he won't make much here at first, but he's saved a bit, and it's a great chance for him. If things go well he may easily be getting forty thousand in five years' time! . . . The management will be generous to us because we were in at the start. Any economies and cuts that may eventually be necessary will be made at the expense of the newcomers."

Germaine was faintly annoyed to hear such figures quoted. "What!" she thought; "forty thousand a year for a porter! And they talk of it as though it were the most natural thing in the world. I was as pleased as Punch last year when Marquis gave me seven hundred a month! And Mareil had to work like a nigger to get me fifty francs a performance, although I'm a well-known actress, a star! But he doesn't seem surprised."

As a matter of fact, Mareil was aware not so much of the social injustice represented by such figures as of the pleasure he got in hearing money speak so loudly in his immediate neighbourhood, in spite of the fact that it was not his, nor ever likely to be. He felt himself more at home with a waiter in a smart restaurant who was stuffed with tips than he would have done with a plumber, although, essentially, one was no more a "proletarian" than the other. He was frightened at the idea that the plumber probably hated him; it never occurred to him to be outraged by the waiter's profits, however absurdly excessive they might be. "There's at least one man," he reflected, "who can serve me without being eaten up with envy." For the most part, however, he gave the matter little thought.

"Who is the big man behind all this?" he asked. "Whose idea was it?"

At first the head waiter seemed not to understand the question. Then: "The idea of starting a watering-place here? . . . So far as I know, it was Monsieur Haverkamp himself."

"Who?"

"But you must have heard of Monsieur Haverkamp!"

Intimidated by the head waiter's rather pitying smile, Mareil hurriedly said: "Oh, of course," though in fact that name meant nothing to him, and his attempt to spell it mentally oscillated between Over-Kant and Auvers-Comte.

The head waiter slipped in a reference to one or two villas which were still available.

"A bargain, sir, I assure you. I've heard that the smaller ones have been going at twenty-five thousand, with every convenience. They must have cost a great deal more than that to build, but they're selling them cheap for the sake of the publicity. You'll see what they'll be fetching in two years' time. You ought to look at them, they're quite charming. . . ."

The head waiter left them for a moment while he attended to a neighbouring table. It occurred to Germaine that Mareil had been rather too deeply interested in this matter of the villas.

"You aren't really thinking of buying a villa here? I absolutely forbid it. Don't you see that it's his job to get rid of them? He gets a commission on them."

"I'm not quite a fool! In the first place, I haven't got the money. . . . But I rather like the idea of coming here for a week or two occasionally, in the autumn perhaps, for a rest, or to finish a play. . . . It'd be rather jolly, so conveniently near Paris, too. I could take the cure at the same time. The ridiculous kind of life we all lead plays the devil with my insides."

The head waiter returned. He was full of information, answering Mareil's questions and venturing spontaneously on several observations of his own.

They learned, for instance, that many summer visitors had already experienced the benefits of the Celle waters, had gone home feeling much better than when they came, and had promised to return.

"The medical side of the business is extremely efficient," he told them. "There is a permanent advisory committee, under the presidency of Professor Ducatelet of the Academy of Medicine . . . you probably know him?" (Once again Mareil gave vent to a confident "Oh yes, of course"; and this time the name "Ducatelet" did vaguely stir his memory.) "Nothing is done, no arrangement made, without the consent of these gentlemen. . . . There are two staff doctors attached to the baths—Doctor Camus, who was formerly house-physician at one of the big hospitals, and Doctor Viaur. Then there's another doctor who's set up for himself in private practice at La Celle; I've heard him very well spoken of."

He told them that plans were well advanced for another hotel, to be opened next season. Like the Thermal it would be owned and run by the company.

"If you came by Saint-Cyr," he said, "you must have noticed a large white building, with a smaller one close to it. It's being made over and modernized; work has already begun."

"But won't that compete with you?" Mareil asked.

"I don't think so. At the moment there's nothing in the way of a second-class hotel, suitable for family parties, big enough to take a lot of people, and thoroughly comfortable without being luxurious. Our prices, I admit, are not high. . . . Let me see, now, what are they asking for your room? . . . Twelve francs? . . . Lunch four francs, dinner five. Very reasonable, I think you will agree, for a hotel of this type; still, high enough to keep certain people away. Not that we complain; we cater deliberately for a fashionable clientèle. . . . The new place will make a point of pension prices, from ten francs a day up. It will be called the Residence Hotel or the Hotel du Parc. . . ."

Mareil expressed surprise that buildings of such a size should already exist in a country place.

The head waiter started on a long and intricate explanation in a confidential tone. He seemed vague about the details, but indicated that it had something to do with a Jesuit College which had been bought back by the Dominicans and involved mysterious difficulties within the bosom of the Church. He was careful to add, however, that everything had been satisfactorily settled, and that intending Catholic visitors need have no scruples of conscience. It had even been rumoured that the Bishop of Versailles was to be asked to some sort of opening ceremony, in order to clear the air of all misunderstanding.

Germaine and Mareil finished the evening in the Casino. Mareil, still in the best of tempers, lost twenty francs or so at boule, and insisted on Germaine trying her luck with five or six. She by no means disliked the excitement of gambling, but she hated to lose money and was still smarting from her memory of the sugar transactions in which she had become involved.

"If you lose, so much the better, my sweet," he said; "it'll bring my play luck."

He was not a great gambler, finding more amusement in the atmosphere of the rooms than in the accidents of the game. But he was perfectly willing to throw away a little money at the tables and regarded it almost as a social duty to do so. He was fond, however, of saying, when, for instance, he was talking of Capus: "I simply can't understand why a dramatist should want to gamble. We've no need of that sort of excitement; we get quite enough of it in our job!"

When he got bored with playing, he buried himself in the newspapers, which he hadn't had time to read since the previous evening. He took an absurd interest in the column of miscellaneous news and commented to Germaine on what he read. They did not, however, share the same type of curiosity. What Germaine liked was the occasional thrill of a really full-dress love-crime, while Mareil was drawn rather to any case, no matter how obscure, which he suspected of being odd.

"They're bringing up that case of 142 A again," he said.

"What case of 142 A?"

"You remember: the concierge of 142 A Faubourg Saint-Denis, who disappeared a month or two ago."

"I thought it had happened quite recently."

"They've only been bothering about it quite recently; the actual disappearance dates back to—to February, if I'm not wrong."

"Have they taken all this time to find it out?"

"You know what people are. . . . As a matter of fact, I've got a theory about disappearances of that sort."

But he did not develop his theory. In matters of this kind he was acutely conscious of his public. Germaine was always ready to lend a fond and attentive ear to anything he might have to say, however trivial, but she was not what he called a "good public" for the kind of leisurely theory he wished to elaborate on the subject of disappearances in general.

At nine o'clock next morning Mareil set off with Germaine for Chartres. He had taken his glass of Celle water and was comfortably conscious of its cleansing qualities, which in no way fell short of the claims made for it in the prospectus which he had read the night before (thanks to a bedside lamp), between making love to his companion and going to sleep. The day was windy but pleasant. Their engine, as they climbed the hills, hummed confidently. Now and then a leaf fell on to the hood of the car and stayed there a moment or two before flying away. There was a feeling of autumn and the countryside in the air—silence, a pleasing melancholy, and the promise of joys to come.

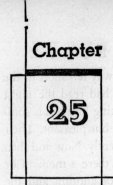
Mionnet did not have his first interview with Mme de Quingey until the beginning of October. It had been found impossible to arrange it by those methods of indirect approach which he loved to employ, and he had been compelled to have recourse, without much enthusiasm on his own part, to the good offices of Canon Desdombs, Director of Public Charities, with whom he had already had several talks about this aspect of diocesan activities. (It would have seemed odd to anyone in Paris that Mionnet, once he was settled at M— and armed with a certain authority, should so entirely have lost interest in the problem to which he owed the beginning of his own good fortune.) Mme de Quingey ran a day nursery for poor children. The Canon arranged that Mionnet should visit this crèche during the month of September, and later, when Mme de Quingey had returned, gave the Abbé's expressed wish to ask her about several details of the work as a reason for bringing them together.

She received him one Tuesday morning, at half past eleven, in the fine old house occupied by herself and her husband, not two hundred yards from the Cathedral and the original Bishop's palace.

She was a tall, thin woman, about forty, and with the figure of a young girl, though rather angular. Her face was long and delicate, with sunken cheeks and protuberant cheek-bones; her fine eyes were black and lively. The Abbé found in her a vague resemblance to the unknown penitent who had accosted him one evening during the winter of 1909 in St. Thomas's Church.

Mme de Quingey wore black and white. She had obviously dressed with greater care than might have been expected at so early an hour and was more elaborately made up than the circumstances of their meeting warranted, more, indeed, than was usual with provincial ladies at that time, and exhaled a strong smell of scent. But there was nothing vulgar in her appearance.

The room, which must have been the great drawing-room of the mansion, was very large, with windows opening on two sides. It was filled with furniture, and the dark, eighteenth-century panelling was almost completely hidden by pictures of various sizes. The dust-sheets which covered the chairs prevented him from getting any general impression, but so far as he could see it was a mixture of fine pieces and the worst possible examples of modern art. The effect of the whole was similar to that produced by most well-to-do houses, giving the visitor an impression not so much of positive bad taste as of a sort of careless eclecticism which gives equal value to all objects above a certain price. It was as though its owners had displayed towards the products of their civilization much the same confident but careless possessiveness as that shown by the rich natives of a colony for anything European.

The conversation came to the point more quickly than Mionnet had expected. Mme de Quingey showed that she was endowed with keen wits, and seemed anxious to show that she was not deceived by the reason he had given for wishing to make her acquaintance.

"Since you are interested in the crèche," she said, "I will put you in touch with a friend of mine, an excellent woman, who is in charge of the organization."

There was no further mention of the crèche.

Mme de Quingey then proceeded to make it clear that though Mionnet's arrival in the town in no way concerned her, she was perfectly well aware of the reasons that had dictated it. Her attitude seemed to him one reason the more for using with her the tactics which he found most successful in dealing with individuals. He let it be seen that he was a man with nothing to conceal, that all he wanted was to confide in his interlocutor. He assumed an air of light-hearted frankness.

"When I agreed to come to M—," he said, "I didn't anticipate anything like the situation I have found. It's terrible! I can see no way out."

He accompanied his words with a sympathetic smile which gave an air of delightful candour to his face.

Mme de Quingey decided that this young priest was altogether charming. She laughed heartily and told him, with a hint of mockery in her tone, that he oughtn't to complain too much about his task, since the rumour went that it would be worth a bishopric to him.

He started.

"But who can possibly have told you that, madame?"

He made as though to protest still more, but contented himself with a laugh, as though to say that so outrageous a suggestion must have been made jokingly.

"No, really," she went on more seriously, "it's common knowledge in M—. People are talking about it all over the diocese. The general view is that you won't be appointed immediately, that you may have to wait two or three years, but that ultimately you're certain to be made bishop."

"Bishop of this diocese? But there's never been any question of such a thing, madame, nor could there be, neither of this bishopric nor of any other. Leaving aside the fact that I could have no claim to such an appointment, the youngest Bishop in France is over forty, and when he was promoted he certainly was not a simple parish priest. . . . I can assure you, madame, that people who talk like that know nothing of the ways of the Church."

"How old are you?"

"Thirty-three, madame."

"Yes, you certainly are very young."

She was at pains to show that she was not one of those who "knew nothing of the ways of the Church."

"They'll find some way of rewarding you. They'll make you a bishop *in partibus,* to keep you from getting impatient. Don't tell me that there aren't any bishops *in partibus* under forty."

The conversation turned once more to the causes of Mionnet's anxiety. She pretended to be surprised at the extent to which he allowed it to prey upon him.

"Do you think it's as serious as all that?"

"It's very serious, madame."

"Aren't you exaggerating a little?"

She hinted that his superiors might have painted the situation blacker than it actually was, in order to ensure his energetic pursuit of a solution. Public opinion in M— was less easily swayed. After all, what was all the bother about? Nothing but rather a cruel accident, which would teach certain proud individuals a salutary lesson. The inclination of the people on the spot would have been to laugh at the whole thing, had not the total of victims been so high. But it was absurd to talk as though it had been disastrous for anybody but a few small tradesmen, and even those who had suffered most could find consolation in the thought that they couldn't be injured with impunity.

He replied that Mme de Quingey's words did not surprise him. They expressed a point of view which he had found to be widespread—unfortunately widespread. No one could call him a pessimist, and, that being so, he felt all the freer to express his opinion that the people of M—, in taking the view they did, were suffering under a grave delusion. The free-thinkers, the Masons, the enemies of the Church—all, in short, who held that it had not been sufficiently brought low, whose one wish was to put an end to the existing truce and recommence an active persecution—would naturally rejoice at what had happened. They, indeed, had reason to triumph in the turn affairs had taken, but for others to do so was a sad sign of frivolity—nay, more, was no less than perverse.

Since he was no longer smiling and spoke in a tone of reasoned concern, Mme de Quingey lost something of her air of assurance. It was still obvious, however, that she regarded Mionnet's anxiety as excessive and as probably due to a certain ignorance of local conditions.

"There is one thing, madame," he said with quiet deliberation, "which I think you have not fully considered. I came here, not from B—, but from Paris. In order to come, I had to cut short my examination work, to interrupt the composition of my lectures for the Catholic Institute, to face the possibility that I might be unable to deliver them. I am in constant communication with the authorities in Paris. Do you really think that with so many serious preoccupations—and Heaven knows they are serious enough, in all conscience—they would have taken so grave a view of what was happening at M— if they had regarded it as of merely local importance?"

Her fine eyes had grown thoughtful.

"What you say worries me," she said.

He continued:

"Please don't think that this attitude of the authorities is in any way dictated by personal motives, by any wish to save the principals in this affair from the consequences of their action. I can assure you —in confidence, of course—that the contrary is the case. If personal questions are involved, it is in a sense quite other than what you imagine. It is not our habit to wash our dirty linen in public. Any action that we may take will be taken when the time seems ripe. We hope that all Catholics, not only fervent Catholics, but those too who are no more than lukewarm, all those who have not deliberately cut themselves adrift from the great family into which they were born —we hope that all such will show confidence in us, and that, pending the final solution of these difficulties, they will do everything they can to help us. . . . They have no idea of the gravity of what has occurred. They regard the whole thing as a joke, as a farce at which they laugh the more because it involves their neighbours. . . . It's really heart-rending!"

He spoke with so solemn, so earnest, an air of conviction that she was speechless.

He saw his advantage and pursued it:

"Do you know where I have found the only genuine understanding of the situation, a realization that what we have to deal with is no laughing matter? I will tell you, madame. I found it among the civil functionaries of the Republic. It is not usual to suspect such men of harbouring any particular tenderness for the Church. Their duty and a concern for their own professional careers impel them rather to tear the prey that is thrown to them. But they have a sense of justice, these men, they are upright and honest, and I take off my hat to them. They realize that the present situation has been produced by imprudence, by ill-directed enthusiasm, possibly by a certain amount of selfishness, but not fundamentally by any calculated villainy. Their training has taught them to take a long view in such matters, to avoid the pettiness of village politics. They find it difficult to understand how sensible people, bred in a long tradition of conduct, conscious of the responsibilities of their position, could deliberately stand by and see a scandal develop, the results of which it is impossible to foresee. They realize that what has happened may be rich in consequences, however distant at the moment those consequences may be, which will inevitably affect all that these people hold most dear: their ideas, their beliefs, their liberties."

He concluded on a colder note:

"That being so, it remains to be seen whether, impelled by a desire to satisfy a private spite, however legitimate, your townsmen will have reason to be proud of their conduct."

Mme de Quingey seemed to have been moved to remorse by his words. She did not wish to appear too deeply cognizant of the situation, nor too ill-informed to play a decisive part in it.

She spoke with an air of timidity. "Have you any idea what can, what ought to be done?"

"Most certainly, madame. I have an idea which could very soon be developed, provided that I was sure of being able to discuss it in confidence, and in a spirit of moral collaboration, with those who are influential in this place and have the means of action in their hands."

"Listen, then . . . I will speak to my husband. He's coming back tomorrow from hunting with some friends. I'm not sure how much he knows, but it can't be difficult for him to find out. . . . I will see what can be done . . . and I will get him to arrange a meeting with you."

Mionnet felt that the moment had come to take his leave. Mme de Quingey, however, began to ask him about himself. Was it true that he had been at the Central Training College, that he had left the University to take Holy Orders, that he had gone straight from atheism into the priesthood?

He replied that he had indeed been at the Training College, and that he had originally intended to become a teacher. He had emerged, he explained, not from aggressive irreligion, but from a period of unbelief.

"How interesting that is!" she exclaimed, slowly turning her fine black eyes upon him.

She tried to find out from him whether some disappointment in love had been responsible for sending him back to religion. Mionnet extricated himself from the question by an embarrassed phrase which he would have found it impossible to repeat two minutes later, a phrase which implied that great sorrows are the means that God sometimes uses to bring men to Him, while leaving it vague how far this admirable maxim was applicable to his own case.

She asked him whether he was happy. He answered that perfect happiness was unattainable by human beings, but that he had certainly recaptured a high degree of tranquillity.

As though in support of this statement, he allowed his countenance to assume once more the expression of good humour which it had worn on his arrival. But a curious eye might have detected now behind the apparent happiness a trace of melancholy which hinted at troubles nobly borne.

She spoke of herself. She said that contact with a new and fervent faith would be of great help to her, since her own, alas, had been sorely tested.

He seemed struck by this confession.

"I, too," she sighed, "have been sadly disillusioned, but in other ways. It may be that I have seen certain things from too near at hand. . . . I know, of course, that one should not confuse an ideal with those who are thought to represent it, and that there *are* situations in life, impossible situations, which demand of those who are placed in them almost supernatural qualities if disappointment is to be avoided, if the pettinesses, the trivialities, of existence are to be prevented from getting the upper hand. . . . It is, perhaps, foolish to indulge in dreams of an unattainable perfection."

She added that if she dared, if she was not afraid to take up time devoted to tasks of infinitely greater importance, she would dearly love to talk occasionally with him.

"I've so often longed to understand myself, but there's nobody here I can talk to, nobody with the least spark of inspiration. To impart the fervour of true faith to another, one must first have it oneself."

Mionnet, while avoiding any appearance of over-anxiety, made it clear that he was at her service. His attitude was that of a doctor of souls for whom the question of his own convenience can never weigh in the balance with the need of his patients and in whose eyes all tasks, where they are concerned, rank as of equal importance.

There was a knock at one of the doors. A butler appeared and announced in a low and deprecating voice that luncheon was served.

Mme de Quingey seemed suddenly embarrassed.

"I would ask you to stay . . ."

He refused with a good grace, saying that he had an engagement elsewhere.

They arranged to meet again the next day, at three o'clock.

"By that time I shall have spoken to my husband about what we were talking of. I'll tell you what he says. And then . . ."—she looked at him with a charming air of entreaty—"perhaps you will be kind enough to interest yourself the tiniest bit in the world in me? I need such interest; indeed I do."

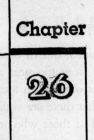
Thus it was that Mionnet suddenly found himself an intimate of the de Quingey household, and its most welcome visitor.

Between the 5th and the 15th of October he had no less than three "spiritual" interviews with Madame and two business conversations with her husband, nor could he avoid accepting one of the three or four invitations to luncheon which the mistress of the house extended to him during that period.

The situation was not without its difficulties. Some of them came from outside. Mionnet made no attempt to hide from Delhostal—who had plenty of other means of finding out for himself—the fact that he had been introduced to the family. But he was not at all anxious that the Canon should be kept informed from day to day of the progress of his manœuvres in that quarter. He had, therefore, to set Delhostal's curiosity at rest and to find plausible reasons to explain why it was that he came late, and sometimes did not come at all, to the midday meal at the Pension Roubier.

In general it was important to prevent the good people of M— from saying, laughingly, as would have been perfectly natural in the circumstances, that the young priest from Paris was Mme de Quingey's new favourite, and that as a preliminary to succeeding Monsignor Sérasquier in the palace he had first supplanted him in a more private capacity.

But it was by no means easy to avoid that particular danger. He could be cautious about how he went to or returned from the de Quingeys', about his use of certain streets, and his entrance at, and emergence from, the door of their house, but he could not prevent the servants from knowing that he was a frequent visitor, or that their mistress was often closeted alone with him. He had no authority to stop them from talking. Apart from these obvious drawbacks—the chief of which was to place him in a farcical situation—such gossip was not without its pleasant side. It flattered his self-conceit, and it gave an agreeable, an almost superstitious, support to the prevailing rumours about his coming advancement. Moreover, it gave those people who doubted his power to act something to think about. But Mionnet was perfectly well aware that these advantages, frail and evanescent in themselves, could be maintained only on two conditions: the gossip must have no foundation in actuality, and those who purveyed it must be left in an agreeable condition of uncertainty. In other words, it was necessary to give the bare minimum of support to appearances, and so to arrange the reality that he would always be in the position to say to an inquisitive superior: "It was all nonsense. Make as many inquiries as you like. It's easy enough to see why people were misled, but, as a matter of fact, they none of them really believed it. Ask them. It was too good a joke to miss, and, to tell the truth, it didn't need much ingenuity to invent it."

Mionnet was not so simple as to think that mere innocence is enough to refute a charge, nor that guilt can ever remain undetected. His point of view was that innocence is a trump card, and that one would be a fool to throw it away except in return for very tangible advantages. And he saw no chance of those until the new dispensation should be an established fact.

But there were difficulties of equal complexity within the situation itself. The most delicate of them was the necessity of keeping his spiritual interviews at the necessary level and degree of warmth. Mme de Quingey was an impulsive lady, an easy prey to self-pity, and apt to let her thoughts run away with her. Without attributing any equivocal intentions to her, he found it necessary to be on his guard against sudden, effusive passages of intimacy and to discount her rather excessive, if rather delightful, consciousness of an audience. Once having agreed in theory to these interviews, he was perforce obliged to accept with resignation the consequences which they involved. But his watchfulness could never be relaxed for a moment. It was essential that he maintain the necessary degree of aloofness without adopting an attitude of coldness which would have put an end to the intimacy. The happy mean, he found, lay in being able to display a sort of impersonal warmth. In other words, what he had to do was to show himself sympathetic to his hostess without involving himself in the process—to achieve, as it were, an abstraction of his individual presence, of that presence which a sensitive creature like Mme de Quingey asked no better than to overwhelm with attentions which might have been misunderstood by an outsider.

The problem of her husband was entirely different, and mainly consisted, for Mionnet, in avoiding saying too many foolish things when they discussed business about the details of which he was ignorant, and in not compromising the success already attained by foolishly counting his chickens before they were hatched. There was always a risk that he might unknowingly touch sore places or rouse his new friend to opposition and hostility. His "social map" of the district was not yet complete enough to give him entire freedom of movement. In what relation, for example, did M. de Quingey stand to Firmin Gambaroux or to the Sermaize Bank?

He set himself, therefore, to feel his way with caution, hinting this, suggesting that. He would mention some name in a colourless tone and watch the result, careful to note the slightest shade of the other's reaction to it.

The results of this method were satisfactory. After their second interview M. de Quingey admitted the necessity of finding locally the capital necessary to set the tramway company on its feet, of so arranging matters that the original stockholders would not feel themselves too hardly treated—above all, of dealing lightly with the small investors. He saw the wisdom of letting the stock-breeder and his friends in on the new concern, though only to a limited extent, and so discounting their hostility which might otherwise have led to dangerous complications.

PROVINCIAL INTERLUDE

Mionnet was left in no doubt as to the extent to which he was helped in his handling of this delicate situation by the spiritual bonds which existed between him and the lady of the house.

Chapter

27

ÉMILIENNE

During these same days of early autumn Mionnet found himself confronted by another problem, of a pleasanter nature, which, so far from adding to his anxieties, came as a welcome diversion.

He had been aware for some time past of the attitude towards him of Mlle Émilienne Roubier, without, at first, attaching any particular importance to it. The young woman was always running across him at odd moments, and at such times engaged him in conversation on perfectly innocent subjects, which she seemed loth to leave. She had a way, too, of coming into his room or of being discovered there when he arrived, for the purpose of seeing to some small detail of his comfort, such as providing fresh towels, cleaning the windows, or mending a torn chair-cover.

This behaviour of hers could, as a matter of fact, be explained in a perfectly normal way. Mlle Émilienne regarded herself as responsible for the house. The number of guests thus dependent upon her was small; in fact, at the moment, Mionnet was the sole inhabitant of the annexe. There was no reason why, just because she was a conscientious housewife, she should not also be gay and talkative. It was natural that she should prefer the conversation of a young ecclesiastic of good education and polite manners to that of the servants, or even to that of some other coarse or ill-tempered lodger who might have taken advantage of the opportunity to treat her with unpleasing familiarity.

It became evident, however, that this companionship between them was becoming less and less restrained and had about it a certain provocative quality. Although she was always careful to address him as

"Monsieur l'Abbé," in her fresh young voice, which seemed to disdain the use of unnecessary words, she never appeared to be conscious of the fact that he was a priest. One day at the end of September she appeared in a pretty new dress of beige and brown woollen. Standing directly in front of him, she said:

"What do you think of my dress? Do you like it? . . . I suppose it would look pretty silly in Paris?"

Mionnet being a Parisian, it was natural that the young woman, when it came to questions of fashion, should set greater store by his opinion as a man of the capital than by the dignity of his office.

The conversation then took a lighter turn. She had more than once asked him to say if any little thing was wrong, and he now availed himself of this permission to remark that the two enlarged photographs which hung in his sitting-room were less attractive to him than they might be to others, owing to the fact that he had never met the originals. He added that though he felt no active dislike for the views of Fontainebleau painted on sections of tree-trunk, he did not find them particularly pleasant.

"All right," she replied, "I'll try to find something else for you."

Two or three days later he heard a knock at the door. Mlle Émilienne appeared with her arms full of picture-frames. Despite the serious expression of her face, she was obviously struggling with suppressed laughter.

"I've brought you more than you need so that you can choose."

There were four large pictures and five or six smaller ones. She propped them up along the walls and against the furniture for him to study at his leisure.

"First of all, you must have two big ones in place of the portraits. They ought, I think, to be companion pieces. These two go very well together, or these. It's all a matter of taste."

"These two" were a "Sacred Heart of Jesus" and a "Madonna," both of the worst possible type of religious chromos and done in revolting colours.

"Or these" were perfectly ordinary lithographs, though not too bad of their kind. Each represented a woman's head, one a brunette, the other a blonde. They were pretty enough in themselves, and in each case the picture included a section of fine neck and bosom which was not so much clothed as draped in a sort of vaporous material. In both the pink tip of one breast waged a winning battle with the folds of muslin which enfolded it. The artist, however, had taken great care to treat this detail rather differently and in accordance with the complexion of his sitter.

The smaller pictures offered much the same alternative. The choice lay between a "Saint Joseph" and a "Good Shepherd" on the one hand and a variety of charming female models, each of whom presented certain portions of their charming anatomy to the eye.

There was nothing indecent about the pictures, nothing that the taste of the times might not quite legitimately admit.

Mlle Émilienne waited discreetly, with but the flicker of a smile.

Mionnet was fully conscious of all that the situation implied. For a moment or two he said nothing. Finally, with some little hesitation, he said in a tone of half-involuntary, half-calculated playfulness:

"I suppose you haven't got a portrait of yourself?"

For the moment she was nonplussed; then she burst out laughing.

"Would you really hang it up?"

"Why not?"

"I haven't got one as big as that, nor, fortunately, in that kind of dress. Besides, if I gave you one, it would only account for a single nail. You've still got to choose something for the others."

"Must all the nails have pictures?"

She laughed again.

"If I ever did give you a portrait of myself," she said, and it was difficult to be sure how serious she was, "I certainly hope that you wouldn't hang it up on the wall!"

The result of the discussion was that the family portraits remained where they were. But the views of Fontainebleau painted on sections of tree-trunk disappeared, and nothing was hung in their place.

In the intervals between these meetings and these playful talks Mionnet thought a good deal. What was this young woman after? Since the Canon's first vague allusions, he had found out nothing definite either about her or about her sister, Clotilde. Delhostal had avoided giving a direct answer to one or two questions, and Mionnet had not pressed the point. He had tried to get Émilienne to talk about the Canon. He could feel that she disliked him, perhaps even had a grudge against him; but he could get her to give no reason for her attitude. He formed the hypothesis that Émilienne or her sister, perhaps both, had been the objects of the Canon's unwelcome advances. Having repulsed him for reasons of their own, they might have suffered a certain amount of persecution, or at least annoyance, at his hands. During one of his talks with Émilienne, Mionnet hinted at something of the sort and gave her an opportunity to explain. But she did not respond. She could be sharp enough in her chatter about trivialities, but she never discussed people and never told him anything that he really wanted to know about herself. If he tried to force her confidence, she pretended not to understand. In the same way she avoided speaking of her sister except in the most superficial terms. "Whatever else she is," Mionnet reflected, "she's not a gossip. She's a clever little thing who avoids complications and is careful of secrets." She would not, he thought, involve him in the sort of indiscretions which, serious enough in any case for a man of his cloth, would be no less than disastrous in his present situation.

"It remains to be seen what it is she's after and why." Mionnet was not sufficiently fatuous to believe that she was the victim of an irresistible passion, nor could he see what benefit she could derive from leading him on. "She must know perfectly well that I'm paid next to nothing, and it must be obvious from my appearance and my way of life that I've got no private means."

But, like many men with an active temperament, Mionnet was willing to admit ignorance about the people he had to deal with, so long as ignorance involved no practical disadvantages. He went to great pains to discover in others the qualities of which he could make use or against which he should be on his guard. But beyond that he wasted no time in attempting to elucidate psychological subtleties for the mere pleasure of the game. And for that very reason he was readier than most to admit the existence of such subtleties. That individuals, especially women, were mysterious, that their feelings and their motives might be obscure, he regarded as a commonplace of human experience.

He was careful, therefore, to examine the possible reasons for Émilienne's behaviour with an eye to those that might conceal dangers for himself. "It would be wise to assume," he thought, "that she is the instrument of people who want to put a spoke in my wheel. If that is so, their object must be to lead me to commit some foolishness or other, so that at a given moment they can provoke a scandal which would make me a laughing-stock and discredit my authority."

He went over in his mind the possible conspirators. Could it be the Bishop? No, that was out of the question, for the Bishop did not even know of Émilienne's existence (he had taken the trouble to find that out). "Besides, he could only act through some go-between, and most of the people round him are unreliable even if they are not actually his enemies. The Vicar-General? That's certainly more likely." This fancy of a plot, of secret meetings between the protonotary apostolic and Mlle Roubier, was all rather like a cheap novelette, still . . .

One day Mionnet said straight out to Émilienne:

"The Vicar-General has been talking to me about you." The "What Vicar-General?" with which she replied was so transparently sincere that his suspicions were laid to rest.

What about the Quingey set, then? Mionnet had already played vaguely with the idea, absurd though it seemed. What little probability it might have had quickly vanished when he became intimate with the family. Had his hypothesis been true, then the period of his intimacy with both wife and husband and the effusiveness of their tone towards him should have coincided with a change in Émilienne's attitude, since the need for her manœuvres would then have ceased.

On the contrary, she had never been more forthcoming.

There remained Delhostal, who was deceitful by nature and skilled in the more subtle ways of injuring his neighbours. The idea was worth examining. True, it presupposed a very carefully arranged piece of play-acting, for it meant the assumption by the Canon of an attitude of aggressive hostility to the young woman and, on her part, the manifestation of an antipathy no less definite if not so obviously marked. It involved, as a matter of fact, even more than that. When it happened that Émilienne served them herself, she always, despite the natural reserve of her manners, showed herself far more agreeable, more smilingly good-humoured, towards Mionnet than towards Delhostal. Now, if the theory of a prearranged plan was to hold water, the Canon should have backed up Mlle Roubier either by affecting not to notice her attitude or by drawing his companion's attention to it and making it the excuse for playful badinage. In fact Delhostal did neither of these things, but made it perfectly clear that he secretly resented her discrimination in the other's favour. This reaction of his might, of course, be a crowning stroke of Machiavellian genius, but Mionnet held to the belief commonly entertained by men of action, that it is never wise to credit your adversary with too great a degree of subtlety. He believed, with them, that in dealing with men, whether as colleagues or as enemies, it is safer to assume that they are much like other folk, and that their power of injury is strictly limited. Armed with such an axiom, a man may sometimes find himself mistaken, but in general it holds true.

"The truth," he concluded, "is probably far simpler. The natural explanation is that she is a young person who likes men, enjoys a sense of mystery, and finds the unusual circumstances rather exciting. It may well be, too, that she has rather a vicious temperament. She finds me not altogether repellent, and the idea of an intrigue with me amuses her, while being obviously free of the fear of embarrassing consequences. Her behaviour only confirms what Delhostal once said to me about the general attitude of a good many women towards priests."

The only other thing to consider was his own feeling in the matter. He held in general that desire led to foolishness and blunders; that it impaired a man's keenness of vision and limited his freedom of action. In his own particular case there was the added conviction that nothing would suit him less than an intrigue entered into at M—. But he drew a careful distinction between desire and the mere satisfaction of appetite. Desire is a fever which definitely puts its victim in a position of inferiority. The satisfaction of appetite, on the other hand, is a perfectly simple operation which fortifies the spirit against profounder disturbances and the assaults of more serious temptations.

He had no idea how long or how troublesome his stay at M— might be, and the prospect of relaxation with so charming a young woman as Émilienne, pursued in the close and pleasant intimacy of the annexe and protected to an unusual degree by the natural atmosphere of secrecy which obtains in provincial towns, was by no means to be lightly set aside.

He even persuaded himself that to yield would, in the circumstances, be wise. It would be foolish to underestimate the danger represented by Mme de Quingey. Stronger men than Mionnet had been caught in the trap of "spiritual talks." Irony is no weapon against such threats. The wretched victim may start by treating the whole thing as a joke, but one fine day he suddenly discovers that it is no laughing matter, and that the woman of forty with the tormented eyes has got him on the end of a string. Not that it would be wise to break too abruptly with Mme de Quingey. The game that Mionnet had been forced to play in the course of his duties at M— might, sooner or later, make it imperative that he should yield to the lady's advances, if these became too urgent or took the form of an ultimatum. But if he found himself faced by the necessity of making some such decision, it was important that he should do so with a mind at ease and with the sense of complete liberty of action, and this would be difficult to ensure in the case of a young man weakened by a long period of abstinence and confronted by an experienced and seductive woman.

Besides, he was more than usually troubled by the sharp pangs of continence. It may be that the rich food of the pension was to blame, the length and regularity of his periods of sleep, the atmosphere of peace and material comfort that weighed upon this country town, or the air, which, in the language of the Directory, was so "pure and exhilarating." Whatever the cause, he had never found it so hard to obey the demands of his professional chastity, nor so little worth while.

One consideration, however, made him pause. He had not forgotten the hint dropped by Delhostal, the sort of half-formulated offer, which he had made shortly after their first meeting.

He had often thought of it since. He had imagined that the subject would recur automatically in the course of their many talks. Perhaps certain words let fall by the Canon had indeed referred to it, but the connexion had not been obvious, and Mionnet had been careful to avoid giving the idea that he had fully understood the suggestion from the first, or that his curiosity was still unsatisfied.

Still, so long as this little mystery remained a mystery, he maintained an attitude of caution in regard to Émilienne. Unlikely though the event might be, he didn't want to discover when it was too late that if only he had exercised a little patience, he might have found, tucked away in this provincial town, an opportunity of even greater secrecy than that offered by the Roubier annexe, and ladies (though Heaven knew where) more discreet, though not more charming, than his landlady's daughter. True, this meant putting himself at Delhostal's mercy; but, after all, the Canon was as dependent on him as he was on the Canon. For all his love of talebearing, it was unlikely that the latter would disclose a secret in which he was himself involved. If he decided to let Mionnet into it, the most that could be supposed was that he was thus anticipating the possibility that the young Paris priest might, in the course of his inquiries, find it out for himself.

28

THE LITTLE CONVENT
IN THE UPPER TOWN

It so happened that one day in the third week of October, while they were seated at luncheon, Delhostal said to him, without any preamble:

"Shall you be free this afternoon between four and six?"

"Yes."

"Well, then, if you like, I'll take you to see the Sisters of the Sacred Heart in the upper town. The Superior is expecting us. She will be delighted to make your acquaintance. I've often spoken about you. I'm hoping that they'll give us a little music."

The Abbé accepted, and they talked of other things.

But though he appeared to be paying attention to what his friend was saying, and managed to answer his questions naturally, Mionnet was conscious, from now on, of a curious sensation of intoxication. There was a sort of buzzing in his head, and he was aware of a curious mental tension. He saw everything about him brightly illuminated, but at a distance. He spoke with pleasure, but gave no thought to what he was saying. He felt exalted, but at the same time indifferent. His condition resembled that of a man with a fixed idea, but the idea remained vague. He had the sensation of being driven on inexorably to some imminent state, to the performance of certain actions in the immediate future which would be entirely independent of his personal volition or of the determination of circumstances. Not that he wasn't surprised by what he felt, for it was something that he had never before experienced. He was perfectly well aware that the intoxicating anticipation of which he was the prey, the irresistible lure of the future, had very little justification in fact and corresponded to nothing that reason could tell him. He was still sufficiently clear-headed to say to himself: "What on earth am I thinking about? I must be mad!" But no previous state of mind had ever been so utterly delightful. Never had he looked forward to a day with so acute a sense of the interest it was to hold.

The Canon came to fetch him at 4.10. Mionnet had more than once walked through the streets they now took, but always in the opposite direction. Very soon they came to the steep, narrow ways that led to the upper town.

He had often felt embarrassed by his clerical garments during his walks at M—, and not seldom even in earlier days, but now the thought of them gave him an odd and secret pleasure. The meditation to which this consciousness was prelude somehow identified itself with the sense of intoxication which for the last few hours had dominated his being. In a curious, oblique way, which only the very simple would have found a cause of scandal, his very real love of his Church was reinforced and strengthened by the ideas that now thronged his brain. A voice murmured deep within him: "Marvellous Church to be so entirely self-sufficient, to be capable of absorbing so completely all the inevitable contradictions of her being. Only believe in her wonderful, her multiple life, and every question will be answered, every trouble soothed. She is the enemy of all violence, of everything that is extemporary, eccentric, or experimental. She is a ripe fruit filled with a thousand blended juices which balance one another with exactitude, stimulate one another with a fine zest, come to a mutual reinforcement, or, on occasion, cancel out to a sure and final flavour. It is not surprising that fools find it hard to understand her. But two courses are open to them: to hate her or to obey, and whichever they do, they do blindly."

They crossed the square by the fountain and passed the blind alley at the end of which the towers of the Cathedral could be seen in the afternoon haze. A little farther on they turned right, into a street where Mionnet had never been. In the first part of its length this street ran roughly parallel to the blind alley and led, like it, towards the escarpment of the plateau, but soon it took a left-hand turn, and continued, like many others in this part of the town, between walls that showed above their tops the thick greenery of trees.

"Here we are," said the Canon.

They stopped before a door of a single panel's width, which was painted a faded blue, pierced by a peep-hole in its middle, and raised by a single step above the level of the pavement. Over the wall, and close at hand among the trees, could be seen the red roof of a small building which was seemingly the porter's lodge.

Delhostal tugged twice at the bell-pull, and an answering tinkle came clearly through the silence from the other side of the door.

They waited for what seemed a long time.

"Won't you ring again?" asked Mionnet.

"No . . . they're always a long time coming. . . . Hark! I can hear footsteps on the gravel."

The shutter of the peep-hole was slid aside, and a moment later the door itself was half-opened.

The woman thus revealed was dumpy, getting on in years, and dressed in lay costume. She greeted the Canon, stared at the Abbé, said something quickly, let them both in, and carefully closed the door behind them.

To their right was the little lodge, and facing them, about thirty feet away, at the end of a gravel path, a biggish white house of two storeys with a mansard roof. All round it stretched the garden, which had been allowed to run wild and seemed to be of considerable extent.

The woman asked them to wait. The sun shone pleasantly. She left them, patting her apron as though to straighten out the folds.

She had spoken with apparent difficulty and with a foreign accent. "A German, or perhaps from Luxembourg," Mionnet thought to himself.

The garden contained a great number of full-grown trees and a quantity of shrubs. Paths led in all directions. There were several narrow strips of lawn and a few flower-beds. The grass was uncut. The general effect was one of neglect, which was not without its charm. It had an air of complete privacy, of being entirely cut off from the outer world.

"They don't keep a regular gardener," Delhostal said. "There's an old man who comes three times a week. . . . It's not badly looked after, on the whole."

The main building dated from the middle of the nineteenth century and was graceful in a rather heavy classic style. It represented the good middle-class taste of its period, untouched by that later exotic suburbanism, born of universal travel and world fairs, which was to penetrate even into the depths of the countryside.

"Are they always so ceremonious with you?" Mionnet asked. "Didn't that woman know who you were?"

"Oh, yes. . . . As a rule I go straight in. . . . It's probably because she saw I'd got somebody with me. You mustn't mind," he added. . . . "They've got used to being a bit over-cautious."

The woman returned with a message that they were expected.

They were shown into a ground-floor room to the right of the entry. It was small and seemed a cross between an unpretentious middle-class drawing-room and the parlour of a convent. Objects of piety stood cheek by jowl with two small tables, a desk, and several chairs.

The door at its far end opened almost at once, and two women came in, wearing the black habits, white cowls, and white crosses of the Sacred Heart. Mionnet was not sufficiently familiar with the uniform to decide whether all the details were in order, but it seemed to him that the two women certainly made as much of it as possible. If they did not actually violate the rule in the matter of cut and material, they wore their clothes with a great deal of taste. He was reminded of his military service with the Chasseurs Alpins, and how certain of his more elegant friends, when they went on leave, had sported "fancy" tunics and breeches at considerable risk to themselves.

One of the two was the Superior; the other was not introduced.
They were about the same age, though it was difficult to determine
precisely what that was. At a rough guess Mionnet would have
placed it somewhere between youth and maturity. Both were fresh-
complexioned, but, of the two, the Superior was the better-looking.
She had become slightly coarsened, but still showed traces of what
must once have been great beauty. The oval of her face, her nose, her
eyes, and the curve of her lips all bore witness to a naturally proud
temperament. She smiled readily and with an air of great breeding,
though it was hard to be sure whether what inspired her was a feeling of kindliness or a faintly malicious humour. Her companion's
face was harder, and she was obviously more curious about their new
visitor. She spoke very little. At first the conversation was restricted
to harmless trivialities. They commented on the weather; on the
white frosts there had been the last few mornings; of the grapes at
the end of the garden which they hadn't picked yet because the gardener had told them not to, with the result that a good many had
been spoiled; of the gardener himself, who was a handful, and spent
most of his working hours smoking his pipe in secluded corners.
Occasional allusions to matters connected with the establishment
meant nothing to Mionnet. Besides, he was listening with only half
his attention, since he was more curious to see how the interview
would develop than to notice how it began.

The Superior spoke and behaved like a woman of the world. Her
conversation was intelligent, and the gaiety and brightness of her
tone might have seemed exceptional to anyone who knew less of the
atmosphere ruling in convents than did Mionnet. What struck him
as unique about her was the way in which she dealt with the flattest
of subjects without any trace of silliness, and he noticed particularly
that this was as true of the expression of her face as of her tone.

She seemed finally to take a sudden interest in Mionnet and asked
him several questions. Did he mean to stay long at M—? Did he like
the climate? Had he found the people welcoming or stand-offish?

He got the impression that the questions themselves were of little importance, and that the Superior, like her companion of the watchful eyes, was using them merely as an excuse to hear the newcomer speak and so to make up her mind about him.

Twenty minutes or so were passed in this way. Then, with disconcerting suddenness, the Superior seemed to consider that it was time to bring the interview to an end. They all got up. The Canon, after a moment's hesitation, and speaking in what appeared to Mionnet to be rather a shy tone, asked whether there was any chance of their being able to hear some music. The Abbé, he added, was very fond of it. The Superior said no—politely, but so definitely that there was clearly nothing to be gained by insisting.

The two priests were about to take their leave when, after listening to some whispered comment of her companion's, she said to Delhostal:

"If you think that Monsieur l'Abbé could find his way back alone, I should like a few words with you. I've had an answer from M—" (Mionnet only half-heard the name she mentioned; it sounded Flemish) "and I should like to show it to you. That affair is not going at all well."

She had spoken with a worried air which seemed genuine enough. Mionnet assured her that he could find his way and took his leave.

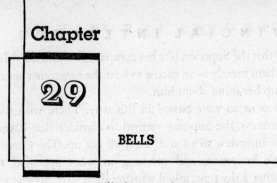

Chapter

29

BELLS

All the way home he kept repeating to himself: "What did you expect? If *that's* the result of prolonged abstinence, you're in a bad way."

When he considered that the whole of this phantasy had sprung from some word let drop by the Canon in July, misinterpreted from the start and ridiculously embroidered in retrospect, he called himself every sort of a fool. His mistake reminded him of the classic stories of his youth, such as the one which ends: "Must they *both* be killed?"

Now that his thoughts had taken a literary turn, he began to quote to himself some verse from La Fontaine's "Heron." Considering how long he had neglected, or seemed to neglect, the delicious opportunities awaiting him at the Pension Roubier, fate, on the whole, had dealt lightly with him.

When he got back to his rooms he found that the shutters had been closed and the curtains drawn. By the light of the lamp he noticed another of Émilienne's playful little attentions.

This time it took the form of a vase of flowers. A few days earlier he had mentioned to the young woman that the little vase that stood on the table in his sitting-room and was filled from time to time with cut flowers was rather too ornate for his taste. He had got tired, he said, of seeing it there, and would rather have anything else, even an ordinary tumbler.

He now saw that the vase had been replaced by an enormous jug of shiny earthenware, stuffed with flowers. The side opposite the handle was adorned with the head of a Zouave, fat-faced and heavily bearded, while the rest of the surface was a mass of turgid lumps and excrescences. The girl must have gone to considerable trouble to find so appalling an object.

He opened the door, took a few steps down the corridor, and called in a low voice:

"Mademoiselle Émilienne!"

She appeared almost at once, as trim and elegant as ever.

"Come here a moment," he said with an assumption of sternness. He made her precede him into the room and closed the door.

The face she turned to him wore a mingled look of mockery and contrition.

"Why, what's the matter?" she said, and repeated the inquiry.

He pointed to the Zouave with its festooned crown of flowers.

"Oh, don't you like it?"

She played her part so well that Mionnet had much ado not to burst out laughing. She, too, was biting her lips.

"Now, listen," he said, giving her a meaning look; "tomorrow I shall probably go for a walk as I did today, but I shall come back rather earlier . . . about half past four . . . before it gets dark. If I find that pot still there—"

He paused.

"What will you do?" she asked with an innocent air.

"I shall call you, just as I did this evening, and then— Well, you'll see. . . . If I punish you, you'll only have yourself to thank."

The next day he timed his walk very precisely, taking his watch from his girdle more than once.

Exactly at half past four he climbed the stairs of the annexe. In spite of himself he felt excited, and was acutely conscious of the smell of beeswax and clean linen. It was already dusk and very quiet.

He entered his sitting-room, which, although he was considerably earlier than he had been on the day previous, was quite dark. The shutters had been closed and the curtains drawn.

He struck a light. Before ever seeing the lamp which also stood upon the table, he was aware of the Zouave with his tuft of flowers.

He lit the lamp, but his hand was trembling to such an extent that he found considerable difficulty in replacing the chimney.

He stood for a moment or two plunged in thought, listening to the silence. Then he took off his shoes and, after removing his cassock, put on a sort of smoking-jacket made without lapels, like the tunic of a Chasseur Alpin, which he often wore in the cold weather when he was alone, and a pair of black leather slippers.

Then he went out again and called softly, on a rising inflexion: "Mademoiselle Émilienne!" in such a way that "Émilienne" sounded as though he had spoken it without a prefix.

The door at the end of the corridor opened at once, and the young woman appeared, dressed in one of her light summer frocks. She was smiling, but she looked frightened and apprehensive.

He made her enter in front of him as he had done the previous day, and turned the key in the lock. He pointed to the fat-faced Zouave where it stood in its place near the lamp.

"So that's it!" he said; "so that's it!"

He took her in his arms, pressing her to him, kissing her face, her lips, finally her lips only. There was a look of rapture in her eyes, but, mixed with it a glimmer of mockery, of reproach that he had kept her waiting so long.

A little later they were in the other room. The lamp, shedding its discreet circle of light, was with them there. The flame shining through the red squares in its shade upon the china of the wash-stand gave it the appearance of a brazier of live coal. Over the roofs of the town the bells rang out, rang out, and went on ringing. There was comfort in the clangour and friendliness. They sounded close, as though they were chiming there within the room, seeing everything, seeing nothing, understanding all, oblivious of all. They were more silent than the silence, more secret than the fields, and such a wealth of purity was in the sound that it seemed to overflow from their high clashing, and drop, second by second, upon the sweet disorder of the bed.

M. de Saint-Papoul, candidate in the second parliamentary district of Bergerac, runs for office. Meeting and schemes of his committee. The election agent Crivelli. Jerphanion is sent for, to draw up speeches and posters on the spot. Jerphanion sends Jallez his impressions of the campaign. Jallez's reply. The Marquis is elected on the second ballot. He entertains his leading supporters at his château. In the morning he takes a horseback ride through the woods of his estate and the neighbourhood. His reflections. The life of country gentlemen.

Laulerque goes on a secret mission to Amsterdam. His meeting with Margaret-Désideria.—Mionnet is summoned to two interviews with Monsignor Lebaigue. Affairs in the diocese of M—. The tramway business. The scandal to be avoided. Mionnet is asked to take an important and delicate part, and accepts.—He sets down a rather odd confession that has been made to him.—He arrives at M—, is met by Bouère, and taken to Mme Roubier's pension; he has lunch with Canon Delhostal. The Canon's disclosures. Mionnet pays his respects to Monsignor Sérasquier. The character of the Bishop.

Paris in July. Increasing heat. Mornings. Storms. Evenings. The holiday of the 14th. Sampeyre's walk. Departures. Germaine's confidences during the fireworks. She has become Mareil's mistress. At the end of July, Jallez and Jerphanion in a skiff.

Stragelius writes to his sister. His melancholy. His thoughts on old age, on success. Hidden greatness. Family cares.

Mionnet tries to unravel the tramway business. More interviews with the Bishop. Various steps taken. The Vicar-General, the lawyer, the banker, the deputy.—Firmin Gambaroux in the market-place at Camboriges. The life of farmers. The cares and pleasures of Gambaroux. Intoxicated well-being. Mionnet introduces himself to him. The cart-ride; Mionnet goes away with his first success. On the other hand, he does not succeed in meeting the de Quingeys and has to remain patient. Appearance of Émilienne and Clothilde Roubier. Delhostal's attitude. He talks about the little convent in the upper town.—Mionnet spends his spare time on walks filled with a feeling for places which is peculiar to him. Émilienne's solicitude.

Jerphanion, invited to Saint-Papoul's château for Jeanne's marriage, sends Jallez an account of his visit. Life at the château. The guests. Arrangements for the wedding.—He writes to Mathilde Cazalis.—Jeanne's wedding night verifies an idea she had received as a young girl.

After a rehearsal of his play Mareil and Germaine leave for a trip in his car; they stop at Celle-les-Eaux. Mareil's enthusiasm for the new resort. The Thermal Palace, the Casino. The papers talk of the disappearance of a concierge in Paris.

Mionnet finally gets an interview with Mme de Quingey. The looks and manners of this lady. Mionnet points out to her the duty of Catholics in the imminent scandal. Mme de Quingey confides to him her spiritual uneasiness.—Mionnet carries on successfully talks on business with M. de Quingey and on spiritual matters with his wife.—Mionnet is intrigued by Émilienne's attitude towards him. The hypotheses he considers. The nature of his scruples. Canon Delhostal invites Mionnet to pay a call with him on the little convent. Mionnet's strange reverie in anticipation. Their reception. Mionnet returns alone and mistaken. Émilienne's teasing. Mionnet decides to give it a friendly approbation, which seems to fulfil Émilienne's hopes. Provincial bells.

INDEX OF CHARACTERS
Note regarding the use of this INDEX

This Index will figure at the end of every volume, and will be extended as necessary.

Large roman numerals refer to the Book.

Small roman numerals refer to the chapter.

Arabic numerals refer to the page.

If there is *no page reference,* this means that the character takes part in the *whole* of the chapter indicated.

When a chapter or a page is given *in brackets,* this means that the character is involved, but does not take part personally in the action.

EXAMPLES

I, x. Refer to Chapter x, Book I, where the character plays an important role.

I, xviii, 149. Refer to page 149, Book I (Chapter xviii), where the character appears only incidentally.

II, (xi). Refer to Chapter xi, Book II; a chapter which, as a whole, involves the character, though he is not personally present.

II, xv, (391). As above; the character is involved only on page 391.

In the case of important events the reference is preceded by a brief summary of the event.

Proper names extraneous to the action, and intended to remain so, are not included in the Index.

INDEX OF CHARACTERS

INDEX OF CHARACTERS

INDEX OF CHARACTERS

Receives an anonymous letter, VII, xx.—VII, xxi, (173).—Has a scene with his wife, VII, xxii. —Goes to see Jallez and is received by Jerphanion, VII, xxviii.—VII, (xxix).—VIII, ii, (321).—VIII, iii, (322).

FARMERS, their life, tastes, and habits, VIII, xiv.—VIII, xv.

FOREST-RANGER OF THE FORÊT D'OTHE, THE, (xx).—V, xxiii, (181, 184–7), 187.

FOREST-RANGER, WIFE OF THE, V, (xx).—V, xxiii, 187.

FORT, PAUL, IV, xx.—At the Closerie on Christmas Eve, IV, xxii.—VIII, xii, (429).

FREEMASONRY, IV, x.—V, xxiv, (199).—VII, ii.—VII, vi, (43). —VII, vii, (46–7, 57).—Rothweil's, VII, xviii.—VII, xxiii, (182).—Discussed by Jerphanion and Laulerque, VII, xxvi, (196–8, 200–1).—As Ardansseaux sees it, VII, xxvii.—As Lengnau sees it, VII, xxxi.— Clanricard's first impressions, VII, xxxiii, (297–8).—VIII, i, (311).—VIII, xxv, (533).

FRIEND OF GERMAINE BAADER, VIII, xi, 413–21.

FRUITERER IN THE RUE DAILLOUD, THE, I, xii.—II, vii.

GAMBAROUX, FIRMIN, VIII, vii, (365).—VIII, xiii, (443, 445–6, 453–4, 456).—Among his friends, VIII, xiv.—His thoughts and preoccupations, VIII, xv.—His

first meeting with Mionnet, VIII, xvi.—Their drive together, VIII, xvii.—VIII, xviii, (479, 480).—VIII, xxvi, (540).

GAMBAROUX, MADAME, VIII, xiv, (459).—VIII, xv, (467, 469).

GENILLÉ, BARON DE, III, x, (115). —III, (xiii).—III, (xv).—III, xviii, (201).—V, xx, (139).— VI, iii, (307).

GENILLÉ, BARONNE DE, III, x, (115).—III, xiii.—III, xiv.— Talks about conjugal beds, III, xv.—VI, xxxi, (528).

GENTILCŒUR, MADAME, V, xxvii, (251).

GENTILCŒUR, and the "perfect life," VII, (xiv).—VII, xv, (115).

GIORDANO, VIII, (i).—VIII, iv, (324).

GIRARD, VIII, xiii, 448–50.—VIII, xviii, (479).

GOUZENNES, VIII, (i).—VIII, ii, (317–19).—VIII, iv, (324).

GRAVISSET, VIII, xiii, (446), 447.

GROUP, LATHUS'S, meet and listen to Haverkamp, V, xxii.

GROUP, LOMMÉRIE'S, V, (vi).—V, vii, (55).—V, viii, (58).—V, (ix).—V, xii.—V, xviii, (126). —Join Lathus's group, V, xxii. —V, (xxvii).—VI, xiii, (376).

"GROUP," THE "LITTLE," I, (x).— II, xx.

GROUP OF IDLERS IN THE RUE MONTMARTRE, THE, I, ii.—Goes on questioning itself about "Accredited," I, viii.—Learns about Alfred's existence, I, xiii.—I, xviii, 149.

viii

INDEX OF CHARACTERS

MEN OF GOOD WILL

A NOTE ON THE TYPE IN
WHICH THIS BOOK IS SET

This book is set in Granjon, a type named in compliment to ROBERT GRANJON, but neither a copy of a classic face nor an entirely original creation. George W. Jones drew the basic design for this type from classic sources, but departed from his model to profit by the intervening centuries of experience and progress. This type is based primarily upon the type used by Claude Garamond (1510-61) in his beautiful French books, and more closely resembles Garamond's own than do any of the various modern types that bear his name.

Of Robert Granjon nothing is known before 1545, except that he had begun his career as type-cutter in 1523. The boldest and most original designer of his time, he was one of the first to practise the trade of type-founder apart from that of printer. Between 1549 and 1551 he printed a number of books in Paris, also continuing as type-cutter. By 1557 he was settled in Lyons and had married Antoinette Salamon, whose father, Bernard, was an artist associated with Jean de Tournes. Between 1557 and 1562 Granjon printed about twenty books in types designed by himself, following, after the fashion of the day, the cursive handwriting of the time. These types, usually known as "caractères de civilité", he himself called "lettres françaises", as especially appropriate to his own country. He was granted a monopoly of these types for ten years, but they were soon copied. Granjon appears to have lived in Antwerp for a time, but was at Lyons in 1575 and 1577, and for the next decade at Rome, working for the Vatican and Medici presses, his work consisting largely in cutting exotic types. Towards the end of his life he may have returned to live in Paris, where he died in 1590.

THIS BOOK WAS COMPOSED, PRINTED, AND BOUND
BY H. WOLFF, NEW YORK